Fire in Heaven

A NOVEL by Malcolm Bosse

SIMON AND SCHUSTER
NEW YORK

This novel is a work of fiction. Names, characters, places, and incidents either are
the product of the author's imagination or are used fictitiously. Any resemblance
to actual events or locales or persons, living or dead, is entirely coincidental.

Copyright © 1985 by Malcolm Bosse
All rights reserved
including the right of reproduction
in whole or in part in any form
Published by Simon and Schuster
A Division of Simon & Schuster, Inc.
Simon & Schuster Building
Rockefeller Center
1230 Avenue of the Americas
New York, New York 10020
SIMON AND SCHUSTER and colophon are registered trademarks of
Simon & Schuster, Inc.
Designed by Irving Perkins Associates
Manufactured in the United States of America
10 9 8 7 6 5 4 3 2 1
Library of Congress Cataloging in Publication Data
Bosse, Malcolm J. (Malcolm Joseph)
    Fire in heaven.
    I. Title.
PS3552.O77F57 1985   813'.54   85-14347
ISBN 0-671-47080-9

To the best, Herman Gollob,
And to Marie-Claude and Malcolm-Scott,
With love

And so it was I entered the broken world
To trace the visionary company of love, its voice
An instant in the wind (I know not whither hurled)
But not for long to hold each desperate choice.
                                    —HART CRANE

Even a wise man acts in accordance with his own nature. Beings
will follow their own nature. What can restraint do?
                                    —THE BHAGAVAD GITA

The call of the wild geese brings no news.
The road's too long for my dreams to reach home.
The grief of separation is like springtime grass:
However far I wander, I find it growing still.
                                    —LI YU

Part One

1 HEAVING OUT OF the muddy pond, a large gray cylinder comes slowly up the bank.

The girl is standing close to the pond, yet doesn't move when the thing climbs toward her on short blunt legs. Beyond the thing and the pond a white face appears in a hut's doorway; an arm from the shadows there beckons frantically, but she doesn't move, won't or can't move. While its four feet, clawing for purchase in the mud, send it forward, the long gray thing grows longer. Its body ends in a thick scaly tail, and its gray snout, held inches above the ground, opens to show long yellow teeth. But she doesn't move, not even when the gnarled tail thrashes rapidly about. From the bamboo hut someone is yelling and waving, but she won't, or possibly can't, move a step. The great muddy thing is close enough now for her to see it's a crocodile. Rising on hind feet in human fashion, the crocodile shuffles toward her. She still doesn't move, although with its mouth gaping wide she can smell the terrible odor from within, a whiff of swamp ground and death, and yet—this she will remember as the most astonishing detail of all— the awesome creature displays one round and gentle eye.

Feeling her own eyes tremble behind the closed lids, she's aware of coming into consciousness. Her heart pounds from the effect of the dream, and the girl tastes sweat on her lips. But rather than free herself completely from sleep, she remains as she is, eyes shut tightly, adrift in the vulnerable region between sleeping and waking.

At last she emerges from one image into the experience of another. This is not a dream, however, but a memory that's been part of her life for a long time.

She is watching two women in bed together, one dark and the other fair-skinned.

She is watching their entwined limbs slide against one another like the snakes she once saw coiling in a nest near the canal. A band of sunshine, falling through the bedroom jalousie, has striped their naked bodies. They move ceaselessly under the light as if being whipped softly by a golden lash. Rising on her elbows, the fair-skinned woman tents her dark companion in her fallen hair. They kiss, make soft noises of pleasure, and remain oblivious to the presence in the doorway.

Sonia sits bolt upright in bed, thoroughly awake.

Her heart pounds, as it had during the crocodile dream, although the vision of the two women is familiar enough. Repetition has drained off the shock of memory, notwithstanding the truth of it: the fair-skinned woman had been her mother.

A gong booms from the wat across the canal, the sound freeing her altogether from the image. With a sigh the girl wipes sweat from her upper lip. Whatever happened between the pretty Siamese woman and Mother, Sonia is not ashamed of it. This decision not to be ashamed is also familiar, but Sonia wishes, as always, for the chance to talk about what happened, to explain it to someone. Often she's tempted to confide in a classmate.

"Are you my friend? Very well, let me tell you something strange. One afternoon I came home from somewhere—I can't remember where —and went upstairs and just as I was going into my own room I saw the door ajar to my mother's bedroom . . ." Once begun, she'd tell it without shame, and if her confidante showed the faintest sign of disapproval or scorn or anything of the sort, why then Sonia would explain still more in the most dignified phrases she could gather.

"I'm sorry, but you see, you don't really understand. During the Russian Civil War my mother walked thousands of kilometers across Siberia, when she was no older than we are. *Think* of it—nineteen, caught in a war, walking through endless snow! On the way she lost her whole family: mother and father, brothers and sisters, aunts and uncles, *everybody*. She nearly froze to death. People by the thousands were dying around her from typhus. But she reached Shanghai, and to keep herself alive sold fruit on the corner. She learned Chinese and got herself a job translating Russian into Chinese. Then she met and fell in love with a Chinese general, believe me a great man, who married her in spite of *everything*. I am his daughter, and when his enemies murdered him, Mother brought me here and raised me, and so I don't judge my mother, whatever she does, because I'm proud of her. And do you think I'm the only one who's proud of her? My stepfather, before he went to war, he loved her like I do, believe me he did, and one of these days he'll be coming back to her. A lot of people love my mother."

The girl has rehearsed this defiant speech many times in her room, when no one is near. Back and forth she walks, declaiming it in a voice of ringing conviction, while her imagined confidante, thoroughly cowed by its logic and passion, agrees there's nothing for her to be ashamed of.

Only the truth is, Sonia has never made this speech to anyone.

She doesn't know why. Maybe none of the girls would be sympathetic. It isn't exactly natural, is it, woman with woman? They talked about such things in the corridors of the convent school, and, for that matter, there were rumors about some of the girls and a lot of giggling, especially among the Siamese. But no one ever suggested that anybody's *mother* could do such a thing. Or maybe she's never told anyone because the facts aren't really clear. That is, had there actually been so much sunlight? It seems each time she thinks of that afternoon the sunlight grows stronger. And her mother and the Siamese girl seem to move against each other more passionately. The details of their touching are more vivid: breast, hip, groin . . .

Sonia runs one hand through her ear-length hair; it's damp, although this is the cool season in Bangkok. She's sweating even before the sun rises.

And a strange thing is, she has never been exactly sure of her age that day, when she noticed the door ajar. Ten? Philip hadn't yet gone to war; he was still living in the house when she was ten, so she must have been older. What happened has a way of moving through her imagination into a vague and tricky past. She used to think it had happened when she was only eight or nine, until it occurred to her that every time she remembers that afternoon, she feels small, standing there unnoticed in the doorway. Then one day she realized that being small in the memory doesn't have to mean being small at the time. Being forgotten in the doorway could have made her remember small. Or something like that. It is all so complicated. Eleven or twelve? It should be simple to remember a thing like that, but she can't, she can't do it.

The smell of charcoal smoke drifts through the screened window. Downstairs, Cook must be boiling rice. It's time to get up.

Twelve? Or even thirteen? Where had she been that day? She had been out somewhere and then she came home and then upstairs the bedroom door, opposite her own room, was ajar. How far ajar? Had she tiptoed over to it? She remembers one thing: For some reason she hadn't made noise. Why not? Perhaps the sounds coming from there told her something strange was happening. Had the door been open a crack or had she pushed it a little? Had she stood boldly in the open space and looked or merely peeked around the door? She'd peeked. That is certain. But how long had she watched? That's important. That's almost vital, isn't it? One minute? Five?

Such questions accompany the memory and remain unanswered.

Lying down again with a sigh, the girl flops over on her stomach. With her chin resting on crossed arms, she looks first at the tiger skin on the floor, then at the teak wall, its grain becoming distinct in the early light. Framed in the window there used to be a young coconut palm to look at when she lay on the bed, its fronds open like strong green arms ready to receive her. Mother had ordered the tree cut down because it was getting too big for the garden. She told Mother not to do it. She argued against cutting such a tree, because the coconut palm is Mother's astrological tree, and it's bad luck to cut down your lucky tree. Mother did it anyway.

"What you don't understand about my mother is this," Sonia now adds to her imagined speech. "Mother was raised in Russia almost like a princess, and so she's used to doing what she wants. If she wants to do something, well, with someone—I mean a woman—then who am I to argue about it?" But if the confidante should ask, "Are you afraid of your mother?" she'd reply without hesitation, "I'm not afraid of *any-one*—" Here she might supply the name of a confidante: Pranee or Lamai or maybe Hilga, who is the daughter of the German Ambassador and talks more about sex than any of the girls. "I'm not afraid of anyone, Hilga. My father stood up to all the warlords of China. He wasn't afraid. Not of Chiang Kai-shek or any of them." The truth is, Mother has warned her not to talk about her father at school in this time of racial tension between the Chinese and the Siamese. But this morning the impassioned speech goes on in her head relentlessly. "The warlords had to kill him because he believed in justice, and he told my mother all about justice and courage, and she's told me. He said to her, 'Don't be afraid.' He said, 'Do what you believe is right.' "

Having taken satisfaction from the conjured words, Sonia lies there awhile listening to a hoolock gibbon in a nearby tree. He's wailing for his mate. The old fellow's there every dawn, peevishly calling for his female, until she comes from the klong after a morning drink.

—Watched them less than a minute. That's probably the truth of it. And then she'd tiptoed downstairs, not wanting to be caught, and she'd waited until they came down together, side by side. Was the woman pretty? She can't remember. She'd stood at the gate alongside Mother and waved goodbye at the woman. Never saw her again, but was she pretty? Her long, frustrating failure to recall faithfully what happened that strange afternoon is the chief reason Sonia keeps a diary now. She has kept one since her fifteenth birthday in a determined effort never again to forget what happens in her life. Locked in a small sandalwood cabinet are four little books, bound in imitation gold with a drawing of bamboo stems on the covers. In the Brahma Jati, the Siamese system of astrology, her element is gold, her lucky plant is bamboo, her sign is the Royal Dragon, because she was born in May, the sixth month. She did the drawings of bamboo herself. Not good, not bad, in her opinion. Not as good as some of the girls can do.

It is now early January, the second month of 1948 according to the old Siamese calendar, and in early May a fifth diary, full of secrets, will be completed and join the others in their cabinet. It's possible that today's entry will be the most momentous she has ever written.

• • •

That possibility gets her out of bed. In his poem *Swasdi Raksa*—she read it again recently—Suthorn Bhu says if on rising you face south, you will be loved. Sonia faces south and with a single decisive motion yanks the cotton nightgown over her head. She picks up a pair of pajama trousers and a baggy blouse from the foot of the bed and yanks them on with the same purposeful ferocity.

She's moving fast now. Perhaps that's why she remembers the lines, "Wisely and slow; they stumble that run fast." Last week, for a university assignment, she read *Romeo and Juliet* in English. To Sonia the play is so beautiful and true that she's put a lot of it to memory. "Wisely and slow; they stumble that run fast." That's a warning, and it brings a flush to her cheeks as Sonia walks rapidly out of the bedroom. Maybe Shakespeare meant the warning, but he was really on the side of Romeo and Juliet. That was the idea, wasn't it? Better to love for the moment than live wisely and slow.

Halfway down the stairway she recalls another line: "My man's as true as steel."

Ah, is he? Will he be? A thrill of dread follows her to the first-floor hallway. She resolves not to think of him, but turns her attention elsewhere—to the air itself. Almost cool, it seems palpable in the hallway, something like the creamy insides of a mangosteen, her favorite fruit. Halting, she breathes deeply to fill her lungs with the fragrance of morning, still carrying as it does the slightly fetid scent of deepest night. A dawn mist, hovering in the hallway, is tinged with blue, and leads her through the door that she now flings open. A wild garden, all tangled and green, lies before her: shady payom trees with white-tinted yellow blossoms, orange jampa, dwarf pikul trees. They're wet with dew, so pristine fresh, it seems to Sonia, they might have pushed through the earth only moments ago.

Chamlong.

Well, it's the first time since waking she's let herself say his name. She says it in a whisper. She says it again, daringly out loud this time: "Chamlong!" The sound of his name on her lips startles her; it seems to boom and resonate through the morning. It's as if her mother, opening the sandalwood cabinet, had pulled out one of the secret diaries and read from it in a voice loud enough to be heard clear across the klong and through the halls of the wat where monks are now chanting.

"Chamlong," she says, feeling the heat rise in her face.

Competing with the spoken name is the shrill cackle of a tokay lizard from somewhere in the garden. The cry of the tokay at dawn is good luck. Passing a hedgerow of red hibiscus and entering the outhouse, Sonia smiles grimly in response to the lizard's cry. Good luck is what she needs today.

The sweeper has already been to the outhouse this morning. Sonia can smell the lye sprinkled liberally down the hole cut in the latrine planking. Another lizard, this one a brown gecko, cocks his head thoughtfully from the wooden roof and eyes the girl, who returns his gaze while removing her pajama bottoms and squatting over the hole. She moves her left foot out of the way of a meandering ant, then looks up again at the lizard. She remembers the brutal mouth, the soft eye of the crocodile in her dream. Blurred in recall, the details of the dream have lost their power, yet their distance in time allows her to consider its meaning. She rarely dreams of animals. Once she flew joyously with a pack of flying squirrels over Bangkok, and once in a terrible nightmare she turned into a cobralike creature attacked by a ferocious mongoose who shook her until she awoke screaming. But the crocodile? It provoked neither joy nor horror. She'd stood there frozen in anticipation while it climbed out of the slimy pond and came toward her. And even when she felt its awful breath upon her, she remained there, unable to move away from the gentle look of its eye. The day has begun strangely.

Which is fitting, she thinks.

Staring up once more at the gecko, whose spongy claws hold it flat against the ceiling, Sonia wonders if what the gecko now feels is what she felt watching the crocodile. But then what had she actually felt?

Something . . . between joy and horror. It was a neutral thing, a waiting. Perhaps nothing more than curiosity.

Finished, she rinses herself with a cup of water scooped from an earthenware jar and dries with her towel hanging next to the door. Putting on the billowy trousers, she glances again at the gecko, who scampers soundlessly across the roof and vanishes in a crack she couldn't have seen had she looked for it.

Leaving the outhouse, Sonia notices a few wasps busy at a corner of the building. They have managed to build a nest with clots of daub. It hadn't been there yesterday, as she recalls. They must have worked hard. But by sundown the sweeper will probably have batted it away with his bamboo broom. She'll ask Mother to let the nest remain, arguing that wasps never harm anyone who leaves them alone. Mother will say that a wasp nest has no business near their outhouse. The nest will come down.

Beyond a bougainvillea bush and some large red flamboyants, Sonia emerges from the garden onto a brick terrace facing the muddy klong. The success or failure of a day is usually determined for her here, on this terrace at dawn, because it's here that she plays Tai Chi Chuan. If she can calm her mind and progress through the slow, demanding exercise for about fifteen minutes without losing concentration, then most likely the day will go well. It happens that way.

Narrowing her eyes, Sonia stares down at the green Chinese tiles in the center of the terrace, seeking a focus of mind that'll enable her to begin, but a nearby crackling of twigs startles her. She lifts her head in time to see Mother between tamarind trees. Only for an instant, before greenery obscures her view, Sonia has a glimpse of short black hair, a turquoise frock: Mother on her way to do obeisance at the Spirit House. Who else in Bangkok but Mother would carry incense and flowers to a Siamese spirit house while wearing a Western dress? Sonia smiles.

There was a time when Mother would be here on the terrace with her, both of them playing Tai Chi Chuan. Mother taught her the exercise, just as Father had taught it to Mother years ago in China. Until recent months the dawn Tai Chi had brought them together. At such times Mother often quoted Father, in Chinese. She always quoted him in Chinese, and Sonia loved her for that.

"To do Tai Chi properly, he told me, you must feel the needle inside the cotton." Mother would laugh. "Easier said than done." And like a scholar she'd say, "Tai Chi is an essay on Yin and Yang. That's what your father told me. Yang solid, Yin empty. Yang forward, Yin backward. He said, 'Tai Chi's a way of feeling that nothing exists without its opposite.'"

Mother's man had been as true as steel.

Yang male, Yin female. "My man's as true as steel." Sonia looks at the empty space between the tamarind trees. By now Mother must be lighting the incense in front of the Spirit House exactly as Siamese women are doing at this hour all over Bangkok. Mother is talking to Father now.

Sonia gazes into the mist rising over the klong. She can just see the muddy presence of the canal through some trees along the edge of the terrace. A dugout passes on its way to the Floating Market. A man in a conical hat sits at the stern, paddling; a woman sits in the stern under a blue umbrella. Produce is piled amidships. Man, woman. Yin, Yang. An essay in movement.

As for herself, she can't concentrate on the exercise. She's thinking of Mother's refusal to play Tai Chi, giving a busy schedule as an excuse. But in recent months Sonia has also noticed, with regret, that Mother rarely mentions the General any more or speaks of his gentleness and strength and vision. It was through Mother's memory, often as they completed the morning's Tai Chi, that they had shared their love of him. It was their time together, the three of them, before she and Mother joined Philip at breakfast for another threesome—pleasant, yes, but not magical!

She can't concentrate, not today. She botched the exercise after only a few postures. There's no sense in continuing, only to forget which arm goes where and then to stand flatfooted, unable to remember, while the hoolock gibbon and his mate look down at her from a tree.

So she'll give it up this morning, go back to her room, and wash before breakfast. Maybe she'll write in her diary before this momentous momentous momentous day actually begins.

Instead of the inside staircase, which Mother put in last year (an innovation that shocked the neighborhood), Sonia takes the old outside ladder up to the second floor. Halfway up, she looks across the garden, past the fence, to the dirt road in front of the house. Trudging along are a group of saffron-robed monks, carrying their big iron pots in both hands.

Seeing them, Sonia turns and goes down again, rushing to the back gate in time to find Cook there, ready with food for the monks. The old woman gives Sonia a frown of disapproval—wanting the merit of feeding the monks all for herself.

Disregarding this rebuff, Sonia gives Cook a *wai:* hands clasped high in front of her nose—a show of respect that usually disarms the old woman. It does now. Old Cook nods with a faint smile, then, unhooking the gate, drags her brass kettle full of steaming rice up to the entrance-way. A middle-aged monk comes along first, shoving his alms pot brusquely forward. The old woman ladles in a few spoonfuls; he shakes his head as a warning for her not to put too much in—other people of the neighborhood will want to gain their own merit by feeding him. Setting the rice kettle down, Cook picks up a cloth and from it adds to his pot some fried pork and pickled garlic, a boiled salted egg, and a piece of salted fish wrapped in banana leaf. Then, kneeling, she does a *wai* with her hands clasped high at her forehead. Without acknowledging the *wai*, he moves on, and a new monk appears at the gate.

He's young and he's handsome, Sonia notices. He's tall by Siamese standards, as tall as she is, and muscular.

"It's my turn," she informs Cook briskly and takes the ladle from her. About my age, Sonia figures, as she ladles a large spoonful of rice into his outstretched alms pot. She can't imagine that he's been a bhikkhu long—maybe not more than a couple of months. Maybe after a year or two, having gained merit for his parents, he'll leave the monastery and pursue another life. What sort of life? Does he go to school? But not at Silpakorn Fine Arts—she'd have remembered him.

Their eyes meet as ladled rice falls into the pot. He holds it far from his body; he means to avoid the slightest physical contact with her, yet the look in his eyes is bright, curious. With the second spoonful, Sonia makes a wish for good luck in love. This is the custom. All her girl-friends at convent school used to do it, and many of them swore that the young monks thought of nothing but love. How did the girls know?

"Your name," the young monk asks softly.

She knows, of course, that he wants her name so he can mention her in his prayers today. Or does he? The question brings color to her cheeks. "Sanuk." She gives him her nickname.

For a moment the young monk looks at her.

Recovering her composure, Sonia gives him a *wai*, one of only moderate respect—her hands clasped chin high—yet a smile goes with it.

Oh, the fellow's surely new in the monastery! She notices he can't help smiling back.

"I saw that," Cook mutters when the monk has gone. "They say good and bad deeds follow you as the shadow follows the body."

"Then you and I have both gained merit this morning." Sonia grimaces at the old woman and returns to the outside staircase, which she mounts slowly, thinking of the young bhikkhu whose bare shoulder possessed the muscles of . . . of a tiger. Like Chamlong. Poor young fellow, she thinks. Supposed to obey 227 rules, to eat nothing after noon, to chant all day, to forget women.

Sanuk giggles at the thought.

Back in her room she takes a key from a drawer to unlock the sandalwood cabinet that sits on top of her dresser. In the top drawer of the cabinet lie a wooden cross and four books. Some years ago Sanuk made the cross by tying together two sticks, pretending it was the cross fashioned from scrap wood by an English soldier and given to Jeanne d'Arc at the Old Market Square in Rouen when she was burned at the stake. Sanuk still daydreams of the Maid, of her spectacular rise and tragic fall in fifteenth-century France. The four books beside the cross are Sanuk's completed diaries—each prefaced by the Saint's motto that flew on her battle standard: "Jésus Marie." Printed in huge red letters. Removing the diaries from the drawer, Sanuk admires the imitation gold covers and her drawings of bamboo (not bad, not good). She thumbs through the pages. How much she has written! From the French desk that Mother bought her last year (she doesn't think it fits with her batik paintings of *The Ramakien*, the Siamese dancing dolls in brocade and rhinestones, and the *ranad ek*, a classical xylophone she's never learned to play that Philip gave her on her tenth birthday), Sonia takes out the diary now in use. In gold letters—the ends of them flourishing over the entire cover—is the word SANUK.

Mother gave her the nickname Sanuk a few years ago. It's a word with a constellation of meanings: fun, well-being, a carefree heart, a joy of living. Hearing the nickname for the first time, Siamese often laugh; they love the word, but they're surprised to hear it used as a name. Sanuk: Yes, it's what she wants to be. And until recently it's what Mother wanted her to be, too. Mother's intent was surely there in the nickname itself. The hope for happiness was there each time Mother pronounced "Sanuk!" But "Sanuk!" is rarely heard these days. Lately Mother has become formal. "Ah, Sonia, you'll love school in America or Europe." These days the house is filled with "Sonia." Sonia this, Sonia that, the name of a Russian grandmother she never knew. A cold name, a flat landscape, a white sea. Here in Bangkok it's a green world that promises joy. Does Mother really expect her to put aside Sanuk for Sonia? As for Mother, she chooses for herself a life *mai sanuk*—a colorless world of work and money, except when Wanna is around, except when the lovely young Siamese woman, an employee in the antique shop, brings a smile, a blush, a warm light to Mother's wintry Russian face.

· · ·

Sanuk unlocks the clasp to her diary with a key hanging around her neck on a silver chain. She turns to the entries for last week, all written in English (the earlier diaries had been written in Thai script).

> Tuesday. Saw him at Wat Phra Keo. We walked in covered gallary pretending to look at Ramakien murals so people would't stare. They stare anyway because Chamlong waves his arms around when he talks polotics. I like to hear him talk polotics, he's so determined. He has made me interested also about what has hapened in Siam since the young king died. It has been year and half since that hapened and nobody knows yet why he was found shot in bed. Chamlong says what is importent is how the Army led by Field Marshal Phibun has used death of king for polotical perposes. Chamlong says Army and Field Marshal Phibun used it as ecuse for attaking Prime Minster Pridi, who Chamlong likes becase Prime Minster Pridi was head of under ground during war—the Free Thai Movment. But Chamlong says the Army and Field Marshal Phibun wanted power again and so blamed king's death on Pridi and that is why Pridi was thrown from ofice and left cuntry. Chamlong says Phibun hates Chinese and will do anything to hurt them in this cuntry. Chamlong says at next genaral election Khuang Aphaiwong will win, but it will onely mean Phibun will be in real charge of govenment, since Khuang is afraid of Phibun and army and will do what they say. Then one of these days Phibun will push Khuang aside and take charge publickly. I asked how he knew, and Chamlong said, never mind. I said at university they like Phibun even if he did work with Japan during war. I said at university they say Phibun and his friends will bring prospirity. Chamlong laghed. He said were they Siamese who like him? and when I said yes, he laghed again. You will not find Chinese who like him, Chamlong said. He said what we must do is think about fate of Chinese in Siam. I asked is it onely Chinese comunists that Phibun hates? Chamlong said Phibun hates all Chinese becase Chinese have most of money and shops and everthing in cuntry. I said how do you know all of these things, and Chamlong said, never mind, I just do becase I have friends. He said both of us are really Chinese, becase when you have Chinese blood you belong forevar to Middle Kingdom. He makes sense. But maybe it's only becase of the way he explains things. He has lighter skin and narrower eyes than Siamese boys and is taller, as tall as me. He is handsome. He has

promosed to teach me Push Hands, a technick for two players of Tai Chi Chuan. Does he really know Push Hands? Even his sister told me, don't trust him. I don't know what to beleive. He was bragging about women again. How he meets them at dance halls like The Cathay and The Silver Palm. I should be desgusted with him, but for some reason I just am not. I have been reading the play of Shake- speare, *Romeo and Juliet*, a wonderful love story. It says "This bud of love, by summer's ripening breath, May prove a beauteous flower when next we meet." I wanted to say that to him, but of course I didn't. "Not stepping o'er the bounds of modesty" also comes from play.

Wednesday. Long day at university. I am not really a good artist. Pranee is much better, so is Lamai. Yet it gives me plesure right now so I do it. It isn't fair though that girls can't go into polotics. I would work for Chinese cause in Siam! Lamai and I talked a lot today about that and other things. Her young brother will be ordained a novuce at Rain Retreet. They will shave his head and make him vow not to make love or drink alchol. Lamai says he is thirteen and will stay with monks all three months of rainy seeson. They will do the sukhwan ritual and seal the khwan inside his body by tying cotton treds around his wrists. Otherwise the free soul can escape if it gets frihtened. Lamai has explained to me the diffarance between khwan and the other soul, the winyan, the self soul. The free soul lasts forevar, but self soul lasts only for your present life. The winyan is yours but khwan can wandar away and if it doesn't come back, you die. It's sad, the way you can lose your life acording to Siamese. Why then are they so happy?

Thursday. Met him again at same place. We talk a long time. I have never had talk like that. He asked me to go some place with him. At first I didn't understand, but then I did. For an anser, I laghed. He was angery and went away, but I'm not sorry I laghed. It was all I could do.

Friday. Went to wat at same time, hoping he would come to, and he did. Again we talked about what he perposed. It was terrable. We argued and walked among the bildings of wat. The glare from sun light was hitting all the glass and porcalin bits and gold of Pantheon and Mondop and Stupa until both of us went giddey. At least I did, and he looked it. And all the time, it's hard to beleive now, we were speaking of trist. He knows where we can go together. I told him no, angerly. But somehow before leaving, we agreed to met here next week on Monday and talk. That's what I told him. We would talk about it. I couldn't beleive later it's what I really said.

Saturday. Nothing happened. Dull all day. Listened to big uggly priest birds in trees with their terrable screech that is suposed to call monks to prayer. Mother worked late at shop. I fought with Cook, I fought with Ah Ngee, it was terrable. Mother said again I must go to university in Europe or America. I didn't argue becase it would do no good. But I won't go. If I go any where it will be to China, land of my Father.

Sunday. I must write down these beutiful words from *Romeo and Juliet* that made me think of dearist Father.

> When he shall die,
> Take him and cut him out in little stars,
> And he will make the face of heaven so fine
> That all the world will be in love with night,
> And pay no worship to the garish sun.

What I am planning is reckliss, stupid. I must not throw away my future on this boy I hardly know and who brags about his desgusting women. Yet he appeals to me wonderfully. He is little taller than me and handsome and I think he's someone with true corage, unafraid. I want to live. My parents did, so why can't I?

Taking up a pen, Sanuk writes under Monday:

This morning I had strange dream about crokodil. It didn't frihten me, because I stood right there, but it could have killed me. Very strange. And then I saw *them* again in my mind. When did it really hapen? I don't know. But it hapened! I came upstairs to my room, heard noizes, took a peak, tip toed downstairs, and never told her, never, and never will, becase she thot I didn't know. But it hapened, and I know it hapened.

Sanuk turns away from the open diary to stare at the window that once was filled with the embracing fronds of a coconut palm. Then she writes again:

Maybe it hapens some times now when I'm out of the house. Maybe Mother and Wanna. I beleive they do. Wanna is very beutiful woman, if another woman thinks of her that way. And Mother can do what she wants. It's her right. Life hasn't always been good to her and any way people should do what they want, and so—

Sanuk pauses, lays down the pen. She'll continue the entry later when the day ends, if this day ever does. Somehow, at the moment, she can't imagine getting to the end of it. From a desk drawer she pulls out a small tray filled with golden finger guards, which curl up at the tips into bright little knobs. Jamming a guard on each finger, which extends them twice their length, Sanuk walks around the room and moves her hands in sensuous designs to imitate the poses of a Siamese dancer. She has always wanted to dance, but, being too tall, Sanuk merely watches while classmates perform. One of them is Chamlong's sister, a full-blooded Chinese, who introduced him to her one day as "my brother who hates me for dancing like a Siamese, even though he's half-Siamese himself."

With a gusty sigh of impatience at her own performance, Sanuk takes off the finger guards, then her exercise trousers and blouse. In an alcove there's a bathroom with a cement floor, a latticed wooden platform over a drain, and a huge earthenware jar that stands waist-high in the corner. Attached to the wall is a long mirror into which Sanuk stares with deep interest.

Her skin is almost as fair as a European's; she could be a farang. Once Mother claimed that people abroad would take her for a European. And it's true that none of the Siamese girls has skin like hers. Of course, Mother's skin often seems as white as an eggshell. Chamlong's skin is fair too, especially for someone with Sino-Thai blood. When Sanuk pointed that out to him, he scoffed and kicked at something in his path.

She looks into the mirror hard. Her hair is cut short, almost of boyish length. It has been ever since that day she cut it on a dare in front of some classmates. They were all Siamese, who wore theirs down to their thighs and watched in utter horror while she snipped the long braids off. "Jeanne d'Arc wore hers this way," she had told the appalled onlookers. Now it is even shorter than Mother's. In the morning light coming through a tiny window, Sanuk's black hair has almost a purplish cast to it. She tosses her head rapidly to help the sunlight enhance the sheen. The hair pleases her, but her shoulders look rangy, too broad, like a boy's; and then with a critical eye she regards her breasts. They seem too large to her. There was a time, at sixteen, when she used to strap them down with a piece of cloth, so the girls at school—particularly svelte Siamese girls—wouldn't stare at her during exercise period. Her teacher, a Frenchwoman, discovered her with the cloth (winding it around and around and around, tightly, like a bandage), and told Mother, who made her stop. And once Hilga, the German girl, whose breasts were even larger, took her aside and declared with a broad grin, "Don't you worry, they're just jealous of us," and stuck out her tongue at a group of Siamese classmates watching them.

But were the Siamese girls jealous? Sanuk has always admired their slim hips, thin arms, long necks, and pert little breasts. Compared to them she feels thick and heavy, earthbound, cloddish. But studying herself with determination this morning, Sanuk concludes that her body is . . . well, all right. Her legs, after all, have a nice length to them. Siamese legs, being so short, often have a bunched-up look. She glances from the top of her head to her feet, getting a swift impression of the body's curve. Her eyes focus on the dark patch centered below her stomach. For a moment this mirrored image, so intricate and mysterious, seems detached from her, an outside thing which she merely observes. Hesitantly she touches the palms of both hands to her stomach. The skin feels warmer than it looks. A little pressure from her fingertips enables her to feel the soft springiness of her flesh.

It feels good. It would feel good to Chamlong too, she thinks, drawing her hands away.

But the next moment she reaches out to brush her pubic hair gently with the pad of one finger. She hesitates again, keeping the finger just there, nestled in hair rather stiff, wiry. But he would like it.

The idea of someone penetrating her body with his own is always strange, as strange as it had seemed when Mother first explained "nature"—perhaps a half-year after schoolmates had given her their own bizarre versions. When she thinks of this act with a man, she wonders why him in me? Why can't I be the one who does that to him? Finally the act seems unpleasant, perhaps frightening. Yes, frightening. After all, he gets into her body and discharges something of himself. She has trouble visualizing the male part that does this. Of course, she has seen the funny little appendages dangling on boys who dive naked into the klong, but she can't imagine such a harmless thing as they possess violating the most secret region of her body. Of course what men have gets large, but how large? She has seen monkeys playing with themselves in the trees, brazenly, making faces as they do it. But she has never taken what they do seriously. How could she? The idea brings a smile to her face: impudent gibbons with their frenzied red stalks!

What she really fears is the—intimacy of the act, the absolute physical closeness. Yet she remains astonished by the excitement, indeed, almost the yearning, that just thinking about it can stimulate in her.

Now there's another question. What happens to the *khwan*, the enduring soul, at the moment of penetration? Does it escape in fear from a woman's body? If that were so, all women would die. Perhaps the *khwan* is only annoyed by this invasion of its privacy. The outrageous idea of annoying her immortal soul by the act of love—like an old amah peeved by the sound of children at play—strikes her as very funny. She puts her hand to her mouth and giggles merrily.

Taking up the large bamboo dipper, she thrusts it into the jar and with a full container pours cool water on her body. Next she soaps down with one of the large scented bars that Mother imports from Singapore. The erotic sense of her body has vanished for the moment; she proceeds to wash herself with a kind of fanatical meticulousness, as if resolved to rid her flesh of the least impurity.

She washes her hair too, knowing that in the low humidity of Bangkok's winter season it will dry quickly. Then with a big towel she rubs her body until the skin tingles, and skeins of pink spread across the light brown sheen of her shoulders, arms, belly.

Again she contemplates the image in the mirror. She's a child of the Dragon. It is said of people of this sign that they often have birthmarks on their private parts—a symbol of their passionate nature. About a year ago Sanuk discovered a slight discoloration of skin near her navel. She has decided the navel qualifies as a private part, so in her case the prediction must be true. And there is more that she knows. For example, she knows that Venus and the Sun together control the hands of Dragon people—result: they enjoy sensual things but hate manual labor. Mercury and the Moon control their feet—result: they like to travel, but often prove fickle in love. Mother, of course, laughs at astrology, but many of Sanuk's friends maintain it has figured in their lives. Sanuk believes that at this very moment, while she holds the towel in both hands, there are many thoughts edging toward consciousness. If she could concentrate on them until they became clear, she'd learn many things. But she can no more concentrate now than she could on the terrace. And anyway, there isn't time, there isn't time!

Rushing back into the bedroom, she picks through a dresser to find something to wear that's appropriate for such a day. There's a light blue pahom and a reddish plaid pasin that look pretty, but a blouse and a sarong of their style will seem too Siamese for Chamlong's taste. Finally she chooses a bright yellow cheongsam with high collar and slit skirt of the kind popular these days in Chinatown. It's a silk dress that fits snugly across her hips. Afraid she might look too wide in it, Sanuk hurries to the bathroom and turns slowly in front of the mirror, studying the rippling silk at her belly, the curve of her exposed thigh. A Siamese girl once said to her with a smile of jaunty fatalism, "It doesn't do any good to dress for boys. They don't care what a girl wears, they only care what a girl will take off. That's the way boys are. Wait. You'll see."

Vigorously Sanuk combs her hair with a tortoise-shell comb from Chiang Mai. It's her favorite comb, and the Northern Siamese claim it's lucky—such a comb brings happiness to the user. Squinting hard at her bangs, she decides they're uneven, and so with a pair of scissors, her face inches from the mirror, she snips a little here, a little there, removing the tiniest ends of a few strands. The line across her forehead might have been measured with a ruler.

Does she look as Chinese as she thinks she does? As she hopes she does? What she likes best about herself is her eyes, because they seem narrow, like those of a Chinese girl. There's nothing in their shape to suggest that half of her is farang. Her mother's eyes are round and big and exposed, unlike her own. Yet staring at the sunlit mirror for a moment more, Ah! fervently for a moment, Sanuk wishes for eyes of a different color, not brown but green, the shade of tamarind leaves she can see from the window, as green as her mother's sea-green eyes.

"Breakfast!"

From the floor below, Ah Ping's voice spirals up like gritty smoke.

"Breakfast!"

Each morning the old voice delivers that same proclamation. Sanuk can picture its owner: the bent little figure in black pajamas, standing at the bottom of the stairway; white hair tied back in a bun; huge freckled pouches beneath watery eyes. For years, this woman from the Teochiu region of South China has served Sanuk's mother.

"Breakfast!"

Ever since the girl can remember, since early childhood in Singapore, she has endured Ah Ping calling her for *something*.

Grimacing in the mirror, Sanuk mouths with perfect synchronization the next words that come up from the stairway. "Are you coming down, lazy girl?" The words never vary.

Sanuk allows herself one more glance at the mirror: immaculate bangs, narrow brown eyes, yellow silk enhancing the fairness of her skin. A Chinese girl?

"Must I," the old voice begins again, "come up and get you or are you coming down, lazy girl?"

By the third word Sanuk has caught up and under her breath matches not only the rest of Ah Ping's phrase, but the peevish intonation as well. They end together—"coming down, lazy girl?" Everything is in place, Sonia thinks, with a sigh of contentment. Or at least everything's in place in the house of her mother.

Now she goes down.

2 AH PING IS waiting at the bottom of the stairs. "Are the cramps gone?"

While the watery eyes, with the great bags under them, study her closely, Sanuk nods.

"It's too tight."

"Cheongsams are supposed to fit this way."

Ah Ping shakes her head. "Too tight." She fingers the dress, roughly pulling it away from Sanuk's hip. "Next time I'll have new medicine you can try."

With a vague smile Sanuk eases past the old woman. She knows the sort of medicine it would be: some horrible concoction of pickled animal innards. She'd rather have menstrual cramps a whole *month* than take Ah Ping's medicine. And anyway, nothing gives her relief; she's doomed to monthly pain.

The teakwood floor creaks underfoot as she walks through the house toward the dining room that faces the garden. She halts at a bird cage and says a cheery good morning to the mynah bird inside. Taksakan, named by Sanuk for a villainous god, puts his black head at an angle and puffs his brown plumage, but makes no sound. He's too old to learn new words; his vocabulary consists of one: *"Choei"—Don't get into trouble.*

Sanuk continues to the unscreened dining room which, open on one side, faces the klong. Her mother, seated at one end of the long table, gives her a bright smile. Turquoise is a good color for that incredibly white skin, the girl thinks, bending over to kiss her mother's cheek. From the corner of her eye Sanuk sees their old Siamese servant, Nipa, watching with distaste. Although Nipa has watched mother and daughter show affection in this Western way for years now, she can't get used to it—they should be rubbing nose against cheek, like civilized people. Even as her lips touch the white cheek, Sanuk can feel Nipa's disapproval at her back; it seems to bore in like something physical. The old servant has often complained about such a greeting—not to Mother, of course, but to Ah Ping, who takes satisfaction from Nipa's outraged response to the farangs' barbarism. One of Sanuk's own pleasures is watching the progress of censure and gossip and intrigue in the back rooms of the house.

As Sanuk draws away from her, Mother asks softly, "Cramps gone, darling?"

"Gone for this month." Sanuk sits next to her.

"Poor darling."

Sanuk weaves her hand cavalierly, as if to dismiss from both their minds the idea of pain. One thing she won't become in this life is a complainer. Seated opposite Mother, she glances at the brown thread of sluggish klong through the greenery. A gardener is coming up from the bank with buckets of canal water dangling from each end of a shoulder pole.

Mother looks up from the papaya she's been peeling. "Going to school today?"

"Not for classes. A few of us are going to sketch along the river."

"Who?"

Sanuk shrugs. "Pranee, Lamai, Sopita. I'm not sure who else."

"In that cheongsam?"

"Of course."

"Isn't it too tight?"

The girl is silent. Mother's now at the age when loose-fitting clothes look better. Not that Mother's lost her figure, she has not, but even so, in a tight cheongsam she might look wide, even chubby. Of course Chinese women don't care if their tummies stand out against the tight silk of a cheongsam; they aren't vain. Mother never steps into sunlight without a hat on.

"Sonia."

Has she been staring at Mother without realizing it?

"Isn't it too tight? I haven't seen you in the Thai ruan-ton we bought." Mother picks up the *Bangkok Times* from beside her plate. "That looks so lovely on you."

"It's pretty," Sanuk observes evasively.

"It's more comfortable than a cheongsam if you're scrambling up and down river banks."

Sanuk's thinking that they bought the Thai ruan-ton before she met Chamlong: a brown skirt with vertical red stripes and a red jacket with three-quarter sleeves cut very wide, and five buttons. But it looks terribly Siamese; Chamlong wouldn't like it.

"I'll wear it tomorrow," Sanuk promises.

Mother lowers the paper thoughtfully. "I just want you to be comfortable."

"I know that." And with a rush of warm feeling, Sanuk does know it. But she also knows that sometimes love isn't enough between them—not on a day like this. What she needs more than love right now is honesty. If only she could say, "Mother, I'm a woman like you are, and that means . . . that means . . ."

But Mother has slipped on a pair of horn-rimmed glasses that have dangled on a black cord around her neck. She's staring through them at the *Bangkok Times*.

Sanuk hates those glasses. They make her mother seem old. Perhaps if Mother wore them constantly the effect would be less noticeable, therefore less disagreeable. As it is, being yanked up to her nose for reading, they emphasize her dependence on something older people use.

"That coconut palm," Sanuk begins without thinking. "The one you had cut down."

Mother glances up from the paper. "The one near your window?"

"It's bad luck to cut down a lucky tree, Mother." Sanuk says this in Thai instead of the Mandarin they've been speaking. "Don't put yourself in danger."

"I thought we settled the matter of that tree. Let's speak English," Mother suggests in correct but heavily accented English. "We both need the practice."

"You mean I need the practice," Sanuk replies in Thai. "You shouldn't have cut the tree down."

"I don't believe in good luck, bad luck. I'm too old to believe in them," she adds with a smile. "Please, Sonia, let us speak in English."

"If you live in a country, shouldn't you speak the language of that country?" Sanuk has again replied in Thai.

"Thai is not like English and French, darling. With those two you can go anywhere. Do you see?" There's a note of strained patience in Mother's voice. Indeed, they've had this conversation so many times that Sanuk has nearly memorized it the way she has memorized Ah Ping's breakfast greeting.

But the girl doesn't want argument today. In fact, she wants to placate Mother, as if to compensate for something she has not yet done. "I know you care," Sanuk says, reaching for her mother's hand. "I know you want me to learn so I can have a good life." She has said the words in correct English.

Delighted, Mother extends her own hand, and they touch. "Sanuk," she murmurs, using the nickname for the first time today. "If we understand each other, the rest will take care of itself."

The girl smiles, feeling uneasy about the deception she's practicing. She wants to say, "We can't understand each other when I don't tell you what I'm thinking, but I can't tell you what I'm thinking when I know you'll hate it, you'll say no, you won't let me do what I think I simply must do in order to be myself, to be a woman, to be—" The speech lengthens in her head, coils around and about, while Mother returns to the newspaper. To cut the string of tortured thought, Sanuk acts—reaches for the fruit bowl. This brings Nipa instantly to her side.

"Take some boiled rice and salted fish, young miss," Nipa suggests in a tone of command.

Sanuk glares at the old servant, who knows full well that she hates boiled rice and salted fish for breakfast. Cook has given Nipa orders to push food on her. That is obvious. Cook wants to gain face in the neighborhood by fattening up her young mistress.

Sanuk gives the servant a sly smile. "Please bring me a small dish of coconut pudding." Then, peeling a mango, she slices it into little golden pieces. In May they'll have mangosteens; the snow-white flesh melts on the tongue like cream. How she'll anticipate that sweetness on future mornings! Life is wonderful. Biting into the sweet-and-sour mango, she watches Mother fastidiously munch a bit of pickled green banana. Mother watches her weight, yet looks thicker than she did a year ago.

I'll look like her someday. The thought isn't unpleasant. After all, Mother is still a handsome woman. But there are touches of gray in the short black hair, fine networks at the edges of those green eyes—the thickening waist. I'm going to stay young a long time, Sanuk vows firmly, and with a smirk accepts a dish of pudding from Nipa, who frowns in response.

• • •

The Russian refugee and the Chinese general: They were once young too, Sanuk thinks sadly. "Tell me again how you met." She leans forward, both elbows on the table, as if preparing for a long story.

Mother lowers the newspaper. "Met who?"

"Who?" Sanuk laughs scornfully. "Tell me again how you met my father."

"What ever brought that to mind?"

Sanuk gives her an encouraging smile. "Please. Tell me exactly how it happened."

Mother's return look is veiled—either impatient or disapproving. "Sonia. You already know that."

"I never tire of hearing it."

"Yes, I know you don't."

"You sound like I *should* tire of it." They are speaking Thai now.

"No, of course not." Mother hesitates, shoving the glasses off her nose to dangle from her neck. "We met at a garden party."

"In Shanghai," Sanuk prompts. "You were a translator."

Mother patiently begins to describe the Defense Commissioner of Southern Shantung Province. A man about forty—

"Not tall but muscular," Sanuk supplies. "Excuse me. Go on."

"His hair was cropped short. He had a very military carriage. But his eyes were the most extraordinary thing." Mother cups her chin in both hands and stares beyond the dining room into the garden. "Tender eyes. Or sad. It was difficult to tell when you looked at him—"

And Sanuk lets the recollected details wash over her like an incoming tide, as she envisions the two lovers married and returning to Qufu; their bliss there in the compound of Confucius' ancestors; their mutual interest in art and poetry; his calling her Black Jade, the name of a heroine in a Chinese romance; the great battle Father fought, Mother's work among the wounded, the warlord intrigues that eventually separated them; his death in ambush at the foot of a sacred mountain. The panorama unreels in front of Sanuk's mind like a movie . . .

"So the day after we met he bought me the Willow Pattern plate."

"The one that's now in the Spirit House."

"The one that's now in the Spirit House." Mother shakes her head in mild disapproval. "You're like a child wanting the same bedtime story. That's enough now. Do eat your pudding, if you're going to be on the river all day."

"And you met Philip."

"Yes, I met Philip." Mother picks up the newspaper and holds it high.

"Was he really in Father's army? It always sounds so strange. I mean, a young American in a Chinese army."

Mother laughs behind the paper. "You know it all as well as I do."

"But wasn't it strange?"

The paper comes down enough so that Sanuk can see her mother's eyes go suddenly blank in the act of memory.

"Everything was strange then. In 1927 there were such possibilities. I think we all felt anything could happen. *Mange ton* pudding."

Sanuk begins eating.

• • •

In a few minutes Mother lowers the paper again and says with a sigh, "Well, they're thinking of changing the country's name back to Thailand. Siam . . . Thailand . . . Siam . . . Thailand . . ."

"Phibun's work," Sanuk says emphatically.

Mother shrugs. Sanuk has come to expect it as Mother's response to things political.

"General Pao's a terrible man," Sanuk continues, shoving a slice of mango fiercely into her mouth.

"Pao?"

"Chief of Police. Surely you know *that*, Mother. He's even worse than Phibun."

"I'd rather you'd not say that out loud. And who's to say who is worse than anyone else?"

Sanuk hates it when Mother goes vague like this; to hold her attention, the girl declares in a loud voice that brings Nipa to the doorway, "Phibun and Pao are doing *terrible* things to the Chinese. They reduced the immigration quota of the Chinese so it's two hundred a year, Mother. *Two hundred a year*. It was ten thousand a year ago."

"Well, I imagine the policy's popular with the Siamese."

"You don't sound concerned at all. Not the least," the girl says reproachfully.

"Darling." Mother's jawline tenses. "I've had my fill of politics. In Russia. In China. And here, during the Japanese occupation. Do you think I care about Siamese politics now?"

"But a country's name *does* matter. Siam or Thailand. People have to know what they are. For example, what are you, Mother? Siamese or Thai?"

"I'm Russian" is the instant reply.

"See there? That's what I'm always talking about," Sanuk says triumphantly. "You know what you are, but what am I?"

"Actually, darling, you're Siamese."

"I'm half-Chinese and half-Russian."

"Yes, but your passport—"

"Yours is Siamese too, only *you* are Russian."

"*Qu'est-ce qui te fait penser ainsi?* Lately your interest in politics surprises me."

"I'm trying to figure out what I am."

"You're my daughter. You live in Siam—or Thailand—whichever it is. And you hold a valid passport of that country."

"It's not enough."

Mother leans forward earnestly. The white skin of her forehead bunches into little furrows, manifesting her age, yet those green eyes of hers, softened by compassion, still dazzle Sanuk. "Each time you want me to talk about your father, I hesitate. Do you know why? Because it usually leads to this—you worrying about where you belong. The thing is, you belong with me. Or if you go abroad for a while, you'll know you have a home here. Trust me, Sonia darling."

Sanuk stares at her plate. It's true that every time she thinks of Father, she wonders where she belongs.

• • •

At this moment Nipa comes in with a bundle of mail and lays it beside Mother's plate. To Sanuk the old servant says, "Boiled rice and salted fish, young miss. A little?"

For reply, Sanuk glares. She feels the day heating up. Once the sun has swung into the trees, even in the winter season, a great change takes place, as if a huge invisible hand has clamped an iron lid on the earth, thickening the air, stilling it. She pulls over the newspaper and idly turns pages, while Mother, starting methodically from the top of the pile, starts to open and read the mail.

An article in the *Bangkok Times* intrigues Sanuk. Last week, in a peninsular town, a young Chinese man married a piece of paper. It was inscribed with the name of a girl who died a year ago. After bowing to the symbol of his deceased bride and offering millions in imitation currency for her good fortune in the land of her ancestors, he lit the paper with their marriage candle. Sanuk tries to imagine the wedding ceremony. The face of the young groom, intent upon his burning bride, becomes that of Chamlong.

To shake off the bizarre image, Sanuk turns toward the garden. One step off the teak floor and she could reach the garden, where, in a kosol bush, a cluster of green parakeets are agitating the leathery, crimson-spotted leaves. Birds are racketing over something, busying themselves like the wasps she'd seen this morning in a corner of the outhouse.

"Mother," she says, turning. She intends to mention the nest there.

"Wait." Sanuk notices that her mother is gripping one of the letters so hard her knuckles are white.

"What is it?"

"Wait. One moment. I—" She turns the paper and reads avidly, then looks up puzzled. "Why—he might come back. Sonia." Her voice has a quietly stunned tone. "I believe he *could* be coming back. I mean Philip."

"Philip?"

"He says here he wants to see us." Mother folds the letter slowly. "He wants to know if he can come."

"Of course he can."

Mother smiles. "Do you want him here?"

"Philip? Of course."

"Well, he was always good to you. In his way," she adds, as if examining that idea for the first time. "But why come back now? The war's been over two years. When did he last write?"

"For my birthday last year."

"That's right. He sent you a doll." Mother sighs. "As if you were still a child."

"And a letter about how much he liked India."

"I remember none of it. And the time before?"

Sanuk can't remember—perhaps the year before that. His letters invariably come crumpled, half torn from too much handling, and with illegible postmarks from somewhere.

"I don't understand why he'd want to come back," Mother says thoughtfully. "We hear from him once a year and suddenly this."

"Let him come back." To convince her mother, Sanuk adds, "Maybe he's not feeling well. Maybe he's tired." Weariness is what she chiefly recalls of Philip Embree, the stepfather whose name she bears: A blond, stocky, tired-looking man with an ugly scar across his forehead. The scar is prominent in her memory, but then she last saw him when she was still a child. She recalls him walking quietly through the house, often gazing at the klong. Even then he seemed like a man who was tired of thinking too much, tired of being alone with his thoughts, tired of having nothing to do that really interested him. And yet suddenly he would come alive. Those were good times. He'd take her on a boat trip through the klongs or to the Pramane Grounds for kite flying. What she remembers of those good times most of all is his continued story of Bright Lotus and Bill. Bright Lotus was a Chinese princess and Bill was a water buffalo. The two of them, great friends, traveled through China and Siam having adventures with dragons and evil wizards. Those were the good times with Philip, but they didn't occur nearly often enough. Aside from memories of Bright Lotus and Bill and eating sweetmeats from the side of a boat on the klong while Philip paid the hawker, she remembers him hardly at all—like someone quietly ill. In the first years after he left for the war, she used to dream up romantic plots for his life: For example, this quiet and mysterious man (mysterious because quiet) suddenly appears at a time of great crisis and to the surprise of everyone rescues a heroine in distress.

Mother is rereading the letter. "He doesn't give a reason for coming back. He merely wants to see us."

In the past Mother has certainly not encouraged him to return— Sanuk knows that. Mother has answered his letters with messages as curt as telegrams. Last year when the doll, Sanuk's birthday present, arrived from India with the letter, Mother had laughed scornfully: "Look at this doll. Does he think you're still a baby? That's Philip— always in the clouds." Sanuk still has the doll; it's some kind of goddess, she thinks, with a gold crown painted above its wooden face and huge painted eyes. She has intended to send him a photograph of herself the next time she gets one taken. Five years ago she sent him a black-and-white in care of a military address. She knows now how terrible she looked then: skinny, with big knees and big hands hanging at her sides, and a long thin face and hair pulled severely back; she'd been something like an ungainly bird. Why had he sent a goddess doll? So she could pray to it for better looks? Sanuk feels good, knowing she's no longer the creature she sent him in the fourteen-year-old picture.

"I just don't get it," Mother says.

"Maybe," Sanuk suggests, "he found what he was looking for in India."

Mother purses her lips. "I never knew what that was."

"He explained it in his letters," Sanuk reminds her. "He said he was looking for the meaning of his life."

"So you remember that."

"I remember he wrote one in Chinese. Remember? Is this one in Chinese too?"

Mother puts the folded letter beneath the pile. "No. *En anglais.* You really want him here?"

"Of course. I think he had a terrible time in the war."

"*Oui, je crois que c'est vrai.*" Mother opens her mouth to say more, but hesitates.

"You still love him, don't you, Mother?" Sanuk hears the rising note of hope in her own voice. She would like Mother to care for a man.

"*Il compte beaucoup pour moi.*"

"I know he means something to you. That's all I meant. I didn't mean love him in the way you loved Father."

"Sonia. You've got a mango stain on your dress."

The girl looks below the round neck, slightly above her left breast, and discovers a fleck of orange fruit.

"*Pourrais-tu faire attention à la manière dont tu manges.*"

Sanuk glares at her mother. "So how do I eat?"

"Like a coolie. *Est-ce que les filles mangent comme ça à l'école?*"

"I'm nineteen, Mother," Sanuk says coldly.

"Do all the girls eat this way?"

"You're not talking to a child."

Their eyes meet. Mother's blink and look away. "You're right, darling. I'm sorry." She whips off the glasses and begins cleaning the lenses with a napkin. "You see, my mother did the same to me, and if you're ever a mother you'll probably criticize your own child, long after you have the right to do it, for whatever he or she wears and eats—"

"And thinks."

"No, Sonia. I don't criticize you for what you think."

"Why don't you play Tai Chi any more?"

Mother puts the glasses back on. "Mornings there's so much to do . . ." Picking up the next letter from the pile, she opens and reads it intently. "Well, this is *quite* a day."

Quite a day: Sanuk repeats the phrase. Is it? Is it really quite a day? A momentous momentous day?

"This is an application form." Mother peers closely at it. "For the Stanford University in America."

"Where in America?"

"The province of California."

"I thought you preferred me to go to Europe."

"I never said that."

"But I've made out the application for the Sorbonne."

"And when the applications come from Grenoble and Montpelier and London and Vassar and the others I wrote, you'll make out those too."

Sanuk sighs wearily.

"Where you go," Mother says, "depends on which school takes you. *Tu es devenue maintenant suffisamment bonne en anglais et en français*, but you must learn to spell. Your spelling in both languages is poor." Mother begins studying the application, her eyes squinting behind the round spectacles that Sanuk hates.

Nipa enters the dining room, bends to stare meaningfully at the bowl of half-eaten coconut pudding.

Sanuk asks mischievously, "Do you have any elephant meat?"

"What?" The old woman's face clouds up. "You don't want elephant meat."

"It's *just* what I want." She watches with suppressed gaiety how the woman grumbles as she carries the bowl out of the room. Nipa once told her that a woman who eats elephant meat will soon get pregnant. I wouldn't be afraid, Sanuk tells herself. In the halls of Silpakorn University girls talk about the rhythm method. She understands how it works all right, but if anything went wrong, Chamlong would do the proper thing; that is, if they became lovers and if anything went wrong, he'd marry her. He's already told her in so many words that he loves her, and if he refused to marry her if anything went wrong, then she'd take care of herself like a girl did in school last year, or so it was rumored—

"Sonia?"

She turns to Mother, who is smiling.

"*Quelle concentration!* I hope you'll have some left over tomorrow morning."

"Why?"

"Because we're going to sit down and make out this application."

Sanuk nods, vowing to herself, however, that she will not go to America or Europe either, until first she's gone to China. Each time Mother has mentioned this plan for her education abroad, Sanuk has made the same vow. She'll see the land of her father first before going elsewhere. In front of the mirror she's vowed it, staring right at herself, watching her lips soundlessly proclaim her destiny.

"Well! *Here* you are! Good morning!"

Sanuk turns from the garden to her mother. It's not necessary to look around to see who has just brought such animation to her mother's face and such an outburst of welcome.

"Good morning, Wanna," the girl says without turning.

. . .

An extremely pretty Siamese woman, coming into view around the table, gives both Sanuk and her mother a respectful *wai*. Sanuk returns it listlessly, but not so her mother, whose skin, that telltale white skin, reddens into a blush as she *wais* back earnestly.

The pretty young woman, perhaps six or seven years older than Sanuk, refuses an offer of tea, but accepts a rattan chair facing the garden. She's wearing a Thai ruan-ton, both skirt and jacket of a soft maroon. The effect is striking yet subtle, the kind of thing Mother likes. And Mother says so.

"The Thai ruan-ton is lovely. Absolutely lovely."

Rustling the newspaper, Sanuk raises it in front of her face.

"Sanuk?"

She looks around the edge of the paper.

"Are the cramps gone?" Wanna asks in Thai.

"Yes, gone. They weren't bad this time."

"Good. Nahng Vera"—the pretty Siamese turns to Mother—"I brought the invoices. Perhaps we can do them here before going to the shop. A few are urgent."

Mother nods solemnly, having lost the fresh color of earnest welcome. "Have you checked the train schedule?"

"Are you going somewhere?" Sanuk asks.

"I thought I told you." Mother pulls off the glasses; they dangle at her prominent breasts. "In a few days Wanna and I are going up to Chiang Mai."

"Why?"

"Pakhoon says he's found some Shan bronzes."

"Which he hasn't."

Mother smiles. "You're probably right. But one of these days he'll come up with something. Then it'll be worth these trips."

"Nahng Vera," the young Siamese woman says, "we can leave from Central Station either at eight thirty or noon. I suggest eight thirty. At noon we'd have the heat."

"I dreamt of a crocodile, Mother." Slapping the paper down on the table, Sanuk is pleased to see both women, who've been looking at each other, turn to look at her. "I'm serious—a crocodile! It was big and horrible, but I didn't run. I stood on the bank of this pond and let it come right up to me."

"That's quite a nightmare," Mother observes.

To Sanuk the remark lacks conviction. Mother would rather stare at pretty Wanna. "It wasn't really a nightmare." Sanuk intends to pursue the subject. "It would have been if I'd been afraid, but I wasn't. But I think you were."

"Me?"

"You were in the dream, too. I can't remember all of it, but beyond the pond was a bamboo hut and you were standing inside, yelling and waving at me."

"I can imagine that's my role in your dreams," Mother says with a wry smile. "Warning and nagging." Now, with Wanna here, she's speaking only Thai.

"Sanuk?"

Reluctantly the girl turns toward Wanna.

"You should read *Chalawan*. It's the story of a princess loved by a crocodile."

"I've read it."

"It's very entertaining, very funny." Wanna laughs. It is the familiar Siamese laugh: soft, carefree, superficial. Sanuk hears it countless times a day in the corridors of school.

"I'm going now." Sanuk rises.

Opening her arms, Mother says, "Come kiss me," and gathers her in.

Sanuk feels warm lips on hers, wishing she could see the expression on Wanna's face.

"Be gone all day?" Mother releases her.

"Until late." She's watching Wanna leave the room. "We want to sketch the river at sunset."

"That late?" Mother, pursing her lips, seems to be visualizing the sun going down on Chao Phya River, on the klongs of Bangkok. "That's pretty late."

"I'll be back for dinner. I'll take a boat most of the way with Lamai."

"Sanuk," Mother says, using the nickname for the second time. "Darling." She hesitates, as if not sure what more she wants to say, as if at this morning separation she wants to make a memorable statement for Sanuk to carry through the day. The girl's accustomed to these parting remarks. Indeed, she looks forward to them, knowing at such moments her mother is concentrating fully on her.

"Once you go abroad and see what's there, you'll understand why I so want it for you."

"I already understand. You want me to have a good education." Sanuk waves her hand to encompass everything. "And to see the world you came from."

"Is that so bad?" Mother asks with a smile.

"Of course not. I want to see it." Sanuk would like to add, "After I see Father's world first."

Wanna has returned with a briefcase, and as she opens it and spreads invoices on the breakfast table, Sanuk comes alongside of her and says, "Wanna, have you read *Phra Ahbai?*"

The pretty woman smiles brightly. It's the Siamese way of showing embarrassment; obviously she hasn't read *Phra Ahbai.*

Pleased, Sanuk explains that *Phra Ahbai* is a romantic poem by Suthorn Bhu. "It's about a prince and the daughter of a powerful giant. You really should read it." Her own malice shakes her, but Sanuk adds anyway, "It's not very funny, but it's one of the greatest poems in *your* language."

Wanna *wais* goodbye. It is never clear to Sanuk if the woman hates or merely feels indifferent to her. Probably indifferent: the Siamese way. Sanuk feels herself smiling tightly.

Turning to leave the room, she glances back at Mother, who is regarding her with a hurt expression—obviously her daughter has just been rude.

Good. Rude. Good, Sanuk thinks, walking through the house. Going past the mynah bird, she waves at it. Taksakan screeches out, *"Choei!"* Sanuk laughs, but then sees Nipa hurrying toward her with something wrapped in banana leaves.

"*Choei,*" the woman mutters. "That's good advice."

"You're the one who taught it to him."

"If that bird says anything, best it says *Choei*. Here." Nipa thrusts the package into her hand. "Gai yang for lunch."

Sanuk shakes her head. Barbecued chicken is her favorite dish. Those two old women will persist until she's fat as a pig. Chamlong wouldn't like that. If Mother goes on a trip with her pretty Wanna, I'll be left in the house with three old women: Nipa, Ah Ping, and Cook. Sanuk leaves the house sighing at the prospect.

Past the garden and terrace, she reaches a stepped dock on the klong and waves at an approaching dugout. It's for hire, so she steps gingerly into it amidships and tells the rower her destination. The sun is hot on the water; the reflection makes her squint, but Sanuk won't wear a hat on the klongs. There is too much to see, even after years of familiarity with them. She wants the sunlight to beat down on her face, the stench of the canal to drift into her nostrils, the noisy activity along the banks to come straight at her, straight at her.

As the rower sets out on the klong at a slow but steady pace, Sanuk grips the gunnels of the boat and looks around. The water has been blackened by pollution to the color and consistency of oil, but some boys are swimming in it, diving from waterside houses built on stilts. Gray tin roofs crowd the banks. Houseboats, tublike with tin roofing, sit like fat worms on the canal, creating an obstacle course for the water traffic. To the left, in the distance, she sees one of the innumerable chedis rising above the greenery, its spire like a huge bright needle. At intervals along the bank she has a glimpse of fields behind the houses, for much of Bangkok is still in cultivation between the broad avenues and the crowded klongs. There are lotuses everywhere, some pink and some nesting on the paddy water like white doves. She notices women through huge windows that allow river breezes to blow through the stilted houses as through tubes. On the wooden verandas women are putting out laundry, washing aluminum pots, ladling water from fifty-gallon jars. She feels a sense of joy in the motion of the klong.

Motion ahead arrests her attention.

A mangy dog is panting on a dock. And to the dock a boat is tied. And next to the boat a woman is standing knee-deep in water with a naked baby in her arms. She squats and lowers the child into the klong for a washing. And at this moment Sanuk recalls something terrible she once heard at school. It happened upriver in a village near Nakhon Sawan. A woman was doing the same thing—dipping her baby into the water. But when the baby screamed and she pulled it out, only the top half was there. The bottom half was clenched in the shut jaws of a big estuarine crocodile, who blinked once at the woman and slid from sight into the river.

For the second time today Sonia Embree breaks into a sweat.

3   "LOVE GOES TOWARD love, as schoolboys from their books."
         As the boat approaches the Chao Phya River, she figures
Shakespeare must have known *everything*.

The klong here is filled with winter refuse, the oily water
stinking, its level low. And it'll get worse, she knows, until the rains of
monsoon flood the canals and freshen them.

"My man's as true as steel."

It's become a refrain, with a rhythm that matches the stroke of the
oarsman. "My man's as true as steel." Sanuk shades her eyes from the
glare to regard the high gray walls of Army Headquarters, which tower
above the waterside huts. Chamlong says the generals' homes in there
are built on tamarind-lined streets. He knows about such things. He
says at the Central Police Station they keep political prisoners in bamboo
cages. Does he make it up? "My man's as true as steel." She notices two
soldiers standing between huts on the canal bank. While her boat passes,
they study her, rifles strapped to their backs. Even after she's some
distance away, Sanuk can feel their male eyes judging her.

In the harsh sunlight what she sees alongside the boat has a kind of
kinetic energy, as if tin roofs, timber walls, hut stilts, and pots and pans
and crockery and woks and charcoal fires and strings of laundry and
spirit houses and bumboats and swallow-tailed *yang-yaos* are glittering
particles held together only for an instant—things interchangeable in
the flow of the canal under a sun that seems capable of shaking everything apart. It's unsettling but a sensation she welcomes. Such moments
absorb her into the life of the klong.

Approaching the end of the canal, her boat slips through a narrow
channel into the broad expanse of the Chao Phya. Other boats, heading
for floating markets, are loaded with fruit and vegetables. Many are
paddled by Siamese girls much younger than herself, their faces a brown
blur under wide conical hats.

"Love goes toward love," she murmurs under her breath, while the
boatman maneuvers along the east bank among water taxis and *rua rew*,
letting the huge rice and sand barges dominate midchannel. Now she
can see brilliant white spires and golden pinnacles ahead, the dazzling
first glimpse of Wat Phra Keo. Her pulse quickens—not in response to
such beauty, but in anticipation of meeting Chamlong there.

When the prow nudges into a dock, Sanuk pays her boatman, gives
him the package of gai yang for a gift, and gets out. Within a few steps
she finds herself in a crowded lane leading up from the river. There are
shops along the way, most of them selling religious articles, because
nearby is the old monastery of Wat Mahathat, where she's heard the
monks not only learn to meditate but to use the black arts as well. Girls
at school told her that. How do they know such things? The same way
Chamlong knows about prison cages and Siamese generals? Two monks

in saffron pass her. Both are young enough to remind her of the bhikkhu novice who took rice from her this morning. Has he remembered her in his prayers? He promised, but young men don't always keep their promises.

Perhaps there are ways to see that they do.

On impulse Sanuk changes her immediate plan and turns down a tiny lane, just before the approach to Wat Mahathat. All along the dirt path are canopied stalls with racks of terra-cotta medallions laid out for display. Shoppers bend over to inspect the amulets, while vendors watch them carefully. Sonia joins them, determined to find something to protect her from lies. After all, every Siamese girl wears an amulet for good luck. But so many rows—how will she choose the right one? Because without the right one, so it goes, she'll not be protected at all. In fact, if she selects the wrong one, she'll be more vulnerable to the lies of young men than she is even now.

Sanuk moves slowly down the row of stalls, hoping a medallion will catch her fancy. There's a surplus of Buddhist images, most of them seated—she knows they're for salvation—and almost as many replicas of former Siamese kings. She doesn't want any of them. Bending down, fingering the image of the god Ganesha, she wonders what its protective power might be directed at. Illness? Accident?

"See what you like?"

Sanuk looks around at the smiling face of a vendor—a dark, mustachioed face, topped by a black cloth tied like a sloppy turban. She returns his smile but withdraws her hand from the Ganesha.

"That's an Indian god, the Remover of Obstacles, Ganesha."

"I know." Sanuk wants to assure him she's not a fool.

But he dangles the amulet in front of her chin. "Indian gods are very popular, very strong. Believe me. What do you want one for?" His smile broadens. "Love?"

She stares at him. His face is too dark, too chiseled for a Siamese, his nose too long and pointed, his eyes too round, although he speaks perfect Thai. Perhaps he's a Tamil from India. Sanuk tells herself to leave, but she keeps looking at the amulets.

The vendor leans toward her conspiratorially. "It's for love. Don't worry, don't be ashamed. Such a pretty girl, worried?" His hand moves swiftly over the display and halts at a rack. With his lips puckered, as if in the effort of deep thought, he picks up something and thrusts it toward Sanuk. "This is what you need. Go on, look. Inspect it."

The small terra-cotta charm represents a woman sitting cross-legged on a lotus, holding a mandolin.

"The Goddess of Love," he tells her.

Sanuk tries to return it, but the vendor retreats behind his stall and raises his hands as if warding off a blow. "It's yours! It's right for you.

With the Goddess of Love around your neck, believe me, you're safe. Know what I mean? It's for you," he says briskly. "Twenty-five bahts."

"Twenty," Sanuk bargains.

The vendor's eyes roll. Then, shrugging in a gesture of hopelessness, he says, "All right. Twenty-three bahts. Here. Believe me, she'll protect you."

"What's her name?" Sonia gives him the money from a little bag tied to her wrist. But the man has already moved toward a new customer at the end of his stall.

Backing away to study the little charm, Sanuk feels foolish for having succumbed to superstition. Yet she halts at a stall farther on that sells gold and silver chains. In a few minutes she's bought a cheap silver-plated chain on which she hooks the amulet and draws it over her head.

A few years ago she wore another chain from which hung a little ivory cross. That was during the time she read some portion of the history of Jeanne d'Arc every day. Once, while looking in the mirror, Sanuk had murmured aloud, *"Finalement elle se décida à obeir à ses 'voix.' "* She didn't have the voice of Saint Catherine or Saint Margaret to listen to, so she listened to her own voice, which told her the fifteenth-century Church had behaved disgracefully in letting the Maid go horribly to her death. In protest Sanuk stopped wearing the cross, and nothing her outraged foreign teachers at the convent school (the Siamese teachers stayed out of it) or her mother could say or threaten had changed her mind. No more crosses, no more crosses around my neck! she declared. Sanuk had kept only the one she herself had made from two twigs—like the cross offered La Pucelle at her death—and it was safely hidden in the locked cabinet.

Of course this amulet is a silly purchase, she tells herself now.

A charm won't protect her, will it? Yet it's possible she doesn't want protection. What she really wants is to live. If living means risk, then she's ready to risk. "I am!" she says aloud and glances around to see if anyone has noticed. Sanuk raises one hand to touch the charm on its chain inside the tight yellow cheongsam.

• • •

There's time to kill before their meeting at Wat Phra Keo, so perhaps she ought to go to the university, as she told Mother. It would be like telling the truth. Sanuk passes by the narrow gateway of Wat Mahathat, where monks plod in and out like old bulls from a paddy field (it's a comparison a Siamese classmate once made). She emerges from the dusty lane onto the vast oval expanse of the Pramane Ground. After the shops and crowds, this broad empty space of the Royal Field is dazzling under sunlight. On weekends most of it is covered by makeshift stalls where peasants bring their produce and thousands come to buy. She's come often with Mother, and they've had fun here, but now it's rare for Mother to take time for such things.

Today all that occupies the parched grass are knots of children trying to get their small bat and dragon kites into the breezeless air. They won't do well until March and April when the wind rises prior to monsoon. Philip once bought her a snake kite, and the two of them, along with Mother, came here to fly it; laughing like crazy people, they never got it ten feet off the ground.

Sanuk smiles at the memory. She wishes for the winds of April, even though they'll be blistering hot. This year she'll definitely watch the kite-fighting contests. If Philip returns by then, she'll bring him along. Maybe the three of them will come to see it all: the hawkers, the bands, the contestants struggling with their kites. Some of the men have partic-ipated for many years. She once met one, an old farmer from Lopburi, here during the kite season. He led a dozen handlers who controlled a huge star-shaped male kite. The farmer had showed her how the little hook on his big kite catches the small female and pulls her back into male territory. He was a nice man. But last year when she and some classmates came, they blushed to hear boys make crude sexual jokes about male and female kites. And then a band played a dirge to express sorrow when the single handler of a female kite outmaneuvered the whole team of a favored male and their kite lost its wind, crashing to the ground. Sanuk and the girls yelled in triumph, but whenever the female kites were hauled in by the big males, no sad song was played for their defeat.

It's a man's world, she thinks. My man's as true as steel. She takes a shaded walk to the university. My man, my man's as true as true as true as steel.

Soon the stone lions in front of a white masonry wall come into view. Why must she go abroad for an education when she can get one here in this lovely, lovely place? But that's a long weary argument with Mother, nothing to dwell on. Not today. It's the ninth day of the month—therefore an auspicious day—but is it *truly* momentous?

Turning into the university grounds, Sanuk glances at the colonnaded gray buildings with their arches and double windows. Inside, in the workrooms, students are sketching from casts or modeling from clay. The thought of going in there on this momentous day is tiresome. What can she possibly say to those giggling girls and those boys whose idea of *sanuk* is to drop insects down someone's back? She feels superior to them. Her own life seems on the verge of great happenings. Jeanne d'Arc—With disdain she glances at the classrooms. If only she could somehow express her feelings! Fortunately, at the end of a brick wall she notices Lamai sitting alone on a stone bench, bent over a book. It's practically an omen on this momentous day: Of all people she could meet, she has come upon one who really matters.

Sanuk rushes up with a shouted hello that startles her friend. A small heart-shaped face looks up squinting from the book. Lamai moves on the bench to make room. "You look breathless. Has anything happened?" She pats the bench.

"Nothing. Perhaps nothing ever will." To emphasize those deliberately cryptic words, Sanuk yanks out the new chain with the amulet. "Look at my Indian Goddess of Love."

"Where did you get it?" Lamai fingers the little piece of terra-cotta.

"At the Amulet Market."

"How much?"

She knows Lamai's a good bargainer. "Fifteen bahts," Sanuk lies.

Examining it more closely, the girl nods judgmentally. "All right for fifteen." Lamai lets go of the amulet. "Why do you need a love charm?"

"Everyone needs a love charm," Sanuk replies airily.

Lamai looks down at her book with a frown.

"Well?" Sanuk regards her friend closely. "Come on. What's wrong?"

Lamai looks sideways at her. "I'm getting married."

"Are you joking?"

"At the start of the Rain Retreat, I'm getting married."

"In a few months!"

Lamai puts aside the book; one hand plucks anxiously at the buttons of her blouse. Her small boyish thighs and hips have plenty of room in the blue sarong she wears. In a matter-of-fact way she tells Sanuk that the boy works for his father, who owns a rice-milling plant. His parents are friends of her parents. She has known this boy since they were five years old. "They live in a house across the klong from us," she explains, touching the book again. "I can see his room from mine."

"How much of you can he see from his—"

But Lamai, who usually shows a Siamese love of risqué remarks, doesn't respond this time.

"You've never mentioned him," Sanuk observes reproachfully.

"I never thought it was important."

Dismayed, Sanuk believes her. "Then you can't love him."

"I've known him all my life. Of course I love him." Lamai turns and glares a moment. "I don't *have* to marry him. I accepted because I just did."

"But why?"

"For one thing, our parents will be happy. And because he cares for me. I know he does. And because if I marry him—" Her voice trails off, as if completing the thought is difficult.

Sanuk waits, not yet able to believe that within a few months her good friend will be married. She can believe it of almost any other girl, especially the Siamese, who talk incessantly of marriage, but Lamai has always laughed at the idea. Lamai has claimed ever since convent school that someday she wants to work in the Archeological Museum.

"Because if I marry him," Lamai starts again, "he promises I can finish my studies."

"He promises," Sanuk repeats. She's been to Siamese weddings. In the morning the couple sign the official register. A priest blesses the wedding house and recites the five Buddhist commandments. People come to see the couple in their ornate crowns that are joined together by a flower garland. Seated, the bride and groom lean forward, elbows resting on a cushion, and clasp hands, over which guests pour water from a conch shell. There it is: marriage. At one ceremony Sanuk was given a pencil that opens like an umbrella and at another a scented handkerchief bearing the wedding couple's names, and today she is sick that her friend will soon wear such a crown roped to that of a boy she doesn't love. "So he promises," Sanuk repeats again, her voice filled with reservations.

"He's always been nice to me."

"But you aren't sure."

"How can anybody be sure of anything? Accept life as it is." She adds, *"Mai pen rai."*

It doesn't matter. The fatalistic shrug that signifies all is transitory. Ah, the Siamese answer for everything! Sanuk figures she must hear it a hundred times a day: *Mai pen rai.* It's an idea separating her with her Russian and Chinese blood from Lamai, a Siamese.

They sit in silence. Sanuk looks at the corrugated roofs of the campus buildings, at beds of red carnations, at the intricate designs carved above windows. She feels angry, helpless. "You better wait," she declares abruptly.

"Then he'll find someone else. And I'll have to find someone else too, and he might not want me to have a career." Lamai looks steadily at Sanuk. "This is 1948. But men still think it's the last century. They haven't got farther than the time when a queen could drown because her servants weren't allowed to touch the royal person."

Sanuk laughs. Spirited words from Lamai! "Your *khwan* is secure." Sanuk touches her friend's arm. "It won't get frightened and run away from *you,* dear friend. It has a good home." Sanuk rises, noticing by the tower clock that it's nearly time for her appointment at Wat Phra Keo.

"Aren't you sketching today?" Lamai asks, shading her eyes to look up. "I thought you and Pranee—"

"No. I have things to do."

"Concerning the Goddess of Love?" Lamai laughs, but almost instantly, as if realizing what that might mean, she starts to frown.

Waving goodbye, Sanuk turns to leave. She turns again at the sound of Lamai's anxious voice.

"Sanuk! Be careful!"

For a moment Sanuk considers staying with her friend. It would be easy. They'd go for tea and meet the others down at the river bank. With sketch pads in hand, they'd spend the day together, laughing and talking. They'd all be safe. Sanuk waves again.

Lamai shades her eyes. "You be careful. On the way home tonight I'll release a bird for you."

"Release it for yourself." Sanuk, turning, waves once more and laughs. "You're the one getting married. You need to build up merit!"

• • •

On her short walk to the Palace Gate, beyond which lie the fairyland pinnacles and pavilions of Wat Phra Keo, Sanuk feels her spirits lift. Her troubled response to Lamai's marriage becomes transformed into the exhilaration of someone who has escaped the unpleasant fate of a friend. Ah Ping calls her willful and, upon occasion, so have Mother, her teachers, her classmates, but at least she's never been accused of cowardice. She is her father's daughter.

In this untempered mood of defiance and optimism, buoyed by faith in possibilities, Sanuk enters the temple compound. Just through the gate, enshadowed in the overhang of a cloister, she halts and looks out upon the sunlit glitter of mosaics and golden spires rising into the depthless blue. Ahead stands the bot, where the Emerald Buddha is housed, and all along the balustrade and entranceway devotees have gathered, carrying long-stemmed flowers and sticks of incense, but Sanuk gives them scarcely a look, not expecting to see him among them. Instead, she turns down the covered gallery that surrounds the complex of buildings. Ordinarily she'd pause in front of the murals along the outer wall. They depict scenes from *The Ramakien*. But Sanuk walks past them with only a glance at one of her favorite murals: the abduction of Sita by the demon-prince Taksakan in his skyborne chariot. It is a brief look, for she's afraid of being late.

When, however, she reaches the closed north gate of the gallery, Chamlong is not there.

Sanuk glances around, bites her lip, and touches the amulet at her throat. Walking to the edge of the gallery, she looks at the passing visitors with their offerings for the Buddha. The curlicue ornaments at the end of the bot's roof beams seem to be wriggling like worms in the flashing sunshine. The roof tiles, reflecting the glare, are tiny explosive bursts of light that threaten, if she continues staring at them, to make her nauseated.

Returning to the gallery's dimness, she paces up and down, attempting to find something of interest in the murals, but they're only so much gold leaf and lovers gawking at each other and so many obnoxious creatures hurling spears from chariots—the foolishness of love and war—that she can't stand looking at them. Back to the edge of the cloister she goes, squinting at the pillars, the bot, the devotees—all of it driving her crazy. Everything looks flat, harsh, unsteady out there, and she's been a fool to come, a fool!

Then she sees him, ambling along the opposite end of the gallery. He's accompanied by another young man, who clamps one hand to the side of his face, as if in pain.

But her attention is all for Chamlong, who wears a plain white shirt and Western-style black pants. As usual, he affects *mai rieb roi*—a fashionable sloppiness. Even so, he has come. . . .

· · ·

The two young men don't increase their pace when they see her. Chamlong shuffles along, holding his companion's free hand, in the Siamese way, and his face expresses studied indifference.

Oh, she knows him! Sanuk refuses to take one step forward to meet them. But when they have almost reached her and Chamlong smiles, she takes a step forward.

"Been here long?" Chamlong drops his companion's hand.

"I just got here," Sanuk lies. She can't take her eyes off Chamlong, attempting to validate the image of him she's been carrying around since last they met, two days ago. His eyes are close together, giving him a haughty look; his entire face, with its straight mouth and nose, seems pared down, only essential lines to it, like faces Sanuk has seen in old Siamese paintings. There's no softness; he has a rather prominent chin, but small ears, a face without curves. And for the first time—the very *first* time, which surprises her—Sanuk notices deep lines at the corners of his mouth, as if the skin's stretched too tight. With relief and disappointment too, she realizes he can't compare with the Chamlong of her imagination.

They've said nothing, and she's aware that the boys have avoided looking directly at her. They're pretending an interest in the murals.

Chamlong's companion, holding his hand against his cheek, exclaims, "I hate them! They're painted with chemical colors, they aren't natural. The perspective is Western!"

Chamlong laughs at the other boy. "He read that. That's what he does. He reads something and makes it his own."

The boy shrugs in acknowledgment of an opinion he accepts.

"This is Somchai," says Chamlong.

The girl stares at Somchai, who stares back. He's shorter than she and Chamlong. "What's wrong with his cheek?" she asks.

"Not his cheek," Chamlong says. "His tooth. Tell her about it."

Somchai grins wide enough for her to see blood inside his mouth. "I went to a dentist this morning."

"A Cantonese dentist," puts in Chamlong. "I told him not to trust those people. He should have found a Teochiu dentist."

Somchai, who wears a pressed sarong with his white shirt, frowns at this criticism. "There aren't any in my neighborhood."

"Go on, tell her," Chamlong says, for the first time giving Sanuk a direct look.

"This Cantonese dentist works out of a barber shop near Triphet Road. He had me sit on a stool and hold the tools he took from this biscuit tin. The stool was propped against a wall, and a good thing too, because when he started to saw the tooth off—"

Sanuk grimaces, holding up her hands. "Stop!"

"Go on," Chamlong tells him placidly.

"My head was going back and forth while he sawed with this little kind of saw he had—"

"Stop!"

"I thought my head was going right through the wall—"

"Stop it! I don't want to hear!"

"When he got it sawed off at gum level—"

Sanuk claps her hands to her ears and glares not at Somchai but at Chamlong, who, starting to laugh, thinks better of it and frowns instead.

"I'm going to walk around," she announces, turning away from them. They follow when she sets out down the gallery. "I want to see the Kinnaris," she tells them, which brings a groan of annoyance and frustration from Somchai.

"I don't like Siamese temples," he declares. "Anything good they copy from us Chinese. Anything bad is their own."

"I want to see the Kinnaris," Sanuk repeats coldly. They have come out from the gallery into the heated light of the flagstoned compound.

"It's too hot," Somchai complains.

Sanuk looks for a reaction from Chamlong, who seems to have none. This annoys, then enheartens her. Perhaps his silence is penitential. Perhaps he's ashamed of having forced upon her the nasty details of his friend's dentistry. So while they head for the marble terrace, Sanuk turns to Somchai. He's dropped hand from cheek, but still grimaces in pain. "Is Chamlong really your friend?"

"Why?"

"I don't know. To be his friend you'd have to be patient."

"Would I?"

"For one thing," Sanuk continues, wanting a touch of revenge for having waited so long, for Chamlong's show of indifference when they met, for the tale of Somchai's tooth, "he thinks he can do everything."

"What does he think he can do?"

Sanuk smiles at him slyly. "He thinks he can play Push Hands Tai Chi."

Somchai narrows his eyes.

Sanuk points a long finger at Chamlong. "He *says* he can."

"Him?" Somchai grins, showing a crimson line of dental blood between his lips. "He can't even get a kite into the air. How's he going to play Push Hands?"

Chamlong yells out, "I'll show you!" There on the flagstones, not far from the entrance to the bot, where devotees are filing in with offerings for the Buddha, the two boys play Push Hands. Standing close to each other, they touch elbows and forearms with the backs of their hands, rolling their arms about in ceaseless motion, until Chamlong suddenly pushes on Somchai's elbow—gently it seems—but with sufficiently directed force to throw him off balance and nearly make him fall.

"Watch out," Sanuk warns, as a uniformed guard starts their way; the two boys stop playing and look. Quickly the trio scoots up the stairway to the platform, vanishing from the guard's view. They stroll over to a Kinnari—a gilded statue of a mythic creature, half bird, half woman.

"Kinnaris live in a magical forest in the Himalayas," mutters Somchai, holding his cheek again.

"See what I mean," scoffs Chamlong. "He reads something and has to tell the world about it."

Sanuk thoughtfully appraises the womanish hips and breasts of the creature, its clawed feet and long jaunty tail. "What do they do in the forest?"

"Make more Kinnaris," Somchai says with a grin. It is, in fact, a leer.

This boy with his anguished expression, with his bloody mouth, and now with his leer is terrible, Sanuk thinks. She wishes she hadn't worn the tight cheongsam. Why did she do it?

But in the midst of morose analysis, Sanuk hears something wonderful: Chamlong is telling his friend to meet them later at the compound entrance.

"You two want to pray to the Buddha?" Somchai replies sarcastically. "Go ahead. Gain merit." He stalks off.

Next thing Sanuk knows, she is walking beside Chamlong down the terrace stairway toward the bot. "Where are we going?" she asks, trembling.

"You know."

"But why did you bring *him?*"

Chamlong frowns as if disappointed by her asking such a question. "You can see how he feels. I couldn't leave him when I saw him that way, could I."

Sanuk is silent, absorbing his compassion, her own selfishness. Apparently, however, Chamlong feels the need of more explanation. "And we're on the same soccer team."

"I didn't know you played soccer." Sanuk has always been impressed by boys who play soccer. Often, from afar, she has watched them in their colorful shorts on the playgrounds of Bangkok, running tirelessly after the pummeled ball. "Do you play for a team?"

"Of course I play for a team. I play for the Bangkok Friendship Society," he tells her with a smile of pride.

Sanuk has heard of the Bangkok Friendship Society—a Chinese gambling club where men go to drink and lose their money.

There's no time, however, for her to contemplate Chamlong's association with such people, because the bot entrance is ahead. Removing their shoes, they're suddenly inside the temple itself, where the small green-jasper Buddha, dressed in its solid gold robe for the dry season, sits high on a stepped pediment above the seated worshipers, many of whom, holding bunches of flowers, are bent forward in prayer with their heads against the marble floor.

Coming from the hot glare of noontime into this dark nave, smoky from incense and lit only by candles, would be enough to bring Sanuk into a contemplative mood, to say nothing of the temple itself, for she has never entered a Buddhist temple without awe (although surreptitiously, when she sits on the floor, feet pointed respectfully away from the image of the deity, she always manages to cross herself and mutter a Hail Mary). Sanuk has always found irresistible the sweet faces of Siamese Buddhas. Their look of calm acceptance draws her deep into her own mind, into a place filled with roiling smoke and indistinct shapes, which she feels must be the enduring self, perhaps the soul known to Jesus or the *khwan* that the Siamese secure to the body with a piece of string. But today, seated on the cool marble floor, facing the tiered mosaic umbrellas and tiny trees of silver, Sanuk has yet another, more personal reason for quiet wonder: Chamlong is keeping his promise; he has brought her to the Emerald Buddha Temple as he said he would.

Glancing at him next to her, Sanuk wonders if his closed eyes and compressed lips really mean that he's dedicating himself to her. It is just wonderfully possible that here, in the presence of the Emerald Buddha, where to lie is to dare eternal damnation, this young man is saying, "I love this woman and promise always to love her."

That is what Chamlong has sworn he'd do today. Sanuk realizes she ought to have brought flowers or at least a joss stick for the Buddha. She has much to be thankful for, not the least of which is the end yesterday of her monthly period. Otherwise she'd not have entered the bot, not even with Chamlong to watch him fulfill his promise as he's doing now.

Once a girl at school, Catholic like herself, had bragged about going into a Buddhist temple while menstruating. Who would know? the girl argued. And anyway, it only counted if you were Buddhist. Sanuk had been shocked, but then the farang girl hadn't lived long enough in Siam to respect Buddhist ways.

Ninth day of the month. Auspicious, Sanuk thinks, as rising she follows Chamlong out of the temple.

For a while they stroll in silence, as grimly focused upon their individual thoughts as people who come for worship. Halting at last, turning to her, Chamlong declares, "I did it."

"Really?"

"Didn't I look like I did?"

"Your eyes were closed. That's true."

"I swore my—what I felt—in front of Buddha."

"So you did it." She's about to add, "I'm happy, I'm proud you did," when something occurs to her. "But you don't believe in Buddha. How can a promise to Buddha mean anything to you?"

She watches the corners of his mouth tighten.

"Don't you think a promise means anything to me?"

"Yes, but—You told me you don't believe in God, in things like that. So what can a promise to the Emerald Buddha mean?" Disliking the rigor of her own logic, she adds quickly, "At least you did it."

"Yes, I did. I did it for you. And I'd do it again, too." Now that his friend's gone, Chamlong seems more communicative.

Sanuk smiles at him. "I'm glad you did."

They stroll, barely glancing at the wiharn with its glitter of porcelain and at the library, at the pantheon. They stroll with heads bent as if deep in thought. At last Chamlong turns, his face contorted by so much emotion that Sanuk is fearful.

"Then you'll come with me today?"

Glancing at the flagstones, then at him, Sanuk says, "I haven't said I would."

"But you will?"

"When?"

"Today. Today, like we said."

"I didn't say anything like that." Sanuk turns away and squints at the tall chedi to the east, covered with gold tiles that seem to writhe in the sunlight. She looks hard and turns farther, as if blotting him out, as if this total absorption in her surroundings will discourage him. She wonders if he'll turn and leave or if he'll stay and argue. Because in truth, now that she tries remembering, she did make something like a promise: If he swore his love for her in front of the Emerald Buddha, maybe she'd go with him wherever he said.

To her relief Chamlong offers no argument.

She has no idea what will happen now, but whatever destiny had in store for them here, in this place, has been fulfilled. She's thinking of the entire day that way—as the special and profound working out of their mutual fate. Without exchanging a word, they return to the main entrance, where they find Somchai sitting on the marble edge of the gallery, holding his cheek with the palm of his hand.

As they approach, Somchai rises and without warning shouts an old Siamese aphorism beloved by drunken men at the gaming tables: "A woman is the hind legs of an elephant!"

Without hesitation Sanuk shouts back through the hushed temple air: "A grown man's a child; a woman's a mother who must care for him!" And the girl wishes that Ah Ping, who once taught her the Chinese saying, could be here now to enjoy along with her the scowl passing across her opponent's face.

4   STANDING AT THE rail of the water taxi, they watch Somchai hurry past the floating dock into a swirling crowd. He vanishes, still holding one hand to his cheek. She wonders if pain made him hate her so much. Or perhaps he wanted Chamlong to himself. The way he took Chamlong's hand, when they left the temple and strolled down to the river, made her wonder if his feelings for Chamlong went beyond friendship. Of course, it's natural enough for two boys or two girls to hold hands, but with Somchai it's somehow different. Usually it's just a lazy holding on to someone as you walk, but she noticed that Somchai twined his wrist around Chamlong's, snaking their arms together, getting more contact. She's aware of her own jealousy, but awareness doesn't prevent her from hating Somchai.

Of course Chamlong didn't seem to notice the boy's interest in him, or at least he was indifferent to it. Maybe he doesn't think it's unnatural. What would he think, however, if she told him about standing in a bedroom doorway years ago and watching her mother with another woman—but she'd never tell.

Now that they're alone, Sanuk glances shyly at him. The river breeze blows his unruly black hair; it's longer than her own. He slouches and ignores her as the crowded boat crawls along the shoreline, its old motor chugging like a weary heart.

Earlier, before leaving them, she'd heard Somchai mutter, "That girl you brought along—*pak talad*." Does she really have the mouth of a marketplace woman? Nobody has ever described the sound of her voice to her. Is it pleasant or is it really harsh as Somchai suggested? Can she ever ask Chamlong what her voice sounds like? What *can* she ask him? And where are they going now?

She notices sweat along his upper lip—it's like a mustache. She could wipe it off, feel the moisture on her finger, the soft wetness of his lip against the pad of her forefinger. What a thought! Anyway, at least she'd like to hold his hand the way Somchai did. But that would cause an uproar on the crowded boat—a boy and a girl holding hands. Two old women are frowning at her right now just for being with a boy. She glares at them briefly, as if to say, "Don't you know this is nineteen hundred and forty-eight?"

On impulse she reaches up and musses Chamlong's already mussed hair. This causes him to draw back, first startled and then embarrassed, as he looks around to see who has noticed.

Laughing, Sanuk says, "See what I'm capable of? I touched your head. Look at those old women. They think I scared your *khwan* so it'll run away."

Chamlong doesn't smile, but remains out of reach. He looks at the old women, at two silent men in farm hats, at a robed monk, all staring at him.

Sanuk is going to persist in the mischief. "Would you be afraid if I touched your head again?"

Chamlong smiles disdainfully but keeps his distance.

"I bet you're worried your *khwan* is scared because I touched where it lives. You're afraid it's run away and it'll stay away till you coax it back with prayers." Sanuk gives the outraged audience a fierce smile. "You'll have bad luck now. Better get the *khwan* back quick. Quick! Quick!"

At last he smiles—and for all her bold impudence she's relieved.

"Where do you get these crazy ideas?" he asks, stepping close again, under the glare of the old women.

"They're Siamese ideas, aren't they? Your mother must have told you about the danger of head touching." She knows from his own Chinese sister that Chamlong is the son of his father's Siamese concubine. This is her way of telling him such things don't matter.

Chamlong shrugs. "She believes those things. I don't."

"I know you don't. You don't believe telling a lie in front of the Emerald Buddha will send you to Hell." When his dark eyes narrow, she adds quickly, "Listen, I'm teasing. Let me tell you about a strange dream I had this morning."

But the water taxi is docking. The landing platform is just opposite Wat Arun on the Thonburi side of the river. The wat's immense prang rises like a glittering mountain; sunlight splinters against shards of porcelain inlaid on the column. People say Wat Arun is majestic, but Sanuk has never liked it. Following Chamlong out of the boat, she glances back at the sculptured gods, monkeys, and demons that clutter Wat Arun's huge sides.

As Chamlong leads the way, she walks fast to keep pace with him. "Do you think Wat Arun is beautiful? I think it's ugly."

"I never thought about it. It's just there." He gives her a smile. "I'm no college boy."

That's something she likes about him. Chamlong's a man of the world, even though he works for his father in a sundry-goods store. Chamlong is also a revolutionary—or so he claims—and the idea excites her. She is heading into the heart of Chinatown with a revolutionary born under the sign of the Tiger. Sanuk has memorized his astrological attributes from the Brahma Jati. Jupiter is in his heart, giving him pride and courage. Saturn and the Moon are in his feet; thus, like herself, he likes traveling. Love is important to him, and the Brahma Jati suggests he too may have a special mark in a private place. . . . The wickedness of such a thought makes her merry for a moment; she smiles at every face on the street. Then, to compensate for her silliness, she tries to think seriously about this boy. He seems ambitious to her and seeks justice. Unfortunately, like all people born under the Tiger, he'll encounter hardships in his life.

As the lean young man leads her deeper into the lanes of Bangkok's Chinatown, she conjures up a speech for her imaginary audience: "He swore his love in front of the Emerald Buddha, then pleaded with me to go with him somewhere, that very day too, but although he was almost in tears, I refused him." In sudden dread, Sanuk plucks at the short sleeve of his shirt. "Where are we going?"

For an answer Chamlong quickens the pace into a crowd that burgeons as they come to an open-air market. There are many tin-canopied provision shops along the way, most of them stocking various grades of rice in large wooden tubs with metal braces. But some of them feature more exotic fare (things pickled in glass jars or withered on cords, looking like parts of a body or like unborn babies) that Sanuk tolerates only when disguised in dishes at a banquet. She follows Chamlong through the crowded dirt lanes, dodging fishy water thrown from doorways. In his haste to get somewhere—where?—Chamlong bumps into a fishmonger who is weighing fillets of grouper on the hook of a hand-held metal pole. The dangling iron balance slides down the rod, nearly spilling the grouper out of the scale. Enraged, the fishmonger shakes his fist at Chamlong, who gives him a low mocking bow.

Sanuk laughs, delighted by his boldness. She wants to take his hand but doesn't dare, not even in a crowd too intent on food to notice what she does. Frogs leap about helplessly in netted bags; live perch, their gills laboring, lie in round bamboo trays; and butchers carve up hog guts for jostling housewives. The air, pierced by shouting, clouded by charcoal smoke, is pungent with the death smell of animals; and for a little comfort in the midst of so much odor and motion, she finally reaches out and grabs his hand.

At first his fingers stiffen in hers. He turns, their eyes meet; the tension softens within the closed warmth of their hands. Sanuk, feeling giddy from sudden joy, lets him lead her out of the market din into a quieter part of Chinatown, where they pass clothing stores, pawnshops, restaurants.

"Won't you tell me where we're going?" she asks.

"There!" Instantly he drops her hand.

Among small restaurants is an even smaller temple, its interior, lit by a single light bulb, is filled with the red color of Good Luck, stacks of joss stick boxes, a lot of folding chairs, some of which are occupied by old men chatting, and farther back, in the smoke, a row of sorry-looking wooden deities. She can't understand why he's taking her there.

But he isn't. Chamlong moves beyond the temple entrance to the next-door restaurant, where sausages and smoked fowl hang in front of the bare-topped tables. On one table lottery tickets, tied in bundles, are displayed under glass covers. Chamlong beckons with a scooping motion at a small boy, who rushes up, holding his round "melon-skin" hat to keep it from falling off his head.

"Give me five, no, six tickets," Chamlong tells him.

"Five's a luckier number," puts in Sanuk.

Chamlong takes six.

So he's stopped only to get lottery tickets. But again she's wrong. Paying for the tickets, Chamlong leads her from the street into the back of this restaurant.

A man, reading a newspaper at a far table, looks up and smiles faintly.

"Am I late, Chin Yin-nan? Sorry I'm late," Chamlong says with an insouciance that suggests he planned to be late. Drawing up a chair, he sits next to the man, who stares questioningly at Sanuk.

"Don't worry about her," Chamlong says. He motions for her to sit down too. On the nearby counter a small radio is blaring tinnily in Thai.

"Notice what's on the radio?" Chamlong says. "A month ago that was a Chinese station." When Chin fails to respond, Chamlong glances around at the empty tables, at the old man asleep in a chair behind the counter, head propped back against the wall. "Listen," Chamlong says, leaning forward and speaking in a lower voice, "she's not like other girls."

At this instant Sanuk wants to embrace him for defending her.

Chin stares at her with cold, appraising eyes.

"Actually, she's a Shantung girl," Chamlong adds.

"My father was born there," Sanuk explains quickly.

His face narrow, his eyes narrow too and intelligent, Chin has turned to look at her closely, without modulation. "And your mother?"

"This girl is all right, Chin Yin-nan."

Sanuk doesn't even glance at Chamlong while he defends her, but stares evenly at Chin Yin-nan. Chin Yin-nan is older than Chamlong, perhaps as old as thirty, with a distinctly southern Chinese face: snub-nosed, bean-eyed, skin almost as dark as that of a Siamese. "My mother is Russian."

"Your father was from where in Shantung?"

"Jinan. And then Qufu." Sanuk nearly adds that her father had been a famous general in the twenties, but Chin might not believe her; the fellow looks skeptical. And anyway, she's ruefully aware that the Nan-yang Chinese of Southeast Asia know little about mainland history. Even Chamlong, with his professed love of revolution and his interest in war, had not heard of General Tang Shan-teh.

But there's no need to defend herself further; she is forgotten as the two men lean toward each other to talk in whispers about politics. On those occasions when she strolled with Chamlong through the covered galleries of Wat Phra Keo, he told her all sorts of things about politics: how Siamese gangs like the Black Elephants and the Tusks and Bud-dha's Disciples were in the hire of the government, which actually paid them to put up anti-Chinese posters all over Bangkok; how the government and the Chinese people were heading toward confrontation in the streets; how the Chinese in this country would have to be militant to survive. Sanuk always wondered if she could believe him. She felt he might be exaggerating the danger when he described such grim possibilities: The Siamese government intending to further restrict the Chinese from buying land; the Ministry of Commerce planning to revise the system of rice trading, so that only Siamese companies can mill and grade rice; Siamese traders taking full control of meat and tobacco marketing once anti-Chinese policies go into effect; Prime Minister Phibun squeezing Chinese merchants dry and then making coolies of them. That sort of thing. But here Chamlong sits with this older man and talks with confidence about similar things. They are speaking now of education in Bangkok. In the future the Chinese language won't be allowed in classrooms. The Ministry of Education will refuse to let new Chinese schools open, and the old ones will be subject to police inspections. That simply means the government will conduct humiliating raids on Chinese schools.

Frequently Chamlong glances at her, as if seeking her response to his familiarity with the older man. Am I important to him? she wonders, picking up odds and ends of their conversation. Something now about Mahachon closing. That's a Communist publishing house in Bangkok.

Once she overheard Mother discussing Mahachon with farangs one evening at dinner. A British banker declared, "Mahachon is a force for anarchy in this country. God knows, Siam doesn't need Red propaganda to add to her other problems." And now Chin says that the government has closed the publishing house and its chief editor may be in police custody.

Chamlong orders tea and sweet-lime rice cakes from another small boy in a black skullcap. Waiting until the child is out of earshot, Chin explains that the *Chuan Min Pao* is still publishing, and although it's not a Communist paper, at least it's against the Kuomintang. The Prime Minister won't shut it down, because Chinese politics in China is of no concern to him. To him the Chinese Civil War is strictly Chinese: Kuomintang against Red or White or Blue makes no difference. What Phibun cares about, so Chin claims, is what the Chinese do here in Siam and only in Siam.

This is politics, Sanuk thinks; this is real. Admiringly she gazes at the two men, proud that one of them is Chamlong, whom Chin insists on calling Ho Jin-shi—in Chinese, the Golden Dragon. Her man as true as steel is the Golden Dragon.

"Where is your friend?" Chin suddenly asks him.

"Somchai doesn't feel good today. He went home. He's got a bad tooth." Chamlong, grinning, makes the motion of sawing at his mouth.

"I don't feel good either," Chin admits. "Something I ate."

"We better forget about Somchai," Chamlong says.

"How so?"

"Somchai won't use a Chinese name. Not even with me. He's only Chinese until he has to prove it. If there's trouble, he'll go back to being Siamese. What's our old saying? 'A thousand friends will eat with you, but hardly one will die with you.' "

Sanuk doesn't say what she knows: that the proverb is not Chinese but Siamese.

Eating a rice cake, she looks idly around the tiny restaurant and smiles at the boy leaning against the wall, his black cap worn in a straight line above his solemn eyes. She hears her companions discussing ex–Prime Minister Pridi, who, it is rumored, has fled to China, where he hopes to regroup his political forces to someday regain power in Siam.

"We need him now!" Chamlong exclaims, banging the table loudly enough to awaken the old man behind the counter.

In a cold voice Chin says, "Watch yourself."

Chamlong glances sheepishly at Sanuk.

"Where Pridi is shouldn't concern you. Don't talk about him, don't mention his name. And don't defend him in public. We don't want you thrown in jail. Is this understood?"

Chamlong nods glumly.

During a long silence Sanuk decides that she doesn't like Chin Yin-nan. He has just bullied Chamlong, who did nothing wrong, who merely showed passionate concern for the fate of a pro-Chinese patriot. With this decision Sanuk feels a new sense of her own understanding of people—enough to judge them by their actions under stress. Abruptly she asks Chin Yin-nan what his astrological sign is. Startled by her sudden intrusion into his world, he nevertheless tells her that he's a Horse. She might have known. The Horse has a bad temper; he won't admit his weaknesses and aims higher than he can reach. He hates traveling. And he is not interested in love. No, she can tell that this Horse is not interested in love.

While she is mulling over the consequences of Chin's sign, the two men talk again, this time of Chamlong's cousin, someone who is coming from Canton. She pieces together some information: This cousin is a journalist who will be writing political pamphlets here as soon as the presses of Mahachon are relocated. When he reaches Bangkok, Chamlong will hide him until the Communist Party can find him a permanent place to stay. It occurs to Sanuk that Chamlong's cousin wants to move cautiously into the world of Bangkok; that's why Chamlong is so important—his cousin will trust him.

Politics. Intrigue. Danger.

Today, Sanuk thinks grandly, I am witness to a meeting between men who fight against oppression. She smiles at Chamlong who has taken the name Ho Jin-shi, Golden Dragon. She watches Chin push aside his plate with a half-eaten rice cake on it.

"Be careful around your father, Ho Jin-shi," he says.

"Don't worry."

"I do worry. If he finds out about everything, who knows what he'll do? How did you get off work today?"

"I told him I had to check the inventory of a ship at the dock. But every day for a week I've been slipping down there after work and doing the inventory bit by bit, so today I'm free. Don't worry. I can handle my father."

"All right, then," Chin says with a sigh. "But if you do something foolish and the police get into it, we won't help you."

"I know that." Chamlong glances proudly at Sanuk. "I wouldn't ask for it."

Chin belches. "It must be the shrimp last night."

Rising and motioning to Sanuk, Chamlong throws down a bhat for the tea and cakes. "Don't worry about me. And don't worry about my cousin either. When he gets here, I know what to do. Once on a visit a few years ago, he said to me, 'Little cousin, you're my favorite in the family. Your father and my father and the rest of them don't treat you right because with their capitalist mentality they look down on people who are struggling.' He said to me—"

"That's enough." Chin looks around anxiously, although the tables are empty. "Don't mention him again."

"Don't worry. I'd carry his name to my death if I had to." Chamlong smiles, as if he has just made this boast to an audience of torturers.

Thrilled by his words, Sanuk thinks of others: My man's as true as steel.

. . .

Leading the way out of the restaurant, he continues down the street without a word until, at the corner, he turns to Sanuk. He's smiling. "Chin Yin-nan likes you."

Sanuk doesn't know what to say. Obviously she'd been brought for an examination; she's annoyed at being appraised by someone she doesn't know. Yet it means that Chamlong is serious about her.

After they walk awhile, this time abreast, Chamlong says, "Chin Yin-nan was a soldier in the Free Thai Movement."

"My stepfather was in the war. He was a hero in Burma." She's not sure this is true, but the words have a ring to them.

"Oh, the farang," Chamlong says disdainfully.

"I think he's coming back to Siam. If he does, you must meet him. Being a soldier, he could help us."

Chamlong halts. "We don't want farangs in this." As if gripped by that bad possibility, he stares down the street. Finally he turns toward her, and Sanuk can see his lips trembling. "Well?" he says.

She doesn't understand what he's asking. Or rather she understands but dreads answering. Ever since leaving Wat Phra Keo, she's dreaded this moment, when he would say, "Well?"

"I'm not sure," Sanuk tells him lamely.

Chamlong moves back from the street, out of traffic, into a covered arcade, along which a series of cubicles serve as clothing stores. "I kept my promise."

Reaching up, Sanuk fingers the amulet. "Not today."

"I kept my promise," he insists doggedly.

"But not today. I have to . . . think about it."

"I meant what I promised."

Lifting her eyes, Sanuk is shocked by the hurt look in his face. "I know you meant it."

"Do you feel the same?"

"Yes. I do."

"Well, then, let's decide on today."

Sanuk looks around, as if fearing that the crowd, intent on other business, is awaiting her decision. Is it late? The sun is still high, a huge wash of light above the two-story buildings of Chinatown. "What do you want me to do?"

"Come with me."

"Where?"

"You know."

"But—do you know a hotel? I mean, do you know how to—" She won't, can't look at him. The amulet gets large against her fingers.

"You mean, do I know how to get a room?" There's sudden power in his voice. "You don't tell a crocodile how to swim."

He's bragged before about women, and she has never known if he was telling the truth. But she wants to believe him, she wants him to be a man of experience. She can feel herself trembling from uncertainty. "I dreamt of a crocodile this morning. It didn't frighten me."

"Come on. Come with me. You got away from home today, so did I. I promised and did what I said I would. Now come with me like you said you would."

"I never said I would."

But when he steps forward, Sanuk comes abreast of him, falling into the quick, decisive rhythm of his pace. She doesn't think, won't let herself think. Mother's going North with Wanna. Philip's coming home. Field Marshal Phibun and his government are persecuting the Chinese of Bangkok. This boy beside her has linked himself with revolutionaries who fear he might do something heroic and get caught. Prison. Bamboo cages. Glancing at him, she lifts one hand and touches the amulet through the cheongsam. It cost too much; she lied about that to Lamai. As the Siamese say: *Mai pen rai.* She mustn't worry. There's no need for fear, and if there is, then she must be brave.

Her mother always says, "What set your father apart from other men in those terrible days was his independence. And he got it from his own father. Your father told me once, 'My father believed in a man doing his own breathing.' It was a dangerous idea in those days, because people weren't sure of themselves. That's what war does to people—destroys their self-confidence. But nothing stopped your father. He went his own way. He did his own breathing."

And a woman should do her own breathing, too, Sanuk thinks. She must show courage worthy of the daughter of General Tang Shan-teh.

• • •

They are standing in front of a three-story building in a lane somewhere off Chareon Krung Road, where signs are in Chinese.

In fantasy, during the past few days, she has imagined coming to a hotel with Chamlong, only it was a large hotel, something like the Oriental, with its name in large, embossed gilt plaster and also in neon.

But this place is grim, shabby—one of those notorious hotels the girls at school giggle about, as they pronounce the English word used by American soldiers in Bangkok after the war: "Short-time."

Chamlong is also frowning at the narrow doorway, at the peeling blue plaster, at the tiny window through which nothing of the hotel's interior can be seen, aside from a fading pink wall and a naked light bulb. Can he also have imagined what the hotel should look like?

Sanuk studies him. His self-confidence seems to shrink while they stand there. She's almost ready to turn and run away when furiously, as if in angry resolve or frantic decision, he grips her arm and shoves her toward the door. His decisive act relieves her. She goes with him willingly, but the sight of the hunched man behind the desk is daunting enough to make her pull back from Chamlong's guiding hand. In an instant she registers the hotel clerk forever in her mind: flaccid cheeks, pouched eyes, liver spots on the loose lips.

In another instant she sees something else, indelible for life: On one wall of the empty lobby—not a table, not a chair in the grim space—is a cheap calendar with a gaudy picture of Kwan Yin, sitting on a lotus, holding a vase and a willow branch. Sanuk feels her nails digging into the palms of her hands. Nothing can relax her. Certainly not when she overhears the desk clerk, in a whining tone of exasperation, demand the money now. Staring at the Goddess of Mercy, Sanuk waits and waits and it seems she's waited a long time before hearing Chamlong's voice, startling in its distant faintness, plead with her to come along.

Not daring to glance toward the desk, Sanuk follows behind the young man's lean figure up a rickety staircase. Chamlong is carrying the room key attached to a foot-long board in one hand, some towels in the other. She remembers hotels in Penang, Kuala Lumpur, and Singapore, when she went to those places with Mother. The towels were always in the rooms when they got there. Here the clerk gives towels at the desk, so anyone can see what's happening.

The humiliating tawdriness of it is almost enough to turn Sanuk round and send her rushing down the stairs, but up she goes, up, up slowly she goes. At the top of the stairs she takes a deep breath, as if the little climb has winded her.

Waddling toward them down the shabby hall is an old woman who, for a moment, terrifies Sanuk by her resemblance to Ah Ping.

"Food, sir? Drinks?" Her blouse is stained, her black pajamas held by a dangling rope around her ample waist. From the sallow light coming through a stairway window, Sanuk can see the woman's eyes: glazed, unfocused, wet. "Drink? What kind, sir?" The woman persists, following Chamlong down the hallway. "Food? Drink for the girl?"

Turning abruptly, with a look of anguish, Chamlong thrusts a few bahts into her hand. "Here. Go."

"You want Mekong whiskey?" The bahts disappear into her pajamas. "Cakes for the girl?"

"Just—go!"

"The key," Sanuk reminds him, as they reach the room door.

Chamlong fumbles with the long board, as the old woman, watching, shows no intention of leaving.

At last Chamlong gets the key in, turns it, and opens the door.

"Sir, let me get you and the girl a bottle of Mekong."

Sanuk follows him into the room, then, turning, she closes the door fast on the woman's boozy face.

Without glancing at Chamlong, indeed, not daring to, Sanuk moves resolutely into the room. It's almost bare, save for a pillowless bed covered by a grayish cotton sheet, one straight-backed chair, and a waist-high old chest of drawers. There's a frayed parchment screen fencing off something in the corner. Sanuk peers around the screen at an open drain—the toilet—and a ten-gallon jar of water and a defective mirror in which her grim face looks like something rising from ocean depths. When she turns back into the room, Chamlong is sitting on the bed, hands gripped in his lap. The way he sits, the defeated posture of his spine and his bent head, suggests to a dismayed Sanuk that maybe he's never been in a "short-time" hotel before. She feels a tremor of sympathy for Chamlong—enough for her to sit quietly beside him.

• • •

In their mutual silence she becomes aware of the noisy street below, the jingling bells of samlors and the cries of hawkers, pots banging, the distant roar of motorized traffic on Chareon Krung Road. Mother's antique store is at the south end of that road, not more than a kilometer from here. What she can do now, she can just get up, Sanuk thinks, and walk out the door past the drunken amah and down the stairs past the soft-looking clerk and the tawdry image of Kwan Yin. She can hail a samlor and within minutes walk into the entrance of Siamese Arts Oriental. She can see Mother, glasses on, look up smiling from a large accounting ledger.

"I don't want to stay here," she says in a low, determined voice. Chamlong doesn't reply, doesn't seem to hear. "I won't stay here." Yet she stays beside him, her thigh almost touching his.

Then she feels something—a warmth—on the top of her hand resting on the bed. She looks down at Chamlong's hand covering hers. She feels the warmth of his fingers steal through her skin; the warmth seems to go right to the bone. She doesn't know what to think of his touch. The intimacy of it frightens her. Yet she feels better too. He is here, really here, beside her. They are here together. Taking a breath and withdrawing her hand from under his, Sanuk points at the door. "I think the old woman's out there, listening. Go see."

While Chamlong dutifully gets up and shuffles to the door, setting his eye to the keyhole, Sanuk wonders what to do now. Yet there isn't time for thinking, because shaking his head Chamlong returns to sit exactly where he'd been—assuming the same hunched posture, taking up her hand again, as if it's an object of comfort.

"My father says," he begins in a voice almost too low for her to hear, " 'Teach them how to eat, but don't teach them anything else—that way you have them.' He means his own people, the Chinese people. That's my father."

Not knowing what else to do, Sanuk squeezes his hand slightly.

"I don't want to be like my father. All I mean to him is the name. I just bear his name, that's all. I told him I'd like some education, but he laughed. 'Work,' he said. 'That's what I have you here for.' He never wanted anything for me." Chamlong glances sideways at her. "Until his Number One son died, he never once thought of me. But when Number One died, all he had was three daughters and me—his son with a Siamese woman he hadn't seen in five years. He came to our house and said to my mother, 'My boy's dead, so let me have Chamlong. I'll raise him like my own.' She couldn't refuse, how could she? So he paid her for me. I work for him. I'm his Number One now, but I hate him. Because you see, I want to do something with my life. I don't want to teach people only to eat so I can have them in my power. I don't want to be my father's son. I want—I don't know what I want." He turns and takes both of her hands in his. "Today at Wat Phra Keo, I meant what I said to the Buddha. I told him, 'This girl is my *khwan fa*. She is my *tee rahk.* ' "

Until this moment they've been speaking Chinese, but *khwan fa* and *tee rahk* he has spoken in Thai, in a soft voice that Sanuk understands must be the voice he used with his mother, a Siamese woman who taught him how to say something beautiful, to say "my beloved, my dearest love." Sanuk leans toward him, resting her head against his, feeling her cheek warm in the curve of his neck. He releases her hands, only to envelop her tightly in his arms. She can feel the tension in his muscles, the trembling in them.

For a time they remain this way, until her heart slows enough for her to think—to decide. "You did keep your promise." She draws away to study his face. "Go behind the screen. Go on. Come in when I call. Go on," she says, pushing him gently.

When he goes behind the screen, Sanuk's chest feels constricted, as if she can't get enough air. Rising, she takes a deep breath before removing the yellow cheongsam. Walking to the door, she listens for any sound;

satisfied, she returns to the bed and lies down. She's not ready to call him. Sanuk won't call him until she feels calm, until what is happening is clearer to her. Clutching the amulet with one hand, she moves the other along her naked hip, up her flank to the curve of one breast. Her breathing is slower and steadier now. She recalls the American movie she saw last year: *Gone with the Wind*. She understood every word of it, and for nights afterward she twisted and turned in bed, cupping her breasts and remembering Scarlett standing in the doorway—it was a doorway, she thinks—before Rhett lifts her and carries her up the long staircase. The amulet warms in Sanuk's hand, her breath slows.

So it's all right now, she tells herself. Trying for a steady voice, she calls out loud, "Come in."

She senses him appearing around the corner of the screen. He has halted to look at her. Slowly she releases the amulet and stretches both arms alongside her flanks. She turns to look at him. He too is naked. She watches, fascinated, as the lithe and muscular young man approaches the bed. Her eyes focus at his groin, at the balls round and tight and shiny, cuddled beneath the man-thing now emerging from itself out of a silky tangle of hair. The flaccid, rubberlike stalk, as he takes a step forward, begins to look like a weapon, a bludgeon, a thing to fear. He's so naked, she thinks, so nude. The momentary fear gives way to curiosity.

He has reached her. He stands beside the bed, above her, allowing the sight of her nakedness to stiffen him further. Without encouragement she reaches out, without thinking about it she reaches out to touch him there, one finger gently behind the head at the slit of which a drop of liquid appears like a glass bead. Her fingers surround him—for *this* is Chamlong, at the moment this is everything he is—and move in the unlearned motion of love, up and down, until she feels in the pads of her fingers a warm life, a deep, pulsing, muscular motion as he lengthens still more under her caress. She is quite ready to bend forward and sense the texture of him on her tongue, but Chamlong abruptly pulls free, impatient for action of his own.

Scrambling onto the bed, with gentle but firm pressure he eases Sanuk upon her back. Placing himself at her center, with both hands he brusquely parts her thighs—willing enough to be parted—and thrusts deeply.

She feels him enter. This is something she had wondered about in her bed on the hot moonlit nights of Bangkok, something she had considered dispassionately as nothing more than the nature of life itself. But at other times, thrashing about in the sweaty sheets of midnight, she had tried to visualize the thing vanishing into her body and thereby to imagine the sensation of it happening. Even so, she's not prepared for the reality, for the mindless, impatient ramming in, for the pain and surprise of it. After a few moments, she realizes that Chamlong has positioned himself squarely upon her, supporting himself on both elbows, his head resting against her right cheek.

Why my right cheek? she wonders, even while becoming aware of the steady tattoo of his body beating against her own. Clearly it is her task now to accommodate herself to that rhythm, but the motion of his body becomes erratic, faster. It's like a gunned motor in those cars that sound their sirens and clear the way for royal princes. His body is like that, a machine letting go. It lets go until she can't stay with it, but she lies there allowing the rhythm to run away with itself. And now, suddenly, she feels herself moving of her own accord, her body seeking its own rhythm. It seems, finally, that she has the rhythm, as if a rapidly beating heart is lodged between her legs, its pulse drilling new pleasure through her loins. But just as the tension mounts into what is unmistakably an ecstasy, just as her satisfaction approaches that which accompanies the watching of anything fill—like water rising toward the rim of a glass—Chamlong, above her, utters a little cry, as if in pain. He stiffens the length of his body and remains motionless. Now, like an emptied sack, he seems to collapse inwardly, and his shoulders, which Sanuk realizes she's been gripping, holding on for dear life, slowly become soft, almost womanish under her clutching fingers. His breath against her ear is gusty now; Sanuk feels his lips graze her cheek.

But he withdraws from her in a single, rapid motion—a thing so physical and definite, it feels to her as though he's ripped something from her self in this attempt to free his body from hers. His face, caught in the late sunlight from a window, is moodily contorted. In that instant Sanuk wonders what the look means. Suddenly she's left alone, far more detached from him than before their lovemaking.

Yet she feels triumphant.

Overcoming her shyness (made easier when Chamlong throws himself alongside her, one arm across his face, his ribs prominent with each quick inhalation of breath), Sanuk slides one finger down her belly to her groin and on the fingertip feels the warm, sticky wetness of her lover.

This is what she has done: She has stepped from one world into another. She knows she has; she knows it! The young man beside her, who has helped her do so, is her true, her steadfast friend, and she glances at him with deep affection. Only later, at least a whole day later, will she ask herself, Does he love me? And when the question arises, she'll recall with dismal vividness the moody expression on his face when he withdrew from her, and she'll brood upon the meaning of it.

But not now, not as minutes pass in the short-time hotel.

Rising, she hesitates in fear of his response to her leaving his side. But Chamlong remains with one arm thrown across his face. Turning from him, she goes behind the screen and splashes water on herself from the jar. Must the mirror distort her face so? She wants to see how she looks. Does she look different? Of course she does. She must.

To her imaginary confidante she says, "I wasn't afraid. Just a little . . . anxious. And I'm happy." If the girl questions her further, she'll add, "I liked it, too. It was wonderful. He's wonderful to me. Where? In a hotel. I can't tell you exactly where, because it's a secret, but a really beautiful hotel. You'd know the name if I told you—"

Will she cry? She feels a deep fatigue; her entire body feels loose and trembling. It occurs to Sanuk, while gazing at the twisted image in the mirror, that she left her cheongsam in the room, that she's naked.

Peering out, she's relieved to see that Chamlong has wrapped the sheet around his waist. He sits on the bed, leaning forward with clasped hands, as if in the grip of an important idea.

She asks him for her dress. Immediately Chamlong rushes to the screen and hands the yellow cheongsam around it.

Dressed, she comes into the room and finds him in the same position of deep thought. Yet turning to look at her, he smiles in a friendly way. Friendly, shy, perhaps grave. Is this what happens to men afterward? Now he, in turn, goes behind the screen and dresses, while she sits on the bed, hands clasped. She knows now why he'd been sitting this way. Like herself, he'd been thinking of the strangeness of everything—of this room, of their bodies, of nakedness, of the simpleness of it all really: Something in something, something in something going in and out. Nothing more. Amazing.

He joins her. Without touching they sit together on the bed, in silence, while the afternoon hubbub grows louder in the street.

• • •

Chamlong suddenly turns and says in a voice faint from shyness, "What are you thinking?"

"I think I'm . . . fine."

"So am I. You are"—he has difficulty forming the words—"different." He adds, "From other girls."

"Have you brought other girls here?"

"I never brought anyone here. I mean, not to this place."

"But you've taken girls other places?"

He raises one hand dismissively. "Nobody I liked as much as you."

Leaning clumsily forward, he kisses her on the cheek, and Sanuk knows in her heart that he's not a man of experience. It's in his clumsiness, in his need to put his clothes on, as she had done, behind the screen. And now she's glad of his innocence. Or rather she doesn't think it's important now. And they've finally spoken to each other, whereas for a while behind the screen, when she looked at her broken image in the mirror, Sanuk had wondered despairingly if they could ever speak to each other again.

"I don't want to hear about the other girls," she tells him.

"I won't mention them, ever."

Sanuk feels a surge of power sweeping her. The power has come to her somehow out of Chamlong's voice, its tone conciliatory and timid. To test this strange new feeling she says briskly, "Don't ever tell me anything about them."

"I won't. I promise."

In his voice she continues to hear her own power. "I hate this place."

"So do I."

"I hate the old woman and the clerk and everything. I hate the towels."

"Next time—" he begins, giving her a worried frown.

He's afraid there won't be a next time, she realizes, and the power surges through her again. "Yes," she says calmly. "Next time?" There's a savoring of the phrase as she speaks it. And her speaking of it, Sanuk notices, makes him smile with relief.

"Next time, I'll find a better place. I promise."

"I'd like that." Taking his hand, she rises and pulls him with her. "It's time to go."

When they reach the door and Chamlong opens it, the old amah is standing there, grinning at them, her glazed eyes attempting to focus.

"Mekong? Spring rolls?"

Chamlong brushes past her, but on impulse Sanuk opens her wrist bag, takes out a couple of bahts, and gives them to the woman.

Side by side they walk down the narrow staircase. Smiling up at them are two old men, but the clerk, waiting for the key, turns sullenly away after taking it from Chamlong.

• • •

The sun's brilliance has faded from the street when they reach it. The late afternoon light has a deep-water cast as it moves upon awning, tin roof, and plaster wall. Sanuk, walking close to Chamlong's side, notices a checker game against a wall opposite the hotel. Men are gathered around, watching the players hunch over a board on an upended crate. "I want to see." Sanuk crosses without doubting he'll follow. After they watch a few minutes, "Who'll win?" she asks him.

"The one on the right. If I had time I'd bet on him."

"Do you bet on a lot of things?"

He laughs, seeming relaxed now. "On everything."

She almost says, "Would you bet that I love you?" but that might be too daring, even for the man who has just taken her to bed. He has taken me to bed, Sanuk thinks in wonder.

They pass a store that sells joss sticks. The back of her hand grazes Chamlong's. Something joyous is happening to Sanuk as she looks above the street at laundry: long-sleeved sam foo jackets; stuck on poles out of second-floor windows, they look like headless birds in flight. Wonderful. Her hand again grazes his. It reminds her of water buffalo in ponds. They stand up to their round bellies in water, blank faces mooning at the world, their flanks grazing each time they shift weight, giving one another a kind of comfort. It's the same now, as she and Chamlong walk through Chinatown—the comfort each time their hands graze.

Everything interests her: the checker game; the laundry; an old man selling cigarettes from the top of a wooden box; deep-fried squares of bean curd strung for sale along a bucket handle. Wonderful. With fascination she watches an itinerant knife sharpener, who wears a battered panama hat, push a wheeled board on which a grinder has been bolted. And inside a little shop, within its shadows, she can see an old woman sitting opposite a letter writer to whom she's dictating a letter, maybe one going home to her family in China. Wonderful! It is all so interesting and wonderful. And at a large intersection, when a platoon of Chief Pao's police march past, Sanuk stares with equal interest, equal serenity, for it is all interesting, each thing in its way, the whole world. It is all wonderful.

· · ·

People did what we just did, she thinks, glancing at Chamlong. They did just what we did for all these people here to be born.

This is what it is, she tells herself, putting the back of her hand against his momentarily. This is love. This is what love means. "Where are we going now?" she asks.

"Let's get something to eat."

"Wonderful!" she exclaims and follows him to a street-side kitchen, where a vigorous man and his little boy are serving people at trestle tables. Sitting on stools, very close, Sanuk and Chamlong eat Hokkien mee. Ravenously she attacks the soupy mixture of shrimp and noodles; when the bowl is empty, her appetite seems greater than before. They order orr chien, but when they've finished every morsel of savory oysters and omelette, they want more—and end with three orders of poh piah, unable to consume the last spring roll.

"And I go home to a complete dinner," Sanuk declares with a laugh.

"How can we eat so much?"

As they smile at each other, Sanuk feels it's their closest moment of the day.

Walking slowly toward Chareon Krung Road, where she'll get a samlor home, they say nothing, but their hands often graze. At one corner Sanuk notices a little temple, beside which a woman is standing with a dozen or so bird cages. She has stationed herself here because people leaving the temple may want to gain merit by giving a bird its freedom.

"Wait," Sanuk tells Chamlong. She halts to study the little bamboo cages filled with birds, most of them finches. Smiling at him, she says, "I want to release two."

When she starts to open her leather pouch, he pushes her hand down. "I'll buy them."

Together they look for birds. "They must be male and female," Sanuk says. She notices a male with rose-pink throat and rump, white belly and wings, a brown-streaked tail. "That one."

Opening the cage, the woman holds its bamboo frame high until, with a blur of motion, a small bird flies out, darting into the air like a fluff of cloud in a storm.

"This one." Chamlong points to a gray-and-brown-streaked female.

When he has paid for the birds, Sanuk says again, "Wait. I have a friend getting married. For good luck—" This time she digs into her pouch, gets the money, and releases another female for Lamai.

Going on in silence, at the main thoroughfare she hails a samlor. Not until the three-wheeler has almost reached them does Chamlong say a word. Then in a voice thin from tension, he asks if they can meet tomorrow.

He does care for me, Sanuk thinks, telling him to meet her at the entrance to Silpakorn University at noon.

"There?" he asks. "Well, all right."

Is he disappointed? she wonders, getting into the samlor. Does he want to meet at a hotel instead? Or is it the idea of school, meeting me where he can't go himself? Love is complicated.

Seated, she looks at him standing in the midst of the crowd. Where can we go? Will he find a better place, as he promised? Does he really keep his promises? Can we do this . . . what we did today . . . often?

Courage. She tells herself *courage*, even while smiling at Chamlong as the samlor sets out. With a sense of deep pleasure she watches him raise his arm in farewell. My man's as true as steel. And Sonia Embree says to herself, in a whisper beneath the cacophony of Chinatown's streets, as she thinks of Mother and Lamai and women throughout Bangkok and the entire world, "Now I have a lover too."

5 Vera Rogacheva Embree stands at dawn in front of the Sal Phrapum, the Spirit House on her property. The wooden building, size of a doll's house, sits on a platform supported by an eye-level post—the Sal Phrapum, according to the Siamese, should be positioned so that people paying homage can look directly at its occupants, at the clutter of horses and elephants and human figures which inhabit the little white rooms, portico, and vestibule.

As usual, Vera brings flowers and a stick of incense for the daily offering. Silently, in the morning mist, she studies the deities or whatever the assemblage is—the Siamese have never explained to her what the Sal Phrapum represents, other than to say the Phi live in it—spirits of the area—some of whom might be the ghosts of people who once lived on this spot, or capricious spirits who come and go, like the one her cook once described: a creature with a mouth as small as a needle and the strange habit of whistling through it while sitting on a person's chest.

Vera has long since gone past the superstitions which accompany the tradition of Sal Phrapum; she has simply accepted the Spirit House as her own shrine, as if once again a girl in Petrograd, happily surrounded by icons purchased and prayed to by her family for generations. In one corner of the Spirit House she has even placed a tiny plaster Virgin in homage to that past, yet within recent memory she hasn't offered a prayer to it, and the daily offering of flowers and incense goes equally to all of them living there: horse, elephant, spirit figures, and Virgin. The truth is, Vera feels, she has finally lost Russia, all of it, even the nightmare of her trek across Siberia—although long habit still impels her to declare, "I am Russian." What she really is is a farang, just another foreigner uprooted by fate and deposited here, in this hot humid City of Angels.

So now she lays the flowers down and lights the incense in deference to the Lord of the Place, who in some mysterious way seems to reign over the destiny not only of the ground but of those who live upon it. What she believes hardly counts in the face of this Siamese conviction: Chao Thi must be made comfortable or else, as chief spirit, he'll bring harm to the household. To placate and honor him Vera had the Sal Phrapum constructed by one of the finest spirit-house builders in Bangkok; it is set sufficiently far from the main house so that no shadows fall across it and disturb its occupants. Vera slips her hand into the tiny doorway to rearrange two small dolls—a boy and a girl—bringing them slightly closer to each other. She has no idea who these two human figures represent; the stories vary. But somehow they protect people from evil on this property. Vera likes to think of them, however, as the General and herself, although she doesn't go so far as to talk to his "ghost"—a charge often made by Sonia, who won't believe for a moment that her mother doesn't stand in front of the Spirit House every morning and hold a conversation with her dead husband.

Vera glances across the lawn at some bushes that lead to a garden and a terrace of Chinese tiles where Sonia plays Tai Chi. Where the girl hasn't played Tai Chi for the last three mornings. It's disconcerting for Vera to look over there and fail to see, through a lattice of vine and leaf, her tall, lovely daughter in the quiet postures of an exercise they'd both inherited from a dead man they love.

No Tai Chi for three days.

Is something bothering Sonia? Ah Ping complains that the door of the girl's room is always closed, and yesterday, when the old woman called up "Breakfast!" without receiving a reply, she climbed the stairs and stood at the door and yelled, "Are you coming down, lazy girl?" and all she got in reply was an insolent "Go away."

Vera turns back to the Spirit House, where a coil of joss smoke whirls into a breeze from the klong. She had the Spirit House constructed so a Chinese *famille rose* porcelain plate could fit inside but not be removed. It's in there now, forming a background against which the human dolls, through their mutual power, cast a spell of protection around this property.

The Willow Pattern plate was once a gift from the General. They had seen it together in a Shanghai calligraphy shop that fateful summer of 1927. She knew the popular story of its design: It described the tragic fate of doomed lovers. She and Shan-teh hadn't been lovers themselves then. Days later, when they'd become lovers, he gave her the plate along with a political explanation for its design: It described the attempt of Chinese patriots to subvert their Manchu oppressors. As, in detail, Shan-teh divulged the esoteric doctrine of a secret society, Vera understood how extraordinary their relationship was becoming: this man was betraying one trust to create another; in a sense he was sacrificing honor for love. Only later would she recognize the whole truth: that Shan-teh considered this disclosure the smallest breach of trust because he had never fully believed in the tenets of the secret society which he'd joined as a young man. In his view the society had evolved from early protector of Chinese values into an organization nearly as oppressive as the Manchu. General Tang Shan-teh would never have sacrificed honor to love. Even so, the memory is still vivid of them sitting side by side on the bed, looking at the plate, allowing it to link them to each other in yet another way.

Thinking of the father brings the daughter to mind. Ever since Sonia learned of the impending marriage of her friend Lamai, she's behaved moodily. At dinner she's distracted, though at times, with a burst of energy coming from a secret hoard young women so often seem to have (Vera recalls it from her own youth), Sonia laughs and blushes and gives the impression of someone standing at the edge of great events.

Vera arranges the flowers in a fluted brass bowl, then taps the trunk of the little plaster elephant for good luck. In one of many incarnations Buddha was an elephant, so it's likely, Siamese friends tell her, an elephant in a Spirit House represents the Lord Buddha. Likely, but not certain. They aren't sure, they don't know, and what is exhilarating to Vera is their indifference to knowing. What can be the value, ultimately, of singling out anyone or anything for special praise, when nothing stands above what is next to it? A Theravada Buddhist once asked her that with a smile of such patience she felt herself to be a child. But later, studying the question without his strong presence there to influence her response, she wondered if it meant anything at all. For these people, at any rate, most distinctions are illusionary. That's the deepest the theology of most Siamese seems to go, in her opinion, and she, a product of Russian Orthodoxy, finds such simplicity both charming and dangerous, a source of comfort verging on sacrilege.

Turning, she faces a little grove of trees, most of them auspicious in a Siamese garden: tamarind, mango, and jackfruit. But to one side of them she's also planted, in an act of rebellion against tradition, a few frangipani trees. Pink, white, and yellow flowers are massed on the thin branches, a contrast of lushness and austerity. Siamese won't put a frangipani in a private garden; it's the tree of sadness because the Thai word for it, *lanthom*, closely resembles the word *rathom*, agony. Even so, King Chulalongkorn planted a whole orchard of them near the monument to his dead wife, the queen who drowned in a boat accident because her retainers were afraid to touch her royal person. Vera has memorized the awkward English written by the king and inscribed on the monument:

> To the Beloved Memory of Her Late and Lamented Majesty Sunandakumviratn, Queen Consort, who wont to spend her most pleasant, and happiest hours in this garden amidst those loving ones and dearest to her. This Memorial is Erected by Chulalongkorn Rex Her Bereaved Husband whose suffering from so cruel an endurance through those trying hours made death seem so Near and Yet Preverable 1881.

Each morning Vera repeats the words under her breath (perhaps this is what Sonia takes for a private talk with the dead) and envisions the plaque on the monument in the palace garden of Bang Pa-in. She has somehow turned those words into a lament for the loss of Shan-teh. Perhaps it's her way of "talking" to his ghost, as Sonia so obviously hopes she does each morning at the Spirit House.

But, of course, not even Sonia knows that the frangipanis are planted here as an act of grief. Grief to be grief must be private, Vera believes. Long ago, on the tundra of Siberia, after she had lost all her family to weather and war, Vera Rogacheva taught herself how to hold back memories, how to knead her grief in silence.

. . .

She has just finished breakfast and discussed with Cook the menu for dinner. Although Cook hates the trip, Vera has ordered her to go to the railroad station, where there's a market that sells the best Malayan egg bananas in Bangkok. Perhaps the most trying time of Vera's day occurs each morning after breakfast, when, as mistress of the house, she must consult Cook about food.

Food.

It's assumed an importance in her life this last year that disturbs her. While eating fruit or fish, she thinks of rich, creamy Russian dishes. There's a hunger in her unappeased by the thin soups and seafood dishes of Siam. Her Russian palate needs the thick bland fatty foods of winter.

On the other hand, her daughter attacks this Siamese food with the intensity of a native, having never seen snow, never felt a wintry wind, never tracked miles of barren plain or heard the sonorous bells of a Russian church. The girl's been blessed with warmth; the horizon for her is broken by green; and what she hears is the tiny tinkling bells, moved by a breath of air, that dangle from the spires of Buddhist pagodas. She's never known hunger, or the dream of black bread and thick beet soup, or the fear of never comforting again a stomach drawn tight as a stretched bow.

Vera is in her bedroom, almost ready to leave for the shop. Still dissatisfied with a spartan breakfast of fruit, she stands at a window, looking down at her property. It seems that lately nothing gives her more satisfaction than this house which she built before the war. It's an elegant house for Bangkok, one to be justly proud of. Part of her satisfaction comes from scrupulous attention to detail. Every board in the building comes from the same forest, so that the spirits in the wood won't, as strangers do, bring quarrels into the house. She insisted that the builders count the number of knots in the main support posts and demanded that they discard any timber possessing two, four, or six knots. Posts made of them could bring danger to the house. She refused to start work on a Tuesday, for that is the day of fever and bloodshed; if the building began on such a day, the entire structure might soon burn down. The earth itself was tested for evil by having a hen's egg buried in black-and-white cloth within it for a month. Dug up, it was inspected and its discoloration judged by soothsayers.

Vera had already bought the land when this ceremony took place, yet she'd been ready to give up the project had the ground proved unsuitable. There were other costly rituals, with geomancers and Buddhist priests attending and with the entire neighborhood turning out to witness, approvingly, the burning of joss sticks and the banging of drums and the recitation of mantras, all of which made her home respectable and safe.

Perhaps only an outsider could have shown such meticulous respect for the customs of a country. Vera has given herself to this plot of earth and the house that stands on it. Orphaned wanderer, she has her own place now, resolutely has it.

The walls are paneled in teak (at this time of year—warm days and cool nights—the house squeaks when the wooden joints contract and expand), and the house is generally open to flying birds who zoom over the Chinese-style railings and race around inside before winging out again to the sluggish klong. To furnish the house she has purchased porcelain taborets, celadon vases from Chiang Mai, inlaid Chinese cabinets, and even a Khmer storm drum to summon rain during droughts. She has installed an electrified chandelier to the astonishment of her neighbors, although to their satisfaction she has resisted putting in a telephone. Aside from money saved for Sonia's education, Vera has fed into this house the profits from her antique shop.

It is with great effort that Vera resists the temptation to go downstairs and summon Cook to make her a snack: a meal of pork roast and creamed vegetables, as much as she can eat. Vera imagines herself bolting the food, her fork moving with terrifying speed.

Turning from the window, she sits at the dressing table and gazes at the mirror. She hasn't slept well lately—of course, *that* is Wanna's fault, isn't it—so there are dark circles under her eyes like big lugubrious bruises. And last night she dreamt that a lightning bolt of white appeared suddenly in her black hair. When she tried dyeing it out, the streak widened until her entire head was a mass of sticky cotton.

But there aren't too many wrinkles—Vera bends close to the mirror—that is, considering her age. She can't pronounce the round number toward which her life is pointing: fifty. It's a strange word, remote, impersonal, yet in a couple of years it will apply oh yes quite intimately to her life.

Something on the dressing table diverts her attention: an envelope. Vera often puts important correspondence here where she must see it on the morning. But the letter inside this envelope is surely something she doesn't want to see again. Yet she must. It's Philip's letter from India, asking for shelter.

Well, not really for shelter.

Vera stares at the creased envelope; the letter inside of it is crumpled, torn from handling.

Why, suddenly, does this man want to come back into her life? Perhaps India has run out of adventures for him. She remembers some of his stranger letters—these she kept hidden from Sonia—disconnected and pathetic wanderings through his damaged psyche, confusing references to someone dead, a friend, Harry, whom he had not saved, whom, for that matter, he seemed to have betrayed.

If true, then Philip still betrays people.

The thought grips her even as her fingers grip the letter. Philip in 1927 betrayed the General by deserting the Shantung army and running away to Hong Kong with her; and then in 1939—fired by the Japanese sinking of an American gunboat near Nanking—he betrayed her too, walked out of the house in a burst of patriotic or visionary fervor or utter exasperation with his staid way of life and ran off to join Stilwell's "China Gang"; and so at last he betrayed this fellow Harry and, indeed, if the chaotic letters can be trusted, also by running away. He means no harm, really, yet whoever crosses his path gets hurt. Long ago she decided that Philip Embree never did bad things by intention, but simply by omission or indifference or—this is worst of all—by a complicated and distorted process of ratiocination. When he acted spontaneously, he was best; when he became deliberate and tried to move into the mainstream of values and behavior, he lost what he really had: the energy, the impulse, the passion—and poor Philip then hunkered down like a toad, awaiting something, awaiting a tumult in the air to force him into the sort of frantic action that gave him sustenance. That's her husband. That's Philip Embree, who wants to "come home," as he calls this wayward desire to enter her life again.

And what is Wanna doing behind her back? Is it a man?

• • •

There's a sharp knock at the door—imperious, familiar, the knock of Ah Ping. Without waiting for permission, the little Teochiu servant enters, her pouched eyes flashing.

"Mistress, she's done it again."

Vera can't help smiling at the furious old face. "Refused breakfast?"

"She stays in her room. She won't even answer!"

"I'll talk to her."

"She writes in that book, too. She's doing it right now."

"Book?"

"Everyday book. She writes something every day."

"Do you look at it, Ah Ping?"

The old woman scoffs. "Nothing in it I'd want to know. It's kept in the sandalwood cabinet."

Vera's afraid of asking more questions. Her own mother once discovered a diary of hers and jimmied the lock open. Vera, at sixteen, never really forgave her mother that betrayal, and so now, a mother herself, she refuses to do the same. "I'll talk to her about coming down to breakfast." Vera adds, after a look at the solemn old face, "And about being rude to you."

"Do you want to see the book? I can get it."

"Absolutely not. Do you understand? I don't want you to touch that book again, Ah Ping."

The rebuke stiffens the features of Ah Ping's mottled face; her lips tighten. "You are the mistress of this house." It's the phrase Ah Ping uses when she feels Vera deserves a rebuke of her own. The old servant turns and marches out.

Vera stares again in the mirror, fearful of seeing in reality the dream's lightning bolt of white in her hair. Then, rising with a sigh, she too leaves. Down the paneled corridor is the closed door to Sonia's room. Strange, but it's the first time Vera has ever felt this closed door could be forbidding. In fact, as she approaches it, Vera feels dread. What will she say to the girl? What, really, is there to say, except please be polite to an old woman who's been faithful for more than eighteen years? Yet at the door Vera hesitates before knocking. What will she call her daughter this morning? Sonia? It's the serious name. But doubtless she'll get a better response if she calls out "Sanuk!" She remembers (one hand halfway to the door knob) that day when she first used the nickname. The girl was in the garden laughing at a monkey looking down at her from a tree. In the girl's face there was such open love of life that Vera, without thinking, had yelled out the Thai word for joy. That was five or six years ago. Life for the girl is different now. Today Sonia's a young woman preparing for the world.

"Sanuk!" she calls out, withdrawing her hand from the knob.

The reply comes cool, thin, distant from behind the teak door. "Come in, Mother."

The girl's room is sunlit. Batik paintings shimmer on the walls; the classical xylophone which Philip gave her stands unplayed in a corner as it has done since her tenth birthday; and Siamese dancing dolls, their rhinestones glittering in the light, sit in a row along the bench where Sanuk used to play with them. Vera glances quickly at the sandalwood cabinet on top of the chest of drawers. Diary there? Daughter's secret life.

"I didn't see you playing Tai Chi this morning." Vera sits on the edge of the bed.

Sanuk wears the pajama trousers and blouse usually worn for her morning Tai Chi. She sits with her back against the wall, an open book (bound in imitation gold, a drawing of bamboo stems on the cover) lying in her lap, a pencil poised above it. "I didn't feel like playing." Sanuk slowly closes the book and holds it protectively against her hip.

"Or for the last few mornings, either."

Sanuk smiles tightly. "Does it matter?"

"Not really." Vera wants to seem casual, yet she can hear a trembling in her voice. Why? she wonders. What am I worried about? I am talking to my daughter who loves me. "No, it's not important. It's just Ah Ping. She frets because you don't come down to breakfast."

"I eat later."

"And she thinks you're rude. When she called this morning, you didn't answer."

"I was busy, Mother."

"Were you thinking about Lamai's marriage?"

"No, of course not. Should I be?"

The girl's defensiveness makes Vera wary. "I would imagine," she says evenly, "a girl your age thinks of a friend's marriage."

"It's not something I want for myself."

"I know you don't want it for yourself. I don't mean to suggest it."

"Weren't you almost thirty when you married father?"

"Twenty-seven." Long ago she'd decided never to tell the girl that she and the General had not married. In his position of authority a Chinese man couldn't marry a Western woman. Once she had said to him, "Is life with me worth your reputation?" And Shan-teh had replied, "I will never lose my reputation. Not as a man who loves his country and fights for it."

To her daughter Vera now says, "We married when I was twenty-seven."

Sonia nods thoughtfully. "I won't even think of it until I'm past thirty. I want to live."

"Some people marry and still live," Vera says, trying to lighten both their moods. But the girl, holding the book close to her hip, seems bound to a determined seriousness. Time to change the subject, Vera decides. The truth is she never feels at ease when they talk of love and marriage—and sex. Vera has often wondered if her reluctance to talk of such matters is a measure of her own scrupulously hidden past: Former whores—she'd heard in her Shanghai days—tend to worry about the slip that reveals everything.

"I'm sorry," the girl says, fumbling with the tie of her pajamas. The diary now lies in her lap.

"What for?"

"For being cross."

"Have you been?"

"I was cross with Ah Ping. I resented her yelling at me. I'm not a child. And when you came in, I was feeling—difficult."

Vera edges closer to the girl. "When people are preoccupied, sometimes they're difficult."

"Do you think I'm preoccupied?"

"I think you've been a little difficult lately. For example, the other day you were rude to Wanna."

"You mean when I told her to read *Phra Abhai?* Well, she ought to know Suthorn Buh is a great poet."

Vera hesitates. For some time now she's been aware of the girl's dislike of the pretty Siamese woman. Natural enough when you're young, she thinks. Natural if you're untried and don't know if you're pretty too. "Wanna's a very gentle person. You must remember that. And she likes you."

"She doesn't like me. And I don't trust her."

"Trust her?" A curious phrase.

Sanuk shrugs, signaling up the kind of inarticulate response her mother knows won't change with prodding. Someday, Vera thinks, perhaps I'll explain what gentleness can mean to someone who knew years of the brutal, the violent. But not now, not yet.

Silence lengthens in the room. Sonia is staring at the rumpled leg of her pajamas. She's doubtless self-absorbed as only the young can be. Maybe someday, but not yet, Vera thinks. I'll admit someday to loving women because of their tenderness. But not yet, not now, when this girl doesn't even know what love between men and women is, except from adolescent dreams of romance. Vera smiles.

"I'll tell you what preoccupies me." Looking up abruptly, Sonia leans forward. "I think all the time about politics."

"Oh, is that it?" Vera wants to treat this lightly too, but the tense expression on her daughter's face demands another response. She composes her own features. "So what concerns you about politics?"

"What the government's doing to the Chinese. People are going to get killed, Mother."

"How do you know that?"

"Everyone knows it."

"Do you talk about such things at school?"

"Of course. Phibun and his gang of army officers want to keep the Chinese down. It's how they hold power. Everything's anti-Chinese now—meat marketing, tobacco trading," Sanuk explains breathlessly.

What fine eyes when she's aroused, Vera thinks.

"The police are hiring men to put up posters in Chinatown. *Stop Chinese Immigration. Close Chinese Schools.* The Black Elephants, the Tusks —those gangs—they're doing it with Phibun's approval. *Under his orders*, Mother. There'll be rioting."

"That has nothing to do with you."

The girl crosses her arms. "It has everything to do with me. I'm Chinese."

"Because you're part Chinese doesn't mean you have to concern yourself with rioting."

"Because, my father would say, it has everything to do with me. Part Chinese is all Chinese."

"Do the students at Silpakorn talk this way?"

Vera can see hesitation in the girl's eyes. The guarded look returns. "Some do. Chinese students do."

"And you sit here with such ideas when you could be down on the terrace doing what your father would *really* approve of?"

Sonia bows her head slightly. Vera understands that the logic of that remark has touched her. Unwilling to gloat or attack further, Vera rises and goes to the door. She turns to face the girl, who has drawn up her legs defensively. "I've gone over your application to Stanford. A lot of words are misspelled. Will you correct them?" When Sonia nods indifferently, Vera doesn't want to leave her daughter in this inconclusive way. Somehow it matters that their conversation end on a better note. They must touch each other this morning. And every morning from now on, because it occurs to Vera with the anguish of love that her daughter is growing up, moving somehow out of focus, going off in some indefinable way. Is it possible they won't touch in the future? Vera clears her throat self-consciously. "Are you going to school?"

"Yes, later. Then shopping with Lamai."

"Tonight we're having one of your favorite things for dinner. I won't tell you what, though. It's a surprise."

Vera notices the girl's hand slide toward the diary in her lap.

Once the door's closed, Vera thinks, she'll pick it up and scribble again—perhaps some romantic nonsense about Jeanne d'Arc and honor and justice in Siam while she dreams of being a warrior like her father.

"Mother, I'll be fine."

"I hope you will."

"Most of what I know I learned from you." In a sudden rush of energy, coming from youth's secret hoard, she opens her arms.

Vera is in them before she knows it. She feels the warmth of her daughter's skin, the brush of young lips against her cheek, the soft words spoken against her ear. "I'm so grateful to you."

Vera pulls back slightly, with a short laugh, to look at the girl's shining eyes. "For what?"

"Oh, for so much. Well, maybe for French." Her grimace means the comment's to be taken lightly. "Maybe it will get me into your American university."

Now it is Vera's turn to refuse frivolity. She means to make a serious thing of Sanuk's remark. "Do you want to go? Just a little?"

Again the guarded look, the withdrawing. "I have to think about that."

"Of course you do." Vera feels the exquisite moment of intimacy has passed, so she rises again and hesitates above her daughter, just long enough for them to exchange smiles. It's all right now; she can leave. That moment of being physically close to Sanuk was what she'd wanted. And Sanuk had known. The girl had understood the need for an embrace. She'd recognized that the distance between them was more than intellectual—and had opened her arms like a woman. That insight accompanies Vera into the hallway, where she pauses to consider it. Sanuk is growing up, and she's aware of all sorts of things. The French, for example. Never before had she acknowledged her mother's help with the language. Yet only Vera herself can ever know how difficult it had been to give such help. Long ago, in 1920, when the French betrayed Baron Wrangel in his attempt to establish a White Russian government, she'd vowed never again to speak that language—the language of betrayal—and for fifteen years she'd kept the vow: not one word of French passed her lips. But one day a customer came into her shop and spoke French. It occurred to Vera at that moment that to deny Sonia a language used worldwide was to deny her an advantage. So on impulse Vera answered the customer in French. Then something strange happened. She couldn't stop speaking the language of her Petrograd childhood, the French of the Russian aristocracy. She followed the frightened customer out into the street, calling out nursery rhymes in French, snatches of song in French, yelling French slang, joyous that through her own skill her daughter might acquire one.

Halfway down the corridor, Vera stops. Can it be a boy? Is her daughter in love? That would explain the moodiness, the lassitude, the guarded look. And yet thus far Sonia hasn't shown interest in men, except for that harmless incident last year: after *Gone with the Wind* appeared for the first time in Bangkok, she had babbled about Clark Gable for days.

No, not yet, not men yet. Lord no, not yet.

Resolutely Vera walks on, shaking the thought away. Not yet. The girl's too inexperienced in the way girls of her class are in Siam. She might as well have been raised in a nunnery as in a Bangkok girls' school. No, not that. Not men. Not yet.

Back in her room, Vera looks again in the mirror; her hair is still black, although a few weeks ago she found some iron-gray filaments on the sink. But that's not what she's thinking about. Vera is thinking about her own poor judgment. Until now it hasn't been clear. She never took to heart her own criticism when a year ago she'd admonished Ah Ping to stop mentioning the General with the kind of extravagant worshipfulness typical of elderly Chinese.

In the girl's childhood, both Ah Ping and Vera had told stories—real and imagined—about the great General who was the girl's father. It had seemed harmless enough, a mother's way of shoring up for her child the memory of a dead father. Married to another man, Vera had spent her happiest moments with Sonia and Ah Ping, the trio imagining the General on his horse in front of an army, the savior of China, snatched away finally by evil foes. How often the three sat deeply moved by the imagined scenes!

"We met at a lawn party," Vera would say, not once but many times over the childhood years of her daughter, with Ah Ping nodding approval nearby and birds chattering in the trees overhead and boatmen yelling at one another on the klong. "I'd been invited by the French or the American Consul General—I forget which one. Yes—"

This always happened in the telling—the forgotten fact remembered. "—the French Consul General. I had done some translating for him. And your father appeared on the lawn, with his uniform bedecked with medals. Everyone turned to look at him. That's how imposing he was. He wasn't that tall, but what held your attention was his eyes. They saw everything—black and quick—and the way he held himself reminded me of guardsmen from my youth. We met in a Shanghai garden, and from that first moment, Sonia, I was lost."

A pretty story that never failed to win the girl's admiration in the safety of their Bangkok garden. The truth, of course, was somewhat different. Vera had first met the General at his army base in Qufu. She'd been taken there by her German lover who wanted her to charm the General and make it easier to sell him munitions. She had been brought there to do what she could—implying anything—that would help seal the bargain. And she had been willing and quite prepared to do anything. Her compliance hadn't been called for, however, because the General left Qufu in search of bandits. Later they'd met in Shanghai, but not at a garden party given by the French Consul, whom she had never met. And so, by twisting facts here and there, she had mythologized for the girl her life with General Tang. Shan-teh had once told her of a Chinese propensity for transforming experience for just such a purpose: "We Chinese deify people who've led important lives. They're worshiped like gods. In this way the gods and the humans both live." So Vera had made him into a kind of Chinese god for their daughter.

But what seemed right for her childhood became something vaguely wrong in Sonia's adolescence. She would not let go of the old stories and begged for their repetition. The girl wanted—indeed, seemed desperately to need—a hero in her life, having got accustomed to it through the years of having a father who was one.

By that time Philip had gone to war, and anyway he'd never offered himself as the image of a hero—the sort of man an imaginative girl might look to as a source of mystery and romance. When at last Vera realized that the desire for a hero had turned a corner of Sonia's mind into compelling obsession, it was too late, and this became obvious: The girl dreamed of a dead father who had assumed the towering importance of a mythic hero.

True, true. Even now the girl lives too much in the idea of her glorious father. True. Doubtless those diaries are filled with him and filled too with a dream of emulation. Jeanne d'Arc riding beside the warrior-king, her father. Oh God. Nor has it helped, perhaps, that Vera had coupled the tales of General Tang to those of her Russian past. In the memories of her own childhood Vera found a source for aristocratic values: honor, truth, beauty came marching out of the mists of Old Russia into the sheltered garden of a Bangkok house.

Vera is staring at her image without seeing it. What, really, is the truth? The truth is that the aristocrats of her homeland fled from a rabble of Bolsheviks, and died one by one in the trackless winter of Siberia. And the truth is that General Tang Shan-teh was murdered by unknown assailants near Tai Shan. At least, that was what a Hong Kong newspaper reported when she, along with Philip, fled to the Crown Colony from war-torn China. Five lines in an English-language newspaper. Local Shantung warlord murdered near Mount Tai.

Vera glances at the envelope on the table. Philip's letter, yet to be answered. What can she say to him? Come along? Stay away? What have they in common, except the knowledge that each betrayed the same man?

Philip. Sonia. And Wanna, too, who surely is doing some betraying of her own.

Vera is wearing a blue cotton blouse with a white, round collar. Leaning toward the mirror, she squints to see if any neck wrinkles show above that collar. They do. They do. To make certain how deep and obvious they are, Vera whips up her glasses from their cord. Why must age do terrible things? It isn't fair. She's done nothing to deserve these wrinkles. Except live.

Vera feels, with some amusement, her own childishness. But what, after all, has sustained her through so many events, so many years, aside from her beauty? The knowledge of it has warmed her psychically the way a fireplace warms a house. It's the one thing she has clung to, her beauty. It's been good to her, has helped her survive with good grace.

And perhaps now she's having the last of it. One day, not too far off, she'll awake to find it truly gone, vanished like smoke in the mirror of years.

It's a terrible thought, bad enough to bring her hands up tightly against both sides of the mirror frame. Does Wanna notice these slight but terrible signs of age? There's no reason to believe she does. And yet Vera often tries to catch her in glances of morbid curiosity. The mirror trembles in Vera's hands.

She wets her lips speculatively. They are still good: full, naturally bowed, even succulent. Yes, that: succulent. She may have a few more years before no one, man or woman, gives her a second glance. Odd, but it's what she used to think in her twenties—that she'd have only a few more years. Vera notices herself smile into the mirror at this idea. Her smile is there as always. Perhaps it'll be with her until the end. And, of course, *Mai pen rai.*

Absently she reaches out to grip the crumpled letter. Poor Philip. She slips his letter into her purse. And now Sonia writing romantic secrets to her father in a diary. And Wanna? Where is she at this precise moment? Rising from a man's bed, having lied about visiting her aunt in Lopburi?

Vera cocks her head, wets her lips, blinks her eyes rapidly to give them a limpid cast. She'll have a little beauty a little longer. That probability gives her a little comfort on this Bangkok morning, when thinking of the trio seems to make their images drift dimly across the mirror's glass. They dwell there, and if she thinks hard about it, which she now does, they stare out at her—taunting, questioning, pleading, enveloping her in their worlds.

6   SIAMESE ARTS ORIENTAL.

Gloomily she stares at the red English letters painted over the entrance to the clapboard building, her shop, which is near the river on New Road. If the government decides, in nationalistic fervor, once again to change the name of Siam to Thailand, she'll have to spend money for new lettering. This is what government means to Vera: an annoyance.

It was hardly more than that during the war, when, as a Thai citizen, she was not incarcerated by the Japanese, as were British, French, and Americans in Bangkok. In fact, for Vera it was a period of business success. After a few initial gifts of Thai antiques to high-ranking Japanese officers, Vera sold steadily to their staffs. In less than four years she unloaded countless fakes, of which the country had a surplus, at prices acceptable to young officers who foresaw the day, soon after victory, when they'd sit in their Tokyo gardens and meditate before images of rare Thai Buddhas.

Next door, outside his tiny shop, stands a short, fat, dark-skinned man in baggy trousers and loose blouse. He grins, she frowns. An Indian from Bombay, he's a money changer who handles any shady deal a visiting foreigner brings to him. For years she has cultivated his friendship in the hope that someday he'll sell his property to her—a fine corner location—so she can expand her own shop onto it. Six months ago she made him an excellent offer, which he countered (matching her friendly smile with one of his own) by asking double the price. They no longer speak. Vera's anger is directed less against him than against herself; she's been a fool to think a coquettish smile can turn the head of a man who arranges an opium buy or a sex show for anyone who comes along.

She opens the door of Siamese Arts Oriental and feels the coolness of a dim interior, sees the clutter of objects on tables and shelves. A thin little man, scarcely larger than a child, rises from a desk at the end of the narrow room. This is her assistant, Prakit Chaidee. He's worked for her ever since she gambled her little hoard of money on the shop. It was Prakit Chaidee who warned her not to put Buddha images on the ground floor of her house. Prakit Chaidee also introduced her to Professor Dhanit Yupho of Silpakorn University, who became her adviser (for a commission) in the collecting of modest relics that might pass for priceless antiques and who in the process taught her a great deal about Thai art. Now her shop contains an impeccable selection of authentic bronzes and fragments of fifteenth-century Sawankhalok porcelains and also—something equally rare—antique silver betel-nut boxes from Malaya and old tapestries from Burma, all purchased from ignorant curio sellers, then sold to foreign buyers at impressive markups.

Prakit Chaidee in soft, rhythmic Thai informs her that a royal prince wants a radio from Singapore. He pulls out a piece of paper on which the make, model, and other specifications are written. She'll have her agent in Singapore buy the radio, then offer it to the prince for a nominal sum, enhancing her reputation for buying goods abroad at very low prices—and protecting her shop from bureaucratic harassment.

Her office has only one window, a serious detriment when the hot weather descends upon Bangkok in April, and yet Vera likes a tightly defined room—a place suited to concentration—when she's writing letters meant for choosy foreign buyers or assessing the real worth of an object brought into the shop for sale. Vera switches on the green-shaded light above her desk. There's a pile of invoices and correspondence. On the far right corner of the desk sits a little figure which, before doing anything else, Vera touches.

It's a *wan nang kwak*, made from tuber root in the shape of a young woman kneeling, with left hand on her thigh and right hand raised in a beckoning gesture. It's a good-luck piece, the sort used by Siamese traders, especially by women in the open-air markets. A few years ago (at Prakit Chaidee's gentle suggestion, during an ominous lull in business) she'd bought a tuberous root at the Weekend Market on Pramane Grounds, had a local sculptor shape it into the proper figure, then paid a Buddhist priest to consecrate it by intoning *Namo Buddhaya* one hundred and eight times over its form. It's now filled with magic capable of drawing customers into the shop as a magnet draws iron filings—so Prakit Chaidee explained—and indeed, since the *wan nang kwak* appeared on her desk, Vera's shop has done a brisker business than before. Each morning—today's no exception—she intones in a low voice the mantra assigned by the priest to this particular *wan nang kwak:* "Om. Lord of the Blue Mountains, bestow on me good fortune, *svaha svahom!"*

Vera isn't sure what it means—the priest warned her that knowledge of the mantra might well destroy its power—and she wouldn't be surprised if the cunning old fellow had tricked her into repeating meaningless jargon each morning, yet she says the words anyway and always before noon places a flower at the feet of the *wan nang kwak*, hoping, as women throughout Bangkok in their fish stalls and trinket shops hope too, for a day's good luck in business.

Having complied with the ritual, Vera sits down and calls out for Prakit Chaidee. When his small face appears in the doorway, she asks for Wanna.

The girl hasn't come in yet. "Perhaps she's gone to Central Station," Prakit Chaidee suggests, "to book tickets for your trip."

"Perhaps." And perhaps, she thinks, Wanna hasn't yet risen from the bed of a man she met last night.

"Mister Thompson came by this morning. He stays at the Oriental."

"Yes, I know who Mister Thompson is."

"He'd be grateful if you stopped to see him this morning. He says it's urgent." Prakit Chaidee steps forward to place some letters on the edge of the desk, then steps back. "And these." Turning, he leaves the room —the step forward, the bending, the turning, each step out of the room, all executed with the balletic grace of dancers she'd seen in her Petrograd youth.

Prakit Chaidee is at least ten years older than she is. A great-grandfather, a casual opium smoker, Prakit Chaidee looks no more than thirty. He wears a few amulets around his neck and on his left forearm a flame-shaped tattoo. If his Siamese magic keeps a person young, maybe she ought to wear a score of amulets and tattoos up both her arms. But probably the spells won't work for a farang.

Vera opens the top letter. It's from Professor Silpa Bhirasri, Dean of Faculty at the University of Fine Arts, inviting her to join a Committee of Citizens to Preserve Thai Art. He outlines a program of six points: to survey old murals; to make photographic records of antiquities; to bind murals to rotting walls with appropriate chemicals; to place railings around threatened old works of art; to cover fragile paintings with glass; to repair leaking roofs where such works are displayed.

There will be only two farangs—the other an Italian archeologist—on the committee of eight, and Vera realizes that her inclusion on it is a veiled appeal for a financial contribution to projects that most likely will be handled with cavalier inefficiency. Even so, it's an honor, and her place on such a committee adds to the respectability of her shop. She has come a long way since the days when tourists hoped her Western ignorance of Eastern art would enable them to buy her antiques cheaply.

The next letter is from Pakhoon Chirachanchai, her agent in Chiang Mai. He's anxiously awaiting her trip to the North, for without a doubt, so Pakhoon declares, the Shan bronzes he has found are good, and there is also an extraordinary work of art—a stone carving from Phayao, a Buddha image from the late Lan Na period. Vera doubts it. Pakhoon is enthusiastic about anything he finds. He sees in every stone or broken shard a commission so large that he can stop working altogether and sit beside the river chewing betel. In the Lan Na period few stone carvings were made, bronze being the favorite medium for sculptors of the time.

And yet, if it *were* true—Vera gazes at the sunlit motes of the little room, indulging in a fantasy of wealth and leisure: a trip to Europe with Sonia, a visit to universities both there and in America that might accept Sonia; a new wardrobe for both of them; repair of the roof; perhaps even a diamond ring, something like her mother's ring that Vera herself removed from the slim white frozen aristocratic finger one wintry night in 1919 and later used as a bribe to get what was left of the family onto the boxcar of a train fleeing Tomsk.

It's time to see Thompson, she supposes. Urgent? What could the man have to do with her that would be urgent?

On the way out of her office, seeing Prakit polishing a small bronze buddha with a rag, Vera says, without thinking, "Has she come in yet?"

Prakit doesn't need to ask who "she" is. Yet he spares Vera a knowing smile. "Perhaps she's been held up at the station. These days it's a fight for bookings."

"Yes," Vera says, "perhaps," and hurries down the small corridor of the shop into the morning sunlight. For an instant Wanna's small heart-shaped face seems to be coming toward her through the crowd. But it belongs to another girl. *Mai pen rai*, Vera says under her breath, trying to believe it.

· · ·

From her shop on New Road it's a short walk beside a klong (black and stinking in the dry season) to the sprawling former palace that's now the Oriental. The old white Oriental is her favorite hotel in Bangkok, although the Trocadero with its iron balconies and the Pacific with its mirrors are both newer. Before the war the Oriental had no bathtubs in the rooms; now there are tubs and hot water in large earthenware jars. On the grounds there's a Japanese garden—built to the specifications of a visiting general—with a red bridge over a stream. At the entrance, saluting briskly as Vera enters, is a uniformed Sikh. The Oriental maintains the style of hotels she'd known in her Russian childhood and those she'd known later in Shanghai, when men displayed her in dining rooms along Nanking Road.

When she asks at the desk for Mister Thompson's room, the Siamese clerk in white gloves directs her to a suite at the top of the stairway, first floor.

Urgent? Vera wonders, climbing the red-carpeted stairs. She has met Thompson only once, and that time perhaps a year ago in the hotel lobby, when he mistook her for a tourist. With three or four swatches of silk draped over the shoulder of his jacket, Thompson had walked up to her and with a rather simpering smile inquired if she were interested in buying a marvelous piece of Siamese cloth. Since then she's had glimpses of him—he lives and works out of the hotel. They say during the war he was a member of the American OSS, was a hero of sorts, and stayed on in Siam for lack of anything else to do. He's liked by people, from what Vera hears. They say he's ambitious, both for himself and for Siam. That's an interesting reputation to have; his urgent request to meet her simply adds to Vera's frank curiosity about the man.

His suite is at the end of a long hallway. When she knocks, the door opens almost instantly, and a man of average height stands there. He's somewhat pudgy, yet with a long Alpine face, a receding hairline, and a startled look in his brown eyes. He greets her effusively, as if they're old friends, but that's what she expects of an American. While he leads her into a large sitting room, to the right she has a glimpse of his bedroom, a mosquito net, a bare sink, and a screen, behind which is probably one of the hotel's new tubs.

"Tea?" Thompson asks when they're seated opposite each other at a teak table.

She ought to refuse, because tea means sweet cakes too; instead she smiles and quite rightly he takes it to mean yes. When he makes no move to call down, Vera guesses that the desk clerk had been instructed to place the order when she arrived.

And sure enough, hardly have they exchanged a few pleasantries about the weather when a waiter enters with a large silver tea tray.

Vera is impressed. Seeing Thompson in the lobby, a rather pathetic-looking salesman with his pieces of silk, she hadn't expected much of him. But here, in this spacious room, with chintz curtains at a window overlooking Chao Phya River, the man seems far more pleasant, perhaps even formidable. Over the first sip of lemon tea, Vera is more curious than ever.

And so she listens intently when, without more prologue, the young American starts to talk business; as he says, "I won't waste your time, Madam. I know it's valuable. I have a proposition you might like to consider." After the war, he tells her, he settled in Siam and through the suggestion of a friend became interested in the local silks. The weavers, all Moslems, worked on hand-operated bamboo looms in a ghetto-like area called Bangkrua. They made sarongs in plaid or brocade; the weaving was superb, but the problem was their use of vegetable dyes that faded after a few washings. Moreover, their silks were too traditional for the taste of urban Siamese, who preferred the subdued colors of textiles made in Europe. The art of the Moslem weavers was dying out.

By now Jim Thompson has smoked a cigarette down to his stained fingertips and has lit another.

Vera takes another sweet cake, abashed to find that she has already eaten half of them. Her attention is divided between her appalling hunger and the young man's story. He tells it leaning forward in his chair, elbows on knees, a cigarette poised in air like the baton of a conductor. What the weavers needed, Thompson continues, was a color-fast dye and better production technique. He had one of the weavers do some typical pieces of this Bangkrua silk, put them in a suitcase, and flew to New York. There he met the publisher of *Vogue* magazine, who loved the design and color. She insisted that everyone on her staff drop by her office and see the silks before leaving that night. She got Valentina, the dress designer, to do an ensemble from the material. It was photographed for *Vogue*. From this response Thompson was sure of a potential market, and so back here in Bangkok he raised enough money to buy some high-quality Swiss dyes for the weavers.

While he tells her how he researched the National Museum for samples of old designs to block-print, Vera finishes off the last sweet cake. Jumping up, the nervous young American grabs a sheaf of papers from a nearby desk and throws them down on the table. They are his own designs, but he doesn't wait for Vera to study them before waving his arms expansively and continuing the story. He learned that Laotians

along the northeast frontier were especially adept at raising and process-
ing silkworms. On a trip North to see their operation, he met and
employed a Laotian who has proved invaluable. They have licked the
technical problems.

Thompson clasps his hands, unclasps them, lights another cigarette.
He talks about marketing and finance. So far, as silk distributor for the
Bangkrua weavers, he's been operating through an independent retail
outlet, but its owner, a Chinese, is untrustworthy.

Vera sips the lemon tea, hoping that the young man will notice the
empty plate and call down for more sweet cakes. It's not that she is
bored by him and therefore turns her attention to food. She just can't
untangle her own physical hunger from his ambition. The fact is she
likes his willingness to risk. Last year she toyed with the idea of found-
ing a celadon company to revive the Siamese art of making stone-
ware.

He is telling her now about the financing of this enterprise, doubtless
the reason for their meeting. Recently he spoke to a visiting Californian
who has encouraged him to incorporate. He needs $25,000 U.S. ini-
tially, to be raised by selling five hundred shares at $50 each. If share-
holders put up only half of their shares at first, perhaps the balance can
be paid later out of company profits. "That's how confident I am,"
Thompson says, lighting another cigarette. The room is filled with a
pungent blue haze. "I'm not just in it for the money either. I want to
make a contribution to Siam."

It's a brash thing to say, yet in keeping with the style of most Americans she has met, and anyway, from this man it seems nothing more
than what he really believes, than what in fact he really is: naïve, energetic, irrepressible. The man can't be more than thirty. Suddenly she
feels old.

"We're paying the weavers only after we sell the silk," Thompson
continues. "But as soon as possible we'll buy the silk outright for cash.
Do you know what I mean? We want to hold this down to a cottage
industry. These people would hate the impersonal routine of a factory
—and it just might lead to inferior silk, a lot of unhappiness." Thompson grins at the idea of his forbearance. "Of course I'm trying to persuade them to use foot-operated shuttles. It would make the work go a
lot faster. What do you think?" Pausing for breath, Thompson sits back;
one hand rests, like a contented child's, on his paunch.

"I think I'm very interested."

"From what I've heard of you, Madam, I thought you would be.
That's why I sent the message urgent. We're moving along rapidly."

"What shares are left?"

Thompson lurches forward, elbows on knees. "I'll be frank. To make
it work legally, the Siamese must have 51 percent. It's nearly pledged. I

have ninety shares and so does Barrie. That means sixty-five shares are left. I have a few probable subscribers—"

"How many can I have?"

Thompson stares at her, clearly surprised. "Well, fifty?"

Vera sits back in her chair. This is a financial commitment she ought to consider in light of her other obligations: there's Sonia's education to pay for, the house to repair, debts to honor, her own business to run. Yet Thompson has fired her imagination. For years she's seen the brilliant patterns of Siamese silk—plaids worn by men, brocades by women —usually on special occasions such as weddings. Each time, in a casual way, the thought has struck her: What beauty! But here, today, this chubby American, who chain-smokes and drapes merchandise on his shoulder in the hotel lobby, has come along with the energy and vision to create more of such beauty—and in the process to make a fortune. It's obvious, so obvious. Vera puts aside caution and with a toss of her head declares, "I'll take the fifty."

• • •

Vera has hardly returned to her office before depression sets in.

It was madness to pledge the money, madness, madness to sign the papers on impulse, to do it then and there. She's committed herself to a scheme that could go bad before getting started; at the very least it's a highly speculative venture, of particular risk at a time when her financial responsibilities are great. Last year's work on the house put her in considerable debt. The roof needs repair, but that must wait until she pays off the construction of the inside staircase. Sonia's air fare to either Europe or America must be taken into account, to say nothing of college tuition and clothes. Business is going well, yet in Bangkok, so the travel agents tell her, the influx of tourists is unpredictable—few people know what to expect from this strange country. She may have to coast for months, and where will the funds come from?

Vera is staring at the small window, oblivious of the heat that invades this room by midday even in the winter season. Why did she throw caution to the wind? There certainly hadn't been a sexual component to her foolishness. The man had no appeal for her in that way at all; in fact, the lack of attraction may have contributed to her vulnerability: Thompson seemed so harmless. But his enthusiasm! When he saw her to the door, a cigarette dangling from his mouth while curiously he managed a little European bow, Thompson had exclaimed, "The weavers of Bangkrua will all be wearing a fez soon. Follow? Wearing the fez means you've made a pilgrimage to Mecca. I want to see a fez on every head in Bangkrua. I want to see happiness!"

Sitting with elbows on the desk, her eyes focused closely on the scrawled address of Philip's letter, Vera feels the panic of financial insecurity. It's a familiar emotion. She felt it in Shanghai during the days when she worked in a house of prostitution, when she was kept by men, when by her sexual labors she managed to accumulate a little treasure—antiques small enough to fit in a suitcase, to follow her ephemeral path through a war-torn land. She felt the insecurity again in Hong Kong, when Philip Embree, better at war than at peace, made scarcely enough in an export company to support the two of them, then the three of them when Sonia was born. Little by little she sold off the contents of the suitcase until, with the sort of abrupt decisiveness she has just displayed today, Vera had gambled the rest of her treasure on a little antique store in Singapore. A few hard years of work there produced funds to get herself, Philip, and the child to Bangkok, where a second shop managed to catch on quickly.

Today it is still doing very well. Yet the shadow of catastrophe falls every day across Vera's shoulder. She can't be sure if it's a real shadow or only the memory of one that followed her across Russia into China.

Having gambled once more with the future, Vera now senses in herself the old fear, the hunger for security, the incipient rise of panic.

She picks up the envelope and slips out Philip's letter to read it again. A phrase arrests her attention: "If given the chance, believe me, Vera, I'll prove to you I have changed." Changed? Can he change? The unique, the dangerous, the edge move him. Life in the center is death for Philip Embree. Yet he's always been generous with whatever he had. Throughout his long absence he sent frequent money orders, appended to hasty, uninformative notes and the curt "Love, Philip."

Has he done well in India? It's hard to tell. To her knowledge he never talks about finances, probably never thinks about them. Whatever he has saved, though, Philip Embree can be counted on to share, to give away in the naïve belief that a gift of money can erase the past. And yet a gift of money is a considerable thing—

Vera picks up a pen from the desk, then puts it down. Something Thompson said comes back to her. After the papers were signed, in a mood of jubilation, the man had kept her a while longer, talking about anything that came to mind: politics, for example. He made expansive pronouncements: Although Field Marshal Phibun collaborated with the Japanese during the war, today his anti-Communist policy is good for Siam. The United States will support him because of it.

And then he said it. He said—what were his exact words?—"I understand you speak Chinese as well as your husband does."

And she said, "Who told you that?"

He seemed flustered, as if, off guard, he'd just said something he shouldn't. "Who? I don't know. It's common knowledge, isn't it?"

And in the confusion and fear that followed her daring act, Vera had forgotten this odd exchange. Raising the pen, however, to start a letter to Philip, she has remembered. It is *not* common knowledge that Philip Embree knows Chinese. It is not, in fact, common knowledge that she is married. Many people in Siam take it for granted that she's a widow —and Vera has left it at that. When she and Philip first came to Bangkok, they knew scarcely anyone, and Philip left within a short time thereafter; none of Vera's present acquaintances ever met him.

Clearly Thompson has other sources of information. She's reminded of stories concerning his war experience and rumors that he's still employed by one of those mysterious American agencies.

Vera picks up the pen again. Very well, next time she sees Thompson, she'll pursue the matter. "What do you know about my husband?" she'll say. "Why do you know it?" And with a laugh she'll add, "Are you one of those exotic spies, Jim?" (She calls him Jim now that he has her money.) "If my husband comes to Bangkok, though, please keep him out of it. He'd like nothing better than something undercover and dangerous. Promise me!" She'll say it lightly, but in earnest. Damn Philip. To have him back would complicate her life needlessly. What would he think of the physical change in her, the aging? Anyway, she wouldn't sleep with him; that is certain. One thing good about his returning, though, could be his influence on Sonia. A man in the house might burn off the intensity of the girl's feelings about a dead, heroic father. And Philip, an American, might encourage her to see the West. But Philip, damn him—just when you think he's only a boy grown tall, a fierce man flashes out of him, an irresponsible dazzler who might walk out on them just when she and Sonia had given him their trust.

Vera, frowning, picks up the pen that she'd again put down. She's written no more than "My Dear Philip: Your letter came as a shock," when she feels the presence of someone in the doorway. Looking up, she sees Wanna there, the lovely face small in the act of concentration. "How long have you been standing there?"

"I was just watching how serious you are when you write."

Just watching how old I seem. "Where have you been?" she asks, amazed at the poignant, somewhat pleading tone of her voice, which ought to sound angry.

"At the train station." Wanna blows out her breath with an exaggerated sigh. "I think everyone in Bangkok's trying to book tickets."

"Prakit says the crowds are terrible." Vera wants to seem agreeable, regretting the little outburst of anxiety.

"Took me the entire morning."

Straight black hair cut in bangs across a broad forehead, tawny skin, flared nostrils, wide cheeks, eyes set wide apart, very wide, and high arched eyebrows, pointed chin. That's her most charming feature—the pointed chin—Vera thinks, and with a bright smile, rising, she says to the girl, "Come, let's go have lunch. I'm starved!"

7 "FEAR RISES FROM the Other."

That's something he read in *The Upanishads* this morning, and until a few moments ago, when he left the tonga and walked toward the Adyar Club, it was still raking his consciousness. Raking it like crossfire.

Strolling up the lawn toward the white Augustan columns, Philip Embree notices a tree that seems heavy with blackened leaves. Getting closer, he realizes the leaves are hundreds of crows as big as bombs. Now and then they explode into the noon air with a ponderous flapping of wings. He halts a moment to watch them; under his floppy Gurkha hat he squints across the manicured grass at an arsenal of crows. What are they doing all in one tree? Blue-black, clattering from branch to branch, they're like machines of tin that merely resemble birds; their thick wings look too unwieldy for flight. He steps closer to see them returning from the air. Cannonballing through the leaves, they shiver each limb down to the trunk when they land. Embree smiles when they try to make themselves comfortable on the slim branches—three-hundred-pound men on toilet seats. He walks to the base of the tree and regards their thick gray necks, their curved beaks and gunmetal feathers, those tufts of hair on their skulls that give them a mad, furious look.

Do they fear the Other?

It's the kind of odd question he doesn't like. Yet similar ones occur to Embree as he stands under the tree. Take that crow on the branch just there, the ugly fellow near the tip. Embree imagines himself speaking to someone. But it won't be Harry. He's done speaking to Harry. It will be one of the English-speaking clerks at the company. Embree will say, "Look at that ugly fellow—does he know himself from his neighbor tilting alongside? How deep is his knowledge of separateness from the other crows? How much of a bird is he and how much of himself does he think is a soul? How does he think of birdness in contradistinction to himself? Does he know when life plays him a dirty trick? Does he blame himself when something goes wrong or does he blame the other birds? Does he blame the Big Bird in the Sky or Abstract Fate or Nothing at All if he's cheated and suffers? Or is he incapable of blaming anything?"

These are not good questions, these are bad questions. Embree knows in himself the signs of impending trouble: odd obsessions, a twisted view of things, the impacted horror of memory. With a final baleful glance at the seething birds, he turns away, marches toward the club. Taking off the Gurkha hat at the front steps, Embree moves briskly across the marble foyer, glad to escape the kinetic assault of a blazing Indian noon. He passes a group of Victorian couches, deep leather chairs, and takes a brief judgmental look at the walls: Raj prints hanging there depict colonial Englishmen administering justice to naked savages. How long will club directors keep the prints up? India has been independent now for half a year. One thing he admires in the British is their doggedness.

Two rangy, sunburned men in bush suits come out of the billiard room and precede him through a ballroom filled with stacked chairs. Embree has heard stories of wild parties at the Adyar Club, of fights and seductions that had their origin on these polished floors, but today, at high noon, the ballroom with its ceiling of painted stars seems curiously innocent, like a deserted schoolhouse.

Three more men, very tall, come by in white ducks, carrying tennis rackets and towels. Five-foot-nine Philip Embree envies them their English height, their relentless composure. Bred into them by a tradition of colonial rule, their confidence has been sustained beyond a capacity to rule. Nothing has changed in the Adyar Club, he thinks, halting to study the bulletin board with its notices of picnics, teas, and meetings. Nothing has touched the club's style and pace: not Gandhi, not Patel, not Nehru, not the Congress Party, not 15 August 1947, not twelve million people in motion across the map of India, a half-million of them dying on the road, not the abduction of thousands of helpless women, not the refugee columns fifty miles long, not babies torn limb from limb in religious and communal frenzy—

A bad sign, this obsession with the post-Independence massacre and the Brits. In fact, his own history says otherwise about his real sentiments. He fought beside the Brits in Burma and admires their valor. And he's not altogether sure their defeat in India will benefit India.

A vague dread. Caused perhaps by *The Upanishads*. Perhaps by his decision to leave India—if he's actually made it. Or perhaps by the boring work he does at the office. Perhaps his unrest is caused merely by living. He likes the last possibility. From what he's read that's a fashionable doctrine in postwar France, and rapidly extending elsewhere. Slapping the felt hat against his leg in a gesture of self-reprimand, Embree enters the paneled bar.

He's supposed to meet Frazer here and so informs the turbaned bartender. Ordering a gimlet (charged to Frazer's club account), he turns from the bar to face an open doorway through which he can see a portion of the veranda. Servants are rolling the chicks halfway down for shade against the noonday sun. Beyond these bamboo curtains, he has a nice view of the expansive lawn, a ribbon of brown river, enormous rain trees. India is beautiful, he thinks. I've accomplished nothing here, but at least I've seen its beauty.

Standing near him at the bar, two men are laughing over their gins.

"Let me tell you another about the old girl," one says. "This particular evening we were sitting with drinks here in the club and someone mentioned the ferocity of the mongoose. And I said, 'That's right. A man can't sleep naked in South India, not when the little bugger might get inside the house.' Bill said, 'Is that a problem? A mongoose is surely nothing more than that—a little bugger.' 'Indeed?' I said. 'It's a little bugger that's been known to mistake a penis for a cobra. Damn thing can rip your organ off in seconds.' So the old girl had been listening to all this. Know what she said then? 'I jolly well can do as much with a few well-chosen words.' "

Embree turns to them: two beefy men attired similar to himself in seersucker and sport shirt—and tie; it's required in the club bar. Their faces are sun-reddened to the purplish tint of meat going bad.

A negative thought, Embree acknowledges. He's definitely coaxing such negative thoughts out of the shadows. Why does human nature gravitate toward misery? Another thought he doesn't need today. He doesn't need *The Upanishads* either. "Fear rises from the Other." That's rot. That's recruit thinking. He'd seen such a thought on young faces new to the jungle, a thought so absorbing to untried soldiers that they tripped the wire, failed to take cover, forgot their antimalaria pills.

Apparently he must be staring at them while thinking negatively, because the two men regard him with sullen curiosity until he looks away.

In loud voices, as if challenging him, they begin a discussion of Gandhi, who, according to the *Hindu*, has begun a new fast. "My mali came in the other day—" One of the Britishers glances past the shoulder of his companion at Embree. "He claimed old Bapu refused to use the Howrah Bridge when he was in Calcutta. Instead, he walked on the Hooghli River."

The other man hoots, motioning for the barman to bring another round.

"And wherever Bapu stepped, according to the mali, lilies sprang out of the water and drifted on the tide." The man makes an extravagant rippling gesture with his large hand. "Filling the stink of Calcutta with their fragrance."

Guffawing, his companion says, "Did the mali say all that? How frightfully clever of him. And what did you reply?"

"I quite nearly said, 'Your Bapu is all well and good, but *our* fellow not only walked on water, he provided bread and fish for a multitude.' "

They chuckle together, and when no challenging stare comes from Embree, they turn dismissively from him.

Sensitive, he thinks. Brits are sensitive these days about Gandhi and the whole Independence thing. But the reference to Christ strikes a chord in his memory. He'd said more or less the same thing to someone, but to whom and when? It won't come to him, so, ordering another gimlet, he walks onto the veranda.

Sitting at a table, he points his rattan chair at the lawn, the rain trees, the river. Above him rattles a revolving fan—he's heard the club installed these electric ones in the last year. Very progressive for Brits. A monkey, racing along the balustrade, is shooed away by a uniformed waiter. Women have recently been allowed to have their lunch on the veranda—still more British progress—so at a nearby table a group of them in broad-brimmed hats and cotton frocks are sipping tall drinks with rounds of lime floating above the ice. They're discussing servants. From their conversation, he gathers they're all rather new to Madras.

Across the broad lawn a brick building is being constructed on club grounds. Shielded from the sun by a huge black umbrella, the overseer squats near the construction site, while an insectile procession of dark-skinned women, with tiered bricks balanced on their heads, climb a ladder of bamboo at the top of which they wait for masons to take the bricks onto the scaffolding. Embree drinks, imagining the terrific weight of hot bricks bearing down on the brainpan of each woman.

A negative thought. But decent.

A woman at the next table is describing what happened to her Swedish neighbor. Ingrid Anderson returned from Bangalore to find the villa's water pump broken, the gas cylinder leaking, none of the toilets working, cook drunk, an ayah sporting a black eye that she said the cook gave her, and a bearer who wouldn't speak to the watchman who wouldn't speak to the cook.

Bangalore.

Embree recalls his own recent trip there, watching mile after rattling mile of landscape pass the train window. He has always loved trains, although in his youth he'd been kidnaped by Chinese bandits on a train bound for Peking. That train is hard to remember after twenty years. He lingers vainly upon the blurred face of a bandit who had prodded him with a gun butt out of the compartment. But the train from Bangalore is fresh in memory. Crows everywhere in the fields. Always crows. Villages with haystacks and white plaster shrines. Crows and shrines. Always. And suddenly he remembers what had happened in the Chinese bandit camp: In answer to the Mongol leader's question about the reputed magic of the Jesus, a youthful Philip Embree had claimed for "our fellow" the power of giving food to a multitude.

Another woman, just arrived, is describing her own problems with India. Last week she got home to find her cook sprawled on the kitchen floor, ants making a trail across his face. She was horrified at first, thinking him dead, but then the snoring suggested he was merely drunk. When she prodded him awake, he threatened to kill her when she wasn't looking. Of course she fired him on the spot. Then he promptly threatened to come back and kill her entire family. Because her husband was on leave in England, she hired a guard service to keep the former cook out of her compound. Sure enough, he returned frightfully drunk, and only a guard's raised lathi dissuaded him from keeping his promise. Now she's standing the expense of an around-the-clock guard. Her companions sympathize. One observes, with considerable heat, that it's all the fault of Independence—these people are simply going wild.

Fear rises from the Other.

From the presence of.

But since the Other is everywhere you are not, you live in constant fear. Is that it? Is it? Is it that? Good God, no, he thinks.

There must be another way, but another way means you must find the Other in yourself.

That, you damn fool, is why you meditate every morning.

He drinks.

Out there in the shimmering brilliance of midday some dark women continue to load and unload bricks. He watches one of them fold a length of cloth on her head, then swiftly wrap the remaining piece into a circle, forming a flat crown on which she places a metal tray. Slowly a companion loads bricks on the tray. Embree counts them: One . . . two . . . three . . . eight bricks. Could he carry as many? A few naked children squat near the construction site, patiently waiting for their mothers to stop work, to cook the noon meal, to feed them.

At the next table they are talking about stomach ulcers and drug addiction among their servants and the alarmingly high incidence of "elephant leg" among South Indians. "Independence has ruined the hospitals," a woman declares with a Scottish burr. "Everyone expected it, though, didn't they. Friends who'd been out before Independence warned me I'd find it worse than they'd had it."

Another nods in outraged agreement. "If you don't tip the nurses now they wind the bandages too tight. I heard of a badly burnt child who lay moaning for two days, while a few beds away some nurses were playing cards or something. They hadn't been properly tipped, you see, to care for the child."

On the train from Bangalore Embree saw a tiny child holding in its arms a still tinier child under the blue shade of a mothering tree. The sight will be with him forever. There are times when human life is very beautiful. Fumbling in his seersucker jacket, he finds a frayed piece of lined paper and reads it once again.

My Dear Philip:

Your letter came as a shock—but a pleasant one. I'm in a rush now, the shop is more demanding than ever, but let me say for Sonia and me that we'll welcome you home any time you decide to come. We've always felt that way. Now, according to your letter, you're thinking seriously of returning. So do. It is just that simple. And never again apologize for your absence. As Sonia says, you've been through a terrible ordeal. You're not the first man who has needed time to sort out his feelings after a war. So come home.

Love, V

What an admirable woman. His wife's letter is sensible, tolerant, generous. Yet the tone is cool, isn't it? Almost, on repeated readings, indifferent. In the last analysis her attitude is withholding, her welcome merely formal. And that's as it should be. After all, he was mustered out two years ago; in all that time he'd never tried to rejoin Vera in Bangkok. It's a wonder she's agreed to take him back. And Sonia defends him! When he left, she was a gangly kid, but now, almost nine years later, she must be a young woman, a pretty young woman. The dramatic features of her Russian mother? Intense eyes of her Chinese father?

"A bearer stole one hundred rupees from my bag," a woman is saying.

Out there the construction team has stopped work. Women laborers crouch around a large iron pot while the rice boils. Hunkered alongside their mothers, the children gleam in the sun's glare like rich chocolate.

The woman at the next table is relating with gusto the tale of her bearer who stole the rupees. Police came for him, and later an officer told her the fellow hadn't yet confessed, though he would after a good beating. Meanwhile the bearer's family had gathered outside her compound, wailing and pleading: a wife, two walking and two carried infants, five other children, a mother-in-law, one brother and three sisters, a variety of cousins, nephews, aunts, and uncles. All of them set up a racket heard through the neighborhood. Calling the police and pleading to drop the charges against a man with such responsibilities, she was told that he'd just confessed; he'd get five years.

"What happened there, the police wanted to exercise power," a woman declares. "It didn't matter what *you* wanted, my dear. That's Independence, isn't it."

Embree turns and smiles at the women, who are too intent upon shared experience, especially the thrill of domestic calamity, to notice a lone man sitting at the next table with a livid scar across his forehead. But Embree, not caring, continues to smile. The gimlets have mellowed him, easing the negative thoughts back into a corner of his mind. Embree doesn't like to think of himself as negative by nature. He takes another sip of gimlet, savoring the icy taste of gin and lime.

India gets used to people. That's the spirit, he tells himself. Optimism.

If you hold on, India eventually accepts you. That's what someone once claimed would happen to him, and happen it did.

Not just someone. It was Harry. Harry told him that. Harry told him. Harry told him he would learn to love India as he'd never loved another place—love it beyond reason, with the blind trust of a man loving a woman.

Embree swallows the last of his gimlet and signals a club boy for another. Three gimlets at midday in Madras is foolhardy, yet he needs to find a way through these bright, bad Indian minutes, through them and beyond the memories.

● ● ●

A woman is telling about her cook who slipped a sharp pin into the evening curry, when a tall round-shouldered man moves in front of Embree's view of the laborers at their midday meal.

"Mister Embree? Sorry I'm late."

Embree rises to shake hands. "Mister Frazer." The hand is firm, the smile formal, and Frazer has gray in his hair.

When they sit down, Frazer places the chair so that his head is backlit by the sun, thereby throwing his face into shadow. A diplomat all right. Don't be negative, Embree tells himself. Yet as they exchange amenities, he feels uneasy about the man sitting this way. While a club boy takes Frazer's order, Embree recalls something: In Burma the Japs tied themselves into trees along the path of an Allied column; they took advantage of the sun, choosing the side that threw glare into the eyes of approaching scouts. Embree blinks a few times, as if by this action he can rid himself of it—Burma, the war, Harry, all of it.

"Well." Turning from the club boy, Frazer puts both hands on the table—the finality of a schoolmaster preparing to start class. "It's a pleasure meeting you. Somehow we've missed each other. I haven't been posted long in Madras, so I don't yet know all of our nationals."

Embree smiles. Actually his attention's fixed on the nearby table where a woman is saying with emphatic conviction, "Never be nice to servants. Strictness is respected, familiarity despised."

"Are you a member of the Madras Club, Mister Embree?"

"I never joined."

"Let me sponsor you."

Such unsolicited patronage swings Embree's attention from the women to his host. He looks at Frazer closely now: the thin, sallow face, horn-rimmed glasses, the receding hairline flecked with gray. Look of college professor or family doctor. Yet in the right circumstances possibly a dangerous man.

"Least I can do," Frazer adds jauntily, "for someone who fought at Yengangyang in 1942." He leans back and narrows his eyes in the effort of recall. "You were Liaison Officer with the Chinese Fifth Army. Under—let me see . . . Sun Li-jen." Shifting, he exposes one side of his face to the light; there's a cast in his right eye.

"No. Sun Li-jen had the 38th Division," Embree corrects him just as Frazer's drink arrives.

Frazer sips thoughtfully, then puts the glass back on the club boy's tray. "I ordered gin and lime, salt. Not gin and lime, sweet."

"Were you in Burma, Frazer?"

"Never got there. You won the DCM at Yengangyang."

" 'Died Chasing Mules' we called it. I suppose where you were they called it something different." Embree is fishing for information; he'd like to know a little about someone who knows so much about him.

"I believe you won the DSO much later." Frazer shows the tips of tobacco-stained teeth before shifting again into shadow.

Embree takes this show of teeth as a controlled smile. "You have quite a dossier on me."

"Am I making you uneasy?"

"As a matter of fact, I'm enjoying myself." Embree lifts his glass in a toast. It's true, he is. There are times for drinking too much, and this is one of them: meeting a United States Consul who has memorized your life.

"I'm glad you're enjoying yourself," Frazer says. "So am I. A little hobby of mine is military history. I envy someone who's met Bill Slim, Joe Stilwell, Orde Wingate. What did you think of Wingate?"

With the aid of gimlets at high noon, Embree remembers the small Brit with his black beard and demonic eyes, with his paranoia and ineffable sense of mission that drew to his crazy schemes many sane men who would go to their deaths without hesitation at his command—and frequently did, there in the jungles. Once when Embree was with the 101st Detachment, in the China-Burma-India theater, they received a radio message from Brigadier Wingate: *Whatsoever Thy Hand Findeth to Do, Do It with Thy Might.* It was a quote from Ecclesiastes that has been with Embree ever since childhood, that has haunted his imagination during manhood, that has shown him the way to bad judgment, that has led him to bravery and betrayal. How extraordinary that the strange British general had chosen the same biblical phrase at a moment of crisis. But Embree says none of this to the American Consul. Instead, he describes Wingate's habit of eating huge piles of onions and giving interviews while stark naked.

"I'd like the benefit of your experience in CBI. Who was the best general there, in your opinion? Stilwell?"

Embree studies his host, who with a gin and lime—salt, mind you, not sweet—sits with lips parted as if interested in an honest answer. "Not Stilwell. He couldn't control his emotions."

"Did you have a run-in with him?"

"Of course I did. You have it in your records. That's why I went to the 101st Detachment."

"Yes, I remember."

"I'm sure you do. Sun Li-jen was the finest military man I met in the war. He was also the second-best field general I ever knew."

"And the first?"

Embree flicks out his hand dismissively. "Someone I knew long ago."

"In China?"

"Yes. A warlord."

"And the worst?" The consul takes a pipe and tobacco pouch from his jacket.

He's going to persist, Embree thinks. "That's easy. Chiang Kai-shek."

Frazer stops tamping tobacco into the pipe bowl. He arches his eyebrows. "That interests me enormously. Why?"

Embree drains his glass. "He couldn't delegate. He exercised field command from GHQ. He cut regimental orders for Burma when he was in Chungking two thousand miles away. By the time his orders got transmitted they were meaningless. Once I met a Chinese commander who told me this story. During a battle he received a message from the Gimo telling him to give the troops watermelon, because it was good for morale. Chiang's the worst. Definitely."

"Another drink before we eat?"

"Thank you."

"Who was the Chinese warlord you spoke so highly of?"

"He's dead." Across the bright lawn the laboring women are back at their brick pile, working like a column of ants at a trash dump. The loin-clothed masons await them on top of the scaffold.

"Was he a Communist?" Frazer asks.

"No. He's just dead."

"When did you know him?"

"In 1927. I'm surprised the dossier missed that."

Frazer puffs briskly.

"Why don't we get this straight." Embree ticks off on his fingers each item in a schoolmasterly way that Frazer might admire. "Yale Divinity School. China, 1927, to be a missionary. Kidnaped on train by Mongolian bandits." He drops his hand with a little shrug. "One thing led to another, I was what you called rescued. Then I joined the rescuers, the Southern Shantung Defense Army. I was in the cavalry of General Tang Shan-teh."

"Sorry, I never heard of him."

"Oh, you would have, had he lived."

The club boy approaches with menus. Arrangements for a bland British luncheon occupy the men awhile. Once the boy is gone, Frazer lights up again. "Extraordinary," he murmurs.

"Kidnaping wasn't extraordinary in those days. Didn't they make American movies about it?" A flippant tone is just right for this interview, Embree thinks. He gives Frazer a fiercely bright smile, but absorbed in his own thoughts the consul doesn't seem to notice.

"An American missionary in a Chinese warlord's army. I call that extraordinary." Frazer inhales deeply and blows out the smoke with a thoughtful look. "I mean, it's not a common thing."

"Not easy to understand."

"That's what I mean. A missionary, a warlord's army."

"A man who said he did a thing like that might be unstable or lying." Frazer puffs hard on his pipe, avoiding comment.

"How I handle it," Embree says, "is by thinking of myself as a dog." Frazer guffaws.

"No, really. You put a puppy in a cage, you keep him there until he's grown. While in the cage, he's been taught to obey commands—you know, *Sit, Roll Over, Stay*. But the moment comes when you open the cage door wide. You give the usual commands—*Sit, Roll Over, Stay*. What will the dog do?"

"Bolt." Frazer, grinning, sucks on the pipe. "He'll definitely bolt. Even so, what you did was extraordinary."

"I know it now. All I knew then was getting free of an extraordinary father."

"He must have been. If he influenced you to do such a thing."

"He spent ten years as a field preacher here in India. Do you have that on file?"

Frazer smiles. "I'm afraid not."

"He had a mission in Bihar, not far from Ramgarh where the 38th bivouacked in '42. I was there after the Japs threw us out of Burma. On furlough I visited the mission, but the Indians had converted it into a village hospital."

"Your father wouldn't have liked that."

"Then you understand. He was a man with one idea. Everything had to fit into it. My mother, my sister, myself, his parishioners, everyone he knew and everything he did had to conform to his idea of what the Godhead was."

"Frightening."

"You understand that too."

"Have you made peace with him?"

"I haven't communicated with my father in twenty years. I have no idea if he's still alive." Watching the club boy come along with the luncheon tray, Embree sighs. "But I've paid the debt I owed him."

"How is that?"

"I came here to find God. Really. That's what I came here for. To see what he'd been making a fuss about all those years."

"And did you find God?"

"Well, I've tried. I've learned a lot about India," Embree says non-committally.

The arrival of food ends that conversation. They turn for a topic to the rumored drought. Some Indian pundits say it will come, some say the gods will prevent it from coming. Temples are doing a land-office business these days because of it: People come in droves to pray for a miracle.

Having agreed that this indeed is India, they discuss the new airplane that can go at supersonic speeds; Jackie Robinson's baseball contract (Embree has never seen a major-league baseball game in his life); the death of Al Capone.

Beyond the club veranda, Madras's air is wavy with noontime sunlight. Out there in the distance the dark women move with their bricks to the scaffold, then away from it, through the dead silence that comes with heat. At the next table the ladies are discussing shops and fashions in England. One voice begins to dominate, speaking with nostalgia and desire of a proposed trip home. Finally Embree turns for a look at the woman, who is speaking with considerable eloquence. Her floppy hat hides most of a youthful face; he sees the tip of a nose, full lips, pointed chin, and beads of sweat trickling down her jawline. He turns almost obsessively in following minutes to glance at the sweat traveling along the shadowed line of her jaw above a throat pallid and soft. How long has it been since he's held a woman? There had been Grace during those few intense weeks in the monsoon. And before that? How long has it been since he held someone close and spoke of love?

Vera must still be lovely, somewhat like this woman, only with broad Slavic cheekbones and wide-set eyes. How long since he held Vera?

"Of course you know Gandhi has started a new fast," Frazer says, putting down his fork, as if to concentrate finally on a topic of importance. "No one thinks it will change things in Delhi. People are calling him Mohammed Gandhi. I think his own Hindu people are hard on him."

"Two years ago in Calcutta they were calling him Jinnah's Slave, but he turned that city around."

"Have you ever seen him?"

"Once," Embree says. "During the Calcutta riots. I was staying off the street because they were throwing kerosene bombs. There was a commotion outside my hotel, so I went to see. And there came Bapuji in his dhoti, racing down the street with a Moslem entourage trying to keep up with him. One interesting thing—" Embree puts down his fork too. "I could see the muscles rippling in his thighs. The old man's frail, all right, but in the way a runner's frail."

"Interesting. What do you think of China?" Lighting his pipe, Frazer gazes steadily through the burst of flame, the rising smoke. "Have you kept up these last few years?"

"Not really. What I know I get from reading the *Hindu*."

"The good old reliable *Hindu*."

"I know that Marshall got nowhere trying to reconcile the Reds and the Kuomintang. And that they're still fighting." He adds after a thoughtful moment, "Didn't Truman issue a policy statement some time ago? Hands off China? Let them clean up their own mess?"

"In December 1946. Then he recalled Marshall, and the mess got worse. This last year has been difficult for the Chinese," Frazer observes.

"For the Chinese most years are."

"Rice riots broke out in the cities. Students demonstrated against corruption. We lifted our embargo against delivery of combat matériel to the Kuomintang."

"After Truman's declaration of hands off. I see. I imagine the Reds loved that."

Frazer ignores the sarcasm. "Chiang Kai-shek ordered general mobilization for war against the Communist rebellion."

"And the fighting?"

"You really haven't kept up, have you. Pretty much a stalemate until last summer."

"Maybe that's why the *Hindu* devoted all of five lines to it every so often."

"Last summer the Reds started a limited offensive north of the Yangtze."

"Now that you mention it, I remember."

"The Reds did well the last half of 1947. Gains in Shansi, Hopei, Honan. Now Manchuria is up for grabs." Frazer hunches his shoulders, a gesture either of mild disgust or mild despair. He has learned the art of ambiguous gesturing. "Chiang Kai-shek had better hold on to Manchuria or there goes his steel and wheat." Frazer calls the club boy over. "Coffee or tea?"

Embree shakes his head. "If you don't mind, another gimlet. I'm finding today's my day to drink."

When the boy is gone, Frazer says, "Your opinion of Chiang Kai-shek isn't encouraging."

"Well, you can discount it. Remember, I was talking about five years ago. You can't make broad statements about anything in China, not even about generals. To know anything you have to be there."

"I couldn't agree more." During a silence that lengthens, Frazer seems to be thinking of other questions.

Well, let him, Embree decides. The fellow's only doing his job. And this luncheon's been a lark. It's compensated for the passage in *The*

Upanishads that's been nagging all day like a sore muscle. This afternoon he's free, because the export house has closed for the festival at Mylapore. Embree feels his mouth lift as the club boy heaves into view with coffee pot and cups and, what is really important, another icy gimlet.

With his new glass raised, Embree says, "To China. May the best man win."

"Are you really that neutral, Mister Embree?"

"I suppose I am."

"Don't you think it matters who wins—Nationalist or Communist?"

"I'm neutral about politics. I don't give a damn as long as the Chinese people come out all right."

"But to come out all right they must have politics. Wouldn't you say?" Frazer puts three lumps of sugar in his cup and stirs with deliberation. "Let me put it differently. Who'll help the Chinese people more?"

"I don't think anyone can help them very much."

"But of the two sides—"

"I don't know."

Frazer relights his pipe and stares through the smoke. Embree smiles: He's with a college professor turned G2. "We've been thinking," Frazer continues, "maybe a neutral view's needed out there right now. For assessment. Maybe our people have chosen sides too quickly."

Embree drinks.

"If an American can be said to know things Chinese, surely you qualify. You speak the language—"

"My Mandarin's rusty. Some dialect. Not that much Chinese."

"Enough to make a living once as a translator."

"What I know about China today I read in the *Hindu*."

"Mister Embree, we could be backing the wrong horse on this one." Again Frazer spreads his hands flat on the table. "Would you be interested in going in and having a look for us? I gather your job here in Madras isn't pressing."

"Do I understand you're offering me a job?"

"I am."

"Flattering." Yes, it really is, Embree thinks. He's in mid-life, with a measly job, without a wife except in name, without a faith he can trust. Yet this scholarly fellow is willing not only to buy him drinks but to stake him to costly travel—and all at the service of his country. Flattering. "Sorry."

"Why?"

"I just can't accept."

The American Consul taps out the ashes of his pipe into his coffee cup; it's a quick gesture of frustration.

"You see, I have a wife and stepdaughter. I haven't seen them since 1939. But you probably know that. Thing is, I never had a leave during the war; then afterward I came here." Embree pauses. "I want to go home now. To Bangkok."

"I can understand that."

With drunken contentment Embree figures the two of them have conducted themselves well today—with the restraint and patience of civilized men. Good for us. The earlier negativism is quite gone. Perhaps he should thank Frazer for that—Frazer and the gimlets.

"So the point you're making," Frazer concludes, "is your duty's to your family."

"Strange as it may seem. It took all this time to see where my life ought to be. Now I have debts in Bangkok."

"You might consider paying your family debt and serving your country at the same time."

"How does that work?"

"We know your Russian wife speaks Chinese too. She's lived in China. You could travel together."

"On what basis?"

"Travel as linguists. Scholars. There are still some in China."

Embree can't decide if the fellow has thought out the plan ahead of time or is creating it on the spot. Foreign service officers have a way of going after what they want, no matter what the cost. Is this spur of the moment or carefully worked out? Either way the plan seems feasible up to a point—the point being that Vera used to say she would never set foot on Chinese soil again. No need to tell Frazer, though.

"Of course," Frazer continues, "she wouldn't accompany you into the interior."

"Where I'd have to go? You weren't offering a stroll through Shanghai and Peking?" He looks at the film of gin and lime in his empty glass. "Truth is, Frazer, she wouldn't go, and I wouldn't try to persuade her. My wife's seen enough of war. Thank you, I'm flattered. But there's no way I'd consider going to China now."

8 THE LUNCHEON ENDS rapidly. Fuzzy from drink, Embree is bewildered by the speed with which Frazer escapes. The stoop-shouldered man, with pipe still in his mouth, seems to be up and out almost before Embree can rise for a cursory handshake. One thing about Frazer, he decides: Man's a poor loser. The brutal swiftness of Frazer's departure takes away from Embree's pride in their mutual civility. It occurs to Embree that he stays too much alone, that he's forgotten the passions of men.

Perhaps the last drink has turned him back to negativism. He raises the empty gimlet. That's what he's left with: an empty glass, a view of women toiling across the vast lawn, a closer view of wilted women—languorous like himself from alcohol—and with an entire afternoon ahead in which to contemplate a line from *The Upanishads*.

Rising unsteadily he moves past the table of women—glancing at the eloquent one who unfortunately hides her face under the wide hat—into the bar, where he orders another gimlet to be put on the consul's tab. Maybe another drink will turn him around again, let him regain the sense of well-being he experienced during luncheon. It had been good, perhaps better than he'd like to admit, to remember the past and talk about it. How odd. Because he'd spoken with ease to a stranger about his youth as a failed missionary. But he'd never told Vera about it. Never. All those years he'd kept it secret. She has always thought he went to China as a language student.

Since 1927 he's carried on the deception. But it hasn't been a gratuitous lie. No. She'd have hated him nearly as much for betraying his God as for betraying the General.

Embree drinks, noting with the satisfaction of a fellow delinquent that the two Brits whom he overheard earlier at the bar have returned to it as well. They've resumed telling stories about India.

Embree grins, and they, in turn—also under the benign influence of midday gin—respond similarly. Encouraged, Embree asks if they had a nice lunch. Indeed they had. Did he? Indeed.

"Good time of day for a peg of gin, isn't it," one says. "I say, I was going to tell my friend this story. Perhaps you haven't heard it."

"I haven't." Embree moves closer.

"A Swami, you see, once asked a Brahman what he wanted next time his wife gave birth—son or daughter? For a change the Brahman wanted a daughter, because he already had sons enough to handle his funeral. 'So it's a daughter you want, is it,' the Swami said. 'You'll have twins.' 'No, I don't want twins if they're going to be daughters,' the Brahman said. 'All right,' said the Swami, 'you'll have what you want; just leave it to me.' So the next time the Brahman's wife gave birth, it was twin girls born dead. The Brahman complained to the Swami. 'Look here, old chap, you did me a bad turn. They were both dead.' 'Indeed?' the Swami said. 'You got your wish, didn't you—no twin daughters.' "

The other man smacks his knee in acknowledgment of a good story, but Embree stands there bemused. He doesn't like it. He thinks of something to tell them. He must tell them. He feels abruptly self-righteous. He senses his companions are not friends, but enemies for reasons obscure.

"All right, gentlemen," he begins, waving his gimlet to get their close attention. "Ponder this, please. Seems there was a Hindu being chased by a tiger. Climbing a tree, he crawled to the end of a branch that hung over a dry well. Mice began gnawing the branch behind him, while beneath him the tiger was waiting for him to fall." The two listeners bend forward, grinning, their faces creased by the wrinkles of good times. "At the bottom of the dry well, into which the poor damn Hindu was staring, there was a nest of snakes. So he couldn't jump into the well for safety. He crawled right to the end of the branch, bending it low from his weight, until he saw a blade of grass growing from a crack in the well. He leaned over and brought his face low, so low he could lick a drop of honey from the blade of grass."

Embree drains his gimlet, signaling the end of his story.

"What in hell does that mean?" one asks in a surly tone of suspicion.

"It means the Hindu knows how to enjoy any moment of life he can get. It's the unearned joy of desperation."

They frown. "All right," says the other, "but what's the point of it? I suppose it's some kind of American idea of the mystic East, is it."

"It must be something like that, gentlemen." Turning, Embree walks away, unsure whether in victory or defeat. Of course he could go back. "Did you hear the one about the missionary?" He doesn't know a story like that, but he could start up anyway. "There was this English missionary. You know the type—a red-faced, wet-eyed, drunken sonofabitch going to fat like yourselves." Which of them would hit him first? Probably the beefier one.

But he keeps walking away, and when he has traversed the ballroom and lobby and had a glimpse of men bending over the pool table in the billiard room, Embree no longer cares. He's thinking of the Hindu tasting a drop of honey when hope is lost. The story, which he'd heard from Harry back in Burma when Harry had still been Harry, draws him into the shadows, where *The Upanishads* continues its grim work.

Before going into the courtyard this morning to meditate, he had read the passage "Fear rises from the Other." And the Other had been there behind his closed eyes during the long dark journey of meditation when, seated in the Half Lotus, he had pursued himself or God as he does every morning. Only this morning, thanks to *The Upanishads*, he had not pursued but had been pursued—by the Other. And it is still with him now, while he's leaving the club.

But he won't have that, Embree decides. Definitely no more negativism. Fatigue is all it leads to. What he's going to do now, he's going to find a rickshaw and go to the festival at Mylapore. He'll mingle with the thousands who manage to get their drop of honey one way or another each day, and he'll lift his hands in homage to Lord Shiva, who as yet hasn't done much for him, and he'll look around for his own drop of honey. By God, that's what he'll do.

Crossing the front lawn of the Adyar Club, he notices the tree where crows had nested earlier. The tree's as empty now as a rifled grave. Not a crow in it. Fear. Of the Other. Fear of the next life, perhaps. Of Vera. Of Vera? Fear of reeling drunkenly into the adolescent mire of his distant past is more like it. And fear of Harry, of that memory.

He wishes he'd stayed long enough at the club to meet the woman whose eyes were hidden by the brim of her hat. He'd ask her, as he'd asked Grace during the monsoon season, if she would have lunch with him. And maybe, like Grace, she would. Perhaps her eyes are spectacular—wide, limpid, filled with depths. Eyes to remind him of Vera's eyes, of his loss of such a woman.

Staggering through the midday glare, Embree reaches the boundary of the club and waves at a rickshaw wallah lounging under the shade of a rain tree. Where's his hat? Left it back there. To hell with it.

Now to Mylapore.

. . .

Cows and people overflow into the stream of traffic surging through Mylapore, past the shops selling tools, food, trinkets, even salvation— for, on closer inspection, some of them are tiny temples with foot-high lingas, with statues of Murugun, Shakti, Venketesvara shadowy in alcoves, greasy from melted camphor and kumkum powder. There are rickshaws, bicycles, a few motor cars heading for Kapaliswarar Temple. But many of the vehicles moving in that direction are jutkas, wheeled slabs drawn by bullocks and loaded with peasants in from the country.

Leaving his rickshaw, Embree joins the crowd—or rather staggers into the manswarm that rends the afternoon air with cries and laughter. Beggars, looking for good fortune on festival days, spot Embree's blond hair and quickly surround him, thrusting handless stubs at his face. He turns on these lepers the blank gaze of Indian survival, brushing past them until alongside some Brahman priests. In their white dhotis, gathered under the legs and tucked around ample waists, they look like fat, rumpled butchers. The heat, the glare, the noise, the motion of thousands heading for the temple, affect Embree like another gimlet. Ahead of him, in colorful saris, Indian ladies are holding big British umbrellas over their heads, making a row of black lotuses sprout above the street.

"Sah! Sah!" Someone, Embree realizes, is trying to attract his attention with a military "sir"—imitating the Gurkhas, who can't be imitated. Embree moves resolutely on, staring at the churned earth beneath his leather shoes and the sandal-clad feet of people bustling toward the steady drumbeat in the next block, where, behind the great temple under a temporary roof of matting, stands the immense chariot of Lord Shiva.

Giddy from both drink and excitement, he moves clear of traffic to pause under a shed with a sign painted above it: SUITING AND DRESS MATERIALS. The tailor has closed for the day. A man standing near Embree spits betel juice, and for a moment, his vision faulty, Embree thinks it's a copious vomit of blood. Scary. It seemed to him for an instant that a man terribly ill or wounded had spilled his guts through his throat, as they used to do in Burma, as they used to do in China, too. But the man was simply ridding himself of the superfluity of pleasure.

Embree steps again into the crowd, letting it propel him toward the sawed-off pyramid of the temple. It rakes the blue sky, offering to incoming spectators the riotous sight of carved deities pulsing on brick surfaces high up in the cloudless heat. Staring at the sculpted figures, Embree sees them for an instant as people joyously dancing and the next instant as insects crawling on a wall. He's drunk, very, and knows it. How do the Indians see those gods? As dancing insects?

Negative. That's negativism.

He surrenders willingly to the crowd, which tightens against itself, and approaches a wooden chariot at least fifty feet high.

It stands beside the temple wall next to a cement ramp. He wants to climb the ramp and reach the top of the chariot, but people massed there won't let others by. Embree yells out, "Shri Sivaramamurti! Shri Sivaramamurti!" He flails his arms and flings himself at the ramp, determined now, with the willfulness of inebriation, to get there.

A white man screaming an important name is sufficient to part the crowd.

Soon he's staggering up the incline, tasting gin, his vision filled with dark-skinned Hindus inching back to give him room.

"Mind your step, mind your step, Mister Embree!" A skinny old man hastens down the ramp toward him. "Thank the Lord you have arrived. I was going to send someone to find you out. Come, mind your step—"

Embree raises his hands, palms together, in greeting.

Mister Sivaramamurti raises his own. "I have been keen on seeing you today. They are bringing the god soon. Come along, please, Mister Embree, sir. Mind your step. I am delighted. The whole Vedanta Society of Madras is here. Every one of them. They will be keen on seeing you, too. A pleasure indeed. Mind your step, please."

They climb the last few feet of the incline to a platform level with the chariot, which has been mounted with pillars and a little house. The whole affair is topped by a wooden umbrella. Workmen are pounding stanchions with mallets, and decorators are draping flower wreaths over the carved sides of the immense chariot, around the shoulders of wooden demons that loom from the vehicle's corners.

"I have been up since half three this morning," Mister Sivaramamurti exclaims, rolling his eyes, bloodshot from glare and lack of sleep. His teeth are stained black by betel chewing. His skin, stretched tight against a small skull, has the tissued look of parchment. Embree wonders how the frail old fellow has managed to stay upright in the pushing crowd. "There has been so much to be doing, my head is eating circles. But what to do? No, no, I don't fancy that." Sivaramamurti flutters his hand at a workman who's trying to strengthen the housing by nailing an extra piece of wood against a pillar. Turning to Embree, he giggles at the naughtiness of a remark he thinks of making. "I had rather the house of the Lord fall down than look makeshift." His clawlike hand grips Embree's shoulder. "I have been so keen on seeing you!"

At this moment Embree can imagine the man as a child. As Sivaramamurti must have done himself, small boys in the crowd below accept the danger of being trampled underfoot—anything if they can share in the fun of parading the god through a few acres of trampled city.

"We have been missing you lately, Mister Embree."

"I was in Bangalore, Calcutta, Benares."

"Ah, Benares!" The name of a sacred city delights Sivaramamurti on this religious day. "My friend"—he looks Embree up and down with a smile—"you have put on some flesh."

Aware the remark is complimentary, Embree smiles in acknowledgment of it. In truth he carries a few more pounds than wanted and thirty more than he weighed coming out of Burma. "You look very fit too, sir," he tells Sivaramamurti, carefully enunciating his words to keep the slur of alcohol out of them.

"No, no, not fit, thank you. I am pulled down some." An aide rushes up to whisper in Sivaramamurti's ear. Taking coins from a small leather pouch, the old man gives them to the aide, who again whispers in his ear. "Indeed, I know," Sivaramamurti says with a nod. "They are rascally chaps. Do what is needful." Turning to Embree, he shakes his head. "It has all gone down, sir, from where it was. Fellows today won't move a step without payment. My blessed father would not have survived in such a world." But a better thought enlivens his face. "I am frightfully delighted to see you, my good friend. We have all been keen to see you. Subramanian, Ramakrishnan, Vasudevan. The rumor is false, is it? You are not leaving the Madras side?"

Breathing the tumultuous air of festival time, Embree has difficulty believing he has ever contemplated such a thing. "I might leave, yes. At least it's possible."

"To where?"

"Siam. If I go. But it's improbable."

"We will not have it," Sivaramamurti declares shrilly. "You will be fetched back from over there, straightaway. You are one of us, sir!"

Embree smiles with pleasure. His mind moves for a moment beyond the crowd, his friend, the compliment. He is composing phrases for an imaginary letter: "My Dearest Vera: Although you have been all too generous in your decision to take me back, I feel we would all three—you, Sonia, and I—be happier if you sold your Bangkok interests and came here. You and Sonia would love India, you would simply love it, I know, because India is—"

Sivaramamurti grips his arm again. "I think the god is coming."

There's a flurry of motion below the ramp, within the enclosed area. There's shouting at the temple's rear door, hidden by platforms on which other gods sit under the matting roof.

All those gimlets are encouraging Embree to be expansive, although he's tried hard for control. He mustn't make a damn fool of himself. A drink or two, yes, but Sivaramamurti and others in the Vedanta Society of Madras would be offended by drunkenness. Even so, he's just been told that they would haul him back from Siam because *he is one of them,* and in consequence, Embree grips the bony arm of Sivaramamurti with boyish eagerness. "Listen! This morning I was reading *The Upanishads,*" he says breathlessly and at the same time trying to keep his speech precise and logical, "and I came upon this phrase—it's stayed with me all day. *Fear—*"

But *fear* is swept aside by a terrific roar, followed by a swirl of white, as a platoon of men in dhotis are running a palaquin up the ramp.

"Ah, the god is coming!" Sivaramamurti exclaims.

A tremor passes through the crowd on the platform, and for a moment Embree is sure someone will topple into the multitude fifty feet below —probably the paper-thin Sivaramamurti—but before mishap can take place, the bronze statue of Lord Shiva has been hauled up the ramp, taken from the palanquin, and placed within the chariot housing. Decorators rush forward to arrange the brocaded robe and gold crown of the two-foot idol that wears on its metallic forehead the mark of Shiva, Lord of the World.

"Let me by, let me by," scolds Mister Sivaramamurti, waving his hands at the workmen. "Come, Mister Embree, have a look here. Do you fancy the gold? I do. Those are diamonds on the robe, and rubies."

Embree stares at the expensive god, looking tiny under its crown, lost in swathes of brocade.

"This," says Sivaramamurti, touching the silk pants which the Lord wears—none save he and the decorators dare touch them—"is very, very dear, sir. The arms and legs move into different positions, don't you see. This is worth more than idols you will be finding elsewhere except at Tirupati," he announces proudly. "Over there, it is true, they have rubies as big as duck eggs."

Embree displays the proper awe. He's been in India too long to be contemptuous of materialistic pride in the splendor of idols. And yet looking at the flagrantly pagan image, he wonders again, as he does each Indian day, what his father must have suffered in the presence of such idolatry—his father who lacked the imagination to see behind a tawdry show a measure of devotion.

"What do you think, sir? Is it splendid?"

"Yes." Embree lifts his palms in prayer and bows toward the idol. "Beautiful and dignified."

"I am delighted to hear you saying so."

There's no more time for talk, however, because people are crowding around Sivaramamurti. Being in charge of the festival chariot, he has, for the moment, more power than a man can want or wield.

• • •

Backing away, Embree leaves his friend alone with responsibility. Gin has hampered his conjuring of the praiseful rhetoric that Sivaramamurti expects. Engrossed by the problem of detaching the ramp's platform from the chariot, the old man has quite forgotten him, so Embree slips into the crowd now starting down the incline. On the way Embree turns for a glimpse of the Lord of the World, whose small bronze face peeks from a skein of flowers. At the bottom of the ramp he can't see the god behind pillars of the chariot.

A murmur greets Embree as he moves beyond the matting roof into the street. A burgeoning sound accompanies the attempt, by pulling on two immense hawsers, to move the chariot away from the ramp. Hundreds of men try to get it into motion. Straining, creaking, the chariot at last leaves dead center. Its thick wooden wheels, a dozen feet high, begin their long circle, and the sight of movement commencing prompts the crowd to yell louder through the afternoon heat. Leaning into their work, the haulers successfully heave the wooden structure into a rattling, constant motion. The chariot shakes. Painted cloth cylinders hanging along the sides begin to sway. A drum pounds out a slow rhythm, joined then by a whining flute.

Embree is pushed forward as the crowd, emitting a long howl of triumph, rushes at the chariot, but is held back by policemen who grip a restraining rope. The great shaking edifice gets hauled into the middle of the street, looking capable of toppling over at any moment. People are prostrating themselves full length on the ground. Others, back near the serried shops, are burning incense and camphor, ritually pulling their ears, turning in circles, muttering prayers.

Carried along beside the lumbering chariot by the ecstatic mob, Embree feels deep within himself an excitement building, as if tons of water were pushing against a dam. His own throat fills with a cry, one more sound augmenting a tremendous roar that drowns out flute and drum. The great hawsers twist and strain with the tensile ferocity of thin wire. At intervals the procession halts to give the pullers a rest. When it does, big wooden levers are set against the wheels to prevent the chariot from easing backward. People stare upward for darshan of the god, but none can see Shiva within the pillared house, his movable arms and legs, brocaded robes, priceless jewelry.

Again the vehicle lurches into motion, with the pullers treading on small fires placed earlier in the street by devotees performing puja. It is dangerous, it is exhilarating, and Embree stumbles along, sensing the unity of everything beneath the cloudless sky. Thousands upon thousands accompany the triumph of the god through the streets. Everywhere he looks there is awe and ecstasy; he can't be sure whether it's the gin or merely the excitement of being here that makes him think of a single filament, tiny and translucent, leading from one ear, through the skull, out the other ear, of each person in the crowd; it connects them in a divine spider web of vitreous thread.

But the strange idea is gone almost as quickly as it comes, and again he surrenders himself to the willful surge of the crowd. Buffeted out of the front rank, he joins the precipitate of onlookers at the outer edge, where hawkers are selling bamboo toys: bows and arrows, peacocks that move along a little pole; and also bangles, sweets, oblations of banana and coconut, and holy ash folded within triangular bits of paper. Sadhus dressed in ocher, clutching iron tridents, their beards and bodies smeared with ash and wide stripes of white and red paint, stride with a blank stare through the crowd parting reverently before them. Along the route of Shiva's procession, devotees push and shove in a panic to see the hidden god in his finery, but back where Embree is, on the perimeter of activity, there's quiet praying.

Here, on the calm edge, as if caught in the eddy of a stream, Embree finds himself with himself. He's alone, as if staring into a mirror at the drunken face of someone who wants, as desperately as anyone here, to believe in God. And so he thinks of his dead friend Harry.

Dammit, Harry, is this what you meant? Is this all there is? You with your guts hanging out like a string of purple sausages, is this what you were trying to tell me? Or is there more?

Questions that Embree has asked every day of his two years in India.

9 As EMBREE RIDES in the battered tonga, Mylapore vanishes behind him, yet the sound from it slaps at his ears like surf. Some minutes ago, when he left that festive district, they were parading half a hundred other gods in Lord Shiva's wake. This evening the deities will be safe again under the roof matting behind the temple. Crowds seeking darshan of the gods will slosh through an enclosure gone muddy from spilled holy water. Embree knows; he saw the affair to its grimy end last year.

He is quietly, drunkenly furious with himself because it's perfectly clear, isn't it, that his religious ecstasy at the festival was faked. He had watched himself pose as a man who almost sees God—a coxcomb glancing sidelong in a mirror.

Embree stares at the back of the tonga driver, who bends from the dickey toward an ancient horse galumphing down the hot, dusty lane. On both sides are wooden shops, each with its painted sign: BREAD HOUSE, SWEET STALL, EGG MART, PROVISION MERCHANT in English, some in Tamil too. There are only a few people on the road. Their neighbors are undoubtedly in Mylapore, following the immense wheels of Shiva's chariot. He can still hear faintly the sound of their rejoicing, as they toss flowers, eat, buy, and jostle one another for a better look at anything that happens.

He's always had a good memory. His sister Mary used to say it was the one thing he really had, but where is Mary now? Alive in the arms of a rich paramour? Dead from alcohol in the streets of New York? For Mary either fate is possible, but he, bastard that he is, hasn't bothered in two decades to find out, although he always loved her.

The self-reproof, a measure of honesty, cheers him. He yells a new destination at the wallah. Instead of going home, he'll head south awhile, near Greenways Road at the edge of the city, where he has friends of a sort.

Sitting back, he feels the sweat dry on his chest as a little wind stirred by the moving horse slants across him. Embree tries to imagine the real Shiva, not that dandified piece of movable metal back there in the Brobdingnagian chariot. Through a continuing haze of gin, he remembers his reading: "Shiva—Mahesvara, Soul of the Universe, the Form and the Formless, Cosmic Dancer, Happy One. His three eyes are the sun, moon, and fire. His breath is air, his body earth. He is bliss."

Embree stops reciting to wave at a tiny boy, standing by the road, with his oily hair slicked against his skull like a gambler in an old daguerrotype. Beyond the boy he sees other children at work in a brickyard—the only people who seem to be working on this holiday afternoon. A dozen children are carrying loads of bricks on their heads, as earlier he'd seen women do at the Adyar Club. Young eyes under iron bowls wearily scan the work site, on the lookout for the overseer of their kiddy labor gang. And the face of one little girl, in its trembling delicacy, is like a morning lotus; her great eyes, seeking the path beneath her rigidly held head, are beautiful enough to make a man cry, to make Philip Embree cry, drunk or sober. It's what he wants to believe. There's too much negativism about India. He won't have it.

He won't be able to leave it, not this scary place of beauty where fear is always rising both from the Self and the Other. He will definitely write Vera and persuade her to sell the Bangkok shop and with Sonia join him here. He'll change jobs, work hard, amount to something.

Or he'll sober up tomorrow and write a letter of abject gratitude to her for letting him return. Either way.

Same result?

But that doesn't matter. What really matters is *The Upanishads*. Good positive thinking. Embree closes his eyes to recite from a Tamil poem.

"Shiva is the blissful terrible one, called Blue Throated because He swallowed poison to save the world." A blue throat. Christ had a bloody forehead from the thorns. It is all real, all of it—salvation and saviors.

Embree opens his eyes just in time to see a beggar alongside the tonga. One leg grotesquely twisted behind his neck, calf against ear, the man hops along on the other leg. Startled, dismayed, Embree stares at the flesh of the immobilized thigh, discolored and shiny. Fumbling in his jacket, Embree finds a few annas and tosses them backward into the dust, where the man is skipping along, trying to keep pace. With a smile, the beggar tips his hand jauntily against his forehead in military salute; then he simply plummets to the road and scoops the coins up where he sprawls, the bad leg extending along his back like a misshapen club.

In the *Hindu* the other day, Embree read that the life expectancy in India is thirty-three years. Life span of Christ. But all these portents and pretty words from poetry and tortuous correspondences in nature ultimately mean nothing. Or they mean everything. Today is a bad day. Today began badly with *The Upanishads* and has not improved. It was only falsely good at lunch, when he spilled a lot of opinions to a man who only wanted to use him. Come to think of it, the day hasn't been good at all, not even in the presence of kind old Sivaramamurti, who has begged him to remain in this wonderful, scary place.

"There!" Embree shouts, pointing at a dilapidated little shop on the road, next to a tea stall. Over the shop's entrance is a board, aslant because the nail in one corner of it is out. In blue letters the English reads: PROVISION AND GENERAL STORE AND FANCY ITEMS.

This is where I belong, Embree thinks.

Climbing out of the tonga, he argues briefly over the fare already agreed upon, then pays what the driver demands. At the doorway he hesitates, peering into the gloom before entering. The only light in the shop comes from sunlight pooling at the entrance. There are three tables, bare, and a few chairs, and behind them a wooden counter and behind it shelves containing canned goods from England. Two men, naked to the waist, sit in dhotis at one table, nothing in front of them but their hands. A curtain parts at one end of the small room, and a man enters. He is wearing pajama trousers, a loose-fitting shirt of homespun, a thick, graying handlebar mustache, a large brass earring in one ear, and a shabby black fedora.

This is Balakrishnan, who owns the shop, who always wears the earring and fedora. Always. Each time Embree has questioned him about the significance of the single brass earring, Balakrishnan replies with a chortling "Oh, my good friend!" as if in explanation.

One look at Embree and the shopkeeper gestures him feverishly back of the curtain into another small room, this one lit by an oil lamp. Two other men are seated at a table. They have glass tumblers of tea in front of them.

"Tea? Coffee?" Balakrishnan asks with a smile, then wags one finger as if catching his new customer up. "I know you, sir! Brahman coffee, is it?" He whirls upon a small thin child sitting in a corner. "Go, go, go —coffee!" Gesturing toward a second table on which the day's *Hindu* is spread, he says to Embree, "How have you been keeping, sir?" When Embree shrugs, he points with a thick finger, gnarled by arthritis, at the newspaper. "Drought." As they sit down, he adds, "No water last year, no water this. Monsoon failed. You read it today?"

This morning's headlines, featuring Gandhi's fast, had caught Embree's eye; he had bypassed an article on the expected drought.

For a few minutes Balakrishnan gives a lecture on a major consequence of drought, as if a white man can't be expected to think of it: Famine will spread over the entire state of Madras. "Here, sir, coffee." And in Tamil to the child who brings the tray, he says, "Mix it."

Holding two brass tumblers in his little hands, the child pours hot milk from one container into the coffee of the other. Keeping the tumblers at arm's length, he pours the liquid back and forth like a long sinuous brown snake until the mixture's frothy and cool enough to drink.

He gives it to Embree with a bow. Balakrishnan beams with pride. "Gopol, my youngest." Watching Embree sip, he leans forward, his face clouded by an idea. "What is it you want today, my friend? I have someone who would be meeting you."

Embree lovingly inhales and then tastes the deep flavor of this coffee, none better in the world. He recalls the last "someone" met here through Balakrishnan: Smelling of chili pekoras, she enfolded him in her fat buttery skin and rubbed her gold nose ring against his cheek. He'd paid her five rupees not to accompany her home. "No one today, thank you, Balakrishnan."

"Then, smoking, is it?"

"Yes, smoking."

This time Balakrishnan calls Gopol over and whispers. Apparently the bhang is secreted somewhere out of the shop. Perhaps, Embree thinks, the old boy isn't paying off the local police well enough these days. Otherwise it would be out in a jar. He notices that the two men at the far table are studying him.

"Your friends?" he asks.

"They are Communist," Balakrishnan explains in the voice of pride he used to identify his youngest son.

Embree remembers the American diplomat asking him his opinion of Communists today—Chinese variety. He doesn't give a damn what these men are as long as they don't interfere with his smoking—and tells Balakrishnan so.

"No, not to worry, sir. They are already having," the shopkeeper declares with a chuckle.

And Embree can see it in them: the fixed, inner look; the dilated eyes. The bhang of South India is as strong as the coffee.

While waiting for the child to return, Balakrishnan explains further that the Communists, who don't speak English, will be attending the conference of the Communist World Federation of Trade Unions convening in Calcutta this February. He has memorized the information as if it bestows upon him a kind of prize.

"Good friends of yours?" Embree asks, just as Gopol rushes through a rear door.

Balakrishnan shrugs, his attention on the child who will prepare the smoke.

Good old Balakrishnan, Embree thinks. Here's a man who won't let ideology interfere with making money. "Tell your friends they can join me if they wish. I'd be privileged." Embree waits until the smiling shopkeeper translates this invitation, then adds, "I have learned to respect men of conviction. No, don't translate that." You are drunk, Embree tells himself. Getting sentimental. For God's sake, watch it.

The men nod in accepting the invitation to join him, then everyone turns to watch the child.

From a small box Gopol takes toke paper out of one drawer, trihedron-shaped pellets from another. He mashes the bhang points on three pieces of paper and rolls each one with a few deft flicks of his hand; tongues and binds the paper of each toke; and distributes them to the three smokers. The shop owner lights a straw from the oil lamp, hands it around, talking all the time. "Maybe from drought the dead not lining the streets Madras way—they are cleaned up. But in villages, hear me, people will be dying everywhere you can look." He translates this English into Tamil, and the men nod in casual agreement, dragging on their smokes.

Embree inhales his, feeling the raw rush into his lungs. This is vijaya, called Death's Wife, and won't wait long before making its presence felt. While the shop owner adds imagined horrors to the coming drought and famine, Embree sits back to await the vijaya, enabled already by the continuing effect of gin to remove himself awhile from the present scene. In China the way was opium, only he didn't use it. In the years of his youth he'd scorned the use of opiates. Perhaps—it's just possible—Embree thinks, a few tatters of his Christian upbringing had still clung to him then. Then.

"Talk English," he hears himself tell Balakrishnan, who has been speaking Tamil to the Communists.

Balakrishnan explains they are discussing the Moslem goondas who last summer at the time of Partition set fire to the homes of the Sikh minority in Lahore—cold-bloodedly burned a quarter-million houses.

"Have him roll me another, please," Embree says, nodding toward the corner, where candlelight illuminates one dark cheek of the boy Gopol.

Sighing, Embree listens to the men drone on self-righteously about Moslem barbarity. Though he can't understand Tamil, he knows this is what they are doing; he can see it in their faces, now outraged, now righteous. The words he can't understand bore him. Mercifully, his mind goes elsewhere, taken away on the wings of smoke. He remembers something in China, something incredible. It happened in Qufu, birthplace of Confucius, where General Tang had bivouacked his army. Vera had been the General's guest then—guest, hell, Tang's concubine. On that particular day, returning with a squad from cavalry maneuvers, he'd watched Vera canter into view on a stallion, her Russian figure magnificent on the best horse in the General's stable. In full view of the Chinese cavalry, near the town square, she'd brutally whipped a man to the ground with her riding crop. He'd been a Soviet agent assigned by the Comintern as an observer to the General's headquarters. For whatever reason, perhaps frustrated by Chinese indifference to his mission in their camp, the Red Russian had turned to opium. On that particular day, rendered helpless by it, he'd cowered under the shifting hooves of the stallion, while the riding crop descended again and again in the hand of a woman who'd fled across so many frozen miles of their joint homeland. She'd seen her entire family die in the attempt to escape from people who shared with this man the conviction that her kind didn't deserve to live. So on that day in 1927 Vera Rogacheva had taken her revenge against communism—her allies a stallion and some pellets of opium.

And myself, Embree thinks. That day I fell in love with her.

. . .

Taking a deep drag of smoke, he thinks of opium, the Chinese Landlord who always collects the rent. Here in India ganja and bhang are less powerful cousins of the Landlord, but even so, he can feel the deep puffs of hemp sludge his bloodstream and slow down the speed of his life.

"And you, sir, what are you thinking of it?"

Embree turns to squint at Balakrishnan. "Thinking of what?"

"Moslems murdering poor Sikhs in Lahore."

Leaning back, feeling the top rung of the chair press against his shoulder blades, Embree smiles and swallows contentedly. "Yes, about that let me say something, friend. Let me tell you about the Sikhs, those poor fellows, the minority up there in the Punjab," he begins. "Translate for my other two friends, will you? Now I want you all to know what I heard from a Subadar of a Gurkha regiment that tried to keep the peace there last summer." And Embree tells them. Each time Balakrishnan translates what he says, during that interval Embree stares at grains in the shop table, at a face emerging out of the wood. In spite of his fascination with the face, he manages to tell them precisely; after all, it's in him as a soldier to be precise about such things. He explains how admirably systematic the poor Sikhs were. Under command of blue-turbaned leaders, they attacked the Moslem districts of a town in groups of eight hundred. First wave, armed with rifles and Bren guns, took care of snipers who might be waiting on rooftops. Second wave threw grenades into Moslem homes. Third wave started fires by throwing spears dipped in burning rags through open windows. Fourth wave, armed with spears and swords and axes, killed the men and children and carried off the women. "That's what the poor Sikhs did," Embree concludes, taking a deep drag of vijaya. "An illustration of equality in violence."

He notices the men at the other table scowling at him. Are they? Or is it the dope? He feels the corners of his mouth stretching into a friendly smile. "Are my companions angry, Balakrishnan?" The shopkeeper is frowning too.

"Sir, am I permitted?"

"Aren't we all?"

"You see, sir, they are thinking you defend Moslems and their freak of natures."

"Freak of natures?"

"Mohandas Gandhi. They hope on this fast the freak of natures will be dying."

"Is that their hope?" Embree shakes his head, puffs hard, as if the hammer of smoke will knock his mind clear. But he merely grins—knows it—stupidly, as he says in a low, lazy voice, "And Bapu once said his desire was to wipe every tear from every eye." A sentimental thing to say. What a drunk might say. And yet he's glad to have said it, and signals his contentment with a broad smile.

Balakrishnan, who hasn't been smoking, pushes the frayed brim of his fedora back, turning more of his sweaty mustachioed face to the lamplight of the close room.

"Well?" says Embree. "Are you going to translate what Bapuji said?"

"They are not liking that freak of natures. They are delegates to convocation at Calcutta, sir."

Embree stares hard at the two men, deciding that the grain in the table has more distinctive facial characteristics than they do. They are commonplace, impassive; they are only two men sitting opposite him and smoking bhang in the hot room, yet somehow they annoy him. Perhaps because Embree's sure he annoys them. "Ask them what they did in the war. Something tells me they were soldiers."

"Ah, sir, you are correct!" Balakrishnan exclaims, then waves brusquely at Gopol to roll another cigarette. "They were soldiers in INA."

Embree, laughing, bangs the table with both hands. So that's it: the Indian National Army. That's what gives them their arrogance—the old INA, that renegade bunch of patriots and political dissidents. He knows the old INA, who joined the Japs and with them tried to enter India through Burma. If he tries hard, he can still hear their rallying cry. *Chalo Delhi!* He also remembers that captured INA officers, brought to trial after Independence, were eulogized by Congress leaders and given suspended sentences. He bears them no grudge in their fight for freedom. If he has a response to politics, it's hatred for oppression and hurrah for independence. Disgustingly simplistic, but his own. What he can't stand about these men isn't their politics, it's their soldiering. He holds such men in contempt for their inept soldiering, as the Gurkha and Punjabi troopers did also. It is now as a soldier, as a veteran fired by gin and bhang into a posture of extravagant righteousness, that Embree will speak to them, because goddamn if he isn't *determined* to speak to them. He knows who he is now, here, in this shop, and who they are, and the majesty of such a clear distinction infuses him as much as the gimlets and vijaya with a sense of elation.

"*Chalo Delhi!*" he calls out sarcastically. "Were they at Imphal?" he asks Balakrishnan.

Imphal. Embree himself hadn't been at Imphal, but friends, a good dozen of them, had died at Imphal, in the malarial valleys, torn to pieces by Jap artillery, left for maggots and vultures. Imphal is a word as familiar to Embree as sleep. "At Imphal? At Imphal?" he repeats before Balakrishnan can translate the question. "Were they, dammit, at Imphal?"

Balakrishnan hurriedly asks and turns back to Embree. "No. Not being there at Imphal."

"At Imphal against the British IV Corps, *now listen up*, the First Division of the INA didn't do a thing. Not a *thing*. Japs did, though. Translate." Embree leans slightly forward, waiting and smoking. A pungent haze drifts in the room, forming a bluish nimbus around the oil lamp. With mild interest he notices that three more men have entered the room and are now also sitting at the opposite table. Glancing at Gopol, he wonders why the boy's eyes look so big and round. Arms and legs, clenched to his body, give him a posture of fear. Embree realizes that Balakrishnan has stopped talking. "Did you translate everything?"

The shopowner nods unhappily.

"I just want to set it straight, if you know what I mean," Embree says. "I mean, when you've seen enough men die, you know they won't ever have anything in compensation for losing their lives except the truth —except having someone set the record straight. If India wants to hand out praise, hand it out to the Gurkha, okay? He won't unsheathe his kukri without drawing blood. Do you understand that? If he shows his knife, before putting it up again he'll nick his own finger. That's the Gurkha. Nobody can make a better single-handed attack on bunkers, machine-gun nests, even tanks. Nobody on God's earth. Translate."

While Balakrishnan speaks to them, the five men sit impassively. Embree feels every eye, however. He doesn't care, though, because he's really thinking of his ax. Hasn't thought of it for a long time, but telling them just now about the Gurkhas' devotion to their knives has reminded him of his old ax. He got that ax in 1927, killed with it in China. Left it in Bangkok in 1939 when he went to Kunming to join Stilwell. Didn't need the ax then. Wasn't going to stay away long. Didn't know six years of war would come between him and Bangkok, then two years here in India chasing God.

Is that what I've been doing? Chasing God?

Balakrishnan has finished the translation. "Japs were damn tough too," Embree says, lifting his finger and in that instant recalling the schoolmasterly way of the American Consul. "Out of a hundred you had to kill ninety-five. The last five killed themselves." He lowers his finger self-consciously. "Anyway, you never found wounded Japs in field hospitals. Buddies killed them so they wouldn't be disgraced by capture. Died in pillboxes with their girls—with their Burmese, Jap, Malayan, and Siamese girlfriends. Whoever came with them died with them. Let's get this straight, too, because pretty soon everyone's going to forget: Those Japanese could fight. They infiltrated, ambushed, set roadblocks. They could do more with a bicycle and a bayonet than most troops do with tanks and cannon. The Brits stayed on the roads, but the Japs, see, roadblocked them and slipped through the jungle, and just for moving like that through such a jungle they deserved medals for bravery, only the Japs never gave medals for bravery—they *assumed* bravery. But they should have given medals for bravery in that damn jungle. You didn't even need to fight to earn medals there. You were brave just to be in it. There were dumdum flies, and tiny buffalo flies that could pass through mosquito netting. And the leeches, the little one-inchers, the buffalo leeches, the goddamn half-foot elephant leeches. The little ones got through eyelet holes in boots and bloated their filthy filthy selves on our feet, so we could hardly get the boots off. You could see leeches on the trail, lifting their filthy heads off the branches, ready to drop. Burned them off or used a hill-tribe remedy of quicklime, tobacco juice, and—let me see—Was it kerosene? Kerosene. You neglect them, they cause this kind of ulcer, see, that can drill right through your body like a corkscrew. Believe it. *Ayo Gurkhali!* That was the war whoop, wasn't it, Harry. We have to walk out. Men cut their finger, died in a few days. People died of a common chill, for God's sake. They died of exhaustion. They died of—of an emptiness. But we walked out. He had a fever of 103 for sure, but I scooped up water in my helmet and poured it over his head, and I told him, 'Come on, Harry, we have to walk out of here.' That's how it was. *Ayo Gurkhali!* Every time I see a dog these days—Balakrishnan, this is *true*—I want to shoot it. I keep seeing them tearing at blown-off arms and legs along the road. Hungry pi-dogs, greedy bastards. They ate corpses till they couldn't get their fat fucking haunches out of the way of a slow-moving tank. But I don't feel that way about Indian dogs. Not at all. Not any more. I feel about Indian dogs, I feel—*pity*, a terrible, terrible pity. . . . Yes, what was I saying?"

Embree looks up from the face that he's been staring hard at, sharply etched in the grain of the table. The men are regarding him from five dark faces. He can't understand the expression: boredom, anger, or maybe just the stunned inward look coming from vijaya. Anyway, they don't look happy, he thinks.

Am I paranoid or high?

"Balakrishnan," he calls out, aware the shopkeeper isn't translating—couldn't have got it all. Probably stopped long ago. Never mind, never mind that. The record is now set straight here, in this place. Good men died at Imphal. Good Indians, too, gave their lives at Imphal—Gurkhas, Punjabis, Sikhs, Nagas, Bengalis, Pathans, Marathas, and others, and Madrasis from this place, right here. But these five want me dead. Am I paranoid? Or is it Death's Wife?

Embree feels himself rising; then his eyes are focusing on the grain of the table. But the face which had dominated his concentration for endless time is gone now, its precise outline fallen back into the haphazard matrix of the wood. Putting both hands out, he steadies himself at the table. What are under him are legs all right, but dead ones. They are there, without feeling to be.

He is speaking to Balakrishnan, asking for the bill. Straightening up to his full quota of height, Embree stares at the five men—five mean-looking crows on a fence—steadily regarding him. "Gentlemen," he says with all the dignity he can muster, "I mean what I say. I'm glad you got your Independence. And I don't care if India goes Communist. Price of rice doubled, cloth tripled, no sugar, right? You're pissed off. So go Red. I know the Brits denied you—" Embree pauses, working hard to pronounce words that come into his mind like fish swimming up from depths. "They denied you freedom, but insisted you fight for British freedom. Sure, I get it. Sure, I understand the miserable paradox of it. Who doesn't? But the Brits taught you the value of freedom, and that's what they left you along with the railroad and post office. And now freedom's yours to do with what you want. Great. I say *great*. I'll fight alongside you if anyone tries to take it away again from blessed India."

Embree pauses, as if looking for the idea he has somehow lost for a moment. He leans forward and bangs the table, causing a brass tumbler to fall off the edge and clatter on the stone floor. "What I was saying, what I meant to say was, Don't tell *me* about the Indian National Army. It wasn't really an *army*. It was a few politicos leading men who didn't want to rot in Jap prison camps. It was Indians from Siam and Malaya who never believed the propaganda about a New Asia under Jap rule but who figured maybe the Japs would rule anyway. Right. Don't you think I know? Anyway, joining Bose and those other harebrained radicals would at least get them out of those camps, where their Brit officers were dying like flies. INA wasn't an *army*. Don't you ever tell me that. It was a rabble trying to act like an army. Balakrishnan?"

Out of the smoke looms the frayed fedora, the brass earring, and under them the dark perspiring face of Balakrishnan, who is desperately trying to smile as he thrusts forward a torn piece of paper. "Here, sir, you are wishing it."

Without looking at the bill, he fumbles in his jacket for money. Rupee notes tumble out. Before Embree can focus on them where they lie on the stone floor, Gopol is there, picking them up rapidly and stuffing them into his outstretched hand. When the money's in his grip again, Embree peels off some notes and hands them to Balakrishnan without a glance. Then to the five seated men Embree says evenly, gratified by the clarity of his pronunciation, "You damn fools, Mahatma Gandhi is your *real* national army."

"Sir."

Turning, he looks into the pinched sweaty face of Balakrishnan, who has put the money away. "Sir, please to be courteous here. These men are delegates to convocation."

Embree shoves the rest of his money into the seersucker jacket, having a sudden sense of danger. They hate him. It's not paranoia or the vijaya telling him that—they really hate him. They don't hate him for being white, for having money, for insulting their army careers, they hate him for his politics, of all things. They hate him for liking Gandhi.

"Don't you fellows believe I know how to kill?" he asks with a bitter smile. "Killing is one thing I do well. Another thing I do well is remember. Balakrishnan, goodbye."

He turns—wheels, actually—and leans forward in a plunging walk past the curtain and through the outer room. Outside, he lurches along awhile before realizing night has almost fallen, only a strip of pinkish light remains at the western edge of huts across the road.

"We have to walk out, Harry," he says in a loud voice and laughs.

10   IN THE FINAL light there's a papery flash of wings. Fear rises from the Other. Glancing over his shoulder, Embree sees only two men riding a bicycle, one carrying a long iron pipe. Ahead of him a number of people are coming along the road, homeward-bound farmers walking out of fields and clumps of woodland. He sees them coming through veils of dusk into the sweet air of falling night. A couple of boys are leading an old bullock, its neck bell tinkling as it sways down the road. In Burma he used to see cows studded with shrapnel wounds, standing in a road somewhat like this one, groaning hoarsely, the sound like a foghorn coming near. Putting one hand out clumsily, Embree pats the animal as it passes.

The light has changed. There are pinpoints of gold within the shops and roadside huts as lanterns are lit. But up ahead there's no light at all; that's where the road moves into countryside. Soon, however, there's another, more pervasive light—a big gibbous moon flooding the areca palms with a whitish glow like poured milk. From somewhere in the growing darkness comes the whine of a solitary flute. Embree pauses, cocking his head to listen. It's what he will put in his letter to Vera: "The sound of a single flute on a village road just as night falls." That sort of thing might even persuade her to come here. Vera's like that—overwhelmed by the beauty of things. A hardheaded woman who can't resist a flower. "*Ayo Gurkhali!*" he calls out and laughs. He told them the truth in there about their damn-fool army. It's like a blessing bestowed when the truth's told; Father used to say that. Except he meant the truth only as he saw it.

Embree speaks aloud to keep himself company. "Hello, Vera darling. Long time no see, old girl. When I write you—well, I don't do much of that, do I—I don't really tell you what I'm doing. What I'm doing is, I'm chasing the God of my father all over the map of India. You never knew about Father. He was a missionary. That's right, darling. And me too. Yep. A missionary. Hard to believe? I find it hard to believe myself." So he'll confess to his religious past, but won't tell her what he did to the General. She just thinks he ran away with her and that was all. He skipped out on the General just to have her. Not so bad, really. What she doesn't know is one little fact—maybe not much in the cosmic scheme of things, but something of some concern: He tried to get the General killed. Can't tell her that, though. Never. Embree hums nervously.

Beneath the moon things are passing him on the road: patches of ghostly white, loincloths passing. Ahead now are a few points of gold—oil lamps, probably a small village. Where am I? Embree wonders. He has gone some distance beyond the limits of Madras, too far to get a tonga for rent. He should turn back, but he doesn't want to turn back. Because this, really, is India: the silent road, the sweet aroma of fields giving off the heated smells accumulated in a bright day; the distant (now) whine of a solitary flute; the big moon shining down on the flat, warm, pungent land edged everywhere with tall palms and their fronds. Ah, fronds like a crown of thorns.

India. A deep pulse in his heart. What India is, what India is, Embree struggles to think clearly, what India is is . . . a presence.

It's what remains of his search for Father's God. It's nothing more than earth under a huge sky, and people walking on a dark road. Drunken sentimentality, of course. Yet India's beautiful in spite of him. India is beautiful anyway, and this too he'll write to Vera.

Ahead are a few humpbacked dwellings that herald a village. Approaching it, he can see that the huts are so overgrown with vines they seem rooted in the ground—vegetable themselves. A few pricks of light invite him farther, but just as he begins the last few stumbling steps into the outer edge of the village, Embree abruptly halts. Stock-still.

Operating from behind the iron gates of vijaya and gin, instinct at last finds him. Embree feels the hair on his arms rise, the faint touch of nausea preceding violent action. Turning his head even before hearing the telltale sounds, Embree has an instant in which to see a few patches of ghostly white and yet another instant in which to follow the course of something coming down at his face.

It's this instant, he'll decide later, that enables him to duck slightly and thereby take the full impact of the board or club or whatever the hell it was upon his shoulder rather than his head, and to save his life, for better or for worse.

• • •

Through the soft haze of early light he's looking into the round, lazy eye of a cow. Moving his head—the motion sends a jolt of pain through shoulder and back—he stares at a ring of naked children: black hair, cavernous eyes, thin legs, bloated bellies. Also in visual range are a copper pot, a rotten plantain, a broken rope sandal, some bits of paper, and a leaf torn from a Tamil calendar. "My, my, my," Embree murmurs, "you have done it now." He moves his head again, again the thrust of pain. He sees a skinny dog with backbone like a bent bow, a trio of scrawny hens, a heap of dead ashes, a small pig rooting in something covered with flies, a bundle of thatch fallen from a roof. He smells urine, bananas, other things. Biting his lip, Embree raises himself painfully on one elbow and looks at a jagged piece of glass sparkling in a mess of banana peels.

Village India all right.

Alive. Somewhere in Village India.

A string of something accumulates under his chin. It takes Embree a few seconds to realize he's drooling. Snapping his mouth shut, he tastes fully the stale alcohol, the acrid vijaya. It's difficult to tell whether the headache or the shoulder hurts more. Yet another grand effort gets him into a sitting position. After experiencing the pain this takes, he notices that the pockets of his coat are turned out.

So he's been robbed.

Before giving that more thought, however, he figures it's time to get on his feet. As Embree moves his legs under him and prepares to try, he hears the sound—his own continuous groan—that has the children staring at him in wonder and dismay. Up he goes, feeling tall and ungainly. The shoulder pain is now a constant, so he accepts the probability that something is broken, perhaps badly.

Never mind. Walk.

But after a few steps he grabs with one hand at the thatch of a low roof. Two goats, their legs folded under brown bodies, regard him with mildly curious eyes. Pottery shards, crumbling brick, paddy hay, broken palm leaf all register visually, then drift beyond his throbbing eyes. Clouds of green and blue flies hover above something—a dog. They gather in excitement around the mangy old fur and swarm at a fresh wound on the left haunch. Embree stares. The dog stands near the side of a hut, as if afraid of sitting down for fear of not getting up again. You and me, Embree thinks. He smiles at the dog, who interprets the smile as aggression; baring his teeth, the dog scoots off with an alacrity that belies his age and condition.

Still wants to live. And so do I.

Embree feels the desire for life with utter clarity, but nausea replaces clarity, and he bends over to retch up all of yesterday: the food, the gin, the smoke, the bravado and self-pity and fear of the Other. Blinking hard to retain consciousness, he stares at the vomit. Suddenly, from among the lumps of half-digested food and slimy bile, he sees movement. A small black pellet shoves its way through the muck, its six legs plowing slowly forward. A beetle, having been caught in the deluge, is going implacably on, motoring with resolve through the puddle.

Embree leans against the hut's wall, takes a deep breath, and continues to watch the insect trundle across the road, past the feet of the staring children. What gives the thing so damn much will? Maybe a churning mass of infant beetles or a sick wife depend on him. In his small black heart a tiny beat is sending him through catastrophe toward insect duty. I'll be damned. He's going home.

And I'll write Vera that too. No, I won't.

Embree watches until the careening shell—the size of his fingernail—has vanished between huts across the road. Looking farther between them, beyond a field, he sees the village tank, a circular pond which the rainless days have nearly dried out. Its desiccated bank looks like the wrinkled skin of the kind of elephant he saw in Burma. Standing at one end of the pond is a tall, caparisoned terra-cotta horse, modeled with a belled harness. It's a Kudarai. He's seen them everywhere in the South: mounts of the god Aiyanar's generals, who gallop down from heaven with their hordes to defend villages at midnight from evil spirits. It's no accident, Embree knows, that the horse is set near the water supply—heaven help the wandering demon who tries to drink from it! On this funny morning, at the start of this strange day, it's fitting, he thinks, to see a Kudarai. It's appropriate, though he has no idea why. If he had time, he'd think about it. And yet he has time.

Once I slept on a horse, Embree recalls dully. He'd taught himself to sleep on a horse like the Mongol cavalrymen whose bandit descendants had captured him in China. Now the Kudarai, a rough-hewn figure of weathered clay, stands at the edge of a tank whose precious cargo can be saved only by cloudbursts, by thunderstorms, by persistent rains—not, surely, by the hosts of heaven. It's nice to think so in this modern world. But what if the terra-cotta horse and its rider actually do beat hell out of demons every night? After all, this is Village India. Perhaps different rules apply. Perhaps rules his father wouldn't understand, much less play by. And I'm here, he thinks. And I'm thinking about what it means to be here. That's positive thinking.

He notices a few people standing in front of their huts, watching him. Feeling abruptly weak, Embree slides down the hut wall against which he's been leaning. He hears a groan come out of his mouth again, feels a sharp pain traverse the dorsal half of his body.

With legs splayed out, he smiles at the somber children who've been joined in their vigil by a couple of toothless old women, who draw chadars over their heads like little tents, so that all he can see are sharp noses, gaping mouths.

He likes it here. Does he like it here? He likes it here because he feels empty here, as empty as those old mouths. If ever there has been a time for him to meditate, the time is now. There were other times in his life when meditation might have worked miracles. They were times when certain events emptied him of the ordinary. They were always times when he'd lost something.

Like the time those bandits captured him on the Peking-bound train in 1927; he left behind a passport, all of his baggage, and the stern Christian teaching that had shaped his first twenty-three years. But he hadn't meditated then. Later, when he betrayed General Tang, whatever conviction and honor he'd possessed were swept away, leaving only his lust for Vera. And when that irresistible desire faded too, leaving in its stead the power of a wanderlust that had already broken the grip of God, he fled Vera too and again headed for China. Each mile that carried him toward Stilwell in Kunming separated him from the woman who had somehow balanced his losses, even when he fully understood her indifference to him. No meditation that time either. And when he walked out of a Burmese jungle, leaving Harry behind, he left with his dead friend whatever else had survived his betrayals, whatever else had sustained his faith in the world. On the day he came out of the jungle there had been nothing left—no identity, no faith, no love, no honor to keep him alive. If any man had been free to go, he, Philip Embree, had been. Or free to meditate. To die or meditate. But he'd done neither.

The irony of his survival sobers him more than the headache, more even than the painful shoulder. Having walked out of the Burmese jungle, in sight of an Allied detachment that would again mean life, the gun barrel cold against his right temple, a withholding of slight pressure on the trigger separating him from death, he'd changed everything at the nadir, perhaps at the last instant of Philip Embree, by making out loud the vow that has brought him up hard against this present moment: *"I will pay the debts, one by one. I will pay them all."*

Even the debt he owed himself. He's been trying to pay it these past two years: here in India, cross-legged, eyes closed, entering the emptiness each morning.

· · ·

Resting his head against the daub-and-wattle hut, Embree closes his eyes. Indeed, he should meditate while sitting hurt and moneyless in an unknown village. It's appropriate too that yesterday brought him to this moment: because yesterday, after taking darshan of Lord Shiva, he let Death's Wife transform him into the kind of foolish war veteran he has always detested, someone garrulous and boastful and unhinged enough to insult a few frustrated men who decided to rob him, which they certainly did, and perhaps to kill him, which they might have done had they taken their time and had not his capricious karma deflected the full weight of the blow.

Fatigue and the events of yesterday have created in him the proper sense of emptiness, the capacity to surrender to the freedom of silence. Yet almost instantly his ears assume the function of sight: A rooster is crowing nearby, and from a farther distance comes a heavy thud— women beating their laundry against rocks. It's initially a whistling arc of sound that ends in a flat, wet deadness. He can't get it out of his mind, a mind which should be concentrating on the motion of his breath, on "You Are That," on the abyss at the end of his unseen nose. His closed eyes make a dim image of women bending over rocks at the edge of a brackish pool, the wet ropes of cloth whistling above their heads at the downswing.

"Oh God. Dear Lord, what has happened to you, sir!"

Embree opens his eyes to stare at a small, thin Indian with prominent cheekbones, a sharp long nose, and the largest of dark eyes—as limpid and large as the eyes of the wandering cow that greeted his return to consciousness a while ago. The young man holds an umbrella over his head as he bends down and studies Embree with a frown.

"Oh, God. Oh, God," he exclaims. "Toughs, sir, have done this?"

Embree starts to nod, but the pain stops him.

"No moving, sir!" the little man warns. Closing the umbrella, he throws it on the ground. He has on a clean white shirt, a dhoti worn long, a pair of dusty sandals. There's a tilak mark on his forehead, so he's done his morning ablutions and with the pad of his right forefinger has placed a red dot of kumkum there to help the day become successful. His black hair curls up at the back like the fur of an animal stroked the wrong way. But Embree is drawn to the enormous eyes, liquid and clear as a child's.

"I do believe I could bash them up myself, sir. What they have been doing to you!" His English is more clearly enunciated than Embree's been used to in the South. It's marked, however, by the final descending tone and drawn-out vowels that give such speech a lilting Indian timbre. Embree likes it. The odd thought occurs to him that he'd never expected to hear English again, that he hadn't let his mind anticipate more than the next few moments in this village.

"I am Rama, sir, at your service. Permit me." Reaching out, the little Indian gently touches the scar on Embree's forehead, as if assuming it's a fresh wound, whereas Embree has carried it for twenty years, ever since a bullet grazed him in the bandit camp. Drawing his hand back, Rama smiles apologetically. "Excuse me. Old, is it. So where, good sir, have you been injured?"

"I think my shoulder's broken."

"Oh, God. Shoulder, is it." Rama leans forward, pulling back Embree's collar with thumb and finger, squinting inside.

"Yes. I've been robbed." While Rama leans toward him, Embree can see within the billowing white shirt a woven brown thread hanging obliquely across the young man's chest; the thread suggests to Embree that Rama belongs to the Brahman caste.

"Robbed. Dacoits on the road, is it."

Embree nods. No use telling him they weren't real bandits, but simply indignant war veterans who needed money.

"Robbed by dacoits." Rama clucks in sympathy.

Now that the young fellow knows there isn't money to reward him for helping, Embree thinks, he'll leave.

And in fact Rama straightens up. "I will go just away to the village, sir, and send someone to fetch transport and then come straightaway back. Please not to worry. Rama is here."

Embree smiles wanly. "Thank you then, Rama. You go on. I won't worry." His words are meant to be a farewell. Actually he feels no anger, but a pleasurable indifference, when the young man rushes off. There's going to be plenty of time now for meditation, and yet for the moment he wants to do nothing. He looks up at the cloudless sky. In this country the sky is rarely interesting. That's an interesting thing to contemplate. Every day dawns without clouds, except in the short monsoon season. A clear blue slate becomes a depthless emptiness once the sunlight of day advances. It lacks anything visually to snag on. It never tugs at the eye; sometimes it seems to him the sky actually withholds texture, as if somewhere behind it there's something resisting being seen. It's openly a blue or blue-white emptiness, no more. It withholds texture. Yes. Just a smooth heaven as characterless as the pundits say that Brahman—the real, the cosmic stuff, the matrix—ultimately is. That's maybe what he sees: the empty blue sky and Brahman.

Embree sighs. Time for everything, sitting like this, afraid to move because of the pain. It's nice in its way.

Lowering his gaze, Embree notices three men squatting in the dust near a hut across the path. They wear dhotis and there are white turbans on their sun-blackened heads. They are watching him out of eyes rimmed red from glare. Crows have begun their monotonous cawing in the village. It's a sound as pervasive as waves breaking on a shore. Embree draws his swollen tongue across lips bone-dry, cracked. The cawing of those crows is like the voice of doom. Where is this place? he thinks, then thinks, It doesn't matter, it's a good place.

Coming along the path are a group of young women, all carrying copper lotas to fill at the local well. Although giving him quick glances, they never pause in their graceful walk. Gold nose jewelry, flower bouquets entwined in their long plaited hair, bangles on their chocolate-brown arms, they pass beyond his vision into the sunlit fields. They are beautiful, but he doesn't like those farmers squatting across the path from him.

Now there are four; they make him nervous.

In Burma the villagers scoured the outlying fields for wounded Allies and Japanese—which kind didn't matter—and sometimes they lined up, just like those four, patiently waiting for a downed soldier to lose the ability to defend himself. When his grip loosened on his gun or he lost consciousness, they went in, hacking with sharp little harvest knives or striking out with broken tree branches. Nobody ever figured out if they did it simply for loot or for revenge against foreigners who had turned their malaria-ridden jungles into a battlefield. But they did it, democratically; they cut up both Ally and Jap.

That was Burma, however, and this is India, he thinks, and this is for some reason a magical day. Embree's certain it is, because the little fellow's umbrella is lying here on the ground. Rama will return for it, meaning that he intended to come back—no Indian would forget his umbrella—and this curious probability helps to make the day magical. But most days in India are magical in some way. Perhaps the magic has kept me here, Embree thinks lazily, much longer than I should have stayed. His debt to Father, for example, was paid months ago, yet here he is, still watching for magic.

And here comes magic, he tells himself, as the young Indian with the wiry hair rushes into view.

"Good news, good news, sir! We are soon having transport." Wiping sweat from his face and belching softly, Rama squats. "God bless you, sir. Can you move?"

"I don't think so."

"They will be helping us." He points at the half-dozen farmers now squatting across the path.

"I think I told you I was robbed. I haven't any money."

Rama moves both hands through the air cavalierly. Embree watches them move. He has always admired South Indian hands, so Italianate in their expressiveness: palms open, fingers spread, wrists twisting. They are something to look at, to contemplate. And there's time for looking.

"Money? No problem," Rama says. His smile reveals teeth stained black from betel juice. "They are dashed honored to be helping."

Embree enjoys the antiquated English slang. "I think we better immobilize my shoulder before you try moving me." At his instructions, Rama goes, aided by a couple of the waiting men, to find a length of cord; they return and secure his left arm tight to his body.

While this is being done, Rama keeps talking. "Yesterday I was to my cousin. The festival, you see, allowed holiday, so I just came over here to him from Madras. He is staying in the next village, around this way rather near." Rama waves his hand vaguely in a few directions. "You will find it there only. So I heard this morning, bless me! a white man was injured, and I told myself, 'Go, Rama. Go to him.'"

"I'm glad you did, sir," Embree replies politely.

"V. S. Ramachandran. But please to call me Rama. Your good name, sir, and country?"

"Embree. Right now, India."

"But you are coming from?"

"I'm American, but I came from Burma."

"American. From proper States, then. You are coming from there before Burma, is it. From Atlantic, Chicago, Florida?" He pauses, seeming to exhaust the possibilities.

"I haven't seen the States proper in a long time." Embree adds, "Not in twenty years."

Rama sucks in his breath to indicate astonishment. "You are staying now in Madras City?"

Embree nods, feeling less pain with the arm secured to his side.

"Are you keen on staying over here, sir?"

"Yes, Rama, I am."

The young Indian gently tugs on the bandage to check its tightness. "You are keen, sir, on India?"

"Very keen."

"Your occupation must be over here. May I ask which is it?"

"I work for a textile company. It's just been transferred from British to Indian ownership."

"Are you keen on transfer?"

"Not any more than I was keen on British ownership." Embree watches the young man react with a smile to the mild witticism. An old woman is advancing toward them with a brass tray. On it is a banana leaf, and on the banana leaf lie some chappatis, a handful of rice, a slug of yogurt.

"Take food, sir," Rama urges, gesturing toward the tray.

"Is this your doing, Rama?"

"I am holding tray. No problem."

Soon Embree is eating, and although he feels profoundly hungry, after a few mouthfuls the desire for food wears off. "No more, please. You finish it," he adds, before realizing what he's said: You don't insult caste Indians by asking them to eat off your plate.

"I wouldn't mind," Rama replies, putting the tray down, "but I took food before. Thank you, sir."

Embree is impressed by the young man's diplomatic handling of a clumsy mistake. Across the way, sitting on a thatched roof, two monkeys are picking lice from each other's head. From the hut beneath them two men haul out an old sewing machine—one iron leg replaced by a plug of wood—and put beside it a stool. They have just set up a tailoring shop.

"I am working for Postal Service," Rama says, while opening the umbrella and holding it over Embree's head. "Our In-charge is a cheeky fellow, though, a Telegu. He could use a bashing up I am sorry to say. Sometime I would like to go in for a better occupation."

Embree figures the young man is angling for a job. To disabuse him of hope from his own quarter, Embree says, and truthfully, "I'm only a clerk in my company. My job isn't important. I do invoices, correct English grammar in letters. That sort of thing. Sorry."

Rama shrugs, as if the idea of asking has never crossed his mind. "Take water, sir."

A child has come along with a glass, its sides blurred from sticky dirt.

"No thank you," Embree says with a smile.

Rama sucks in his breath. "Ah, forgive me, sir! You take boiled water only. I know that, I know what gentlemen need. No problem." He speaks Tamil to the child in a voice that enjoys giving commands. "It will be getting boiled five minutes."

"Please—twenty!"

Rama shouts additional orders, which bring smiles of amusement to the faces of the sun-darkened farmers aligned across the road, along the front walls of some huts. Embree smiles back at them. The Burman-type scavengers have suddenly become harmless. They squat there in their huge white turbans and loincloths like prospective fathers in a maternity ward who've gone through the experience many times: patient, agreeable, confident of a happy outcome. Some wear mustaches, and their teeth, like those of Rama, are black from chewing pan. One fellow with canines elongated from overbite suddenly gets up and almost immediately returns with a short wooden flute. Soon he's playing, and Embree wonders if this is the same flute that played last night.

Now down the dusty path come a gang of men pushing an automobile. It has no headlights, no windows, and as they push it closer, Embree can see it has no engine. They are struggling to get the empty metal shell deeper into the village, like ants bringing what they've foraged back to the nest. What can the village do with such a thing? Embree wonders. Where did they ever find it? There's not enough left to identify the model. This must be an extraordinary event for the village, yet none of the men sitting opposite him do more than give the chassis a brief glance of curiosity, much like the goats had given him earlier in the morning.

"I am definitely on the outlook for another occupation," Rama says, shifting the umbrella handle to his other hand. "I cannot make my both ends meet on such wages. Are you keen on stories, Master? Excuse me, this one is a bit green, but two men are heading to temple when—"

Two women, at this moment, emerge from between the huts lying just ahead of Embree. Bitterly arguing and waving their hands around, they seem ready to fight. For a few moments Rama and the waiting farmers listen intently—all except the flute player, who continues to embroider a nasal wail with pert little figures of rhythm.

One of the farmers, turning to the women, calls out sharply.

Rama sucks in his breath and grins. "Now they will come away." And in fact the two quarreling women, instantly silent, move together as one down the gutter between the huts and head for the water tank. Embree notices three boys astride the terra-cotta horse, the Kudarai, while a fourth is beating the weathered flank of the Demon General's mount with a long stick.

Embree, turning his head slightly, can't keep up with all that's happening within the limited range of his vision. This isn't a lazy little village, this is a huge metropolis in frenetic motion.

A small girl, racing up, speaks rapidly to Rama, who carefully props the umbrella against Embree's unharmed shoulder, so that it still gives shade. "Good news, Master. Our transport is coming just over here." He wags his head, South Indian style, to give emphasis to his optimism. "I told you. Listen to Rama."

His skinny legs under the dhoti flash a moment. He's gone.

Master? Embree repeats the word. He called me "Master"?

Coming into sight now is a crow; it waddles boldly across the path— a big creature with a blue-black sheen. It has the dark arrogant look of a pirate. Halting, it cocks its yellow eye and regards Embree critically until, at the shooing insistence of two women who balance iron bowls on their heads, it must take to the air. The great wings flap heavily, like brooms, before they raise it from the village path.

Snotty-nosed tots come along, gnawing peeled sticks of sugar cane. Across the way some of the farmers are smiling either at him or at thoughts evoked by the wailing of the flute.

Master? Does he think I mean to keep him, employ him? Embree wonders. But another, greater thought wedges Rama out of his mind. Back against the warm wall, smiling at the patient men, he tells himself he won't leave India. Definitely not. Vera will bring Sonia here, and together we'll work out our destiny on Indian soil. That's what we can do—as a family, as the family we never were. I'll pay the debt to Vera here. Pay it in India. She'll love this country as I do. There's nothing I won't try in order to make her happy. There's nothing a man can do for his family that I won't do. There's nothing to fear when the world moves along as it's doing now. Is there, Harry? You told me to walk out, and so I have, just as you said, Harry. I've stayed alive and come to this.

Rama rushes into view, holding a bottle before him. It is an unopened Coca-Cola bottle, so dusty that the dark liquid inside has a gray cast. Marshaling the help of a few watchful farmers—five men crowd around it on the ground like surgeons in an operating theater—Rama manages to lift the cap off with a knife. Holding the opened bottle proudly aloft, Rama approaches.

"Take soft drink, Master." He wipes the bottle swiftly with the end of his dhoti.

Embree takes the bottle, feeling a thrust of pain accompany the motion. But swept up in this moment, with the flute wailing and the two women quarreling again in the distance near the sacred horse ridden by boys and switched like a recalcitrant cow, with the black-faced farmers crouching patiently along the wall, and with the young women on their return from the village well singing a Tamil song, with the kids gnawing their sugar cane and pigs ecstatically wiggling their corkscrew tails, and with the beetle no doubt still resolutely trundling home, Embree drinks deeply of the warm vapid liquid and thinks of nothing but being alive.

"Good, Master," Rama murmurs like a parent with a sick child. "You are shaping very well."

From the distance comes a rasping sound that grows louder, that becomes a thick grinding cough, as if a multitude of crows cawed in unison.

"Rama, I swear to God this is magic," Embree declares between chuckles, feeling giddy and foolish.

"Pardon, Master?"

"I said"—Embree has to shout over the approaching noise—"this is India!"

"Oh, yes, Master. India," Rama agrees with an uncertain smile.

As Embree lifts the bottle to drink again, feeling another sharp pain travel across shoulder and back, into sudden view rattles an old car, or what is left of one. It's a convertible chassis with a truck mounting—a 1938 Crosley: the overhead canvas half shredded, a single headlight, most of the truck slats missing, without windshield wipers or door handles. Nevertheless, unlike its compatriot hauled earlier through the village, this vehicle has a motor that spits, coughs, and drags the whole rumbling thing along the path until not five feet away it comes to a shimmying halt.

"Do you see, Master? Here is transport! Please not to worry when Rama is here." He picks his nose, triumphantly regarding the old car.

Indeed, Embree is not worrying. He has not felt better in days, weeks. And as the patient farmers rise to come help him into the old car, he remembers his reading yesterday of *The Upanishads*, and for an instant to stay with him for the rest of his life, Philip Embree is convinced that, when all is said and done, there is no Other.

11 WHEN YOU FALL in love, most likely you aren't thinking of the flux of time, you're thinking of permanence, of this moment lasting, and then something happens that makes you think of love as nothing less than a function of time, an insidious expression of change and perhaps of mortality. Such a grim philosophy has followed Vera into consciousness on a drizzly morning in Chiang Mai.

Wanna sleeps beside her in the hotel bed: that small mouth like a cracked red bead, that umber skin as smooth as lam yai, the plum of this region, called dragon's eye.

A crack of thunder, a bolt of lightning zigzags obliquely across the window. Vera lies there naked, although at this time of year, in the dry season, Chiang Mai is usually cool until midday. But for twenty-four hours the region has been overcast, a thick cloud cover holding the temperature steady from noontime on, as if the next three months have already passed and the monsoon begun. Rain is pelting on the hotel roof —a tin roof—clattering like something alive up there in a panic. Vera stirs, throws the sheet off her belly, and turns toward the girl.

A familiar statue in Siam is that of the young Earth Goddess, Thorani, wringing water from her hair—a lovely image of divine self-absorption. Here, Vera thinks, in this bed lies Thorani.

Wanna comes from nearby Lamphun, renowned for beautiful women. Two days ago they went there to see the orchid farm where Wanna grew up, where every morning in sarong and broad-brimmed hat her mother watered the plants in their beds of charcoal, suspended waist-high in openwork wooden boxes under bamboo arbors. To Vera, standing beside her lovely young companion, the wet petals—white, pink, yellow, purple—seemed to throb like hearts beating on the stiff long stalks. Hanging in the mist, disembodied above the ground, they brought bursts of orchidaceous color into the still morning.

Even so, Vera's reaction to the beautiful farm surprised her; she felt alien there, uneasy. Dry, ropy roots were tangled under the boxes like the cast skins of snakes; those flowery rows possessed the strict order of a military march; and silence accentuated the forbidding sense of controlled beauty. In vain she tried to share Wanna's past. She wanted to imagine a pretty little girl playing in the checkered light that slanted through the arbor, long braids tied up with silk, black eyes studying the edge of an orchid blossom. What came instead was the image of cool wet silent mornings and the hanging plants, each tended with more care than little girls receive. She sought in vain for a pleasing image of Wanna's childhood. The thought of those silent mornings and cool mists and watery dots of color took Vera into a region of shifting perspectives, a world of ominous perfection that might even hide the poison of scorpions.

Vera reaches across the bed to touch, fondly, the girl's slim, brown, hairless arm. When she thinks of Wanna she often thinks of jasmine, of its sweet, almost cloying fragrance in a room where necklaces of the white flowers have lain all night. Jasmine and orchids. The goddess Thorani absorbed in drying her hair. Enchanting, evanescent, and— cold.

Yes, that—cold.

Vera feels hungry, ravenously so, and for a moment recalls the kantoke meal eaten last night: the glutinous rice and hot curries which she bolted as if loving them. The truth is, she'd eaten like a wanderer on the road, filling her stomach with whatever was at hand, in fear of not eating again for a long time. And now she wants breakfast. Saliva fills her mouth at the thought of durian, in season now, that strange fruit the size of a human skull, spiny outside, emitting the odor of stale onions, yet with yellow flesh tasting cool, creamy, subtle.

Yes, cold. Wanna's cold. There's something too direct in the girl's lovemaking, something functional and explicit, which reminds Vera of herself as a youthful prostitute in Shanghai. The thought is appalling— that there is a similarity between herself then and Wanna now. She loves the girl. There is nothing in their relationship remotely like that of a prostitute with a client. Yet sometimes it is difficult to match Wanna's ethereal face with the crisp economy of her sexual performance. She can be brusque, even crude, sometimes indifferent, and, worst of all, overtly skillful. Vera thinks disconsolately that it's what men must have thought about her own lovemaking in the Shanghai days. What a bitter irony to contemplate such a fate: that she is playing the role of buyer to Wanna's whore.

Foolishness.

They are lovers in the true sense, as true as lovers ever are. With a firmness typical of her, Vera puts the pessimistic thinking out of mind. But another sad thought enters, brought in by the look of her own naked body under the dull gray light. The marmoreal breasts of her youth have become less firm, the nipples darker. But that's not all. There are the other signals of age that her eyes dare not dwell on. None of this, of course, should matter, Vera tells herself impatiently; she's always believed that women as lovers are less concerned with physical perfection than men are. Wanna is not her first female lover. There was a Chinese girl, Yu-ying, whom she loved to desperation when they sought comfort in each other's arms during off hours in a Shanghai brothel. And there was Malee before Wanna, and a few others, women who gave her less reason to fix upon aging than male lovers surely would have. Yet there must come a day when no one escapes time.

Vera can't turn to look at the girl; not now, not yet. She'd rather feel the hunger intensify than succumb to it. If she gives in, she'll wake the girl and gaily suggest breakfast, only to have them stare at each other in silence. That's what Vera now imagines: she, awestruck, exploring the beauty of a young body, while the girl studies the sad vestiges of beauty. Vera imagines the girl's clear pragmatic eyes looking downward, a witness to the sag of breasts, the thickening of hips—dispassionately recording the pull toward the earth, the grave.

It is no good thinking about such things. Better think about the good things. The last few days have been wonderful, filled with images Vera now tries to conjure: spectacularly tall yang trees with their leathery green crowns that poke above forests; pong grass in the valleys, and along the mountain ridges thick stands of pine; and kapoks with long dangling pods, ready to split and let fall their white woolly innards; and the heart-shaped leaves of the bo, hanging down as limp as dishrags in the still air; and on the train from Tak she saw a green-striped heron in the brown stubble of a rice field. And the splendor of these northern temples: ancient bronze Buddhas; golden umbrellas of majesty and *cho fa* ornaments at the end of eaves that catapult the mind beyond roofing into far reaches of the air; the carved Wheel of Law on boundary stones housed in tabernacles; gabled wiharns, public chapels fashioned from imaginations cooled centuries ago in devotional texts. And the climax of their five days in the North: the climb to a hilltop monastery dedicated to the white elephant who died after lugging a mysterious relic up the steep ascent (Wanna did a respectful *wai* there); and then, within the cloister itself, a gilded chedi surmounted by a five-tiered umbrella; and a courtyard shaded by a breadfruit tree with a vista as wide and green as her old Russian landscape come alive in spring. It is good to be in this place. It is worth working for, Vera thinks, content that her mind has turned to such gentle, pleasant things.

But her breasts, when she cups them, have the spongy dead feel of cotton, whereas when she touches those of Wanna—as she did last night in passion—the flesh beneath her palms, her fingers, her lips has the texture of young life: resistant, elastic, mutable. Is there no hope?

Again a foolish question. Assailed by sharper pangs of hunger, Vera turns again toward the girl, prepared to waken her—but only after drawing the sheet up shoulder high.

Before Vera can touch the thin brown arm, a gentle but insistent knocking at the door turns her once more, this time in the direction of the other room of their suite. Rising, she slips a cotton robe over her naked body and cinches up the sash. The knocking continues until she reaches the door, opens it.

• • •

Standing there, grinning, is Pakhoon Chirachanchai, and behind him, glum and withdrawn, a tiny hill-tribe woman with a sleeping infant slung to her back.

The appearance of Pakhoon Chirachanchai at this early hour at her hotel room annoys Vera almost to the point of slamming the door in his face. The Shan bronzes, which he'd sworn were authentic and which Vera had come to Chiang Mai to see, had proved so worthless that she couldn't risk selling them to the most innocent of collectors as anything but the cheap imitations they were. And, as she suspected, the great prize he'd written about, a Phayao stone carving from the late Lan Na period, can't be much older than Pakhoon—and he's younger than she is by ten years at least. In fact, he had brought her nothing she could use, and the trip would have been a business disaster had she not discovered, on her own in a local bazaar, something unearthed by a farmer and brought into town to exchange for a harvesting knife—a bulbous, dull-brown porcelain lime pot with the eyes, beak, and tail of an owl: a Khmer design of an Angkor Wat type, possibly fifteenth century, and in itself worth the entire trip. Moreover, she found some antique opium measures, little iron weights in the form of elephants and birds; and in Phitsanulok two silver betel sets, consisting of four boxes, a horn-shaped case, and a tray, each item covered with wonderful reliefs of Burmese gods and demons. And what has she gained through Pakhoon? Nothing but a headache.

Pakhoon, Pakhoon.

Yet she likes this tiny whippet-like man with the large, froglike mouth and sparkling black eyes and Adam's apple that thumps each time he speaks.

"Tell me it's important," Vera says. "Don't tell me you came up here so early with another story of Lan Na treasures that somebody carved last week, Pakhoon. And what's this woman doing with you?"

"She's a White Karen."

"I know she's a White Karen." Vera stares briefly at the woman in the green blouse and striped sarong; within a flat, wrinkled face, below a huge red towel wrapped sloppily into a turban, are ageless, watchful, unperturbed, wide-set eyes. Similar are the eyes of the infant, whose round face appears over her thin shoulder. On other occasions Vera has visited the settlements of hill people—the Yao, the Meo, and the Red and White Karens. Appalled by the poverty brought on by opium addiction and by the aggressiveness of stronger neighbors, she walked quickly through their hopeless villages of bamboo and laterite. They spin a little cloth, grow a little cotton, process a lot of opium, beg, and scavenge. Their broad Mongolian faces peer above V-shaped red robes, and they stink from lack of bathing, since they fear the Water Spirit more than their own odor. Pigs root in their dark rattan huts to which clings the sweet, rather burned smell of opium. If they come down from the mountains and stay in the plains, they die of malaria, and so, resisting governmental welfare, they remain in the chill heights, embattled against evil spirits and bureaucrats, the old prey of new generations. Vera can't remember if it's the White Karens, but one of these tribes murders newborn twins and exiles the guilty parents. Some of them eat black dogs for spiritual power.

Vera backs off a few steps, having had a good whiff of the Karen woman. "Tell me, Pakhoon. Tell me there's a good reason for coming here so early."

Pakhoon motions fiercely at the woman, who takes a sack from the shoulder not occupied by the baby's sling.

"You will not believe this," Pakhoon says to Vera, beaming. He holds the sack up high, like a trophy. "She came down from the hills only last week, and in a field, digging for roots to eat, she found it. I still can't believe it."

"Pakhoon," Vera says impatiently.

"You'll see, you'll see! Our luck—I still don't believe it! Here, this is what she found: a Lan Na bronze!"

When he pulls it grandly out of the sack, Vera leans forward to get a better look in the gray light. The object is a small bronze Buddha which displays the *bhumisparsha mudra*—fingers of the right hand pointing downward to symbolize Buddha calling on Earth to witness his Enlightenment. The Buddha, seated in the lotus position, has a slight paunch. The end of his robe ends in a stylized fold above the left nipple of his massive chest. The eyebrows meet, and there's a rather decadent shape to the face—plumpish, almost effeminate—along with a look of profound melancholy.

It could be Lan Na. Surely it's been cast in Lan Na style. The exposed nipple differentiates it from later Northern Thai sculpture, which covers more of the chest.

Pakhoon is cackling.

It could be Lan Na, she thinks, turning the bronze slowly in both hands.

Pakhoon thrusts his small face between hers and the sculpture. "Can you believe it? This is a miracle! A Karen found it!"

Vera turns the piece of metal as if it were spitted above a fire. It could be Lan Na. It has all the external characteristics. Professor Dhanit Yupho must take a look at it, confirm or reject her judgment. If it's authentic Lan Na, then she'll contact some important European collectors. By now she can hardly think, because of the animal noises of triumph emanating from the little man, who persists in insinuating his grinning face—the froggish mouth, immense Adam's apple—between her eyes and the bronze. She must actually pull the object back, to one side, and even this doesn't deter Pakhoon, who moves around until his pulsating Adam's apple is no more than inches from the Buddha's left foot.

"Can you believe it?"

"I'm not sure what to believe," Vera says coolly and turns to the woman. "We'll discuss it later. For now, give her some money."

"But—"

"Money to buy clothes for herself, something to eat for the baby, fare on a cart home. And then give her double that amount." When he stares at her, Vera adds, "Oh, well, there, get me that, please." She points to her handbag, and when haltingly Pakhoon gets it from the table and brings it to her, she finds enough bahts to meet her goal. But instead of handing the money to the woman, she gives it to Pakhoon. It must come from him. The hill tribes are accustomed to getting paid by Pakhoon. "Give it to her," Vera tells him.

Reluctantly he does.

"You mustn't take it from her once you leave this room, Pakhoon."

"No," he agrees dejectedly. "Isn't it Lan Na?"

"We don't know yet. But you've done well," she adds with a smile, again raising his hopes. "I want to take another look in better light. Then we'll see."

From Pakhoon comes a quick peal of laughter signaling his relief, his faith too in success. This is what Vera likes about Pakhoon Chirachanchai: his belief in a benign fate. "I told you," he cackles and playfully points a finger at Vera. "It's Lan Na! No doubt about it! Nine this morning? Ten?"

"Come back at noon," Vera says, but holds the bronze when he moves to take it from her. "No, it'll be safe with me."

"Of course." He nods eagerly.

"Noon," Vera says, motioning for him to leave. As the door closes, giving her a final glimpse of the dirty-faced infant and the stoic woman and two pair of ageless eyes, she again orders Pakhoon to let the Karen woman keep that money.

After the door shuts, Vera wonders if, by the time Pakhoon reaches the landing, he will have roughly snatched at least half the money away from the woman. It's impossible to tell, although Vera has done business with him for years. She won't even hazard a guess, having lived in this country long enough to know how unpredictable the Siamese can be.

• • •

Instead of returning to the bedroom, Vera sits on the worn couch in front of a window; Asian rain, as soft as down, slides along the open shutter, accumulates in great fat drops and finally gives way, falling heavily into the gray air. She watches. And she thinks, Unpredictable. Yes.

Six years ago she came north with a Siamese girl, Malee. First they went by train to Phitsanulok. She recalls to this day her exhilaration in the company of Malee (shorter than Wanna, with a rounder face, a sweeter smile), as they stood on a quay lined with areca palms, touching hip to hip. They watched the tin-roofed river boats plod slowly down the brown channel. They knelt together in front of the great masterpiece of Sukhothai art—Victorious King, the large bronze Phra Buddha Jinaraj. And then by rattling old car over a dirt road they traveled to Sukhothai, seeing along the way dozens of tall white poles with outspread nets to capture large flying cockroaches—a delicacy stewed or fried. And she'd held Malee's hand most of the eight-hour journey, turning the short pudgy fingers around, her captured prize, and altering her gaze from distant teak forests to the small round face not a foot away, with its clear eyes. And Vera will never forget entering the dreary little town of Sukhothai, not expecting to see at a sudden turn in the road the majestic ruins of Wat Mahathat: broken walls of reddish brick, vast temple complexes set in patches of grass, awesome in neglect, the huge buddhas smiling impassively into a thin veil of falling rain. Malee had gasped too. And they had walked endlessly among the bell-shaped stupas and rain-glazed shrines, looking from columns and pillars and bas-reliefs to each other's faces, expressing in a glance both admiration for the ruins and love. No man, save Shan-teh himself, had ever shared with Vera such moments as Malee had done that afternoon. It meant to

Vera that she'd been right to fall in love again—and with a woman. And of course it had not necessarily meant that at all, because two months later Malee was gone.

She remembers with clarity their last day together. Sonia had been sent for the afternoon somewhere with Ah Ping, so Malee came to the house; usually they met in a cheap hotel. Cook had left a cold lunch, and Vera arranged for the other servants to go on various errands. Lunch on the veranda was good. They often touched hands during it. And afterward they went upstairs to her bedroom. "Your daughter?" Malee was discreet, typical of the Siamese. "She'll be gone for the afternoon." "You arranged it?" "Of course I arranged it." And then the bedroom awash in sunlight. It lapped at their bodies like water, hovered around them like something alive and protective that afternoon. There had been ecstasy, oblivion in the sunlit confines of their little world. To bring Malee here had been right. Later, when they went downstairs, Sonia was home. They came down the stairs together, and Sonia gave them a strange wild look. "Did you just get home, darling?" "Yes, just now." But Sonia kept looking at them that strange wild way. "This is Malee, a friend. I've been showing her the house.. She loves that porcelain vase. You know the one on my dresser?" And the girl kept looking at them in a strange wild way, until Vera wondered if by their expressions they conveyed to her something of their happiness. Plainly the twelve-year-old girl was mystified and had no idea why. Vera remembers smoothing Sonia's hair while they stood together at the gate and watched Malee turn to wave goodbye. "Do you like Malee?" "I guess she's pretty." They saw her disappear down the lane, and never again was she mentioned in the household.

That was the last time Vera ever saw Malee. No message sent, no final farewell. Overnight the young woman gave up her job in a nearby shop, vanished, and that was the end of it. But no recriminations either, no tears, no anger. Perhaps Malee had been right. The Siamese are adept at falling in and out of love.

Getting up from the couch, Vera walks to the window, postponing the moment when she kisses Wanna awake. She needs more time alone. There was Philip's cable—that witless and insulting request for her to drop everything she has labored for, to throw away years of accomplishment and like a dutiful wife join him in his damned India. His cable ran two pages long—a jumble of boyish enthusiasm for a country which, in some way known only to him, seems capable of compensating a woman for surrendering everything to rejoin the man who deserted her. Ah, Philip!

At least the length of his cable suggests he has money in his pocket. Not a noble insight. Yet Philip seems worthy of it, oblivious of her life outside of his own. Lack of sensitivity is a cardinal sin in Vera's world —worse than mendaciousness.

She wipes her forehead—sweat? At this time of year in Chiang Mai? It isn't that warm, certainly, and yet she feels sweaty. Come to think of it, a little nauseated, faint. She needs to eat, but continues to postpone her meeting with the earth goddess in the next room.

Malee had a broader nose, fuller cheeks, a broader forehead than Wanna. Malee's skin was fine, with a translucent quality in the proper light; her hair, cut straight across as Siamese girls so often wear it, was pulled back into a perky bun, with little fringes of black hair, poignant as a child's, displayed all along her temples. Vera had wonderfully enjoyed tucking back the wayward strands that defied complete imprisonment, bless them, ah bless them for their beauty and rich color and mortality.

Vera has fixed her gaze on something happening in the rain-drenched street. Along the side of a house, two young men, wearing black shorts and dirty undershirts, are splashing big words in red paint across the gum-tree wall.

CHINESE GO HOME

The paint, mixed with rain, drips out of form, yet the message persists, and the two boys with their paint can lope away into the gray dawn. Politics interfering with the world even before it awakens.

Will she leave me with a pretty wave of goodbye as Malee did? Just vanish one day?

Vera feels a slight constriction in her chest. It's really time for food, but not yet time for her to confront Wanna. Her handbag lies on the front-room table, so she picks it up and takes out a little vial. In it are black pellets made of frog-gland extract. They cure almost anything. Vera learned that in Shanghai, when she used them for colds and flu and earache and once for dengue fever and they never seemed to fail her —at least, they did no harm—unless, of course, she includes that time when she took them to abort: On that occasion they made her sick, and she had to do it manually anyway.

That's no memory to pursue. Taking out a cigarette, she lights it and sits down, overwhelmed by sudden fatigue. She is sweating. On the table lies a heap of striped silk of a native design, woven in the weavers' village of San Kamphaeng. She'll give it to Jim Thompson for his opinion of its quality. For a while she stares at the intricate patterns of the silk. Really quite nice. Surely Jim will like this work. Vera sighs; the sitting down seems to ease the constriction in her chest. Sweat is cooling now on her forehead.

She saw Jim just before leaving on this trip. They talked about silk, and the meeting deepened her impression of him as a gifted designer, a man of energy enough to match his ambition. Their project will work. But she'd felt uneasy when he mentioned Philip again. "When's your husband coming to Bangkok?"

"How do you know he's coming here?"

"Didn't you tell me?"

"I did not."

"Then I must have assumed it, right?" And his cherubic face broke into a boyish American smile.

What is all this? She recalls again the rumors in Bangkok that Jim Thompson had been—still is—a secret agent. It's not exactly the sort of business partner Vera has envisioned. And Philip: Is he mixed up in another foolish adventure?

Vera puffs furiously on the cigarette. The constriction has gone away, the faintness too. She is still terribly hungry. And yet she remains there on the couch, alone, unwilling to awaken the girl in the next room. Ah, love. The fearful eventuality of Sonia's falling in love occurs to her. It has often occurred to her lately. Vera had counted on the convent school and then the conservative university and the sheltered girls whom Sonia has known all her life to protect her from that eventuality.

When will Stanford University decide on Sonia's application?

Philip might know such things. Vera contemplates the curt refusal she sent in answer to his desperate cable. Perhaps she ought to have been more friendly, and it occurs to her, with mild surprise, that perhaps he should be encouraged to come to Bangkok. At least for a while. But she won't sleep with him. Rising, she walks to the bedroom.

She halts in the doorway, arrested by the sight of Wanna asleep. For countless minutes now, on this gray morning, she has been thinking, thinking, turning around in her mind any stray thought that came along. But the beauty of the girl focuses all Vera's attention on a single desire: to love and be loved. Hardly has she sensed the depth of this desire than Vera tells herself the girl will leave her.

Wanna's going to leave me. Vera clutches the door frame while gazing at the girl, whose skin, in the aqueous light of a rainy day, seems luminous, unearthly.

Mai pen rai, Vera says under her breath. In a few quick steps she's beside the girl, kissing her cheek. One slim arm comes up and circles Vera's neck, and for the instant this motion takes, the girl displays to Vera's sidelong view a chunky silver bracelet purchased yesterday. The comparison asserts itself cruelly to Vera: her past and Wanna's present. I'm buying the girl's love as men bought mine, Vera thinks, even while her lips touch the dewdrop of Wanna's ear. With a little moan Vera gives herself to the sensation of feeling with her tongue the firm convolutions of that ear, the cartilaginous arc leading to the utter softness of a lobe she nibbles now like a calf nuzzling its mother's teat.

Mai pen rai.

"Darling," she murmurs in Russian. "Darling," she repeats in Thai.

12 MADRAS IS AWAKING. In the east, beyond the Bay of Bengal, appears a line of blue somewhat lighter than the rest of the sky. In the nighttime merging of sky and ocean it's as though they switched places to break the monotony of systems, and the ocean turned upside down, leaving its darker part on the surface, its lighter in the depths. The line of lighter blue now lightens further and starts to inch its way toward the shoreline of the city, a thousand miles south of Calcutta.

What catches the first light immediately is the spire of the old Portuguese Cathedral of Saô Tomé, a dull white cone high above the waterfront. North stretches the flat wide beach of the Marina, all the way to the brick mass of Fort St. George and farther to the High Court and the Sea Customs House as well, squatting by the harbor where ocean vessels anchor in the tranquil blue.

An edge of sunlight breaks over the now defined horizon, sliding like oil across the Marina for rapid movement inland, past a rim of urban greenery and the moldy fronts of old mansions nestled within groves of palm, to lap thickly at the high walls of Government House.

The sun is now fully up, a round ball with its upper half brilliant crimson and its lower half mottled a dull bronze by the ground mist still floating along the bay. Light eases down the lanes, hovering around the cupola of the Adyar Club, around an obelisk dedicated to a British officer killed in Indian battle. Colonial mansion and junk shop in Moore Market are scoured by a new light buffeting everything out of nighttime depths into daytime sky, until chickens, dogs, and cows assume their animal shapes, their living edges defining the dawn, as do those of the ragged field laborers who'll be heading soon for palm groves where they'll gather coconuts through the morning to make a venomous toddy for evening sale in the slums.

Elsewhere, in better districts, Brahmans are sitting in the gardens of their rambling homes, having finished their prayers long before the sun came up. Now they sip their cups of steaming Madrasi coffee and read the *Hindu* or discuss with wives the management of their households.

• • •

Philip Embree has also risen early, matching his austere Brahman neighbors. Long before ocean separated from sky this morning, he left the house with a rolled mat under his arm and spread it under a huge bo tree in a far corner of the courtyard. Here he can't be seen by the next-door cook, who bangs pots around every morning and hums popular Tamil tunes and doubtless wonders why the foreign gentleman would try to do things only Indians, by the grace of God, can do.

Yoga, for example.

Every morning, for half an hour, Embree struggles through asanas. A lifetime of physical activity has not prepared him for such an effort—not his youthful days on the Yale crew or his rigorous service in a Chinese cavalry regiment or his wartime experience in the jungles of Burma. He has learned from Hatha Yoga what internal combat really is: For two years now he's fought a war of inches to arch his back and bend his legs. The battleground is laid out on his practice mat.

Today hasn't gone well. Of course part of the trouble is his broken shoulder in a plaster cast. He couldn't attempt many asanas, and others, demanding balance and suppleness, made him feel like an insect enclosed in chiton. Even so, he went through what exercises he could, emphasizing the stretching asanas like *Urgasana* and *Janu Sirsansana*. He attempted to do each one without the hectic effort a yoga teacher once described to him as "noise." Finally he reached the end of his morning course, arriving at the reward.

The reward was *Savasana*.

For this asana it was necessary for him to lie like a corpse full length on the mat, with hands, palms up, slightly away from the thighs. In this comfortable position, with eyes closed, his task was to visualize each part of his body, starting with his feet. When relaxed properly, he'd felt his mind let go of his body and wander through the past, as if muscle and bone could free memory as an opened door can free a caged bird.

During these calm moments, with his eyes closed and the beat of his pulse lizard-soft, he's learned to accept into his mind certain visualizations of water: rivers and bays, the Charles where he and the Yale crew defeated Harvard, lazy memories of water, of light upon water, of stream and eddy at the shore, of beach-front houses licked by the sea, of spume bubbling at the metal strakes of an ocean-bound ship. He has always loved water, yet until *Savasana*, he's never known how much.

This morning he drifted back in memory to a beach long ago: His mother (always a shadowy figure; she died when he was in his early teens) was there sunning herself; and Father, a tall robust man, read in the blazing sunlight; and his sister was there too, wearing a bathing suit considered risqué by their father, yet wear it she did in full view of admiring young men. Embree recalled himself looking at the long blue waves rolling in, just as earlier this morning, while doing *Jathara Parivartanasana*—rolling the belly around—his gaze had been fixed overhead, where sunlight rolled across filaments of white cloud, tingeing them pink. He thought he remembered the exact tone of light on the beach those many years ago. The exact light, the look of waves. Of course he could be imagining such detail. He is forty-three now; the memory's more than thirty years old. It's difficult to recall the mind of a model boy who served as his father's acolyte and harbored secret anger, who once in a short-lived adolescent escape from Father's bastion of rectitude called himself "Nameless No Name."

• • •

After the asanas, Embree did breathing exercises, the pranayama. It is said that a yogi's life is measured by his breaths, not by his days, and Embree believes—well, sort of—that regulation of the breath helps to check emotion. And checking emotion, so the yogis say, leads the mind toward the still point, the source, the zero of mystery.

But the exercises are hellish. Worst of all is *bahya kumbhaka*—long restraint from taking a breath after full exhalation. *Bahya kumbhaka* has often wrung from him emotions proper to the battlefield—desire for flight, struggle for control, panic—as he craves a single inhalation, just one life-giving intake of breath.

This morning, during pranayama, he noticed that his right hand counting the in-and-out movements of breath was clenched and there was pressure around his eyes, as his entire body mobilized for the kind of physical effort he associates with combat. Even so, he managed to spend a full fifteen minutes (he can't rid himself of the habit of wearing a watch, checking the time) at the task of controlled breathing.

• • •

Finished with asanas and pranayama, he turns to the last segment of morning yoga, to what he calls "the real thing."

Stretching out both legs while sitting on the mat, Embree draws in his left leg against his right thigh. He pulls firmly on the foot to turn its sole upward. It should look like a narrow plate you can put your food on, a yoga teacher once told him. Next he stretches his good arm out, placing the left hand on the left knee, with thumb and forefinger touching each other. He feels good, he feels strong, his spine like a post drilling into the warm earth of Madras.

Eyes closed, he begins to watch his breath. It's easy to do this morning, pleasant, simple. Not the struggle it so often is. Embree is certain he'll move farther into zero today than he's ever gone before. He knows it as he feels the air touching the membrane of his nostrils, as he watches the breath spilling like a waterfall into the recesses of a body made calm by everything he's done this morning. Embree feels wonderful, confident; whatever he is is working in concert: breath, body, mind, and will.

Breath goes in, breath goes out. "Nicely," as the Indians say. Breath in breath out breath in . . . Except for the cook banging pots around next door.

Banging pots . . . Breath in, breath out.

He wriggles again, seeking better contact with the ground. He adjusts the pressure of finger pad against thumb. Breath in, breath out. A crow cawing overhead, someone singing. Not that fool next door but a woman on the street. Perhaps she's hawking something. Pakoras?

Breath in, breath out.

He tries to go deeper, but suddenly it seems as if everything is on the surface: body, breath, mind, and will. He feels something . . . Opening his eyes, Embree discovers a solitary ant making its way across the blond hair, mixed with patches of gray, that mats his chest. He flicks the insect off, readjusts his position, concentrates again on breathing, with a small panic edging into his mind.

Sound of pots banging, crows. His shoulder's itching under the cast. And then the second letter from the American Consul begging him to reconsider the China deal.

Steady.

Breath in, breath out. Watch it curve—throat to lungs like a drawn bow. Like a drawn bow: breath like a drawn bow. A teacher told him that. Which one told him that?

"Dear Mister Embree. I do hope you have reconsidered your decision concerning the matter we discussed recently at the Adyar Club." Steady. Breath in, breath out, a thread curving from nostrils—into the mysteries. His own words or a teacher's? Words again.

Steady.

Goddammit! *You're doing it all in words!*

Steady.

Steady.

The post of spine no longer supports him; he feels his back giving like a reed. Embree stiffens, but no longer feels anything drilling into the ground, anchoring him. He feels unhinged, in pieces . . . impossible, he thinks, and opens his eyes, closes them.

Time to dive, he tells himself. Dive, dive! But *calmly*. The pressure between finger and thumb is terrific, as if he's trying to smash a hard-shelled tick between them. For a few *very* long moments he works to get the pads of thumb and forefinger into sensibly soft but firm contact.

Breath in, breath out. Breath in, breath out. Breath in, breath
out   breath in   breath out   breath   in   breath   out
breath   in   breath   out   breath   in

He begins to feel it, a calmness moving into the blank screen of his
closed eyes. Amorphous forms circle, are churning gently, leading him
onward, inward toward zero. He reaches that strange point where it's
possible to watch the breath while at the same time focusing his closed
eyes on the screen. Practice has taught him that when this happens, he
can move quickly toward zero. But his left foot needs adjusting. He can
manage it without opening his eyes, yet he opens them, glancing blearily
at the wall behind which the cook's singing.

For a moment he had been at zero.

Coming back to the blankness, he feels his mind go instantly into zero
—it's like a muffled blow altering the sensations he feels, a tap, a turning
that draws him into zero, no mind outside of it for a few strong moments.

But the monkeys come along.

Steady.

Monkeys are running through his head, tearing the darkness into
shreds of raw light. Monkeys and the next-door cook at the damn pots,
at the damn pots, and crows cawing in the trees, and now the weary
repetitious ideas knocking hard for attention: Well, what about this
young Indian who calls you Master? Did he really send the cable or did
he pocket the money?

No, he brought back the postal slip.

Steady. Yet why hasn't Vera answered? She has to decide; of course,
it's a big decision to drop everything—life, business in Bangkok—and
come here to India, but by now she should have—*should* have—

Steady. Rama sent it. Works for the postal service, doesn't he, but
postal workers peel off stamps and sell them unless you get the letters
franked. Cables aren't letters, though; Rama doesn't work in the cable
section. Rama sent the cable.

She'll definitely come. Works for postal service, so you can trust him.
Steady. Don't think.

That's it.

Steady.

Breath in, breath out. Breath in, breath out. Breath in, breath out
    breath   in   breath   out   breath   in   breath
out   breath   in   out   in   out   in

He attempts to move his consciousness like a lump of dough far back
into the blankness, toward the immense black zero, and plunge it down
there, big, amorphous, quiet, as dumb as earth. And indeed, through
the mercy of long practice, he's able to draw his mind into the blankness,
to go far into it, deeply into its space, and move through its soft black

jelly toward the zero, until all left to him is the faint but nagging hope that the zero will take on color, a blue a pink a purple, and slowly twist like something in water. Breath in . . . breath out . . . breath in . . . He's getting it.

His guru is the light, his salvation and soul the lumpy bit of turning light in the middle of the blankness . . . his guru, his teacher, his guide the pulsing light where everything is: himself, the others, the Unity, all everything in essence within the orange drop of light. No more words. Or not those words.

Steady.

Tat Twam Asi. You are that. That. Everything. You are all of it. Inseparable. The pots, you, the cook, you, the tree, you, the clouds, you. *Om Tat Twam Asi.* Thou art that. And *nothing else.*

A slight rustling sound causes Embree to open his eyes. A mongoose is making its clumsy but swift way across the courtyard. Embree hates these animals, having seen them at fairs and around temples, with leather collars and leashes restraining them from tearing to pieces the pathetic cobras, risen in their baskets, mouths sewn shut, hoods flared in a hopeless attempt at intimidating the little killers—

Embree moves his tongue around to seek moisture in a dry mouth. The meditation is going badly. His ahamkara, the I-maker, the thing inside which says I know this and I know that, dammit, has shamelessly taken charge, while next door the cook bangs those fucking pots around and sings a popular song off-key, and overhead in the bo tree crows are scolding one another with a stream of grating caws, and under the damp plaster his shoulder itches mercilessly.

So he'll try another way. He picks up his Rudrakshi beads which lie on the ground near his right toe. There are one hundred and eight beads, a Hindu rosary called the mala. Holding the mala by the tip of his ring finger and thumb, Embree is careful to keep his index finger clear of the beads, because it's the outcast finger, used to accuse and threaten, and therefore the instrument by which mankind expresses duality. So there it is: the way you hold something is a philosophical statement. It's the kind of fastidious symbolism that first drew Embree to Indian thought and that now often annoys him. Even so, running the rosary through his fingers, he finds the large starting bead and keeps his index finger free of it.

He begins to say his mantra: Tat Twam Asi, prefixing the mental phrase by the universal Om, then easing a bead between the pads of finger and thumb.

Om Tat Twam Asi. Om Tat Twam Asi. Damn pots. Om Tat Twam
Asi   Om   Tat Twam Asi   Om   Tat Twam Asi
Om   Tat   Twam   Asi   Om   Tat   Twam   Asi
Om   Tat and that insipid song he's singing, the plaster damp and the

skin itching Twam Asi   Om Tat Twam Asi   Om Tat TwamAsi
Om Tat TwamAsi   Om Tat TwamAsi   Om Tat Twam Asi
Omtattwamasi

Saying it too fast.

He tries to establish a rhythm in his mind: Om   Tat   Twam
Asi. No need to panic. No need to push aside the random thoughts
either; patiently let them come and go.

That's it. That's what he must think. Let the pots bang, because they
are you, because you are the mongoose, the cook singing, the pots
themselves. Breath in, breath out. Rama calls him Master. Since their
meeting in the village they've been drawn together. Rama would doubtless say that their karmas are responsible. And what would I say? Embree wonders. We need each other. Om Tat Twam Asi.   Om Tat
Twam Asi. I give him a kind of hope; he brings charity into my own
selfish life. It's a good thing. Om Tat Twam Asi. And has Vera aged?
That question pushes through the four droned words. And Sonia in the
old photo—skinny, knees like fists, thin serious lips. Girl grown now
into a woman? Of course. Almost twenty. Rama sent the cable, and
Vera will come because Rama sent cable Rama sent cable Rama sent—

Steady. He tries now to concentrate on the world behind his closed
eyes. On the screen, earlier, there had been the orange light, but it
faded, and then a wad of cotton, and then a wriggling string within the
zero, and now nothing. Steady. But his thigh aches, his foot feels numb,
and another question intrudes, slips between the spaces of Om Tat
Twam Asi: How long have I been sitting?

That's a poor question, so he attempts to count his breath, to get back
to zero. Breath, touching the membrane of nostrils, curves down into
lungs. Breath in, breath out   in   out   in   out
in curving   out   in   out writing a letter
means they want you—sure, for dirty work.

Breath in, breath out. Steady. Vera   girl coming steady
consul   breathinbreathoutbreath in breath out

Steady.
Steady.
Well.
Steady.
Well.

Well, for a while he had it—breath going right, hurtling into zero, a
sweet orange universe—He had it just right.

He may even have had it for a minute.

Embree opens his eyes, hating himself not so much for his failure at
meditating but for his interest in the defeated: I, I, I, the impossible
parasite.

A habit of mind has attached him terribly to the concept of himself.

If he'd started young, if he'd given himself to such morning combat back in New Haven—

The idea of Eastern meditation in the strict evangelical house of his father diverts him for a moment from the pain in his legs, which he now stretches and rubs. Father in his Christian certitude would have been horrified at the sight of his own son sitting like one of the Indian fakirs he had tried, during a score of years on the subcontinent, to convert to the true religion. Poor Father, preaching God in the midst of malaria and typhoid, willing to sacrifice health and even his life if he could bring the One God to these ignorant creatures.

Embree smiles, gets unsteadily to his feet.

Everything seems distant, a bit wavy, as always after a bout of meditation. How long today? He checks his watch: thirty-five minutes. Not bad if they'd been good minutes, but they hadn't been. Monkeys skittered through every damn one of them, chattering and pinching and grab-assing, while he choked on Om and watched his breath shatter like glass in the desperate mind.

• • •

On this gentle misty morning in Madras, as he returns to the house through a courtyard under mango and palm trees, Embree recalls a strange experience he had a year ago.

In the company of a young Indian student of Vedanta philosophy, he'd gone to Tiruvannamalai, where the famous Hindu mystic Ramana Maharshi maintained an ashram. Embree had heard the usual stories about the saint—his ability to read thoughts, his indifference to physical comfort, his hypnotic gaze, and all the rest of the mystical foolishness —and so, upon entering the ashram hall, Embree had been puzzled by what he saw: a little man in a homespun robe leaning against a small bolster on a raised platform at the far wall. Forty or fifty people seated in front of the platform were simply looking at the little man. That was all. Infrequently someone would rise and approach the mystic and ask a question, which was usually answered by a crisp word or two or merely a nod, a smile. That was all. There was no ceremony, no lecture, not even a little speech to the assembly. Letters were brought and the little man would read them, then whisper to an aide who came forward, head bowed, to receive the replies. That was all. And a benign glance now and then around the hall, a tiny smile, which, it seemed to Embree, could very well be interpreted as a smile of amusement.

After about an hour of sitting in the silent hall, Embree had felt a kind of breath blow over him, something like the slightest of breezes, and this rustle of air carried with it something very strange; he hasn't forgotten it to this day, the memory of that small vibration of air within the silent hall. Maybe it contained nothing more than silence itself, but in memory he's convinced that it carried peace, as if peace were not a state but a substance, an invisible yet very real agitation of the atmosphere; and this something moving across the bent backs of the devotees and across his own cheek and forehead was actually peace itself.

On impulse he had then risen and gone forward to the dais where shocked Brahman priests, waiting on the saint, stared in helpless confusion as the foreigner leaned forward and said to Ramana Maharshi, "What am I to ask?"

And the little man, with a white grizzled beard and ears too large for his small head, had also leaned forward to ask sharply, "Who are you?"

"My name is—"

"No, no, I don't mean that. I mean, who *are* you? That is what you should ask." Lifting his head slightly, like an animal sniffing the air, he addressed the hall in a high, thin voice. "People would know who they are in a single instant if only they'd become simple." That was all he said; with a smile, he looked at Embree and then, as if with indifference, out into the hall.

Later that day the young philosophy student had introduced Embree to one of the acharyas in the ashram. This was a jolly, middle-aged man with a potbelly—typical of temple priests fed on great mounds of rice and dal. They sat on a veranda with a view of the twin-peaked sacred hill of Arunachala.

"What, really, was he trying to tell me this morning?" Embree asked.

"Exactly what he said." The fat man rubbed his sweaty face with a soiled handkerchief. "If you know who you are, then, when you act, what is really acting is not you but the world."

"Yes, I understand the words, but what I don't like about them is their insistence on *me*. It's what I don't like about meditation: always the insistence on *me* sitting, *me* quieting my mind, *me* getting in touch with the universe. Sometimes when I think about it, I think what *arrogance* this is: I am important enough to get in touch with the universe! What I don't like about religions is the self-absorption they encourage. Religions say to us through them we lose ourselves, but what we really do is end up thinking of *me, me, me*."

The fat man laughed. "When you meditate, you are not really doing it. You are giving God pleasure by letting God meditate. He's having a bit of fun through you, and at the same time you are having a bit of fun as well, because, after all, you are all there is. You are meditating in your role as God."

Embree had gone away that evening filled with the subtlety of an argument which linked him so indisputably to God. Harry had said many of the same things, but in a callow way, with the untempered enthusiasm of a neophyte. His experience at the ashram had convinced Embree that Harry really had been on the right track. That night, for the first time, Embree had faced these ideas without hostility. The body and I are not the same, he thought. The sense of I arises from the body, but isn't caused by the body or, for that matter, by the mind, which is part of the body. Embree thought such propositions through. The sense of I comes from the world stuff, from the Cosmic I. And what, therefore, am I? Part of the Cosmic I.

On the train ride back to Madras, he'd been exhilarated by the notion that all of this, the entire world, was something like a game, a huge universal bit of fun, and at the center was the I which contained all the other I's, his own included. Surrender to this precept, the fat man had said, and you free yourself. If you carry a heavy load while riding in the car, you don't help the car go forward, you are wasting your effort. Why think *you* do something, when, in fact, God is doing it? Getting rid of yourself makes life lighter, and you can play through it along with the Cosmic Player. The world outside is real; it is the Self, even as you are. Sit back and watch what is real and be free. Remember, only the I has a destiny. The Self is always now.

Those phrases of the fat acharya carried a breathless new Embree back to Madras, and they stayed with him for days like a half-forgotten melody. Now and then they returned to his consciousness with the thrill of discovery, and at those brief but splendid times he sat with faith the way an old man sits with a cat: serene, fulfilled, listening to the smallest pulse of life.

But a few months later Embree heard that the fat acharya, along with two others, had left the ashram in disgrace for having plotted against the great Maharshi. Six months ago Embree had learned that the three dissidents had set up a rival ashram and with the help of advertising were doing quite well. Damn the fat man, Embree had thought then. Cosmic play, is it? The whole affair had thrown him into a depression for weeks, abetted by the infuriating equanimity with which his Indian friends accepted the fat acharya's defection.

• • •

Crossing the courtyard and leaving the garden behind, he brushes aside the fronds of a banana palm to see the hard morning light glittering against the gray stucco of the two-story Victorian house in which he has lived nearly two years now.

Before buying this house, Embree had lived in a hovel near the beach, aping the impoverished Indians whom he couldn't know without living among them. Now, of course, he's confident that had he lived among them even for many years he'd not have known them. Not to the core. Not to the nightmare and dream of their lives. But he'd tried for three months in the beach shack, eating their food, drinking their water until he came down with dysentery, followed by a recurrence of the malaria he'd picked up in Burma. In this weakened—and indeed nearly fatal—condition, he'd realized that any search for salvation without a concomitant interest in hygiene might lead him nowhere but to the grave. Indians concurred with this judgment and finally convinced him that few foreigners, no matter how devout, can deal with Indian microbes.

When Embree recovered sufficiently to put his folly in perspective, he'd straightaway searched for a house rather than for the Truth, and found this sprawling old place tucked away in vegetation just north of the Cooum River near Spur Tank Road.

He had purchased it (with mustering-out pay) from an old Anglo-Indian lawyer, who was needed in Bombay to take care of a sick brother. The old advocate sat one night with Embree over tots of gin and angrily denounced the Indian bid for independence, predicting no good would come of it. Without the Empire, the old fellow argued, corruption and disorder would inevitably result. He was a legalist gone cynic. He was also a Brahman gone atheist and heartily scoffed at Embree's interest in Indian religion. When Embree suggested that perhaps you can never get the religion out of a missionary's son, he declared proudly, "My father was religious too, but that didn't stop me from facing the truth."

Yet toward the end of this ginny conversation the old man confessed to a sentiment his otherwise Western intellect held in contempt: In spite of his belief that religion is nothing more than rank superstition, when his father died he had erected a small temple in the family name and attended the ceremony at which Brahman priests dedicated it to Ganesh, Remover of Obstacles, his father's favorite god.

• • •

Embree has reached the kitchen doorway at the same moment the neighbor woman from her own kitchen stoop (on the opposite side of the pot-banging cook) glances in his direction. Their eyes meet. She is grossly fat, with hair pulled back in a severe bun; already, before the day has heated up, there are thick drops of sweat beading her forehead.

Sure her neighbor has fully savored her disapproval, she turns abruptly away. She's a Brahman woman who has never forgiven Embree for hiring a low-caste cook, a harijan. Often he's seen her stare in horror at the garbage, as if proximity to food prepared by the outcast might pollute her beyond redemption.

From the entrance of Embree's kitchen, Cook steeples his hands in greeting. "Good morning, Master. That boy dropped by when you were out back and left some bananas. I think he was keen on bothering you, but I sent him down his way."

Embree steps into the kitchen. Cook is referring to Rama, whom with obvious contempt he calls "the boy," although Rama is twenty-three—a fact Embree has noted, since twenty-three was his own age when he left America for China.

Is that why I have him around? Because I was his age when my life really began? Embree wonders. Or to reward him for getting me out of a fix? Embree smiles at the thought of the young man cheerfully announcing that everything's all right because "Rama is here." Embree is aware of smiling. That, perhaps, is why he likes to have Rama around: there's a joy in the young man that he misses in himself. Sometimes he wonders if the Hindu gods have given good fortune to Rama as a reward for obedience, loyalty, persistence. Indeed, Embree has often heard him mutter "Narayana," a name for Vishnu; it's surely a habit of long standing, because pronouncing the word for God has become for him as natural as breathing. It's merely a formula, of course, and yet Embree wonders if it's also, somehow, the source of Rama's good humor and zest for life. Does the young man meditate? All Indians do, one way or another. It doesn't work for all of them, but for Rama perhaps it does. On this bright morning Embree suddenly wonders if he doesn't want Rama around so that one of these days, quite accidentally, he might learn from the young Indian something about God.

"I told him," continues Cook, "never come here bothering Master when he's out back. I don't care how keen you are on bothering him, I am telling you. You cannot and there's an end of it." Cook is a thin man with a crown of white hair. Since Independence he's become a local expert on politics. Embree has seen him squatting in front of neighborhood bearers, explaining to them how the government has created all sorts of committees and these committees will solve every care of the people.

Embree sits down at the table in the large kitchen, which has a brick-sided well in the middle of it and an open-air ceiling for ventilation. In front of him, on a palm leaf, the cook sets half a dozen rice-lentil cakes along with spicy sambar to dip them in, some hot pickled fruit, and lime chutney.

"I saw him this morning!" Cook exclaims suddenly, while pouring a mixture of coffee and milk back and forth in brass bowls.

Embree looks up from the piece of iddly held in his good hand. "The cobra?"

"He was coming home from journey."

The cobra lives in a rat hole under a mango tree. Embree has not called in the Irula—members of a snake-hunting tribe—to take it away. For many months he has simply avoided the mango tree, especially at night when cobras go abroad. Being a cannibal, so an Indian friend has explained to Embree, the cobra will keep a compound free of banded kraits and saw-scaled vipers who are at least as dangerous. Moreover, removing the snake would result in the loss of his cook and bearer, both of whom are Naga worshipers and would consider the act disastrous. The cobra—this had been explained to Embree by Cook many times—can hear people plotting against it and the punishment for such intrigue is swift and terrible: boils and bloody discharges from penis and anus. Parenthetically, the cobra will curse pregnant women who speak against it and their children will be born with scaly skins. People find gold when they drink a brew made from its boiled entrails. Cook knows all about cobras.

"I did puja and lit a candle," Cook declares proudly, content with his homage. With a theatrical gesture of distaste he throws Rama's bunch of bananas into a trash basket. "Master won't be wanting these. I know where the good ones can be getting."

Embree figures there are no more jealous people in the world than Indian servants when another Indian threatens to join their establishment. And it's true that Rama has made a conspicuous attempt to find employment here ever since he took Embree to the hospital in that old car. Every day he appeared at the hospital, a bouquet of flowers in hand, ready to run any errand possible or impossible—"Don't worry, Rama is here!" And when Embree left the hospital, Rama was there with a taxi to take him home. Since then, sometime during the day Rama shows up, bearing in one hand a bunch of flowers and in the other his rolled black British umbrella.

Slowly Embree eats his breakfast. It's said that japa yoga done badly leads to restlessness and bad temper, but this morning Embree is in a calm, almost stunned mood, as his gaze roams across a shower of sunlight pouring down through the open ceiling. There's a glint on stone jars of pickled fruit, a brown glow on gunnysacks filled with short-grained rice. The kitchen, for a few moments, achieves unity, is itself and everything. Cook is praising the local government for creating so many wonderful committees that will bring in prosperity. The high-pitched voice continues, while above them in the bo tree noisy crows are joined by other birds whose warbling spreads like sunlight through the compound. Embree feels at peace. The yoga was therefore worth it.

. . .

He mounts the narrow staircase to the second floor, a large barren maze of rooms which the retired advocate had used to store bundles of old newspapers, a defunct Telerad radio, peeling chests, heaps of torn mosquito netting, broken tables. There are no decorations on the walls painted an institutional green. Overhead in one room is an electric fan which sometimes works—if there isn't a power outage in the neighborhood and often without a little shock when the switch is thrown.

Because of the fan, Embree has put his brass bedstead in this room.

Also occupying space is a huge dusty armoire, stacks of magazines tied with twine, and a clothes rack. Through the extravagant emptiness of the second floor he passes to the bathroom; it has a pull-chain toilet, a bucket, a drain, and a sink over which hangs a small mirror.

Embree pours hot water from the bucket (brought up each morning by the mali) into the sink and lathers for a shave. He has a tough, vigorous beard—once all blond, now streaked gray. Briefly he studies the face in the mirror: the still livid scar across his forehead; a square jaw which adds to the general impression he gives of a stocky, somewhat powerful man; a set of good teeth in spite of dental neglect; a generous nose with flared nostrils. The face looks remarkably smooth for a man in his mid-forties, perhaps in part because of the light blue eyes, a notably young color, like the sky. He has always wanted darker eyes— or rather he wanted them when youth demanded an air of mystery and his appearance really mattered to him. Studying this face, he's overtaken by a sense of irony: The morning exercises had for their aim a surrender of interest in the thing he now stares at, yet he stares at it with interest, as if the exercises had prepared him for nothing more than a look at himself. That's negative. He nicks his chin with the razor.

Embree has nearly finished shaving when the mali appears.

Shrinivas is young, dark-skinned, bony. He wears a jaunty mustache that doesn't match his dirty army shorts and grease-stained undershirt.

Shrinivas clutches a few pieces of mail in both hands—an awkward way of carrying so little, but a way of saying, "Look, I hide nothing; both my hands are working for you."

Embree takes the mail, which Shrinivas holds out at arm's length. The extreme deference no longer unsettles Embree. A harijan, Shrinivas is sensitive about coming too close to another man's space. Embree has lived long enough in India not only to recognize the results of injustice but to live with them amiably. He too has been humbled by tradition deeply felt. When the long thin dark hands reach out with the letters, Embree accepts their fear and respect.

"Seeing him this morning, Master!"

"Yes, Cook told me." Embree shuffles rapidly through the mail; a few pieces he sets aside—invitations to dance and music concerts in Madras, to a monthly meeting of the Vedanta Society.

"Cook and I doing puja."

"Yes, he told me." A letter from the consulate, the third one. A Christmas card. Embree's pulse quickens—a letter postmarked from Bangkok.

"He is watching."

Embree looks at Shrinivas, who stands there with a broad grin on his angular face. "*Watching*, Master." The mali raises his hand in imitation of a cobra flaring its hood. Next he flicks his tongue rapidly between his lips in chilling mimicry of a snake sensing the air; the pupils of his eyes dilate and fix. Shrinivas looks enough like a snake to shift Embree's attention from the Bangkok letter. "So he was watching, was he?"

"Watching!" Shrinivas exclaims proudly.

Embree knows what he wants. "Tell Cook to take ten annas out of the household account and have you buy a puja garland for the cobra."

Shrinivas whips his arm up to give a smart salute, then turns and scampers away. This afternoon a garland of flowers will lie next to the rat hole under the mango tree; it will have cost four or five annas; the rest Shrinivas will use to buy a shot of arrack.

Before opening the Bangkok letter, Embree studies the handwriting, disappointed to discover that the script is not Vera's, not that series of long, looping strokes which she'd perfected through a study of Chinese calligraphy. This writing is square, hesitant, almost childish. There is no return address. Opening it, before reading a word he looks at the close: "Very sincerely yours, Sonia (Sanuk, that's what people call me now)."

> Dear Philip:
>   Please excuse my English. I speak it better than I write, Mother says. But I am trying, even although I would perfer to go to school here than abroad, as she wants. Of course I would like to go to Europe and America, but not now. There is too much to do here now. I am writing because Mother says you are coming back to Siam. I hope you do. It has been so long since you left for war. I was just a girl then. You probably won't recognice me now. I am now a woman. Do you know Shakespeare? But of course you do. We are reading it in school, although my main subject is art. I wish it were polotics because there is so much to do. About that we can talk when you come here. I am looking forward to it, since I remember we always had wonderful talks when I was a child.

And the close. Embree feels himself smiling at such open enthusiasm. He's pleased by her memory of him—had he really talked much to her? The thought surprises Embree, but then everything that happened to him for years prior to the war surprises him. What happened happened in a dream, and that long stretch of time reminds him of the second floor of this house: bare, grim, with memories tied up in bundles.

Obviously the letter was sent before his cable arrived, because the girl doesn't mention the possibility of coming to India. What's this about politics? He smiles again, while tearing up Frazer's letter from the consulate.

The next piece of mail he doesn't read until returning to his bedroom, where he sits down on the edge of the mattress and holds the Christmas card in his left hand. He holds it a long time before looking at the verse on the reverse side of a Flemish Virgin and Child. He skims through the atrocious rhymes to the two signatures: *Grace Pollack. Matthew Pollack.* And the scribbled little message in a tight hand: *May 1948 bring you peace.*

He had first seen Grace Pollack in Spencer's General Store and Provisions at the beginning of the last monsoon. She was having some trouble making herself understood in the pharmacy. He helped her. They stood under the portico watching the early rain come down. Grace was slim, round-shouldered, a woman in her thirties with a cupid face, bobbed blond hair, and the wide-set pellucid eyes of a cat.

Within ten minutes he understood everything: She was new to India, brave but confused, and with a husband engrossed in his own work. In the short time that he stood with her on the tiled portico of Spencer's, while the rain pattered into pools soon to become great lakes of water, Embree realized that this attractive woman was looking for an affair—though she might not know it. For almost a decade his encounters with women had been limited to brief sexual bouts with Burman and Yunnanese girls accustomed to serving soldiers for cigarettes or chocolate. Without thinking (later he scrutinized the impulse, for it reminded him of other impulses that had governed his life, thrusting him off center) he asked her to lunch at his house.

"At your house?" she'd asked nervously.

"Yes, I thought we might have lunch at my house. I have a fine cook."

She pursed her lips a moment. "Give me the address." She memorized it instantly, and Embree got the impression it was like a piece of wood to a drowning man. He was excited by her desperation, then by his own.

"Come tomorrow."

"Tomorrow?" Her eyes were merry, expectant. "All right, tomorrow. At one?"

"Make it noon."

And so it began.

Thinking of Grace now, as he holds the Christmas card delivered weeks late, Embree can't remember much of what they said, not even much of what they did each time they met. His image is of them lying side by side in midafternoon while the monsoon rain pounded on the tiled roof above them and the animals thrived. Perhaps he remembers them, the animals, better than anything. House lizards, pale, almost translucent, hugged the bedroom walls and grew fat on flies that multiplied in the dampness like a miracle. The lizards dropped tiny turds on Embree's bed and on their flung clothes and skittered through their lovemaking like little dragons of the mind. A drowned scorpion, its deadly tail curled under it like that of a whipped dog, brought a shriek of fear from Grace one afternoon as it floated past the front door when she opened it to leave. Even in as short a time as an afternoon, when they rose from bed to dress, their clothes were covered by a chalky mildew, and the smell was dank, cold, like something moldering in a cellar. Sometimes they stood naked at the window (the greenery was too thick for anyone to see them from either neighboring house) and watched the heavy rain agitate the palm leaves and slide like syrup down the sides of jackfruit. At another window, dressed, they could see a coconut godown with a thatched roof and thousands of opened coconut shells strewn around. Like human skulls. He'd shared that image with her; her shocked dismay convinced him his psyche was nothing she needed.

Grace needed physical love. She was married to a missionary (Missionary! The idea never ceased to amaze Embree: He was violating the wife of a missionary. The Freudian aspects of the affair, given his own history, were obvious, yet no less fascinating for that) whom she loved —in her own way.

She once said, "I like being a missionary's wife. I like to meet all sorts of people. And we travel. And though I don't have the need to serve God like he does, I believe in God and so I'm not really faking anything." She never faked in bed either, but proved to be a generous, considerate, grateful lover. Often, when leaving, she turned to Embree and murmured, as if amazed by her good luck, "Ah, thank you, Phil, you really can *do* it."

They saw each other two or three afternoons a week during the monsoon, while the insects and lizards made of the world a great teeming womb, and rain clouds swept across the rooftops of Madras to lash the city without ceasing. But after a month the daily rains tapered off a little, as did their passion. Myriads of tiny brown frogs—brewed in the miniature lakes of gardens and driveways—began to appear. They made their hopping way across cement walk, floor, bed sheets, food, and the naked bodies of the lovers. And then came an invasion of cockroaches. One afternoon a few of them, at least three inches long, flew like birds across the bedroom. Grace became hysterical, for her maid had told her that cockroaches fly only when escaping their mortal enemy the scorpion. It was their first and only crisis. When Grace calmed down, she whimpered against Embree's arm, "I love my husband." Holding her with a mixed sense of relief and sadness, he murmured in agreement, "I know you do." They kissed while the toads plopped around their feet, and courteously they thanked each other and that was the end of it. Three days later the day dawned pristine blue. The monsoon was over.

. . .

With a sigh Philip Embree picks up the final letter, the one he'd kept for last, as if marshaling the courage to read it. The return address reads Stubbs, Barnsley, Yorkshire, England.

Dear Sir:

I thank you for your faithfulness in writing to us. My youngest, Dora, says, "Mister Embree is like one of the family." And I told her, indeed he is.

We have finally decided to set up the gravestone here on our little property, in the back yard. We can't think what else to do. You tell us it is impossible to find where he lies, and the Imperial War Graves Commission agrees with you. Yet we still hope he might be found, so that we can bring him here or let him stay there with the other boys. Either is all right with us, you see. What saddens us is not to know where his remains really are. But let that be. You have been so kind.

We wish, respectfully, to count on that kindness once again. In your last letter you mentioned that you might be moving out of India. If that means you might be going through Burma, we would like to request some moments of your time. You see, other boys who served with Harry are buried there in a place called Thanbyuzayat. It is an Allied Cemetery. Boys captured by the Japanese and taken to work on their railroad are buried there. Some of the mothers of Harry's Koylie Division meet now and then to exchange thoughts. We met recently and I told them about you and your kindness. Now they all want you to see the graves of their sons for them. I am sorry for making such an inconvenient request, and believe me, sir, if it is not possible, we will understand. I only make it now because your past kindness encourages me to do so. If you are there in Burma at some future time, if you could just see those graves, the mothers would be deeply grateful. I am enclosing six names. I suppose you knew these boys or heard of them. They were all known to Harry.

Again, our enduring gratitude for your kindness and sympathy for our sorrow, which has not diminished since the day we first heard of our dear boy's death.

Yours truly,
Katherine Stubbs
Mrs. John Stubbs

Embree clutches the letter. Where is Harry lying? He doesn't know. He didn't know a week after leaving Harry there, against the tree.

After rereading the letter, he still clutches it. From what Harry had told him of the family, no one could have written such a fine letter. Mrs. Stubbs must have had help in composing it, and that makes it the more touching.

Dammit, it does.

What she wants is more about her son, much more, and he can't, mustn't give it to her. He can't tell her the truth. For that matter, what he has told the Stubbs family thus far is vague at best: that he'd met Harry in a Koylie unit during the retreat from Burma; that later, during the 1944 campaign, he'd met Harry again when the Allies were trying to take Myitkyina; that they'd been on a mission together. It hadn't been necessary to describe the Harry he'd left against the tree.

Now he can't really explain to them why Harry is not to be found. They wouldn't believe or want such an explanation. But this is the truth: A week after he left Harry there, the jungle itself must have changed—brush and trees, thrusting from the earth, would have brutally pushed away other brush and trees in the fight for breathing room. The ground must have looked like a heaving sea of green waves.

He can't make the Stubbs family understand that nature moves in the Burmese jungle with a velocity incomprehensible to people used to flower gardens and lawns. Within a few months the birds and insects would have carried Harry away—flesh, muscle, bone—bit by bit until nothing was left except perhaps a belt buckle or some buttons. And the pistol with which Harry killed four Japs that final day would be rusted now, as fragile as dandelions.

If you set me down within a mile of that spot, Mrs. Stubbs, I could never find it.

Embree looks up from the clutched letter. There's a commotion in the hall. Shrinivas fairly skids into the room to announce the arrival of someone. "Man waiting, Master! Man waiting!"

Embree rises, still clutching the letter. Carefully he folds it and lays it in a drawer. He places the card from Grace next to it, Virgin and Child up. Rapidly dressing in khaki pants and a bush shirt, Embree goes downstairs.

13 MISTER NAGARAJAN IS sitting in the little study that faces the veranda. It's a cluttered room where the old advocate spent most of his time among the glass paperweights, among the rattan chairs set so close together that to traverse the room meant moving sideways, and among tattered books and calendars on every wall, the most recent one five years old.

When Embree enters the room, the short, heavy-set Indian jumps to his feet, hand extended for a Western greeting.

"I hope I have not come too early, sir?" Nagarajan's English is rather good; he wears seersucker, an open white shirt. Two heavy gold rings catch the light flowing in from the veranda.

Long ago Embree learned that Indians make business calls before working hours. This call is not too early. "I always welcome a visit from you, sir," he says, matching Nagarajan's courtesy.

They have not seated themselves long enough to comment about the possibility of drought before Cook enters with a tray, cups, and tea. Cook is good about entertaining guests, which is one reason why the cobra has maintained residence under the mango tree.

After tea is poured, Mister Nagarajan smiles (he has two gold teeth in front of his smile) and clears his throat. "Sir, I wish to invite you to concert on February the fourteen. Kanthimathi Santhanam and party will sing bajans, and the Madras Society of Culture is honored to play host to Shri Rudra Jagannathan for that evening." After a pause he adds, "Shri Rudra Jagannathan is our greatest violinist."

Embree knows this and knows further that Nagarajan knows he knows.

"I have taken liberty," Nagarajan continues, "to reserve a pakka seat for you. Have I presumed too much?"

"I'd love to attend. The problem is my family might be here." Embree likes the sound of "my family." He lived with Vera and Sonia for more than a decade, yet during that time he never felt they were his family. Now, at this moment, they are. He feels proud enough of it to emphasize the fact to Mister Nagarajan. "You see, I expect my wife and daughter from Bangkok shortly." Well, he thinks, maybe not Sonia—Sanuk, as she calls herself. Sounds like a wild thing, full of political ideas of some kind; she may want to remain in Bangkok and work them out. But Vera will come, surely Vera will come. I have a debt to pay—

He looks up abruptly, aware that his eyes have fixed on an old calendar of the goddess Sarasvathi. "Would you repeat that, Mister Nagarajan?" A rooster is crowing nearby; he waves his hand to indicate that it disturbed his concentration.

Nagarajan fidgets, puts the tea cup down. "I wish to point out, sir, our situation now is very delicate."

That's the one word Embree has heard through his musings: "delicate."

"With British out, everything is confusing for us. Rumor has Congress intent on punishing the South. They are going to insist we accept Hindi as national language. We Tamils cannot do that, sir. No, never."

"I'm sure you will never do that."

"Then there is rumor about searches." Nagarajan grimaces to make sure Embree realizes this is what he's come to talk about. It certainly isn't about tickets—last week he sent a note indicating that, as a director of the Madras Society of Culture, he'd reserve a ticket to the February concert for his good friend.

"We cannot be certain, but it seems, sir, quite obvious now. A particular group of local politicians are beastly fellows, who are bent, sir, on cooperating with North in plan to destroy the solid values of our country."

Embree is aware that Nagarajan has lost out in a local political struggle; the man must pay for losing—doesn't he realize that?

Nagarajan is fidgeting violently now. He has rather fat fingers that seem to be turning invisible beads. His face is sweaty, the fixed smile has vanished, and creases show about his bright black eyes. "The problem is, sir, the problem can well be, sir, actual private searches of property." He waves his hand dramatically, dramatically through the air, encompassing this and all the taxable compounds of the city. "They will call these searches a way of protecting tax system! Protection? Robbery!" His eyes lose their light. "Authorities will be digging up lawns, gardens, and taking what goods they find."

"Digging up gardens?"

Nagarajan smiles in acknowledgment of Embree's surprise. "People are nerved up, sir. They have been burying goods in their gardens, and these tax fellows threaten to dig up property—at expense of taxpayer. No good keeping goods in safes. We understand these fellows will confiscate safes."

"Are you sure of all this?"

Nagarajan opens his hands in a gesture of frustration. "What to do? It is rumor we must respect."

Thoughtfully Embree drinks his tea. Were he an Indian he'd be as troubled as Nagarajan. The air has been filled with ominous rumors lately, and indeed, after the horror of Partition, to exercise good sense is to assume anything is possible. Up north there have been a number of Communist-inspired strikes. A few weeks from now the Asian Youth Conference—Red organized—will meet in Calcutta, and a month later the Second Congress of the Indian Communist Party will also meet there. The rich and miserly Nizam of Hyderabad, who controls an area as large as England, Scotland, and Wales combined, has refused to join the Indian Union, although his Moslem loyalists are a minority in the state. And every day there is heated debate by Hindus over the Bill for Codification of Hindu Law, a remarkable piece of social legislation. Embree has overheard men on trains, in tea shops, at temple entrances discuss it in varying moods of acceptance and fury. If passed, it will equalize inheritance of sons and daughters, safeguard a woman's dowry, ensure the right of a testator to will his property as he chooses. Embree follows the debate closely, a rare thing for a man who abhors politics.

He is fascinated; such changes stand at the edge of a history five thousand years old, threatening, like explorers, to stare into the abyss below and then with a single leap cross it.

"Sir." Nagarajan, having respected Embree's thoughtful silence for a while, breaks in timidly. "Sir." He clears his throat. "I was indeed hoping you might grant me particular favor. That is, since you are foreign gentleman and beyond reach of these tax collectors—"

Embree interrupts. "For the moment."

"They would never turn up *your* garden. Perhaps your safe—they might demand to see what is in it. But, believe me, it is not the Indian way to be so discourteous as to bring spades and pickaxes onto property of foreign gentleman and dig through flower beds."

"So you're asking to bring your goods here?"

Nagarajan smiles hopefully. "You have hit nail on its head, sir. I have a few goods worth a while. I would trust you fully with them."

"Mister Nagarajan—"

Both hands go up. The portly Indian leans forward expectantly. "I know your objection, sir, but rest assured I would not hold *you* responsible. All I want is tiny corner somewhere on property. Just few feet. And believe me, the digging would take place in secret, at night. I would not even inform you of exact location if that would cease your fears. You see, I have traveled. I know what it means to be gentleman. I lived one year in England. I traveled in America. In 1936. New York, Chicago, Salt Lake, San Francisco—I know them all."

There is a poignancy in Nagarajan's appeal to his American heritage that makes Embree wince. He doesn't know Nagarajan that well; the man runs a foodstuff enterprise. Once he'd discussed with Embree the possibility of sending refrigerated frog's legs to France. Because Embree could speak French, he'd been offered a job by Nagarajan if the deal went through with a French importer.

"Look, my friend," Embree begins slowly, "I understand your dilemma, and I'd like to help, but as I told you, my family's coming to India. I don't want them involved in such a thing."

"Believe me, sir, you are absolutely safe. I would not consider this if otherwise."

Of course, Embree can't be sure of it. Even so, it seems reasonable. Experience has taught him not to trust people too far but if possible not to deny them either. "Let me think about it," he says, expecting Nagarajan to take his pronouncement as an end to the interview. But the man continues to sit there, fidgeting with his hands, swiping a palm across his sweaty forehead.

Embree can't look at such anxiety but turns toward the veranda, where a huge black crow, sitting on the balustrade, is eying him with an audaciously judgmental look. Turning to Mister Nagarajan, he says abruptly, "Do you practice yoga?"

"Of course," Mister Nagarajan replies with a smile that suggests he's been asked the question before by foreigners.

"Do you ever get in touch with the zero?"

"I am not sure what you mean, zero."

"It's what I call it. I mean the point of concentration."

"Excuse me, Mister Embree, but there is more than one point of concentration."

Embree is exasperated. He knows only too well that in matters of philosophy and religion the Indian, otherwise pliable and eager to please, becomes fiendishly pedantic, aloof, arrogant. He's sorry that his own preoccupations have led the interview in this direction. "Yes, of course," he says lamely. "I agree with you, sir. More than one point. I've thought of the phrase *continuous fixation*." Fully aware this is no time to pursue the subject, Embree is prepared to do just that. "At least I think it's one way of describing what happens in meditation."

"Yes, now if you would be so kind, sir, this is matter of pressing urgency, believe me—"

Embree understands, with a jolt of recognition, that they both have matters of pressing urgency: one man to find a hiding place for his valuables and the other man to find whatever it is he is.

"Urgent, yes. I believe you," Embree says. "If by chance my family doesn't come, perhaps you can put your goods in my compound. Of course, if they don't come, I may very well have to go see them." He nearly adds, foolishly, "You see, I owe a debt to my wife, a very important one. I must pay it one way or another."

"If you are not on premises, that is not essential." Nagarajan waves his hand to dismiss the importance of Embree's continued existence. "Just so property is in your name," he says bluntly.

There's a callousness in Nagarajan's words and manner that relieves Embree from feeling sorry for the man. Yet a few minutes later, when Nagarajan reluctantly gets up to leave, Embree gives him his word—if the family doesn't come, the digging can take place. After all, Embree thinks, waving goodbye to the heavy-set man who heads glumly for the front gate, we are both desperate men, each in his own way.

• • •

Wearing a floppy Gurkha hat (he abhors the large Cawnpore Tent Club pith helmets worn by many Westerners), Embree leaves the house. In the full sunlight he can feel the weight of heat that will grow burdensome by midday, although the hot season won't begin for another three months. Then on the veranda Shrinivas will throw water against the lowered bamboo chicks to keep the house cool. Now the chicks are rolled snugly, like green tubes, against the top of the portico that runs along the building's front.

Turning at the gate, he gazes a moment at his property; it's the first he has ever owned. It really isn't much; for the past twenty years an old man shuffled through its decaying rooms with a ring of unused keys swinging on his belt. Even so, Embree is proud of it. Somehow it signals his intention to domesticate himself seriously. Flowers sit in pots; a baobab tree in the front yard is blooming, its pink blossoms giving color to the drab expanse of swept clay. It's a place that has possibilities. Not even the predicted drought can dim his enthusiasm for the house this morning. God is good. Or something is. Embree wonders if in fact his life is now beginning. This, at least, is true: He is happy to be in India, to have, moreover, the chance of introducing it to Vera and Sonia, to his family. Indeed, his family. And in India. Living here has regained for him a love of the music of vast lands, a music he hadn't heard since leaving China. There's a wind right now in the palm leaves that shakes out of them a series of clattering percussive notes. The music of India. He must tell Vera about it, but then, if he knows Vera, she'll hear it long before he thinks of mentioning its existence.

Whistling a nameless tune (has he learned it unwittingly from the next-door cook during meditation?), Embree starts down the dirt lane toward a main road where he can find a tonga. He feels a sudden hope. The yoga must have gone better than he realized this morning. And he likes himself for having promised treasure space in his garden to Naga-rajan. That is, if Vera doesn't come. But she'll come, that is certain. She must come, he thinks warily. He has never been much of a husband; now he will do it, he will pay off that debt too. First Father, now Vera.

As a lonely child, he used to carry on imaginary conversations with a boy named Wilbur. As a young man in China, he carried on such illusory interviews with his rebellious sister who lived a fast life in New York. Then for years he spoke to no one but people who were present. Since Burma, he has talked to Harry.

Today, walking down the lane, he imagines meeting Vera at the Madras pier. She gets off the ship, walking gingerly down the gangway. She wears something pretty; Vera always does. Will she be a little thicker than he'd remembered, will there be crow's-feet around her eyes? Of course. But it won't matter. She's alone. Sonia has decided to stay awhile in Bangkok; a rather grown-up girl, Sonia wants to study art and politics.

Yes, so he brings Vera back to the house, where he's installed Rama as a kind of steward. Rama steeples his hands in honor of Memsahib's arrival. Even Cook smiles. Shrinivas gives her a military salute. This is really a nice place, a sort of Garden of Eden if looked at properly. "This house is yours now," Embree will tell her, as they stroll from room to room. "It's not much, but by Indian standards it has style. And the thing is, the property's large enough to put some kind of addition onto it—perhaps another room or two along the west wall. Labor's cheap. With a little effort I can rise in the company. The Indians still need Western ideas, especially in business. You'll see. If I set my mind to it and forget my religious fantasies—I'll explain them later, I'll explain *everything*—I can do well, I can provide, I can make you proud. I can make it all up."

Embree imagines the words rapidly, with such concentration that he nearly bumps into an old cow ambling down the lane. "You'll see, you'll like India. You can't possibly know how much it means to me that you're here. I have lived with, I have been haunted by, Vera darling, things of the past you never knew. For one thing, during those days in Peking, when I was representing the General and he'd sent you up there to be out of the way during all the turmoil—do you remember? Well, of course, you remember—I looked at you and wanted you more than anything in my life. I was young, remember that, *please please please*, just remember how young I was, and inexperienced and passionate. Perhaps that's why I gave him up to his enemies. Perhaps? No doubt about it— that's exactly why I told his enemies where they could ambush him. Told them, wrote the exact information on a piece of paper. Judas, my father would say. Well, enough of that. What I did—and almost without thinking—I wrote down the arrival time of a train he'd be on. And I did it knowing, when he got off the train, his enemies weren't going to greet him with flowers of welcome. I knew damn well I was signing his death warrant. Because his death was what I wanted. That he survived the ambush doesn't get me off the hook, does it? Of course not, no. I'm aware, Vera, of everything now. What matters was my desire for his death so I could have you. And that's it. It's all the truth we need. It's what stood between us all the time. And now you know it. And we can begin again. Because this time it has got to be right, honest and open, Vera. Darling."

He tries to imagine her response to this terrible revelation (but his sincerity coming through?) and runs possibilities through his mind, as the lane curves from his house, leaving its peeling stucco and veranda behind, and bringing him closer to the main thoroughfare: She slumps down, disconsolate; she strikes out at him in a rage, with hands and feet; she turns and runs through the house into the garden. Ultimately the vision breaks down; he sees only her mouth rounded into a horrified O of disbelief and fury. Then he can't see her any more; his mind flees the imagined scene.

An old woman, sitting in front of a begging bowl at the side of the lane, starts to call to him, "Ma . . . Ma . . . Ma . . ." an insistent sound of a mechanical timbre, a demanding quality to it like the quacking of a duck or a phonograph needle stuck in a groove. It is the mindless, nerve-racking sound that Indian beggars have perfected through centuries to shift toward them the attention of passersby—so he's been told by Indians. Embree looks at her white flowing hair, her toothless mouth, one eye gone opaque from cataracts. Fishing a few annas from his pocket, he drops them in the bowl. The old woman nods approvingly and puts her hands together in prayer.

Perhaps he's begun the day with false hopes, Embree thinks gloomily and trudges on.

Two men come along, pushing a wheeled slab piled high with iron rods. The men are skinny in their loincloths; the strained muscles of their thighs look like wet rope. One of them wears the sign of Vishnu on his forehead. A laborer taking his god to work with him. Religion is everywhere, Embree thinks. It's quite literally everywhere he looks in this country: in the newspapers, in the cheap posters sold in bazaars, chalked on walls, sounded in the bajans sung at open windows, in the lecture halls, in music, dance, in advertisements for clothing and radios, in the gestures and conversation of anyone anywhere, in the roadside temples, hammered on gold bracelets, in the thread woven into saris, in processions and festivals, in the cinema, everywhere except in his own heart.

What about it, Harry? I came here to find God, but instead I've found a house and a way of paying off another debt. It's not as nice a day as I thought.

Embree halts a moment to stare up at some clouds passing. They are white explosions in the blue sky—clouds like bombs frozen at the moment of impact, great bursts of mortal smoke, bulbous as growths of fungi, woolly and terrible, ballooning into the air: clouds, bombs, an aerial attack, a cold white battlefield in the heavens.

"Harry," he says aloud and walks on.

A young girl passes on the lane; she wears a blood-red sari, has a purple flower stuck in the sleek black bun of her hair and a nose ring and a large red tilaki mark in the center of her dark forehead. Her eyes are magnificent. They make him think of Grace, of the Christian card of the Virgin and Child that she and her husband sent him. Grace will have children someday; of that he's certain. He saw her husband only once—and this too was at Spencer's General Store. Matthew Pollack and his wife were shopping. He was about as tall as Grace, a thin, balding young man with a trimmed beard and horn-rimmed glasses. He walked stiffly, like someone who had gone to military school. His thin lips barely moved as he spoke of things he pointed at, and Grace nodded in eager agreement. They were a family. How Embree had envied the missionary that moment!

Just ahead he sees a tonga waiting by the side of the road. It has a round hood, a yoked bullock with horns wearing half a dozen bronze bells around its neck. Embree heads for the rear step to mount the carriage. "Here, Gentman, here!" the driver calls out, doffing an old felt hat full of holes.

· · ·

Embree gets out of the tonga on a teeming street near the waterfront. Around him swirls India, the hawkers and bearers and shoppers, the cows and dogs. One of the latter, tail between its legs, skitters just ahead of Embree as he walks toward the low-slung MAHALINGAM EXPORT COMPANY (heretofore BROOKES EXPORT LIMITED). For no reason that he can discern, he recalls some lines from Tagore: "The bird wishes it were a cloud. The cloud wishes it were a bird."

He is staring at the dog, who gives the illusion of leading him through the crowd toward the company's entrance. What would that mangy creature rather be? Better a cockroach, better anything than what it is. Embree can't keep his eyes off the animal, for something truly Indian, he understands, is now happening: Life is becoming a symbol, behaving like the sign of something beyond what we know as life. The dog is telling him this. Embree knows, even during the experience (he's deeply conscious of such things occurring in this country), that the symbol is nothing more than a creation of his own mind. He knows this but doesn't altogether believe it, because the damned dog is talking to him about something very important, something crucial.

Damned dogs of India. They are everywhere. He sees them every day as they lie panting and unwanted by the roadside. Carts, trucks, rickshaws, tongas run over their scrawny legs, not killing but maiming them, so they limp pitiably on three legs, the fourth often held high off the ground at a gut-wrenching angle, their eyes squinting in the sunlight for a glimpse of something to scavenge.

He remembers with particular horror the dogs of Benares. In the lanes and on the riverbanks, where Shiva is worshiped as the black god-dog Bhairon, they congregate and fight. There on the ghats of the Ganga he has seen them: the Benarsi dogs with their suppurating battle wounds and their ugly tumors and their frightened eyes. He has seen even the pups fight savagely. He halted, fascinated, in the tiny lanes to watch the canine rituals of domination: the stronger dog holding the weaker, defenseless on its back, by the throat. One yip of pain would bring a dozen on the run, snarling in their hearts of hell. Moving underfoot, oblivious of humanity, they mastered one another by their own fierce logic. Better a cockroach than an Indian dog in the next life, he used to think in Benares, and now the thought returns.

The dog ahead is his witness—but to what end? Embree feels a shiver of dread, as with a few long steps he reaches the green door of Mahal-ingam Export—and watches the dog turn quickly away to disappear among the feet of advancing bearers, who are bent nearly double by the gunnysacks they carry.

Entering the office building, Embree slows down to get his bearings in the dark corridor, which seems positively black after the dazzling January sunlight. Slowly, from the dimness of the east wall, emerge scribbled words: *Jai Hind!* Not even linguistic fervor prevented the Tamils from using that Hindi slogan during the push for independence. Now, however, all over Madras he's seen those chalked and painted words removed.

He smells the paper even before reaching the office. Rounding a corner, he comes upon it: a large, high-ceilinged room with desks in rows, each hardly visible because of paper bundles lying on them, towering sheaves of orders and requisitions in triplicate, prepared to rot slowly in damp Madrasi heat, to provide meals for a variety of insects, ultimately to fall apart like the fluff of dead flowers.

As he enters, two men at front desks look up from dusty ledgers. He hears the rackety whirr of electric ceiling fans—so they're working today; they've been broken for the last two weeks. Embree nods, the clerks nod, and he passes between them to a little cubicle at one side, away from the window that overlooks the sparkling Bay of Bengal. As a Westerner, he still has certain privileges. One is coming to work a half-hour late; another is having a private office, although his position is scarcely higher than those of the clerks outside. His desk, like theirs, is piled with frayed bundles tied with string. The top one is wrapped in a green strip of paper marked URGENT. Embree gives it a cursory glance, then turns on the overhead light—a naked bulb shines weakly under a round shade that hangs from an exposed wire. He could have a desk near the brilliant window, but that would cost him his privacy—something needed in this office, which is often possessed by the dizzying atmosphere of a train station.

At the moment three clerks have gathered around one desk to chat. He can hear their melodious Indian voices (the language is English right now) as they discuss Gandhi's triumphant fast (a holy man, that is sure, but wrongheaded, they agree, to give in to the scheming Moslems), and then they analyze the latest cricket match.

A bearer comes in to place a note on his desk. It's a phone number; beside it is scribbled *consulate*. Embree shoves the note away and begins to open the URGENT bundle. Halfway through untying the string, he looks up and stares straight ahead through his open office door at the window beyond the desks.

Sunlight leaps against the windowpanes slanted open. From his angle of vision he can see a long flat ribbon of blue water at the edge of a long flat ribbon of brown sand. There are places in India where the eye can't rest for an instant on any space near ground level without catching within this circle of vision something human—the whole body or part of it: foot, hand, shoulder, head. And then there are vast stretches of landscape which seem empty of man, going on without such consciousness, nothing but vegetable and mineral rolling toward infinite horizons. It is now the latter, the humanless world, that seems to pour into him through the window, flooding his mind with a white silent void, perhaps eternity—perhaps, comes the odd and terrible thought at eight-thirty A.M., with his own death.

I have tried hard, he tells himself.

It's true. For two years he tried to square a debt, and he did, he squared the one with Father. I tried to find something of his life in mine, Embree tells himself. Tried. Paid. And I'm done with it. If I'm a dog next time, so be it.

That's what the dog was trying to say: This is what you'll be next time. You'll be me, so take a good look.

Embree moves the string in his fingers without untying it. Was Father ever afraid of destiny? Father used to say, "When I serve people I serve Jesus Christ, who told us, 'Inasmuch as you have done it unto one of the least of these my brethren, you have done it unto me.' " He sees Father in his mind: the rugged, erect old man with stern visage, shock of white hair, judgmental eyes. Father used to say of his mission in India, "I gave the life of Jesus Christ to the poor and the maimed." Just like Father to speak in phrases from the Bible. What Father gave was himself, not Christ; his failure was not to see that. Saving souls was his business, so he thought, but giving succor to the damned was what he really did. And that was good, good enough, that was wonderfully good.

It's not the first time Embree has seen his father in a positive light. Father did more than sit with eyes closed, legs crossed, trying to rid himself of I. Father went out and did what he could—pushed away the I by sheer effort and in the process did some good.

Father. That's what he did.

Coming to such a conclusion is like forgiving. But is it possible, Embree wonders, to forgive after so many years?

No good comes of such questions. They turn you around and around, they go nowhere.

Embree realizes he holds the string tautly between both hands, less to untie it than to grip something; thoughts beat in at him from the intense window.

I've not been my father's son. Whatever his faults, he tried. I've only blamed him for mine.

Said to himself, these rather formal words make up a formal confession. In the past, during periods of anxiety, he's confessed in the same precise way: "Whatever his faults, Father tried. I've only blamed him for mine." Yet until now the words leapt along the surface of his mind, like flashes of comfort. Now they seem to surge up from the depths. Has meditation done this? That wasn't the purpose of it. He hates to think that instead of ridding himself of I he's discovered a way to enhance it. He feels tired and he's sweating. But it isn't that hot in the office.

Outside, the flat landscape of sea and sand and sky assaults him; he needs movement to concentrate on, something to distract him from the void. It's as if he is meditating against his will, diving into a blue zero. I, I, I, the impossible parasite.

It's stupid to think so, but because of the way he has lived this life, in the next one he'll be a savage, frightened, hideous, and tormented dog.

Embree is still holding the string when one of the clerks saunters to the doorway. "You have a phone call, Mister Embree." The other employees call one another by their first names, but to them he is always "Mister Embree." Even the Managing Agent (they have not yet changed the nomenclature of authority from colonial rule). The MA, as they call him, is a self-confident man, who daily proclaims his patriotism by supporting legislation for the establishment of prohibition to offset the debilitating effects of Western vice (these are his words, rolled through his mouth with a British fullness), but who calls his shipping officer, in a voice muted with unconscious respect, "Mister Embree."

Embree, feeling slightly nauseated, goes to the main office, picks up the receiver, and hears the incessant crackling of an Indian phone.

"Embree here!" he shouts into the mouthpiece and grins at the clerk, who doesn't try to hide his curiosity but leans forward to make sure not a word is lost.

"One moment, please!" Embree hears a female voice through the crackling.

In a moment he hears another voice, which he recognizes even through the auditory maze. "Mister Embree, did you get my last letter?"

"Yes, I did! Thank you!" Thanking the consul is a bit foolish, but Embree still feels unhinged by the thoughts of moments ago.

"Well?"

For an instant Embree can't recall what he did with the letter; ah, he tore it up. "I can't hear you!" he shouts.

"I want to know what you'll do!"

"I'm still not sure!"

"Don't wait too long! Plans have to be made! Estash your we'll make it worth your while!"

Embree strains to hear, figuring the garbled words were "rest assured." Bastards are eager, aren't they. They want him badly. China.

For a moment he feels his pulse quicken, a familiar message telling him, "Here it is, the danger, the excitement, the way out!"

"I won't wait too long!" he yells into the phone.

"The offer won't last forev—!"

"Sure, I know!"

Something more comes through the crackling. ". . . and make it worthwhile, believe me, Mister Embree!"

"I know, I know!" Embree can hear the irritation in his own voice. Why that? Do I want to say yes? Is that it? "Thanks for calling, Frazer! Goodbye!"

Back in the cubicle, Embree sits a few moments with head in hands, as if exhausted. No more of that life, no more running.

．．．

One of the bearers employed by the office comes to the entrance of the cubicle.

"Putting up!" the bearer says in triumph and holds up for display a large poster, which he has brought on orders of the MA. It is a printed indictment of alcohol in garish red, featuring both English and Tamil. Among other epithets used to describe this foreign vice are The Cruel Tempter, The Vicious Seducer, The Demoralizer of Mankind, and The Western Plague.

"So put it up," Embree tells him, hearing from outside some voices raised in heated discussion. There's to be another organizational meeting to discuss the formation of a union; three such meetings last week resulted in a new mound of tied bundles on each desk this week. For a moment Embree catches phrases and tone—pride, confusion, anxiety, eagerness are all in the voices. "Of course," he says with a smile, "put it up."

The bearer is securing the thin poster onto the wall with three-quarter-inch nails, when suddenly Rama appears in the doorway, waving a piece of flimsy paper.

"Cable, Master! Got from friend in cable section and am bringing you."

Embree stares at the young Indian, those large ears and shining eyes, and the rolled umbrella clutched in a bony hand.

The cable is short, not like the rambling, expensive one that Embree had sent to Bangkok.

APPRECIATE OFFER STOP BUSINESS PREVENTS
COMING   V

Embree slumps down. It seems clear now that everything today, including the meditation, has been focused on the I in him that wanted her to come here.

Vera, I had somehow counted on you. I had counted on your saving things.

Glancing up, he sees Rama still there in the doorway. Embree has the odd feeling that Rama would remain there forever, a faint expectant smile on his dark face, unless ordered otherwise. He cares what happens to me, Embree thinks in wonder. This concern is so Christian. It is the thing his father had preached but not practiced, at least not with him.

"Rama, do you meditate?"

The young man narrows his eyes to a squint. "Meditate, Master?"

"Sit cross-legged, concentrating."

Rama shakes his head. "No, Master, I am not doing like that. That is for yogis. I am not being that patient. But I pray to God. That I am doing."

Embree has not heard this explanation. He has forgotten Rama. What he is looking at, all that matters, is the light in the window. Staring at it past the little Indian's shoulder, he feels the morning's events fade into the broad expanse of whiteness. The light is a void and into it seems to flow the I, I, I that has plagued him since his waking moments today. So the light is a relief; but then, appalled by its vast emptiness, he fears death. For an instant he has a vision of Harry propped against the tree with a gray coil of intestines bubbling in his crimson lap. Turning abruptly from the window, Embree says to Rama in a voice overloud, "Thank you. You brought me what I wanted to know."

14 SHE'S PACING IN the hot little room, can't keep still. Chamlong has left her alone in this foul, insect-ridden hotel for hours. He's gone to see his uncle, who runs a Chinese store filled with herbal medicines, kitchen utensils, bamboo toys, calendars. Sanuk knows the sort of cheap, shabby place. They're all over Bangkok now. And apparently they've come to the South too, competing with stores that traditionally specialize in one product only. She knows from Mother about the marketplace economics of the Chinese in Siam, but that doesn't make the subject less boring.

Everything bores her in the tiny room with a tin roof in the Chinese section of Songkhla.

For diversion she sprawls on the rumpled bed and opens her diary. A drop of sweat falls on the last entry, to which with a sigh she now adds another: "It's not so much his leaving me this way as it is me not having something to do. He is not always thotful. But he is brave fighter for Chinese freedom." She can't think of more to add, although the entry leaves her dissatisfied. In fact, Sanuk feels everything she's written lately has been dull and stupid—and dishonest. Because she hasn't put down what really happened. She hasn't explained how Chamlong urged her to come South with him while her mother went North; how he was going to carry an important message to a Communist group while taking account ledgers to his uncle in the Songkhla store. She hasn't admitted to the diary her fear of losing Chamlong if she refused to go along. Nor did she write down the details of her deception: a note left for Mother saying she was spending the weekend with Lamai, because it was the last time they'd have together before the wedding. Of the lie and the fear scarcely a mention appears save for "I am kind of panick trying to figure out what to do. I love them both, yet I must betray one of them. Is this what love comes to? I wanted to ask Lamai, but she would never be of help in such thing. Except I got her word not to say I was not with her. That took a full hour! I worry about you, she said, and cried. But her mind is on marriage. I am alone." It's an entry Sanuk is proud of. It has the ring of tragic drama, of despair almost religious in intensity, hasn't it, like that of the Maid facing the Burgundian tribunal, when doubts assailed her, and she wasn't sure her voices told her to do what was right.

But the other entries are dishonest. They aren't worthy of either her Chinese or her Russian blood. It is the Russian side of her heritage that worries her now. What would her grandparents, honored citizens of Petrograd, think of a girl who lied shamelessly? It is less the idea of running off with a boy than of sneaking off. Mother has explained to her the Russian code of honor—break it and face a duel or ostracism, the second alternative much the worse. You didn't lie, you kept your word, you didn't cheat, you answered up for what you did. Mother laughingly and proudly called it "our antiquated Rogacheva sense of honor." Sanuk's grandmother, to the final days of a long life, walked five miles every morning through the grounds of the *dacha*, rain or shine, singing lustily; she once contradicted the Czar about the facts in a story by Gogol. Would such a strong woman tolerate a grandchild who sneaked around instead of announcing to the world she loved a man?

Another drop of sweat smudges the page, causing Sanuk to close the book. If only she'd brought along her Shakespeare, she could read *Romeo and Juliet* again. Or if she had something to read other than the Siamese romances she found in a Songkhla market: filled with wicked landowners and innocent maidens and bold adventurers and bad dragons, the sort of story (so cheaply bound that the glue usually parts by page six or seven) that Mother forbids her to bring into the house.

Had it been this way for Mother while waiting for Father to return from his troops? The restless loneliness? The inability to concentrate? Not with Mother. She'd translated Chinese poetry.

Sanuk goes to a window shuttered from afternoon heat and sunlight. Flinging the shutters open, she looks down at the sunlit street. In the glare she squints at a tram stop where students are waiting, girls of thirteen and fourteen in blue skirts, white blouses, black sailor ties. The sort of uniform she herself wore at school. Fourteen. A century ago.

Absently Sanuk touches the amulet at her neck, squeezes the Indian Goddess of Love between her fingers. At sixteen she and her classmates at school were already talking about the rhythm method. Each kept track of her menstrual cycle, working out the arithmetic that made the difference between freedom and bondage. Giggling naughtily, each girl calculated when intercourse was dangerous for her, although none of them—to Sanuk's knowledge, at any rate—had cause to worry about that in those days. Now that knowledge comes in handy for her. The eighth day from the start of her period through the seventeenth day— beware! She won't consider the possibility of an irregular cycle, although hers are often off a few days. Touching the amulet again, Sanuk gets rid of the thought.

Yesterday at a Buddhist temple she and Chamlong shook the fortune sticks in a box, and her number came up five, a lucky number. He got a nine, also lucky. They'd returned to the hotel in high spirits, ready to make love.

The memory brings a flush to her cheeks.

Only two weeks ago she'd been a virgin. Now she's a woman capable of running off with her lover, telling lies along the way.

The transformation, if amazing, is not really unpleasant. The memory of the past few hectic days brings a smile to her lips. Sanuk turns from the window and gives the room a curious survey: the rumpled bed, the cheap bamboo dresser, the overhead fan creaking plaintively, the peeling walls— If she looks at a wall for a while, inevitably something will crawl across it. Most likely one of those cockroaches of the South.

To her imaginary confidante Sanuk says, while pacing, "We went down on the train. Two days after my mother went North with her girlfriend. I wish she would come out with it, instead of making excuses about Burmese sculptures up there to buy and all of that. She could just tell me. I'd understand. What she does is fine with me, more now than ever. Maybe once I was ashamed of Mother's love for other women, but not any more. Because love is love. Isn't it? Do you understand? Because now I know what the need for love is."

This conversation completed to her satisfaction, Sanuk halts and buttons her blouse, which, in the heat, she's let flap open. Along with the blouse she's wearing a sarong: plaid sarong, red blouse, a nice combination for the South, although he never notices what she wears.

Barefoot, she goes to the door, opens it, peers down the grim narrow hall. Light shines from an open doorway. With a sigh of determination Sanuk pushes strands of sweaty hair back from her forehead and pads down the hall, toward the light.

She looks through the open door at a window in whose brilliance is framed the featureless silhouette of someone lying on a bed. A soft voice speaks out. "You there. Come in and talk."

Sanuk takes a step into the room. Once out of sunlight, she can see the girl, stretched out, naked to the waist. Nipples point upward from little breasts. "Don't you stay down the hall?" the girl asks pleasantly.

Sanuk nods, sitting on the edge of a rattan chair.

"You're with the Lukjin?"

"How did you know he's a Lukjin?"

The girl shrugs her thin shoulders; she can't be more than sixteen or seventeen. "A lot of Lukjins come around here. I do business with them, so I know. He's tall like Chinese but dark like Siamese, and anyway, he looks half and half. He has that look." The girl has a flat nose, long hair, alert black eyes. Her left cheek is pitted—a scar from a wound or from disease. "Are you from Bangkok?"

"Yes."

"I thought so. You have the accent. You're Chinese?"

Sanuk smiles. "Yes, I am."

Appraising Sanuk thoughtfully, the girl says, "But you're not all Chinese."

Sanuk is disappointed. "I'm Chinese," she insists.

The girl points to a bottle and two dirty glasses on a small table. "Have a drink."

Sanuk rises and picks up a glass. After hesitating a moment, she pours a tiny drink of Mekong whiskey.

"Go on. Have a real drink."

Sanuk pours a little more in the glass. She's never had whiskey in her life. But with determination Sanuk swallows the brown liquid now. The bad taste and the burning startle her, bring tears to her eyes. But fortunately the girl hasn't noticed—she's up getting her own drink. Sanuk watches the girl's breasts lift slightly as she arches back to knock down the whiskey in one gulp. What if men come down the hall and see her half naked? Does she cross her arms or just stand there?

The girl pours another, sips it. "It kills the pain of my toothache," she explains, shuffling back to the bed and flinging herself down. "Maybe next week I'll have it pulled, only I hate to do that." Opening her mouth she points to a front tooth. "I hate to have a hole there."

Somchai and the bad dentistry—the saw, the blood. "I'd hate that too," Sanuk says, holding the glass and sitting on the chair again.

From the bed the girl regards Sanuk. "Is he paying you?"

"Who?"

"Your Lukjin." The girl rolls onto her stomach, cradling her head in both hands. "Isn't he paying you?"

"For what?"

"Even if it's love, for coming all the way down from Bangkok with him, he should pay you. I went to Bangkok once with a soldier and he paid both ways, along with buying me a necklace, and at the train station he gave me a hundred bahts," the girl says proudly. "Who do you take care of?"

"Well, myself."

"You're lucky. My mother's sick, so I have her and then two sisters who aren't old enough to work yet. I'll bring one of them here next year, though. She'll be thirteen." Sitting up and flicking her left nipple with one finger, as if testing its resiliency, the girl says, "Her tits are already as big as mine. Is the Lukjin good to you?"

"Yes, he's good to me."

"I had someone like that till a month ago. He kept telling me we'd marry. Of course I never believed him, because he was a Moslem and anyway he couldn't hold a job. But how he could talk! You know that saying: His tongue was so long he could wind it around his ears." She laughs briefly. "You don't talk much, do you."

"Sure I do." To prove it Sanuk asks for the girl's birth date, then explains the astrological importance of it. "You were born under the sign of the Monkey. The Brahma Jati says a monkey person is a good talker."

The girl leans forward, showing interest. "Do you know all that?"

"A demon rides on your back."

The girl grimaces.

"But that can mean good luck. Your element is iron, your lucky plant the jackfruit."

"I like jackfruit."

"The moon's in your mouth, so you like to learn things."

The girl nods vigorously. "I do."

"Being born a Monkey is good for monks." When the girl laughs, Sanuk laughs too.

"Have another drink. It's hot in here."

Sanuk, rising, pours another whiskey. "Because Venus is in the feet of Monkeys, they don't like traveling."

"That's right, I don't. Except that one time to Bangkok I've never been anywhere, and that's fine with me." Rising too, she gets herself a drink.

Sanuk nearly adds that Monkeys are often addicted to sexual vice because Saturn is in their loins, but instead she explains that Monkeys are careful workers because Mars is in their hands.

"That's me. Have another. Go on, your glass is empty. I've got another bottle under the bed."

Sanuk feels the whiskey, yet, anxious for the girl to like her, she pours another.

"Tell me about Monkeys and marriage."

"Stay clear of men whose element is wood."

"Which are they?"

"Men born under the Tiger and the Hare."

The girl hits one fist against the palm of her other hand. "That's it. I remember. Once he told me he was a Tiger."

"See?" Sanuk feels vindicated.

"You know a lot," the girl says admiringly.

"So do you."

The girl scoffs. "I can't even read."

A daring question, swimming up through the Mekong whiskey, occurs to Sanuk. "I bet you can tell me this, though. Why do women make love together?"

"That's easy." The girl gathers a pillow under her chest. "They like gentleness. And one woman knows another woman better than a man can know a woman. Isn't that so? That makes it more comfortable."

"But sometimes men make love together too, don't they?"

"Sure they do."

"But are men as gentle as women?"

"Not that I ever knew."

"Then what do they get out of love together? If they could find more tenderness with women, why not make love with women? Come to think of it, if women are more tender than men, why don't men and women both want to make love only with women?"

The girl shakes her head. Both of them, humbled by the question, stare into the sunlight.

"Another drink?" the girl asks after a while.

"No, I'll be getting back." Sanuk rises.

Turning face up to the ceiling, her sharp nipples rising from flattened breasts, the girl murmurs, "You're afraid of him."

Sanuk turns at the doorway to look at her silhouetted in the blazing sunshine. "Do you think so?"

"Of course you are. Listen." She turns her head; it's only a dark round spot on the sunlit bed. "In the next life I'm going to be a man. I pray for it. I take flowers every day to Lord Buddha. I'm gaining merit, so next time I'll be a man."

"Why do you want that?"

"So I can come to places like this and pay and then leave. So I don't have to stay here."

"I wish you luck," Sanuk tells her with enthusiasm.

"You too. Keep your eyes crossed in a cross-eyed town."

The old Siamese saying follows an unsteady Sanuk down the hall to her room. Throwing herself on the bed, she tries to think of what it means, but falls almost instantly into sleep.

• • •

He awakens her with his body.

And almost before she can separate the states of waking and sleeping, he has entered her forcefully, his breath gusting against her cheek. Soon they're both sweating in the close little room, and the cool sensation of moisture between their bodies enhances Sanuk's pleasure. She feels thick, heavy, a slippery thing, something amphibian and deep, a thing sliding into a warm gelatinous bog. It feels good to feel this way. And aside from his gusty breath and the sweaty smell of him, all she really knows in their lovemaking is her own body. It is hers, hers, it is her own body, not his but hers that she feels during these tumultuous times, lifting her again toward ecstasy, toward the brimming cup that fails to overflow at the last moment.

Later, watching him dress, Sanuk wonders, as she always does, if he loves her. How can he, really? Afterward his face withdraws, forgetful of what's just happened. How can he mean it when he says, "I love you"? Or are all men like him? Is this male love?

That girl down the hall, praying to be a man in the next life.

The thought hangs there, because she feels him looking at her.

"You drank whiskey when I was gone," Chamlong says reproachfully. "I never knew you drank."

"I don't."

"You did today."

"A girl down the hall—"

"I don't want you talking to the whores around here."

"I was restless. You were gone a long time." He's handsome, she thinks. Later she'll savor the memory of this moment when he'd seemed so handsome, so heroic, so inaccessible that she'd felt both sorrow and admiration.

"I don't want you talking to whores." He is standing at the window, looking out of it. The lowering sunlight frames his sharp features.

"We just talked awhile."

"And drank whiskey." Turning, he frowns at her.

"She was born in the year of the Monkey."

Chamlong says nothing. She isn't sure he heard her, because he turns back to the window, looking down at the street as if expecting to find something there.

There's a long silence during which she rises and puts on her sarong. The bathroom down the hall is near the girl's room, so Sanuk wonders if she ought to go there to wash now. Chamlong might think she'd gone down there to talk with a whore again.

Now he's talking, with his back toward her, his eyes fixed on the street. He tells her a story of intrigue and danger. There's a Chinese plot to disrupt governmental communications in the South. That's why undercover police are prowling the streets of Songkhla. Any moment now violence could erupt between Chinese radicals and Siamese agents.

Chamlong's face is shadowed by incoming sunlight. That she can't see his features makes him more powerful and mysterious to her—like a warrior. "The people here in Songkhla trust me," he is saying, eyes still turned to the street. Now he turns with a smile. "I can tell you what I've been doing here, because I'm finished now. I brought pamphlets from my cousin."

She knows his cousin Wan-li has just returned to Bangkok.

"I brought them pamphlets he'd translated from Marxism and philosophy," Chamlong explains proudly.

"What do they say?" She wants to show interest.

Chamlong shrugs. "I haven't read them. But they're important. They're revolutionary. Do you have any idea what Phibun's gang will do to me if I get caught?"

Torture, death. Those ideas heighten her sense of him as a warrior. He steps back from the window, freeing himself from the web of sunlight and letting her see his actual features: small ears, prominent chin, eyes set close together, straight sharp nose. There are firm lines of determination around his lips, giving him a face without softness, without dreams too, a face meant for action. Such a look frightens but elates her. Minutes ago this hard grim young man had been thrusting into her, his breath fierce on her cheek.

He's coming toward the bed, and for a moment she thinks Chamlong is going to embrace her again. But instead, sitting down, he takes a small wad of money from his pocket. Smoothing the bills carefully, he counts them aloud, despair in his voice.

Last night they'd gone to Haadyai to the bullfights: two huge animals with their horns locked in a pushing contest that Sanuk found brutal and meaningless. Chamlong had bet on the loser. On the bus back to Songkhla, he'd claimed the winner's handlers had rubbed hog-badger fat on their bull's nose, an illegal maneuver that made the beast invincible. Chamlong had lost nearly all their money.

"We have enough for the train home," Sanuk points out.

"Yes, but I have to buy dinner for two Party members tonight." He hesitates. "And I wanted to go home a winner. I wanted to show them in Bangkok I know how to bet on the bullfights. I do know how, but I wanted them to know I know. Don't you see?" he asks desperately.

Sanuk touches his hand, but he withdraws it to stuff the bills, crumpled again, into his pocket. "I'll show them," he mutters. "Someday I will."

. . .

Now there are two men, strangers to her. One, the shorter, has the dark flat features of a Malay. The other is Chinese, with light skin, Mongolian eyes.

Seated in the outdoor restaurant, at a table facing the beach, Sanuk looks beyond them toward the Gulf of Siam, sparkling in twilight as if the blue waters were crashing splinters of glass. It's beautiful here. The white beaches and lush casuarina trees draw her away from a conversation Chamlong is having with his guests, two local Communists. Unlike Chin, who had spoken freely in her presence, they're guarded because she's a woman.

Sanuk thinks of the half-naked girl praying for manhood next time.

Across the table from her the Malay is chewing a tiger prawn. He has large white teeth in a wide face; such prominent teeth give him an animal look. There's an old saying she recalls: In the South the Malay Moslem is the lowly rubber tapper, while the Siamese Buddhist holds government office and the Chinese Taoist controls the marketplace. She would never repeat it to this primitive-looking Malay. When their eyes meet, he smiles, mangling the white prawn flesh in his open mouth until she looks away.

It's beautiful here, beautiful in the South. With prows facing inland from the beach, the brightly painted *gorlae* rest side by side in the sand. In front of them on attap platforms the day's catch of silverfish are drying. After a half-year of fermenting, the fish can be mixed with chilis to make nam pla. She likes nam pla with kra-phong, a pungent fish of this region. She's just eaten a whole one while the men have been discussing the national elections. Phibun's gang is certain to win; no argument about that. If the rumor proves true, so the Chinese man suggests, Field Marshal Phibun will come forward and take the premiership for himself instead of pretending to work behind the scenes. Chamlong agrees heartily. He's been drinking. The Malay eats more prawns, masticating them with a slow open-mouthed obscene pleasure.

The girl, naked to the waist and with a toothache, prayed for manhood next time.

Sanuk smiles at Chamlong's two guests, as if they've accepted her presence. Chamlong only brought her to show them he could have a woman too. That's a sad thought, but maybe a true one. Maybe the thought a woman learns to have, and it draws her mind beyond the trio into the beauty of this Songhkla beach. She looks past their heads at the gulf and two humpbacked islands, one small, one large: the Cat and

Mouse Islands lying off Songkhla. It's not Chamlong's fault. It's the need for him to be a warrior in a time of revolution.

Someday they'll return together to the South and enjoy it without a sense of danger. Just the two of them journeying through uncounted days along the Siamese Peninsula. Together, safe, they'll travel past the stucco houses with bird cages hanging from porches. How the southerners love birds! And they'll look together at passing banana palms, pine trees, limestone cliffs where the monkeys clamber and in whose caverns the nests of swallows are collected. They'll eat the expensive soup made from those nests. Together they'll come here and sit at this same beachside restaurant and order fish curry wrapped in banana leaves and coconut-curd milk on top of gelatin. When the moon rises above the gulf, just as it's doing now, together they'll walk slowly to their hotel, a good one without cockroaches on every wall, and it will be set back in the casuarina trees just like the hotel over there, and until the dawn breaks over the wide beach unhurried lovemaking will keep them awake.

Such pleasant thoughts occupy her until the men rise to leave. They disappear into the dusk, just as a waiter comes along lighting the beach torches.

Chamlong is looking at her critically. It's not an expression most people would recognize as critical, but she's learned to read him.

"Women don't know what trouble is until it falls on them."

Sanuk smiles. What else can she do? But it seems to anger him, because he adds harshly, "You wouldn't be smiling if you knew the truth."

"Please tell it to me." She leans toward him. His face has little hollows in the flickering torchlight.

"Those men, their lives are in danger."

"I didn't know that."

"That's what I'm telling you. Women don't know such things. And mine too. My life's in danger."

Sanuk leans closer, studying his face for a better sign. Is it true? Or is he bragging? Should she be as afraid as he wants her to be? Confused, she waits for Chamlong to say more. When he doesn't, Sanuk decides to talk, only what she wants to talk about isn't danger; it's something equally important, though. "Did you really want me to come with you?"

"Why ask that now? Of course I did." Chamlong looks around quickly, as if checking to see if they're being overheard. He studies a waiter who's carrying a platter of seafood from the charcoal fire set back on the beach. "I just want you to know how serious this is."

"I know how serious this is."

"This afternoon I heard three members of the Party have already disappeared around here. I didn't want to worry you, but now you better know."

"I know how serious this is. But I came anyway."

Chamlong blinks at her in obvious confusion. He doesn't know how to reply. His regard—his love, Sanuk decides—prevents him from saying more. He wants to impress her; at the same time he doesn't want to frighten her. Love confuses him. Good. How handsome he is, and brave too, because it really is dangerous here. He's right to insist on a recognition of his bravery.

Minutes later, after paying the check with their last money, they take a stroll on the beach. Tomorrow they return to Bangkok—Sanuk has the tickets pinned inside her sarong—and the idea of leaving here saddens her. The moon is full, a freshening wind coming off the gulf. She wants to tell Chamlong how right he was about everything, about taking her that first time to the Chinatown hotel, even if it was a run-down "short-time" place, and about persuading her to come South with him. But it seems wrong to break their silence, which is something intimate between them, a special sharing. She won't speak, not even to compliment him. She's staring at the water in moonshine, when his voice startles her by its intensity.

"Someone's following us, but I don't want you to look. Don't look, don't turn around. Just keep walking."

"I won't look." But the temptation to glance around is almost unbearable.

They have walked another hundred yards before Chamlong whispers tensely again. "I know who it is. I saw him in a tea shop this afternoon. He was watching us."

"Watching who?"

"Party members I was with. They told me he might be an agent."

"Is he still following?" She lets him do the glancing back.

"Closer now."

Sanuk realizes with surprise that Chamlong has never sounded more confident. This is what he wants, she thinks in awe, dread.

"Closer."

"What do we do?" She turns slightly, then checks the impulse.

"I'll take care of it."

We're slowing down, she thinks. Ahead there's a limestone outcropping that projects from a cliff to the water's edge, breaking through the beach. It's like a wall they'll soon come to. We're slowing down. I won't look back.

Suddenly he's turned and is rushing through the sand, is almost instantly grappling with someone there, behind them. A man taller, heavier—Sanuk can see that, in dismay she sees it. The two men lurch into the shallows of the gulf, twisting in each other's grasp for better purchase until both of them fall into the water. Up, staggering, they embrace again and stagger farther into the gulf; it drops off suddenly, bringing them waist high into the ocean.

Sanuk can hear their breath above the hiss of surf. Then Chamlong, who seems to buckle and heel to one side, calls out in alarm, "Help me! Help me!"

Who's he calling? she wonders. Not me! Me? Appalled by his situation, she slogs into the water. Beneath the milky moonlight Chamlong's handsome face is circled in the gulf, like a face on a plate. It goes under, resurfaces, his mouth gasping, "Help me!" before the man pushes him down again.

Scrambling out farther, Sanuk reaches them and wraps her forearm around the man's throat. She has to stand on tiptoe to accomplish this: it lets her know how big he really is. His flesh against hers feels warm, and the configuration of his laryngeal cartilage presses against her arm, warmly, while a sound comes from his mouth, a little grunt of annoyance until more pressure from her cuts it off.

She's flung off. He's simply swept her off his back. She lands spread-eagled in the gulf.

Thumb. Stabbing pain.

But she's not thinking, she's moving through the water. Leaping back on him, Sanuk wraps both arms around his neck, pulling him sideways, and now Chamlong, having managed to pull free of the man's grip, is helping her. Both of them entwine him and wriggle their hands from shoulders to neck to the vulnerable throat. Sanuk feels her fingers dig deep into his flesh, even though her left thumb hurts terribly, and it's with surprise and terror and finally with exhilaration that she realizes her hands, what they are doing, are causing him to whimper. Alongside Chamlong she watches their two pairs of hands crowd the man's throat. They have heeled him over into the gulf, and she watches his water-slick head go under, fight up under their hands, go under again, fight up into the moonlight until she can see, horribly, his wide frightened eyes, a milky light gleaming in their pupils. Face and hair, streaming water, go under once again—she can feel him wriggling under four hands like something alive, as if he hadn't been really alive until this moment when every muscle of him is straining to push them away. He comes up one final time, his mouth stretched into a black oval of terror, and his Siamese eyes enormous as if ready to roll out of their sockets, twin terrible moons reflecting the big one, and then at last all of him goes under a last time.

What's alive under her hands slows down; she can feel him dying in her fingers. It feels like something dying within herself, as if this slippery twisting thing under the water is somehow an extension of her own arms, hands, fingertips.

Bubbles rise from the swell of the gulf. The dead thing they mutually hold collapses in their straining arms.

. . .

At the railroad station, where they board the train for Bangkok, hawkers are selling dried squid, kanom sweets, roasted cashews. Chamlong asks her if she'd like something. She's not hungry. "I'll buy something any-way," he tells her. "I'm not hungry," she tells him angrily when he offers her some roasted cashews. He finishes them himself while the train heads north. As it rattles through the hot glare of morning, Sanuk stares at passing farmhouses on stilts, shrouded heavily in gardenia hedges and hibiscus. Sleepy towns go by, then globular limestone hills and rice paddies and sometimes a golden pagoda and once a huge stucco Buddha seated in the Sukhotai style with a black flame bursting from the top of his head. Mother would like that, she thinks. Don't think of Mother, she thinks.

Resolutely Sanuk's attention is fixed on the countryside: resolutely, although what really interests her is Chamlong. He sits opposite her in the train compartment. They haven't spoken since leaving the station. Resolutely she faces the window, as if trying to maintain some kind of interest in the hot flat light of midmorning. Her left thumb is throbbing, but she can't even think of it. She can't even focus properly on the pain she's feeling.

We killed him.

Each time she's capable of having that thought, the memory accom-panying it returns with tremendous force: supine in the water, the man bobbing as they stared down at him, at his death. She won't forget his hair. It spread like a fan from a tiny white spot on the top of his head and moved in the tide. Because of it he seemed more plant than human, a thing growing out of the gulf, rooted up out of it like sea-weed.

They pulled him through the shallows along the shore to the lime-stone headland. He felt incredibly light, nothing more than a child, buoyed as he was by the ocean swell. They dragged him to a crevice of rock half submerged. After removing the man's clothes, Chamlong jammed him headfirst into a curve of limestone that would hold him in its grip unless a storm came up. Sanuk gawked at the buttocks and the genitals, for aside from Chamlong she had never seen a grown man naked. On the beach Chamlong searched the pants pockets. Nothing except fifty-eight bahts. Chamlong put that in his own pocket. But there was nothing else on the man. No official papers, no document to identify him as anyone, let alone as a government agent. As they dug a hole in a thicket beyond the beach, Chamlong claimed that the man had attacked first. As they stuffed the clothing into the sandy hole, Chamlong swore that the government agent had meant to kill them.

Sanuk can't remember it starting. Her memory of what happened seems secondhand now, something she's heard but not experienced herself. Except for her thumb. The pain and swelling are real. They confirm the horror of last night.

"You're shaking."

It's Chamlong speaking from the opposite seat, but she won't turn to face him, can't. Resolutely Sanuk stares awhile longer from the train window, then shyly, as if glancing at a boy for the first time, she looks at him. His eyes, meeting hers, have a look of anguish in them, surely duplicated in her own. They share what had happened, truly; her own memory is recognizable in his troubled face. Sanuk's heart goes out to him. Their suffering links them. That's what she tells herself. I am linked to him in a way I've never been linked to anyone else—not to Mother, not to friends at school, not even to Chamlong when we make love.

"You're shaking," he repeats.

"I'm all right."

"I know you are. Only—" His voice drops, although they're alone in the compartment. "You mustn't shake that way. You're shaking. Look at you."

Sanuk glances down at her hands. It's true. They're shaking in her lap like the palsied hands of an old woman. Gripping them together, she tries to smile. The swollen thumb sticks out awkwardly, as if it doesn't belong there. "I'm all right now." Resolutely she stares from the window, fleetingly aware of the beauty—pine forests, white sand, sparkling gulf. There's no chance, though, of enjoying such beauty. Will she ever enjoy anything again? Don't think of last night, think of something else.

Think, she orders herself. What she'll do, she'll retrieve the note left for Mother with Ah Ping. If Mother isn't home yet, this can be done. Something can be salvaged. Something can be made right. Bribe both servants. Mother won't ever know she left the house. Ah Ping will resist the idea at first and fret and mutter *choei*, but finally she'll accept the bribe. And make Nipa accept a bribe too. Those old women will stay as mum as the grave. Think of that. Don't think of it, think of that.

Or think of the thumb, of its throbbing. Broken? Well, think of that, don't think of it.

Hair fanning out like seaweed from the top of his head.

"Stop shaking."

Sanuk turns from the window. He's glaring at her or pleading with her; she can't tell.

"See? You're shaking. Look at you. Stop it!" Chamlong hisses at her.

Sanuk is appalled to see her hands shaking again. Clenching them harder, even though the pressure increases the pain in her thumb, Sanuk tries to meet his anxious eyes. Her own are blinded by tears.

"Stop it," he repeats gently.

In a voice so faint it frightens her, Sanuk says, "I'm all right now. See? I've stopped it."

15

CROWS MUST BE the happiest of God's creatures, Rama thinks as he jiggles along, legs dangling over the wooden slab of the jutka. One hand holds his rolled umbrella, the other a bunch of fat red roses wrapped in newspaper. He bought them at the Kumbakonam train station, near the Tiffin Shed, where he ate the highly spiced upma that has given him gas ever since the farmer agreed to let him ride in the jutka for three annas.

Crows must be the happiest of God's creatures; they can eat anything.

As the farmer's old bullock draws the jutka down a rutted road, Rama watches half a dozen crows picking at something in a dry ditch. He cranes to see what it is they're busy at. Two weeks ago, when last he made this journey home, the ditches were filled with fishes and frogs. Now the crows are jabbing their curved gray beaks into something that gives off the odor of rot. He can see now—they are gulping down the carcasses of frogs dead from lack of moisture.

Drought coming, he thinks, and sneezes once. The sneezing must be caused by dusty straw that's strewn in the cart. After waiting apprehensively, he's pleased not to sneeze again. That's good luck, one sneeze. Two is bad.

There are rice fields on either side of the road. The brown grain, almost ripe, droops on the brittle stalks; tall poles with pieces of cloth serving as scarecrows loom above the fields nearing harvest. There used to be ponds choked with lily pads around Kumbakonam, but not any more; they have vanished into the thirsty earth. It could be drought coming. The idea brings Vishnu to mind. "Narayana," he says aloud. Of all the names of Lord Vishnu, he considers this the most auspicious. To say it is better luck than sneezing once. Narayana, among other things, is protection.

The jutka ambles past a field of banana palms, their leaves rattling like paper in the sighing wind. Then mango and nim trees. The nim leaves will be falling soon. Rama belches.

Harvest soon. In another month along this road he'll see knobby-kneed farmers walking in their rapid rolling gait with 57-kilo—exactly 57-kilo—sacks of paddy rice balanced on their heads. There is no sight more wonderful than the 57-kilo sacks moving down a harvest road, and yet the water shortage is sure to bring death by July or August. By mid-August at the latest, in his opinion. Rama opens the umbrella over his head to keep out the intense sun; it will wilt the flowers before he gets them to his uncle.

Master once said, "You can't be dead and live in India." What did it mean? Was it just white talk? Not from such a man with his terrible scar and smooth face and blue eyes. Master walks like a man who knows. Master sits in meditation and finds wisdom, even though his cook and bearer cheat him on weekly receipts. Master doesn't talk nonsense like white people usually do. He doesn't sit on the veranda at tiffin time and swill quantities of gin, although on their first meeting he'd smelled awfully of alcohol. Every man has his weakness. Master once said too, "Whatever weakness you are hiding, India will find it." That's a wise thing to say. That's what a swami might say. Master is not like the noisy memsahibs and the angry Britishers in their pith helmets. Master is from America, Land of the Free.

A thick flapping sound, like tents blown in a stiff wind, turns his attention once more to the ditches. The crows are frantic over the leathery corpses of the frogs. There should be water in the ditches now, and there should be ponds all along this stretch of road, with frogs peeping everywhere. It's too early, isn't it, for the water to go away? How will the buffalo keep cool in the hot season, if they can't find a water hole? Can't cook rice without water. And the autumn crop will dry up. Narayana, he says with a low whistle of fearful awe. Drought coming. The signs are here.

Rama belches, wishing he had a quid of betel to freshen his mouth, foul-smelling from the spicy upma. Father used to say, Never eat in tiffin sheds in train stations unless you must. Father was right, of course; no one knew more about railroads and train stations. For a few moments Rama senses a presence nearby, that of a rather portly man with a bad cough. It is Father. Father had been a conductor on the Delhi-Madras line for sixteen years, always on the same train, with nineteen hours on duty, five off, then two days free. That was his schedule for all those years until a heart attack between Jhansi and Bhopal, southward bound, took him on another kind of journey. Narayana. The presence vanishes into afternoon sunlight.

Rama wishes for betel or coconut water or something. The idea of drought has soured his trip home today. Usually the anticipation of seeing his two boys and of sleeping with his wife has Rama in an elated mood at this stage of the trip from Madras. Along about now he always remembers his childhood in the farmland of the South. Whether he takes this road by foot or cart, the same thoughts come back to him: leading the cow home with a staff in his hand; washing his teeth with a peeled stick at the village stream; eating sugar cane. Along this stretch of road the memories come like clouds, like monsoon clouds that come through heavy with rain to rustle the lotus leaves like pages of newspaper, the drops exploding on the flat brown ponds and the roll upon roll of thunder overhead, as if a great shawl had been snapped out like Mother used to do in front of the house when she was cleaning, only this one is a huge dark cotton shawl that the heavens throw on the land to cover everything in a damp warmth. The thunder, the rain, the mist everywhere, the smell of it, and Mother sewing a new shawl by lamplight while the drops hit forever on the thatch. Such things have made his life a good one.

Narayana.

He had a pet goose once that waddled through the compound with its neck stretched out, its beak held so high and haughty that Rama couldn't understand how the creature knew where to step. And the dog. She was thin, with a ratlike tail—it had a white tip—and long, pointed ears, and a sharp muzzle that poked into places it didn't belong. Rama smiles when he thinks of this dog, whose belly grew big one summer. She had puppies that sucked on her pink dugs while she lay panting in the shade. He can't remember, though, her name or what happened to her. Narayana, he says under his breath, while the familiar countryside jerks by.

He never loses his interest in the rice paddy, never, although he's given up farm life for the life of a city man, an employee of the Government Postal Service. He still yearns for what he sees, and yet years ago, after his graduation from English medium school in Trichy, he began to dream of traveling far from here. He'd worked then for a shipping company in Madras, for a Mister Henderson, who pulled out when Independence threatened. Rama recalls the red-faced Britisher shouting in the corridor, "If the bloody fools want to destroy themselves, let them! I won't stay around to watch it." Rama had been exultant then, proud of being an Indian who could send this white man packing. Yet a Sindhi took over the firm and promptly fired half the staff; they were unnecessary, he claimed. Rama was among those fired, and he left the company with two thoughts in mind: He would still like to see the places whose names appeared on the labels of parcels that arrived each morning from the pier; and he was no longer so sure about the glory of Independence. Now at the post office he is followed by the same two thoughts, which haunt him more each day in the huge echoing hall where mail is sorted from abroad with all the exotic postage stamps and where the caste rivalries, held in check by British agents heretofore, run rampant among the workers.

"Here you are!" the jutka driver calls out, and halts.

Rama jumps off the wooden slab and runs his hand through a wild shock of black hair. The driver takes a south fork of the road; he's heading for a village famous for musicians. Half the Carnatic musicians of the South, both singers and instrumentalists, come from that single village. For an idle moment, for the uncountable time at this fork in the road, Rama wonders why it is so.

He proceeds on foot, holding the umbrella over his head, seeing from beneath its black circle the fields stretching into the distance. After staring at the ripening grain, he decides the second crop of paddy will yield better than usual. But then the drought coming.

Pretty soon the gunnysacks will be filled; then the goats will be tethered in the paddy fields to eat away the remaining stubble. It is a beautiful thing, it is a wonderful place here. But the drought coming.

For an instant Rama is startled by a distant sound; then he recognizes it: firecrackers set off to frighten birds away from the crop. Soon the wooden basins and the great stone jars will be filled with rice; after a few months of mellowing, it will be ready for eating. Those first days of eating a new crop of rice are wonderful, Narayana. Narayana.

But the drought coming. Madras people never realized last fall that the monsoon wasn't good enough. City people always think if the streets are flooded and pools form in the roads, everything is all right. They never imagine the water seeping into the earth, escaping there, leaving a terrible emptiness at the root of things. The gods didn't listen this year. Maybe they listened to prayers for the spring crop, but obviously they won't do anything to prevent a disaster next fall. Maybe they have other things to do. Maybe the pundits didn't advise people well in their pujas. Gods are sometimes accessible, sometimes not. For example, maybe he prayed to the wrong god concerning this matter of drought. He had done many pujas at a Murugan temple, because a Madrasi pundit had told him that Murugan is especially merciful to those who pray for good crops. So, experimenting, Rama had given the priests there some money and brought offerings to Murugan and concentrated upon Murugan's spear, the powerful three-pronged Vel, but look now, the ditches have dried up, the ponds of a month ago have vanished, and the feeble monsoon is leading straight to a terrible drought, so nothing came of the pujas. It will be a long time before he beseeches Murugan for anything again, Rama thinks crossly.

He sneezes. Once. Narayana. Looking at the roses, still erect and blood-red, thrusting from the newsprint, Rama feels a surge of good cheer. The sky is blue, the fields are ripening, and tonight he will lie with Usha.

But the drought coming.

. . .

And coming along the road, toward Rama, is a very dark-skinned man wearing a dhoti pulled up between skinny shanks. Rama knows who he is, a Chakkiliyan from his own village. They pass, exchanging a barely perceptible glance of recognition. Unlike many of his friends and other Brahmans in the village, Rama doesn't mind the idea of low castes coming into a Brahman home or entering temples, but it's an opinion he doesn't often voice. Not that he's afraid to talk up; he simply doesn't want the backward castes to think that Independence gives them the right to do anything they want—for instance, to draw water from Brahman wells or sit on the same floor with high-caste people. It is said Bapuji will share food and water with anyone. And up there in Delhi right now he says prayers from the Koran every day along with slokas from the *Gita*. Such a thing is wrong, wrong, Rama thinks, and glances balefully over his shoulder at the retreating shoemaker. There must be rules or life falls apart. Rama decides to express this opinion to Uncle.

"So you're home on a visit again."

Rama turns to face a sparely built man in homespun khaddar, who also carries an umbrella. It's the grain merchant, Mani.

"I admire you," the man says with a smile. "You're not afraid to travel on Tuesdays."

"That's a superstition," Rama replies coolly. This Mani is a Chettiyar who, during the war, bought up village crops. The inflationary market for rice, caused by the loss of supplies from Burma at a time when Indians in uniform needed to be fed, resulted in the kind of speculation that made men like Mani rich. Throughout the country there was wholesale starvation among the peasants; twice as many villagers died because of the speculation as men in uniform. Fortunately for Mani there was enough food in the village to offset his hoarding, and no one died. Even so, few people speak civilly to him. The wonder is that Mani doesn't seem to care.

"I understand," says Mani, who seems in the mood to talk, "your uncle bought an Ongole bull last week. I haven't seen it, but I suppose it's a fine animal."

"Ongoles are the best." Rama looks at the fields getting brown under the January sunshine. "Will the drought come?" Although he dislikes the man, he knows that Mani has purchased the finest house in the village not only by being an opportunist during the war but also by knowing more about rice than anyone in the neighborhood.

"Of course there'll be a drought. And a bad one."

"You really believe that?"

"I know it," Mani declares. "I tell that to everyone who asks me. I want everyone to know. That way, when it happens, no one can say I kept the truth from them. I am honest, let no one say otherwise unless he can prove it." Delivered of this speech, Mani smiles again, complacently. "Is it true the water carriers at the train stations no longer have to be Brahmans?"

"No, it's not true yet. But I've heard the rumor. It's only a matter of time." Rama is civil, having been impressed by Mani's outburst.

"If it happens, what are we to do? I won't take water from a low-caste fellow."

"That's the price of Independence."

Mani shakes his head grimly. "Gandhi's Children of God will rule us all before he's done."

Rama nods. They steeple their hands in respect and go their ways. Politics has brought them together for a moment in something like friendship. It is indeed true that Gandhi's harijans will assume terrible power if people aren't careful. Master's servants are harijans and look how they rule that house. In Father's time, Rama thinks, they would be turned out of a British house for speaking disrespectfully to a Brahman like himself. But then the Raj had some faint notion of caste, even if they pretended to sniff at it. The thing is, an American like Master has no feeling for the days before Independence. He lets harijan servants, who cheat him, create a very bad impression in the neighborhood. A pity. Rama decides to have a word with Master about this some day. It's a fine idea, and the force of it causes his hand to lift the umbrella higher above his head, just as the road curves toward the village.

• • •

There is more greenery now, as the road parallels a tributary of the Coleroon River. Trees slant over the bank toward the sluggish, brown water. On the other side of the road are mango groves, chili patches, cashew trees, and small tethering spaces for goats. People appear in outlying huts: teeth stained by betel, eyes red from glare, mustaches, and nose rings. He folds the umbrella, now that tamarind trees rise over him. A boy, pissing alongside a house, holds his attention for a moment —looks like his older child, but no, too small. Hari is big for his age, Rama decides with satisfaction. He breathes deeply without a glance for the footpath that leads around the village to the west where the low castes have their houses. Swinging the umbrella like a cane, he smiles at women brooming the dirt away from their stoops. The smell of a village is sweet, he thinks. Some fruit ripening, flowers in bloom, the sturdy odor of a wood fire, the earth itself—all as fresh as the world on the day when Brahma awakened from his sleep and created another eon. Narayana. *Om Namo Narayanaya.*

He passes the village well, and for an instant almost yields to the temptation to throw a stone down it and listen for the interval between the throwing and the plunk. But he won't think of the drought. Some young girls are gathered now in late afternoon near the well, their brass and iron pots lined up on the wet cement. One girl regards him with a faint smile, and he thinks of Usha, of tonight with her alone after the boys are asleep. But that's a thought to avoid now, he tells himself severely. Think of Uncle.

He passes a small temple, then the village tank in which a few buffalo are soaking and some women are doing late afternoon laundry on the stones—slapping their wet clothes on the flat surface, expelling their breath in loud percussive grunts. The water level in the tank is low. There's no mistaking it.

Beyond the tank is another temple. This is his favorite; in the sanctorum stands a foot-high bronze Krishna, and through the camphor smoke he has sometimes seen the god dance. So have other people, because the living god is pleased to be here. Narayana. There isn't time to go inside, but Rama drops to his knees, touches his forehead to the dust, and rapidly says a mantra.

Up again, he turns down a path and enters the main thoroughfare of the village. Ahead is a two-story brick house with shuttered windows, the kind of house he sees everywhere in Madras but rarely here—there are only three in this village of a thousand. One belongs to Mani, one to the Headman, and one to Rama's uncle.

A fence separates the compound from the dirt road. Carefully Rama unhooks a piece of wire that holds the gate. When he is through it, carefully he rehooks the wire. He recalls on each visit to his uncle that time when he was eleven that he forgot to hook this gate. His father had to come back with him and explain to Uncle why so many goats were able to get inside the compound and eat an entire sack of grain. Rama swept the yard like a common mali for six months before satisfying his uncle that the debt was paid.

Wriggling his feet from his sandals, Rama calls out at the entranceway, "I am here! V. S. Ramachandran!"

• • •

An hour later he is on the street again, shaking with rage. But then that is usually how an interview with Uncle ends. They argued as usual about Rama's future. Ever since Uncle's son died of typhoid three years ago, the third largest landowner in the village has bargained for his nephew's services, with the vague promise that if Rama will work for the family, someday all the land will be his. The proposition has never really tempted Rama.

First, he doesn't trust Uncle, who long ago cheated Father out of his share of the family land. He might very well work—it would be as a slave—for Uncle, only to have the old wretch deed over the land to one of three sons-in-law who live in neighboring districts. Rama knows the daughters are always badgering the old man about their inheritance. And second, Rama doesn't want to stay in the village. Like Father, he wants to see something of the world. One of his fondest memories is of sitting in the corner and listening to Father describe the train trip between Delhi and Madras. From his earliest days Rama has had a vision of the red and green flags held by stationmasters in their white suits, the flags signaling the trains onward into the vast countryside of India. And this vision has been compounded by his service in the import company, then in the post office, where daily he sees evidence of the outer world in postage stamps, return addresses, billing forms that send things to Singapore, Hong Kong, New York, London, and Paris.

During today's confrontation Uncle had been particularly aggressive. Sitting in his study, he had appealed to Rama's worst fear: that the Congress Party would pass legislation to establish quotas for competitive central government services, including the post office. "They will kick you out," Uncle predicted brutally. "They will give your post to a Handi Jogi or a Dom. They will toss you on your ear and put a low caste in your place!"

Rama was thirsty but knew better than to ask Uncle for a cup of tea. For his pains he'd get nothing save a lecture on thrift—after all, tea costs money—and a warning not to follow the path of his wastrel father, who after so many years on the railroad had nothing to show for it because of gambling debts. Somehow at every interview Uncle managed to get that reference in, a cruel thing for Rama to bear because it was true.

"You must be prepared for the new world, Nephew," the man continued. Uncle was built large and solid, more like a Punjabi than a Tamil. He sat in the cluttered study, filled with ugly overstuffed chairs purchased in England, and rummaged, as he spoke, through two or three little suitcases in which he kept documents and keys and herbal medicine. Piled one on top of another upon a small desk, they served as his filing cabinet. "Now that Independence is here, you must know who your leader is. This Nehru is a Moslem at heart. He doesn't believe in God." Uncle coughed and rummaged for something, which he didn't find. Rama has always been surprised by how little his uncle can locate in the suitcases.

Uncle grumbled awhile about a recent wedding between two of his field hands. He had to give a larger gift than usual, because his foreman insisted that Independence required extra. There was always a reason for giving extra, the elderly man said, while both hands felt around in a suitcase among papers and tiny vials and packs of jingling keys. "You think since I've remained in the village all these years I'm an ignorant fool, but I know the world." In fact, he took a trip to England every decade to buy things for his house and for his wife, at least until last year, when she died. "If you had a European superior at your work you would get up early, labor all day, go home tired, and sleep. Now that you have an Indian superior, you must get up early, labor all day, go home tired and not sleep, because you lie awake wondering what intrigue's afoot to turn you out and put someone else in your place. You will deny it to me, but in fact it's so." And it was so, although Rama did deny it.

Walking now down the street, having left the roses on a table—forgotten by Uncle—doubtless to be thrown out by a servant, Rama feels a rush of defiance. Like his father, he won't sit forever in the village where nothing happens, where nothing has happened for centuries. He will keep his family here until there's money enough to take them away, but he won't come back himself. He won't. Of course, if the drought comes, then they are better off here. Uncle will help them, won't he? They are family to him too, so he must help. But it won't come to that, Rama thinks quickly.

Possessed by these gloomy thoughts, Rama has walked down the main road almost to the end of the Brahman part of the village. Here on the outskirts of it are the homes of poor Brahmans, his own among them, and ahead now, almost startled by the sight of it, after such intense thinking, he sees the familiar coconut palm angling over the roof as if pushed askew by an invisible hand and the jackfruit tree with a couple of large fruits hanging down like beehives, and then the small daub-and-thatch house.

God will provide, he thinks, and turns into the tiny front yard. Sweeping aside the homespun curtain at the doorway, Rama goes inside his house. There's enough light from the back door for him to see. With a sigh of ownership he looks around at the little stone goddess garlanded with flowers, a kerosene lamp, a few brass puja utensils, a thin mattress on the dirt floor strewn with bamboo mats, a couple of posters of gods pinned to the daub walls, and a calendar for 1948 featuring a pretty Marathi girl who is advertising silks from Bombay.

Sitting down on a mat, Rama wipes the sweat from his forehead and wonders where she is. The smell of food drifts from the back room, but she is gone. Annoyance and anxiety fill him. He had been seventeen, Usha fourteen when they married. The next year she'd had their first son. The second was born dead. The third is now six, nearly old enough for the ceremony of Upananyana. It's hard to believe the little fellow is almost ready to wear the sacred thread. Rama sniffs the smoke; it is odorless, the smoke of burning dung, but the heady smell of cooked spices drifts into the room. He's hungry, no longer suffering from gas caused by the upma at the Tiffin Shed. Where are the boys? Playing in the fields? Of course. As he used to do. Rama's mind drifts like the smoke, settling an instant on the memory of combing his hair with a heavy wooden comb; Mother slapped him when he couldn't flatten it down, then embraced him with a little groan of loving frustration. Where is Usha, where is she? Their horoscopes meshed very well indeed, and the village pundit claimed they would have a good marriage. He was right. Narayana.

Where is she? From a small chest of drawers that he can reach from his sitting position, Rama takes a box of kumkum powder and carefully draws on his forehead the V-shaped urdhvapundra, mark of Vishnu. This is an act that always makes him feel at home. Father, returning from the railroad, would do the same. Rama stares at the opposite wall, the plaster streaked from monsoon rains. Hung there is an open cardboard box between two plastic roses, and inside the box, still in its cellophane wrapper, is a Western doll, a blond girl with long eyelashes and fiery red cheeks, that he'd bought Usha for Devali last year. If Master had a child it might look like this. Where is she? Has she forgotten I'm coming home today? Impossible. Rich odors from the kettle in the back room assure him. And yet she ought to be here, he thinks nervously.

Unable to sit longer, Rama leaves the house and walks down the lane to a tea shop, where he slakes his thirst with a double tea. The strong tannic acid content makes him grimace, and he tells the tea wallah it's a terrible brew. "You're getting a hundred cups out of the leaves instead of ten like you should. That's why it tastes this way," Rama declares angrily, aware he's made the charge before. And the reply coming back is familiar too: "If you like it better in the city, go back to the city."

On his return home, Usha is there to greet him. His heart lifts when he sees her: full-bodied in the brown cotton sari, her thick hair pulled back from a broad forehead in the middle of which she has put a round bindu mark, her eyes immense, the pupils black in startling contrast to the pure white around them. He can smell the cleanness of his wife, for it's obvious she has just come from a special bath in the river. She has stood in the stream and massaged her body under a plain shift with gingelly oil, then soap, then water. The smell of gingelly pervades the small room as she kneels down and salutes him with steepled hands.

He has good tea now. Three times a week Usha hikes five kilometers to the banks of the Cauvery River for the water there, which is considered the sweetest in the South. Basin people say that drinking it brings good luck. She makes tea with it every time Rama comes home. He has spiced nuts to eat with his tea. Given his hunger, he'd have asked for dinner straightaway but for his desire to talk. He speaks of his Master in Madras, the rich American hero who fought against the Japanese (Rama has long since forgotten that during the war he'd shared a popular Indian hope that the Japanese might well be the saviors of Asia). "Maybe someday I'll consent to work for him," Rama says, sipping the tea loudly, while his wife watches and listens, holding the bowl of nuts toward him. "I am sick of the post office, the cheating, the lies. Telagus are getting control of it already. Telegu Reddis will take over, mark my words." He pauses to make sure the warning takes full effect, and it does—Usha's mouth curls down, her eyes narrow. "But you mustn't worry. You're safe here. I have seen to that," he says vaguely, wondering if he should bring up the subject of a drought coming. "I will probably work for my American Master now. He needs me." Rama doesn't mention, however, the promised arrival of Master's family from Bangkok, as he usually does. Since they aren't coming, he can no longer use them as the reason why Master will hire him. "Master can't control his servants. You should see them cheat him." He watches, satisfied, as Usha shakes her head sadly. "I will box the cook's ears if he doesn't stop cheating. He submits weekly food receipts at least ten rupees too high!" It is an extravagant guess that has Usha looking horrified. "*More* than ten," Rama says, catching from the corner of his eye something peeking around the doorway leading to the back room.

It is Hari, his older boy; Rama speaks loudly, more arrogantly now, of the cook and what he will do to him. "When I act as steward for Master, that house will run smoothly. I will pull up Cook, believe me, and if he still cheats, then I will turn him out myself, and Master won't say a word, because he trusts me. He has trusted your husband from our first meeting. And after I've worked for him awhile, perhaps you can come to Madras." It's a possibility he has never mentioned until now, and doing it surprises him. Perhaps it's because he glimpses the single bright eye peeking around the door frame. His son, Hari.

"Is it true?" Usha asks in a breathless whisper.

"Of course it is. Master is an American. He is a rich hero from the war. He has this on his face—" Rama wonders if he's mentioned the scar earlier, as, with his hand, he draws an extravagant line across his forehead, going right through the crimson urdhvapundra. Usha nods in awe. "Working for a white man like him would guarantee good money." Rama pauses. Has he spoken too hastily? He glances at the bright eye, the thin line of a small dark face, the half of a keen little nose.

Looking back at Usha, he says, "But as for you coming to Madras, it will take time."

"But someday?"

"Of course, someday. Until then, you and the boys remain here where it's safe. I don't want you in a big city until I can provide."

Usha smiles.

"Come in here, Hari! Let me see you!" the proud father cries out.

• • •

Before the evening meal Rama sits outside with the boys (the little one had rushed in yelling "Amma! Amma!" but upon seeing his father home had stifled the outcry for his mother and slumped down respectfully to touch his father's feet). Rama questions the older boy about his work at the district school. Next year, in Standard Four, Hari will begin the study of English, and it's all Rama can do to control his own pride. The boy has not yet been promising. In infancy he suffered from skin rashes, the dust inflamed his eyes, he has always developed a bad cough during monsoon. But Rama feels sure the boy will distinguish himself well enough to go on to secondary school in Trichy, just as he himself did. While admonishing Hari to work hard, Rama is recalling his own school-days: the large colonial building with balconies and terrace; the playground of red dirt; a few trees for shade; two swings; the pink shorts and white shirt he wore; the classrooms facing a courtyard; wooden benches and desks, a blackboard, shuttered windows; a murmur of voices in recitation; a cage for rabbits; and above all, the after-school pilgrimage to the railroad tracks where, with comrades, he waved at the passing trains, although it was not Father's line.

He is now telling both boys that bettering one's moral nature is the goal of life. "God's right hand is gentle, but terrible is his left hand." Rama can't remember who told him that, but his boys are respectfully solemn. Then he shows the younger one how to spin a top. There's a secret to making the top spin a long time, and Rama teaches the child how to release the string with a final snap. The boy learns quickly; he is the brighter, but Rama is partial to Hari, perhaps—and he knows this too—because someday, as the older son, Hari will light the funeral pyre. He will pay for the recitation of slokas while the flames go up (my feet will last longest, Rama thinks idly; nothing of the body is as tough). And afterward Hari will lead the little procession of mourners to the river bank for a ritual bathing. Yes, of course, Hari is his favorite.

Rama has put off hunger long enough. By oil lamp he eats from a large palm leaf, while Usha looks on, ready to serve additional mounds of steaming rice and curd, which he'll mix with his right hand to the consistency of gruel. She's prepared an okra curry too, along with pickled mango. Before eating, Rama places a few kernels of rice along-side the leaf to appease hungry ants that might happen along. He takes a deep draught of buffalo milk from his cup—it is thicker and sweeter than cow's milk and makes better curds. Usha watches attentively while he slurps the mixture of rice and curds. He belches and nods for more, which she ladles onto the palm leaf—placing the rice carefully on the tender left frond. Into a sweet-and-sour sauce Usha breaks up a nim leaf for him to munch as a digestive that they say prevents malaria. Rama regards her closely as he eats; there's a bead of sweat under her left eye. He remembers as a child seeing Mother brush sweat from her eyes with the end of her sari. Mother used to fan Father with a leaf while he swirled the rice and dal and sucked up gobs of it from his funneled fingers. Usha doesn't fan her husband, but at the end of evening meals she often rubs sandalwood paste on his shoulders to cool the skin and keep mosquitoes away. Mother didn't do that. He's telling Usha that with the new Constitution there'll be quotas for jobs. Brahmans will suffer, because in the new world it's not quality of lineage but quantity of votes that is going to count.

He is telling her many things, babbling away, yet his eyes steadily view the moisture on her skin. Rama has always been proud of her light skin, lighter than most Tamil girls'. She's of good family. Their lineages are equal, which of course makes them compatible, even though she was never taught to read. Well, he'll teach her when there's time. Sometimes he's ashamed of the emotion she causes in him. Women can do that: Parvati even seduced Shiva when he was supposed to be meditating upon the creation of the world, his world; and Lord Krishna couldn't remain away long from the lovely Radha.

A line from Jayadeva's *Gitagovinda* drifts into Rama's mind, a mind not so long removed from student days that it can't remember an erotic poem that he and his friends used to snicker over: "My beautiful loins are a deep cavern to take the thrusts of love—Cover them with jeweled girdles, cloths, and ornaments, Krishna!" And "Lover, draw kohl glossier than a swarm of black bees on my eyes! Your lips kissed away the lampblack bow that shoots arrows of Love." It's unmanly, he knows, to let the mind wallow in such thoughts. Lust is surely destructive of good karma, but the way she looks now, the moisture on her skin, takes Rama's breath away. Rama talks; he is relating a story told him by a postal colleague: In the world of Independence a family should have a doctor and a government servant among its sons: one to heal and the other to obtain permits. Rama giggles, Usha smiles and withdraws the ladle from over the palm leaf when he signals he's had enough. He can hear the boys in the other room trying to settle down for sleep; if only they would hurry!

• • •

The room smells of gingelly oil, sandalwood paste, and okra curry. As if watered milk has been poured into the window, there's a sudden glow in the room; the moon has just shifted around the edge of the house, past a mango tree whose leaves make a tangle of shadow within the pool of moonlight. Usha has gone outside, soundlessly, so as not to wake the boys.

Rama anticipates her return to the mattress. This is the best time of year for lovemaking. In a few months it will simply be too hot, even though he does enjoy the smell of Usha sweating, the feel of her warm pulsing body when the little room is like an oven. But they don't last long in such heat. For a moment he fears what will happen tonight. The village pundit says a man is allotted so many shootings, and if he exceeds the limit, he dies. How can a man tell when his portion has been reached? The guru says the limit is known only to God, but of course a man showing restraint will live longer.

Usha has returned, her figure full and supple as she crosses the pool of moonlight in a cotton shift. She is talking now, her voice low, melodious. Usha always seems to talk at such times, before they lie together on the mattress, like a nervous girl—and his own excitement is compounded by her own. She says a neighbor woman, pregnant, saw a cat the first thing this morning—what bad luck! And will there be a drought? People say yes.

Rama speaks softly into the night air. No drought, he tells her.

Usha stands beside the mattress, facing east, the good luck direction, and removes the shift. When they were first married, she would remove it only at his insistence once they were lying together, but after the passion of marriage gripped her, Usha started to take it off beforehand, and now in the moolight she displays her body shamelessly for his pleasure.

Usha is telling him about the three jungle scorpions she saw today. People tell her so many scorpions at this time of year are a sign of drought. One was bigger than her hand, with two pincers as long as her fingers, and the tail with the stinger was like a curved knife.

He tells her to keep the boys out of brick piles; that's where the scorpions go when it gets hot. He speaks the words, but his mind is fully attending her movements: the thrown shift, the brief wobble of young breasts as she kneels, the sliding of her thighs against the single sheet on the mattress.

As a child in his family's house, Rama used to hear from the next room certain noises, and took them at first for quarreling between his parents, who in fact often quarreled about money. Then, in the darkness, a little older, he listened breathlessly to the groans and stifled cries that separated him from his parents forever.

Now, embracing the warm body of his wife, fired by mutual passion, Rama lets all thoughts go out of him—Narayana, Narayana, he repeats soundlessly as he enters his beloved woman and the pleasure mounts.

Later, hearing her begin to snore faintly, Rama crosses his arms behind his neck and watches the moonlight shift and vanish, leaving the little house utterly dark, and he wonders how is it possible for a man to show restraint, even if the length of his life on this earth is at stake, when such as Usha offers herself to his arms.

16 WHEN RAMA HAS finished his morning ablutions and released his sacred thread from around his right ear, where he'd placed it while squatting, the sun is already level with the lower fronds of palm trees that line the fields. He carries a brass pot, now empty of water. Passing some mango trees, Rama tries to envision their large heavy white flowers in March bloom. Nothing like mangoes in March.

Shading his eyes, he watches some farmers trudging down paths to their paddy fields. Each season is marked by what they carry: plow, harrow, seed drill, pick, gunnysack. Today they're carrying pulley wheels, because it's time to let the ripening grain drink from gravity pumps. As he enters the village, Rama halts at the well. Leaning over it, he peers down at the water level. Two, maybe three feet deep. At this time of year it should be eight or ten.

A woman comes along, waits for him to step aside so she can lower the bucket.

"It looks very low," he says.

When she throws the bucket down, it splashes with a hollow clunk. "God will provide."

"Narayana."

Walking toward home, Rama thinks again of working as an assistant to his uncle. That way he could get the family past the drought. Uncle wouldn't let a nephew, at least one working for him, starve in front of the village. Rama yanks the knot of his dhoti to tighten it. It would mean hauling those suitcases from field to field, while Uncle jots down the anticipated yields and bullies the laborers. Rama pauses to watch a villager pour milk and cold rice on an anthill. A waste, Rama thinks. The ignorant villager hopes by this offering to placate cobras, who often live in anthills. The worship of snakes is not modern in Rama's opinion.

Near the anthill some boys are playing tic-tac-toe with a piece of chalk on a flat rock. They remind Rama of his childhood, of his own boys, and for a moment he watches them play, feeling sadness creep into his mind. The sadness remains when he says goodbye to his wife, and it gets worse when he takes the road for Kumbakonem.

Pigs are running free, tethered goats bleat, chickens cluck along, when he leaves the village. Briefly he looks back at women grinding kernels of rice into a powder.

When he returned to the house to say goodbye, his younger boy had been there, getting his hair combed. Usha used the same kind of thickly toothed comb that Rama's mother had once used on him. The comb seemed useless in the little boy's coarse hair, and Rama was reminded of his own trouble in keeping his hair down. When the boy scampered away, Rama felt ill at ease, troubled, and roughly admonished Usha not to worry about the drought. "God will provide," he told her sternly. "And your husband is always here. In the sense of caring for you. Do you understand?" And she'd nodded in acknowledgment of his good advice and promise. But he'd carried away discontentment, and now on the road he becomes critical of his wife, whose superstitions derive from her inability to read. No one in Madras would believe, as she does, that a mounted god rides through the village every night to drive off evil spirits.

He becomes aware of his right eye throbbing. That's a good omen, and for a while he walks along the road absorbed by a little pain that brings luck. Everyone will need luck with the drought coming. Even Uncle. Money's what's needed if the drought comes, and it will surely come.

The village well. It'll be empty before the hot season is half over, and then life will depend on rupees. But where to get rupees? You can't pick them up like nuts.

Rama nearly turns and retraces his steps, feeling dread. He touches the black stone sacred to Vishnu that he wears around his neck. "Narayana, Narayana," he says aloud, touching the saligrama each time he says the name of God. He could never sit and watch his boys die a little each day. He'd rather thrust his hand into a rat hole inhabited by cobras than see a boy with wiry hair get weaker each day, the eyes grow opaque, the belly distend, the arms shrivel, the skin become scaly—like a snake's—and the terrible sounds, the whimpering . . . no, no, he couldn't live with that.

The image of his two boys and Usha, too, panting and dying of thirst, of starvation, in the little house of love wrenches his gut. Rama feels nauseated, appalled by a vision that won't leave him, not even in the light of noon.

Golla men, riding a jutka with their tubs of milk, approach on the dusty road. For an instant he thinks of drinking milk from a brass bowl and having his mother wipe his mouth when he's finished. In a few months such milk will dry up in the udders. Famine after the hot month of Chaitra.

White men have money, Rama thinks bitterly. He remembers Father describing a drought once, especially in Madras and Trichy—the panic, the death, the money in hands of grain speculators and dairymen. Famine, money. Nothing but money can help, either in cities or in villages. Cities suffer worse. That's what Father said, and a man who traveled so much should know.

As Rama comes closer to the Golla men and their dairy cart, he sees distinctly in his mind three people: his own little family. They are smiling, innocent, vulnerable. The sun swings round in the heavens for an instant, making him feel giddy from the dreadful motion. Narayana, he says frantically, in the desperate hope that God effulgent in innumerable suns, carrying in four hands a conch shell, discus, club, and lotus, will spring out of the sky to bring his little family under the protection of the Lord.

Golla men, passing in the jutka, eye him curiously as he yanks hard on the saligrama and chants in a loud voice, *"Om Namo Narayana."*

He'd intended to go straight to the Kumbakonem train station, but anxiety turns him elsewhere. Rama is going to pray for deliverance from trouble.

• • •

In the center of town is a rectangular pool, a good six acres in extent. This is Mahamakham Tank, famous throughout South India, and especially dear to Rama. Shuffling alongside the sheet of calm water, Rama regards the women washing their clothes on the brick sides of the tank. On the tank's surface are reflected the blue pillars and pink roofing of sixteen mandapams from which a profusion of sculpted gods and goddesses gaze down at the brown water. Rama halts and stares too into the pool that should be higher at this time of year. Four years ago he'd been here with a million other people. What a day that had been! The celebration of Mahamakham takes place here every twelve years on a day chosen by astrologers when the moon comes into conjunction with the star Makham in the Tamil month of Masi. Rama knows this as precisely as the day of his own birth.

Squatting beside the granite steps of the tank, Rama remembers: idols of river goddesses placed in the mandapams; the tread of myriad feet muddying the waist-high water, as devotees filed into the pool for a few precious minutes before an anxious multitude behind them pushed forward; the tumultuous noise of worshipers raising their voices in prayer as water from seven sacred rivers, some of it coming all the way from the Himalayas, converged magically in the tank, magically, and washed all sins away. People died from drinking the polluted water, and Rama recalls, as a child entering Kumbakonem after one such festival, that the whole town stank of urine and defecation and rotting food left by a crowd that swelled the population to fifty times its normal size, and tons of waste paper had blown down the streets and across the outlying fields and trampled greenery, as the entire area struggled to regain its strength after such an overwhelming assault by the forces of God. Narayana. The power of it.

Rama remembers.

Rising to his feet again, briefly glancing at the washerwomen, he continues on his way past the drab shops lining the square. At the south end of the tank sits the small ancient temple of Shri Kasiviswanatha-swami. It is a Shaivite temple, yet because of his memories of the Mahamakham celebration, it is nonetheless one of his favorites and therefore powerful. At the entrance, disregarding the line of seated beggars with their hands stretched out, Rama buys flowers and a coco-nut for an offering.

It is dark inside, save for two lamps of brass nearly three feet high with oil floating in their large bowls and long wicks. As Rama enters, he hears the shrill cry of a bird from somewhere. This is more than coin-cidence, he thinks, this is an omen. The possibility so excites him that the hair on his neck rises.

Ahead, in the small temple, is the God. On a pedestal stands a foot-high bronze of dancing Shiva.

After setting down the offering, Rama touches the floor with his hands, then touches one hand to his forehead, then steeples both hands respectfully. He turns toward the sanctum gate to the right, where a pujari waits to receive his offering. Rama holds out his right hand for holy water. As the pujari pours, Rama sucks up the drops passionately, and dries his fingers by running them through his wiry hair.

Approaching Nataraja, he turns in a circle three times with hands high over his head, then touches his left ear with his right hand. After dipping his knees three times, he moves to the left of the God to another representation of Shiva, this one a stone linga. Here he prostrates him-self full length on the cool marble floor, trying to remember that Shiva is God here and therefore would not take kindly to an accidentally muttered "Narayana."

The universe is immense, he thinks. It's a linga which expands infi-nitely in both directions, just as the pundits say. There's no need to push too hard in this life; there's time to do better in the next life and the next. The chakra, the wheel of fire, goes round and round, with its center motionless. That's what to focus on, and yet his little family's back there in the village, defenseless against the cruelty and callousness and anger that come in the wake of a drought.

"Narayana."

The word escapes him, so instantly he adds, *"Om Namah Shivaya."*

Without a lot of money he can't take them to Madras; and if they stay in the village, can he really count on Uncle unless important money changes hands between them? God will provide. *Om Namah Shivaya.* He tries to think of his head under the feet of God. Can the truth be that God doesn't care if the drought's coming, if his little family will suffer? The truth is we can't know what the truth is; we just live whatever the gods give us to live. Isn't it so? In February the large bats come at sunset; then after a month they disappear. The ants return home in columns at sunset during March and April, and they move underground until autumn. And so it goes through the year, with everything thriving and waning and reviving and going under and coming up again. *Narayana. Om Namo Narayanaya. Om Namah Shivaya. Om Sri Ganeshaya Namah. Jaya Hanuman. Sita Ram Sita Ram Sita Ram.* The names seem to diffuse through him like water through the earth. He feels calmer. What is truth but a shifting thing, like a river, a cloud, a change of season? It is God's business, not his own. Rama stretches his arms out with hands steepled in prayer. Who has faith in this or that truth has the truth. Who doesn't doesn't. Isn't that so?

Feeling he's answered these questions, contented, Rama rises to his feet. He has done his duty here, and with a parting remark for Lord Shiva—Grant me my request, Lord Nataraja, that the family won't suffer in the drought, and I'll do many pujas for you—Rama bows low and leaves. Having drunk consecrated water, having made an offering, having pulled his ear and turned the right number of times in obeisance to God, he feels absolved of worrying more about the future.

Except that he hopes Lord Vishnu will forgive him his promise to make prayers to Shiva, but of course the merciful Lord of the Universe will surely understand that desperation has brought him here to another god. As Rama emerges from the temple to blink in the hot reality of a South Indian noon, he's comforted by the thought that, anyway, somehow the gods are all one.

• • •

While waiting at the Kumbakonem train station, Rama buys a quid from a betel wallah. He watches critically while the wizened hawker smears slaked lime on a betel leaf, adds grated areca nut, some spices, folds the leaf deftly, and hands it over. Placing the quid between cheek and gum, Rama feels the saliva bubble up instantly. As he masticates the leaf, a slightly bitter flavor accompanies the salivation. He spits, his expectorate already red from the action of lime on betel. The alkaloids in the grated nut give him a moment of mild dizziness, as if he'd knocked down a thimbleful of arrack. Having just eaten a marsala dosai in the Tiffin Shed, he counts on the betel mixture to protect him from gas, and to sweeten his breath when he goes to Master. Because today he is going to Master. Today.

Two men in crisply laundered dhotis come alongside him on the train platform. They are holding hands, and both carry compartmented lunch pails for the journey. On a wooden skid a legless beggar scuttles among the waiting passengers. Along come porters in red shirts and white turbans with heavy suitcases balanced on their heads, each hand holding packages or bedrolls. Women with jasmine sprigs in their hair are dragging sacks and luggage onto the cement platform; from the exertion their bright saris have dark half-moons of sweat at the armpits.

Rama looks upon the other passengers with satisfaction. The idea of travel, even the few hours from Kumbakonem to Madras, provides him with more optimism than his prayers have done today. He spits, he sniffs the air redolent with the smell of frying oil, hot tea, spices.

He will go directly to Master and say, "I am Brahman, so I fear Telegu castes will gain prominence in post office, Master. I am not wanting to bother you with trouble, sir, but not mentioned yet is family. If I am leaving post office, what will happen to them? I cannot make my both ends meet."

Rama pauses. Should he reveal so much to a white man? He starts again. "I am not wanting to bother you with trouble, sir, but I am prepared to take new position. You and I mix well together. I can do any work. Have no fear of it—Rama can do what you are requiring." This is better.

He glances again with satisfaction at the crowd assembling on the platform: men with folded umbrellas like his own, porters and hawkers, children and beggars. It's a rush and bustle that his father must have witnessed countless times. His eye catches a painted notice in English and Tamil over a wooden trough: SPITTOON HERE. He leans forward and spits a copious amount of blood-red saliva at the track, whose sparkling iron rails run parallel, as he squints at them, until they converge in the far distance. Soon he'll be where they converge, except there they'll be parallel again when the train reaches them, and he'll have to look from the bogie window to watch them converge again and so on and so on as the miles jiggle past.

A man with a Vishnu mark on his forehead is standing nearby with a newspaper. Rama glances at the headlines: GANDHI TO PAKISTAN.

"I can do any work," he tells Master in the imagined interview. Perhaps it will be a good idea to change the subject for a moment—let the white man consider what he's been told. "Did you see the flash in newspaper, Master? Bapuji is going to Pakistan to pray for Moslems.

Such a god man! We must all be listening to him; it will tone up our ways." This will predispose Master to give him the job, because Master seems to like Gandhi's policies. White people, except Britishers, do.

A stationmaster in a billed cap is walking through the crowd now, calling out the train for Madras. Briefly Rama studies him and instead of this skinny fellow sees his own father, a short, rather pudgy man with a flourishing mustache. Others on the platform move closer to the track and look toward the south, where the train from Trichy will soon appear, but Rama looks north, in the direction he'll be going. The rattling bogie will soon be drawing him away from his troubles into the limitless countryside, where he can watch the black pulse growing and the banyan trees spreading their immense limbs to shade little streams. And the earth is red where it isn't planted, as deeply red as the betel juice he spits, and the white plaster of farmhouses will show through patches in the greenery that surrounds each village, and all of it, everything, will pass lazily before his eyes in a rhythm as steady and lulling as the sound of an evening flute. That is the best of the world—the seeing of it.

• • •

Getting off at Egmore Station in Madras, he goes briskly in the direction of Master's place instead of heading for the boardinghouse room which he shares with two other postal employees. He buys a bunch of yellow flowers at a little stand and at once is swallowed up in the crowd streaming out of the station. Madras excites him. During Rama's student days in Trichy, a friend of his went to Bombay hoping for adventure. This fellow rented the corner of a room, found temporary work, saw the cinema now and then, took a stroll on the beach and looked at the Arabian Sea. This he did almost every day, and little more. Yet he wouldn't go home for a visit for fear of missing something in the city.

Rama feels the same fear when away from Madras. Here things happen. Days are filled with time, whereas time rushes into the village for only a few weeks during planting or harvesting and then rushes out again, leaving everything empty save for the passage of day and night.

He sees another headline: BAPU GOING TO LAHORE.

On the train two men were discussing Gandhi. They were merchants from Madurai, and one of them quoted Bapuji as once saying to the British, "Leave India to God; if that is too much, leave her to anarchy." They called it defiance and called Bapuji idealistic.

Yet when Rama heard the words, he admired them. India for Indians. Even though he might lose his job for being of the wrong community, he likes the idea of India for Indians. Today, seeing Master, he will stand up. "Give me a job, Master, and you'll see things hum. You'll be home and dry!" Rama says the English out loud with a grunt of satisfaction.

But as he passes the ghee and curd and rice shops along the way, Rama feels the heat begin to weigh. It isn't too heavy now, but within a few months the heat will bear down like an immense snake, whose coils have the power to strangle anything that moves. The *Hindu* will feature a black-bordered column listing daily how many died of sunstroke and heat exhaustion. And the drought coming along with it will let loose a two-headed snake in Madras. And in the countryside. In his village, in his house.

Absorbed as he is in these thoughts, Rama has turned without realizing it into the lane leading to Master's house. Then he sees a familiar group of trees along the way—gulmohar trees in bloom, their blood-red blossoms as red as betel juice.

For a moment he halts to recite a few lines from his imagined speech. "I would not be bothering you, Master, with trouble, but yet to tell about is my family. I have wife, two boys. Boys eight and six. I can do any job. Not to worry about that, Master. You and I mix well together, so I wouldn't mind working for you. I will come away from post office tomorrow if you are wishing it." Satisfied, Rama straightens the lower edge of his dhoti, grips the umbrella in one hand, the bouquet in the other, and walks confidently forward, past a line of stately asoka trees which stand like tall guardians in front of the high-walled homes of rich Indians and of a few foreigners like Master.

Approaching the gate, he sees the young mali inside, sweeping the clay yard with a bamboo broom.

Shrinivas looks up with a frown when the gate swings open.

"Is Master home? I've come to see him," Rama explains coolly.

The mali wipes sweat from his brow. "He's at home. You better see him now. It's your last chance."

For an instant Rama sees Master dying in bed: right in front of his eyes the scarred face of Master going blank. "Is he sick? Is it fever?"

"He's leaving."

"Leaving Madras? Where to?"

Shrinivas shrugs and makes a lazy swipe at the yard with his broom.

"Leaving for good?"

"That's what Cook says."

"When?"

"I don't know. Soon." Shrinivas grimaces; his mustache gleams with sweat. "A Sindhi came today. If he buys the house, I won't work for him. Sindhis are worse than Moslems."

Rama drops the flowers. Leaving? For good? Soon? Rounding the side of the house, he rushes for the kitchen, having never dared to enter the house from the front. Without his customary caution, Rama bursts into the kitchen, surprising Cook, who's up to his elbows in dough at the flour board.

"What are you doing here?" Cook shouts.

"Where is Master? Upstairs?"

Wiping dough from his fingers, Cook says, "Get out. Master has enough on his mind without you bothering him."

"*Me?* What about *you?* Did you cheat him so much he decided to leave?"

Cook reaches for the cleaver near the flour board.

But fired by anxiety beyond caution, Rama yells at him, "What have you done to Master! He *can't* leave!"

Cook takes a step forward, the cleaver held chest high in a flour-smeared hand. "Get out. You're not wanted."

There's a small table between them, and Rama takes advantage of it —sliding by and scuttling out of the kitchen before Cook can decide whether or not an attack is worth it.

Behind him, as he mounts the stairway to the second floor, Rama hears the cook's voice in diminished volume calling out to him to stop. Rama touches the river stone at his neck. Narayana. At the top of the stairs, he can see through the empty rooms to the veranda with its rolled chicks and lounge chair and rattan table. Master's blond head is visible above the chair. The sight of the living man enheartens Rama. For the past few moments he's thought everything was lost, as if he were seeking out someone already dead.

Master turns as he reaches the veranda. "Well, I'm glad to see you, Rama." The white man holds a glass. In the late sunlight his unwrinkled face takes on a golden color. The livid scar on his forehead looks suddenly to Rama like one of the lines of a Shaivite mark. "You've heard the news?"

"Going from India, Master?" Rama can't wait for confirmation. "Staying where then?"

"Siam."

"Ah, Siam. Is hot there, Master."

"My wife needs me there." He adds, "I'm needed in Bangkok."

Rama remembers the cable that he'd brought to Master from the post office. Panicky, he wonders if his understanding of English is so faulty that he missed a plea for help in the curt message. It had seemed to him no more than the woman's refusal to come to India. Master needed? White people ask for help in strange ways. "Are you keen on going, Master?"

The white man considers a moment before replying. "No, Rama, I'm not. I had counted on staying."

Why, then, doesn't Master *demand* that the woman come here? If help is what she wants, Master can give her that right here in Madras. For a moment Rama's spirits lift. All he needs to do is warn Master how unmanly it is to let a woman make such decisions.

Master is saying something that gets in the way of a warning. Master is saying, "You never told me anything about yourself, Rama, except you're unhappy at the post office. Are you free?"

Rama doesn't understand the question. Instead he mumbles phrases from what he can remember of his speech. "I am not wanting to bother you with trouble, but we mix up well together. At the post office I can't make both my ends meet."

Before Rama can say more, the white man holds out the glass for him to take. He rushes for it.

"Please put it on the table, Rama." Master points with his good hand to the sling. "It won't be easy traveling with this, especially since I'm stopping first in Burma. I have business in Burma too."

Rama nods listlessly. He had counted equally on Lord Shiva, Lord Vishnu, Uncle, and Master to save his little family. Now, abruptly, he feels lost. There is nothing to do but sit down and let the night come.

"I've been thinking," Master says, cocking his head to appraise Rama. "We get on together. I wonder, will you come along?" Master lifts his slinged arm. "The devil, traveling with one arm. Especially in Burma. If you come along, I'll pay your fare round trip. And of course you'll get wages. You'll handle the arrangements—luggage, transportation, that sort of thing."

Rama hears the words, but he's not sure of their meaning. They mean too much to be understood quickly.

"I want to leave in a couple of days. I'm sorry for the short notice. Forget it if you're not free."

"Burma? Siam? Wages?"

"For that matter, I suppose I can manage alone. Don't let it worry you."

"Free?"

"Yes, I thought of it today."

"Come along? You are meaning Rama?"

Master frowns, as if impatient. "Yes, free to come along and help me out."

Although he knows Master is impatient with his slowness of understanding, Rama can't put these facts together. "Free? I am not seeing how—" Suddenly he remembers the bird calling out just as he was entering Shri Kasiviswanathaswami Temple. That was a good sign, or at least, he hoped it was. Has Lord Shiva answered his prayer? Turning away from Master for a moment, for a moment more in which to consider what is happening, Rama looks beyond the balcony toward the neighboring tiled roof. On the road beneath the house a dhobi is hurrying along with a basket of laundry on his head, going somewhere, moving out of sight. Turned away from Master a moment longer, for one last moment in which to think, Rama stares at a mango tree. If he goes to foreign places, if he travels far from the village, he won't be here in the month of Chaitra when the mangoes bloom. He won't see the mangoes bloom or the drought coming.

"Well, all right, Rama," Master says with a shrug of regret. "It seemed like a good idea at the moment."

Not to see drought coming and boys getting sick and then there would be money coming from Master and Siam isn't too far away but far enough so he would not see drought coming but he would see foreign places and for money that he could send home and they wouldn't starve although she would be angry at him for not telling her he was leaving and for not coming home one time more and yet in the end it would be all right. Narayana.

"Rama? Don't worry about me. I'll be fine."

He looks down at the seated white man, who is squinting up at him. "No worrying, Master." Rama takes a deep breath. "I am going," he says, reaching for the river stone that dangles from his neck. He touches the stone. "Rama is going with you, Master. I am free."

Part Two

17 STEAMERS FROM ALL over the world are plying the muddy roadstead of the Hlaing River. Standing at the rail of one of those steamers, Philip Embree, alongside his companion, V. S. Ramachandran, gazes at the harbor scene. In a lug-sail scow people hold umbrellas over their heads for protection against the burning noon sun; they look like black mushrooms sprouting amid-ships in the old boat. On the opposite side of the river a profusion of huts balance crazily on their stilts, scarcely distinguishable from the vegetation and mud banks they cling to. As the steamer turns into its berth, Embree has a final glimpse of the waterside huts, of an old woman smoking a maize-leaf cheroot on the slanted porch of one of them. The noise is now deafening from barges and launches and from stevedores yelling on the pier. Nearby, like the weathered side of an ancient whale, part of a rusty hull rises from the water—a Japanese cargo ship sunk there in 1945, when the Allies retook Rangoon.

Embree watches the docking: Great hawsers rattle their way through deck-side chocks down to bollards on the pier. From a neighboring godown—a low-slung building of thatch and bamboo—coolie laborers, most of them spindly-legged Indians, are carrying hundred-pound gun-nys of rice down to the steamer. They'll be loaded as soon as the spices and hides and cottons and agricultural tools are unloaded that came aboard in Madras. Embree glances at Rama to see if he's spotted his countrymen. Of course he has. On the South Indian's face is a look of intense scrutiny.

Along with laborers carrying sacks of rice from the godown, there are stevedores pushing drums of oil into position in front of the steamer. The oil, Embree figures, must come from the fields at Yenangyaung, where, in the spring of 1942, engineers of the Burma Oil Company had smashed generators, pumps, drills, and shafts, burned the entire stock of petroleum, and blown up the power station for central Burma, thereby denying oil to the Japanese invaders.

It was at Yenangyaung that he first tasted combat in Burma.

For a moment he looks beyond the dock to the city, recognizing the High Court and City Hall buildings, brick models of classic Victorian architecture; other colonial structures are in the process of restoration, because Rangoon was razed in 1942 by the retreating British and incoming Japanese and bombed by the Allies three years later. But Embree's attention is riveted now on the grand treasure of Burma, the Shwedagon Pagoda, whose stupa, gilded by tons of gold leaf, towers on its hill far above the streets of downtown Rangoon.

Yet the present spectacle is no stronger than memory. Yenangyaung, the oil fields, the retreat from Lower Burma.

"What in the hell are you doing here, Yank?" a group of British soldiers asked him when he drove into headquarters near Twingon on that April day six years ago. They gave him raised eyebrows when he explained that he was Liaison Officer for one of two Chinese armies coming down the road from Mandalay. "What's a Yank doing with Chinamen?" These soldiers were from the King's Own Yorkshire Light Infantry—the Koylies.

In the distance, while they looked curiously at the Yank who'd come to represent a Chinese army which for days had been expected to help the First Burma Division out of a bad show and had somehow managed never to arrive (the Chinese being what they were—shirkers, inscrutables from the East, a bunch of thieves and coolies), while they studied this strange liaison officer in a Chinese field uniform, they could still hear the wells blowing up and still see an immense dirty cloud of orange smoke hovering above the petroleum fields there, twenty-five miles away, and they could still feel the sting in their nostrils of combusted oil, wafted over from the devastation on winds almost as hot as the scorched earth of Yenangyaung.

He now watches the stevedores pushing oil drums from Yenangyaung and feels an odd moment of tenderness for the oil itself, sloshing in metal enclosures. The oil of Yenangyaung. Kept it out of the hands of the little fuckers in 1942.

And now dock workers are springing the steamer in alongside the pier, where a small group of Burmans, attempting to look official in the midst of so much vertiginous activity, are waiting to welcome someone from the arriving ship. Each wears a gaung-baung, a fancy headdress of bright silk wrapped around a frame of cane.

Embree's attention shifts to some boys playing chinlon near the go-down. Standing in a circle, they keep a ball of woven thatch in the air by striking it with every part of their bodies except their hands. Their skill at the game is matched by their enthusiasm. So here's an example, Embree thinks, of the Burman's renowned vivacity. He had seen precious little of it during the war. Now, coming once again into a Rangoon he'd left by troop ship in 1945, Embree stares with interest at the gaiety of a people who in the Yenangyaung days had murdered the retreating Allies.

Below him, not far from the forward spring line, stands a boy wearing nothing but a greasy blue shirt that scarcely covers his belly. He's all knobby knees, save for a gathering of genital flesh at his groin. The child's thin right arm is raised, two fingers spread in the V for Victory.

The war has been over now for three years, yet the boy remembers.

When the Japanese lost, all over Burma the V had appeared—along village paths, down roads, on rivers, from windows, and the doorways of temples.

Embree straightens up from the railing. His left arm is still immobilized in a sling, but he raises his right hand, slowly opening the space between his first two fingers, answering the boy's salute with a V of his own.

. . .

The V was not a ubiquitous sign of defiant hope and ultimate triumph in early 1939, when Philip Embree left Bangkok and joined Colonel Stilwell's "China Gang." Along with a handful of other American adventurers-cum-servicemen, he was stationed at remote outposts in China while the Japanese purchased scrap metal from the United States to make into the bombs they dropped on Nunning and Chungking. His friends were the Flying Tiger pilots of Kunming and the engineers for whom he translated Chinese on the Burma Road—men mostly forgotten in the backwaters of a nasty foreign war. Pearl Harbor changed that, and brought Stilwell, promoted to general, from training-camp assignments in the States back to China. In early 1942 he attached Embree to the Chinese Fifth Army, which was entering the Burmese theater of operations. That spring Embree was responsible for liaison between Chinese and British units operating in the western sector of Lower Burma. In this capacity he was ordered to join what was left of the retreating British Army—not much more than the tattered remnants of the First Burma Division and the undermanned Black Cat Division. The British high command made no effort to disguise their contempt for Chinese troops, yet during the retreat from Lower Burma, the 38th Division broke through a Japanese blockade and saved the British from annihilation. As an old China hand, Embree had been proud of them, but their heroic performance was not repeated. While he marched northward with the British troops—now called the Burma Corps—the Chinese forces, moving eastward, fell prey as much to poor leadership as they did to Japanese attack. One division, the 55th from the Sixth Army, was so harassed that one day it simply disappeared, vanished. As General Stilwell remarked, "It's the goddamnedest thing I ever saw; last night I had a division, and today there isn't any."

Some of those panicked troops drifted back into China, but most of them died of starvation or disease along the road, were captured by Japanese patrols or murdered by bands of marauding Burmans. Other

Chinese divisions, poorly equipped, met defeat again and again at the hands of a mobile, fiercely aggressive enemy. Stilwell, nominally in charge of the Chinese troops in Burma, soon realized that Chiang Kai-shek had tricked him, because in reality command still resided with the Generalissimo two thousand miles away in Chungking. Orders from Stilwell were either ignored or misinterpreted or interminably postponed by Chinese commanders.

Although Stilwell had lived in China and spoke the language almost as well as Embree did, he had nevertheless forgotten something important in his desire to succeed: the Chinese propensity for hoarding things —in this case, artillery and troops. Chiang argued that his troops shouldn't go into combat unless they had a numerical advantage of five to one over the Japanese. He further expected Stilwell to honor the Kuomintang philosophy of "defense in depth," which meant a column of divisions should be strung out one behind another across the countryside like widely separated beads—easily isolated, therefore, and cut to pieces by an enemy who never protected his own rear but attacked, attacked, attacked ceaselessly. And so the badly trained and under-equipped Chinese armies reeled daily under the Japanese blows.

As a liaison officer traveling with British troops, Embree became slowly but steadily isolated from the Chinese army that he'd come with to Burma. Two streams of retreating forces moved north toward Mandalay and Lashio: the Chinese to the east, the Imperial Army of Britain to the west. Units of Chinese battalions and regiments and finally entire divisions, following the example of the doomed 55th, simply fell apart, like shards of a cracked bowl; troops scattered, wobbling through jungles and over mountains, hoping to find a way out of this Burmese hell by heading northwest, in the direction from which they'd come.

The 38th, the only healthy Chinese element left in Burma, was still following the British route northeastward toward India, but having its own LO, the division didn't need Embree. Like so many soldiers during that chaotic period, he found himself cut off from his own command. Unable to rejoin the Chinese Fifth Army, Embree remained with the Gloucesters and West Yorks from England, with the Cameronians from Scotland, with the Inniskillings from Ireland, with the Punjabis, the Garhwalis, the Sikhs, and the Gurkhas from India, and with the loyal tribals from Burma itself, the Kachins and Karens and Chins—a great horde moving forward on traffic-choked dusty highways while Japanese troops and Burman dacoits struck at their flanks daily, ambushed them from roadblocks, strafed them from the skies.

Embree spent most of his time with the Koylies, fresh from England. He rode with them, and when the Willys Jeeps and Land-Rovers broke down from overheating and lack of petrol, he walked with them. He walked with Harry Stubbs, a sandy-haired corporal from Leeds who was young enough to be his son. Harry came from a coal-mining family. At seventeen he'd won a scholarship to London University, and at the time he joined the army he'd been reading philosophy for two years.

Harry was a complicated lad, the other young infantrymen said. And he was. Surely about war he was innocent, but around campfires Harry Stubbs, all of twenty, displayed the erudition that often comes to someone who represents a family's first ascent into the world of opportunity. What surprised Embree was his own tolerance of this callow young Englishman, who reminded him of his own days at the Yale Divinity School and of his father orating at the dinner table: windy excursions into ontological proofs for the existence of God, long journeys through definitions for Truth and Reality and the like.

On the road, thirsty and frightened, plagued by firefights and strafings, trembling at the thought of contracting the typhus and malaria that were taking a horrible toll of the retreating army, Philip Embree still found time to wonder about the mental constitution of this young Englishman. Indeed, sometimes on the march Embree wondered if the strange kid actually knew what was happening, so engrossed did he seem in questions that had no place here: questions out of Plato and Aristotle, Descartes and Locke, Hume and Kant that belonged in a tomblike library or drowsy classroom. And yet Harry's excessive intellection didn't make him the fool that Embree had thought him to be at first encounter. Perhaps sheer enthusiasm saved him from that fate— enthusiasm and at times a toughness left over from ancestors who'd suffered out their lives in the coal mines of Yorkshire. The kid had courage when it was needed (he pulled a wounded man out of the road into a ditch during a Zero's strafing), and the ability to pitch in, say, when a lorry was stuck in the sands of central Burma. Sturdily built, a good four inches taller than Embree, the young scholar had a penchant for action that made him acceptable to his mates.

As for Embree, he was more than acceptable to them. Although he was an officer and nearly twice their age, he walked toward Mandalay with them, the young Koylies, most of whom had never been as far as London until six months ago. During the day there was no time for conversation, no energy for it either, as roadblocks and snipers from the dusty bushes kept them thinking of death, but at nighttime, along the starlit roadside, Embree told them stories of China in the old days, when warlords roamed a countryside almost as chaotic as the one they were retreating over. He spoke of General Tang Shan-teh, a warlord whose troops surpassed in discipline and skill any of the Chinese forces seen here in Burma. "He was the best man I ever knew," Embree claimed. When asked how well he'd known such a chap, he told them, to their astonishment, that he'd served in the General's cavalry. When the Koylies protested that their General Slim was better than any Chinaman could be, Embree explained Tang's tactics, as daring and aggressive as those the Japanese were using against them now; and there, in the hot dry evening of a devastated country, the young soldiers listened solemnly to the exploits of a man for whom this terrible retreat must be only another episode in a lifelong adventure.

After a vicious dawn firefight, in which the Koylies suffered twenty percent casualties, they came often to Embree for advice about their weapons, about firing positions, about survival under fire.

The retreating Allies were near Mandalay by then. As they slogged toward the Ava Bridge, to the north they could see the city, under Japanese bombing attack for weeks, sending up columns of gray smoke. Embree was reassigned to the Indian Black Cat division to coordinate its movements with those of the 38th, whose LO had been killed. These two groups, along with the Seventh Armored Brigade, were to fight a rear-guard action against the oncoming Japanese. This would give the Imperial Army a chance to cross the Irrawaddy River and head for safety in India—the battle for Burma was obviously lost.

Embree said goodbye to the little group of Koylies he'd come to know on the march, and then for three days saw action at the Ava Bridge, having his first look at Gurkhas, who lived up to their reputation for courage and ferocity. After a few spans of the bridge were blown, halting the Japanese advance temporarily, the rear-guard units of the retreating army followed the main body to Monywa on the Chindwin River, thence north to Yeu and Shwegyin. By the time the rear guard caught up at Shwegyin, Slim's army was in desperate straits. The British had been roadbound, too dependent on lorries and tanks and jeeps, whereas the Japs moved comfortably off the beaten path, taking advantage of help from lowland Burmans. Welcomed in villages that the British could enter only by force of arms, the Japanese were well fed, while their fleeing opponents lived on bully beef and biscuits.

The Imperial British Army, lacking petrol and spare parts, had abandoned most of its tanks and lorries. Lost from following maps that featured nonexistent roads, units were ambushed and decimated; men captured were often tortured before getting the final bullet or bayonet thrust. Infiltrating Japanese squads lobbed harmless firecrackers along with Mills bombs into Allied command posts at night, letting no one rest, and sometimes, when a Very light burst overhead, machine guns clattered immediately, riddling ambulances and command tents.

And there was always the silent killer: mite-borne typhus, beriberi, malignant tertian malaria, amoebic dysentery. As the army entered the jungle areas of North Burma, bloodsucking leeches found them, and poisonous kraits and leaves as sharp as knives, and they encountered vast wastes of stinking mud and trees with huge, knotted, exposed root systems that made walking among them almost impossible. Up into jungle-clad mountains and down into valley swamplands, the army faced exotic new dangers—parasites and viruses causing schistosomiasis, Naga sores, nameless but lethal fevers.

Slim made a final stand at Shwegyin, where the cart path his ragged army had been following came to an end. It was here, at a ferryboat landing on the Chindwin River, that Embree again met up with the young Koylies—what was left of them. Two ambushes had decreased the twenty or so men he'd known a few weeks earlier to just five, no longer young. Indeed, as he stared at Harry Stubbs, while they stood on the river bank watching ferries load up with wounded and a few salvageable heavy guns, Embree could scarcely recognize in the heavily bearded face, the lusterless eyes, the matted filthy hair, anything of the ebullient young scholar who blithely, in the midst of war, had discussed the categorical imperative.

In the ensuing battle, Embree stayed close to the Yorkshire kid who, to his battlewise eye, seemed ready to crack. Yet during the long artillery duel and subsequent attacks upon the staging area, Harry Stubbs did not crack. Instead, he carried wounded on his back down to the ferries under fire—slogging patiently along the mortared beach and going back for another trip. He did this five times, although the Basin, as the landing was called, became blanketed by small-arms fire. Embree watched this extraordinary performance from the cover of desert scrub, as did other astonished veterans, who made bets, each time, on the kid's chances of making it.

By using everything he had, including Bofors AA guns against Japanese fieldpieces, Slim managed to fight the enemy to a standstill and ferry the remnants of his army six miles upstream to Kalewa. Once into the jungles of the west bank of the Chindwin, his troops disengaged from the Japanese, who chose not to follow. The reason was clear enough: they felt the malaria-infested jungle would finish off the survivors for them.

The monsoon had begun in the Kabaw Valley, turning it into what the struggling British called the Valley of Death. Brutal rains pelted them night and day. Weak from dysentery, they trudged through knee-deep mud while there was light, then slept in it when darkness fell. The air, laden with moisture, became fetid and heavy, so heavy it was difficult for the enfeebled men to breathe. Their clothes rotted on their bodies during the nightmarish ninety-mile march. Harry had contracted malaria in Kalewa.

"Come on, Harry," Embree muttered to the feverish boy, "we're walking out of here. We're walking out, Harry."

While Harry shook, Embree half-carried him along the path.

"Let me rest," Harry panted.

"We're walking out, Harry."

And two weeks later, both scarcely alive, their boots disintegrated from jungle rot, they staggered into an outpost near Tamu. They were in India; they had walked out.

. . .

We did it, we walked out, Embree thinks while staring down at the Rangoon dock.

The boy in the ragged blue shirt has disappeared in the crowd waiting for the gangway to lower. A few minutes later, with Rama and porters ahead of him, Embree is descending the gangway. He observes with amusement how boldly Rama takes charge of the porters carrying the luggage. If the young Indian slips easily into a role of borrowed authority, Embree is glad of it. It proves his decision to bring Rama was a good one.

He swears to himself that what he told Rama is the truth: Vera needs him in Bangkok, and he's going there to help her. The fact is, she may very well despise him for coming. She made it perfectly clear in her cable that business in Bangkok was more important than joining him in India. And therefore his, to himself at least, quite reasonable decision: If she won't come to him, he'll go to her. He'll do this with the aim of discovering what she doesn't know—that she needs him, even if he doesn't yet know why.

Embree is jostled by the welcoming crowd on the pier: the hawkers and porters and businessmen, both foreign and Burman. A half-dozen boys circle him, grinning. They raise their V's for Victory and yell out in perfect English, "Hello, Brit!" One of them, pushed forward by the others, displays on a slab of wood a crude chalk drawing of a big-breasted girl with her legs parted to reveal an enormous, spiky-haired vagina—a couple of little girls nearby, seeing the board, join their laughter. Looking above their heads into the crowd, Embree sees an old man waving newspapers for sale. They're in English, and the stark black gigantic headline comes out at Embree across the swirling dock:

GANDHI ASSASSINATED!

. . .

Minutes later he knows the bare details: A Hindu zealot, enraged by Gandhi's concessions to the Moslems, had shot the Indian leader dead at Birla House in Delhi on 30 January 1948, just at evening, before a prayer meeting in the garden.

So it's finally happened, Embree thinks, holding the newspaper.

At his side, Rama is reading the account. Breathless exclamations escape the young Indian as he bends close to the newsprint, too absorbed to realize that his master must now peer around him at the following words:

"Over the microphone of All India Radio, the Prime Minister, Jawaharlal Nehru, said to the grief-stricken people of India, 'The light has gone out of our lives and there is darkness everywhere. Our beloved leader, Bapu, as we called him, the father of the nation, is no more.' "

India's fortunate it didn't happen sooner, Embree thinks. So Bapuji is gone. Embree has this sudden image of him scurrying down the ravaged streets of Calcutta with a covey of Moslems at his heels. About world affairs the little man from Porbandar was naïve. He domineered over those nearest to him and shouldered a load of prejudice as heavy as most men carry. He was therefore human. He was also brave, compassionate, and energetic beyond belief. Such men, Embree thinks, don't appear each generation or even, perhaps, each century. Their names leap out of history in isolated brilliance.

A loud wailing shifts his attention to the godown, where, to his surprise, he sees Rama, who is running up and down the lines of Indian coolies, shouting out the news in Tamil. And then, to Embree's further surprise, Rama flings himself on his knees and steeples his hands, one of them holding the salagrama stone that hangs around his neck. The coolies, following his example, fall to their knees too, and work stops on the pier, despite the efforts of Burman stevedores to get them back on their feet. They mumble their prayers for Bapu on the Rangoon dock, while Burmans stare at them with undisguised contempt.

Embree watches with interest how fervently Rama participates in ritual mourning for a man whom, on the steamer from Madras, he'd criticized so often: "Ah, he is good man, a god man too, but with wrong head, Master. Gandhi gives too much away to Moslems. His head is wrong, do you see. It would be better for us if he died now—God help me for speaking truth—because when Bapu takes on a fast, Moslems are better off for it, but we Hindus lose."

What is Rama thinking now? Embree wonders. The young Indian kneels on the dock, oblivious to the stevedores yelling at him, to his Master awaiting him, to the porters he must command. Is he ashamed now of his criticism of Gandhi? Does he still feel justified in having made it? Nevertheless, his prayer is certainly sincere: taut jaw, closed eyes, trembling mouth. At this moment Rama is wonderfully alive—just, Embree thinks, as I was during those first days in China two decades ago.

Patiently he waits for Rama to finish the prayer. His decision to bring along the young Tamil was indeed a good one: he is traveling with someone with a heart.

· · ·

From the third floor, where he has a room, Philip Embree takes the lift —a cage of paneled teak, containing an ashtray on a waist-high stand and a mirror in which ladies might inspect themselves before going down to dinners of roast beef and champagne, that is, until the war brought such elegant living to an end—strolls down flowered carpets strewn on marble floors, pauses at the dining room to peek at white Doric columns there, continues past the ballroom, along wide corridors above which slowly revolving fans unsettle the evening air, and comes finally, beyond a row of potted plants, into the bar of the Strand Hotel.

Embree was last in it in 1945. There had been crowds of soldiers drinking beer then in the hot, spacious room, everyone jubilant in victory, eager to go home. Now only a few rattan chairs are occupied and these by quiet tourists and ship's officers from visiting liners.

Embree steps up to the half-moon bar and places one foot on the copper rail. He's alone, Rama having requested permission to visit the Thein Gyi Zei on Anawrahta Road. "I don't mind if I go to look at it," the young Indian had said nonchalantly, affecting no more than slight curiosity about the market there, with its stalls of goods and spices: the red chilis and cardamon seeds and magazines in Tamil and rows of carved Hindu deities that might bring him closer for a time to the land that he—how obvious to his master—is already homesick for.

Embree orders a beer, looks around. Two men, nearby, smile and he smiles back, recalling a recent encounter at the Adyar Club in Madras. But tonight he's not drunk, not belligerent, although memories besiege him now as then, and for a few moments after smiling at the two men, he recalls *The Upanishads:* Fear rises from the Other. But not tonight; he won't have it. Lifting his glass, Embree stares at a wood carving of Karaweik, the holy swan of Burma, sitting on a ledge behind the bar, above a row of bottles.

"Excuse me, sir."

Embree turns to the two men, one of whom is dressed in a faded green bush jacket, khaki cord breeches, and a British officer's felt hat with badly worn cord band—a castoff uniform. "Have we met, sir?"

"I don't know. Have we?" Embree asks with a smile.

"Kohima, June of '44?"

"I wasn't there."

"But you were here in Burma," the ex-soldier declares.

"Oh, yes."

"Don't mind me. We're all mates now, aren't we, who were here then? What was your year?"

Why not talk about it, Embree thinks. He smiles again, aware of his excessive good will. "The first time—1942. I was attached to the Chinese Fifth Army."

The Englishman whistles. "I say, that's odd. Speak Chinese?"

Embree nods, swinging into the mood of easy revelations. "I was LO for the Fifth. Ended up the retreat with the Burma Corps."

"One of Stilwell's Yanks. Thought so. Not many of you in on the retreat. That was our own mucked-up show." He shakes his head sadly. "Second time?"

"With you British again. With Slim in '45."

The man laughs. "Slim. Jolly well best damn general in the British Army. Were you with the 33rd Corps?"

"No, with the 19th." Embree says nothing about his other assignment, with OSS Detachment 101. Although it's no longer necessary to keep that secret, by force of habit he never mentions the 101st.

"The 19th. The Daggers. Then it was Mandalay." The ex-soldier guffaws. "That's where we met. I was with the Second Seventh Gurkhas."

Embree raises his glass. "Who took the Hill."

"Not really, I'm afraid. That honor went to the Fourth Gurkhas. We covered them on the south while they went round. Name's Kemp."

"Embree." He moves along the bar and clasps the ex-officer's hand.

"This is Mister Teleki."

Embree extends his hand now to Kemp's companion, a short heavyset fellow at least ten years older than Kemp, around fifty.

"Come now, what are you drinking?" Kemp asks, pushing Embree's beer glass away. "You shan't have that here. How's a tot of gin for old Mandalay?" Turning to Mister Teleki, he claps both hands on his hips, like an officer giving commands. "Time for a bit of celebration, Teleki. This chap remembers old Mandalay."

Old Mandalay. It's strange how fresh some memories remain. Even while Embree stands there, one foot on the copper railing, his gaze fixed on the man who has just offered him a drink, so much of old Mandalay returns in an instant: Tramping past the Hill, its Japanese guns now silenced in the broken temples on its slope, his own battalion is approaching the gates of Fort Dufferin in the middle of Mandalay; "toad in the hole"—a Jap crouched in a roadside crater—detonates a large aerial bomb by striking its nose cap with a stone: tank commander and gunner are blown out of the turret in myriad soaring pieces; and beyond the fort's gate, he and a half dozen Sikh machine-gunners are crouching at either side of a tunnel while an infantryman blasts the steel door with a PIAT and then, when it caves in, an engineer tosses a beehive charge inside where the Japs are and then when that doesn't dislodge the defenders a couple of other engineers roll in kegs of gasoline and set them afire with tracers, and after that the Japs come out wrapped in flames and screaming, but by God shooting their rifles.

Embree shakes his head, partly to rid himself of such images, partly in response to the Englishman's question. "No gin. Beer will do fine, thank you. I can remember Mandalay on that."

"Then beer it is, old chap. I say, you've been hurt." He gestures at Embree's arm. "Not a good practice out here—getting hurt. Remember the Naga sores? Just a little boil at first, Teleki"—he turns a moment to the older man—"but then it goes deeper, bores into the skin right to the bone. Right *through* the bone. A lot of chaps had it." Kemp laughs; he has a slightly drooping black mustache, and bad teeth, and very bright eyes, one of which diverges toward the left. That eye makes it difficult for Embree to look at him head on. "Break it here?" he asks pleasantly.

Embree shrugs. "No, in India. Madras."

"I like Madras. Next to Delhi I prefer it in India. Not an accident, I'll wager."

Embree can't help but smile at Kemp, a man resolved to find violence where he can.

"Dacoits?" Kemp suggests enthusiastically.

"Well, in a way."

"Rotten thieves and murderers. I knew it," Kemp crows, ordering gins for himself and Mister Teleki and a beer for Embree. "But you don't have the dacoits there you have in Burma. Crime here's highest in Asia, most likely in the world, isn't it. Never understand these people. Fun-loving all right, but can't hold their palm toddy. Loan you their shirt, but kill each other over a cockfight bet. I say, Teleki"—he turns again to the stout older man—"don't you think they're worse now that independence has made everyone here quite mad?" He answers for Mister Teleki. "Independence has brought the dacoits out of hiding, let me tell you. Now that they're the Union of Burma—when was that, Teleki?"

The older man speaks gruffly. "On 4 January at 4:20 A.M."

"That's it. They had one of those astrologers set the time for declaring independence. That's your Burmans. I was there that day. Aung San's body—mind you, the man had been dead six months—lay in state in a flag-draped hall. Governor and staff and people like myself saluted while the Union Jack came down and they played 'God Save the King' and that five-starred flag of theirs went up and their national anthem was played and they blew conch shells. It was all perfectly mad." After another short laugh, he squints at Embree. "On holiday?"

"Yes. Or, that is, I'm on my way to Bangkok. That's where my family is." He adds, "They're expecting me," hearing the foolish note of pride in his voice.

"Bangkok. That's a bit of all right, isn't it. Bangkok's quiet at least, not like it is here. Isn't that so, Teleki? You're in business there?"

How difficult my life is to explain, Embree thinks sadly. Instead of trying to untangle a lifetime of ambiguous goals and lost opportunities for this garrulous ex-officer, Embree says, "Yes, in export."

"Export's a jolly way to make one's living these days. Teleki here exports gems. As for Anthony Kemp, I retired from the army last year. Thought of going home, but it all seemed—" Kemp's easy self-confidence escapes him; he looks confused, unsure. "Well, you know. Live half your life out here, you just can't pick up and go back there, can you. I know lads who've gone home and suddenly they've got the Jungle Happiness—go quite mad. Stark raving." Kemp gives a hearty guffaw. "If I go that way, I'd much rather do it out here among the Burmans, who're all quite mad themselves. Well, it had to be Mandalay."

"Maybe it was around Fort Dufferin."

"That's it then. But we met. There's no doubt of that. I never forget a face. Dead or alive, they're all in my memory."

"There's a cemetery at Thanbyuzayat—"

Kemp stares hard at Embree a few moments, then his features soften into a look of compassion. "Ah, you've chaps there you came to see." He adds, "They keep it trimmed, hedges and all. Won't let the jungle in. It's tidy. Yes . . ." His voice trails off. "Actually it's located about sixty-five kilometers south of Moulmein. You can go by train now. Remember the trains?"

Embree remembers them: During the retreat the Burmese Railway Administration evacuated its personnel; lacking engineers to throw switches and give signals, trains couldn't proceed without fear of collision. A lot of men died because they couldn't get out by train.

"Teleki here doesn't know about those trains. He wasn't here during the war. Got out before the Nips came in." Kemp says this in a tone of disapproval.

Embree, however, smiles at the stout, aging man who'd had the good sense to leave a doomed city. The smile apparently pleases Mister Teleki, because he starts to talk in a strongly accented but correct English. He is originally from Hungary. At the start of World War One he had the good sense to go to Brazil. Then he drifted east and settled in Rangoon, where he opened an export house for gems. "Finest rubies and sapphires in the world come from Burma," he declares in a voice that startles by its certainty.

"He got out on the last steamer," Kemp explains. "Three more," he says to the barman.

"Not for me," Embree says. Tomorrow he's going to the Allied Cemetery in Thanbyuzayat. He will not go there with a hangover.

Kemp shrugs. "Will you join us for dinner? We eat here every night. Food's frightful, but cheap. At least what you tuck into here won't give you dysentery. Remember that, Embree? Chaps cutting the seat of their pants away?" His own memory of it brings a rueful chortle from Anthony Kemp, late of the Gurkha Rifles.

• • •

The food in the Strand Hotel dining room is indeed frightful, but it's served by turbaned waiters in starched white uniforms, and a saing orchestra of drums and gongs and bamboo clappers, flute, and xylophone hints at the luxurious life that foreigners enjoyed here in the prewar days.

"Did you know, Embree," Kemp says while they're eating, "the Nips used this hotel for a whorehouse during the war?"

Embree is staring at a wall portrait of Warren Hastings, symbol of Britain's colonial success in this part of the world. It won't be on the wall much longer. First India, now Burma.

He glances at Kemp in the faded khakis and bush jacket of a British officer. The droop of Kemp's mustache, the glitter of his strabismal eye, the desperate confidence and good cheer all attest to his life here in Burma: disinherited, unwanted, at odds.

Embree tries to show more interest than he feels in Kemp's stories of the Second Battalion, Seventh Regiment. Although at Indian Independence the Seventh had gone to the Crown, Kemp hadn't wanted to retire in India, so he claims, with the memory still fresh of the Gurkha Brigade splitting up: "The Regiment was raised at Thayetymo here in Burma in 1902 as the Eighth, then the Seventh. So I've come back to the source of things, in a manner of speaking. Burma's where the Regiment belongs. And it was here in Burma we fought our best." Kemp is drinking brandy now. Three of them go down fast, while he reels off the names of Gurkha heroes: Subadar Majar Pirthalal Limbu, who won four Northwest Frontier medals, including the Kabul-Kandahar Star; there were also Lance-Naik Bahadur Gurung and Havildar Gambir Rai, who with kukris in hand rushed a Nip machine-gun nest and decapitated the whole crew before a mortar killed them.

Teleki smokes quietly, a far-off look in his eye which suggests he's heard these stories many times.

"Did you ever handle a kukri, Embree?"

"Yes, a few times." He remembers the delicate balance of the heavy-bladed, curved Gurkha knife. "I prefer an ax," he adds.

But Kemp either ignores or doesn't believe the remark. His divergent eye fixed on something past Embree's shoulder, he sighs and declares, "We were the best in the Brigade. Everything we did was different from the way everyone else operated, you see. In our regiment the chin strap of a Gurkha's hat was worn at point of chin instead of under the lower lip. Jolly well individualistic."

Teleki belches.

"Nothing like our Nepalese Gurkha. Never saw his like for seeing great distances. Especially from the Gurung and Limbu tribes, though I know officers in other battalions who swear by the Rai or even the Sunwar. Beastly hard decision to make—who could see farther. I suspect this talent came from living in the mountains. All of them could see a whisker on a goat's chin from a hundred meters. There was this Subadar—what in the devil was his name now—"

Embree orders another cup of coffee; so does Teleki, who seems bored. Why, Embree wonders, does the man come here every night to hear Kemp's stories?

The ex-officer suddenly rises. "Join me at the WC anyone?"

When he leaves, Embree turns to the stolid Hungarian and says, for want of anything else, "It's a shame about Gandhi, isn't it."

"Well, we must be prepared out here for such things. Consider the way Bogyoke Aung San and his ministers were gunned down before Independence." Teleki seems glad of the opportunity to speak while his companion's gone. "Two men with automatic weapons rushed into the room and assassinated the Prime Minister and seven cabinet members. Aung San was only thirty, with a great future ahead of him." Teleki shakes his head, pulls out a cigar and lights it. His full lips wet the tobacco leaf as he spins the cigar in his mouth. Then in precise, rather studied English he speaks of Burmese politics.

It's a grim analysis, a display of the sort of unadorned pessimism that Embree has learned to expect from Europeans who survived the wars of the first half of the century. There's something about Teleki's distaste for hypocrisy and violence that reminds him of Vera, who always brought to discussions of political affairs the same kind of acute but somber, almost despairing judgment.

According to Teleki, the expulsion of the British in 1942 by the Japanese marked the end of colonial rule in Burma. It was the actual end, although the Churchill government tried to hang on here in the postwar period. The colonials hung on because they didn't understand: The Burmese were no longer afraid of Europeans. The natives had seen colonials blown sky high with Asian bombs, had seen them tortured, had seen them plead for their lives, while little Asians hovered over them, laughing, with the power of life and death in a yellow hand. Burmese intellectuals came to the speakers' platforms in Rangoon without fear.

The problem was, however, few of them had a goal in mind except winning independence. It's the problem revolutionaries always face: What's freedom for? Teleki accompanies this comment with a wry, hapless smile. As a consequence, when their charismatic leader fell under assassins' bullets, various Burmese factions fought each other viciously for the right to proclaim freedom from colonial rule. And none of them had a plan for what might follow Independence.

Kemp, who's returned from the WC, breaks into Teleki's monologue. "This is what I say. We should never have taught these people English. The old policy was best. You learned their language but you didn't teach them yours. That way you could say what you pleased in front of them, whereas they couldn't do the same to you. Promotion in the British Army in India depended on an officer's ability to speak languages. I say that's a jolly good idea."

Without so much as a twitch of acknowledgment of these remarks, Teleki continues. "There's a ferment of activity these days. The Red Flags, for example—a hotheaded group of young people—they are sending a delegation to the Communist Congress in Calcutta this month—"

Embree recalls the bhang-smoking Communists in Balakrishnan's tea shop: They too were going to the Congress.

"What will come of all this?" Embree asks.

"Warfare among the Communists, the Socialists, the veterans, the army. Weaker groups, the losers, will take over villages in the countryside and control their own little kingdoms."

"Like China in the twenties. The warlords," Embree says.

"You see, they no longer have a mutual goal. On 4 January, when they got independence, they lost the last thing that held them together: the *desire* for independence. But they'd learned something too. What the Japanese taught them was the importance of the gun. If the Japanese could oust the British from Burma with the gun, then they can oust one another."

"Is it that simple?"

"I think so. You see, they have no other experience in politics. Everything's elemental at the moment. Ideology won't determine things here. Personal ambition will. At least for a time. But I suspect ultimately they'll turn to some form of socialism."

Embree glances at Kemp, who sits across from him moodily drinking another brandy. It seems that between Kemp and Teleki almost no communication exists; each delivers a monologue, then lapses into self-absorbed silence.

"And I suspect," Teleki continues, puffing on the cigar, "the tribals like the Chin, the Karen, the Shan, all of them, will cause political trouble for years. They have their own languages and customs and territories, so they have an eye on independence too. This is one of the most turbulent countries in the world."

Teleki draws a deep sigh, then puffs on the cigar. "The people of Burma are politically reckless. At this moment nearly half of the members of Parliament are jailed or in revolt. Yet we must understand the reasons why." He pauses a moment. "Not until 1923 did a Burman become a member of the Indian Civil Service. The British"—he pauses again, but without looking at the British ex-officer across the table from him—"waited a very long time to acknowledge that a Burman had the intelligence, let alone the right, to serve the Empire. There were a series of strikes, much rioting and boycotting of English goods. A major uprising took place in the early thirties. A fanatical monk convinced his followers that British bullets couldn't hurt them. Three thousand died. Although Burma became a separate colony in 1935, agitation for more autonomy continued, and young patriots were jailed. Well, there was much more. But for a tiny personal injustice that must have rankled terribly, I think of the Burman who at Oxford University had been a Rugger Blue—" Teleki turns to look at Embree. "I believe that's membership on the rugby team, a distinguished honor. Yet when he returned to Burma, he could not enter the clubs where his former British teammates toasted Oxford victories." Teleki puffs hard and gazes at a white wall in the sultry room. "I wonder how the Asian, I mean the common man, the peasant, must have felt after Pearl Harbor and the early Japanese successes. He must have thought, 'Here is one of us who can beat the whites at their own game. Bully for him.' Of course Japanese brutality ruined that initial impression, but it must have been there, don't you think?"

"I do," Embree agrees emphatically.

"Well." Teleki sets his cigar down in an ashtray, sighs, and motions for a turbaned waiter. "It's time for me to leave."

• • •

After the stout Hungarian has gone, Embree continues to sit at the table with Kemp, who is having yet another brandy.

"Teleki's an extraordinary man," Embree observes.

Kemp guffaws and drinks. "He's an extraordinary chap all right. Learned his English in Brazil. Had a tutor come in every day. Not that he expected to use English then. Simply learned it, as he's learned a half-dozen other languages. His wife died last year of relapsing fever."

"Really?" That explains it, Embree thinks: the lonely widowerer coming here every night for a drink, a dinner with someone who bores him.

"Yes, they were close. No children. Spent their time together. Taken it well, though. Teleki's not a bad bloke, but frightfully tight."

"Tight?" Now that Kemp has drunk deeply, the divergent squint seems more pronounced. Embree has trouble choosing which eye to concentrate on.

"Tight with money, lad. Of course he's made a fortune here with Burmese gems. Absolute fortune. Wealthy as Croesus. And childless, and now that his better half's dead, old Teleki can't know what to do with it all. Yet when I hit him for a bit of a loan, what did he do but refuse me. Not 'perhaps, old chap,' or something polite at least. Just a flat Hungarian no." Kemp shakes his head in extravagant bewilderment.

There's a long silence, during which Embree decides to leave. Teleki has left money for his part of the bill, so Embree takes out his wallet and puts down an equal amount of kyats. With a questioning look, he turns to Kemp, who smiles faintly and lifts his brandy glass, as if in a toast.

"Look, old fellow, I'm a bit short."

"Perfectly all right." Embree starts to add enough to cover Kemp's share of the bill.

"By God, I've *got* it now!"

Embree looks up at the man, who is pinching one end of his mustache in agitation.

"Wasn't Mandalay. You were at Kalewa."

"Yes, I was there."

Leaning forward, Kemp plants both forearms on the table, decisively. "We met on a ferry there. Took a hit forward. Blew up a few Gloucesters huddling in the bow together. Remember that? We were in the stern of it. You were taking care of a young lad—"

"A Koylie."

"That's right. Coming down with malaria. You were taking care of the lad. Did he make it?"

"Yes—" Embree hesitates.

"But chucked it in later?"

"That's right."

Kemp shakes his head gloomily. "It was what I bloody well never got used to: chaps managing one bad show, chucking it in the next. If there was justice, don't you see, he'd get it the first time. Well . . . well . . . that's Jungle Happiness, I suspect." Kemp utters a broken laugh of dismay, then, clearing his throat, leans closer to Embree, as if to confide. "I won't muck you about, Yank. I'll put it straight to you. I need money. I gambled with a few Burmans some time back and lost too much. Much too much. I owe them, and take my word for it, they're a nasty lot."

"How much?" Embree says quickly, unable to look at the ruddy face, its features awry from the effort of confession.

"Do you think I'd ask you—"

"It's all right. Please. How much?" Embree has his wallet out, wanting to avoid more of this scene.

"No, you listen to me. You're not listening," he says in a low voice of annoyance.

"Yes, sorry. I'm listening."

"I just want to say, well, you see, I wouldn't ask simply *anyone* who walked in here. I thought we had something in common."

"We do. Kalewa."

"You're not listening to me. Sorry, but I mean to have you, a comrade in arms so to speak, know why I'm . . . I'm humiliating myself this way. As I said, it's an emergency."

"Yes, I realize that."

"Do you? I'm glad you do, old chap. I really am. Because if I thought you didn't—"

"I do." Embree has kept his wallet out in both hands.

"Well, if you put it that way, Yank, I could dearly use fifty quid."

"I don't have English pounds. And I can't afford fifty."

Kemp shrugs, leaning back in his chair. He looks older than earlier in the evening. The strabismal eye adds to the impression of weary age. So do the faded green jacket, the faded khakis, the worn band on the old felt hat.

They agree on twenty-five British pounds in Burmese equivalency. The evening is over. Once the money has changed hands, both look away from each other and rise. Then, standing by the table, shaking hands with quick little jerks, they say goodbye. For an instant longer Kemp squints at Embree. "Made too many blunders now to do anything about it. Asked to leave the service. Given the boot. That's the truth of my life. I'm a drunk and a gambler. But we all did something back there in '42, Yank. We covered nine hundred miles through enemy territory. Armies have done similar things, of course, but in that retreat we British carried our weapons out. Most of us did. Had my .303 SMLE rifle in my hand when I got to Imphal, though I was vomiting worms, a whole tub of them. Had my rifle. Brought it nearly a thousand miles, and whatever happens, they can't take that away from me. Good night, sir. Thank you, sir, and good night." Turning, with a rapid stride, Anthony Kemp, late of the Gurkha Rifles, walks out of the Strand dining room.

• • •

While Embree ascends the lift to the fourth floor, he's thinking loneliness brings people together who should remain apart. And yet, perhaps each night at the bar they find something in each other's company. And sometimes, perhaps, Teleki has a chance to display his correct English. And perhaps Kemp extracts from an old veteran enough money to bet on the cocks.

When Embree opens the room door, he sees Rama leap off one of the twin beds, as if caught in a criminal act. Embree is startled by the young Indian's behavior—standing in the corner, bowing his head, naked save for a loincloth. At the outset Embree had decided that although Rama would be in his employ, he'd not be an abject servant. What the hell, this young Indian ought to learn what independence really means. So Embree thought. But at the desk of the Strand Hotel a clerk had obviously been disgusted by an arrangement allowing this servant, an Indian servant at that, to share a room with his master. Now Rama is perpetuating the old colonial relationship.

"When I come in, Rama, you don't have to jump up as if scared out of your wits."

"Yes, Master."

"Remember, I asked you to come along as my assistant, my companion. We're traveling together. You're helping a man with a broken shoulder get home. Understood?"

"Yes, Master."

"You insist on calling me 'Master.' I suppose it makes you feel better, I don't know. But no more of this jumping around as if I'm a maharaja. Understood?"

"Yes, Master."

Embree notices some prayer beads on the rumpled bed. "Have you been praying?"

"Yes, Master."

Embree smiles and with his good hand starts to unbutton his shirt. "For Gandiji's soul?"

Rama comes forward. "Let me, Master." He helps Embree get out of the shirt.

Kicking off his sandals, Embree walks over to the chest of drawers, warped and cracked through the years by humid heat. "What's this?" He's looking at a foot-long plaster doll, with blond curls, red lips, a white dress of tulle.

"I have bought in market," Rama says proudly.

"For whom?"

A cloud passes over Rama's face when he says, "For niece. Sending it to niece in Kumbakonem."

For a girlfriend in Madras, Embree thinks. "And these?" He picks up one of two metal toy soldiers: Highlanders wearing the khaki Balmoral of Scottish regiments. Doubtless these prewar figures had belonged to the British child of a provincial civil servant.

"For nephews, also in Kumbakonem."

Embree turns, before entering the bathroom, and asks, "Did you really pray for Gandiji tonight?"

Rama nods emphatically. "Gandiji had wrong head, but was god man." He adds after a pause, "And gave us our country."

18 IT'S A BEAUTIFUL Sunday in Bangkok, one of those cloudless balmy days that precede the blazing heat of late spring, the torrential rains of summer. In celebration of such a day, she has come out with Wanna for a stroll, as people do in this city, beside the Grand Palace, perhaps through Wat Phra Keo, and finally to the market erected each weekend on the Pramane Grounds.

Although Wanna shows little enthusiasm for it, Vera brings them first to Wat Phra Keo. She takes a long look at the *Ramakien* frescoes in the covered gallery of the temple, but Wanna can't or won't look at them if there's anything else in the area—anything alive: a child, a family, a few schoolboys, a man. A handsome man. Indeed, Vera herself is diverted from the paintings, wondering at whom her pretty companion is looking, head cocked pertly, mouth parted in what Vera can only call an invitation. It's a tribute to the murals that they can compete at all with the girl for Vera's attention. Two loves vie here. But for a time the great epic compels her to move along slowly, as the *Ramakien*'s story unfolds through more than a hundred large panels: The battles feature golden chariots and golden bows; the elegant warriors outdo one another in stylized combat; and demons are the creations of artists with a sense of humor. If only war were fought as it is in the *Ramakien*; if only good and evil, Vera thinks, were a matter of art.

This morning she read of the death of Gandhi. Political events rarely interest her, yet this news is troubling, not only because the man was great but because it is a harbinger of more violence. She has a strong hunch that Communists were behind the killing. Someone told her recently of a coup d'état in Czechoslovakia. Bolsheviks again. Vera won't give up the outmoded term for the people who made her family flee Russia. Bolsheviks are stirring up the world, and everyone will soon know what she and the Whites recognized two decades ago: that the Reds are by nature a bloody and ruthless coalition of ambitious men who want only power. Next there will be assassinations here in Bangkok. Bolsheviks are on the klongs, passing out propaganda leaflets. And there are rumors about young men roaming the riverbanks, looking for trouble. She's told Sonia to stay clear of the river area, but the girl just laughs—a high, almost hysterical laugh.

What's happening to her daughter? While Vera was on the business trip up North, Sonia had broken her thumb.

Arriving home yesterday from Chiang Mai, Vera found her sitting at the breakfast table, glaring at a plate of boiled rice and salted fish, which Nipa claimed was good for a pain in the thumb. Pain in the thumb? It was swollen to banana size, angry red, shiny and tender.

"How did this happen?" Vera turned first to Nipa, who threw up her hands, and then to Ah Ping, who shrugged. "What did you do?" she asked Sonia.

"It's nothing. I fell. I won't eat boiled rice and salted fish. Nipa knows I hate it."

How does a girl break her thumb, except through utter carelessness? Vera can't imagine being a girl again, as she strolls out of the *Ramakien* gallery.

Glancing at Wanna, she notices a line of sweat on the girl's forehead. It makes her fragile-looking, vulnerable. It's the way young women are, she thinks sadly. Wanna is wearing a white blouse, a plaid sarong, very plain, and she is beautiful. Twenty years ago, Vera thinks, I could have worn the same thing with the same effect.

Across the hot marble courtyard, in the blue-tiled *bot*, the Emerald Buddha is housed. Vera would like a look at him in his seasonal robe— solid gold now—but Wanna grimaces when she suggests it. The grimace is enough for Vera. "Then let's go, darling." This is said in Thai, except for the English "darling." For terms of endearment they often use English. Once she'd called Wanna "honey," something that Philip used to call her. It surprised her that the girl knew what it meant. In fun they began using other English terms—my dearest, my sweetheart, my honeybunch, my beautiful doll—mostly supplied by Wanna. Vera begins to realize where she got them. Doubtless, from American GIs who crowded Bangkok when Wanna first came here after the war. That Wanna might have been a prostitute in those days is of no consequence to Vera; prudently, however, she never speaks of her own past in Shanghai.

They leave the temple, and at the entrance she pauses for a final look at upswept cho-fa eaves and roofing tiles that overlap like fish scales.

"Nahng Vera!"

She turns to Wanna's pinched and cloudy face.

"Can we go *now*, Vera? Haven't I been here long enough, waiting?"

Vera is surprised by the girl's open anger. It isn't Siamese; it isn't the Wanna she knows either. "I'm sorry. Let's do go."

"You are like a tourist, Nahng Vera. You see everything for the first time."

"Yes, it's what I hope to do. But please, don't call me Nahng." To be called "Mrs. Vera" makes her feel like an old matron, and, of course, Wanna is clearly aware of that.

• • •

It's like a refugee camp, Vera thinks. They are passing beneath shady tamarind trees at the outer fringes of the weekend market on the Pramane Grounds near the Grand Palace. Everything has been heaped here —clothes, food, household goods—under haphazardly raised tents, canvas awnings, umbrellas. She smiles at Wanna, who returns it. We're in love, Vera tells herself, moving into the crowd beside the girl. Together they'll experience the market with its pythons for sale and herbal medicines devoted to long life.

She insists they stop for o-liang, an iced coffee, and watches happily how much Wanna enjoys it. I won't expect too much of her, Vera thinks, sipping the o-liang while the girl orders another. She's young, and if . . . by any chance she takes another lover, either man or woman, I can handle that too.

"Are you happy?" She touches Wanna's arm with a fingertip. *"Tee rahk."*

The girl nods, a response too cool for Vera, who adds reproachfully, "You call me Nahng, but I call you 'sweetheart' in your own language. Can you also call me *Tee rahk?"*

"But I do." Wanna looks at her over the rim of the glass.

That's not what I want, Vera tells herself. Yet *mai pen rai.* The girl's young.

"Come, let's see what they have to eat," she calls out in a voice of tense gaiety and leads toward the center of the immense market, where food stalls are arranged. What bothers her, as they shoulder through the crowd, what continues to bother her is the Siamese penchant for drifting from one lover to the next in a succession of easy affairs. It isn't her own way. It hadn't been even in Shanghai. She hadn't minded the nightly sailors in a pleasure house so much as living with one man for some time, then moving on. And when finally she'd come to Shan-teh, no power on earth could have wrested her from his arms, except fear. Fear alone made her inconstant. Wanna, she says without uttering the word. Turning, she leans toward the almond-brown ear. *"Tee rahk."*

But the girl's attention is elsewhere. She's looking across the sea of people and crates and utensils hanging from tent poles, across the drifting wok smoke. She's looking for something, perhaps for anything at all, Vera thinks. They come out of the narrow path momentarily and see a crowd gathering around a man who has a couple of small wicker baskets and a battered suitcase. She knows what it means and swerves therefore down another passageway. He has cobras and mongooses in the baskets, patent medicines in the suitcase. Vera won't watch him torture the creatures in order to sell a potion that'll give visiting farmers a bellyache for days.

Ahead she sees the jerry-built counters laid out with a dozen varieties of whole fish, dried strips of fish, and prawns stacked in decorative designs. Beyond them are the sections for meat, vegetables, spices, all displayed elegantly—like battles on the *Ramakien* murals. This is the season for asparagus, as long and thin as skeins of twine; here tables are piled high with them. There are good things frying in immense woks beyond the grocery area. Indeed, the aroma of spiced pork drifts toward

Vera, and she feels instantly the overwhelming hunger that has gripped her recently. It's as if the craving itself were a memory of the Siberian steppes, when the memory of dinners she'd eaten had kept her refugee feet moving through the snow.

"Let's go first to the flowers!" Again with excessive gaiety. She wants to avoid the food or at least delay that moment when she lets go of caution and eats too much. It mustn't happen this afternoon. She wants to feel young and carefree. "There!" She points to a distant awning from whose tent poles baskets of orchids are hanging.

Wanna smiles when she sees them.

Why can't I make her smile so happily?

This time Wanna leads, her boyish saronged hips supplely missing contact with bodies coming toward her through the crowd. She moves ahead of Vera, then halts suddenly. Halts in the stream of traffic, gets jostled.

What's happened? Vera wonders. Has she seen a man she knows? Vera lurches forward, reaching her. "What is it?"

Turning toward her, Wanna says something in a low voice.

There's so much noise. "What is it?"

Now Wanna speaks louder. "Your daughter. I saw your daughter."

"Sonia?" Vera smiles. "Good. She can come with us."

"Very well, Nahng Vera."

Stepping out of the traffic, craning her neck, Vera looks past the heaps of boxes and steaming woks, past the stacks of clothing and the teapots strung on tent cords, seeking her daughter.

"There she is," Wanna says calmly. "There. See? Right over there."

At last Vera sees.

It's Sonia, all right, wearing a red cheongsam very tight across her chest and slit far, far up her thigh. Beside her is a thin young man in slacks, a white shirt. He's as tall as she is, although he slouches. He could be—what could he be, who is he, what is he doing with her at the market, walking along unconcerned, as if they're a couple like the countless couples who come every weekend to look at things they can't buy? Who is he?

Turning to Wanna, she says, "Who is he?"

"I don't know who he is, Nahng Vera."

"Is he Chinese?"

"He could be, Nahng Vera."

"What's he doing with her?"

"Walking, Nahng Vera."

She turns quickly enough to catch amusement in the girl's eyes before they go blank. "Probably he's a boy from school," Vera suggests.

"I'm sure he is, Nahng Vera."

"Will you stop calling me that! Yes, he's a student. I think I recognize him."

"I'll get them." Wanna steps forward, but Vera catches her arm.

"No."

"Are you sure, Vera sweetheart?"

"Leave them alone. They have art to talk about. He's one of the students. She's mentioned him."

"Shall we go to the orchids first or the food booths?"

"Whatever you say."

"Then it shall be the orchids," Wanna declares.

When the girl steps out, Vera follows, determined not to look again in the direction of her daughter. As they approach the orchids, she feels perfectly in control, because, after all, there's no reason for a girl Sonia's age not to stroll with a fellow student. But she might have told me, Vera thinks.

The next moment she halts, swept by a dull pain in her chest. People nudge and prod her on their way through the narrow passage, but she can't move from the spot, as if the pain has sent roots into the ground beneath her feet. For a few moments she can concentrate only on the pain, which isn't traveling earthward but outward, spreading across her chest into her shoulder.

"Are you all right, sweetheart?"

She turns to Wanna, who doesn't seem altogether in focus.

"You're sweating." She plucks at Vera's blouse as if to test how wet it is.

"Yes. I . . . feel a little faint." She hears her tiny voice as Wanna guides her by the elbow out of the pathway. They stand between counters piled with cheap sandals and pants. Vera gazes dully at the bustling world out there, outside her pain, while her mind concentrates on what is happening inside her body. It has happened more than once recently—the feeling of pain that halts her, that makes her think, Can it be my heart? No, she's too strong. Didn't she march over frozen tundras?

"Feeling better?" Wanna asks with a smile.

Vera turns to regard the dark eyes that have no love in them. She will leave me, Vera thinks. And if she's anything like I was at her age, she'll wait until she has someone to replace me. Vera notices she has balled her hand at her chest.

"Better?" Wanna asks again.

"Oh, yes. Better." In fact, it is. The radiating pain has collapsed in on itself, coming to a small zero in her chest, then disappearing. She takes a handkerchief and wipes her forehead. The sweat is cold.

After a minute more, she says again with false gaiety, "Let's go. It's just the heat," she says. "Thank you," she says as if appreciative of something Wanna might have done. And she adds in English, "Sweetheart."

. . .

In late afternoon she's waiting on the riverfront terrace of the Oriental Hotel for Jim Thompson. They have an appointment, and in spite of fatigue and that little scare in the weekend market, Vera means to keep it. She won't give in to fainting spells the way women did in her grandmother's day, when smelling salts was a means of ending an unpleasant conversation. Aside from hemorrhaging after a botched abortion, she's never been seriously ill in her life. No one survived the trek out of Russia in 1919 who wasn't made of the strongest stock. She won't coddle herself.

What she needs is peace of mind. Perhaps she'll take up calligraphy again, as she did in Shanghai, or the translation of Chinese poetry. All those habits dropped away, like possessions discarded on a grueling march, when she ran away to Hong Kong with Philip Embree and left behind everything dear. Everything except the suitcase filled with antiques she'd accumulated over the years in China—items of worth paid for by her body and charm. It had been those antiques, none too large for the suitcase, that proved to be her salvation, for by selling them she managed to set herself up in business. She had Philip to thank for that chance. Until then she'd depended on men to see her through hard times, but Philip—ah, Philip, stunned into sloth without a war to fight, translator of bills of lading, married to a woman still in love with a dead man—poor Philip, by drowning in his dreams, he'd allowed her to flourish.

She has become proud of her own practical nature, although from whom she inherited it is a mystery. Perhaps from her mother's family, about whom she knew little because they'd all died in a black fever epidemic at a Caspian Sea resort when she was very young. Surely not from the Rogachevas, her father's people, who valued nothing that failed to draw from them declarations of piety or patriotism and who eschewed a commonsensical approach to anything.

Now and then she finds in Sonia symptoms of the Rogacheva disease. She'd first noticed it a few years ago, when the girl was in convent school. There had been the scandal about the cross. Sonia refused to wear hers because the Church had betrayed and abandoned Jeanne d'Arc. The girl didn't think this protest against something that had happened five hundred years ago was unreasonable. That sort of whimsical idealism was characteristic of Sonia's grandfather, who spent a lifetime tilting at windmills until he died while fleeing the Bolsheviks, died because he fled too slowly, not wanting to appear as though he were fleeing. As Vera used to tell herself on the long march across Siberia toward her own practical freedom, "Poor Father died of anti-quated Rogacheva honor." Maybe she has given her daughter too much Russian as well as too much Chinese legend—filtered through a proud mother's imagination.

Sometimes in the garden, having temporarily exhausted her fund of stories about the General, she has told the eager girl about the old Russia of huge fireplaces and rolling lawns and handsome guardsmen. "Your grandfather was so noble in bearing that people seeing him ride down the street instinctively bowed. And your grandmother was a saint, a fearless one. In public she once corrected the Czar. They were discuss-ing a story by Gogol, and she told him he had the name of a character wrong. His Highness stared, and you could hear the swish of excited fans like wind through trees. That's how my aunt described it, and she was there. Your grandmother insisted that he was wrong, while ladies beat the air with their fans. Finally His Highness said, with a smile, 'You're right.'"

Perhaps such stories, every one of them tainted by heroic boldness, encouraged in Sonia a foolish pride, a dangerous desire to emulate the valorous characters of her mind, such as her father and Jeanne d'Arc.

And so, Vera thinks ruefully, I played a role in the girl's acquired passion for the contrary, the singular, the rebellious. Because Sonia *acquired* daring; it had not been part of her character as a child. In her early years she was solemn, watchful, timid, a little girl shuttled from one place to another. But here in Bangkok, settled, surrounded by shel-tering trees, Sonia learned from intemperate stories how to follow a path of defiance and risk.

How much risk? Is she rebelling against me or the norms of Bangkok society or against some hidden fantastic rule of her own devising? Wear-ing such clothes, walking with such an awful boy.

Vera orders a lemon squash, trying not to think of Sonia and that boy. Nothing wrong in a pleasant stroll on a lovely afternoon. Sonia can't go through life without meeting men. The idea is preposterous, looked at head on. Yet Vera realizes how deep her apprehension about Sonia has become. God knows, her own life has prepared her for such fears.

Not a day goes by without her recalling one detail or other about some man who made love to her. He might have been nothing more than a customer at the House of Madam Lotus or a man whose mistress she'd been for some time. What she recalls is often irrelevant—a tattoo, a limp, the cloying smell of hair oil—but sometimes her day is shaken by other images: brutalities and humiliations flashing before her eyes.

Vera notices that her fingers, curled around the glass of lemon squash, are trembling. She pulls her hand back into her lap and looks across the hotel lawn to the river and the opposite shore. The sun is beginning to set over the river boats and waterfront shacks. The river is narrow here, choppy in the winds that blow briskly across Bangkok in the cool season. Few people have yet taken tables, so Vera has the view to herself. Across the river now, the blood-red sun drops behind a rain tree. Vera sighs, filled with the joy of experiencing this simple thing, a sunset. Red roses are blooming in shallow troughs along the terrace's edge, and baby's breath is there, and spiky little palms. A motor barge chugs along the river, spewing oil upon a surface now blue, now pink.

This is one of Vera's favorite places in Bangkok; she's glad that Jim Thompson chose it for their meeting. Sipping the lemon squash, Vera smiles at an elderly couple in evening clothes. They don't smile back. The sun itself, vanishing behind the jumble of huts on the Thonburi side of the river, leaves in its wake a line of dusky pink. Vera smiles at them again anyway, and turns to the dusky pink, the color of weathered roses.

She notices the evening orchestra of gongs and xylophones is setting up to play on the lawn. But her attention quickly shifts to the sky. She watches intently how the fading light continues to diffuse, as if it too is water, poured sluggishly across the sky. And the river beneath it turns a yellowish gray, a shiny metallic hue, while southward a quarter-moon —she thinks of the Islamic scimitar her father had mounted on the wall of his study—hangs as if ready to drop with a clang on the iron surface of the water.

"To watch the moon washing its soul." That's what Shan-teh once said to her. It was through him she'd changed her attitude toward the moon. For years she'd hated the cold silvery light which had illuminated the faces of the dead on the wind-swept tundra of Siberia. The moon had meant death until Shan-teh brought her back to contemplation of its beauty, of its allusions to love. How he loved beauty: the severely classical paintings of Ni Tsan, the vigorous poetry of Lu Yu. And together they had sat in moonlight before the towering intricate Tai Hu stones of a Chinese garden. That memory is good, calming.

It's good to be alive, she tells herself. The fading day has eased her into a mood of receptive calm. More people are now being seated, foreigners on business or tour. She wonders if her own expression is similar to theirs: studiedly bored, withholding a world of experience that the years have bestowed and bestowed graciously, like a blessing.

She'd tried hard to convince Sonia that the little ivory cross could be worn without disloyalty to the Maid, but the girl had been adamant. Was this a measure of spiritual commitment, as one of Sonia's teachers —a timid Frenchwoman—had suggested? Vera doesn't believe so. The girl acted like a soldier defending a position, not like someone possessed by God. As for herself, Vera understands she has given little time to things of the spirit. Perhaps this is so because her belief has always been steady, unaltered, a low pulse beating in her heart, a given of daily life like eating and sleeping. Much of her life has been tumultuous—surely her young womanhood was—but her sense of God has never faltered.

Sonia as a child was told to believe in Christ, but in these Asian lands, without the sights and sounds that make the belief of a Christian easy and plausible, how difficult it must have been for her, how artificial it must have seemed, surrounded as she was by a plenitude of Chinese gods, by Siamese images of Buddha. Vera had hoped the convent school would be the solution, but the staff, mostly Siamese, recoiled from difficulties about doctrine, and the foreign teachers, succumbing to the languid pace of Siam, did little more than pray at assembly.

Have I ruined my child? But the question seems false. Indeed, Vera laughs at herself. She must pull in the reins or become a fool; that is clear. She's still attempting to find in her operatic fears the humor of exaggeration, when a waiter informs her that a messenger is waiting in the lobby.

When Vera reaches there—or rather beyond the entrance where the doorman has positioned the messenger—she finds Ah Ping, whose baggy eyes glitter from curiosity as they shift toward anything moving in or out of the hotel.

"Ah, Mistress, this came for you. I brought it here myself. Came as fast as I could."

Vera takes an envelope from the old Teochiu servant, whose white hair is neatly arranged in a bun and whose black pajamas are smartly creased. Ah Ping must have spent an hour primping for her arrival at the great hotel.

"Is my daughter home yet?"

"Miss not home yet."

Vera gives her money for the boat ride home, although Ah Ping has an allowance for such things. The old woman waits to see if she will open the envelope in front of her, but Vera sends her on. Back at the table on the hotel terrace, Vera still doesn't open it. The dusky pink in the sky has changed into a flat sheet of orange, a heavy, serious color suggesting the clash of something, of earth and atmosphere far away, and in this embattled light certain silhouettes appear on the river. Clutching the envelope—a sealed cable—Vera looks at them.

This must be from Philip. He's furious I won't come to India. Good, she thinks. Yet she feels sad, because this is surely the end of their relationship. The end is something she has not really contemplated. Not even during the war, when she failed to hear from him for long stretches of time. Somehow they are linked; Vera has always believed that. She holds the cable, letting her pulse slow, for she can feel it racing now, thumping in her chest.

Vera stares ahead at the shadowy figures on the river, at the boats and the rowers standing in their sterns. The air is cooler now; it releases the scent of flowers. Jasmine, roses. The river itself. The smells of evening are coming in. Carefully she opens the envelope.

The cable has been garbled, so it takes a while for her to make sense of the message. IF YOU CANTCON TO ME I WLL CON TO YOU STOP WLX WIRE XRRVAL FROM STOPSTOP OVERR BURA LOD PILLIP

It is like Sonia used to write English—and almost still does. Vera smiles. She feels happy. He is coming. If I won't come to him, then he'll come to me. What's he doing in Burma? And why, really, is he coming, when plainly I told him there was nothing between us to salvage? Or did I? she wonders. She can't sort out the feelings this unexpected response from him arouses in her. She won't sleep with him, if he does show up. That is certain. But her feelings are more complicated than the refusal to sleep with a man with whom, after all, she has not slept in a decade.

The truth is, she has need of him.

The revelation comes just as the sky turns darker, a bruised red now, the purplish red of a wound. The angry red of Sonia's broken thumb. The girl won't go abroad and study, she falls down somehow, and today she was strolling in a whorish dress with a boy who slouches. Perhaps Philip is really needed here. Sonia herself has expressed a desire to have him back. Those two always got along. Of course he'd never been a father, but a friend or perhaps an uncle. They talked easily together, as Vera recalls, and in a childlike way probably shared secrets. He may help, but she won't sleep with him.

Waiters are now lighting flares on poles along the edge of the terrace. Very soon now a descending blue depth will encircle the whole half of the world above Bangkok. Stars have joined the scimitar moon, and Vera sits back with a new lemon squash in one hand, the cable in the other, as if to protect it from harm, and she tries again to capture the magic of a sun setting. But of course the sunset is gone; it won't come back.

· · ·

Looking up from her glass of lemon squash, she recognizes Jim Thompson, balding and stout, coming across the terrace. He's wearing a seersucker outfit with tie; obviously he's been with important people. Vera is aware of his pleasure in being with important people. Jim's artlessness is something she likes about him.

Bending, he kisses her cheek, as she would expect an American businessman to do: really kisses, leaving a cool wetness on the skin.

"I have news," he says happily, and because he's bursting to tell it, Vera sits back to listen, glad to have him interrupt her obsessive thoughts. Jim tells her the silk project is "going ahead by leaps and bounds." It's a quaint idiom unknown to her, just the sort of extravagant phrase this young American would use. But what he has to say transcends boyishness. It really does look as if her money is safe. On schedule Jim and his Laotian assistant have introduced color-fast dyes into all the weaving shops of Bangkrua. Moreover, they're showing the Moslem workers how to use foot-operated shuttles. And Jim's financial adviser has obtained still more backing in recent days. That's the Californian.

California. She wonders if this Californian can help Sonia get into Stanford University.

"Believe me, your fifty shares are safer than the Bank of England," Jim boasts. "Within six months the Jim Thompson Silk Company will be more than a going concern."

"I'm glad of that." She wags a finger at him in mock threat. "I have a daughter to educate."

"Give me a few more years, you can educate a dozen daughters. I'll have a Scotch," he tells a waiter and sits back, thumbs hooked under his belt, a picture of self-contentment.

Good for him, she thinks.

"I'm getting together new designs for the block printing too." Lighting a cigarette, he looks directly at her. "Did she come?"

"Who?"

"That American woman. To your store. She was looking for antiques, so I sent her along."

Vera laughs. "Oh, yes, the American woman. She did come. First she wanted to see Ban Go Noi pottery from Si Satchanalai—but only perfect pieces. I thought that was interesting. Where did she think I was going to get fourteenth-century pieces like that? I'd give my right arm —isn't that what you say?—for a piece of perfect celadon from that period. Of course I could let her have fragments of Ban Go Noi from a later time. Costly, but I have them. I have three, ranging from dark green to light green. But when I said I had them, she waved her hand. She wasn't interested. And then I knew what she was."

"What was she?" Jim Thompson asks amiably, puffing his cigarette.

"Someone who goes around picking up a fact here, a fact there, and what's learned in one shop she recites in the next."

"Selling isn't easy."

"Then she changed to Burmese bronzes. She wanted to see only Burmese bronzes. I must tell you, Jim, she was difficult. I got rid of her only by explaining that you can distinguish many styles simply by looking at the eyebrows of the Buddhas. Whether the eyebrows are separate or meet and how they meet. I went through Chieng Saen, Lopburi, Sukhothai before she had facts enough to take away. Then she left."

"I'm sorry I put her onto you."

"Please don't be."

"When our project takes hold, Vera, I'll be your best client. That's the truth. I love art. I respect your judgment. You'll definitely have me as a client."

His enthusiasm and confidence prompt her to equal boldness. "But for sending the American woman, you can—how is it said?—make amends, if you wish."

"Tell me."

"Ask your friend in California if he knows important personages at Stanford University. For my daughter, you see."

"You're sending her to the States?"

"I want to."

Jim Thompson thumps the table. "Done. I'll write George."

"I worry about my daughter," she continues impulsively. "I worry about her on the streets of Bangkok. The rumors of violence—"

"Well, I think those rumors exaggerate the situation. Nothing's happened yet. The Communists hand out leaflets. The government threatens. Frankly, I think the Siamese are too satisfied with their way of life to jeopardize it."

"You're an optimist, Jim Thompson. You've never seen the world around you go to ruin."

"Yes, that's true. But I think I know the Siamese."

"Do you know the Chinese and their gangs? I worry about my daughter. Today I saw her walking in the weekend market with a young man. He seemed to be Chinese, but I don't know what he was or who."

"How old is your daughter?"

"Nineteen."

Jim Thompson smiles. It's a condescending smile. "Well, I think she's old enough to take care of herself. Don't you? Especially in a city like Bangkok? I'd worry more in New York or Paris."

Vera doesn't respond. Will no one understand a fear that carries with it a feeling of premonition?

"By the way—" Jim Thompson begins.

He wants to change the subject, she thinks.

"What ever happened to the statue you found in Chiang Mai?" He lights a cigarette from one already half smoked.

"It's not from the Lan Na period. It's a fake. Clever enough, according to Professor Yupho, but definitely a recent piece. I'll sell it for the imitation it is."

"You don't cheat, Vera." Jim Thompson nods emphatically to his own statement. "It's a pleasure to do business with you." Shoving his chair back, he prepares to rise. "Can I get you a samlor or a boat?"

"No, I'll sit awhile." She wants to delay going home. Not that she expects a confrontation—in fact, she won't even mention today to Sonia. Definitely she won't. But it's pleasant here on the terrace with torches illuminating the river.

"So I'll bid you good night," Jim says. "I've enjoyed it, Vera, as I always do." This is his American attempt at formality. Still, she likes him enormously, even though he has no understanding of a mother's fear.

As he turns away, Jim Thompson looks back over his shoulder. "By the way, have you heard from your husband?"

"Yes. He's coming to Bangkok, I think."

"You think?"

"It's hard to tell what Philip will do. What do you want him for, Jim?" she asks in a bold moment. "One of your secret American missions?"

He laughs, but moves away a few steps, thinking before he replies. "Anyway, I'd very much like to meet him when he does get here."

Vera thumps the table, imitating him. "Done!"

She watches the heavy-set man climb the terrace steps. He's one of the lucky ones, she thinks. Events haven't taught him too much caution. He's all expansiveness, and by this trait he'll succeed. She is sure of it now. In spite of his tendency to find the best in people. Does he honestly think that she's always scrupulous in her business dealings? That if given the chance, she won't tell a rich and stupid collector something is "really very old" when it isn't? Dear optimistic Jim. Yet she can't forgive his easy dismissal of her fear. Is her anxiety worse because Wanna was there today, enjoying her confusion?

Mai pen rai. What matters is the safety of her child.

Something hovers at the edge of her consciousness, then moves forward. It's the memory of an old dream. She'd had it two or three times during her pregnancy. In this dream Shan-teh told her of his own dream in which she carried his child; then her dream shifted to the infant in her arms, and shifted once again to her holding this child toward Shan-teh, as he approached, smiling. She had needed Shan-teh then, desperately. But he wasn't the man to accept back someone who'd betrayed him as she had done. So she'd needed him in vain.

Again she needs him, almost as desperately. They have a child, a daughter she'd have held out to him had she been able. Sonia is their mutual dream. It comes to her with the force of despair that she needs Shan-teh's advice.

19 I CAN NEVER go back to a dull life now, Sanuk tells herself. She's walking with Chamlong near the verge of the Pramane Grounds market, a jungle of cartons and tent poles. She feels as if in the last few weeks a great distance has been put between herself and the daily world. None of these people swarming through the market can ever know her now. Looking down at the prominent splint on her broken thumb, she has a quick, bad vision of the man on the beach, his head slick from cascades of water, choking in the moonlight.

She notices a couple of youngsters studying her red cheongsam. It's tight, of course, but Chamlong likes her to dress this way, especially for a meeting, when the other men look up from their tea and study her more thoughtfully than these boys do, with their stupid grins and whispering. Earlier, on the street, a boy had yelled at her, "I like double-jointed women! They're the best! Are you double-jointed?" and might have continued to bray and bully her if Chamlong hadn't come out of a shop, bringing her a snack of roasted cashews.

As he now turns away from the market, Sanuk glances shyly at him: his small ears, sharp nose, prominent chin—the pared-down look which seems more powerful to her each day. Through him she's learned about love and death.

He's so different from the young guardsmen who courted Mother in her Russian girlhood. Mother has described them so often that Sanuk can almost see them in their regimental uniforms. "They were so handsome, Sonia, with their blue eyes and curly hair. At the balls they wore knee-high leather boots and red demikaftans and gold shoulder straps and their coats of arms were braided on their sleeves and curved sabers clattered at their sides, and when they lifted you into a carriage they doffed their lambskin kolpaks and smiled at you with the snow falling round their long pale faces." It has always sounded to Sanuk like a Siamese romance without the dragons.

Now she is living in the real world—with Chamlong, who has been accepted because of his famous cousin, the journalist from Canton, into the inner circle of the Siamese Communist Party. She has gone to their teahouse meetings in Chamlong's company. Nothing could be more exciting than the talk of young revolutionaries plotting the course of freedom.

Only yesterday they discussed the late King's death. Ananda Mahidon was found shot to death in his bed on June 9, 1946. It was a fateful day for Siam, and yesterday, in the teahouse, Sanuk felt for the first time what an impact one event can have on the destiny of a nation. When the King was discovered sprawled on the royal bed with a pistol near his left hand, three explanations for the tragedy made the rounds: His death could be the result of suicide, accident, or murder. (At the time, in Sanuk's last year of convent school, girls had worn long somber faces for one day and then the next had been back to giggling—Sanuk had been no different.) Yesterday, in the teahouse, she leaned forward to hear each of the theories discussed. At the time of the King's death, suicide had been quickly ruled out; the Buddhist Siamese considered it a spiritual impossibility for a king of the Rama line to commit such a sin. Accidental death—the King, known to like guns, might have been playing with the pistol—had been a logical explanation, but not satisfying to a nation in mourning. Murder was therefore the explanation most likely to take hold. This was especially true when the government failed to provide an alternative explanation for why a King of Siam, such a young man and only recently returned from school in Switzerland, should be found with a bullet in his head in his own bedroom. Who could have killed the King? (Sanuk can't remember any such question arising at school.)

Yesterday, seated at a round table in the back of a smoky teahouse, the young Communists debated the question with the fervor of just having heard the news. Someone claimed a prince had killed his brother to gain the throne. But the majority, including Chamlong, saw the murder as the result of a conspiracy engineered by Field Marshal Phibun. They reasoned that Phibun, in disgrace for collaborating with the Japanese during the war, wanted to discredit his political rival, Prime Minister Pridi. What better way than killing the most sacred person in the land and putting the Prime Minister—by Siamese tradition completely responsible for the King's well-being—at the very least under profound criticism and at the worst under suspicion? And that's what happened, according to these passionate young men, smoking cigarettes and drinking tea together: Public opinion ousted Pridi from office and put Field Marshal Phibun's party in control.

For Sanuk it's like the good and evil of *The Ramakien:* The good man is Pridi, the embodiment of heroic Rama; the evil man is Phibun, the avatar of evil Taksakan. The good man is good to the Chinese. The evil man is bad to them. That's it—the stark moral drama of a great epic. In Sanuk's eyes these young men are warriors in the camp of Pridi-Rama. Warriors gathering in teahouses to plot the course of a new world.

• • •

It's to one of those meetings that Chamlong is taking her now. "We're going to a tea shop near Wat Khemasiri," he tells her. "We'll have to take a boat, but I haven't any money."

"You spent the last of it on my cashews," she reminds him. "I'll pay."

"That's the third time you've had to pay." His tone is not apologetic but factual. "But in the new world, men and women will share equally. That's in a leaflet Wan-li is writing."

"Who'll be there today?"

"Chin Yin-nan."

She says nothing. Sanuk hasn't seen him since that day of days, when she first went to a hotel with Chamlong. He'd criticized Chamlong to make him seem a fool. Everyone who knows Chin says he'll become an important leader in the Party someday.

"What happened," Chamlong says abruptly, "I lost a bet at the Friendship Society on a soccer match. Took everything I had, which wasn't much. If I had given him one less point, I'd have won, though. It was a good bet."

"Don't worry about the money," Sanuk tells him, wanting to touch his hand. "Whatever I can do, I will do," she says. "Never forget that."

With a nod Chamlong lifts his head and searches the klong they're coming to for a sampan.

• • •

Wan-li is powerfully built but much shorter than his cousin Chamlong. He dips his head in welcome when Sanuk and his cousin approach the tea shop table.

Chin Yin-nan, seated next to him, does not acknowledge them at all.

"Sit down, please." Wan-li speaks Teochiu with a strong Cantonese accent.

Sanuk feels his eyes intimately on her when she pulls up a chair in the little room. She feels his look as if it were a hand on her thigh.

"You're late," Chin finally says to Chamlong. To Sanuk he says, "Remember me?"

"You're the sign of the Horse."

"What's this?" Wan-li smiles at her.

"The Siamese say people born in that sign have a bad temper." She turns directly to Chin. "Won't admit their weaknesses. Aim higher than they can reach. And they aren't interested in love."

Wan-li cackles.

She doesn't like Wan-li. In part it's because he looks unappealing. His face is square, his hair spiky—a mad halo around his head. Moreover, he has a habit of flicking his tongue against his lower lip, keeping it perpetually wet. On the other hand, he obviously likes her. This attraction accounts for her being allowed into these meetings. Wan-li is becoming known by the dissidents of Bangkok. He writes leaflets for Mahachon, the underground Communist press.

"I've ordered a little food," he says to her. "Do you like salted fish and rice?" he asks solicitously.

It excites her to know that this man, whom the others so admire, is anxious for a smile from her. "Very much," she tells him, glancing at Chamlong to see if he notices. He seems oblivious to his cousin's interest in her, although when men look at her on the street he's proudly alert to their interest, aggressively protective too. Now, however, he seems oblivious to her, although at the crowded table her thigh moves warmly against his. He wants men to covet her, yet at times he seems indifferent to what it is about her that appeals to them. Sanuk withdraws into herself with this mystery, thinking about it.

"So far we've held off the government," Chin is saying. There are altogether eight people at the table, leaning toward its center. "That's because we stopped the troublemakers"—he looks directly at Chamlong —"from making trouble." He goes on to say the Siamese gangs are furious because of the quiet acceptance of anti-Chinese posters in Chinatown. There hasn't been a single incident, and the police are baffled, for they too had hoped for a show of violence, allowing them to rush with force into the area. "What I'm saying is this: They're frustrated. They won't wait much longer. We can expect an attack soon."

"Do you know this for certain?" Wan-li asks.

"I know nothing for certain. I only know it makes sense. The government has to act against the Chinese."

"No. The government can show patience. It's something the Siamese admire. Isn't that true?"

"Phibun will *demand* action," Chin maintains. "If the cabinet won't act against the Chinese, he'll call them incompetent. He'll throw them out and take charge of the government."

"That doesn't make sense."

"Why doesn't it?"

"Because he's already got what he wants. He brought the anti-Chinese posters into Chinatown and they weren't ripped down. He proved to the Siamese he has enough power to handle us. What more does he want? Phibun has won."

Chin shakes his head. "Phibun has not won yet. What he wants is total victory, and he'll have it if we make the wrong move."

"And what's that?"

"To react violently. That's his aim—to get the Chinese to do something violent. Then he'll have an excuse for martial law. His troops will overrun Chinatown. If we fight now, he'll break us."

"I don't agree. He'll break us if we don't fight. Phibun doesn't want violence. All he wants is submission," Wan-li argues. "We should not give in. We should have rallies. We should stir up unrest in the unions. We should let Phibun know the Chinese won't sit back and let his government do what it pleases to them. My pamphlets will help." Wan-li looks proudly around the table. "We can distribute them everywhere, not only in Chinatown. We must show Bangkok that the Communist Party is strong." Wan-li glances at Sanuk, flicks his tongue over his lips. "We Chinese must stand up to the government."

Chin laughs scornfully. "You talk like you write, and that's dangerous. Put those ideas in a pamphlet, and that's fine, but don't try to live by them here. You don't understand the politics of Bangkok. Phibun doesn't care about the Chinese or about the Communists either. What he cares about is having complete control of the government. The Chinese, especially the Chinese Communists, are a means to that end. And if the Chinese don't give him an excuse to use the army, Phibun will make his own excuse. If the government can't stir up trouble in Chinatown, he'll say they're easy on the Chinese. If the government succeeds in stirring up trouble, he'll say bring in the army—of course, with him at the head of it."

"You're saying Phibun's political future lies here in Chinatown?" Wan-li looks skeptical.

"That's what I'm saying. If you listen, you'll understand it." No one but Chin speaks to the journalist from Canton with such impertinence. "He must convince his own people that they need a strong leader like himself to control us. And this is the point he'll make: Proof of the treasonable attitude of the Chinese population in Bangkok is their support of Communists. That's it. He'll take over control of the government to suppress the Communists who threaten it." Chin looks around triumphantly. It has been a studied, brilliant speech.

After staring into his teacup, Wan-li glances sideways at Chin. "What about the Party then, its future?"

"That's what I'm saying. Right now it's uncertain. Living in Canton hasn't prepared you for life in Siam. Here you can't appeal to Chinese tradition, much less use ideas coming from Europe. Here you must be subtle. Here everything is patience—or you're dead. You can't go around shouting and waving your hands. Not if you're Chinese. You can't tell the Siamese to believe in Marxism because you, a Chinese, believe in it. The Party must be cautious."

Wan-li, cowed by the trenchant argument, looks down at his hands, then glances quickly at Sanuk.

In his moment of defeat she gives him a smile. Rice and salted fish come, set down heavily by a waiter. Everyone leans forward to the steaming bowls. "It's cheap food," Wan-li says to her. "But it's all we can afford."

What she won't touch at home Sanuk now devours. She is happy here among men bent over their simple food, linked together by danger and purpose. This is the world of her father, this is life. Avoiding Wan-li's eye, she smiles often at her lover, who hardly seems to notice.

• • •

She's in her room, furious, having left Chamlong in the street yelling at her to go home.

After the meeting, they walked a long time while he expressed his ideas about the meeting. His cousin Wan-li was right, Chin was wrong. Wan-li, coming from the mainland, was bringing the confidence of real China to Bangkok, but Chin represented the weakness of Southeast Asian Chinese, who won't fight for their freedom. Here in Bangkok the Party must stand up for the People; the People must stand against Phibun and the government. Isn't that clear? None of this patience, none of this waiting, none of this cowardice. And then in mid-sentence he asked her to go to a hotel. Had that been on his mind all the time instead of politics? Sanuk wondered as she refused.

It's hard in retrospect for her to understand why she refused. Maybe desire wasn't there for the first time since they'd become lovers. Maybe Wan-li's continual staring in the tea shop made her self-conscious about her body. Maybe she felt tired. Had she felt tired? And it was late in the afternoon. Since returning from the South, she's been careful not to stay out too long, especially since Mother has become apprehensive lately about violence in Bangkok. In a Chinatown alley, she and Chamlong argued about the hotel. They didn't care if people noticed them, they were arguing so intently. And then Chamlong accused her of being childish, and when in turn she accused him of being selfish, he accused her next of having *pak talad*, the mouth of a market woman. It was very unpleasant, and has left Sanuk in a bitter mood.

Unlocking the sandalwood box on top of her dresser, she takes out her current diary and opens it. Lately, not only has she been writing more, she's been spelling the English correctly. Now, when she writes, a dictionary is by her side. Of course she can't tell Mother about this odd change in her habits. Mother would want to know why, and she can't say, "I want to spell correctly because what I'm writing now is important. I'm a woman now like you. I have my own lover, and what I see and do and feel deserves something better than the sloppy treatment of a schoolgirl."

Opening the diary, she begins to write, with the aid of her dictionary, under *Sunday:*

> I dreamt last night I bought a new pair of shoes. Nipa said at breakfast that means I will be traveling soon. Both servants are still angry because I got them in trouble about my thumb. They say it wasn't their fault for not knowing it was broken. And they're curious about how it got broken. Worse than Mother. If only all of them really knew how it got broken. What would they think? What do I think? Sometimes what happened is beyond my understanding. Sometimes I am sure it never happened at all, but then I look at him and want to cry. But I won't because he would hate that and so would I.

Sanuk looks up the word "comprehension"; then, scratching out "understanding," she replaces it with the fancier word.

We had our first important fight. He wanted me to go with him somewhere, but I said no. And it wasn't the wrong time of the month, either. I just didn't feel like it. I don't like his cousin, who is always looking at me. It is strange how one man can look at you, like Chamlong does, and it's nice, but another man can't. And yet I don't understand Chamlong. Does he love me? Around his friends he ignores me. Well, that is comprehensible. Men are all like that, except Wan-li who doesn't seem to care if his interest is obvious—and except Chamlong who doesn't seem to care either if Wan-li is interested. Confusing. Saw Lamai yesterday. Soon she'll be married. They say it is better to be a Siamese wife than a Chinese wife, at least after the first child. In either case, the first wife manages the household. Is she happy? I have not met her boy yet, but Lamai swears she likes him. I don't know. I couldn't marry someone like Wan-li, even though everyone admires him. I suspect I won't like many men in my life.

Today I thought about great women of history. I hereby list them in order of importance: Jeanne d'Arc, Eleanor of Aquitaine, Elizabeth of England, the Rani of Jhansi, and someone new I have discovered, Yu Hsuan-chi. I have discovered her while trying to read some Chinese poetry. (That is my passion these days, doing better in Chinese, and I admit Mother was right long ago when she said I must practice each day memorizing characters.) This Yu Hsuan-chi was a woman of the Tang Dynasty (and I believe, though Mother won't answer me, Father could have traced his ancestry all the way back to Tang emperors, one thousand years ago). She was a courtesan who died before thirty. She was a poet too, and some of her poetry is in a book. Because I can't understand the characters well enough, I had a man in Yommarat Market translate a poem into English for me. He's that old Mandarin who speaks many languages. He wrote it out for me, and the part I like best is: "Lovers should learn from the river how to flow. I know we won't meet again in the season of flowers." I have changed his version, because he leaves out English articles and plurals and I am careful of them now. It makes me sad to think of Yu Hsuan-chi, alone in the world, parted from her lover. I thought of Chamlong. If we are ever separated, will I feel the same as Yu Hsuan-chi did? I hope so. It would be terrible not to feel anything.

It has taken Sanuk a long time to complete this entry, considering she has stopped every third or fourth word to verify the spelling. But finished, she is proud of the result. As an old woman, she'll read about herself as a young woman in love.

Soon Mother will come home, and Ah Ping will shout up that dinner's ready. Yet as she puts the diary back into the sandalwood box, Sanuk withdraws it again. There is more to write, more. Without something else in the diary, it will be a false record. To get it down fast, Sanuk pushes aside the dictionary.

> There is reason to beleive the man was harmless. [Pausing, she decides to hide the truth, in case someone ever peeks at the diary.] I am talking about man I will write story about. That man and two people who kill him. It will be murder mistery. So this man, why was he harmless? Because after they killed them, they found no wepon, not even knive on his body. Why would he attack them on lonly beech at night unarmed? He was big but not that big. They must have made mistacke. You might argue he had overtakken them on the beech. But maybe he just walked faster than they did. You see there is no reason to think of him thretening them. And idea of him being a govenment agent, that is no good either. Govenment agent would not try to overtakke them all alone. He would have help. He would be armed. No, he was not govenment agent. He was just big man walking on

There's a sharp knock at the door. Quickly she closes the diary and returns it to the sandalwood cabinet, just as the door opens and Mother walks in.

"You're in pajamas? No cheongsam?"

Sanuk is startled by her mother's aggressive tone of voice.

"That's a lot different than a cheongsam slit up to *here*— Each time I see you in a cheongsam, it's slit higher on the leg."

"It's the style, Mother. This is 1948." Trying to smile, Sanuk regards the woman in the doorway, who stands braced against it with both hands, one holding a cigarette. At first she wonders if her mother's been drinking. The tone, the stance, the absence of civility, the sullen look of confusion suggest it.

"Where did you go today?" Sanuk asks casually. "Did you see Mister Thompson?"

"Where did I go today? Where did *you* go today is more to the point," Mother says, walking into the room. Instead of sitting down, she begins pacing. "I can remember so many things." Puffing on the cigarette, she turns to stare at Sanuk. "I mean, when you were young. Things we did together." Pacing again, she talks to the air. "You were never trouble. Did I ever tell you that? Never. You were beautiful and joyous and I thanked God. I'll never forget the day I was coming down the path and saw you alone in the garden, so beautiful and joyous—I called out without thinking, 'Sanuk!' Remember?"

Sanuk leans forward in the desk chair, grasping her hands together. "You never call me that any more."

Her mother doesn't seem to hear. She's pacing again, smoking.

Sanuk grips her hands tighter around the bandaged thumb.

"I exaggerate, of course. I'm making a fool of myself. I never meant to come in here, but look at me. I've come upstairs and walked right in. Maybe it doesn't look like it, darling, but I'm trying hard not to make a stupid scene, even though it seems I will. In our family, when I was a child, no matter what happened there were no stupid scenes. It's called aristocratic restraint. Stupid mistakes, stupid lies, stupid attitudes, but no stupid scenes. What I'm trying to say is, I don't want this to be stupid. But the truth is—" Mother halts to look at her. "The truth really is, Sonia, I expected too much of you. I never thought we'd grow apart." Again she starts pacing. "Today I saw this girl at the weekend market. She was wearing something outrageous. Look at her, poor thing, I thought. Certain she's lovely in the dress of a whore. And with that boy. Just a boy, any boy. The two of them pitiable really. I wouldn't have laughed at them although some people might have, but I wouldn't have cried either, figuring it was their business how they looked and what they were, and yet crying's what I wanted to do when I saw the girl was you. Do you understand? Do I make sense? It's not that you were with a boy. It's that you never told me. It's the deception, it's the lack of trust."

Sanuk, gripping her hands tightly, stares at the floor. So it's happened. Recently at odd times of the day—washing her hair, reading Chinese, writing in her diary—she has envisioned it happening, a bad event overtaking her in partial payment for that night on the Songkhla beach, when she and Chamlong strangled an innocent man.

She's looking hard at the floor, like someone staring at a wall in preparation for being lashed by a whip. And then into the circle of her vision comes a face—her mother has bent down, knelt in front of her. There's something so physically unexpected about this action, something like a plea or cry for help, that Sanuk feels abruptly frightened. By preparing for this inevitable scene through the imagining of it, Sanuk has negated its actual effect until now. And Mother knows it. Their faces are a hand's-breadth apart.

"Sanuk," Mother whispers gently. "Do you understand? Can you understand me?"

"I understand."

"What I understand too is you don't want to hurt me."

"No, I don't want that." Her mother's green eyes seem to bore into her, seeking her heart. Sanuk tightens her hands. "I just want to live my life."

"This boy, who is he?"

"He's not a student."

"I didn't think he was. He didn't have the look of a student. Does he row a sampan? No, he's not that powerful. Does he sell vegetables? Is he a wok cook on the street?"

"Don't."

"Don't? You think I'm unreasonable?" On her feet, Mother's pacing again. The cigarette is hardly more than a stub in her fingers. The back of her blouse is drenched with sweat. "Well, am I? Just seeing you with a boy wouldn't have brought all this on. Don't you understand? I'd have been a little annoyed, but not . . . bewildered, crushed, the way I'm feeling now." She turns in her pacing to Sanuk. "Don't you know, darling, the servants will protect their jobs before they'll protect you? I just talked to them. When I was in Chiang Mai, you were gone for three days—maybe longer, because I'm sure they don't tell me the whole truth. *You were with this boy.*"

She has no choice, wants none. The full force of what is happening is what Sanuk wants. "Yes, I was."

"You were with him. You slept with him."

"I'm a woman now."

"Oh, are you. Then bring him here so I can meet him."

"He won't come."

"Why?"

"He just won't come." She's never asked Chamlong if he would, yet she knows him well enough to answer for him: Chamlong will never set foot in this farang house and justify himself to a farang woman.

"Sonia, if he won't meet me, I want you to stop seeing him. Otherwise our lives are senseless. Can you see that? A worthwhile man wouldn't be afraid of me. He'd face me for your sake. If this boy fails to come into my house, he can't see my daughter. Is that unfair?"

"Yes."

"All right, it's unfair. You won't go out of this house alone, you won't leave it without me. Not until this is straightened out between us. You're my daughter. This may be 1948 and you're nineteen years old, but I have more power than you can imagine." Her mother sits down on the bed, bending forward and clasping her hands as if to hold on.

Leaning back, Sanuk realizes where her own habit comes from—they hold on the same way, they clasp hands.

"What do you do, Sonia? I mean, to take care of yourself?"

Sanuk thinks she understands, but it's been a long time since her mother talked about "nature," as they'd called it during those two or three after-dinner clinical discussions of sex—sitting far apart from each other on the veranda with their faces mercifully hidden by the Bangkok darkness.

"So you won't get pregnant," Mother adds coldly.

"I count."

"You *count*." The tone is heavily sarcastic. "Where did you learn to *count*? From your classmates?"

"You're making fun of me." Sanuk almost adds: "It's what you should have explained to me yourself." Instead she says, "We all understood the rhythm method."

"Such knowledgeable girls."

"Well, you asked."

"Let me ask this, too. What do you tell him if the time's not right? Do you say, 'please' or 'I can't' or 'maybe next week'?"

Sanuk grips her own hands hard.

"Tell me what you say," Mother insists.

"It hasn't happened yet."

"But it will. And what will you say? Will he pay attention? Will you?" Mother adds hoarsely, "Don't you think I've ever faced such things myself? Don't you think I know anything?"

Sanuk won't look up from her clasped hands. Won't.

After a long silence, Mother says, "All right, I'm calm now, I won't be foolish. I won't make a stupid scene." White knuckles. Eyes intense. "I'm going to tell you a story, young woman. And it's a *true* story."

Sanuk listens. The story her mother tells is simple enough, uncomplicated and believable after Sanuk accepts the premise that everything her mother told her about the old days in Shanghai was a lie. When Mother got there from Siberia, she didn't sell fruit on a street corner to survive. She didn't have money to buy fruit to sell; and anyway, Chinese vendors would have laughed a penniless refugee off the street. She never went to language school and learned to translate Russian into Chinese for a living. She would live for years in Shanghai before knowing Chinese fluently. To survive she worked in a pleasure house, as did many Russian women pretty enough and young enough to get the chance in those days. She learned how to abort herself with chopsticks. She didn't have the luxury of sitting out the "dangerous days" of her menstrual cycle. The pleasure house was her world, like it or not. And later, when fortune smiled on her, she became the mistress of a man who took her out of there and kept her until, tired of her, he introduced her to another man. And in this manner she lived until she met General Tang Shan-teh, who, contrary to the story told to a little girl, never married her—not even an unconventional Chinese general would have dared marry a foreign woman—but who nevertheless kept and loved her. Loved her. That was true. That was part of the true story. He loved her.

At this point Sanuk interrupts, sharply. "Did he know?"

"That I was a whore? When we met he knew I was another man's mistress. I suspect he must have guessed what I'd been earlier, but he never asked me. He never brought that between us."

"This is the truth?"

"It is. At last."

They sit through a long silence. "Why didn't you tell me before?" Sanuk asks softly.

"I never expected to tell you at all."

"I'm glad to know."

Mother shakes her head, unclasping her hands. "You are glad to know I've been a whore in a foreign land. But I began life in Old Russia. I knew royalty, I lived in the civilized world. That's the part of my life I wish you were glad to know. But you aren't. I've failed."

"I'm glad to know all of it, everything."

"You say that now, but when you've thought about it, you'll change your mind. Do you have any idea why I've told you something so painful to me?" Mother rises, face haggard, lips trembling from exhaustion. "I know men. I know what they do. What I did I had to do, but you have a choice. My God, child, make the right one! Don't let a foolish boy ruin your life."

Sanuk rises too, expecting an embrace, but Mother has turned away and walked, staggered from the room. For a moment Sanuk thinks of running after her and saying, "I'm glad you told me, I'm glad!" But something holds her back. Sanuk sits at the desk and gazes around the room of her childhood: at the batik prints, the Siamese dolls in their glittering rhinestones, the shelves holding her schoolbooks. It all looks smaller, as if viewed from a distance. Reaching forward, she pulls the diary out again. She writes one sentence.

> I will not give up Chamlong any more than Mother would have given
> up my father.

She's tempted to write more. There's Mother's story to tell. Is there? After holding the pen above the diary a few moments, she puts it down. That is Mother's story, not hers. To write down Mother's secrets would be a betrayal. Mother's secrets. Sanuk tries to imagine what must have happened to her mother more than twenty years ago: men tramping up a stairway much like those in the shabby hotels she has gone to with Chamlong. She can imagine their faces as they came toward her mother: Wan-li's face, all of them.

Once again she picks the pen up.

> I am changing order of my list. Next to Maid I put Yu Hsuan-chi,
> the prostutute. And my faverite line of all poetry is hers: "I know we
> won't meet again in the season of flowers."

From the stairway below comes the high whining sound of Ah Ping calling her to dinner.

Sanuk is amazed to realize that life will go on, much like before, that she will sit at the table with Mother, just as usual, and eat and perhaps even talk. What will they say? Harmless things, surely. For it is true that at heart Mother is an aristocrat from Old Russia. It's called aristocratic restraint. Sanuk will ask Mother again, "What did you do today?" And she will ask Mother, "Is it true Mahatma Gandhi died?" She will ask questions and receive decorous replies.

20

KEMP'S RIGHT ABOUT this place. Embree is looking across the vast Allied Cemetery outside the little town of Thanbyuzayat: The hedges and lawns are tidy.

In these graves lie thousands of prisoners who died while building a railroad for the Japanese. Other thousands lie at the other end of the track in Thailand, 250 miles away. In a Madras newspaper Embree once read that each mile of track cost the lives of 400 men, including native laborers. He looks now at the headstones—six of which he must locate—neatly laid out in rows as straight as a plumb line.

He can remember having known only three of the half-dozen young Koylies listed at the bottom of Mrs. Stubbs's letter. He can recall only one face, that of a pale young man with big ears and a perpetually runny nose: Arthur Wiggs. Wiggs had been captured during the retreat—if Embree remembers correctly, around Nyaungu—when a Koylie unit got caught in a fire fight. God only knew what his condition had been by the time the Japs trucked him here to work on the railroad. Arthur Wiggs, a haggard kid with a bad cold. He'd joined the other prisoners from both Malaya and Burma—a mélange of sick, weary, half-starved young men who proceeded to work with axes, shovels, even elephants, at the task of felling trees and clearing debris from the slowly extending track of iron rails and wooden sleepers, and whose headstones, skillfully carved, here attest to their fate at such labor.

Like them, young Arthur Wiggs must have unloaded countless wicker baskets of earth onto the train embankments, doing it on starvation rations, in spite of fever, dysentery, and abuse. Maybe he contracted typhus or died in one of the cholera epidemics. Maybe he was beaten to death by a guard or simply wandered off into the brush and gave up quietly one afternoon. How is such a fate determined? Embree asks the sultry Burmese air. He studies the immaculate rows within the green lawn.

Embree had heard rumors about the death camps before actually seeing the survivors, who were trucked into Rangoon one day in early June 1945. He was there with the victorious Allied army, under General Slim. The Allies—British, Indian, and Chinese forces supported by American air power—had swept down from Mandalay in time to beat the monsoon rains to Rangoon. The Japs were putting up isolated resistance, but the war was won. It was won, and men like Embree were waiting for transportation out of Rangoon. Throughout the hot, muggy tropical city, Missouri mules were hauling pack howitzers; Sherman tanks rumbled along the boulevards with platoons clinging to gun and turret; drunken soldiers from the Fourth and 33rd Corps elbowed natives off the sidewalks; village girls on the covered passageways to the Shwedagon Pagoda negotiated to exchange themselves for cartons of Lucky Strikes; Buddhist priests solicited funds for their temples outside the Strand Hotel; and All India Radio, now beamed into Burma, hourly announced more Allied victories throughout Asia. And above the tumult the sky was filled with B-25s and P-51 Mustangs buzzing the rooftops in farewell before leaving for other bases.

It was in the midst of so much noise and commotion that the trucks sputtered into Rangoon with the pitiful survivors of the Japanese prison camps. Embree stood there silently with other soldiers and watched them disembark—those who could walk, those who had to be carried. Their stench filled the street. Their sunken eyes had a dead, oily look; bystanders backed away.

Arthur Wiggs had been with such men.

Standing in the immaculate graveyard Philip Embree tries to understand that. How strange it must have been for a coal-mining lad from Yorkshire. There must have been many odd visions shored up in that innocent head before they leaked out of Arthur Wiggs along with his life's blood. There must have been for Arthur Wiggs a wooden trestle over a shallow gorge somewhere and a river twisting blue in its sandy channel, just like Burmese rivers Embree had seen, and prisoners no older or experienced than Arthur Wiggs must have chopped a railbed out of rock and putrescent vegetation and then slept on rattan in bamboo sheds, listening to the termites eat their way through the wood. Yes. That might have been one of the kid's experiences, unlike any he'd have known in the mines of Yorkshire.

That day in 1945, watching the unloading of trucks in Rangoon, Embree had overheard a survivor speak of it in a way Arthur Wiggs might have done too, had he lived: "Termites in the bamboo," the man had muttered dreamily. He repeated it again, again, again, while a medic jammed a hypo into his arm. "Termites, they made noise in the bamboo. You could hear them all night, like a bloody band. Chewing it. Termites making a bloody racket in the bamboo. That's what they did. They made noise in the bamboo."

Now, with the cemetery in sight, Embree concentrates on that. It's his duty, it's what Mrs. Stubbs and those other women mean for him to do. He has to think of exhausted men like Arthur Wiggs lying awake in the darkness, listening to the ghostly avaricious sound of termites in the bamboo, the ticking, ticking, ticking all night next to their sunburnt ears—

"Here, Master."

It is Rama, carrying an armful of flowers he'd been sent to buy in town.

Sighing, Embree tells him, "All right, let's get on with it."

Half an hour later, they have located three of the six graves and placed a bouquet on each.

"There are men under these rocks, Master?" Rama asks, staring down at one of the headstones with the inscription:

V. W. WILSON
THE ROYAL NORTHUMBERLAND FUSILIERS
27th May 1943 Age 25
A Voice We Love Is Still
A Place Is Vacant Which We Can Never Fill

Embree turns to the young Tamil. Men under the rocks? What a question. And then it strikes Embree that it is, for Rama, quite sensible to ask. As a Hindu, he's probably never seen a grown man buried. Children when they die are buried or put gently in a stream; holy men are stood upright, wedged between mountain rocks. Otherwise the Hindu dead are cremated. "Yes, Rama, there are men under the rocks."

"Narayana."

"I suspect you think it's rather untidy," Embree says with a faint smile.

"Burning cleanses the soul. Prepares it for next time." Rama kneels beside a headstone. It's a simple concrete block with a brass plaque set into it, bearing a regimental crest and a carved message:

Happy Memories, Ray Dear,
Till We Meet Again.
Momma, Dad, Ken, and Elsie.

"Till we meet again. Very good. These good people are thinking, Master, of next time. That is good, indeed. Though it mustn't be expected we shall meet again as we were being. Pundits tell us such is not way of Brahman. For getting words to carve on rock, does each family say what pleases them?"

"That's right. What pleases them."

"Narayana."

A. L. WIGGS
THE KING'S OWN YORKSHIRE LIGHT INFANTRY
Age 20
In Loving Memory of Arthur
Sadly Missed by All at Home

Now it's Embree's turn to kneel as he lays a bouquet of flowers on the headstone. Goddamn world, he thinks. Here they are: lance corporal, gunner, driver, fusilier trooper, bombardier, sapper, sublieutenant, the lot of them underground in this alien land.

But we walked out, Harry, he thinks. At least we did the first time. At least we got to India.

• • •

He carries this thought with him during the forty-mile journey from Thanbyuzayat northward to Moulmein in an old Nissan truck now used as a bus (during the war he'd seen many of them bombed out along the road, their red hoods buckled, their wooden planking as blackened and charred as their Japanese passengers). He and Harry had walked out of Burma all right, then gone their separate ways.

Embree had returned to Stilwell's command headquarters at Ramgarh in Bihar State, India. In this flat dry dusty land the camp had initially been used to intern German and Italian nationals caught in India at the beginning of the war. Ramgarh had since then become part of Stilwell's dream: to retake Burma and to do much of it with Chinese troops. He had organized the remnants of the Fifth Army and the 38th Division into a new fighting element called the X Force, adding to it whatever troops Chiang Kai-shek would spare from the Chinese mainland.

It was here in Ramgarh that Philip Embree, along with other Americans who spoke Chinese and some who did not, undertook the training of soldiers newly arrived from China—undernourished, dispirited young men, without motivation or knowledge of modern warfare. He taught them the simplest things first: to take their quinine pills with the same zeal that they chewed buds of garlic for their general health, to sleep inside a mosquito net, to cut weeds before pitching a tent in tick-infested jungle, to bathe as often as possible—and never to lie down in a sweat-drenched shirt, never, never, never, no matter how exhausted, because the dampness most likely would bring on a chest cold leading to pneumonia that meant death in the trackless vegetation of Burma.

The irony of his position was not lost on Philip Embree. Not far from this base where he taught men how to survive in war, his missionary father had taught men how to worship God. It was an irony his father would not have appreciated, which made Embree appreciate it more.

Chinese officers and veterans, especially of the battle-hardened 38th Division, were difficult to handle at Ramgarh. From their point of the view, the British had behaved treacherously by retreating from the announced line of defense in Lower Burma, thereby leaving the Chinese to take the full brunt of Japanese attacks. Stationed here in India, it was clear to them that the British had reluctantly acquiesced to American demands for Chinese participation in this war theater. It was also clear that the British wanted to keep China out of her colony: The Chinese had long expressed territorial claims to regions of India, and if they wedged one foot in the door, they might be hard to dislodge. This British attitude, plainly apparent in the High Command at Delhi, had a disquieting effect upon Chinese morale at Ramgarh.

The Chinese veterans felt betrayed too by their own commander in chief. Chiang Kai-shek had interfered for political reasons in the daily tactics of forces two thousand miles away from his headquarters. Such interference had resulted, more than once, in heavy losses of men and matériel. Chinese officers privately confided to Embree their disgust and disillusionment, for it seemed to them that everywhere they turned—surely the Indians didn't want them on Indian soil any more than the British did—they met hostility, suspicion, contempt, and in compensation for such treatment received from their homeland only empty promises, poor leadership, indifference.

Meanwhile, throughout India there were riots and patriotic uprisings, as the Congress Party stirred up resentment against Britain for expecting the colony to fight against Japan without the reward of immediate freedom. More than fifty British infantry battalions were assigned policing duty in an effort to restore order in the countryside, where track was torn up, telephone lines cut, signal devices destroyed, supply dumps periodically raided, and isolated Europeans butchered. Embree figured the Koylies, after their losses sustained during the retreat, might have earned such duty. It was surely better than preparing for a return to Burma. But he never heard from any of them, not even from Harry, once the Koylie wounded moved out of field hospitals in Imphal.

When his R & R finally came, Embree decided to take it in Calcutta, simply because from Ramgarh it was the city most easily reached by train.

• • •

East Bengal emerged aqueously from the deep mists of dawn like an ocean reef at low tide as his train slid past the heavily wooded suburbs of Calcutta. Through the smudged dirty window he could see a landscape come out of the night. All along the railbed early fires appeared, around which figures wrapped in blankets huddled for warmth. Soon it would be stifling hot, but for these precious moments at sunup the air was crisp, almost chill. Embree leaned toward the window, fascinated, although the compartment was astir with soldiers like himself on R & R.

He had been in India more than a year, yet without seeing much more than the hospital at Imphal, the barracks at Ramgarh. Looking through the filthy glass from the train constituted his first real contact with the country. Life was coming out of the dawn. Hobbled goats knelt to crop some patches of grass; bulls chained to trees stared into swampland; women bearing brass pots on their heads returned from the water tanks. Nothing in this bucolic scene hinted of what was taking place in the hinterlands of Bengal during those autumn days in 1943: More than a million people were starving to death. The rice crop had failed last year; that loss, coupled with the loss of Burmese rice because of the war, had strained the capacity of Bengal State to feed its people. Moreover, seeing profit in this situation, businessmen from Calcutta had bought up village reserves to sell at inflated prices to the Allied army. Many times the number of military deaths suffered by India in the war would be suffered by the peasants of Bengal that year—so Embree had read in a British newspaper—and yet, as the train shuffled into Calcutta, no sign of the tragedy, occurring in places only a hundred miles away, was at all visible. He had read that nothing stirred in some of those villages except vultures, yet within a short while he was to discover that Calcutta itself had the frenetic look and feel of a city in which anything was possible.

• • •

By his second day in Calcutta, Embree had had enough. Nothing worked in his hotel, not the toilets or fans or lights, but that was the least of it. The city possessed the character of a big unruly village. Everything was out of control. In a maze of streets and alleys, people went about the business of basic survival—eating, sleeping, washing, defecating, working, begging, dying, and all of it in the infernal heat of Calcutta. It was a wet, suffocating heat, so thick that the betel sellers and sidewalk barbers and limbless beggars seemed awash in it, as if the air itself were a watery, pervasive gelatin. He hated it. He had not walked out of Burma's hell to enter another, more dismaying inferno. There were ruptured sewage mains throughout the city, and a gray mass of humanity slithered through a gray mud that stank like a corpse-strewn battlefield.

He shared the muck and noise with thousands of other soldiers on

R & R, brought here doubtless as he had been, because of accessibility by train. He saw them—their faces furrowed like his in the shock of experiencing this place—elbowing along the thoroughfares, trying in their pressed uniforms to fend off the beggars, some of whom thrust handless stumps up from the sidewalks where they lay. Trucks, jeeps, old trolleys that were nothing more than boards and strips of tin, horse-drawn wagons, rickshaws, all streamed steadily through the gray streets, until Embree felt everything was coming at him through the heat, coming at him and going through him and emerging into the hot wild city again, where construction seemed perpetually both under way and delayed, the coal piles and sewage pipes and stacks of bricks and bamboo scaffolding scattered everywhere, lying about like the discarded playthings of a gigantic, willful child.

In bars and restaurants, during those two days, he exchanged with other servicemen stories of what had been witnessed in these terrible streets.

"Nothing compares with Calcutta," he was telling a Royal Hampshires NCO in a bar off Chowringhee Road, when he heard a familiar voice call out.

"Say there, Philip! Philip Embree! You ruddy Yank, it's me!"

It was Harry Stubbs.

It was Harry, no longer young. Before the Koylie got through the crowded room to him, Embree saw the old eyes and drawn features of someone transformed forever by war.

They had a drink. Harry was here on R & R too. Because of his heroics during the river evacuation at Shwegyin, he'd been reassigned to Orde Wingate's Chindit raiders. "What they do with heroes," Harry observed with a laugh, "is feed them bloody raw to Wingate."

"The truth is you volunteered."

"Well, I couldn't stay with the Koylies. The battalion's split up. We lost eighty percent of our chaps. Did you know that?"

"Yes. I suppose everyone does." After a brief silence Embree asked if he was still reading Kant.

No, he was not. Harry Stubbs was reading Vedanta philosophy. Moreover, from a Madrasi sapper in the Chindit training camp he was learning how to meditate.

And as he listened to Harry's enthusiastic espousal of Indian spirituality, Embree realized that the Englishman was still young, pathetically so, the perpetual convert to whatever ideas drifted by. Out of their joint struggle to survive, Embree still felt an affection for Harry Stubbs, however, and when the young Englishman insisted on taking him somewhere "important, because by saving my life you became responsible for it," he reluctantly agreed to go along.

They hired a rickshaw and rode northward out of Calcutta.

"I'll show you, old chap," Harry said gaily. "I have found what I want."

"Lucky you. Not many people ever find that. Surely not during a war."

The sarcasm seemed to elude Harry, who had never been sensitive to disapproval. Perhaps his Yorkshire mining blood gave him the toughness required to go his own way. Embree felt in himself a deep measure of annoyance that was augmented by Harry's youthful exposition of karma and moksha and vivarta-vada, a veritable tumbling forth of Indian terms newly acquired, surely, from the pages of a textbook.

"Here we are!" Harry told the rickshaw wallah to halt at the end of a muddy road in a field. Ahead was a series of buildings with white plaster facades. "Dashineswar Temple!"

Leaving the rickshaw, they walked toward the entrance. To the right of the temple they could see the Ganga, a brown ribbon of water bending northward.

"Ramakrishna lived here," Harry said.

Embree nodded without comment. He didn't have to be told who Ramakrishna was. He knew of the Bengali saint because one of his disciples had once come to America. A swami named Vivekananda. Embree's father used to declaim against Vivekananda at the dinner table. Father never got over the mad fervor with which the good-looking swami was received in Chicago, Detroit, Boston. That Indian fakir, Father called him.

Beggars surged around the temple gate. A blind man to one side of it was playing a harmonium, accompanied by a woman clanging cymbals and a boy beating on a big clay pot. A glance at Harry told Embree that the young man never saw them. Was Harry thinking of karma and his immortal soul?

Suddenly Embree said, "You're a bloody fool."

"Come on, old chap. Let me show you around."

Inside the temple compound Harry, who obviously had been here many times, pointed out its various features: twelve small shrines along the western wall; the room at the northwest corner of the courtyard where Sri Ramakrishna had lived; the two main temples, one of them devoted to Goddess Kali.

"Isn't that the goddess," Embree asked, "with her tongue hanging out and a belt of skulls around her waist?"

"My dear fellow, that's not all. She has her own bed and her own fan to be fanned with when it's hot. They have a splendid statue in there— of course, we aren't allowed to see it—but I understand she is standing with one foot planted on Shiva's chest as he lies stretched out beneath her."

"And Ramakrishna worshiped her?"

"Oh, indeed he did. He called out her name incessantly, with tears streaming down his face. He sang songs to her, and the sight of that statue could throw him into a trance. His eyes would cross, his breathing stop, his chest become red. All of this is documented."

"You damn fool."

"If you hadn't got me out of Burma, I wouldn't bring you here and tell you such things. But by saving my life you incurred a debt. And so did I. Let's stop here."

They sat on a marble step, watching devotees cross the hot courtyard, and Harry described his practice of meditation back in camp. There was a place he went to behind a rubbish heap. He would sit with eyes closed and watch his breath go in and out, just as the Madrasi sapper had told him to do. One evening when he was meditating behind the garbage heap, he heard a word in his head. Not actually spoken, but somehow a word was repeated again and again: Ramakrishna, Ramakrishna. Then a light appeared behind his closed eyes, small at first and a bright yellow. But the more he heard the word the lighter the light became until at last it filled the entire space behind his closed eyes. It frightened hell out of him. When he opened his eyes, he was bathed in sweat, panting. But the next day the same thing happened. When he meditated, the word came into his mind, and this time he stayed with it, didn't let it go, and the light and the word remained for a long time. Ramakrishna had been with him.

"Stop there, Harry. I can't let that go by. When did Ramakrishna live?"

"He died in 1885. I know. Bloody awful, isn't it. I told the Madrasi sapper about it, and he said not to worry—Sri Ramakrishna has contacted you. It means you're meditating well, and he's come to encourage you."

"Harry."

"And now when I come to this temple, I stand between two of those small temples over there and close my eyes and the word comes."

"And the light too."

"Yes, that too."

"Let's go back to Calcutta." Embree turned toward the entrance.

"You don't believe me."

"Let's go back to Calcutta."

"Very well, old chap. Sorry. I felt I owed it to you for saving my life."

Embree knew that Harry meant it, that the young Englishman sincerely believed what he'd said. But during their silent ride back to Calcutta, all that Embree could think of was his hatred for this sort of delusion. And hatred for Harry too. Glancing at the sandy-haired young Englishman, he could see the implacable fervor, the souped-up ecstatic determination of someone convinced of being on familiar terms with God. Harry and Father, Embree thought bitterly. A vast chasm separated him from them. Back in the city, he jumped out of the rickshaw waved his hand without a glance at Harry, and vanished into the crowd. The next day he returned to Ramgarh and proceeded to get into trouble.

21

"UNCLE JOE WANTS you," he was told by an aide to General Stilwell. "And be careful. He's on the warpath."

Minutes later, standing in front of the General's desk in the small, airless, unadorned staff room, Embree saw immediately that the aide had given him good advice. Stilwell sat in a straight-backed chair, wearing GI pants and jacket with no insignia of rank, on his head a stiff-brimmed campaign hat from World War I, secured beneath the skinny throat by a shoelace instead of a leather strap. On the desk, next to a pile of papers from which the General was reading, sat a tin of half-eaten C rations. He continued to read for some minutes, leaving Embree at attention. Pushing away a memorandum, at last he glanced up sourly. "Goddammit, Embree, stand at ease."

Embree did.

"You're a damn good officer, Embree, but you've got a big mouth."

"General?"

"You've been talking to people. You've been saying we ought to put supplies and payroll directly in the hands of Chink commanders."

"Yes, sir, I have."

"Well, dammit. Explain yourself."

"Sir, these young recruits, they won't follow a commander who doesn't pay them directly, who doesn't parcel out supplies directly. They're used to the Chinese way. They don't know what chain of command is."

"Don't lecture me about the Chinese. I know them as well as you do. I speak the lingo just as well. I like them. I respect them just as much. So don't get sanctimonious with me."

"Yes, sir, General."

"We're going to keep control of the finances, and I don't give a tinker's damn if a few Chink officers lose face. It's their own fault for squeezing us. I want you to keep your mouth *shut*, Embree. You hear that? Well?"

"General, we'll lose a lot of morale in the Chinese ranks, if we don't let them do it their way."

Stilwell picked up a cigarette holder, jammed a cigarette into it, and lit up, puffing furiously while regarding Embree with cold blue eyes. "I've had enough. Chiang Kai-shek's been fouling up again, the little sonofabitch. He's holding back another division. He's stalling. He's a vicious little peanut bastard and here *you* are lecturing me how to handle the Chinese. This is the army, or supposed to be. I think a lot of people forget that." Stilwell rose in one swift motion, displaying the kind of physical ability—unsuspected in a man of his fragile appearance—that had enabled him not only to walk out of Burma on foot, but also by sheer force of will to bring along with him more than a hundred men and women, civilians and soldiers. "I don't want a single damn word about this from you again, Embree. You're good, damn good. Too independent, but you're tough, you're a fighter, you've got the heart of a soldier—there's no denying *that*—and you've been with me a long time, but god*damn* if I'm going to let you or anyone interfere with my handling of the Chinese. Now, get out of here."

Before nightfall, new orders were cut for Lieutenant Philip Embree. He was being sent to an obscure new unit called Detachment 101. "I want him out of here," Stilwell was known to have told staff members that afternoon. "I don't want him stirring up my Chinese boys."

Two days later Philip Embree joined Detachment 101. It was a clandestine guerrilla unit designed to operate behind Japanese lines in Burma. The force would be following a pattern of long-range penetration already established by Brigadier Wingate, whose quick-striking British raiders, the Chindits, had for their unit symbol the chinthe, a Burmese temple gargoyle.

Within a week Embree had been sent, along with other "volunteers" for extremely hazardous duty, to participate in joint training with Chindits at a camp near Imphal. No sooner had he debarked from the truck than again he heard the familiar voice: "I say, Philip! Look over here, you chap! It's me!"

• • •

"Here, here I am!" Rama, his dhoti gathered about his thighs so he can come at a trot, appears around a corner. "I have checked, Master. Ferry to Martaban will not be leaving on schedule."

Embree moves away from the shaded wall against which he's been standing. He's been waiting for Rama near the bus stop in a market area of Moulmein. "How long will it be?"

"Three, four hours. I am sorry, Master." Rama holds up one hand, as if prepared to count off the hours on each finger.

Three, four hours. Embree hasn't the patience to wait. Time to keep moving, time to go, see, do, dammit, not to wait and think. He's staring at some barley cakes near his feet. The pasty surfaces are so covered with flies they look like orange cakes dotted with raisins. He has to do something, go somewhere, run.

"Then I'm going there." Embree squints in the sunlight at a winding road leading up a hillside.

"What is up there, Master?" Rama leans forward slightly, as if to give his sharp nose a sniff of what is up there.

"One of these Burmans told me a monastery."

"Buddhist, is it, Master?"

Embree nods. "Will you go up?"

"Oh no, Master. I'm thanking you kindly, but I will wait here. No Buddhist monastery for me, Master. I would not be caring for it." Rama glances around the little market square. A war-vintage Garant ambulance, it too now a bus, stands next to the Nissan truck. A local scribe has set up shop nearby with a stool and a little table; he has an old, clattering British typewriter on which he's writing letters for people who wait in a long line. A hawker comes along, tries to sell Rama a papier-mâché owl, a fake antique Buddha (Rama raises his hands as if to ward off a blow), and a replica of a pagoda umbrella. "Not to worry, Master," Rama declares, backing out of the mainstream of market traffic and waving his umbrella at Embree. "I will be waiting right here." He moves against a wall, beyond a group of women passing by in their htamein skirts pulled high under their armpits. "I am waiting here, Master!" Hunkering down against the wall, he opens the big black umbrella and, grinning, holds it over his head.

Waving goodbye, Embree starts out of the busy marketplace. Food is laid out on wicker trays at his feet. Burman merchants stare impassively at him as he starts up the dirt path. It is hot. He feels the heat intensify within the plaster cast on his upper arm and shoulder. A man beside the path is selling ice water; a block of ice is suspended over a canvas bag, and he's banging a cup on a wooden board to attract attention. Embree is abruptly thirsty, but doesn't dare take such water, although more than once in the old Burma days he drank it out of stagnant ponds, risking death. Once he drank from a pond choked with corpses. He checked first, however, to see if fish were swimming in it, figuring if they were, the water was still good. A specious argument. But the idea of testing the water gave him a sense of control over his destiny for a couple of seconds. And he survived the water, didn't he, even though he hadn't seen fish in it, dead or alive.

The ice-water seller gives him a smile; Embree smiles back but plods on. He can give up this little expedition, of course. He can find a café somewhere and sit in the cool shade with Rama, or he can simply join Rama under the umbrella—it's big enough. But from the moment he learned that the building half hidden in foliage on top of the hill is a monastery, Embree has wanted to go there.

He needs to go there. Fear rises from the Other. The terrible idea has gripped him once more; it began on the Nissan truck ride into Moulmein.

From a winding hillside road he'd been lazily watching the Salween River flow by, the lovely islands set within its channel, the cargo ships positioned in Moulmein Harbor. And suddenly it hit him, wedged among the others inside the uncovered Nissan truck: Something was there, aside from himself and his companions, riding along with them, wedged too among them. A delusion, of course. Yet India has taught Embree never to take delusions lightly, as they might be part of a reality otherwise too odd to meet head on.

You're damn right they might be, he tells himself.

Embree is taking such thoughts up the steep path toward the monastery. High above the business section of Moulmein now, he has a panoramic view of the harbor. Rafts made of bamboo are down there, poled or paddled or under the power of sputtering prewar engines, all of them hauling teak logs that are strapped to their undersides. He can see the stately sinuous Salween River and beyond it the large island of Bilugyun in a blue-white thermal haze. He could go down there right now and watch buffaloes grapple the teak around with huge timber chains—enter the eighteenth or nineteenth century down there. He could stand on the river bank and lose himself in the dust and sunlight and harbor motion. Or stay right here on the hillside, looking down as he's doing now. It's beautiful here, spectacular, yet he'll go on to the monastery. Because the feeling prods him forward: Fear is walking alongside him, taking each step he does, accompanying him with an intimacy a gentle soul like Rama can't match.

Harry's doing it.

Harry's doing it, he tells himself, just as the path opens upon a series of buildings set along the hillside. Naked children, seeing him, run. He has a glimpse of a couple of saffron-robed pongyis eyeing him and running too into the shadowy interior of the monastery.

Embree stops, considering whether he ought to retrace his steps. There's nothing for him here. What is he looking for?

Suddenly, out of the shadowy entrance to the monastery, comes a tiny man wearing a pork-pie hat with a green feather in it. In lilting English he calls out, "Welcome to our kyaung, sir! Welcome, welcome!" Approaching Embree, he extends his hand, and when Embree takes it in his own, pumps vigorously. "It is very pleasurable to meet you, sir. Please, this way. I fear you won't see our abbot. He has been in deep meditation now for three days. No one in Burma," the tiny man says proudly, "can meditate as long as he does. No food passes his mouth, though we do wet his lips. And he will come out of it refreshed. It is true. I have seen it. How pleasurable it is to speak English! This way, please sir."

A dozen yards farther on the right there's a thatch-roofed building of teak, standing on posts amidst a tangle of bougainvillea, tamarind and mango trees. "We will have tea," the little man announces and, to prove it, speaks loudly to a turbaned Burman who waits at the top of the wooden stairway.

"Your English is remarkable," Embree says politely, when they reach the dining hall, a large open-air room without furniture, except for low, round tables.

"Not so remarkable when you consider I studied three years in England. Yes." He nods proudly. "But when I returned, there was no place for me. Politics." After a pause to let Embree comment if he wishes, the little man in the pork-pie hat continues. "So I came here as manager of the monastery. It is quite pleasant. We have a holy man for abbot. I have spent nearly forty years of my life on this hill. I have no wish to go down it. Or at least, the wish doesn't come too often."

The faint humor and self-deprecation of this last remark relieves Embree. He hasn't come here for sanctimonious lectures. Why have I come here? he wonders. The turbaned Burman comes along, bearing a tea tray with a dish covered by a wire cage. Soon on the low round table are all sorts of things: egg curry, squash and potato, chili sauces, pickled tea leaves, corn, and peanuts. "Please," the little manager says.

Embree introduces himself as Philip. The manager is Ko Kau Reng. While drinking tea and eating, they let the conversation meander pleasantly. Philip explains that he's stopping over in Burma on his way home to Bangkok; his wife and child are in Bangkok. He has been to Burma before, but never to Moulmein, which he finds lovely. They agree that the harbor of Moulmein is spectacular, far more interesting than the one of Rangoon. It's a lovely day, not too much humidity, but the haze, as usual, impairs the river view.

Ko Kau Reng takes out a cigar, offers it to Ko Philip, who politely refuses. Ko Kau Reng lights it up for himself. Blowing out the smoke, he shifts his position—they're sitting cross-legged on the floor, with a cotton sheet under them. "You were in Burma during the war, Ko Philip?"

"Yes. Yenangyaung. Kalewa. And Upper Burma. And Mandalay. Back down to Rangoon."

"Oh, my, you have seen Burma!" Ko Kau Reng pulls on the short brim of his hat and smiles broadly. The dining hall's almost empty now, save for two pongyis at a far table, reading newspapers. In the open-air room Embree can see, a few feet away at the end of the floor, sunlight dappling a mango tree. A temple bell is ringing nearby.

"I did not see Burma," he says abruptly. "I saw only the killing."

Ko Kau Reng nods.

Why am I telling him this? He's not even a pongyi. Maybe he robs the monks, sneaks down into Moulmein for women, gets drunk. Ridiculous hat with its green feather. Yet I'll tell him. "Listen, Ko Kau Reng, I'm having trouble and that's why I came here."

The manager doesn't seem surprised. "I will get one of the monks to speak to you. Don't worry. I will get a good one."

"No, wait. Listen. In the war another soldier and I were on a mission. Do you understand?"

"I do."

"And during this mission he got sick. I think it was typhus, I'm not sure."

"Where were you?"

"North of Indaw somewhere."

Ko Kau Reng nods. "That is the worse typhus country in all of Burma."

"We were cut off, but I knew a base lay about fifteen miles away. So I set out for it, but then I discovered a Japanese force going east of there. I followed them a day, then another. Finally, I went back to my friend. His name was Harry."

"You feel unhappy about him to this day."

"Yes—unhappy."

"You feel you shouldn't have followed the Japanese. Your duty was to him. But in war wasn't your duty to follow the Japanese?"

"I have not been altogether candid."

"Candid? I know the word but have forgotten."

"I have not been altogether truthful. When I started to follow the Japanese, it was clear I couldn't do anything about them. I had no weapons except a rifle and a knife, and no radio, so I couldn't send a message. I was alone. All I might do of value is get to that base and report their presence at the same time I got help for my friend."

"That does sound reasonable." Ko Kau Reng pours tea and puffs his cigar.

"Yet when I saw them on the trail, I felt I must follow them. There was always the outside chance I might do something . . . something . . ."

"Unusual," Ko Kau Reng supplies with a grin.

"Exactly that. I had discovered a bunch of Japs and the question was, What could I do about it? It was . . . an adventure I couldn't give up. I forgot my friend in the excitement of it. Do you see that?"

The manager nods somberly. "Of course I do."

"But that's not all."

"Ah, I thought not."

"I went back to him when it was clear I'd made a mistake. A Jap patrol had found him. He'd killed four men, but they'd wounded him badly."

"You could not get him help then."

"There was nothing to do."

"Was your friend aware of his condition?"

"Absolutely. But he was . . . unafraid. Now, I've watched a lot of men die, but not many—perhaps none—with his kind of acceptance."

"He was an old soul. In past lives he learned how to die, how to accept it. You were lucky to have such a friend, Ko Philip."

"But that's not all."

"No?" At last Ko Kau Reng seems surprised.

"We discussed his condition and agreed I ought to . . . put him out of it. He was very logical. No need to let the Jap patrols have him. And he insisted it was time for me to get back to base, if I was to get back at all. Harry was a soldier as well as . . . your old soul."

"He was a religious man."

"I suppose you could call him that."

"You are also a religious man, Ko Philip."

"I am not a religious man. I have tried—well, let's get on with it. It was arranged I'd go off into the jungle a little way, then come back and shoot him. He was propped against this tree. So I walked off and began to think—perhaps I could get help for him at the base."

"But you knew you could not."

"You understand perfectly. I knew I could not, but by heading out, I could avoid shooting him. My leaving him earlier had led to his wound. If I put a bullet into him, I'd merely be ending what I had begun."

"That is . . ." Ko Kau Reng, searching for words, pushes the pork-pie hat back on his head.

"We call it rationalization."

"Regrettable. I have forgotten the word."

"We call it escaping a commitment. We call it cowardly."

"But that is not all either, Ko Philip?"

"No. After walking through the jungle a couple of hours, I finally looked at the truth. I had to go back and finish him. So I went back, but by then he was dead." Embree, who has been staring at his teacup, looks up suddenly.

"And he is with you still."

"Then you know that too."

Ko Kau Reng relights the cigar that's gone out. "It is no special knowledge in Burma. If someone dies violently, without justice, he remains on the earth to plague those who get in his way. Especially the one who did the violence to him."

"That's not Buddhist doctrine," Embree says. He's annoyed by superstition coming into a discussion of human guilt.

"No, it is not. But we have taken the old belief into our faith. We believe in Nats."

"Nats are spirits, aren't they?"

Ko Kau Reng laughs. "What you think of them, Ko Philip, is on your face. Westerners don't seem able to understand the Nats. But I suggest you consider them. They are like your Christian saints and devils."

Embree smiles at last, feeling relief for having told his story, even if it's been to this tiny man with a pork-pie hat who isn't even a monk in this place. "Why do you think I should consider Nats?"

"Oh, simply because, Ko Philip, your friend has become one."

Had Embree not lived in India so long, at this moment he would have laughed. Instead, he dips his head in a gesture of respect. "Thank you for your advice."

"I see, Ko Philip, you understand too. Now I will tell you please to go somewhere and summon your friend."

"Summon him?"

"Have a talk with him, settle it."

"I can't believe that's possible—to summon him and talk."

"Go to Pagan. Sit there. Pagan is a good place to sit. It will put your friend into a receptive mood. I am surprised how well my English is doing today. A little practice does it." He gets to his feet, ending the conversation.

• • •

On their return to Rangoon from Moulmein, once again Rama asks permission to go to the market.

"You haven't found a woman there, have you?" Embree teases.

The young Tamil throws up his hands in horror. "Oh, no, Master. Oh, never, Master!"

Embree watches him walk away in his white dhoti, carrying the rolled black umbrella. "There goes my sanity."

Turning from the crowded station, Embree looks across the rooftops of Rangoon at the massive stupa of Shwedagon Pagoda, its golden dome beckoning. So he'll go to it. He'll climb the steps and stand on the high, broad terrace of the largest pagoda in the world, from which vantage point he'll consider the world of Ko Kau Reng, the cigar-smoking business manager of a monastery, who for a few minutes convinced him that the dead come back to haunt the living.

As he walks through the late afternoon, people pass him on the road. The women are lovely. Two slight young girls come along, bearing bamboo water buckets on shoulder poles: jasmine in their hair, their faces marked with the chalky-textured yellow tanaka-root powder that cools the skin in hot sunlight. He recalls his first trip to the great pagoda at the end of the war. The profusion of spires induced in him an over-whelming sense of soaring. But that night he drifted toward the water-front, where in a scruffy brothel he copulated with a Burman girl; his savagery and meanness had appalled him. In the morning he paid her double the price and slipped guiltily into the street, never once raising his eyes toward the dominating spire of Shwedagon.

He now knows why. Or thinks he does. He'd been swept up suddenly in his father's world of the spirit. Now he can handle such an experience; India has taught him how. But then it had been impossible. And so the girl suffered. And so he will never touch a Burman girl again.

• • •

Embree comes to the pagoda entrance. It is guarded by two enormous chinthes, whose duty it is to see that none enter the terrace ground with shoes on.

Looking up at them, Embree is reminded of the Chindit commandos who took this mythical name—chinthes—for their own. In 1944, dur-ing Operation End Run (an Allied plan to take Myitkyina), Embree's unit in 101 had been given by Stilwell to Wingate's Chindits for harass-ment strikes against Japanese units between Myitkyina and Indaw. It was during the operation that Embree met Harry Stubbs once again. It was somewhere between Myitkyina and Indaw that Harry died.

Craning his neck for a long appraisal of the chinthes, Embree sees nothing but painted plaster and the sort of extravagant image—a kind of lion-and-griffin creature—children might draw. So much for chinthes. Climbing the covered southern approach, he passes the shops lining the stairway that sell incense, flowers, and cheap replicas of Bud-dha. If Ko Kau Reng ever gets tired of managing a monastery whose abbot, being in perpetual ecstasy, is never available, he can set up busi-ness here, selling pork-pie hats. A negative thought, Embree thinks while climbing. Demons, evil spirits, Nats. Bullshit. Yet during his own meditations he has seen colors and on the edge of his vision certain shapes that startled him into opening his eyes. Bullshit. And yet—

He enters the compound. It's immense; a terrace paved in marble surrounds the central stupa and scores of other spired pagodas that cluster under it. Everywhere he looks there are Buddhas in bronze, plaster, wood. Even in late afternoon he's dazzled by the colors, by the spires, columns, upturned finials. Embree feels overwhelmed here.

He sits on the marble ledge of a pavilion.

A family sets up nearby for the afternoon; they have brought maga-zines, mats, and cooking utensils. Behind them, against a column, sit two young lovers in earnest conversation; the girl modestly holds a handkerchief to her face. And a small child, wearing only a shirt, carefully lifts a cup to drink from it, then just as carefully puts it down. In an act of intense concentration he quite roughly pulls the foreskin of his penis, as if it were a rubber band, lets it go—wap!—and picks up the cup again. Embree smiles. It is human here; he'd forgotten that; he'd remembered only the profusion of spires.

He walks again, this time paying more attention to people than architecture. An old monk, sitting in one of the temples, is doing his rosary with one hand, while with the other he holds a cigarette. In front of a small pavilion along the ambulatory, two men are methodically pouring water over a Buddha from two large silver bowls. Another man, carrying an infant, comes along. He picks up a cup and dips it into one of the silver bowls, then pours water over the Buddha's head in a series of three motions—perhaps, Embree thinks, for himself, for baby, for wife. It's nice to think so. All three men then tip the attendant who keeps the bowl filled.

Again Embree sits, facing a pavilion enclosed in glass. The statues of two men, ornately dressed and draped in organdy, smile out at the passersby. But the smile on the plaster faces isn't serene or welcoming. It's a pained smile, perhaps neurotic. Embree can't stop looking at this glassed pavilion and finally, after some minutes, accosts an elderly man who is strolling with elegant precision around the ambulatory.

"Sir, excuse me. Do you speak English?" Embree asks.

With a haughty stare at Embree the man says, "I do."

"Can you tell me who those figures represent? Those two?"

Following Embree's gaze, the man says, reluctantly, "Bo Bo Gyi and Thagyamin."

"I see. Are they Buddhist saints? Are they Arhats?"

"They are Nats. Bo Bo Gyi is guardian of Shwedagon. Thagyamin is king of Nats."

"Then they aren't Buddhist?"

"Nats," the man declares, and, with a last contemptuous appraisal of Embree, strolls on.

Nats. Ridiculous.

He continues his own walk around the terrace. The sun is lowering, and with it a breeze is coming up, churning the wind bells on hundreds of spires into tinkling music. He comes upon two large plaster figures dressed in green with gold trimming. Their demonic faces have up-swung tusks, and they carry long curved knives. Doubtless Nats too. Nats, spirits, demons. Like Harry. Embree laughs outright at the idea, bringing hooded glances from people arriving with paper umbrellas to insert in flower bowls. Funny, but he'd learned in India to accept anything. And now after tolerating all sorts of belief, Philip Embree has come up against something—these damn Nats—that he can never believe in or condone as worthy of the belief of others. Even though the monastery manager claims that Harry is one of them.

And yet.

It's a good thing I'm going home. Am I? Will she have me? Vera never loved me, never, not even during those first beautiful times in Peking, when I persuaded her to leave with me. She left because of fear. Not because of me. I know it, I know it.

Head down, Embree walks along the marble terrace. Abruptly sensitive to where he is, Embree halts and looks around: The final light of day is catching against the surfaces of spire and statue, creating shadow and glint, disembodying the Buddhas so they seem to float in pieces— arm, nose, forehead, shoulder. He stands there, motionless, while a squad of women come along with bamboo brooms to sweep the terrace at the close of day. He moves out of their path, gathering in for himself the immense calm and beauty of this moment, when the sun, purely round and glowing moltenly, swings into its last curve. As darkness falls, little points of candlelight flicker in front of shrines, and the great spire of the pagoda takes on a soft glow, a golden liquidity as if it were ready to pour down in a warm, sweet river and set awash these people who have lifted their hands in prayer and turned their beads in the world for their Lord.

Believe in it, he tells himself. Maybe in the Nats too. Or maybe not in the Nats. But something is here. Everything here, at this moment, is not for nothing. You have not wasted the years in India, the hours of meditation. You were right to do what you did.

• • •

Back at the Strand Hotel, he decides to eat elsewhere, having no desire for another session with Kemp and Mister Teleki. And yet curiosity guides him toward a quick look at the hotel bar. Standing at its entrance, he sees at the curve of the bar Kemp's faded green bush jacket, khaki cord breeches, and officer's felt hat.

Embree remembers something he saw on the road to Shwedagon today: Two girls were sitting on the porch of a house set back from the road; they were combing each other's hair to find lice—he'd seen the same thing many times. Then they'd oil the strands, so their hair would glisten like wet ebony. But Mrs. Teleki hadn't located and rid herself of the louse that carried relapsing fever. Poor damn Teleki.

Kemp, shifting his stance at the bar, meets Embree's gaze. They stare at each other briefly, then Kemp changes his stance to look elsewhere. For a moment Embree almost enters the bar to join him. But it wouldn't do any good, and of course Mister Teleki will show up soon with his intricate Burmese politics about which Embree recalls almost nothing now. Only that men have complaints, that they commit violence, that they have dreams of justice none but themselves can realize.

He goes upstairs to his room and sits down at the rickety desk there. Soon he is writing.

Dear Mrs. Stubbs:

How kind you were to write me. Your letter came just in time, because I was setting out to join my family in Bangkok. You see, it has been a long time. [Embree pauses; should he go into such an explanation, should he lie to this woman?] I had been living in India to improve our finances, but now it is possible for me to return home. [He pauses again; God, this is terrible.] You can imagine how wonderful my reunion with wife and daughter will be for us all.

At any rate, I was privileged to carry out the wishes of you and your friends. I have stopped in Burma. I have gone to the Allied Cemetery, and I have seen each of the six graves. Believe me, each of them. And let me report that the [he pauses again for the word] setting is splendid. The lawns are green and tidy, the hedges too. It is a lovely spot [he pauses again; should he get sentimental?], worthy of such brave young men. [Enough, he thinks.]

I do hope you will keep in contact with me, Mrs. Stubbs. [He pauses again; Can I say this? Must I?] I too feel like one of your family.

With warm regards,
Philip Embree

Two matters are missing from this letter: He didn't mention the whereabouts of Harry's remains; he didn't give his forwarding address in Bangkok for fear that Vera, when he arrives, won't want him to stay there.

Soon after he's finished the letter and sealed its envelope, the door opens.

A slight, dark young man in khaki bush shirt and pants—GI castoffs —stands grinning in the doorway.

"Well, Rama, I see what you've been doing in the market."

"Do you think I am looking ideal, Master?" Frowning with anxiety now, Rama slips into the room, a bundle under his arm—the discarded dhoti.

"Definitely ideal."

"You are meaning it?"

"I am. You look now like what you are: a world traveler."

"Ah, I am happy, Master." Rama beams.

Embree rises. "Now let's go eat. If I remember correctly, there's a small restaurant just north of here. The Palace."

"Indians allowed, Master?"

Ignoring that question, Embree says, "They serve monhinga there. You'll like it: a fish curry with rice noodles, and a sauce made of all kinds of things—duck egg, chili, onion, banana stalk. I don't know what else."

Fiddling with the buttons on his bush shirt, Rama says shyly, "I won't be caring for it, Master. I'll just be having a vegetable curry, thank you. I am looking ideal?"

"Ideal, Rama. But you may want to wear a dhoti where we're going next. It's hot and dusty."

"Going, Master, where to next?"

"A place called Pagan."

22 He is desperate for money.

There were the bullfights when they went south to Pattani. He doesn't know anything about bullfighting, yet he bet heavily and lost. He knows something about cockfighting, yet last week he bet heavily and lost there too. Because he was born in July he's a Royal Tiger, Sanuk tells him, and because of his age, twenty-two, he's ruled by Mars with Mercury as the sharing planet—riches should come to him from the north, south, and east. All that is good, except he was born on a Tuesday, which for the House of the Tiger means anger and ferocity.

Of course a man's a fool who believes a woman.

If he's angry at anyone right now, it's at himself. He just bought a ticket for the boxing match tomorrow night. Because it's an important bout, the tickets are expensive. Yet as desperate as he is for money, not only did he buy a ticket, but he bought the best, in the pit. Well, he shouldn't be angry about that, because if he decides to do any betting, the pit is the place to be. Betting? With what?

Coming toward him down the alley is a snack vendor in a broad-brimmed palm-leaf hat, a plaid sarong. The old woman is carrying a shoulder pole with baskets dangling on each end of it. In a wailing voice she advertises her delicacies: *"Kanoom mah laew! Kanoom mah laew! Kanoon mah laew!"*

"Here," Chamlong says to her roughly. "Let me see."

The old woman sets the woven baskets down. One of them contains bowls, cutlery, pots; the other holds food already prepared: sticky rice, sweet barbecued beef shreds, and a salad of beans, shrimp, papaya, peanuts, lemon juice, fish sauce, and chilies. He adores this som tam; therefore it doesn't seem extravagant to have some. So he asks her for a bowl and watches her ladle the salad in. "I want my mine hot." He supervises the addition of a few extra chilies.

"A fifteen-stang piece," the old woman says, holding the bowl.

He reaches for it, but she slips it between arm and breast. "A fifteen-stang piece."

"That's expensive."

"A fifteen-stang piece."

He pays. The snack vendor waits patiently as he leans against a wall and finishes the som tam. Giving her the empty bowl, he says, "I've eaten better."

"But not as cheap." She walks on, whining out, *"Kanoom mah laew! Kanoom mah laew!"*

For a moment he watches the old woman maneuver her baskets through the crowded alley. Old people are too serious, he thinks. Like his father.

Only a few days ago his father had thrown him out of the house, shouting at him, "Where have you been? I send you on errands, you're gone all day! You disappear a whole afternoon without telling me! It's the Siamese blood! You aren't my son, you aren't a Chinese son! I've had enough of you! Go on the streets!" Well, he had. He'd stayed one night with this friend, one night with that. It is said, "Yellow money is plentiful compared to white-haired friends," and he believes it, because some of his old gang won't even give him a corner of their rooms for a night's sleep. His father often says, "You are a lion with money; without it you are a dog." Yet his father threw him on the street without any money except the few bahts he had in his pocket. Sanuk has brought him rotten luck. It's her fault that he went bad on the job. He'd been pleasing Father with his steady work, but not after Sanuk came into his life. She is beautiful. He can't stay away from her, and then, when he's run off from work to see her, his first thought is a hotel. But now, even if she were with him, he doesn't have the money for a room.

If only he had rich friends, but none of his are. And anyway, they quit lending him money long ago, because they say he never pays back. Well, he does if he has it—that's what he tells them and that's what he believes.

He's staring at a poster across the alley. It's a large smiling portrait of Khuang Aphaiwong, who has just won the general election for the Democratic Party. That means nothing, of course. The Democratic Party bows down to the military, and the military bows down to Phibun. Politics is no good. And anyway, Chamlong thinks as he strolls down the alley, he hadn't been eligible to vote. Even though he was born in Siam, he can't vote because his father is an alien. Well, he could vote if he'd been educated in Thai through the Sixth Level, but who wants to go to a Siamese school? Before his father took him into the household, when he'd lived with his mother, Chamlong had disliked the Siamese school where he learned to read. He didn't want to read Thai. The only worthwhile language is Chinese, and anyone with sense knows it. When he went to live with Father, his half-sisters laughed at his bad Chinese. He won't ever forget how they giggled when he spoke. He hates school. Having decided that, Chamlong turns out of the alley into a broader street lined with stores.

He hates the government too. They think they hurt the Chinese by rules and regulations that keep the Teochiu and Cantonese out of political office. How wrong the Siamese politicians are! They don't seem to realize that when you're Chinese, it doesn't matter where you are born —Siam or Malaya or Singapore or any place—*you are Chinese*. And the thing is, the Chinese take care of their own. The Ang Yee societies are always policing the marketplace, so everything goes smoothly, and now the Chinese Communists of Siam are going to expose the corruption of Phibun, the military, Khuang Aphaiwong, and the worthless Democratic Party, and finally convince the Siamese of their inferiority.

That's what he told her, but who can tell if a woman understands?

She sits at the meetings, she smiles and sometimes talks when she shouldn't, but who can tell if she makes sense of it, and if she does, does she care? It is said there are three things never to put your trust in: a male elephant, any crocodile, and a loving woman.

He's wearing khaki shorts, and both hands feel around in the pockets for coins. All he has left is a couple of salehng, hardly enough to get him across town to pick up the leaflets. But he has plenty of time to get there.

If only Sanuk would come to him, they might go to a hotel; they'd have time. But yesterday, when he went to the Bangkok Friendship Club (to lose what little he had left at cards), he found a note from her. "*Tee Rahk,*" it began. A woman calling him "Beloved" still disturbs Chamlong, although their first time together he'd called her the same. That seems different, however, a man saying it. A woman saying it suggests the promiscuity of the Siamese, who will say it to any man any time. This is known. "*Tee Rahk.* I have come down with fever. Can't see you until better. Never forget me. Your Sanuk."

Chamlong misses her. He admits it. She's almost as cheerful as a Siamese girl, and a lot more faithful. At least he hopes so. Since yesterday Chamlong has wondered if she's trying to get rid of him, if the note is a way of saying goodbye. Girls like her can find a man easily. She has only to wear the red cheongsam. But she really isn't like most girls. After all, she's given him money three times, but of course that's because her mother's a farang and lives in a great house. Even so, she's not like other girls, and she's been good to him. The image of her with him in bed slows Chamlong's gait. He's hardly aware of people jostling him, while he thinks of her slim legs entwining his. But he must be careful. Chamlong remembers the old days, when he lived with his mother, and the men coming into the shack. While he played and slept in one room, the men were with her in the other. It maddened him to think those arrogant strangers could draw from his mother such sounds of pleasure. But that's what women are. Aside from Sanuk, he's had only two girls, although no one knows, not even Somchai, that he's had so few.

One girl he met a year ago in Chinatown, not far from where he's walking now. She was looking at him out of a second-story window. He can remember to this moment how she laughed at him, how the little curtain by her face was moving from a breeze. They talked. She called him up. She was a brazen girl, but of course she was Hainanese and that explains it. Her parents were working. She was alone up there in a messy room with two little brothers, one of whom hardly walked yet. She claimed to be sixteen, but she couldn't have been older than fourteen. One of her front teeth was broken, and her face was dark, square, with some kind of darker mark on her chin. She told him to sit down and so he did, right beside her on the bed. He had nothing to say, and after a while she pouted her lips and told him he didn't know anything, but she took his hand. He squeezed hers, and then he reached out and put the palm of his hand across her blouse until he felt a prominent nipple on the flat chest. Instantly she got up and hurried both children into the other room. Hooking the door on them, she turned and without looking at Chamlong removed her clothes. "Hurry, before my parents get home," she told him and jumped into the bed. But, of course, she was Hainanese. A girl with Teochiu or Cantonese or Hakka parents wouldn't have been so brazen.

And then the other time he'd gone with three other boys, one of them Somchai, to a Siamese house, where a dozen girls sat on benches under a single light bulb.

He hates Siamese. They're loose. None of their women can be trusted. Everyone knows the Siamese women envy Chinese wives, because a Chinese man may have a girlfriend or two, but eventually he comes home, whereas the Siamese man drinks and whores to the exclusion of much else, neglecting his wife except to beat her. Everyone knows this, Chamlong tells himself. It's common knowledge.

Ahead of him, on a footpath curving off the street, he sees two boys drawing circles in the dust. They're going to fight. How often, when he lived in the Siamese district with his mother, he had fought—and often about her reputation. The boys are intent upon drawing the circles, which represent their heads, the sacred part of their bodies. If one boy rubs out the other's drawing with his hand, they will fight. And if the foot is used to do the rubbing, they will fight until one or the other is really hurt. What, after all, can be worse than to insult the spirit dwelling in the head and to do it with the most degraded part of the body? This is known. One of the boys, now that the circles are drawn, extends one leg, ready to drop his foot on the drawing. Chamlong rushes toward them. "You two stop it."

"Who are you?" one asks defiantly.

Chamlong sees himself ten years ago in that boy: dirty-faced, sullen, a creature of the streets. In a gentler voice Chamlong says, "What is there to fight about?"

"He owes me money," the other boy says. "He bet me on a kite fight and lost."

Chamlong looks from one to the other. "You're betting at your age?"

"Is there an age you're supposed to start?" scoffs the one who reminds Chamlong of himself.

"How much do you owe?" Chamlong asks.

"A salehng," the other boy declares.

"That's a lot of money." Chamlong fishes in his pocket and brings out a coin. "That's enough to hire a boat for a trip on the klongs."

"We know that," says the one who reminds Chamlong of himself.

Flipping it into the air, Chamlong says "Here" and tosses the coin to the other boy. "Now. No more debts. No more fighting. Is that right?"

He turns quickly not to see their faces. Not to witness the sudden bewilderment that'll precede a minute of good luck before the world presses in on them again.

Once again Chamlong realizes how much he misses Sanuk. He really does. He would have liked her to observe his generosity just now. It would have been nice to bask in her approval. Chamlong feels good as he turns toward the klong, where he can get a boat with his last money. A man must follow his instincts or he's not a man. No matter what the odds say, they are always even, because either you win or you don't.

• • •

Chamlong's boatman is a talkative old man. To the stroke of his oar he gives a running account of activities on the klong. But Chamlong is thinking of the leaflets he'll be distributing today. Wan-li is sending a squad with these leaflets into a Siamese neighborhood; it could be dangerous. That possibility excites Ho Jin-shu, the Golden Lion. Again he wishes for Sanuk so he might say, "The Siamese have no spirit. If the government says do something, they do it. But we Chinese don't care for laws we haven't made ourselves."

Now the boatman is talking about the boxing matches scheduled for tomorrow night, so Chamlong listens to the high, nasal Siamese voice.

"Best fighters come from the Northeast. Have you noticed that? Sometimes you get a clever fighter from the South, but it's the Northeast that has the power. Tomorrow I would bet on Torapee the Black Bull."

"I was thinking the opposite," Chamlong says. "I like the boy from the South."

"The Songkhla Demon."

"That's him."

The old man shakes his head in disagreement. He has a large mole on his cheek, a wispy beard like shreds from a burst kapok pod. "I've been following it for twenty-five years. Believe me, Torapee is going to win. If I had the money, I'd bet on him. *Sai!*" he yells, taking his left hand off the oar and striking out with it. "*Sai!* Two or three blows like that, the southern boy will go down. And he won't get up, either. Not when the Black Bull hits him."

It occurs to Chamlong that the boatman is so familiar because he takes his passenger for a Siamese. To make his own Chinese identity clear, Chamlong says, "I don't care much for your boxing. I bet on mah-jong."

"Ah," the old man grunts. "*Mai pen rai.*"

The boat is silent now, so Chamlong can hear distant temple bells, a siren, a pervasive chorus of samlor bells jingling in the nearby boulevard like crickets praying for rain. He dips his hand idly into the water along the boat's gunnel, then withdraws it when some garbage floats by— meat, paper, vegetables, all mushy and mixed together, not unlike a decomposing corpse. It's true the klongs are unpleasant in the cool season, because they dry out and collect debris. They become sweet again with the monsoon rains, but right now they smell, get scummy. It's the fault of the Siamese that so much trash is dumped into the water. In their village huts they throw garbage between the floor slats; it piles up under them, but they don't care. They care only for their phi, because of what those spirits might do to them.

A large red car speeds down the boulevard alongside the klong. Bullock carts, samlors, trucks appear to scatter out of the way like geese. As it passes, Chamlong can see a chauffeur in white behind the wheel. Royalty. The red tells that. Chamlong spits into the turgid klong. He turns from the vanishing automobile and looks at the opposite bank, where some little girls in white blouses and blue skirts are marching in a column of twos, with their teacher leading them. Did Sanuk look like them when she was a child—knock-kneed and skinny? Chamlong smiles to himself at the possibility. He admits it; he misses her.

. . .

He's on the fringe of Chinatown, in a side street notable for its crumbling buildings and twisting passageways. Suddenly this soi is familiar to him—just ahead is the Siamese pleasure house where he went with friends a year ago. Chamlong passes it slowly. He had no idea it was so near the leaflet distribution house. There are a couple of beggars squatting outside the brothel, which is called in Thai THE PLEASURE CLUB and something else in, he supposes, English. The foreign words are lit in neon. He remembers the inside of the house perfectly. There's a cashier's stool, a desk, a fan, a little bar. On one wall is a big calendar of a farang girl in a Western bathing suit; her blond hair is flung back with one hand; she is standing on a beach, with her feet planted wide apart, making her long legs seem even longer. And one wall is a glass panel through which the girls can be seen, lounging on chairs. To the right of the glass wall is a door and beyond the door a hallway lined with rooms. A red light goes on over a room when it's occupied. A rumpled bed, a chair, a copper basin on a stand. The girl said, "Come here and let me wash you."

Because, without thinking about it, he has slowed almost to a halt, a girl comes to the brothel entrance. Wearing a black Western skirt and a white blouse, she slouches against the doorway. "Come on in," she coaxes, gesturing to him. "What's wrong, no money?" she says in English, which he can't understand, "No money, no honey." And then in Thai again, grimacing playfully at him and bending forward, so her breasts lunge against the blouse, she brays loudly, "Don't be sad, you funny boy! You look sad, funny boy! Don't you ever laugh?"

He won't look at her, but increases his pace, feeling heat in his cheeks.

At his back he can hear her: "What's the matter? If you laugh a lot it will rain! Don't you want rain?"

He can hear her until the soi curves away from the house. Siamese, they are loose, he thinks.

Within a few minutes he has reached a new soi that leads off this one. Just as he turns into it, from the opposite end of the alley comes a green truck, almost too wide for the narrow passage. Fortunately, there's a little vegetable shop opposite him, with a long dirty awning, so Chamlong slips under it and stands at the piled fruit. He watches in terror a group of men in khaki leap out of the truck and, with guns held at the ready, trot into the squalid two-story house that had been Chamlong's destination.

He wants to run, yet curiosity roots him to the spot. "Do you want something?" a young girl asks him, coming down the aisle between the wooden bins holding mangoes, bananas, papayas.

"Not yet, not yet," he mumbles, straining to hear. The men going in there are from the elite corps of the Metropolitan Police. He's seen them before in their floppy hats: the Asawins. He's heard stories of Asawins smuggling jewels and opium and gasoline, of running for themselves illegal cigarette factories. The general population fears them.

"Not yet," he says when the girl comes forward again. And he hears it, halfway down the block, a thin piercing scream, and now shouting, more screams. The girl comes from the shop to stand in the alley. There's enough noise, emanating from the ramshackle building in the middle of the block, for people to come out of houses all along the way.

I can run or stay, he thinks. The crowd gives him the chance to stay. Losing himself in it, as the throng builds from both ends of the soi, he's not twenty feet from the building when the first Asawins appear in the entranceway. They have armloads of leaflets, some of which flutter to the ground, carrying a message of revolution. The Asawins in their khaki uniforms and brown belts push back the gathering mob, making a path for the prisoners.

People gasp.

There are four prisoners, each bloody from beatings with truncheons, which some of the Asawins are brandishing to keep the crowd at a distance. Chamlong can't help himself—he leans forward, straining for a better look at Chin Yin-nan, whose mouth seems crushed, like a ripe fruit, and whose closed left eye is oozing blood and a gray gelatinous substance. His hands are tied behind him; his hair is being pulled from the back by an Asawin. And he's yelling. He's screaming defiance. "Long live China! Long live the Party!" Handled roughly, kicked as he plunges to his knees, Chin continues to yell, "Long live freedom! Long live China!"

And yet it was Chin who preached caution, Chamlong thinks. Such bravery frightens him.

He strains to see the last of the prisoners. It is Somchai. They were supposed to have met in the street before going into the house; Somchai must have arrived early and gone inside to get his quota of leaflets.

He's sobbing.

His hands are also tied behind him, and one of the Asawins has him too by the hair. He's not as bloody as Chin, although an ugly welt has risen on his cheek, and there's a gash along his jawline. He's sobbing, glancing wildly around.

Chamlong moves back, but not quickly enough, and their eyes, for an instant, meet. Chamlong feels his body grow cold with fear; he can't run, yet he must. But Somchai is passed roughly along by the Asawins until he too is shoved into the truck.

Somchai didn't point me out. He let me go free. He could have told them, "See, there! Get him too!" in the hope of better treatment. It's what Chamlong would have expected of him, and yet Somchai showed courage.

"Clear away! Clear away!" an Asawin yells at the crowd. Three stars on his epaulettes identify him as a captain. For a moment the officer seems to look directly at Chamlong and then climbs into the cab of the truck; the driver roars off, scattering the crowd. Chamlong stares at the truck receding down the soi. He can't see Chin, who must be down, but Somchai is there all right—back arched by the position of his arms, his bloodied face pale and frightened.

That is what Chamlong is left with: Somchai, huddled among the Asawins, looking with wild eyes into the air, as if unable to comprehend what sort of fate the gods have in store for him, as if incapable of understanding anything except the dull, pervasive throb of his own fear.

Yet he didn't betray me, Chamlong thinks in wonder.

· · ·

But Somchai and the others, even Chin, can't hold out for long. It's what worries him as he hurries away.

Bodies will start showing up in the klongs, eyes gouged out, bones crushed in what will be a prolonged, messy, humiliating death.

Party members—that means his cousin too—talk about that possibility if they get caught. They shrug and call it bad luck. Bad luck?

The public won't care if we die for them, Chamlong tells himself. The Siamese will be happy; the Chinese like his father, with business to protect, care only that the police keep order. Somchai, Chin, and the others will never get out of Khlong Prem Central Prison alive. That's certain.

He thinks of the fear on Somchai's face. When they hold a tube of running water down Somchai's throat, swelling his gut like a melon, the poor fellow will talk. Certainly he will, even though the others will hate him for it. But Chin won't talk. Not for a long time anyway. And if Somchai tells everything he knows and they let him live, he'll spend the rest of his life on Ko Tarutao, that prison camp on a Straits island. Worse than death. Somchai's wild eyes, they will get wilder when the CSD straps him down for torture. They say the Crime Suppression Division is worse than anything, worse than the Asawins.

How long do I have? Chamlong halts, leans for support against a wall. People hurrying through the dusk are happy. Isn't that strange? That they're going home to noodles and pork, while I try to save my life?

During teahouse meetings Wan-li and the others had talked about hiding out. They said, if you are caught and imprisoned, give your comrades one day, a whole day in which to make arrangements for hiding out. Give them one day, try to at least, then tell the torturers what you must.

Will Somchai hold out a whole day? From the look in his eyes he won't. Yet when they were dragging him to the truck, he didn't betray me.

Thing is, Chamlong tells himself, beginning to walk rapidly again, I need money. I can't go anywhere or do anything without it.

The Golden Lion swerves in another direction, looking for help from Chinatown friends.

· · ·

Hours later he is hurrying elsewhere.

It's been a frustrating time, for some of his friends are nowhere to be found and others had excuses and still others laughed at him. They called him Jianghuke, the carefree rogue. In the old days Chamlong enjoyed the idea of being Jianghuke. From his boyhood he's always done what shocks others. There was a time in adolescence when Chamlong went around desecrating statues of Buddha by touching their heads, an act of such outrageous impiety that some of his friends, who might drink beer and smoke cigarettes and steal, were horrified. He liked the idea of being Jianghuke, a man who gambled, loved women, kept free. But this evening the word "Jianghuke" appalls him, for it means "no money for you," it means "a merry hero must take care of himself," it means "death."

He argued in vain with them, sitting in tea shops, leaning against walls. "Aren't we Chinese? Don't the Chinese help one another? I'm in a little trouble. No, don't worry about what kind, I'll tell you later. But I really need money. When? As soon as I can get it. I'll pay you back. Aren't we friends? But I paid that back, didn't I? Well, maybe not. I just forgot. Then I'll add that on too, when I pay you back this time. Come on. We're Chinese."

Now, walking through the darkness, Chamlong is exhausted. He hasn't the money for a sampan or a samlor or even a handful of sticky rice. Something comes to him from his Siamese childhood. "If you betray me, may you never understand the teaching of Buddha in this or future lives." In his neighborhood that had been the most serious of curses, and a man died in a knife fight for having uttered it against his enemy.

Chamlong stops in a lane filled with the burned cinnamon smell of opium. Oil lamps flicker in the upstairs windows of Chinatown houses. He thinks of his friends, one by one. Most of them still go by their legal Siamese names, so he names them: Thavi Indradat. Udom Prinyarjun. Pisoot Sudasna.

And then there is Huang Yu-luan, who claims he will no longer be known by his Chinese name, but by Luan Wongwanit.

And then there is his oldest friend from school: Hai Hong.

Chamlong does not include those acquaintances he couldn't locate.

Standing in the lane, he takes a deep breath and says out loud, although people are passing on both sides, "You have betrayed me, so may you never understand the teaching of the Buddha in this or future lives!"

Satisfied with having sworn the worst of maledictions, Chamlong hurries off. He's tried every way to avoid it, but there's no longer a choice. Seeking a reconciliation with his father is the only way out.

. . .

Home is down a narrow lane near Yaowaraj Road, deep in the heart of Chinatown, where Hakkas have their tailor shops, Cantonese their machine shops, Teochius their pawn shops. There is also, in the next soi, a group of turbaned Sikhs who offer bolts of silk from sheet-covered platforms on which they sit cross-legged, their dark eyes brilliant in the assessment of customers. Many of the stores have shut down, with iron bars across their entrances. But Father's hardware store is still open—he can see light shining from it across the alley wet from dishpan water—and he feels his heart racing.

It's with relief that he sees Muang Song in the store, instead of Father positioned just inside the entrance on a rickety chair.

"You!" Muang Song cries, throwing up his hands.

"I have . . . come home. I'm sorry. I have disgraced my ancestors. Is my father here?"

"Good, good, that's good. You should come home and made amends. You're a good boy. This is very good," Muang Song says. "But your exalted father is at a meeting of the Yu-yi."

His father is a past chairman of the Sundry Goods Business Association, and if he's attending one of those meetings, he will stay late, smoking and drinking tea with his friends. If Chamlong knows him, he will talk politics, on every point defending the government. In the name of freedom, he will strike out at the Communists. He will claim that repressive measures against the Chinese schools in Bangkok are good, because it's within the schools that Communists get a foothold. Chamlong can hear in his mind the rapid, emphatic voice denouncing anything that might affect business.

"No one else is here either," Muang Song volunteers. "They have all gone to see your Number Three Sister perform. The servants got a holiday."

Chamlong knows about the concert; he disapproves. His younger sister has a Hakka mother, is therefore pure Chinese. But for years now she's chosen to dance like a Siamese. She's come to look like one of them: hipless, splay-footed, always moving her neck to find an angle of beauty. There is only one important thing about that sister: She'd been Sanuk's classmate in school. Introducing him to Sanuk, in his opinion, is Number Three Sister's only worthwhile act on this earth.

Chamlong glances around the shop, at the clutter he'd seen every day until Father threw him out. Now it all seems alien to him. So much is here. Indeed, when Chamlong first came to live with his father, he thought everything in the world was contained within the bottom floor of the building, inside the four walls of this store: cattle bells, laundry irons, kegs of nails, glazed cast-iron urinals, copper lanterns, bell-shaped lighting fixtures for temples, inlaid furniture, rosewood screens, appliances of every kind, bicycles imported from Hong Kong, tins of turpentine, paint, magazines in four dialects from Singapore, cheap household china, bags of soybean flour, bags of quicklime, bags of hard candy from Manila, all of it stacked precariously on wobbly tables and warped counters, so that no one, except Father, knows where everything is.

"You're still open?" Chamlong asks.

"As your exalted father says, at New Year's time, that's when to stay open. Don't you listen to him when he explains? People will be paying their debts soon, so they buy something for themselves first—a reward for paying up. That's what he says."

Chamlong looks at the assistant's square, beaming face. Years ago Muang Song had been one of numerous coolies who drift into Siam to work in rice mills, tin mines, on the docks. Father had taken him in to sweep up. Muang Song learned to use the abacus and to do accounts. Chamlong has never heard him call Father anything but "exalted."

"You see?" Muang Song lifts his chin to indicate a man coming into the shop. "Your exalted father's never wrong."

"I'll wait for him in the back."

But Muang Song doesn't hear, having already moved a few steps toward the front, hands folded placidly on his paunch, feet apart, heavy chin dipped almost to his throat, as he judges the possibility of a sale. Chamlong has seen him take this stance countless times, and wonders if Father himself gets as much pleasure from selling goods as Muang Song does.

Shuffling down the narrow aisle, Chamlong goes into the back room, an office as cluttered as the shop. Father has always scoffed at neatness in a business establishment, because it arouses suspicion in customers. Neatness where you eat, sleep, pray—that's another matter, according to Chukkrit Napaget, who beats the women of his house so they'll keep the domestic quarters scrupulously clean.

On the red-lacquered Cantonese desk, here in the office, so many objects (among them two empty bottles of orange squash, his father's favorite drink) and so much paper are scattered around that the writing space is no larger than a hand. The accounting done by Muang Song takes place in a cubby behind the next room, a toilet-squat of concrete.

Chamlong sits down. Forlornly he looks at the cluttered desk, wondering what to do. Will his father forgive him? More important, will Chukkrit Napaget—Father uses his Siamese name exclusively—help someone wanted by the police? Chamlong shifts in the chair to regard a tall cabinet in the corner. On it stand a pair of cut-glass vases holding paper flowers in front of a stiffly posed, tinted photograph of his dead half-brother. To this pale boy, Chamlong thinks gloomily, with the narrow face and hair that won't lie down and large ears, he owes his good fortune. What there is of it.

Although it's been years since he was scooped out of that Siamese shacktown and brought to live here, Chamlong doesn't know Father well enough to judge what he'll do. Of course Chamlong knows his history, but that's because Father likes to tell it.

Father was born in the village of Chao An in Kwangtung Province. He was sent to middle school in Swatow, but never finished because his family was too poor to maintain him there. He married a Teochiu girl from his own district, just before leaving her to work in Singapore as a laborer. He left Singapore in 1910, a year before the fall of the Manchu Dynasty in China, and worked his way through Malaya to Siam, where he swept floors in a salted-fish factory. After starting as a dishwasher at Bangkok Christian College, he got a janitor's job there and learned some English. That enabled him to find better employment. He was hired as a shipping clerk for a rice-milling company that did most of its business with a British firm in Hong Kong. Meanwhile he brought his Teochiu wife to Bangkok and by her had one son, two daughters. He saved, made connections, joined associations, and won the trust of the Teochiu community, so that when he wanted to go into business for himself, he secured the necessary loan. He had one little shop, then two, then three. When the Teochiu wife died, Chukkrit Napaget ignored the advice of friends and married not only out of his own hsien but out of his language as well: a Hakka woman who at least brought along a dowry. By then he had shaved off his queue and joined the Chamber of Commerce. His most memorable achievement followed the death of his mother back in the Kwangtung village where she was born. In two leading Chinese newspapers of Bangkok he published an obituary notice along with a eulogy signed by seventy-five prominent Chinese businessmen, as well as Teochiu and Hakka associations and the Chamber of Commerce.

He talks about it to this day from the head of the dinner table. He talked about it the day before throwing Chamlong out. "No woman had a better son," he exclaimed. "And she cooked all her life for laborers in the fields." Chukkrit Napaget often used the commemoration of his mother's death to lecture his son. "If I hadn't worked hard, my mother wouldn't have had such a notice, signed by seventy-five important men. You should model yourself on such men. Think of Leader Chou—think of my friend, Chairman of the Chamber of Commerce. He's held the top executive post in four of the six most important organizations we have here. Prince Athit himself selected a Siamese name for Chou. He was decorated by Chiang Kai-shek a year ago. You could be like him, Chamlong, but instead you play soccer and gamble. There's no substitute for work. It's in the Chinese blood to work. Did I give none to you?"

Sitting in the cluttered office, hearing Muang Song and the customer softly discussing something beyond the door, Chamlong suddenly knows: His father will forgive him, but not help him, especially when a criminal act is involved.

Father will walk away from him and count upon his new mistress, a robust Siamese farm girl, to give him a new son.

Chamlong thinks of his Siamese name: Copy. And of his father's name: The Sword. He's supposed to be a copy of the sword, yet he's only managed to bring disgrace upon the old woman whose name appeared in two newspapers, along with a eulogy subscribed to by seventy-five important men.

"Lost," he murmurs.

. . .

And I have killed a man. What surprises him is the fact of having forgotten it all day. Sanuk lied to him when she said the sharing of Mars and Mercury in his stars would bring him wealth. His problem with her is she knows too much about him. Their first afternoon together he'd told her his family troubles. That's wrong for a man to do. When a man tells a woman too much, bad luck follows. Everyone knows it.

Following his train of thought, Chamlong has swung around to look again at the photograph on top of the cabinet. The narrow, stupid face stares back at him. Behind that photograph, with its paper flowers and vases, is a silver incense burner. He has seen Father fumble inside of it many times and come out with a folded piece of paper. Long ago he realized it must contain the combinations for his safes, because Father takes it away somewhere and returns with a stack of bahts. The entire household is aware of his safes; they are all over the house. The idea—Father prides himself on it—is to cut his losses in case of theft.

Chamlong gets up and takes a few steps toward the doorway. Now there are two more customers in the shop. Exalted father is always right, he thinks bitterly.

Turning, after a pause he goes to the cabinet, reaches over the photograph, and pulls back the hinged lid of the incense burner. At this moment Chamlong realizes his life will be changed forever by what he's doing.

He takes out the piece of paper and unfolds it. There are five sets of numbers written in columns. Sitting down again, he studies them. One column has five numbers, the rest have four. So the five-number column must belong to the big safe, which stands opposite the desk. He looks at the old steel-plated box on which dozens of ledgers have been piled, and on top of them at a little ivory cage, empty now, which used to house fighting crickets when Chukkrit Napaget fancied the sport.

The other columns belong to safes in the building or perhaps elsewhere. Chamlong knows of three. One is in the Hakka woman's bedroom; now, as Number One Wife, she must check it herself daily. A small one sits under the main counter, and he's often seen Father bending there, squinting at the dial, then spinning it rapidly. There's one upstairs, too, in the study where Father entertains his friends.

Slipping the paper into his trouser pocket, Chamlong goes to the door again. Broad back toward him, Muang Song is holding a can of turpentine high, while a turbaned Siamese customer eyes it skeptically. In this moment Chamlong slips out of the office and quickly mounts the short, narrow flight of stairs to the next floor. The boards creak. Did Muang Song hear down there? Not when a customer's in the shop.

The rooms in the living quarters are small, close. Chamlong doesn't bother to look into his own room with its bed, chair, battered wardrobe. The hotel rooms he takes Sanuk to are better. Near the end of the hall is the study. Chamlong halts in front of it, takes a deep breath, and opens the door. He switches on the light, a single bulb with a conical black shade. There are bulky pieces of ornately carved teak in the room —straight chairs are set along one wall; a round table with a large flowered vase dominates the middle. There are no books in this study, no desk, but another small cabinet with another tinted picture of the dead half-brother, this one draped in a red-velvet cloth. There's a faint after-smell of incense; probably Chukkrit Napaget said a prayer before going to the Yu-yi Association meeting. On a table in an alcove there's a forest of joss sticks jammed into bowls of sand; a porcelain figure of a bearded man wearing Han Dynasty robes stands on a small pedestal, with vases of paper flowers on either side of him. This is who Chukkrit Napaget usually worships: Lao Yeh, a god favored by crafts and guilds.

But what interests Chamlong is sitting under Lao Yeh. Drawing aside the curtains of the alcove's table, he locates the little safe. It's hardly big enough to put a pineapple in. Taking out the paper, he spreads it on the floor and tries to remember what Muang Song had once told him about opening a safe. "Boy," said Muang Song, "you spin it, then go right, then go left past the first number, then right again. Maybe someday you'll have a safe of your own to open. But don't practice with your exalted father's safes. I'm telling you how it works so you won't be stupid like the street boys you run with."

Spin it. Right, left, right. What is it? To get the second number going left, you must pass the first number?

Hunching up close to the dial, he squints in the poor light. Starting with the first column, he works the dial as Muang Song once told him

—or he thinks told him. Spin. Right, left, right. Nothing happens when he pulls on the safe's handle. Chamlong tries the next column, but that doesn't work either. Lost, he thinks. He's forgotten what Muang Song told him, or else this isn't the right piece of paper.

Chamlong sits back, cross-legged, and stares gloomily at the gray metal dial on the black box. There's nothing he can do except wait for Father to return, but already he knows what will happen. After a stern lecture, Father will accept him back into the household on condition that he give up gambling and soccer, that he be on time for work and never miss, that he act in all ways like the son of an important leader in the Teochiu community. That's not so bad, that's possible. But tomorrow, if the police come, Chukkrit Napaget will renounce him publicly. Chamlong can hear the strong, familiar voice: "Get out of here! You are not my son! Criminal! Get out!"

Father will betray him. No doubt of it.

Picking up the paper again, with a deep sigh Chamlong tries the next-to-last column of numbers. This time, when he's set the third number into place, he can hear the click inside the lock as its tumblers align themselves, freeing the bolt to move to the unlocked position. He hears it! Pushing the handle down, he yanks the door of the safe open.

• • •

Minutes later he's walking rapidly down the alley. In his pocket are five thousand bahts. When he opened the safe and saw the pile, Chamlong estimated there must have been ten thousand. He meant to take only a thousand or two, but his hand pulled out more than half the bills. And with the money safely in his pocket now, he's glad of it. After all, he can put it back later without being suspected. That's because the safe up there is not opened every day. The working safes are in the shop, he reasons.

Chamlong smiles at the memory of his escape.

Turning out the light, he crept down the hall and waited at the top of the stairs until he could hear Muang Song busy with the demonstration of a radio—"very cheap, but the best Hong Kong has to offer." Then he went rapidly down the stairway and turned into the shop. Without rushing, he went soberly past Muang Song with the casual promise to come back tomorrow. "It's too late for me," he said in parting.

Muang Song continued to hawk the radio, banging its side to diminish the static.

Chamlong pats his trouser pocket, bulging with bank notes. Who now is The Sword of the family? he asks himself. Swaggering down the soi, Chamlong feels giddy from the change in his fortunes. The world opens up with possibilities. What he'll do now is find a little hotel out of the way. He has twenty-four hours to make a plan; and he has the money to carry it out. Maybe he'll take a look at the boxing matches tomorrow night—his last fling for a while. Maybe he'll just go there and bet this money, because by doubling the amount, he can pay Father back without anyone being the wiser. Chamlong guffaws, and in the light thrown from houses along the soi, passersby stare at the young man laughing to himself.

I'll win, Chamlong says aloud. At his age, the Royal Tiger is ruled by Mars with Mercury sharing. Therefore riches will come to him from all directions except the west. The boxing stadium is in the north of Bangkok, facing north. Tomorrow I will win.

23 THE SIAMESE BOXING matches are held in a large, circular auditorium with broad cement seats in tiers. Halfway up there's a ten-foot wire screen that prevents movement from cheaper to better seats, especially in the pit near the ring, where the chief bettors sit. Chamlong has always sat behind the wire screen with his friends until tonight. Now he has a folding chair alongside men who gamble heavily.

Chamlong pats both pockets. They're full of money, as he won two of the three fights just wagered on. The first two bouts went by before he summoned the nerve to bet with money stolen from Chukkrit Napaget, but then he told himself, "I'm not a copy of anyone." Chamlong put down a bet with the first man who looked his way—and won.

Sanuk was right: His stars have brought him luck, even if women can't be trusted to give good advice. What he'll do after leaving here is slip back into the house and return Father's money. The combination to the safe is still in his head, so he can sneak into the room, spin it, go right, go left, go right. Then he simply leaves. How will he do it without getting caught? The house was left unattended last night only because of his sister's performance—that's the second worthwhile thing she has ever done in her life. Usually the house is bustling with servants and women. How will he get into the study?

That's only a detail, Chamlong tells himself in the full bloom of success. He glances with a proprietary smile at the square ring with its red, white, blue, and yellow ropes, and at his companions here in the pit with whom he wagers tonight, and then up at the cement seats and the wire screen, beyond which he'll refuse ever to sit again.

Anxiously he awaits the main bout—sixth of a scheduled ten. What the sampan rower said yesterday is true: Torapee the Black Bull from the Northeast will destroy this upstart from the South! Chamlong's own judgment about Siamese boxing has always been good and is especially good tonight. He supposes that the soccer playing has given him insight into the way a boxer moves. For example, he watches a boxer's stomach to detect a shift in the muscles—that can mean a change in weight for a roundhouse kick. No one has ever told him such a thing; he's figured it out for himself. Chamlong is considering the depth of his judgment when a roar comes up from the crowd.

From opposite sides of the auditorium, to the cry of *EEE EEE EEE*, in come the main fighters of the evening. Each is barefoot, in silk trunks that almost reach the knees. Each wears the mongkhon, a headdress of rolled silk-covered rattan that circles the head in an "auspicious wheel," jutting out behind in a long tube of rattan from which a colored tassel dangles.

But only Torapee the Black Bull wears a full garland of flowers, which distinguishes him as a winner of more than fifty matches. Chamlong joins in the shouting for Torapee. He glances triumphantly at three Siamese nearby, wearing identical white shirts and baggy brown pants. He heard them earlier making great claims for the southern challenger, with only eighteen wins to his credit out of twenty fights.

Chamlong is not impressed by the Songkhla Demon. The boy looks sullen, keeping his head down as two trainers lead him through the yelling crowd. Perhaps he's afraid, Chamlong thinks. Overhead spotlights illuminate the white ring as both fighters climb through the ropes. On impulse Chamlong raises his right arm, holds one finger up. Turning, he looks at the three Siamese in their white shirts. "Torapee!" he shouts. "Ten!"

One of the men nods. "Eight!"

Chamlong nods too, a dip of his head self-consciously casual. He's just bet on the champion: one thousand bahts to eight hundred.

"Good bet," the man standing next to him declares. "He didn't get the odds he should from you."

Chamlong is proud of himself. "They must be from the South," he suggests knowingly.

"Well, let me tell you about the South. They have fighters down there."

Chamlong is vaguely disturbed by this comment. Yet he's encouraged by the look of the champion standing with his trainers. "I don't think anybody can beat Torapee tonight," he maintains.

"You're right," the man says. He's a short, dapper Chinese in a flowered shirt; he wears a Western fedora pulled down to his eyes. A gambler, Chamlong suspects—glad to be near such a man of experience.

Gloves are being tied on the boxers' hands. With the flower garland removed, Torapee looks good, Chamlong tells himself. Then the music starts. In a bleacher sits an orchestra: Four weary-looking old men play a pair of two-headed drums, cymbals, and a naga horn. As the percussive and wailing sounds permeate the smoky atmosphere, both fighters hold their gloved hands in the attitude of a *wai*. They move to the center of the ring, drop to their knees, and pray. The Songkhla Demon does so mechanically, whereas Torapee leans close to the mat, touching his forehead to it. And then he's on his feet, performing a dance in the classic way.

Shuffling in a path along the ropes, Torapee does a pantomime of searching for the enemy—head slightly cocked, gloves rotating at his chest in little circles to the rhythm of the drumming. Then he raises one leg off the mat, thrusts out his chest, and brings his arms slowly forward, fluttering the gloves like wings. It's a pose of Garuda, the bird-god whom Lord Vishnu rides.

Chamlong can feel in himself a surge of emotion as a memory of childhood sweeps through his mind: In the Siamese area where he lived, many people worshiped not only *phi* and Buddha but Brahman gods as well, and his mother kept a small wooden Garuda on a tiny stand, and in memory, while Torapee holds the pose, he can see her kneeling, with a *wai* made high above her head in obeisance to the bird god.

Most of the boxers tonight have done their dance of prowess, but none with the skill of Torapee. When the Black Bull has finished, he returns to his corner, where his trainer blesses him with a *wai*. Then the youthful southerner merely walks around the ring, giving a brusque salute at each corner.

In an instant Chamlong has rushed to the three Siamese in their white shirts and baggy pants. They see him coming through the milling crowd of bettors, and they smile. The one who's already bet with him says, "No more." Chamlong holds up his hand, as if it's a trophy. He sticks two fingers out.

"You'll bet that much on old Torapee?" one of the Siamese scoffs.

"He's only twenty-six," Chamlong shouts over the noise in the pit. "Come on." A third finger sticks out.

The Siamese who hasn't yet spoken nods. He says something and Chamlong nods too.

But on his return to the folding chair, just as the referee has waved the two fighters to the middle of the ring, Chamlong realizes he has bet three thousand bahts against fifteen hundred. Two-to-one odds. Rotten for this fight, and he knows it. Where's the man in the Western hat? Chamlong sees him angrily gesticulating at a man up in the cement seats. The man finally waves his hand, the man in the hat nods.

Chamlong is glad the gambler didn't see him bet again. It's a foolish bet. But when the bell rings, excitement takes over from apprehension. He leans forward, nearly as tense as the men in the ring. The fighters, their headdresses removed, approach each other, gloves held open at face level, as if ready to deliver a playful cuff. Tentatively they kick and punch from a distance, shooting for thigh and bicep to slow each other down. The music has stopped, so from ringside Chamlong can hear the little explosions of breath that accompany a thrown blow. Torapee often raises one leg as if to knee his opponent; it's a defense against the Song-khla Demon's aggressive crowding.

Noticing that the gambler in the Western hat has returned to his chair, Chamlong says to him confidently, "Crowding won't work. To-rapee has got him."

The gambler doesn't comment, but pushes the brim of his hat slightly up above his eyes. Chamlong notices scar tissue at the edge of the left eye. Was the man once a boxer too? Or was he cut in a gang fight?

His attention shifts back to the ring when a roar of *"EEE EEE EEE"* comes up from the crowd. "What happened?" he yells, seeing both fighters in their lazy shuffle again.

"Torapee got him with a kick," the gambler says calmly, without looking at Chamlong.

"I thought so." He glances at the three men in white shirts, who are watching with calm faces. He starts to add up his profits thus far in the evening, when suddenly Torapee whips out with a roundhouse kick, misses, and whirls completely around; with the leg still extended, he catches the Songkhla Demon this second time with a terrific blow to the back of the head. Chamlong saw him do it last year and knock his opponent out, but this time, to Chamlong's surprise and dismay, the southerner merely backs off a couple of paces, then bores in again.

"He almost went down," Chamlong says to the gambler.

"He takes a punch."

The round ends.

Both men, unhurt, go to their corners, where trainers slide out big metal trays on which the ring stools are placed. As a handler massages Torapee's biceps, Chamlong studies him. He is sweating, of course—with nearly a full crowd, it's hot in the stadium—but he's not even breathing hard.

"It was the Bull's round," Chamlong tells the gambler, who nods without comment. Behind them Chamlong hears a man claiming that Torapee's getting old, he can't kick, he's flabby. Turning, Chamlong glares at this man and his companion, who are passing a bottle of Me-kong whiskey back and forth. He feels indignant, as if his judgment has been called in question. And in a way it has. Chamlong has bet four thousand bahts on his judgment of boxing. He turns now toward the trio of judges at ringside who'll give a decision if it goes five rounds. But they might as well go home, Chamlong thinks. The Bull will get him by the third.

When the second round begins, each fighter holds the other by the neck, and with the free hand batters at the other's ribs. Each uses a raised knee to seek the groin or, by swinging the leg wider, to rap the kidney. Close contact seems to arouse more energy in both men, and they flail away in earnest.

Half the people in the pit—Chamlong among them—are on their feet, and along with people on the cement benches and those behind the wire screen are yelling *"EEE EEE EEE"* rhythmically after each blow. Adding to the noise is the orchestra, which has started playing again at the first sign of real contact. Holding each other in a sweaty embrace, circling, the fighters jab and knee-kick, while the referee stands back to watch.

"The Bull's holding his own!" Chamlong yells at the gambler.

The gambler nods.

"Isn't he?"

"He's a little tired."

Tired? Chamlong stares at the champion, who has finally been separated from his opponent by the referee. The Bull is breathing hard, but so is the Demon, who now seems less straight, almost as much in a crouch as the champion. They are circling again, cautiously, as if the blows each delivered have earned respect. Chamlong glances around. The pit is seething with people who no longer sit calmly in their chairs. Men are shouting, lifting fingers up, waving their spread hands. The betting has increased, but Chamlong can't tell how it's going. The cry of *"EEE EEE EEE"* goes up as the fighters exchange kicks and punches. Torapee hits the younger man with a right—*"KWAH!"* the arena yells in unison, *"KWAH!"* urging him to throw another right hand. And he does. *"KWAH! KWAH!"*

"See?" Chamlong yells at the gambler, who nods.

Torapee continues the attack, but the Demon counters with left jabs to a new chorus of *"SAI! SAI!"* The Bull comes forward, however, looking heavier than his hundred and thirty pounds. His eyes, pillowed in scar tissue, seek a weakness in the taller challenger. A few desultory kicks follow, then the two men back away.

"He'll win this round too!" Chamlong shouts.

"Maybe so," the gambler says.

The music, which had stopped, starts again, and the whining sound of the flute coils through the smoky arena. Suddenly the southerner whips out his foot to catch Torapee on the left hip, then, following with a left hand, snaps the Bull's head back.

The crowd roars. The stadium echoes with an encouraging *"SAI! SAI! KWAH! SAI!"* but Chamlong finds a yell frozen in his own throat. The Bull is backpedaling from a rain of blows when the round ends.

Turning to the gambler, he says, "Even?"

The gambler nods and walks away.

Chamlong anxiously watches the handlers work over Torapee, who sits breathing heavily on the stool. One trainer fans him with a towel, another whispers in his ear while rubbing his neck, arms. Glancing at the three Siamese, Chamlong is furious to see them returning the look —and smiling.

What he can't understand is Torapee's failure to watch the challenger's stomach muscles. They're the key to his tactics. Each time he's ready for the combination his stomach, just below the navel, bunches up like a small twisting rope. Chamlong's sure of this. If he can see it, why can't Torapee? It's so *easy* to see from here.

Something else bothers him too. At the end of the last round, instead of going quietly to his corner, the Songkhla Demon raised his arms in premature victory.

It's impolite. It's rude.

The Chinese household has drummed tradition into Chamlong, but until tonight he had never really felt it. Now he has, looking at the Songkhla Demon, who pushes aside the water bottle and grins at his trainer. Before the fight he never prayed respectfully or performed a dance as he should. Now that he's had a good round, the Demon's smirking arrogantly. Chamlong's only sorry that the gambler isn't next to him, so he can say, "What do you think of this southerner? Don't they teach them respect in Songkhla? It's an insult to the stadium." Chamlong feels the indignation of righteousness; he has never felt so old, so conservative, so Chinese.

When the third round begins, everyone in the pit crowds close to the ring, pushing Chamlong shoulder to shoulder with men drinking whiskey. They're still making bets with other gamblers standing in the bleachers.

Supporters of the Demon are no longer getting odds. The side bets made now, Chamlong notices uneasily, are even.

Both fighters waste no time circling, but engage with a quick series of punches. The music for this round has already begun, and to the drumbeat the Songkhla Demon dances back and forth on his toes, while Torapee, flat-footed, stalks him. After another short exchange, they both kick at once—their right legs smack together in midair with a sound heard through the large stadium. The Songkhla Demon is expelling his breath loudly with each punch, encouraging Chamlong to hope he's all rush and arrogance, but no sooner does Chamlong register this thought than the southerner connects with a powerful left hand, then a kick that sends Torapee back against the ropes. For an instant Chamlong fears the Bull will go down: he is staggering on rubbery legs, eyes glazed, gloves held waist high. Fortunately for the Bull, the Songkhla Demon dances in triumph rather than continuing the attack.

Chamlong hates him.

Watching the champion shuffle forward, head lowered between his gloves, Chamlong thinks of himself, of the injustice that hounds him tonight. Nothing is fair, nothing is the way it should be.

When the round ends, he turns away from the ring. Men are mopping their foreheads in the heat, swigging from Mekong bottles, opening their shirts a button. Most of the men at ringside wear trousers, but a few are wearing sarongs, like the majority of spectators in the cement bleachers and behind the wire screen—they pinch the cotton away from their legs and flail a little to move some air inside.

He sees the three Siamese standing alone, out of the turmoil. They're reading the program, as if they've decided how this bout will end. As if they're bored with it now and look forward to the rest of the card.

She said five, he thinks. Sanuk told him since he's a Royal Tiger five is his lucky number.

Walking up to the three men, he holds up five fingers outstretched from his hand.

They all smile.

"I mean it," he tells them. "But even. I won't give odds."

"No more," says the man with whom he'd made the first bet of a thousand bahts.

"You Siamese."

"What's that?" asks the one he hasn't bet with.

"This is *Siamese* boxing, isn't it? But you won't bet when the stake's high. Don't you Siamese have *pride?*"

"Who ever bet on pride."

"What are you, a Lukjin?" another asks.

"I'll cover that bet. Five thousand. Even," says the one with whom Chamlong has already bet three thousand.

Chamlong nods without a word and returns to the crowd along the ring. He has bet five, the Royal's Tiger lucky number, and the thought of it thrills and frightens him. Watching Torapee rise from the ring stool, he tells himself that victory is theirs. Together they'll show everybody.

In this mood of optimism, Chamlong watches the first blows exchanged; they are tentative, as if the previous round had wearied both fighters. Torapee yanks his blue trunks up and raises his left leg as if to take a giant step, but this time the Demon ignores the defensive maneuver and bulls in, catching Torapee with a left hand, jarring him back. "*SAI! SAI!*" mounts to a new pitch, suggesting there's a new mood of expectation among the spectators. "*SAI! KWAH! SAI! SAI!*"

Torapee, aware of being in trouble, gives up the flat-footed stance to pedal backward around the ring, making the challenger follow him.

Backing away, running. It's not his style, Chamlong thinks in dismay. And then for an instant he forgets the fight, although his eyes continue to watch it. He's thinking of the money in his pocket. He isn't sure how much is there. Perhaps a little more than nine thousand or a little less. If only he could think clearly. So many people making so much noise makes it impossible for him to estimate if he has enough to pay them. Or should he pay them? Of course, everyone knows a bet made within these walls must be paid. That's the rule. But what if someone breaks it? he wonders, just as his eyes register yet another terrific kick from the Demon. What if I pay part of it? Will that satisfy them? They hadn't wanted to bet anyway.

"*EEE EEE EEE*" rings through the arena as the Bull staggers against the ropes.

The orchestra is playing full tilt now; the chorus of yells is accented by the deep throb of the drums, the figured wail of the horn, the clang of cymbals. Craning his neck, Chamlong tries to locate the three Siamese in the crowd, which surges around the ring. Where are they? Well, they are there. But not seeing them gives him a sudden rush of hope. It is going to be all right. We will win.

And as this thought enters his mind, Chamlong watches the Bull move out of a covering crouch and strike the Demon squarely in the stomach with a roundhouse kick.

The challenger goes down to one knee, then bounces up again almost before the referee has reached him. Another kick by Torapee is intercepted by the Demon's gloves, which thrust his leg away, making the champion lose his balance and stagger back against the ropes.

"*EEE EEE EEE EEE EEE!*"

Both fighters fall into a clinch, giving Chamlong time for another searching look around the crowd. His eye catches that of the dapper gambler in the Western hat. "He'll win!" Chamlong yells. Appalled, he watches the gambler cross his hands rapidly in a gesture of hopelessness.

But he will, Chamlong tells himself, turning to scream out "*KWAH! KWAH!*" as the champion connects with two quick rights to the cheek and heart. They come together in a clinch, but the taller challenger wrestles Torapee to the mat, kneeing him in the chin as he goes down.

"*EEE EEE EEE EEE EEE!*"

The Bull rises slowly. His chest and shoulders are visibly red, as he runs into another clinch. The Demon holds his glove flat against Torapee's face while kneeing him in the stomach, and follows with a hard left to the jaw. Chamlong can see the champion's eyes go wide, go narrow, his mouth open. The Demon lands a straight foot to the heart. The arena seethes like an angry sea; men cluster here and there, pushing one another to get unobstructed views. The champion, plainly hurt, keeps his gloves high, against his cheeks, legs bent, wobbling. The Demon, at last flat-footed too, gasping for air, swings wildly with both hands, kicks Torapee in the ribs. The champion sends out a light left jab but, retracting his arm too slowly, leaves his head exposed for a kick —And it comes: a full swinging kick that catches him on the temple. He goes down.

The crowd screams until not even the drums can be heard.

The left leg of the fallen champion twitches, his chest heaves in quick gusty jerks. The Songkhla Demon circles the ring, holding both gloves high.

Eight, nine thousand? Chamlong is thinking. More? Or less?

. . .

There's a swirling crush around the ring, as bettors seek one another out to settle wagers. Chamlong yanks the bank notes from one pocket. Rapidly he counts, stuffs them back, takes money from the other pocket. He has nine thousand and . . . although he just counted he's not sure how much more—a few hundred. Putting four thousand alone in one pocket, he bends over and jams the rest between his right foot and sandal. Rising up, he looks around quickly, but the mob is thick here, milling and shouting. It would be hard for anyone, he thinks, to find him in the turmoil. Men are reaching down from the cement benches to give or take money, as Chamlong slips through the crowd, watching balefully for the three Siamese.

They see him first, but wait where they are, letting him come to them.

"The fight was fixed," is the first thing Chamlong says. "That southerner couldn't take Torapee in a fair fight."

"No?"

Turning, Chamlong sees the Bull's two trainers helping the half-conscious man to his feet. "It was fixed anyway."

Glancing sideways at the men, he sees they haven't moved, but regard him coolly. "I can pay," he tells them. Taking the money from his pocket, he turns to the man he'd first bet with. "Here." The man takes two five-hundred-baht notes. "Here," he says to the second man, handing over six five-hundred-baht notes. "Now," he says, clearing his throat, "I haven't got the other five thousand with me."

"Where are they?" one asks.

"I have to get them tomorrow." He smiles at each man. The arena is calming down now. Both fighters have left the ring, and bettors are moving around the pit, looking for new wagers. "Tell me where you'll be tomorrow or write your address."

"You can find us here," one says.

"I promise to pay. I'll pay," Chamlong assures them. What unnerves him momentarily is their passive acceptance of the arrangement. He has expected some bullying and threats, although nothing can make him surrender what he has left.

"You'll be here tomorrow night?" one asks.

"I promise."

"Because we don't want to lose what we fairly won."

"I told you. I have to round up the money tomorrow and I'll be here. Everyone who comes here pays up, don't they?"

"They do."

"Then—tomorrow." Chamlong smiles in farewell, raises his hand, turns quickly, and moves through the crowd without looking back.

• • •

The thing to do, he tells himself on reaching the entrance, is take a samlor to the hotel. The memory of their white shirts and open collars has followed him through the packed auditorium. They looked harmless and neat in those white shirts, but somehow in memory the shirts remind him of the open-collared khaki shirts of the Asawins.

Why do people pay their debts at the stadium? Because gamblers enforce the rule. It's known.

Chamlong has always known it. Behind the wire screen, high above the ring, he and his young companions used to speak in awe of the Bangkok gamblers, who'd slit your throat for a wrong look.

He has known it. Why, therefore, has he taken such a chance? Having arrived outside, Chamlong stares at the long line of samlors parked near the entrance.

Bending down, he takes the money from his sandal and puts it in his pocket. He'll go back and pay them, Chamlong decides. But no sooner has he taken three steps toward the brightly lit entrance of the stadium than he sees the three Siamese men in their white shirts.

Trying to smile, Chamlong calls out to them, "I was coming back to see you!"

"Why is that?" one says. Chamlong notices for the first time he has a tiny tattoo on his right earlobe—one of those magical designs that ward off evil.

"Well, I just found in my back pocket the money I thought I had to get tomorrow. It was with me all the time." He smiles painfully, looking from one expressionless face to another. "I forgot." He plunges one hand into his pocket. "I was coming to find you."

"Let's go talk," the man with the tattoo says.

"I'll just pay you and—"

The other two men have gripped Chamlong by his upper arms. He can see their lips trembling. Fear courses through his legs, weakening them until he can hardly walk, when the trio leads him away from the lights of the stadium into an alley.

There they push him gently against the wall of a shack. This is a poultry market, and the sweet heavy smell of chicken blood pervades the area. Opposite them, in a two-story house, a light is shining, its flare angling across the narrow lane, an arm's-breadth away from where they've put Chamlong against the wall.

"I was coming back." He hears the high, faint pitch of his own voice. "I was . . . afraid."

"Yes, I believe that," says the tattooed man coolly. "You looked afraid."

"Are you a Lukjin?" another asks.

"My mother was Siamese."

"A whore?"

"Never mind that," says the tattooed man. "You," he says to Chamlong, "are a fool."

"Yes, I know that."

"You know it only now, when you're here with us."

"His mother was a whore for the Chinese, so now he thinks he is Chinese."

"Never mind that," repeats the tattooed man. "I don't think you'd be that foolish again," he says to Chamlong.

Hope rising, Chamlong agrees. "You're right. I won't be, I promise."

"Look at him," one of the others declares in disgust.

"We could cut you," the tattooed man tells Chamlong in the same tone of voice he's used all the time: not harsh or threatening, but too neutral to be pleasant, like someone giving a direction.

"I know that." Chamlong feels the fear go through him again, numbing his legs like poison. "I won't be a fool again. I promise."

"You're lucky you were coming back. Or looked as if you were coming back. That's lucky for you."

"I hope so."

"Let's have the money."

Chamlong digs it out of his pocket again and hands it to the tattooed man, who calmly takes it, then hits him very hard in the stomach, very hard.

On the ground, smelling the strong odor of chicken blood, Chamlong feels them kicking him hard in the stomach, groin, arms, and legs. But the pain is less than the fear. He hears himself whimpering and pleading, but fear is what settles hard and solid in his brain. Not even the numbing blow in his groin, bringing up a well of nausea, can overtake the fear that's telling him rapidly, at incredible speed, now will they cut now will they bring out the knife cut you stomach throat eyes balls anywhere they want they can do it do it do it—

The men step quietly back and regard him lying there in the dust of the alley, retching, clutching his groin.

The man to whom he owes the five thousand bends down to Chamlong. "Say you are Siamese."

He opens his eyes, looking into a face silhouetted in the light slanting down from the opposite building. I say it, Chamlong thinks, then he kills me.

"Say you are Siamese."

Chamlong doesn't understand. He asks, "What?" and the word comes out like a groan.

"I said say you're Siamese."

Chamlong groans.

"You better say it."

"I am Siamese," Chamlong mutters.

"But the Siamese don't want a coward like me. Say it."

"But the Siamese don't want a coward like me."

"So I pretend I'm Chinese."

"So I pretend I'm Chinese."

The man he owed money to rises.

Having counted the money, the tattooed man stands over Chamlong and lets some bank notes drift down on his curled body. "That's yours."

"I think we ought to cut him," one says.

"Never mind that," says the tattooed man. "Let him do himself in. He will." Leading the other two away, he strolls out of the alley, turning in the direction of the stadium.

Chamlong lies there a long time, moving only when a street dog comes along, sniffing. When he sits up, Chamlong realizes they didn't really hurt him—thanks to the tattooed one, who probably saved his life. It's strange, but he's glad to be alive at the same moment he's filled with deep humiliation. Glancing around he finds the discarded money, counts it: two hundred ten bahts. That's something.

Rising unsteadily, he feels nauseated again and has to lean against the wall. When the feeling subsides, he looks around. From the opposite building comes the sound of laughter, male and then female.

The one he owed five thousand to was the worst, Chamlong thinks.

Taking his hand from the wall, he judges his ability to walk, then takes one step, two, three. He's all right. Someday he'll be a man no one dares to humiliate or call a Siamese. He is Ho Jin-shi. He vows in a tense whisper that no one will dare to humiliate Ho Jin-shi ever again. The oath gives him strength enough to stagger out of the alley.

Now his only hope is Wan-li.

• • •

This thought carries him—the Golden Lion, Chinese revolutionary—into the Bangkok night. But the problem is finding his cousin, who surely, after the raid, left the room where he had stayed since coming to Siam. Every leader has a contact address assigned to him in case he goes into hiding. A message left there will reach him.

With the new plan in mind, Ho Jin-shi heads straight for the Chinatown laundry shop assigned to his cousin. By the time he gets there, his head's clear, his body sore but nothing broken. The tattooed Siamese was right about him—he's been lucky. The truth of it keeps him hopeful, while his mind races through the possibilities awaiting him at this laundry shop in a soi near Sua Pa Road: Wan-li is there; Wan-li is not there, but someone knows where he is; no one is there, the shop having been raided.

One thing Ho is sure of: He can trust Wan-li. They have something in common. Both have been disowned by their fathers. It happened to Wan-li when he returned to Siam from Canton, where he'd been living with a radical uncle who supported Mao and the Liberation Army fighting in the North. As soon as Wan-li's father learned of his activities as a Communist agitator, the old man went to a local temple and publicly denounced the memory of his son, who according to him was dead.

We are now like brothers, Ho thinks as he turns into the soi. Along the way are tailor shops, a couple of herbal stores, a silversmith. The laundry, as he suspected, is still open, even though it's almost midnight. Steam issues from the doorway, and Ho can see an old man bending over a laundry iron filled with charcoal.

"Old Father," Ho calls from the open doorway.

The man, squinting, puts aside the iron. "Well, bring it."

Entering, Ho says, "I haven't brought laundry. I'm looking for my cousin. Everything depends on finding him." For emphasis he repeats it. "Everything."

The laundryman looks at him.

"Did you hear me, Father?"

The man nods.

"Wan-li is his name. Ho Wan-li."

"I don't know him," the laundryman says in a dry, faint voice that seems to come from a place high in his throat.

"I'm his cousin. If I don't find him, everything is lost. Do you understand, Father?"

"What people say, divide by five." He picks up the iron and returns to the skirt he's pressing.

"Let me leave a message then."

The old man responds by shoving the iron firmly across the cloth. Ho takes a square little piece of paper used for billing and a pencil stub lying on the counter and writes: "Ho Jin-shi must see Ho Wan-li."

It's a long chance, but the only one left. "Please," he says.

The old man looks up briefly from the iron.

. . .

Next morning Ho can't wait, but hurries back to the shop, where his heart sinks, for the old man isn't there. A younger man and two girls are working in the laundry, from which great puffs of humid steam surge into the alley.

Yet when Ho introduces himself and asks if they have anything for him, one of the girls wordlessly hands him the same square of paper on which he'd written the message last night. Under his own are the words: "Wat Benchamabopit. Two-thirty."

Promptly at two-thirty Ho Jin-shi enters the temple grounds and nervously glances at people strolling there. No Wan-li among them, as they admire the ornate marble bot.

From the moment of reading the message, Ho has feared it's a trap, yet there's no other choice. Sun is beating down on the gold tiles of the bot, flashing as if the building were on fire. The light is harsh, piercing, and when Ho steps through the entranceway between guardian marble lions, he's momentarily blinded. Then out of the cool darkness, by candlelight, eternal shapes emerge: Straight ahead is the main Buddha, big-bellied, with a round face in the Sukhothai style, his fingers of equal length; small buddhas, both seated and standing, flank the large bronze. There are wall niches that hold pictures, but Ho turns impatiently away, once he's made sure that none of the worshipers, kneeling on the floor, is Wan-li.

Passing between the two singha again, Ho watches a courtyard of pigeons swirl up, then plummet down, fix themselves to the marble yard.

He won't come.

This panicky thought carries Ho farther into the temple complex. He stares at the little canal; it's filled with turtles released by people who want to gain merit (even in his fear he recalls coming here with his mother when she slipped a turtle—bought for the purpose—out of a sack into the water). Beyond the canal is the monastery, not a monk in sight. Turning back, he squints through the afternoon brilliance at the bot again, glittering white and gold. No one but old people, young couples, skipping children—no one that counts. No Wan-li.

Remembering there's a back courtyard, enclosed from the rest of the temple, Ho rushes toward the door leading to it. He glances at a carved marble gable of Vishnu riding Garuda. Garuda. It was the memory of the god-bird's little statue in his mother's house that had blinded him to Torapee's aging incompetence.

In the enclosed courtyard, within a covered gallery, stand more than fifty Buddha images, both originals and copies of famous Siamese bronzes. They represent every period of art: Davaravati, Khmer, Lop-buri, Sukhothai, Ayutthaya, and Bangkok, among others, both small and large, sitting and standing. But Ho doesn't see them. Or rather for an instant he stares at the raised hand of one of them, palm outward, signifying "Fear not." Fear not. Where is Wan-li? Only a few people are dragging from sculpture to sculpture, looking into time that has nothing to do with them, and not one of them remotely like his cousin. Lost. He remembers again coming here with his mother to release the turtle. How many years ago?

Lost.

He is lost unless there's help, yet the world supplies none. Ho studies his watch, as if there's something wrong with it. Father gave me this old watch, Ho thinks, when he got a better one. The dials behind the scratched glass say three o'clock. That's not so late, only a half-hour late. Wan-li might yet come.

Wan-li owes it to him to come. Arriving in Bangkok from Canton, tired and suspicious, having forgotten most of his childhood Thai, Cousin Wan-li had depended upon him a few months ago. Ho had got him a hotel room in a safe part of Chinatown. Ho had tried hard to convince him of the efficiency and good will of the local Communist Party members. Patiently he had explained Bangkok politics: how the government was harassing the Chinese people in Siam; how the Red publishing company had relocated and awaited inspiration from the great journalist from Canton; how everyone would support Ho Wan-li from China because he alone could lead the Chinese people, through his Communist writing, to resist the evil Siamese government. Outdoing himself in inventiveness, Ho had flattered his cousin, along with bring-ing him food and taking his laundry and buying him paper and correct-ing his Thai and encouraging him, as if he were a child, to have faith and courage. Ho had never tried harder with anyone in his life. He'd missed work in the store and Father had cursed him for it. And after a few days, when Wan-li mustered up the courage and trust, Ho had brought Party members to the hotel room. He had done all that for Wan-li in the spirit of family and of revolution too, so both as a cousin and a Communist Wan-li owes him the same loyalty, the same consid-eration. But will he get them?

Returning to the front entrance, Ho looks in every direction, trying between the tall pickets of the iron fence to see his cousin coming along. Then, returning to the canal, he looks thoughtfully at the low-slung buildings where the monks live. Would Wan-li—? No. He wouldn't go into the monastery.

Turning, Ho must exert control not to run back to the enclosed courtyard. That's where Wan-li must be waiting. Must, must be waiting! He walks rapidly, looking to both sides, and reaches the courtyard only to find it empty save for two children and their mother, who carries a parasol.

Lost.

And then he sees a figure moving near the east wall, slipping into the covered gallery.

When Ho reaches his cousin's side, Wan-li is studying a large Sukhothai bronze, its arched eyebrows meeting at the bridge of a hooked nose.

"I've been looking for you," Ho begins breathlessly.

"You don't have to let everyone know it."

"You're late," Ho observes reproachfully.

"I'm not late. Careful." He regards the woman with her children. "Chin Yin-nan is dead."

"Ah. How do you know?"

"His body was found in a klong this morning."

"Somchai?"

"We don't know. But the Asawins have our names. That we know."

"Mine too?"

Wan-li turns slightly to regard him. "Of course yours. What is that?" He points to a large purple bruise on Ho's bare arm.

"Nothing. A samlor bumped me on the street."

"You can't afford a stupid accident."

Ho nods. "What happens to us now?"

Wan-li explains the Party goes underground. It has happened before elsewhere; it will happen again to people bent on changing the world. With faith there's nothing to worry about.

Faith. For Ho Jin-shi the word seems to resonate in the cool gallery, though it was spoken in a whisper. His cousin is a cold man, yet he talks sometimes like a bhikkhu, like one of those who used to lecture in the temple when Ho was a boy and went there with his mother. Wan-li is like that sometimes, which is why Ho trusts him.

"Are you all right?" Wan-li asks.

"Yes, of course I am. Why?"

"You look sick."

"Well, you see, I did something." Ho pauses, not having thought out what he'd tell or not tell Wan-li. "I needed money. I was desperate for it. You understand? So I took a little—not much—from one of Father's safes."

Wan-li chuckles. "Why not? He's exploited others, including you, for a lifetime. If the money helps you, good."

"But he won't rest till I'm found. He'll have all the Teochiu organizations helping him. Father knows everybody."

Wan-li purses his lips, considering this development. "What do you want?"

"I want to get out of the country."

"Well, you could go South awhile."

"Not South. No." He's thinking of the man stuffed in the outcropping on the gulf, white as a dead fish.

"Does she want to leave the country?"

"Who?"

Wan-li wets his lips. "Have you thought about this carefully?"

"Yes," lies Ho, having just thought about it.

"All right then. Let me think about it too. Come here tomorrow at the same time."

"Please don't be late. I went crazy waiting."

"Now that I know it's you, I won't be late."

• • •

When his cousin arrives at Wat Benchamabopit the next day, Ho looks at his watch. Only three minutes late—that's a good sign.

And indeed, Wan-li has brought good news. Last night at a meeting of the Executive Committee of the Chinese Communist Party of Siam, it was decided that Comrade Ho Jin-shi would be entrusted with a message of great importance.

He is to take this message to China and give it personally to the exiled Premier of Siam, Phanomyong Pridi, who's accepted the protection of revolutionary forces there. The former Premier is planning to return to Siam. His return will mean an invasion of Bangkok. It will mean an overthrow of the present imperialist regime.

"So you see," Wan-li concludes, "you've been given an important mission."

"I'll go up in the Party," says an overwhelmed Ho.

"No doubt about it."

"I owe you everything," he says impulsively, but Wan-li waves his hand to ward off gratitude.

"Since you robbed the old thief," Wan-li says, "you have money to pay your way to China." With a smile, he adds, "Well, isn't it true?"

"Yes, it's true."

"Then *you* pay. The Party can't afford it. Not when we need money to hide out like this."

"I understand."

"Here's the name of someone who'll make you forged papers. He's one of us, so he won't charge much. Not that *you* can't afford it." Wan-li looks him over coolly. "Are you well?"

"Of course."

"You look worried. Don't do that when you're on the run. Don't look like you're running."

"I won't," Ho declares. He can't understand his cousin's sour attitude.

But then lately everything has bounced against everything else: good joss, bad joss, luck swinging from pole to pole, good following bad and bad following good with blinding speed. Here his cousin has brought wonderful news, but delivers it bitterly and then turns critic.

"One other thing. Leave the girl here. Don't take her along. You were thinking of that, weren't you?"

"No," he says honestly.

Again Wan-li smiles. His lips glisten as his tongue plays over them. "I'll watch over her. Don't worry."

When they part, Ho sits with a cup of tea in a Siamese shop. No one knows him in this area, so he's safe unless by chance an old acquaintance should happen upon this shop, recognize him, and run for the police. Ah, it can happen, he thinks, sipping the dregs of his tea.

Although his fortune has changed swiftly in a short time, good bad good bad, it has finally become too bad to turn good again. The planets are definitely against him; Sanuk has been wrong about his horoscope all along. The thing is, he can't tell his cousin the stolen money is gone. Wan-li would want to know why. What would the Party think? They wouldn't let a gambler carry an important message to the exiled Premier. Who knows, they might even turn him over to the police. But maybe not, because he could betray them, just as Somchai must have done when they put the poor fellow to torture.

Sitting there, brooding, Ho lets his thoughts turn to Sanuk. Lately he hasn't had time to think of being in a hotel room with her. Bad luck alternating with good luck has drained him of desire. But since his cousin mentioned her at the wat, her presence hasn't left him: the young woman who has walked beside him, accompanied him to meetings, given him money, assured him she would always help. Like an animal stalking its prey to a final moment of decision, Ho follows this presence of Sanuk through his mind until, bolting the tea shop, he too must act.

First he buys a broad-brimmed rattan fisherman's hat at a stand. Assured that it hides his face, Ho takes a samlor down to a section of river front lined with fishermen's shacks. This area, because of crime, is often patroled by the Metropolitan Police; therefore it's dangerous for him. And yet, leaving the samlor, Ho Jin-shi tells himself he must take a chance. Fate hasn't left him another choice, not one. Taking a deep breath, he strides toward a cluster of huts standing in muddy water on thin pilings. Warily, from under the wide brim, he looks around for khaki uniforms. Ahead is what he's looking for: boys kicking a ball near a garbage dump smelling of fish.

"Where is Sopon?" Ho calls out commandingly.

Only one boy turns from the game and points.

Past them, along the stinking waterfront, he walks quickly, keeping an eye out for khaki. Ahead of him some women are crouching around a large wicker basket, cleaning river fish, and beyond them there's another pack of boys. Approaching, Ho can see between the onlookers two boys brandishing wooden swords at each other. And among the onlookers he sees Sopon, a boy of ten or eleven, naked save for a cut-down pair of ragged khaki shorts.

Ho feels a moment of open tenderness at the look of Sopon, his own look a dozen years ago: matted hair gray from dirt; knees huge in the middle of skinny legs; hands huge too at the ends of sticklike arms.

When Ho calls, the boy turns with a sullen glance, then continues to watch the playful duel a good minute before peeling off from the group and joining Ho.

"I have a message," Ho tells him, then realizes in the rush it hasn't been written. "Get me a pencil and paper."

Sopon regards him narrowly. "Why the hat?"

"Just get me a pencil and paper."

"You don't look like a fisherman, if that's what you want." Sopon extends his hand. "Ten satang for renting the pencil. They won't give it to me if I don't pay. Come on, what's ten satang?"

Impatiently Ho digs into his pocket. Sopon will keep the ten satang and borrow a pencil from one of the whores up there, who may or may not be his mother. Watching the boy scamper off, Ho's afraid of getting turned in. Sopon's a clever boy, a tough boy, just like he himself had been. Given the opportunity to turn in a wanted criminal, would he, at Sopon's age, have gone for the pencil or for the police? Ho doesn't know. He won't know either until someone comes down from those whore-houses that line the wharf area like festering sores.

But he breathes freely when Sopon appears, running lightly across the muddy waterfront, carrying a pencil like a small torch.

Ho writes carefully, laboriously, with the paper on his knee, and Sopon, who can't read, peering over his shoulder. "Are you better? I hope so. Must see you. Important. Call at Laemtong Hotel or send message. Come soon."

He feels it's an act of wisdom not to sign it. But will she know enough to ask for his new Chinese name? You can't trust women to figure out such things, so he adds, after "message," another phrase: "to my friend Ho Jin-shi." That will confuse anyone who might intercept it, he thinks happily.

Giving it to Sopon, he hauls out a baht and hands it over.

The boy shakes his head.

"What's wrong?"

"Not enough."

"You took a note to her last week for a baht. It was enough then."

"The price has gone up."

"Why? She'll send the answer herself. You'll only do one trip."

The boy shakes his head. "I have to go there and throw the pebbles and throw them right, so they hit on the second floor near her room. That's not easy. I have to pitch them from across the street under this tree or someone'll see me. If I throw them wrong, against another part of the house, one of those women will hear it hit and come down. Or if they don't hear and she does, then I have to wait under that tree until she comes down to give it to her. That can take time, because those women might be around, watching. Let me tell you they know how to watch, the old Chinese woman and the cook and that Siamese who I heard them call Nipa. And if they catch me, at least they'll beat me for mischief or maybe take me in there and ask a lot of questions and I'll have to keep my mouth shut, won't I. All of that's worth more than a baht."

Ho fishes out a salehng.

"Make it another." Sopon looks up at him with a hopeful smile. "Come on. That's only two bahts altogether."

After giving the boy another salehng, Ho watches him tear off to deliver the message.

• • •

Ho doesn't sleep that night, and when the dawn rises over Bangkok, he stands at the small open window of his hotel room, telling himself again and again, Lost, I am lost. The day drags forward, each second of it oozing out of a small tight hole, until late in the afternoon, there's a knock at the door.

It's a young girl, about thirteen, with breasts starting to bud. She looks up at him from wide, fearful eyes. "Ho Jin-shi?"

"Who are you?" he asks suspiciously, looking into the narrow hall behind her.

"Ho Jin-shi?"

He realizes the girl's been told to pronounce those words, nothing more. "I know him."

"Ho Jin-shi?"

With a sigh he tells her, "Yes, I'm Ho Jin-shi."

Reaching between her blouse and the top of her sarong, the girl picks out a folded paper and hands it to him.

When he unfolds it, he reads with relief: *"Tee rahk."* She hasn't forgotten him. But what follows only confirms his bad luck. "Still the fever. Doctor came today, but doesn't know what it is. Nothing serious, though. Don't worry. Your note sounded urgent. I worry for you. As soon as I am better I will come. You know me. That is my promise. I will send message to this hotel unless you write otherwise. Don't worry. Trust me. Your Sanuk."

"Message?" the girl asks faintly when he's finished reading.

After staring at her, Ho Jin-shi says, "Yes." He closes the door and sits on the bed with a nub of pencil, a torn piece of newspaper. Trust her? I must, he thinks. In the clear space at the top of the paper, he writes: *"Tee rahk.* Come soon. I need you." When he's given the folded paper to the girl waiting outside, Ho begins pacing in his squalid room. Perhaps her fever is real, and after it has passed she'll come. But when she learns I need money, will she help? Her farang mother is rich, but what does that mean? After all, I have a rich parent too. It's a strange thing to put faith in a woman, he thinks solemnly. The thought brings him to a halt in the little room. Can I trust a woman? The stars have deceived him into thinking they were lucky stars. Someone must help him, and soon, or everything will be lost. Everything. Lost.

24

AN EXTRAORDINARY PLACE, he thinks. Right for what I'm here for.

Standing beside the horse-drawn tonga, Embree stares at the hundreds of red-brick temples—those visible from this vantage point—of the thousands that still stand here at Pagan, after weather and looting have done their work for eight hundred years on the dusty plain of Central Burma.

Rama has remained in the little guest house they've taken in the village of Nyaung-Y. The young Indian claims he has a headache, but Embree suspects the real reason for staying away from the ancient temples of Pagan is otherwise: Such testimony to Buddhism, lying in ruins though it does, offends Rama's Hindu sensibility.

The last time Embree looked at this sagebrush plain, studded with spires, was during the last months of the war. A main Allied crossing had been made at Nyaung-U, and as the columns poured southward, many soldiers took a final glimpse over their packs at sunlight slanting down into the shadows of terrace, porch, and finial on the Pagan temples. Embree took such a last look, and the next day barely escaped death when someone detonated a Japanese land mine.

Today he has had another contact with the Japanese. It was on the plane from Rangoon. He and Rama and a half-dozen other passengers boarded a twin-engined Armstrong Whitsworth Albemarle. During the war it had been a specialized glider tug converted for transport duties and now, ruthlessly patched and hopefully retooled, it performed as an ex-RAF pilot's ferrying service between Rangoon, Pagan, and Mandalay. It was a very strange flight for Philip Embree, seated as he was on a bench opposite two Japanese men, dressed casually in slacks and open-collared white shirts. Last time he'd seen a Jap was in a Burman village three years ago. Aware the Nips were losing the war, the Burmans had decided to ingratiate themselves with the Allies by capturing and killing a Jap soldier. A villager, smoking a cheroot, was wearing the soldier's pot-shaped steel helmet; another his fatigue cap. Still another sported his waraji straw sandals that did better in mud than GI boots. These villagers had severed his genitals and stuffed them between his teeth. He was bloated in the heat, when Embree saw him; his arms and legs were as round and smooth as a baby's.

On the plane today one of the Japanese passengers made frequent trips to the cockpit, a map in hand, while the other, an older man, sat impassively, staring somewhere off Embree's right shoulder.

The younger Japanese finally came back from the cockpit in great excitement. The older one grabbed the map, and together they studied it. Then after a few minutes both leaned toward the small cabin window and peered down at the landscape advancing under bits of cloud. At a gruff command from the older one, they moved back from the window, stood at attention, and saluted stiffly. When they sat down again, tears were welling up in the older man's eyes.

Embree couldn't watch the man crying. He looked beyond the left shoulder of the white shirt into his own confused memories of war. He found them elusive and chaotic. Had his life been less eventful, would his memories be more coherent? It's one of those questions that only a fool wastes time on.

And yet what troubled him on the flight, as it has often troubled him recently, is this way events, particularly battles, fuse in his mind, so that he is fighting under General Tang at Hengshui in 1927 in the 1942 uniform of a British infantryman. The Japanese soldiers coming at him wear the arm bands of a Chinese warlord, and the dead face staring up at him that belonged to his friend Fu Chang-so, a cavalryman in Tang's army, becomes that of a Gurkha killed at Fort Dufferin. Perhaps a simpler life would have given him the comfort of orderly recollections. As it was, on the plane ride his mind seethed with images that came from all directions, out of different times. What he wanted was peace. Wasn't that true? Wasn't that why he'd crawled away to Madras and hid himself there, seeking God with crossed legs and closed eyes? Of course that's what he has told himself all this time, but is it *true?* Sometimes the terrible memories carry with them the awful beauty of men experiencing their most intense moments. Life lived on the knife edge has an appeal that's hard to put aside.

After the plane landed, he'd gone to the ex-RAF pilot and asked why the two Japs had been allowed to fly around Burma this way.

The pilot pushed the bill of his cap back. "You're asking me, Yank? Word I got, the Nip was a bloody colonel. The young one's his aide. Your MacArthur's given them permission to fly over a battlefield and salute their dead lads. I don't know, though." He pulls the bill down again. "Seems like this lot shouldn't be given favors."

"No," Embree said, without adding that the route they'd flown over today was one he'd fought through, mile by mile, and it was just possible he might have lost friends to troops that the former colonel, sobbing over a span of jungle, had once commanded.

So now he stands beside a tonga on the plain of Pagan, which in the thirteenth century had been a metropolis of half a million, a city of culture, which had finally fallen into the hands of Kublai Khan. It was the Golden Horde who defeated Pagan, the Mongols whom Philip Embree, during his early China days, had so admired that to emulate them he'd learned to sleep, as they'd done in their campaigns, on the back of a horse.

From where he stands, he can see Ananda Temple, its terraced sides whitewashed, its stupa golden. He picks out other great Mon and Burmese temples on the map he carries. The tonga driver, hunched beneath the canvas roof of his carriage, waits patiently in the silence. There's an eerie silence here, on the Pagan plain, yet a rush of centuries too, a rush of sadness and grandeur that seems discernible to Embree in the wind moving through the thistled bushes. It's the place a Nat might come to, he thinks. That's an amusing idea, a terrible one. He won't try to communicate with Harry. He hasn't tried that, really, has he? That would be insane. Now and then, for a joke, for . . . company, in the exercise of a rather silly habit, for something to do, for something in bad taste to do, he speaks out to the air, as if Harry might be hovering in it. It's a game. He doesn't try to get in touch, he doesn't try anything phony.

Embree calls out to the tonga driver. It is late, and the plane ride was hardly relaxing. Tomorrow he'll come back and see the temples, nothing fancy, just look at them. And then he'll get the hell out of Pagan and go to Bangkok, where he belongs or where he might learn to belong. Good. Settled. There is something from *The Gita* he remembers: "The self-controlled man, moving among objects, with his senses under restraint and free from both attraction and repulsion, attains peace." Of course. How easy it is.

• • •

After a dinner of noodles and vegetables, he goes down to the river with Rama and watches fishermen bringing in their sturdy flat-bottomed boats. They build fires on the mud flats and eat before going out again, this time for huge catfish, perch, and spade-headed river shark. Their nets, while they eat, are piled like bundles of clothes in the bows. They finish and push the boats off the mud flats into the turgid expanse of the Irrawaddy that lies there, in the final splashes of twilight, like a sullen gray cloud.

Rama and Embree watch. Then, silently, they watch some pinpricks of other light appear across the black line of the river. The air is almost cool and carries an indefinable aroma—perhaps a mixture of wet wood and river and flowers holding out on the spiny little trees that edge close to the banks. Abruptly, from across the river, comes the sound of laughter—a hollow sound at this distance. Above the two silent men the belt of Orion emerges from the blackness, pointing to Sirius and Aldebaran in Taurus and the faint cluster of the Pleiades to the west and the Dipper's handle pointing eastward, where Arcturus, cold and remote in such a warm oceanic sky, has risen crisply above the horizon. Embree is glad to be alive. He turns and says to Rama, "I'm glad you came with me."

"Ah, Master, I am keen on it myself."

"What do you think of Burma?"

"I wouldn't want to lodge on this side long."

"Because it's Buddhist?"

"Ah . . ."

In the darkness Embree can't see Rama waggle his head in an ambiguous gesture that ultimately means yes, but he knows the young Indian's doing it. Embree wonders if, in fact, Rama is getting much out of the trip. It's hard to say.

"You know, Rama, someday you'll marry and have children and you can tell them about the American you rescued and accompanied on a long journey." When Rama doesn't respond, he continues, "It's a long journey. Do you know why we're taking it?"

"Memsahib needs you."

"Well, yes. That, of course, is the main reason. But there's another. You see, things happened to me in the war here."

"Yes, Master. I know."

"You know in a way, but it's . . . difficult." In the midst of his struggle to explain himself, Embree suddenly blurts it out. "I talk, Rama, to this man, a soldier, who isn't really here. That is, he's dead, but I find myself talking to him. Oh, not much, but I'll say things like 'What about that, Harry?' or 'Is this your idea, Harry?' "

"Yes, Master," Rama says when Embree pauses.

"By that I mean I talk to myself. But the things I talk about are for him, that is, if he were alive, and so I . . . imagine he's here."

"Yes, Master."

"It's not easy to explain."

"Yes, Master, not easy."

"Do you understand what I'm saying?"

"Yes, Master, I understand."

He doesn't understand, Embree thinks, and they both fall silent.

That night, lying on a thatch cot, with moonlight shredding through a bamboo chick at the window, Embree has a dream. He is watching a girl removing her clothes. He realizes her behavior has been caused by some kind of military situation, and hers is the placating gesture of a woman, perhaps a refugee, who is trying to save herself from worse treatment. She beckons, actually implores him to come to her, as she sits back—she is sitting, legs wide apart to make access easy. The girl watches dispassionately as he approaches and frantically enters, beside himself from the lust that comes from his knowing how vulnerable she is, how powerless she is to stop him. But then, quite calmly and devoid of passion, together they watch him work in her, as if a common machine piston is in operation, moving at a brisk mechanical pace at her center.

Embree awakes, sweating. It's a nasty vision, but contains a power that pushes him back into the memory of a girl he'd nearly killed in China. His army companions were raping the women of a landlord, and this girl was with him in the courtyard near the pig trough. He had selected her, but shyness and uncertainty made him incapable of performing. She, however, was ready—called him "hairy boy" and asked him what he had down there. This playful ridicule infuriated him. He held a knife to her throat, terrifying her until she satisfied him by crying. Something had emerged from him for a few moments, something cold and brutal and heartless, and now, lying here in Nyaung U, haunted by memories of the war, he has had a dream that conjures the worst of him again. You don't escape, he tells himself. You never do. You don't, do you, Harry. It was you who did it just now. It was you, Harry the Nat, insinuating that dream into my sleep. I am not insane. But I'm scared.

• • •

This time Rama goes with him. The sun is not yet high enough to generate much heat, although Embree has streaked his face with tanaka powder to protect it from the sun's rays. The two men ride a tonga out among the pagodas and temples, most of them no more than piles of crumbled brick. With map in hand, Embree leads the way to the Htilominlo Temple, set back from most of the others on the plain. Embree has selected the Htilominlo to climb because of its view, which the guest house manager claims is the best in Pagan.

As Embree walks toward the stairway of the two-story temple, he turns to Rama and says, "Come along this time."

The young Indian shakes his head. "I won't be caring for it, Master.

You will be going, thank you. I shall wait over there—" He points to a spindly tree a few yards from the base of the temple.

Embree shrugs; yet as he starts up the uneven brick stairway, he can feel himself trembling. He wants someone along. But how, possibly, can he turn now and say to the little Tamil, "I'm afraid to go alone"?

Delaying the climb, he wanders through the main eastern vestibule, looking indifferently at the carvings on pediment, frieze, and pilaster. It strikes him that Vera should be here with him. Art has meaning for her; to him it is nothing compared to the evanescent color of sky, of water. The paintings and sculpture that create in her a sense of excitement have always seemed rather stiff and pompous to Embree. Static. He always wonders why one thing takes precedence over another, and suspects that, ultimately, artistic judgment comes down to the exercise of power. And artistic enjoyment? That's a mystery; he has never found the key to open that door. So in a spirit of alienation Philip Embree has looked at the twelfth-century moldings and stood in front of the Buddhas placed at cardinal points in the Pagan temple. They are stone. What else they are eludes him.

He recalls how General Tang had been moved by such images. Twenty years ago Embree had climbed Thousand Buddha Mountain in the Li Shan foothills outside Jinan—the whole winding way not ten feet behind the General, who was heading for a temple on the summit where a meeting of warlords would take place. Perhaps the fate of Central China would be decided at that meeting, yet throughout the ascent General Tang halted to study old Buddhist sculptures carved in the rock, as if their beauty and not his fate and that of thousands of other people was what had brought him here. Square body motionless, square face as hard-looking and blocky as the granite he stared at, the General gave himself to a world denied to Embree to this day. Whenever he recalls the General, Embree sees this square figure strolling past Tai Hu rocks or ancient sculptures, hands clasped behind his back, a solitary man in contemplation of the timeless, the mysterious, the beautiful, all of which he had shared with Vera Rogacheva. Embree remembers the General not as a warrior but as a philosopher. In Embree's memory of those days the man in battle dress is himself, seated on a horse, whereas the General is vanishing in the mist, romantically, with Vera beside him.

"All right, Harry," he says out loud. "It's time to go up." He climbs a dark narrow staircase to the upper terrace, which puts him farther than a hundred feet above the ground with a view of the great temples, most of them grouped to the southwest. Later in the year much of the land below will be corn and peanut fields, so he's been told, but now it's quite barren, save for a few palms that line the paths leading to the large temples. It's silent, dusty, lunar in its lifeless breadth. Embree stands at the brick parapet and looks southward first, then, turning clockwise, regards the Sulamani and Dhammayangyi temples, the Shwesandaw Pagoda, and turning a little farther sees the two giant temples, white-washed to look like snow-covered mountains in the Himalayas: the stately Ananda, the taller Thatbyinnyu. There are others, dozens, scores, hundreds, all dotting the vast plain under a day without clouds.

Turning away, he looks at the curve of the Irrawaddy and a battered sail leaning into the river wind, and Philip Embree tells himself this is the place. A powerful place. The monastery manager was right; Pagan is the place to sit.

And Embree does.

. . .

He has no plan, not really. He has simply plummeted down here, has sat down cross-legged on the brick terrace with little tufts of weathered grass and weed pushing up through myriad cracks. Will he meditate? Why would he do that here? He could do that in the tiny room in the guest house—send Rama out to look at the world and get himself settled in a corner somewhere with beads and mantra.

Has he really come here to confront a Burmese Nat who shuffles through time awaiting justice?

"Harry," he says aloud.

"Where in hell are you, damn you, old chap, Harry?" he says in a louder voice. There's a touch of laughter in that voice. This is a joke.

"Harry!" he shouts defiantly.

The sound of his voice reverberating in the walled terrace is a weird reminder that he's just called out to a dead man. It's only a joke, gro-tesque and morbid, but a joke. Yet he feels excited. Something will happen here. It's the excitement that India has prepared him for: Often, when settling down on the meditation mat, he's felt the excitement of a journey. Usually nothing happens; he goes to breakfast disappointed, listless. But he knows what the anticipation is, what it can sometimes bring: a sense of cleansing, a glimpse beyond the cage.

Breath in.

Breath out.

Breath in.

Breath out . . .

No, that won't do. He can't conjure Harry the way Harry conjured Ramakrishna. The monastery manager said to summon him. "Harry, I'm here waiting!"

Silence.

Breath—

No, it won't work. All that preparation for this moment, all those mornings under the bo tree with the cook banging pots around next door, all those exercises, all the concentrated madness behind closed eyes, all of it worthless here on the terrace of Htilominlo. None of it applies. Meditation's not the way, is it, Harry.

Harry. He doesn't say the word out loud this time. He is waiting now, really waiting.

Harry.

He waits. The silence rises like another parapet around him, and through it he hears the buzzing of a fly. It's the only sound he hears. But something else is edging into his consciousness, and he widens his eyes to avoid it. Getting to his feet, Embree paces back and forth. He tries to keep his attention on the plain, on the brick ruins that seem to smolder in the rising heat waves, but his eyes won't stay put. He looks at his feet. Pacing, he looks at them, at nothing, because at the edge of his vision now are remembered images. Well, they are there, they won't go away, they have been there almost four years now, in bits and pieces, in flashing recollections, in isolated lineaments that come and go too quickly to hold, like a flying insect seen at the eye's edge. But here on the parapet of Htilominlo Temple, for whatever reason, he feels something is forcing him to recollect it all coherently, in sequence, without interruption. Before summoning Harry, he must get it all straight in his mind. Again he sits down, closes his eyes.

It was May 1944. Vinegar Joe Stilwell was pushing his Chinese X Force south toward Myitkyina; circling behind Lieutenant General Shinichi Tanaka's 18th Division were Merrill's Marauders. Farther south were Chindit battalions whose responsibility was to cut off the 18th from reinforcements at Indaw. The 101st Detachment was operating between the two Allied forces, harassing the enemy's supply lines and bivouacs. Embree's patrol consisted of five men: three Kachin tribesmen of the Jinghpaw clan, a Gurkha trooper, and himself.

Their mission was to help a small group of Chindits who'd been cut off from the main force. The radio transmission, having given coordinates, cut out—from either design or mishap, the patrol didn't know. But they did know it would take perhaps two days to get to the Chindits. What appeared on their map as twenty miles might be double that in actual travel, depending on the jungle trails. The Gurkha and Embree speculated, as they sloshed through the muddy undergrowth, on what lay ahead. The Chindit group must be holed up in bad country or else a plane might have taken them out. Or maybe there were too many of them. How many were they? And what could five men do once they found the Chindits, especially if the Nips had contact?

It was the sort of speculation the Kachins never bothered with. They just fought. Long ago the Burmans had tried to drive these hilltop dwellers back into their ancestral Tibetan lands, but the Kachins outbattled them and took undisputed control of northern Burma. When the

Japanese arrived, they made the same mistake, attempting to intimidate the tribesmen with rape and executions. The Kachins fought back. They wore black cotton pants, white shirts, black turbans. Many of them carried a dah the length of a saber, with the end squared and the single-edged blade thick and heavy; the two-handed grip was often ornamented with silver and topped with a silver knob. They put such fearsome weapons in fine-grained wooden scabbards, banded in silver. Embree had learned enough Jinghpaw to talk with these short, squat, dark men whose features were more Chinese than Burmese, their hair often matted, their teeth broken. They loved American D ration chocolate and DelMonte canned vegetables and tins of lemon cream wafers from Messrs. Huntley & Palmer of London when the limeys gave them gifts. The Kachins hunted anything—tiger, barking deer, civet cat, boar, pheasant, Komodo lizard, snake, paddy rat, monkey, termites, and white bees. They were adept at laying *panji*—two-foot bamboo slivers, planted by the thousands alongside trails and slanted in the direction of the road, so Japanese soldiers, in case of an ambush, would impale themselves when they dove for cover. They rigged crossbows with a pull of 150 pounds across trails: when tripped, such a weapon could transfix two men walking in file with a single poisoned arrow. Along with the Gurkhas, the Kachins were the most fearless warriors Embree had ever seen.

But they were not immortal. Half a day's journey toward the rendezvous with the Chindits, the leading Kachin was blown up. When the patrol got to him, they found a smoking heap on the trail. His two Kachin companions knelt in the rain and inspected the booby trap with professional interest. They explained to Embree that the device had been a bamboo cup, holding a grenade with an instantaneous fuse. They showed him how the grenade had been pegged to the ground and the cup slipped over it, with the pin removed. The trip wire had been stretched taut a few inches across the trail, here scarcely a foot wide. With a few exasperated shoves of their feet they rolled the corpse of their comrade into the undergrowth. They were ashamed. He had been stupidly tricked by a device the Japs must have learned to use from Kachins, even though Embree and the Gurkha argued that, after all, the trail was very narrow here, and the rain must have diverted his attention.

The rain was furious that day, Embree remembers. Visibility was less than six feet, and after a while the pelting against cap and shoulder seemed cold, sharp, like pellets of ice. But then, during an hour of respite, the heat descended upon them like something alive. It surrounded and clung to them, sucked up the air they breathed. So they halted off the trail on a little knoll. They were too exhausted to use their Kohler pack stove, and anyway it was too wet to keep a fire going. They ate date bars, Spam, hard biscuits from their K rations, and smoked Cavalier cigarettes. Embree remembers an odd fact: He remembers wondering if the Gurkha missed his spicy dal and unleavened bread; it would do no good to ask, because the trooper would exclaim, "No, sah, Bara Sahib!"

They had one mule, not in good shape: Her fetlocks were crawling with maggots, dumdum flies zoomed in and out of her nostrils, her ears, her anus: both Kachins had to burn at least a score of buffalo leeches from her bleeding sides. The next morning, when they started at dawn, she was down. They couldn't shoot her because of the noise, so Sabaw Gam, one of the Kachin rangers, slit her throat.

The rain began soon enough. They had to hack through the undergrowth with knives; the Kachins always won Embree's admiration for their tireless work with the dahs. He watched them swing at the sinewy vines and wondered where in hell they got the energy; his own arms ached from the effort, became as heavy as logs, lost sensation; his hand twitched spasmodically on the GI machete he carried. Often he thought of his old ax that he'd used during the early days in China. He'd never been without it. He'd slept, eaten, and killed with it. He often thought, hacking away at this Burmese jungle, what a strange young man he'd been: wild for adventure, wild for breaking out, undaunted, foolish and heartless.

By noon—under the circumstances they'd come fast—they were in the designated area. Along the trail was evidence of a recent firefight: bloating corpses, expended shells, both equipment and flesh already inextricably mixed in the monsoon mud of the jungle. In a few weeks no one might have known which force was which, but for the moment, in the unrelenting downpour, the patrol could distinguish Chindit from Jap: the lion-headed dragon device on Chindit sleeves, the Sam Browne belts, the jungle-green drill which was the battle dress of the British; and the rubber, webbed-toed boots, the Shinto amulets, the silk scarves (painted with Rising Suns or scenes of copulation), and kidney-shaped mess kits of the Japanese. These last never failed to interest the Kachins, who would have carried the kits along except for the extra weight. There were guns, already rusting in the mud: the Number 5 Mark 1 Jungle Carbine, the 9-mm. Browning FN pistol, the Japanese 81-mm. mortar and the Nambu 88-mm. pistol. Haversacks and ammo clips and binoculars and map cases and raincoats, cans of corned beef, biscuits, clothing were all scattered about in the soupy mud, sinking down into larva land, into the liquid bowels of the Burma earth. The stench rose into the patrol's nostrils, until even the Kachins grimaced and held kerchiefs to their faces.

In dead center of the area they had to break radio silence. On his SCR, having rare good luck, Embree managed to raise the Chindit unit within a few minutes. In another half-hour the 101st patrol came into the Chindit perimeter on a mountain ridge; a nearby stream burbled maniacally from the torrents of monsoon rain pouring in from high ground. Embree was amazed to find only a dozen men (until he learned that the Chindit company had been almost annihilated by a strong Japanese detachment three days ago). He was even more amazed to discover that one of the Chindits was Harry Stubbs.

So then there were sixteen men on the ridge, and with keen prospects of being attacked again, although the Chindits had enjoyed a respite for two days. All they could talk about was the lad who had gone for help and apparently made it back to base camp. What they refused to believe was Embree's insistence that this sorry-looking patrol from Detachment 101 constituted the rescue team.

"It's that bugger Stilwell," a Chindit said. "He don't care if we live or die. Likely wants us dead, the bloody bastard. We been out here nearly four months. What's Churchill and them blokes in Whitehall thinking about, letting a bloody Yank take charge."

Embree took in their condition at a glance. Save for Harry and two other troopers, they were all sick. He noticed they didn't bother to put Halazone in their canteens any more; they just washed the pills down when they drank, without waiting for the chemicals to work. One of them, too weak to move, had fouled his clothes from dysentery—they'd cut out the bottom of his pants for him. They had fever, cramps, rashes, headaches. Two of them had jungle ulcers on their legs; the length of their shinbones was filled with putrescence, with blackened and shredded flesh. One of them muttered, "I need a ruddy great sleep," and everyone knew he'd have it soon. Another, his fever spiking, chattered endlessly about Mayfair, a place called Hay's Mews, where there were flats over garages, and nearby Chesterfield Hill with its spiked iron fences and flower boxes. Another could not let Stilwell go. "Bloody fucking bastard," he kept mumbling. "I'd pour petrol on the sonofabitch and light it, that's what I'd do, you can jolly well put that in your pipe and bloody smoke it."

Night fell. It was too dangerous to light a fire. A young Chindit lieutenant was ranking officer, it was established, and he set up a defense perimeter for the night: Three Chindit troopers took first watch. Embree suggested that a Kachin ranger might stand with them—Kachins could hear a twig snap at twenty yards—but the lieutenant ignored him.

In the wet darkness (a drizzle ceaselessly fell) Embree and Harry talked. Through the black night Harry's voice had a soft, wavering quality, so that Embree, had he heard only the voice, might have taken the speaker for an old man. Yet in his depthless weariness Harry seemed free to say anything. He didn't talk about the Chindit operation or his long time on the line or even his desire to go home, as Embree had heard other men often do out here in the jungle, but about a desire for enlightenment. That was it: desire, yearning. It was the sort of thing Embree's father had often spoken of as the source for Christian faith. Such desire was therefore something that Embree had assiduously avoided, even in divinity school, where he substituted curiosity for desire, bringing his energies to focus upon intellectual conumdrums at the sacrifice of commitment. But here, in the Burmese jungle, he listened with attention, not because Harry Stubbs inspired the same deep yearning but because the young man so manifested his own. Perhaps at another time Embree might have turned away from the aphorisms which Harry recited like a dutiful student, but in the damp blackness, hearing only that ancient, trembling voice, and in circumstances of such danger, he listened humbly, fully, and remembered them.

He remembers now on the terrace of Htilominlo Temple.

That night, while someone was moaning in his sleep, Harry said, "Ramakrishna knew, I believe he really did know. Once he told his disciples: 'The water and the bubble are one.' Are you listening, old chap?"

"Go on," Embree said, pausing a moment to hear movement nearby. Someone was shifting position in the mud, a mushy sound.

"The water and the bubble are one. The bubble has its birth in the water, floats on it, and finally goes back into it. So also—do listen, this is the point—the individual ego and the supreme spirit are one and the same. The difference is in degree. One dependent, the other independent."

"You really still meditate?"

Nearby a soldier awoke, yelling out, "What? Where is that?"

"Shut up, mate, for godssake," someone whispered.

"Ah, God, I'm burning up."

"Let me see. Well, I've got something here. Take it."

"I want bangers and mash. I'd like to beat some of that into me."

"Now you're talking, mate. Washed down with beer."

"I still meditate when I can. I will after the war," Harry said. "I'll be staying out here."

"India?"

"Yes. I'm going on with it."

"Sure?"

"I'm going on with it."

Later, as Embree recalls, he must have fallen asleep. What awoke him was gunfire, the light popping sound of Japanese rifles. He can't follow exactly what happened next—impossible in a night attack. No coordination, no defense. They were overwhelmed by a sudden assault in strength. The young Chindit lieutenant cried out, "Run! Get out of here!" And then somehow Embree was alongside Harry, their shoulders touching as they scrambled through the undergrowth on the hillside. The racketing fire was intense from every direction.

Now, on the parapet of Htilominlo, he believes that he saw that night, just ahead, the Gurkha spun around by a burst of automatic fire—a wide-brimmed hat was blown back and knocked against Embree's chest, a Gurkha hat.

There were screams, explosions, and blasts of light by which he and Harry managed to find their way through the undergrowth, to plunge downward in the slick mire until suddenly Embree fell against something—it clutched him, he fired his pistol, it let go. Something else was there; he fired again, it was gone. And they kept sliding in the mud, crashing down, fighting branches and vines away, their lungs gasping for air, hurtling their bodies into trunk, limb, bush in the muddy descent.

And then they were at the bottom, slipping in deeper mud. Something was coming through the darkness. Harry fumbled with a grenade hanging on his belt, got it, pulled the pin, threw it, and the explosion illuminated the nearby cascading stream. They dove into it, were washed into its swift current and out of the area so quickly that within minutes the crackling of gunfire seemed distant. Tumbling, rolling, bumping against the crumbling banks of the stream, they were carried a long way, until at last Embree yelled, "Get out! Get out now!"

25 AT DAWN THEY struggled to their feet, went on. By compass and map grids Embree estimated they were thirty miles from a Chindit base—to get there would be pushing it, but surely within their limit of endurance. In this dense jungle it might take three, four days. Harry had rations in his fatigue pockets, both had pistols, and Embree had his machete. Between them they had one canteen. That was the worst part. No matches between them to build a fire and boil water.

They went steadily northward that first day, then changed direction to the northeast. Embree took the lead when it was apparent that Harry lacked the strength for cutting through the undergrowth. "I don't understand it, old chap," Harry said apologetically. "I'm a bit down."

"Are you sick?"

"Some dysentery. But I'm as good as new right now. Just a bit tired."

Twice during the day they heard planes, but they couldn't see anything through an overgrowth that shut out the sun, when it was shining, and provided some protection, like a huge continuous umbrella, from the savage rainstorms. That night they shared a few drops from the canteen. Neither had a raging thirst, but both knew it would come.

Around noon of the second day, just after crossing a narrow but tumultuous river—Harry lost two tins of rations, leaving them only three—they came to a village. Ordinarily they'd go around it, but their need for water and food outweighed their fear of the natives. The rain had let up, and for a while the sun shone, hot, searing, bringing out iridescences in the moisture-laden air. They went past little patches of barley, snake gourds, chili bushes, expecting by now someone, perhaps a child, to come look at them. There was a strange, pervasive silence. A few dogs barked as they moved cautiously past the outlying huts, but otherwise there was no sign of life. Something caught Embree's eye as he went at a half crouch deeper into the village. Under one of the stilted huts he could see forms moving. Dogs. Peering closely, he brought from them low threatening growls, but a quick swinging motion with his pistol scattered the animals away from something. He knelt under the hut and looked into the shadows.

It was a half-eaten child.

"Philip!"

He followed the sound of Harry's voice to the opposite side of the village path. Harry had climbed into a hut and was crouching at the entrance, staring at a platform on which lay three people, dead. They were clothed, but the platform stank of diarrhea, and green vomit streaked the mouths of all three corpses; flesh seemed to have melted from their bones; their skin was deeply wrinkled, mottled, a gray-brown.

"Cholera," Harry said. "We've seen a lot of it around here. Survivors must have gone off into the hills."

"What are they?" Embree asked, looking at a man wearing a huge black turban and baggy blue trousers, a girl in a bright petticoat. "Shan?"

"I think so. Shan."

They looked around the hut; there was a hand-operated sugar-cane press, bananas rotting, knitted shoulder bags of the Shan style. Embree found a box of British matches. Now they could make a fire, boil water. In a corner, where the attap roofing hung down into the open-sided hut, they discovered a Japanese helmet covered with hessian netting, a pair of cross-gartered puttees, an identity disc—Embree turned it in his hand: the Japanese characters, the numbers that once stood for a living man. Next to the Japanese articles lay an empty Flit can. Harry picked it up and tossed it into the air a few times. "These tribes love Flit. They keep the empty cans for barter. You find these cans in all the villages."

It was perhaps Harry's factual tone of voice, in the midst of this stink and death, that set Embree off.

On the Htilominlo terrace, that's what he thinks now.

"Dammit, Harry," he said angrily.

Harry turned to stare at him, the young British face heavily bearded, of a yellowish cast from years of taking quinine tablets, but the light brown eyes still boyishly questioning. "What's up?"

"What's up? I don't mean to sound goddamn sanctimonious, but here we are up to our ankles in green vomit, and you're talking about empty Flit cans. Jesus, Harry."

He jumped off the hut's platform and started down the path, with Harry after him.

"I don't understand, old chap."

Embree turned, just as a stray cloud let down a short, fiercely pelting rain. "Let me quote *you*, Harry. You say the ego is identified with the universe. We're all one and the fucking same. Well, leave me out. I don't want any part of it. Who wants to be identified with this weird goddamn world? With green vomit? *Identity. Soul.* They're words, they're *phony*. Don't you see? Let's get out of here."

They walked in silence through the village. In another month, Embree thought, the vines and insects would have it all to themselves. That's one thing about the so-called civilized world—it keeps records. It writes down its disasters, it commemorates its sufferings. It scrutinizes its mistakes, it dates and documents them. But these poor devils, alone out here in the jungle, they catch something and die in their own stink, and nobody will ever know about it, because within a short time there won't be any record left of them, except a Jap helmet, a few Flit cans.

And Harry looked at it all without flinching. Like Father would look at it. Because in some strange way both men found order in chaos, purpose in horror, being content with the hidden Divine Plan.

Embree's final glimpse of that village was of a Russell's viper, called a *daboia* in India or a *tic polonga* or a *mwe-boai* here in Burma—or bad news anywhere—its fat slick venomous coils undulating out of a doorway. It's what he last saw in the village, a viper.

They walked in silence for hours, while fresh rain beat down on them. The jungle filled their noses with the heavy cloying smell of leaf mold. Bamboo pierced their arms and legs like needles. Swarms of black flies, seeking entry to the warm wet interior of their bodies, nearly drove them mad.

• • •

That night, while they lay beneath a teak tree, with lianas hanging down around them like a ship's hawsers, Harry abruptly said, "You don't understand, old chap. I have seen maybe a dozen villages like that. They strip Japs who died of cholera and wear the clothes around and eat the rations. In a week they don't have a village. That's the way it is."

Embree said nothing.

"You're asking me how I can believe in God after this?"

"Have I asked you that?"

"You're asking it, aren't you?"

"Well, maybe I am."

"I thought so. I believe in God because I don't ask anything of Him. How can I? In a certain sense, I *am* God. So are you, so are the dead Shans, the dead Japs, the bloody rotten dogs back there eating the bodies. It's all God."

"Bullshit, Harry."

Now, on a terrace of Htilominlo in Pagan, Embree realizes what he had been stupid enough to expect from this young Englishman: the wisdom of a holy man, the wisdom his own father had done no more than mouth in words, not live. Poor damn Harry. He was only doing what he could do, thinking what he could think, in the midst of war, pain, death. Too much had been expected of him.

Sitting with eyes closed on the terrace of Htilominlo, Embree says Harry in his mind.

He waits.

In the jungle they hadn't spoken any more that night, but next morning Harry woke up complaining of chills. Malaria, Embree thought—Harry had had it before, on the retreat. But the young Englishman opened his shirt and felt a small oval ulcer covered by a black scab. "I have this too."

"It could be a jungle sore."

"That's what I'm thinking, mate."

But it could be, Embree knew they both knew, a sign of scrub typhus.

By noon Harry had a fever, back pain, an excruciating headache, yet somehow he kept moving—staggering, really, through the brush. Once again the rains had stopped, leaving the jungle to envelop them like a huge, wet, heated tarpaulin. They could hardly breathe. Opening Harry's shirt to the belt, Embree noticed a rash developing across the chest and abdomen.

"How are you, lad?"

"Lovely." The young man's hands played restlessly in his lap; on his face was a blank stare of apathy.

They went on, and by the time they halted that day, Harry seemed disoriented. Once he said, "One hell of a way to train us chaps, isn't it."

That night a fierce thunderstorm raged for hours, as they huddled beneath some fronds. Harry was wracked by a deep, railing cough.

Embree noted with distress there was an accumulation of pus in the Englishman's eyes. And at the height of the downpour, Harry began to talk excitedly, without ceasing. Much of it was about his family in Yorkshire: how they counted on him to do something with his life, how they had sacrificed for him so he could learn enough to make the university. He mentioned a professor who had encouraged him. He had been ashamed of his accent, of his Yorkshire slang, and worked to get rid of it. He talked about a girl he knew. He talked about a friend he'd played rugby with. He didn't talk about God.

But in the morning, when Embree awoke after a short restless sleep, he found Harry smiling at him. Propped against a teak tree, Harry was bathed in sweat, pale, but apparently in better shape than the night before.

"I have something to tell you, old chap," he said. "You're the best mate I ever had."

"After my outburst yesterday?"

"Suspect I had it coming. Must have seemed cold-blooded after all my talk about God. Matter of consistency, isn't it. I mean, having faith. One moment I believe, I know exactly what the belief is, I have it quite pat. Next moment I'm acting against the belief. Or seem to. Is that it?"

"Let's talk about it later."

"Let's talk about it now."

"Look, Harry, if you have faith, good for you. People who have it win two ways. If there's nothing after death, they don't know they were deceived. If there really is something, they can say, 'I told you so.' "

"You bloody well know that's not the faith I mean." Harry coughs hard. "You play the devil with me, old chap. But that's because you suspect I may be on to something."

"How are you feeling?"

"Oh, much better. It's a bad cold. Or maybe a touch of malaria."

"One of the two."

"Philip."

"Yes?"

"You got me out once. If you don't do it again, don't blame yourself."

"I'll get you out."

"Philip, I say, I'd appreciate very much, under the circumstance, if you'd tell me what really happened to you. Someone in my shoes ought to have such a right—to ask for the secret."

"I don't understand."

"You not only saved my life, you've been a mate. We've shared a lot, haven't we. Is it getting hotter or am I getting hotter?"

Embree hadn't felt a rise in temperature, but said, "I noticed it was getting hotter some time ago."

"Really? Well, you see, old chap, there's something I want to know —call me cheeky—but I feel I ought to know. You've done something in your life you regret awfully."

"So you know that."

"I do."

"All right then. It happened a long time ago, in China. In 1927—you must have been five or six. I was serving in the army of a warlord."

"I remember you telling that."

"What you don't know, what no one knows, is what I did to that warlord. His enemies approached me with a proposal to betray him. In exchange they'd get me out of China—and along with me a woman who happened to be the General's mistress, who also happened to be a woman I wanted beyond reason. So I betrayed him. I never told that woman what I'd done. We married. It wasn't a good marriage, though I loved her—maybe still do. The General was assassinated by other enemies soon after we left the country together."

"Yes. One hell of a thing, isn't it. I'm sorry."

After a long silence, Embree said, "Here's the way it stands. The base is within a day's march now, if I've got my bearings. But you can't make it. Don't argue. You can't walk one kilometer more. So the plan's simple. When I get to the base, I'll have them send people to get you out." Embree unhooked the canteen. "Keep this. I have the matches, so I can boil water."

"No."

"We'll divide the ammo. I'm not coddling you." Embree took out Harry's pistol and inserted a new clip. He took the rations left and laid them in Harry's lap. He stuffed his own kerchief in Harry's pocket. That was all he could do. Rising to his feet, he looked down at a pale but smiling face.

"I'm thinking of *The Gita*," Harry said. "In the long run, what is it really saying? Just: Do your duty. We're doing that, old chap."

Embree nodded, cinching his belt tighter, checking his pistol, securing the machete in its scabbard.

"In *The Gita* a warrior refuses to fight because he's decided war is wrong. But God tells him he must fight. It is his destiny to fight." Harry paused to spit up phlegm. "He must go on with his life as it is. You see? We can't change what happened in the village. We must go through whatever is there, *The Gita* says, with detachment, with—respect for events. I think that's it. *Respect for events.*"

"Save your strength," Embree told him gruffly. "You're talking too much."

He'd seen plenty of men in a bad way, but none reacted quite like this. With medical help Harry's chances were fifty-fifty or almost that, but survival wasn't on his mind. Other matters occupied the mind of

Harry Stubbs: the morality of duty, the inconsistencies of faith, the nature of God. Matters that had occupied Embree's own father and had haunted his own world since childhood. In this helpless feverish man, Embree saw an awesome manifestation of what Father had always preached about, hoped for in him: Harry believed.

· · ·

Hours later, slogging through the jungle, Embree heard something up ahead. The sound came through the heavy rain—a metallic clink, rhythmically repeated.

A column marching: no doubt of it.

He skittered to a small rise and, through the interstices between heavily leafed branches, was able to see them: Nips heading east with mortars, Bren guns, pack howitzers on mules—he estimated two companies, perhaps even battalion strength. Embree stared at them as if unable to get enough of looking at their haversacks and pot-shaped helmets and blankets rolled in shelter halves. When the column had slogged out of sight on the narrow path, Embree moved with them, following close along their left flank, not a hundred yards away. His excitement grew as time passed: an hour, two. He didn't reason it out, but followed. Now and then he remembered Harry back there, waiting, but Harry had his God to take care of problems. Harry could wait and think of *The Gita* and how everything happened the way it must happen and so to hell with trying to change it, to hell with pain and death, because they were part of the whole thing, this big stewpot into which every thought, hope, horror, and joy could be tossed and stirred and brewed up to nourish us all. Let him wait.

Something might happen here along the trail; that's what Embree thought. This was adventure. He was the Philip Embree who'd turned his back on a Christian mission in Harbin and joined a band of Mongol bandits, then a Chinese cavalry. He was true to himself once again. That possibility excited him as he trailed the enemy column.

Where were the Japs going? It was just possible they were heading for an important objective. If so, his information would be valuable.

Harry would have to wait; Harry had his God to keep him company. Harry would have to wait until the Japs hunkered down and provided the real world with information.

Abruptly the rain stopped again, and sunlight streamed down on soldiers churning through the mud, their muscular calves bulging in leg wrappings. Often they wiped their sweaty faces with the kerchiefs tied around their necks; they turned their soft caps around with the bills facing backward. Sometimes they laughed.

Harry would have to wait until they made camp. When finally the column halted for the day, Embree could assess their strength properly:

their weaponry, ammo, transport, supplies. He'd have their coordinates on his map. There was a good chance for him to contribute something important, so Harry would have to wait.

Through the brush he could see the Japanese moving on the path, like sections of a big sluggish snake. He followed them most of the day, moving farther from the Chindit base, farther from where Harry waited. He scrambled through the wet brush, cutting himself on the bladed leaves, collecting on arms and legs a host of leeches, their bloated bodies glistening. He couldn't burn them off, either, because Jap scouts might pick up the flare of a match. He was on a mission, wasn't he. Harry would have to wait, too bad, fever and rash and all. Too bad, Harry, it's not my fault. Just hold on to your God till I get back. I'm coming, but not yet.

Once this Jap column was taken care of, Embree told himself, he'd take care of Harry. But right now there was work to do. He felt a rush of adrenalin, the familiar sense of adventure that he'd lusted after as a young man. He was riding again through the wind-swept fields of China, ax in his belt, wild men beside him. This was living.

Embree decided to move ahead of the column, and for that purpose he needed to travel faster. So he veered off, putting a good four hundred yards between himself and the Japanese. At this remove he could use less caution in getting through the brush. Suddenly he heard engines overhead, a flight of aircraft, and so did the Japanese, who dove into the undergrowth—yanking mules off the path, squirming into bushes, making themselves small in the mud. He saw the planes at the same time they did: P-51s coming in low over the trees, guns firing. Five P-51s. And then came two B-25 H bombers, the kind assigned to the Chindits, with 50-cal. machine guns and a 75-mm. cannon beneath the pilot. All along the trail plumes of fire and smoke rose up as if to lick the bellies of the swooping planes. Huge balls of orange rose out of the massed greenery. The earth shook. Embree sat cross-legged in a bamboo thicket, holding a flaming twig against the swollen leeches on his chest, while four hundred yards away the explosives sucked up mud, tree, and soldier into the sky. Then out of nowhere, it seemed to Embree, a huge cloud swept in, unloading a thunderstorm to go with the bombs and AA fire. The attack ended abruptly. The planes swerved off, perhaps threatened by tremendous updrafts caused by the storm.

Embree waited and listened, when it was over, to the screams of wounded Japs. That had been a deliberate aerial attack, headquarters directed. And when the clouds lifted, planes would be back, hammering away. The position of this column had been known for some time. And why not? It was a big enough unit. He knew that. He had known it from the first sighting. Nothing he might have done would have changed the status of the Japanese column—except getting back to base as soon as possible. He had been following it needlessly. He had been having an adventure and making Harry wait.

• • •

Harry was much closer than the Chindit base, so instead of heading for help Embree headed for him. Struggling through the dusky jungle, Embree felt desperate to get there, to save Harry—

Now, seated on the terrace of Htilominlo, he tells himself what he really wanted to do. He went straight back there not so much to save Harry as to confess. That's it. He knows it now for sure. It had been there at the edge of his mind all the time, but it's front and center now: Harry, dammit, I was angry at you for playing the role of father with me, telling me what I should and shouldn't believe, loading me up with your half-digested ideas about the spiritual life, and so . . . so out of spite—not out of a desire to *really* harm you, believe me—but out of the desire to let you suffer a little while, a short while, with ideas that seemed nothing to me but evasions, lies, hypocrisies, I trailed the Japanese senselessly and let you wait. I'm sorry, sorry, it was a terrible thing to do, a viciously childish thing, and I apologize, I do, I apologize, Harry, for letting you wait.

"Harry," he says into the morning air, opening his eyes, closing them again.

But the hoped-for passionate confession didn't take place the next day, when after a few backtrackings he at last found the path, then the location where he'd left Harry, propped against a tree.

Harry was still there.

So were two Nips, lying crumpled on the footpath, flies already swarming over the quiet meat.

Harry smiled—

Embree remembers to this moment how he turned into sight, halting briefly to look at the dead Japs, then at the young Englishman against the tree, smiling out of a deathly ashen face. As Embree rushed up, he saw another Jap bent over a liana vine, as if his hurtling progress had been frozen in midair. Harry moved his head slightly, indicating another direction, and following that gaze Embree saw yet a fourth Jap, this one splayed out in the underbrush, like a drunk snoozing on a summer day.

He stared at Harry's lap, where both hands were placed, bright red. "In the stomach?"

When Embree bent down for a closer look, reaching to take the hands away, Harry said weakly, "It'll fall out."

"Ah, lad, I've got to look." Carefully he pulled back Harry's hands, and a purplish coil of intestine slid partway out of the gaping cavity. "Ah, Harry."

"Came this morning," the young man panted. "Two on path, got them before they saw me."

"Don't talk." Embree had seen men, gut-shot, chatter on and on, so numbed by shock they hardly knew they were wounded.

"Got the third too, but the fourth—" He paused, breathless. "Glad you're here."

"I'm glad too. We'll get you out." Embree had nothing more than chlorine sulfate tablets in his pocket. Wonderful aid for a man with his abdomen shot away. He started to remove his shirt—Harry was shaking from chill, one of his legs jerking.

When Embree leaned toward him with the shirt, Harry shook his head. "Don't muck about. There's nothing to sort out here."

"Ah, lad, come on now."

"I mean it."

Embree stood there, the shirt bunched up in his hand.

"Let me be, old chap. I'm dying. I feel it in my legs."

Embree knelt down, tears heavy in his eyes. "I met up with some Japs, chased after them, it was stupid."

Harry gasped, his eyes became round. "Really hurts."

And then Embree did what he remembers now on the parapet with terrible clarity. He leaned forward and asked curiously, "Are you afraid?"

Harry turned slightly to meet Embree's eyes. "Afraid? No."

"Is that true? Is it, Harry?"

"Not afraid. But it bloody hurts."

"And God?" Embree persisted. "Are you thinking about God now?"

"Afraid I can't think. Thirsty."

"But you're not afraid? Do they still mean something?"

"Can't follow, mate. Thirsty—"

"Your beliefs—"

"Beliefs?" His voice was dreamy.

"Do you still have them? Do they still mean something? Right now? Are they still more than words?" Embree asked rapidly.

For a moment Harry closed his eyes, then ran a dry tongue across his lips. "Come on, water. It can't matter now."

Embree gripped his arm. "That'll make the pain worse. Hold on, Harry."

"All right. Then shoot me."

Embree withdrew his hand, sat back.

"Come on, shoot me." He licked his lips again. "I'm ready. Bloody well do it."

"I can't do it."

"Scruples? You're already forgiven." When Embree didn't reply, he said, "Be a good chap, for godssake. Do it. Can't myself. Can't reach my gun."

Embree rose.

"Philip? Go to India."

Pain was clouding Harry's mind, Embree thought.

"Come close," Harry said weakly.

Embree bent down to his mouth.

"Damn you, go to India. Or you'll go mad."

That's exactly what Harry said, Embree tells himself on the second terrace of Htilominlo.

"Promise," Harry said.

To placate him, Embree said, "I promise."

"Say it all."

"I promise to go to India."

"And find myself."

"And find myself. Look, Harry, if I can just bind the wound—"

"Don't muck about. I'm ready." He coughed, the pain of the effort twisting his lips. For a moment he seemed to be losing consciousness. "Do it. Christ, man. Ah, it hurts—"

Embree backed away, resolved to do it, but not while facing Harry. He moved in a circle around the teak tree, coming behind Harry, so he could see the back of his head. He unholstered the pistol, raised his arm, aimed.

Then, in a panicky voice—

Now he can recall perfectly the sound of it.

—he said, "No, Harry, I'm going for help."

Minutes later he was crashing through the undergrowth.

• • •

He can't remember now how long he ran, but finally he collapsed from exhaustion, lay prostrate in the mud, while a fine new rain drifted down through the banyan, teak, and nim leaves.

He didn't get up for a while. His mind struggled to cling to something, anything, except Harry back there, waiting for the gift. He saw a kapok tree, its fruit hanging upside down like green bats; someday it would burst, the pods giving the tree the appearance of a line of white laundry. Interesting. Think of the kapok tree. But then he was on his feet. What if the Japs found Harry alive? He hadn't thought of that. The possibility sent him reeling back through the jungle. Japs would play with him awhile. There was the story of a Shan village that Embree once heard. The Japs played a game. They set fire to an old man's hair, then poured boiling water over his head when he yelled for them to put it out. Then they poured gasoline over the roasted scalp and relit it.

Then while he writhed on the ground, they politely offered him a boiling kettle of water to put out that fire. It was their way of passing the time. What would they do with a wounded Chindit, lying defenseless?

It seemed to take him much longer to return, however, than it had taken him to escape from Harry. He broke through the final vines and saw in front of him the tree, the side of the wounded man's head. Again he took out the pistol, aimed. But there was something in the angle of that head that caused him to lower the gun. Going forward, he saw that Harry was dead. Like a string of sausage, the guts had rolled out, cascading down his thighs. In and out of his open mouth, winged insects were already journeying. Harry's eyes were open too—staring straight ahead, flat, dull, already of a gray opaqueness.

Embree slumped down, talking for the first time to dead Harry, but not for the last. "Ah, Harry," he said. "I did it for sure. I betrayed you is what I did. Listen to me."

He stopped talking then, said no more.

He has said a lot since then. But only today has he tried to recall everything, the whole terrible sequence, exactly as it was.

Harry, he says in his mind.

"Harry," he says aloud.

"Harry!" he shouts, hearing the echo reverberate over the plain of Pagan.

"Harry! Harry! Harry!" The echo shoots back lugubriously. In a lower voice he says, "You're here, you're listening, you've got reason to hate me. So tell me so! *Tell* me, Harry! Harry!" Again the echo, followed by the vast silence of the plain, as if the air in it had been sucked up by fire, leaving a dead vacuum.

Harry, he says in his mind.

Harry.

And the silence.

Harry.

There's no answer, there will be no answer. There is no Harry. Harry is dead.

And it occurs to Embree for the first time that he's disappointed. He had wanted Harry the Nat to exist. What a miracle it would have been had the manager of the monastery been right—Harry swooping down from another dimension, thirsting for justice, ready to right the wrong done him. Now Embree knows how deeply he'd wanted a confrontation with dead Harry—enough to turn his back on reason. He had wanted to beg forgiveness.

Embree rises and leans wearily against the parapet. The bad words from *The Upanishads* come at him again: Fear arises from the Other.

But if there is no Other, he thinks, then fear arises from nothing.

Or arises from thoughts.

But if the thoughts are true—sometimes they must be—the Other exists. But sometimes they can't possibly be true.

Embree stares down at the rough brick of the parapet, the fingers of his good hand spread over it. Slowly he grinds his hand hard into the textured brick, hard hard hard, until the fingers are scraped raw and bleed. Good. He feels the reality of the world.

"Harry," he says aloud once again.

Still no answer.

So there really isn't a Harry any more.

Embree stands away from the terrace wall and looks across the dry brown expanse of Pagan. He feels cleansed, but like a terminally ill man, who's had all the medication possible and now must go it alone.

26

THERE ARE SOME things white people don't know, Rama tells himself confidently. For example, they don't know how comforting a quid of betel is. Up there, on the terrace of that crumbling Burman building, Master is talking to himself—shouting out Hari! Hari! For what reason, who can tell? Probably he doesn't even know that Hari is a sacred name of Vishnu. Narayana.

Having justified to himself the value of betel, Rama proceeds to make a quid, while sheltered from the intense heat and sunlight by a scraggly tree on the Pagan plain. He bought the areca seeds, slaked lime, and betel leaf yesterday in the village of Nyaung-U. He pops the quid into his mouth, next to the gum; instantly saliva begins to flow. That's something the white men don't seem to understand: how betel sweetens the breath, relieves gas, keeps the gums strong. He'd asked Master to chew and Master refused, saying blood-red gums and black teeth didn't appeal to him. Why not? Usha has them, and she is beautiful. But right now Rama would like some aniseed and cardamon to give the quid a little more pungency. He spits a stream of red juice on the dusty ground. Not bad for Burmans.

But their betel is the only good thing about them. In Rangoon, at the market of Thein Gyi Zei, he'd met a great many Tamil merchants, who returned to Burma after the war. They were an unfortunate lot. Forced by circumstances to come back here, having no funds or interests in India, they still lived with the horror of the war. That is something the white men can't realize either. Squatting beneath awnings in the market, he had listened, horrified, awe-struck, to the tales of these sad men.

Every one of them had lost family. Every one of them bore on his person the scars of escaping from Burma in 1942. At the time of the Japanese invasion, half of Rangoon was Indian, one of the Tamil merchants told Rama, as they chewed betel together under an awning. "Indian servants were left on the dock by British masters fleeing the Japanese. The poor creatures were hacked to death by Burmans right there, while the ships were still in the harbor. I saw it with my own eyes. The British sahibs and memsahibs were standing at the ship rails, watching their servants of many years being decapitated and shoved into the water."

And Rama heard the tales of the long, incredible exodus: A million Indians took to the road, less afraid of the Japanese than of the Burmans, who hated them—especially the Nattukottai Chattiyars, who as money-lenders had for decades maneuvered the easygoing natives out of their property. All along the escape route, toward the Tamu Pass in the Chin Hills, they felt the harassment of dacoits and village toughs. Partisans of the Thakins, who with Japanese approval led a nationalistic movement, began tattooing themselves with images of demons and magic signs, ready for arson, looting, and the murder of Indians, in the name of a free Burma. Dacoits nailed bamboo ladders against trees, so they could scramble up at a moment's notice to see if Indians were coming down the road who might be robbed, tortured, butchered. Soon, along the path of exodus, oiled-silk umbrellas on bamboo frames—favored by rich Indians—lay broken near corpses. At night, afraid of attack, Indian refugees drew their ox carts together beside the road for protection. There were fires everywhere, Rama was told. Night and day there were fires and screams, while the long, sluggish line of Indian refugees pushed northward on what they called the Black Trail, across saw-toothed ridges and through malarial jungles on a handful of rice, on berries, weeds, tree bark.

"Believe me, young man," said an old clothing merchant, "on that road a canteen was as precious as gold. So was a blanket, a can of food, a sun helmet, a mosquito net." He described the dust, the flying sand coming at sick, weary people carrying bundles on their heads. He told of pots hung from sticks over a bonfire, of boiling onions, of the cholera that came, as it will, to humanity helpless on the road. They lay on the roadside, in ditches, with foaming lips, unable to get water, and when they died, their limbs pointed skyward until they rotted or buzzards ate them.

"We had no time to burn them," he told Rama. "We left them where they died. We watched the vultures nesting in low branches along the way. They became too heavy to fly. They flapped their wings helplessly. And the dogs too became fat, but completely wild as they tore at corpses." Women died while nursing their infants. Men went amok with knives, fearing someone would steal their last possession. "I remember in April of '42, we reached the Irrawaddy near Shwebo," said an old man who'd been born in Trichy. "There must have been twenty thousand of us there, and of course, the military, who got the first barges and paddle-wheel steamers. When our turn came, a lot of the boats—manned by Burmans—never came back to the riverbank. People couldn't go farther. They lay in the sand, unable to help themselves when dacoits came along. These outlaws ripped bracelets off women, slit the throats of men. You cannot imagine it."

"Narayana," Rama said. "But why were the Burmans so cruel? The Chattiyars had rightful deeds to the property, didn't they?"

The old merchant laughed. "Men who lose their land forget about rightful deeds. But Chattiyars weren't the only problem. When this country became part of the Empire, the British brought in Indians to help run it. They understood one another through the colonial system. And the Burmans were known to be lazy, unreliable, without skills. The British brought in Indians for their servants. Indians joined the Burma Civil Service in droves, leaving the Burmans out. Burma was Indian as far as wealth was concerned. And then suddenly . . . British protection was gone. The Burmans took their revenge."

Recollecting those conversations, Rama spits some juice and touches the salagrama stone around his neck. Terrible, terrible. It is said, "God's right hand is gentle, but terrible is his left hand." White men can't know. They have no understanding of life and death. At that place, for example, where Master went with flowers—men buried under rocks! A strange, unsanitary, quite barbarous custom. But Rama tells himself to be charitable. They are a young people, not very spiritual yet.

But these Burmans should know better. They're an older people. How can they deceive themselves by following the way of Buddha, as if there were truth in it? Buddha is nothing more than a manifestation of Vishnu. The great God came to earth disguised as a fraud, with the desire to ruin human faith by handing out false ideas. This destruction Buddha failed to accomplish (of course by Vishnu's design, since in fact he was Vishnu), and by this failure taught man to follow the truth. This is known by people in Rama's village who can't even read. So, looked at properly, Buddhism is a way of strengthening Hindu devotion to the true God. It's simple when looked at properly. Rama spits.

What is Master doing up there? It's silent up there again. And through the silence Rama can hear a bat chirping inside the dark, cool interior of the temple. What is he doing up there? And yelling out Hari! so the whole countryside might hear him? The quid chewed, Rama considers preparing another. He wishes he had one of those Burman snacks of pickled tea leaves, roasted soybeans, and an oily mixture of sesame seeds and corn. Tasty. Not bad for Burmans. But nothing can compare with Usha's morning coffee. This very morning she must have prepared it. He can imagine her squatting over the brazier, with water bubbling in the pot and her strong slim arm turning the bean grinder.

Rama tries to dismiss the image, but it remains, even though he opens his eyes wide into a heat haze squirming at the edge of his shade. Eyes opened or closed makes no difference: Usha's still there.

By now, of course, she knows everything, because someone who knows English (he hopes not Uncle; he told her not to ask Uncle) must have read the letter to her. There are five people in the village besides Uncle who could have done it. In Rangoon he wrote another letter, telling her to be brave and not worry. He repeated his reason for leaving without notice: Traveling with the Sahib was an opportunity that might not come again, so he had to take it for the family's sake. When there was money enough, he'd send for them. Meanwhile, they must be brave and guard against the drought coming. Be nice to Uncle. Don't contradict or displease Uncle, who would be their source of welfare when the drought came. Meanwhile, be brave. It may not take as long as they think before his fortune is made and they can join him. "Narayana," he wrote. And then: "Love to you all." And then: "Sincerely, V. S. Ramachandran."

Often he thinks of them in the village. Hari has just come in from playing. The younger boy is already seated on the floor, watching his mother ladle rice onto a palm leaf.

I'll prepare another quid, Rama tells himself nervously. He has done the right thing, leaving. It is God's will. Otherwise, when he went to see Master that day, why had he been offered this chance to travel and see the world and by extension of such an opportunity to make his fortune as well? It is definitely God's will.

What's he doing up there?

Rama squints into the sunlight, seeking the broad-shouldered figure along the parapet. But Master has gone around the other side, doing whatever he is doing there—shouting out the name of Vishnu and Rama's own son.

I must be patient with Master, Rama thinks. Finishing the preparation of the quid, he slips it between cheek and gum. White men go through strange sufferings. For example, Master has been speaking to a dead man, or so he thinks, when most probably he is in communication with a god or a saint who is trying to help him. But can a white man be told that? They have no stomach for that kind of truth, but the truth is that things are there, behind what we see, ready to speak if only we listen. Whites can't listen. They don't know how, Rama tells himself with certainty.

Delivered of this judgment, he leans back against the tree and lets the mild stimulant in his mouth draw him out of Burma to consider again the good sense of leaving his family in the path of drought. I am trying, he thinks. No one is perfect. We are imperfect. God is perfect. So what can we do? Submit to God. Meanwhile, being imperfect, we must do what seems best at the time. It is all quite clear. Rama closes his eyes, hoping for a nap, but something in him is still restless. He sees the two boys, his wife grinding coffee beans.

Narayana.

On the train, sitting beside Master, he saw rice fields that reminded him of home, but he didn't tell Master, because how could a white man share the joy of looking at good rice growing any more than a white man could understand why someone had to leave a family behind at the time of drought in order to seek his fortune? He must be patient with Master, but it will never do to tell him what a white man can never absorb. Rama nearly confessed when, in the hotel room, Master picked up the pretty doll and the soldiers bought for a song in the market. Thank the Lord, Rama thinks now, he had not confessed. Master would not have understood the necessity for him to hide the fact of a family, even of a wife, because travelers to foreign countries must not be burdened with responsibilities. Of that Rama is certain.

He wiggles against the tree trunk to get more comfortable. Closing his eyes, he wants to sleep and dream of home, but instead he remembers the rice fields between Rangoon and Moulmein. It was on that very ride that Master asked him if he'd ever seen anyone there who is not actually there. And Rama had said, "Yes, Master. Of course." And Master had said, "Who?" "My father," he'd told Master. And it was true; he has seen his father often, coming out of the fields on a paddy path or from a morning mist or at dusk appearing around a distant tree. And Master had asked him, "What happens then, how close does he get, what does he do?" White questions. And Rama had told him, "Father comes just around here. Not too close, though." And naturally Master had persisted. "Does he speak?" "No, Master." "What do you think about it?" "I am not thinking too much about it, Master." "But why not? Don't you think it's strange, seeing a dead man?" And he had told Master, "No, Master, not so strange if it happens. I am glad he is coming to see me."

White men can't know about these things.

Rama opens his eyes long enough to see where he's spitting; he doesn't want to stain his new Western clothes with betel juice. With his eyes closed he dreams again of the rice fields passing the train window, one after another, all day long. It had made him homesick, for the sight drew him back into a memory of his youth, when Father still lived, and the village fields encompassed Rama's world. In those days the paddy yielded only twenty-five kilos per acre. Lorries came in now and then, taking a hundred bags, but most of the harvest was hauled by bullock carts. Rama used to play around the bullocks until the drivers shooed him away. Best crop is the fall crop. Not many white men in India know that. Master wouldn't know that.

Rama dreams of the harvesters attacking the field from windward, armed with sickles shaped like billhooks, the edges serrated. Squatting on their heels, grasping bundles of rice stalks with their left hands, they sever the sheaf near the ground and place it gently behind them. They work without wasted motion, with a rhythm like the dancing at festival time in honor of the gods who let them have their harvest. Narayana.

. . .

The sun has moved southwesterly in its arc, so Rama shifts out of the rays that slip through the least shady side of the little tree. He opens his umbrella and props it in such a way, between his back and the trunk, that his face is out of the light. He doesn't want his skin to get darker. When the steamer came into Rangoon, the first thing he'd seen was the Tamil dockworkers, lugging bales through the sunlight, their skin as dark as Africans must be. Master wouldn't like him darker; that is certain. A white man wouldn't want to be traveling with someone too dark-skinned. Rama knows such things. And Master is so fair-skinned. The wonder of it is Master's insistence that they're companions and can share a room together. Well, so be it. It is God's will.

It was also God's will to take away Bapuji. Rama spits. Gandhi dead: wrongheaded to make so many concessions to the Moslems, yet still a god man. It had taken Rama's breath away on the dock when he'd seen the newspaper. He had written that in the letter to his wife: "You can well imagine how it was for me, coming into this strange city where so many of our people met their fate during the war, to see the flash in the paper about Bapu's death. I tell you, it unsettled me properly."

The quid has been masticated and dissolved. Maybe he has time for another, because there's no telling about white men—Master might be up there with his dead friend or a god all day. Rama takes the makings from his shirt pocket; there is something to say for these Western clothes with their pockets here, their pockets there. He'd put that about Gandhi in the letter and about being in a foreign city to arouse in Usha a little sympathy for his plight. He admits it. No one is perfect. Narayana.

With a new quid in his mouth, once again he tries to settle back for a nap, and once again the images insinuate themselves that recall harvest time in his village. He sees men in the fields, sifting rattan trays of chaff and grain. The village is a good place, really. If only there weren't droughts and famines and moneylenders and landlords, everything would be good for his family in the village. His father understood the problem, loving the village, yet working on the railroad. On the last anniversary of his father's death, Rama had hired two Brahmans to bless a little statue of Lord Krishna. He bought them new dhotis, gave them food and other gifts, and in two days' time their prayers had infused the dead stone of the idol with the heavenly spirit of the Lord. Then Rama prayed to the Lord inside the stone for his father's soul.

The idea of it fills Rama's eyes with tears. To be homesick is a terrible thing, terrible. He hadn't known it would be.

His little family will be all right; God will see to that. Usha is plucky, and if the boys misbehave, she knows how to pull them up. He thinks about it. Yes.

Where is Master? Rama wonders apprehensively. This master is not a common man. Rama will never forget the look on his face at the burial ground for soldiers. Is he capable, up there, of doing himself harm? White men don't know how to talk to the dead.

The possibility so upsets Rama that he bends forward, causing the umbrella to keel over into his lap. It is best to go up there, even if it is a Burman temple. As he climbs, he must consider that it is not a living temple, not with priests and devotees, but an ancient temple, half in ruins. Such a place can't harm him, especially when he has his amulet and the Lord's understanding.

Leaving the tree's shelter, Rama steps reluctantly into the blazing light of Pagan. Ahead are the rugged steps of Htilominlo, the ravaged brick walls, the feathery trees growing from cracks along the terraces. He goes up. Narayana. It is a long, frightful journey, made worse at the second story, which must be climbed within the stone interior. He hears bats flapping around in the vaulting. The smell here is stale, cool, old. Narayana. But he comes out into the sunlight again and sees Master at the parapet, leaning on it.

"I am coming," Rama calls with relief. "I am here, Master!"

The white man, turning, smiles.

That, too, is a relief. Rama hurries up, but halts briefly when he sees the bloody hand. "Ah, sir, what is coming off? How did this happen? Let me do something."

The white man shrugs, but with the bloody hand takes a handkerchief from his back pocket and gives it to Rama.

While wrapping and tying the cloth, Rama looks anxiously into the cool blue eyes. He thinks better of asking again what happened.

"Thank you for coming, Rama."

"I was worried, sir. Your not coming down upset me nicely."

"Remember I told you I talked to a dead man? Well, it wasn't true. He doesn't exist."

Rama waits, unsure of how to respond. He would like to say, "Don't worry, Master, he may be waiting. He may not be wanting to speak today." But there is something forbidding in Master's manner. He seems shaken, perhaps bitter, the way white men get when thwarted.

"Rama, you've seen your father."

"Yes, Master."

"But you've never talked to him."

"As of now, sir, not talking."

"And you believe you've seen him?"

"Yes, Master."

The white man seems to consider the answer deeply. Then with a sigh he looks at his bandaged right hand, at his left arm in the sling, and laughs outright. This laughter also relieves Rama. It will be all right now.

"Look at me," Master says, shaking his head. Then, returning to the parapet, he's serious again. "Look out there, Rama. Eight hundred years ago a half-million people worked, loved, worshiped there. They had a great civilization there."

"Yes, Master," Rama says without enthusiasm for the Buddhist dead.

"I'm glad we came. This was the right place. What are you thinking, Rama?"

"Master?"

"What are you thinking?"

"It is best to die in the hand of the Lord."

They go down. Walking toward the waiting tonga, Rama wants to offer a quid of betel to his master, but that wouldn't be the comfort it should be, so he keeps the makings in his pocket. White men don't know as much as they think they do. Poor Master never has the benefit of a quid, simply because his mind is closed to its comfort. That is a pity. And he opens his mind when it should be closed—up there, feeling sad for a city of dead Buddhists.

But Rama tells himself it's best to be charitable. Touching the amulet, he says under his breath, "Narayana," as they get into the canvas-roofed tonga. When they're seated, he glances at Master, who is grimly silent, perhaps living out in his mind whatever happened to him up there on the Burman building. One thing is certain: who Master was counting on for help didn't come. And yet Master seems more relaxed now, as if he survived a great battle. Was it battle up there? All the shouting? Calling out to Hari Krishna? A battle of a magical kind? Not that Rama believes in magic. He is a modern man, cautious about what can and can't be. And so it's best not to think of what took place up there. What concerns him is one thing: Master must be looked after. These white people need someone to help them, Rama decides. Proud of himself for having the responsibility, he lapses into a reverie. He is in a large temple, maybe Srirangam Temple, where Father once took him when he was a child. The idol of Ranganatha, seated in a golden-domed palanquin, is brought from the inner shrine for all to see. But it is not Srirangam; it is another temple, one only vaguely remembered, and yet he can still feel the sudden coolness of the covered galleries after coming from the heat of a courtyard, the water splashed on the stone floors to cool them, the smell of melting camphor as the priests held prayer dishes toward worshipers, and then the deep recess where, in a dark niche, seen dimly, he saw the god draped in rich clothing, dark-complexioned and passionate, the image of universal power.

"Rama."

He turns toward Master, who is smiling now.

"I'm glad you came with me."

"Yes, Master. Thank you, Master."

"You're a patient man. Tolerant."

"Oh, yes, Master. I am always those."

They bounce along, as the old horse, his traces painted in bright colors, clip-clops down the dusty road.

"We are going to Bangkok now, Rama."

"Yes, Master. Very good, sir." But he wonders if in fact it will be good. Will Master send him home, once the destination is reached? It is not yet time for him to return home; there is so much to see, and anyway there is yet his fortune to make. He must reason with Master and point out the logic of his remaining in service. He will do that, Rama tells himself confidently.

As they pass along the ancient boulevard, scruffy trees line the way. It's almost time now for the mangoes to bloom in Kumbakonem. But Rama won't think of that. Now is the time for him to anticipate those pickled tea leaves. Not a bad dish, considering who made it. But he must be charitable to the Burmans. Narayana. The prospect of that acrid, spicy taste puts him in a good mood all the way back to Nyaung-U.

27 SHE'S ONE DAY out of bed, and her period begins. Even so, the abdominal pain isn't as severe as usual, and she isn't nauseated, and anyway it's better than the daily fever, dull through the day, spiking at night.

It's been a mysterious fever, but then they often are in the dry season of Bangkok. The German doctor had no idea what it was. In his heavily accented English he'd put the stick on her tongue, taken her temperature, listened to her heart, and muttered, *"Ja, ist F . . . U . . . O,"* as if calling it a fever of unknown origin solved anything. Hers began the morning after what she calls "the talk about men with Mother." Her man, Mother's men.

While confined to bed, with time to think about that confrontation, she hasn't yet thought about it. She has discussed it with her imaginary confidante, but that's not the same. Each time her mother's confession comes to mind, Sanuk feels another thought edging it out. The details of it are there—the truth about Shanghai—but something lies behind them. What has she felt? Sadness, anger, bewilderment. All those things, yet none of them seem to answer what it means that Mother lived such a life or that she herself now knows it. Perhaps the fever got in the way. Surely it's kept Mother and her from continuing what they started that evening. Mother has not once mentioned their talk. It might never have happened, as she's bent to kiss her ailing daughter and to ask in a voice Sanuk remembers from childhood, "Are you better, darling?"

But now everything will happen, Sanuk tells herself. At last she's on her feet again, feeling strong in the first hot morning of the year. Even the cast is off her thumb. All's right with the world, she thinks in English. It's such a nice simple line of poetry. Whoever wrote it must have been happy writing it.

Sanuk looks out the window at a rain tree across the lane. In a while now the monsoon will come, drowning this lane, making the leaves glisten. She has lost two weeks. It has not been all bad. A few days ago Lamai visited her, and they discussed the wedding plans. The family astrologer had picked the exact hour for the wedding. Lamai will wear a sarong of solid blue, the color of devotion, and a shawl of pink, the color of love, when the priest recites the Five Commandments. Lamai had seemed interested in these details, but wary of discussing the consummation. Yet when Sanuk persisted, Lamai put up only token resistance. "You mustn't say those things."

"But there's something wrong here," Sanuk told her with a laugh. "What's marriage to a Buddhist? I mean, someone once told me—let me see: 'Marriage simply acknowledges the hated flesh must be served.' "

"Who told you that?"

"That clever boy, Suchat."

Lamai threw up her hands in mock despair. "He can't draw, he can't paint, he can't model clay."

"But he's clever. Now, the point is," Sanuk went on, glad to have company besides the women of this house, "the flesh is hated, but everyone knows the Siamese love love."

"You shouldn't say those things. Anyway, who's everyone?"

"You must sleep on the left side and never cross your feet."

"Tell me why!"

"It prevents a difficult birth. But only as it applies to the fifth waxing and the third waning moons. Nipa told me."

"Nipa tells you things you shouldn't know," Lamai says, trying to sound judicious.

"Let me tell you how to know if you're pregnant."

"Enough now."

"This is true. I read this in an astrology book. Pranee once lent it to me. You subtract your age in months from his in months—"

"Enough!" Lamai pleaded gaily.

"—and then divide by seven. I mean your age in months when you think you might . . . you just might be . . . because something has happened between you—"

Lamai was laughing too hard to protest, as Sanuk, her eyes glittering from the last of the fever, leaned forward from the pillow. "Now, after dividing by seven—listen, you aren't listening properly—if you have a remainder from one through six, there's a good chance. If the division comes out even, forget it. And nothing positive ever results from a seven through nine. It's true. I read it in Pranee's book." And in fact Sanuk had, but Lamai, a literal girl who never wasted time on foolish things, had not believed her.

Nor would she have believed I have loved a man, not only once but often in the beds of terrible hotels, not only here in Bangkok but in the South as well where we traveled together, openly. The raw details shock her, as Sanuk thinks them while standing at the window. What makes the reality difficult to accept is the absence from her life of Chamlong, who after this long separation—more than two weeks—seems almost shadowy in her mind, a tall, a very tall and vaguely handsome presence against the bright sunlight. He has a prominent chin, too prominent, and very small ears and skin as taut as a sail. Things about him are exaggerated in memory, and what isn't exaggerated doesn't exist for her. Absently she touches her breasts, enlarged and slightly tender from the period. Then her hand moves to the Hindu goddess on the chain around her neck.

We killed a man together.

From below comes Nipa's whining voice as she complains to someone Siamese—perhaps a delivery man—of the *Jeen*, the *Jeen*, the impossibly stupid and mean-spirited *Jeen*, encompassing the entire Chinese race in her daily denunciations of one old woman. In truth, Ah Ping is a household tyrant. Each day Nipa waits for her to go on an errand; then the litany against the Chinese begins.

Sanuk listens without hearing the words. She only hopes that Nipa keeps bringing her niece around to do odd jobs. In fact, last night at dinner—her first downstairs in two weeks—Sanuk had praised young Lalawal's efficiency. "It's hard to believe, Mother, the girl is only thirteen."

What worries Sanuk is the possibility that the household doesn't need this child, who unbeknown to anyone else has become her own personal servant—and messenger. She truly likes the girl: open, honest, fun-loving, loyal. And malleable. Lalawal's main handicap is timidity, but Sanuk's been working on that, ever since she persuaded the girl to take the note to Chamlong.

The deception doesn't please Sanuk, but there's no other way to maintain contact with him. Mother is adamant. In the sickroom she'd been tender and loving. Yet sitting on the edge of the bed with Sanuk's hand in hers, Mother will suddenly blurt out what has been on her mind all the time: "He's not for you" or "You must understand you're not old enough yet to judge men wisely, so please, for me, give this boy up" or "An attachment of that sort, darling, can only bring you grief."

To this last declaration Sanuk once added, "I know."

Since the illness, she's felt differently about her mother. For one thing, Mother seems younger. Mother is indeed attractive, even now, although gaining weight from an appetite she can't seem to appease. Sanuk has always considered her mother's life tragic because of her father's death, but the revelation of Shanghai has deepened the girl's fascination as well as her sympathy, as she might feel similar things for heroines she admires: Jeanne d'Arc, the noble Rani of Jhansi who died fighting for her people against the British, and other women of spirit doomed to a tragic fate. To her imaginary confidante, while lying feverish in bed, Sanuk has said, "So there it is, a lie I've believed all my life. I wish she'd told me earlier about Shanghai; it's the thing I regret most. But I suppose she's always felt I was too young to understand. Now, of course, I do. I really do. Some girls would hate their mother for being a prostitute. Especially girls at convent school. But I've sinned as much as she has, and I don't hate myself for it. I don't hate myself for what I've done with Chamlong"—she has never mentioned the murder to her confidante—"so why should I hate my mother for doing only what she had to do? The Buddhists are right: What counts is why you do something, not what you do. Those were bad times, you know. She was only trying to survive, and I know my father forgave her. So what I'm saying is, we all have faults in this life. We must be tolerant." This pleasant homily, delivered to the imaginary confidante, merely emphasizes her own dissatisfaction with Mother, who is being so intolerant of Chamlong. Sanuk is developing the idea that it is Mother, not herself, who misunderstands men. No wonder her mother has come to hate men, indiscriminately. Chamlong. Philip. The good ones lumped in with the bad.

During long days in bed Sanuk often imagined the sexual degradation to which countless men had submitted Mother. It is horrible, it is thrilling too, and Sanuk sometimes feels ashamed of a tendency to imagine herself in Mother's place. She herself is there in Shanghai hotel rooms much like those paid for by Chamlong, except with cruel, faceless men.

Lately, Sanuk has been trying to read Chinese poetry, especially that of the courtesan Yu Hsuan-chi of the Tang Dynasty. Dead at thirty. Jeanne d'Arc dead at nineteen—her own age, her very own. And Mother struggling to survive in callous Shanghai. The images build in Sanuk's mind, shifting and fading and returning: men, swords, orange blossoms, a raging storm and battle cries, two people by a lake, a fist raised in a dark room, bare light bulbs, the silken swish of a robe removed, a burning pyre, a cross held tight to the bosom, the cry of Jesus!, the sorrow of women.

During the illness, such images made her entire body tremble, although Sanuk wonders now if the fever caused it. These last two weeks are already uncertain in memory. But of one thing she's certain: She will go to Chamlong no matter what Mother says.

Yet Sanuk's defiance is tempered by a general anxiety, the residue of illness. And this morning an insect fell on her left shoulder, a little bug she wouldn't have noticed had she not been looking in a mirror when it fell. That's a bad omen, really. An insect falling on your left shoulder, Nipa once explained, means the death of someone you know. If only it had fallen on the left arm—that's just a quarrel. Once she saw a flying insect light on Chamlong's ear. It means he secretly fears a woman.

She will see him. Mother keeps coming in with portentous rumors about Siamese gangs roaming the waterfront, about Communist gangs threatening the peace of Bangkok. It's yet another twist of reality for Sanuk that she's sat in tea shops with many of those Communists who threaten Mother's peace of mind.

. . .

She is turned from this irony by a knock at the door. It's Lalawal (she's glad to see the girl in the house), announcing a visitor.

Sopita, Chamlong's sister, walks in.

There are amenities, a short discussion of the dance concert at the National Theatre. Sanuk has always been jealous of Sopita, of the aloof Chinese girl's ability to dance the classical *khon*. And as they talk, Sanuk regards critically the petite features, the long neck, the graceful fingers that she's seen bend backward almost to the wrist. She had almost forgotten Sopita's arrogant beauty. They haven't seen each other in a long time—not since Sopita introduced her brother.

Their conversation has meandered to a halt. What has she come for? Sanuk wonders, as they sit through an awkward silence.

Finally Sopita looks up from hands folded in her lap. "Do you see my brother?"

"No, how could I?" Sanuk replies coolly. "I've been sick."

"I tell you as a friend. You shouldn't see him."

"Why?"

"I can't say. But if you know where he is, I wish you'd tell me."

"What did your brother do?"

"The longer he stays away from home, the worse it'll be for him, Sanuk. You'd be doing him a favor by telling me."

"I have no idea where your brother is." Sanuk watches the girl rise, visibly annoyed.

When Sopita leaves, Sanuk goes to the window. She waits there until the young woman emerges below and begins walking, with exceptional grace, down the lane. Watching her recede into the haze of a hot morning, Sanuk feels triumphant. My man's as true as steel. Did Sopita think I'd betray him? We have killed a man, she thinks. What we did together binds us like a rope of steel.

• • •

Minutes later she's down in the kitchen, where Cook and Nipa are sitting among pots and pans, near a cold stove, with Burmese cheroots in their mouths.

Cook merely stares, Nipa slowly rises, as the girl comes in. Everyone calls Nipa an old woman, yet actually she's younger than Mother. She just looks old, with her stringy hair, her dumpy figure, her perpetual expression of weariness. "Does Miss want anything? Coconut pudding?" Said with a great sigh. Though she always looks tired, she's as energetic as a bee.

Politely Sanuk says, "Thank you, I'm not hungry. I don't want to bother you." She smiles at Cook, who frowns.

"Isn't your niece here today?" she asks Nipa, who nods. "Can the girl sew?"

"My niece is a fine, good girl who can cook and sew and do what is asked," Nipa declares proudly.

"Then I have work for her. Please send her to my room."

Minutes later, waiting impatiently by the window, Sanuk is startled by a knock on the door, although she's been expecting it. When the girl comes in, Sanuk tells her to sit on the bed. "Go on, sit down," Sanuk insists when the girl hesitates. "Lalawal, I have a note for you to take." Picking up the folded paper from the desk, she gives it to the girl, who sits glum and reluctant. "Come now, you've done it before," Sanuk tells her soothingly.

"But if I get caught."

"Who will catch you?"

"My aunt." The girl's pretty face is tense at the jawline.

"Don't worry about your aunt." She gives Lalawal a piece of thread. "If she stops you going out, tell her I sent you for more of this thread. Then, when you return, tell her you couldn't find it in the market, if she asks."

"She'll ask."

Regarding the girl's evident distress, Sanuk sits down by her and takes her hand. Turning it over, then spreading out the palm, she says, "This is a good hand. The lines are silken, as they should be."

"Really?" Lalawal bends to inspect her palm too.

"You have a warm hand. Good." Holding the hand up and inspecting it carefully, she continues, "The back of your hand's arched like a turtle's back. That's very good. A bad sign would be hard, dry palms, and flatness. That would mean riches but a sad heart."

"I don't want a sad heart." Lalawal smiles; it's like a blossom opening.

"According to your hand, you won't have. See the lines here, how deep and narrow and unbroken they are? You're a clever girl."

"No, I'm not."

"You must be. Your hand says it right here. And see how these lines go straight up into the fingers? You can finish any work you undertake. There now." Patting her hand, Sanuk rises to get money from her desk. Something strikes her. Turning, she says to the girl, "When you saw him that time, what did you think of him?"

"I don't know."

"Really. What?"

"Well"—the girl smiles broadly—"he's a handsome fellow."

"Hurry now." Like shooing a small child from her room, she rushes Lalawal out.

The girl carries a short message: "Tell me when I can come."

· · ·

The next two days will be among the strangest of her life.

First, Lalawal returns with the same piece of paper, under which is printed: "I will be here waiting. Come soon." Again that sense of urgency. And with the memory still fresh in her mind of Sopita's cool but insistent attempt to learn his whereabouts, Sanuk can understand why: People are searching for him. Poor Chamlong! Doubtless the Party has run into trouble, although the nature of it is frustratingly obscure. Recently the news has been heavily censored; the newspapers contain little but references to the royal family, Buddhist councils, cultural events. Mother's rumors must be discounted—a hodgepodge of market talk about raids and gangs and trouble of some kind, any kind, in Chinatown.

She can't wait any longer. Dressed, feeling weak and crampy, nevertheless Sanuk marches downstairs and out the front entrance. As she fully expects, a voice calls her name from the house. Turning and shading her eyes, she informs Ah Ping with all the dignity at her command that she's late for an appointment with her friend who's getting married. Immediately the little Teochiu woman rushes from the house, words preceding her like guard dogs: "You are still sick, you have the cramps too, you're not supposed to run around town with these gangs in the streets, Miss, and until your mother—are you listening to me—are you coming back here—"

The words grow faint, as Sanuk's wobbly legs stride through the hot, dusty afternoon. When she hires a boat at the end of the lane, Sanuk steps wearily into it. The klong, scummy from months without rain, reflects her pale, worried face as she bends over from the thwart and stares at the passing water.

She has not expected a good hotel, surely no better than the ones they'd gone to together, but Chamlong's hideout is an appalling place. When he opens the room door after her insistent knocking, Chamlong's appearance is a worse shock: He looks wild, haggard, aged beyond his years. Instead of embracing her, he backs off and slumps down on a fetid mattress lying on the floor. Worrying his tousled hair with both hands, he looks down and mutters, "I am lost. Everything is lost."

It takes some minutes for her to piece together his story about the raid on the leaflet distribution building. The death of Chin, the imprisonment of Somchai and the others affect her deeply. Poor Chamlong! No wonder he's sunk in despair—his friends and comrades have been taken, while he goes free. When she tries to console him, Chamlong waves her away. "No, no, you don't understand," he says. "I have to get out of the country, or I'm lost. I haven't any money—"

Sitting beside him, Sanuk asks if he has papers. He has papers. And where is he thinking of going?

Without looking at her, he says, "China."

The word seems to run through her like fire. China—he is going to China!

"But it's only a dream." He turns to her with his eyes wild. "I can't get out of here without money. And they've given me a mission."

When he explains the nature of it, Sanuk puts her arm around him. "But if they give you such a mission, they'll provide the money to go."

"Not when everyone's hiding out. The money's needed here."

"Ah, I see. But you must go. It's your duty."

"Not without money," he says rapidly, as if annoyed by her lack of comprehension.

"Don't worry about money," Sanuk tells him. "I'll get it."

Chamlong raises his eyes to her. "How can you get it? Not from your mother. She's like my father." He looks between his legs at the floor. "No, you can't get it."

Sanuk lays her head against his cheek, smelling the rank odor of his unwashed body. It makes her pity him more. Poor Chamlong! "Remember what I said? I said I will always do what I can."

"Yes, I remember."

"Trust me."

With her head resting against his, she can't see his expression when he replies dully, "I can't trust anyone."

Sanuk moves away from him to stare. "You can trust me. You can trust your friends and the Party."

"Maybe I can trust Wan-li," he suggests in a faint tone of hope.

That is one man she can't trust, but to encourage Chamlong she agrees they must both trust Wan-li. Then, holding his hand, she explains she'll get the money in a day or two, so he mustn't leave here. From her beaded money pouch she gives him what money she has, save for the fare home. He bends over and counts it twice. Poor Chamlong! But when he reaches for her, touching her breast, she pulls away, explaining it's her time of the month. A ripple of disgust crosses his face; she sees it. But maybe all men are like that, she thinks. At the door, she squeezes his hand like a sister. "Trust me," she tells the haggard young man and leaves him peeking at her, door slightly ajar, until she goes down the hallway stairs.

• • •

Sanuk fully expects a quarrel when she arrives home late that afternoon. By now Ah Ping must have described her departure from the house with spirited embellishments. Rather than wait for trouble to find her, Sanuk decides to seek it out. That way she'll free her mind for the main problem: how to get Chamlong the money when she has none of her own. In this both fearless and troubled mood she locates her mother in the garden, sitting under a tamarind tree. As Sanuk approaches, she can see on the woman's face a look of rapt concentration. A piece of paper is gripped in her hand.

"I suppose Ah Ping told you I left," Sanuk begins boldly. "Lamai wanted me to come around when I could, because there isn't much time now before the wedding, and so this afternoon I just decided to do it. I felt well enough."

Mother waves her hand dismissively. "Yes. But don't be rude to Ah Ping. She loses face with Nipa and Cook."

Sanuk can feel Mother studying her.

"You haven't seen that boy, have you?"

"No."

"Because I trust you." This is said, however, almost indifferently, as a matter of form rather than conviction. Something else is consuming Mother's attention. "Here. Read this." She hands over the piece of paper.

It's a cable from Philip. He's arriving the next day by steamship from Rangoon.

28 IT'S LATE AT night. As far as she knows, everyone is asleep, although Sanuk suspects that Mother may be lying awake, just as she herself is, thinking of tomorrow.

Touching the amulet at her neck, she tries to picture Chamlong in her mind, only not the one she saw today, but the old Chamlong, with his grudging smile and face of angles. She tries also to recall poor Chin's face, but all that comes to her is disembodied lips set in a scowl. And Somchai. She remembers vividly the first she ever saw of him: his mouth full of blood from butchered dentistry. She had learned to like him. His swaggering way with unimportant facts had only hidden a lack of confidence. What are they doing to him in prison? All those young men with their ideals and anger—scattered now, like ducks off a path. Clearly the Communist movement has collapsed in Bangkok. Not that she cares that much. She's never understood the political theory of communism, except insofar as it's against the rich and for justice. Only Wan-li and a couple of others knew more, spouting their Marx and Mao. But she cares about the fate of Chinese people in this country. This is true. Isn't she the daughter of a great Chinese general? People forget that. Chamlong does; none of the Party members have ever bothered to remember it; and sometimes even Mother seems to ignore their linked circumstances: They are the wife and the daughter of General Tang Shan-teh, late Defense Commissioner of Southern Shantung Province. And more than that—the potential savior of China. But how could Mother forget for a moment?

In the garden during late afternoons, when she returned from school, Sanuk often sprawled on the lawn and listened to Mother describe the General's horse, the General's songbirds ("he was partial to a frosted-opal bronze cock and a broken-capped gold female"), his love for the art of Ni Tsan, his hatred of footbinding. He defied the notorious Green Gang in Shanghai, and got away with it, because the Green Gang knew that in dealing with him at least they dealt with an honest man. He admired Christianity for preaching against idleness, yet could say something cryptic and noble (noble: Mother's word) such as: "We Chinese can speak seriously without speaking of God; we don't need God to explain man's actions on earth." He kept his hair cropped short; it went with a rugged face, a sturdy torso. And yet he laughed with his eyes (Mother's description); and his long earlobes, according to Chinese belief, meant he was spiritual—which he was, Mother said. He used to talk about the "impossible heart of Confucius," which is the five virtues of kindness, honesty, dedication, knowledge, faith. He had them all, Mother said. His men worshiped him, Mother said. He went to war because of honor; fought the great Battle of Henshui because a rival general questioned his integrity. He wore a big pistol. Men snapped to attention, Mother said, when he passed. Mother never seemed to realize that in describing Father she described a man of war—the sort of man she otherwise abhorred. When Mother spoke of him, on those lilting afternoons, Sanuk had envisioned him in front of his troops, mixed somehow in her mind with Jeanne d'Arc, the two warriors leading their men into glorious battle, swords in hand, galloping . . .

If only she had known him, even a day, an hour, even just long enough to see his face and watch the way he walked and held himself, Sanuk would consider herself lucky. Denied that chance, she's always felt an emptiness, as if in the making of herself something was left out.

Now Chamlong is going to China, where her father lived, fought, died.

Mother once said in the garden, "When we met in Shanghai, we fell in love. But how could anything come of it? He was a Chinese general, I was a foreign woman."

This dramatic way of putting the dilemma has never ceased to thrill Sanuk.

"He asked me to marry him and return to Qufu, where his army was. I told him it was impossible."

How could she refuse? Sanuk always wondered.

"I told him we came from different worlds. His was China. Mine was Russia—or had been; at least it was not China. And then one day he said—"

"Where were you?" Sanuk always asked at this point in the narrative.

"In the Garden of Yu the Mandarin. We were standing in front of a famous Tai Hu rock. And your father—he was wearing a Western suit—"

"Why?" Sanuk always asked.

"To please me, though he looked wonderful in uniform."

Wonderful. Sanuk pictured him with epaulettes and a bandolier and that pistol in a black holster and a billed cap and gold buttons up the front of his jacket and medals of honor along one side of it.

"And your father said, 'Where you belong is a state of mind. The things of China are yours, if you want them. China has a place for us together.' That's what changed my mind—his words in the Garden of Yu the Mandarin. I accepted him."

It seems that lately Sanuk's own life has drawn closer to China, to her blood's inheritance. During the Party meetings, she's noticed how the leaders, people like Wan-li, have begun to link Siam with China, the underground activity here with the civil war there. They are similar events, for in both cases Chinese are fighting for justice and freedom. That's what is said. She's heard Chin say it and Wan-li and the other leaders. So it is true.

Getting off the bed and turning on a light, she gropes for her diary in the sandalwood cabinet. Soon she's writing rapidly:

> I beleive you must act quickly in life. If you wait, you never get the chance again. If I cuold breath the air he breathed, I know I cuold find him in my mind.

Closing the diary, lying down in the darkness again, she shuts her eyes tightly. Her lips are trembling, she can feel them, and her heart pounds. Something is going to happen.

The Siamese are always claiming that outside forces control our lives. These forces can be karma accumulated during a past life or *phi* functioning in this one or ghosts or other spirits hovering at the edge of this world. Whatever they are they control us. Stubbornly skeptical until this moment, she's resisted the idea of outside forces controlling her life. Now she feels the truth of it. There are no choices presented to her. Her only choice is to realize there aren't any. It is clear now. She needs only to look at the facts, and they'll show the way. Chamlong, her lover, to whom she's bound by an act of blood—this is *true*—must leave Siam. The fight for justice here is temporarily halted. He's leaving for the land of her father, who never stopped fighting for justice until he died. That is true. And now she has the chance to help her lover, but in doing so, may never see him again.

There's no choice. She must go with him.

• • •

Next morning there is bustle in the house, as everyone is preparing for Master's arrival—that's what the servants call it, and Sanuk recognizes her mother's forbearance in not correcting them. What will happen in this house when I'm gone? Sanuk wonders, even while smiling at Nipa, who brings mango juice to the table. Mother has gone out, so they won't have breakfast together. This is disturbing. They may not eat together again for a long time. The idea is odd, compelling, terrible.

But what there is between us will survive this, Sanuk tells herself. Events, fate, God has put this in my path.

She hears something. "What?"

"I said, Miss, do you want coconut pudding this morning?"

"Fine, fine. When will my mother be home?"

"Soon. She must go to the boat for Master. You are going too?"

Sanuk shakes her head. Maybe, she thinks, I could wait until Mother comes home, then eat breakfast. Recognizing the danger of such comfortable thinking, Sanuk calls out, "I'll have the pudding now!"

In her room, packing a suitcase with the door locked, she hears some time later the sound of Mother's voice rising anxiously from below, giving orders to Ah Ping. Sanuk puts the suitcase under the bed, unlocks and opens the door, walks to the landing and looks down.

Her mother is wearing a white blouse, a red skirt, red sandals. Her hair is combed up around her head like a soft black cloud—she's been to the hairdresser—and her face is wonderfully animated. Wonderfully, Sanuk tells herself. She wants to remember her mother looking so wonderful. Is this going to happen?

"Sanuk." Mother is smiling. She has used the Siamese nickname. That's a good omen. Mother's gloomy response to the cable has given way to acceptance. Will she accept Philip back? Mother has never seemed to realize what a fine man he is.

"Will you come to the pier?" Mother calls up.

"I'm not feeling well."

"What? Fever?"

"No, the usual—cramps."

"Nipa told me you had your period."

It occurs to Sanuk that her mother, worried about the boy, must have asked the servants, must have nervously sought information on *that* subject. Mother's desire to protect her strikes Sanuk as so poignant she nearly cries. Yet with composure she waves goodbye, returns to her room, and finishes packing behind a locked door.

• • •

Her room doesn't face the klong, so she can't watch Mother take a boat from there. Sitting on the bed, she strains to hear any sounds in the house. From below comes a dull clang—Cook and her pans. She's preparing a banquet for Master's return and no doubt is in a seething artistic rage. An outside door creaks open; Sanuk rushes to the window to see Lalawal heading down the lane. Nipa has sent her on an errand. Later, will they suspect the girl and punish her for her part in what happened? Or will they care?

Unlocking the door, Sanuk glances around. There is Mother's door, ajar, and the guest room door, closed. Perhaps Ah Ping is in the servants' bungalow, taking a nap now that Mistress is gone. Stepping out of her room, Sanuk crosses quickly to Mother's and shuts the door. Her heart is pounding. Usually when she comes into this room, Sanuk regards with curiosity the chintz curtains, the lace everywhere, the airy feminine mood that Mother has created out of a memory of Old Russia, when such things surrounded the women who went to balls and took sleigh rides and shopped in boutiques that imitated Paris. But today Sanuk looks only at the vase standing on an elegant teak dresser.

It's rose porcelain from the Ching Dynasty. Quite probably from the Ching-te-Chen factory, third decade of the eighteenth century—Mother claims she will have it authenticated someday. She found it in a sundry goods shop in Singapore years ago, and Sanuk remembers it from her childhood. No one touches it but Mother, who used to lift and turn it for Sanuk to admire: some ladies in blue dresses with rose-pink collars; a stag in canary yellow with a pink neck; branches of fruit blossoms in various shades of pink; all of these figures contained in a glowing field of white.

For the first time in her life Sanuk touches its cool glazed curves, then lifts it, as Mother does, for inspection. There are other things in the house, but most of them are Siamese: heavy bronzes, generally Buddha images. Dealers have them in abundance. This, however, is a rarity in Bangkok. How often, when a guest from the university or a visiting collector has come to dinner, Sanuk has been bored by Mother's lectures about this vase: "You see, in Yung Cheng porcelain what's so wonderful is the delicacy of the drawing. There's no crowding of the figures. The open spaces are the glory of Yung Cheng, really. The *juan ts'ai* are the most beautiful colors you'll find in porcelain. And the glazes: so glassy, blue-green, almost transparent in the light." Sanuk can recite Mother's analysis, just as she recites Ah Ping's morning call to breakfast.

As she turns the porcelain beaker, Sanuk tells herself there's no choice, none.

Another object on the dresser catches her eye. It's an ink stone of white jade. The plain oblong with the indentation at one end has never been used, never been stained by ink sticks. Nor has Mother told her where she got it or its value, but Sanuk can see the hard mineral is highly polished, finely grained. She takes that too.

•   •   •

This time she gets to the lane before Ah Ping shouts. Turning to squint in the noon light, Sanuk waits patiently until the old woman in black trousers reaches her.

"Not again, Miss. You mustn't leave the house." Her puffed eyes regard Sanuk reproachfully. "Mistress will be angry. She's not forgiven me for your running off to the South." She lifts a mottled hand and points with a trembling finger. "What is that?"

She looks down at the old woman. "My suitcase, Ah Ping."

"No, no." Her white hair, pulled back into a bun, has a sheen in the sunlight. "No, Miss," Ah Ping says, moving her head from side to side. "You must give him up."

"I'm going, Ah Ping." She hears the weakness in her voice, feels the tears rising. If she stays another moment with this old servant of her childhood, she'll cry and Ah Ping will grab the suitcase with one hand and with the other guide her by the elbow back into the house, haranguing all the time.

"I'm going, Ah Ping." Turning, the girl steps out. She expects to hear at her back a high whining scold, but none comes, not a sound. Not until reaching a klong at the lane's end does she look back. Ah Ping is standing there in the wide black trousers, arms limp at her sides, head cocked slightly, hot sun beating down on her white hair.

• • •

The shop she's looking for is on a soi near Chulalongkorn University. Sanuk feels faint; the heat of spring has clamped down on Bangkok like a great iron cover. After crossing a bridge over one klong, she comes upon another meandering stream, too narrow for traffic, and turns at last into the soi, which is lined by hardware and machine shops.

ANTIQUES OF ASIA is a neat sign in front of a tiny store at the end of the street. Mother has often spoken of the Dutchman, a fine man and a rather good dealer, who would do better in a better location, such as hers, near the hotels and the embassies. Her tone has always been apprehensive, however, as if the Dutchman might move closer and take business away from her. Whatever Mother says, the Dutchman is the best-known foreign dealer in Bangkok; his clients are museums and world-famous collectors, a fact that Mother has always attributed to his honesty, not his judgment.

When Sanuk enters the little shop, a bell tinkles above the doorway, alerting the man seated behind a desk at the back of the room. His wooden counters contain many objects beneath covers of glass; nothing stands on the tops. It is a clean, spare, unobtrusive shop, which seems to match the tall man who approaches her.

Putting the suitcase down, Sanuk opens it and takes out the beaker and the ink stone. "I have these to sell." She makes an effort to meet his cool blue-eyed gaze. Mother says never look weak when you negotiate.

She has spoken English, and so therefore does the Dutchman, who stands back and looks at the objects she has placed on a glass-topped counter. "You wish to sell both of them?" He picks up the jade ink stone and studies it a moment. "I have no use for this," he says flatly and hands it back to her.

Their eyes meet. Sanuk concentrates on holding her facial muscles firm. She won't look worried or uncertain, she won't.

· · ·

The tall antique dealer lifts the vase carefully and turns it in a beam of sunlight coming through a small window. He squints. "May I?" Motioning to the door and waiting for her nod of permission, the Dutchman takes the beaker outside for a better look.

Following him, Sanuk observes enthusiastically, "You can see the glaze, how glossy and blue-green it is. Almost transparent."

Turning from the vase a moment, he stares at her. Then, holding the beaker to the light, he turns it slowly, like a pig on a spit. His inspection is close, minute, patient. Returning to the shop, he puts it down, again carefully, and stands back, one hand cradling his chin.

"The shape isn't perfect," he comments after a while.

"It shouldn't be. Not if it's Yung Cheng."

He gives her a faint smile. "So it's Yung Cheng, is it?"

"You can test it." She tries to remember: You put some acid in water, then dip the porcelain in it a few moments; after that you wash the porcelain, wipe it dry with a soft duster. But she can't think of why. It's to prove something. "You can test it with acid."

He nods.

"Do you know what I mean?"

Again he smiles. "Added clobber will peel but the original enamel won't. Do you think I need help, young lady?" He walks slowly back to his desk and returns with a magnifying glass.

"That's a good test too," Sanuk maintains eagerly. "When you look at the pinks, they're clear pinks. The forgeries look violet."

While he's studying the beaker with his magnifying glass, the Dutchman says, "Who are you, young lady?"

"I'm passing through Bangkok." Having anticipated the question, she's prepared for it. "I'm Chinese-American. We live in Shanghai and I'm on my way to Europe to school."

"Where?"

"The Sorbonne. And I was supposed to sell this beaker in Europe, but, you see, I've lost all my money, so I've decided to sell it here."

Still holding the glass, he regards her thoughtfully a few moments. "That's quite a story."

"Well, it's the truth." Sanuk meets his gaze without faltering.

"Did you wire your parents and tell them what you're doing?"

"I did. They agree." She feels her spine's as straight as a tree.

Again he picks the beaker up, turning it in the light, studying the sheen, the lines. "The base is covered with little punctures," he comments finally.

"Of course."

"You know quite a lot about porcelain, young lady."

"That comes from living in China."

Again their eyes meet, and this time the Dutchman lowers his with a little sigh of decision. "I don't know if this is genuine Yung Cheng. You don't have authentication papers with you, do you?"

Sanuk shakes her head, trying not to look annoyed or worried. She hopes her face is composed into an expression of impassive confidence.

"You see," the Dutchman says, "that's the trouble. Without papers I can't be sure."

"But you are sure," Sanuk says boldly.

"I'll have to think about it." He picks up the vase and extends it toward her.

Sanuk makes no effort to take it. "I can't wait."

"No? Why not?"

"My ship leaves tomorrow. It goes to . . . Rangoon. I lost my ticket too. I have to buy the ticket from here to Rangoon and then to Europe, you see. I can't wait. I have to sell it now."

The Dutchman shrugs. "Very well. But I can't make the offer now I might make after a few days of studying this vase. I am honest with you."

Sanuk nods. "I know that. What will you give me?"

Again cradling his chin in his hand, the Dutchman turns his cool blue eyes to the window. "Ten thousand bahts."

It is this part of the negotiation that Sanuk has feared. Whenever Mother talks business, say, with Wanna or Prakit Chaidee, the subject of price always bores Sanuk—the numbers float in and out of her head, finding no place to rest.

The Dutchman, seeing her hesitate, volunteers more information. "I know it's only twenty, maybe thirty percent of what you might get in Europe, even for an imitation, if that's what it is. I'm telling you this before you decide whether or not to accept the offer."

"I have no choice."

"Young lady, you *always* have the choice to accept or refuse an offer."

"I have no choice. I'll accept."

• • •

The next few hours are spent in the steamship lines near the waterfront of Bangkok. Looking back on that afternoon, she will always be in awe of the girl who trudged from one office to another, seeking fast passage to China for herself and Chamlong: the Messageries Maritime Company, China Navigation, Isthmian Steamship Company, American President

Lines, British Straits Steamships Company, and finally the Norwegian line, Duket Shipping, whose agent in Bangkok was Ngow Hock Limited, Charterers. At Ngow Hock she was able to get third-class passage on a steamer laying over a day in Singapore, with Shanghai as final destination.

In a samlor headed for Chamlong's hotel, she faces yet another problem. She has a passport issued last year, when she accompanied Mother on a two weeks' trip to Singapore, but it won't do, not if Mother checks the passenger lists of vessels and planes leaving Bangkok for "Sonia Embree." To the steamship ticket agent she gave a false name, conjured at the moment: "Tang Yu-ying." She will carry her father's surname into China; that she must do. As for "Yu-ying," it popped into her mind —the name of a great lady her mother once knew in Shanghai. "Tang Yu-ying" has a pleasant sound, and she repeats it aloud to herself while the samlor heads for the hotel. At the dock, she'll have to support her new name with a passport. But that's a problem that must be put aside until later; Sanuk is learning that sometimes a problem can't even be thought of for a while.

Squinting into the heat of this spring day, she feels abruptly old. Until now she's not considered such matters as transportation, money, and passports. Other people did it for her: Mother did it. But now, on the threshold of this adventure, she feels older, more like a woman, in fact, than she did after leaving the hotel with Chamlong that first time. As a Royal Dragon, she has her feet in Mars and Mercury, and that means she's a traveler at heart. Indeed, it seems that way, for in spite of sudden jolts of conscience and regret, Sanuk's mind is firmly set on one of those ships out there on the river, waiting to take her and her lover to sea.

. . .

When she knocks on his door this time, Chamlong answers it quickly. She's relieved to see an improvement in his appearance. Of course he's pale and drawn from nearly three weeks in this tiny hovel, but there's a new alertness about him that reminds her of the Chamlong who played Push Hands Tai Chi against Somchai at the Temple of the Emerald Buddha.

"You have it?" he asks, when she enters the room and closes the door.

"I have it."

Smiling, Chamlong puts his hands on her shoulders. The touch comforts Sanuk enough for her to place her cheek against his. He smells of strong soap. Pulling back to look at him, she says. "Do you still mean what you said at the Emerald Buddha?"

"What?"

"The oath you took in front of the Buddha. Do you still mean it?"

"Of course I mean it. Tell me what happened today. Come." He pulls her along to the mattress.

In detail made vivid by pride, Sanuk explains how she left home and what she took and how much she got at the antique store.

"Ten thousand," he muses. "And you still have the ink stone."

"If we have trouble, we can sell it somewhere—perhaps Singapore or Shanghai."

Chamlong frowns at her. "What do you mean, 'we'?"

"I'm going too."

"Oh, but you can't," he tells her quickly. "Wan-li said you can't go along."

Coolly Sanuk looks at him. "Wan-li doesn't need to know. He isn't providing the money. I am."

He considers the distinction. "If we have the money, well . . ."

Taking his hand, she says, "Do you want me with you, Chamlong?"

"Of course I do." He looks toward the window; it's growing dark now. "As long as we have the money, we can go together. It's an important mission. Two are better than one."

Jumping to his feet, as if energized by the new idea, Chamlong begins pacing. "We must get tickets and think how to go."

"I've got tickets for Shanghai."

Turning, he smiles. This is the Chamlong I love, she thinks.

"There's one problem, though."

He stops pacing.

"I need new papers. I can't use mine with my name in them."

"Never mind about that," he tells her expansively. "The man who did my papers can do yours. And it's cheap."

"But soon? The ship leaves in three days."

"Tomorrow. I know about these things. All you do is follow my directions to his house. He's one of us. You have a photograph?"

"I can take it from my passport. Chamlong—"

Whirling on her, his voice tinged with annoyance, he tells her she must no longer call him Chamlong. "I am Ho Jin-shi, now and forever," he says dramatically. At the window he looks down at Bangkok from the second-story room. "It's getting dark. There's a boy downstairs who'll get us food. Do you want to go down and tell him?"

Sanuk rises from the mattress. When she reaches the door, Ho stops her by gripping her arm. "*Tee rahk*," he says.

"*Tee rahk*." And Sanuk tells herself, stepping into the squalid dimness of the hall, there has been no choice, none. Fate has put this squarely in her path.

29 Taking cover from the hot sun beneath a transit shed, Vera looks beyond the dock at a small freighter standing in. That's the Apcar Lines steamer bringing Philip Embree back into her life.

She touches her hair, mussed by the boat ride to the harbor. It's been nine years. Has he changed? She remembers thinking in the Peking autumn of 1927 that no matter what happened to him he'd always look boyish; experience would fail to alter his features. How he courted her in his American way, both awkward and bold! And how ineffably awed he was when finally she took him to her hotel room, poor fellow, not realizing that the seduction she allowed was simply a way of getting herself and her unborn child out of China's chaos. Perhaps too often in her life she's outsmarted herself.

Never, really, has she been honest with Philip Embree. If she couldn't tell him she was pregnant before leaving China, at least she could have told him once they reached Hong Kong. But in her wisdom she kept postponing it, and when her condition became obvious, she led him to believe it was his child she carried. Only when she gave birth to a girl with Chinese eye folds did he finally know the truth.

At the time Philip made a single comment: "She's his." In retrospect the passivity of his acceptance seems incredible. That's all he ever said about it. Yet through the decade they spent together in Hong Kong, Singapore, and Bangkok, what he really felt—the anger, the disappointment, the frustration—was manifest in everything he did. Throughout those years he moved through his life like a ghost. He translated from Chinese to English for export firms; he took walks; he read the paper; he made love to her in sudden frenzies after long intervals of sexual indifference.

Am I to blame for his failure in life? she asks herself as a freighter turns into the approach channel. She must refuse that guilt. Fact: He ran away when the chance came, as finally it did in 1939. Once again, too, China with its interminable wars provided the excuse. He packed one morning and went to war, not returning even when peace revoked his excuse for staying away. She won't accept blame.

Turning away from the river, as if by this action ridding herself of Philip, Vera stares at new godowns built back of the quay. They are ferroconcrete buildings with a flat distempered paint, a muddy cream with green trim. They don't look sturdy in this tropical setting, not the way brick does.

And she thinks suddenly of Sukhothai, the great mass of crumbling brick that has withstood nature for seven hundred years. Vera remembers him at Sukhothai, when they visited the ruins of Wat Mahathat. Sitting on a stone in front of a shattered old temple, Philip stared at a stucco frieze of walking monks—stared at it long enough for her to circle the entire ruins.

"Don't you want to look around?" she'd asked him. "There are marvelous Buddhas over there. Khmer style."

He had turned those eyes on her, those startled blue eyes. "How wonderful for people then. They lived completely in the midst of their beliefs." And how like him to think so. That it was wonderful.

A tendril of hair has fallen across her forehead, and in pushing it back Vera is disheartened by its wetness. By the time he arrives, she'll be soaked in sweat.

The freighter is standing in. It's a cluttered, shabby little ship with peeling paint and cargo stacked everywhere. On the cabin deck, passengers are lined up along the rail. Vera moves into the sunlight, shades her eyes, and when she can't recognize him, moves back into the shade of the transit shed.

It occurs to her with shattering clarity that they'd have been better off never meeting.

Mai pen rai, she mutters aloud.

But Sonia matters. This is one certainty in Vera's mind today. She must live long enough to see the girl settled. The German doctor who came to see Sonia for the fever examined Vera too, and confirmed her fears—she has heart trouble. Well, according to him, not too serious, a little angina. But of course, as he made clear—with much throat clearing —his diagnosis was based only on a house call and therefore without a complete examination . . . and on and on. She won't put up with his Germanic qualifications. It's enough that he gave her some little white pills in case of chest pain. All she must do is let one dissolve under her tongue, and the pain will go away. It's that simple, although he tried to make more of it: Of course, in the event . . . certain complications . . . and on and on. The German is a big, tall man who reminds her of a former lover, a munitions dealer in Shanghai. His name for a moment escapes her—Luckner, Erich Luckner. She's almost lost the name of a man with whom she lived a year. So many men.

Leaning against a stanchion under the corrugated tin roof, Vera squints into the sunlight, but can't see Philip yet.

Oh yes, Sonia matters. The fever interrupted what she and Sonia had started that night. Now that Sonia's better, they must talk more, go beyond confessions and mistakes into a new kind of understanding. The prospect of it brings a smile to Vera's lips, buoys her in the intense heat. And if honesty does have value, they'll be the better for having gone through the confrontation. Already she feels better. This morning, while preparing to leave the house, she'd glanced up and discovered Sonia on the landing, giving her a pensive look, much like the girl used to do years ago, when Philip had gone and they were alone together.

So lost is Vera in these thoughts that she's unaware of the woman approaching, until the pretty young face looms in front of her eyes.

Startled, Vera says, "I thought you were at the shop."

Wanna pouts her lips and shrugs. She's wearing a Siamese dress—Thai chitrlada—much too formal for the docks. The silk sarong has a little design on the lower border; the long-sleeved jacket is buttoned up the front to a stand-up collar. Vera studies every detail of the pretty girl in lime green and blue. "I said I thought you were at the shop," Vera repeats sharply.

Wanna dips her chin, accentuating her upward glance at Vera. "*Tee rahk*, I've finished the work you had for me today and Prakit Chaidee is there, so I thought you'd want me with you here, when you meet Master."

"You needn't call him Master. Call him Philip."

"Oh, I can't do that."

"Yes, you can," Vera says evenly. The girl has put her into a difficult situation. Difficult, ridiculous. How can she welcome a husband who in effect is no longer a husband, while in the company of a lover who perhaps is no longer a lover?

There isn't time to worry the situation, however, because the Apcar freighter is coming alongside the dock. She turns to the activity ahead of her. A large dockside crane, mounted on a gantry, slews along the quay, and stevedores are yelling at the ship's crew to send down the lines. Vera shades her eyes again, searching for him among those at the rail. Did he change his mind and not come? She can't determine what this possibility means to her—relief or regret.

• • •

But he's there. When the gangway lowers and passengers begin to descend, Vera recognizes him first from his shoulders—at once broad and hunched, a combination of strength and timidity—before she can see the square tanned face under a solar topi he's wearing.

"Where is Master? Philip? Do you see him yet?" Wanna asks eagerly.

She doesn't answer, but watches him come down the gangway in his white duck suit, one arm in a sling. She wants to watch him very carefully as he seeks her in the waiting crowd. What will her appearance do to his eyes?

And he sees her, waves with his good arm.

"That is Master?" Wanna asks.

Vera waves back, relieved to see him smile, but the topi puts the upper half of his face in shadow. His eyes, what do they say?

Fortunately, as he approaches, Philip yanks off the sun helmet.

Young.

The years have scarcely touched him, Vera thinks grimly. His hair's still blond, not a touch of gray. In the moment before they embrace, she can see nothing troubled in his blue eyes, no withholding, and in the brief contact of her body against his, Vera feels glad that he's here. In the next few minutes of chitchat—a good voyage, the sling can go in a day or two now, nothing serious, the food was pretty bad, I'm not really tired, you look wonderful—Vera understands that her initial assessment was wrong. There is something much older about Philip, although aside from a few wrinkles (fewer than her own, really), his face remains youthful. She can't define the change, but it's there. Perhaps in the mouth, a pinched, almost down-curving set to it, as if an effort has been made over a long period of time to control outwardly what he feels. Yes, that's a direction Philip might take: to limit what people can know of him.

"You look wonderful," he repeats, putting the topi on again. Unable now to see his eyes—again thrown into shadow by the sun helmet—she wonders if perhaps Philip has aged more than she has. It's in the deep lines around his mouth: nearly a decade of war and of India, whatever might have happened to him there. Looking at him, Vera feels the excitement of mystery.

But Wanna has been standing so close that their shoulders rub, their arms touch. The insistence must finally be rewarded, and so Vera introduces her, noting that under the topi Philip's mouth turns up in an appreciative smile. Well, why not, Vera thinks. The girl's lovely.

"I am pleased to meet you, Master." She says it in English. "Nahng Vera, I will get Master's baggage." She says the phrase so perfectly that Vera knows the girl must have rehearsed it all the way to the harbor.

"That won't be necessary. Here comes Rama."

Vera follows his gaze to see a young Indian guiding some porters with a steamer trunk and a few suitcases through the crowd. "Come, come now. Don't be laggard," he admonishes them in musical English.

"Rama has been invaluable," Philip explains. "Of course, now that he's got me here, he'll be going back to Madras."

Vera notices the young Indian glance sharply at them when he overhears Philip. Poor fellow, she thinks. He doesn't want to go back. Years ago, when she first came to Bangkok, she'd offered to pay Ah Ping's return to Hong Kong. The little Teochiu had wailed piteously until assurance came that she could stay.

• • •

A half-hour later they're all in a water taxi, a bumboat fitted with an ancient motor that at each heave spits a little oil into the water, leaving a greasy wake behind its slow progress through the crowded harbor.

Vera is sitting amidships with the girl, Philip on the thwart opposite them, and Rama up in the bow.

It hasn't taken them long, Vera thinks. Of course, Philip at least tries to hide it by looking away at intervals at the tramp ships and the shore cranes, but Wanna steadfastly regards him, even when Vera turns sharply to her to make a comment of some sort. Even when Vera tells her in Thai (Philip admitted on the dock he's forgotten what little Thai he knew) not to say "Nahng"—surely he remembers that—and not to call him "Master."

Immediately, leaning forward in the boat, Wanna asks if she may call him Philip. At his pleased assent, the girl coos, "Oh, good!" in English.

Vera has raised a parasol, but the heat is still fierce, and she can feel, along her forehead, matted tendrils of hair. Thank God she didn't wear makeup except lipstick. But Wanna needs nothing, and with the sun beating down on her black hair loose in the wind, she looks utterly fresh, perfect. And Philip, beneath his damn sun helmet, has missed none of her beauty. Perhaps he's not matured after all. Perhaps he brought with him from India only the appearance of a man, remaining in essence a boy. And yet she knows from the past that a fiercely sexual man is capable of emerging suddenly, like a capricious storm, from the boyhood he lives in. He's older now, of course. Perhaps more fighting than even he could relish has turned Philip Embree into a permanent man—no longer fierce, but wiser and sadder, a little bent, but more charming and therefore potentially more dangerous to women.

But not to me, Vera tells herself, even as she understands that what she feels is jealousy. Well, they are rude, exchanging looks even before Philip has got to the house, and not to his house, to *my* house, she thinks.

"I brought a few things from India and Burma," he shouts above the harbor noise. "I didn't know what to get Sonia. I didn't have her sizes."

Vera smiles. Poor Philip trying to make mundane conversation, while the girl next to me rudely continues to enchant him. It is rude, rude.

Turning away in the attempt to shut both of them from her mind, Vera gazes intently at the shoreline, as if until now she has never seen these houses on wooden posts and the flower pots and the attap walls battened down with strips of bamboo. The bumboat turns into a klong, clattering past coconut groves and orange orchards. Priests in saffron have rowed alongside, intently studying the farang in the solar topi. Two girls in a sampan paddle by; their boat is piled with kitchen utensils for sale. They are very young and wear broad wicker hats that sit high on their heads, allowing for air to circulate underneath. They're not as pretty as Wanna, though, and the thought forces her to glance sideways at the girl, who is smiling smiling smiling at the man whose face is half hidden, but who is smiling too.

. . .

The water taxi is in view of the house before Vera, confused throughout the ride, can even form the question, much less answer it: Of whom is she jealous? But the quandary at least moves her to action when the bumboat comes alongside the house dock. Watching Philip and his Indian servant and the boatman lift the steamer trunk up to the ground, she turns to Wanna. "You keep the boat." At the girl's perplexity, Vera smiles. "Yes. I want you to recheck those invoices at the shop. I know you've done it already, but I'm worried about them. They're complex." She doesn't wait for the girl to answer, to grimace, to set in motion a new chain of events which will have her inside the house, smiling and smiling at him there too.

Almost before Wanna knows what's happening, she is motoring on the klong again, looking back at the trio waving from the dock. Vera waves the longest.

She is still waving at the girl, whose head cocked at an angle betrays surprise, frustration, when Philip says at her shoulder, "Wanna's your secretary?"

"Yes. Pretty, isn't she?"

Philip and Rama carry the steamer trunk from the dock, through the garden, into the house.

He has come with everything, she thinks. He has come to stay. The thought is annoying; he might have cabled for permission to bring all his worldly goods. This is *her* house. "Nipa!" she calls when they stand in the foyer. "Nipa!"

"I will be getting her, Mistress," Rama offers.

"No. She will come." These men are taking over. Vera gives a baleful glance at the steamer trunk, the suitcases, the two men standing in her foyer. Then Nipa appears, looking sheepish and worried, wiping her hands on a apron.

"Cutting things for Cook."

"We'll want tea in the garden."

Nipa is looking past her at Philip, bobbing her head deferentially. She has never met him before, having come to work for Vera a few years after he'd left.

"Tea in the garden. And where is Ah Ping?"

The Siamese woman opens her mouth, closes it. "Lalawal is here."

"Have her help with the luggage. Where is Ah Ping?"

"She is not here now, Mistress."

"Anything wrong? You look strange, Nipa."

"Ah Ping has gone to her temple. I don't know anything." And she is gone before Vera can pursue this. What have the servants been doing? No doubt quarreling about authority or money. She takes Philip up the stairs to show him the guest room. Watching him glance indifferently at the furnishings, Vera recognizes the old Philip, who has never had much taste. Yet he's changed.

"There's a servants' house," she tells him, "but the women live there. Your Rama can have a room next to the kitchen. It's small—"

Philip turns from looking out of the window. "The house is lovely. I'd forgotten." He smiles and tests the mattress of the bed. "Haven't slept on anything that soft since leaving Bangkok. Vera, you've done a wonderful job."

He means it, she knows. Good fortune for others has never bothered him. His is the generosity of someone who wants little. "I'm across the landing," Vera says, pointing to her room with its door closed. That she's even mentioned her own bedroom surprises her—as if she needs to explain where she sleeps, as if sleeping arrangements are on her mind. This is precisely why she doesn't trust herself now—confusion brings on blunders. "I'll let you freshen up," she tells him like a good hostess and gets out of there.

On the landing Vera takes a deep breath, goes downstairs, and tells Rama where his room is. She watches him carry one suitcase into the kitchen, while Lalawal comes out of it to carry two suitcases up to Philip's room. Vera goes to the garden. Plummeting into a deck chair, she looks at the orange jampas which stand like sentinels at the garden verge. Ah, she'd forgotten to tell him where the outhouse is. But won't he remember that?

He's changed, but even if he'd changed enough to attract her, Vera would have none of him. The timing's wrong. Perhaps love is always a matter of timing. When she fell in love with Shan-teh and he with her, they were both vulnerable. He was facing a possible military defeat; she was facing a possible breakup with the German arms dealer she was living with. But today she's not a kept woman lost in China; she's a woman of some means.

"*Choei! Choei!*" she hears from the house. It's Taksakan screaming out the only word he knows. Sonia's bird. Where is she? Nipa is coming with iced tea, banana fritters, and other sweets. "My daughter," Vera says, while the servant puts the tray down on the lawn table. "Where is she?"

"Gone, Mistress." Nipa has already taken a few steps away.

"Wait." When the woman turns reluctantly, Vera says, "I thought she wasn't feeling well. Where did she go?"

"I know nothing, Mistress. Ask Ah Ping."

At this moment Philip appears in the garden, having discarded his suit coat.

378 ·

"I forgot to tell you where the outhouse is."

"I remembered that." He laughs and sits down. "Vera," he begins. His face clouds up with an expression she recalls now: There's so much effort inside of him, she thinks, so much turmoil trying to take shape. "I had to come." When she chooses to say nothing, Philip continues, taking heart, it seems, from her silence. "There's no way to explain myself. Not yet at any rate."

"Then don't try." She wants to put him at ease.

"In a few letters I attempted a kind of explanation, but I suppose it was useless. Yes. Well. I can't explain. It would sound pretentious. Or false. Take your pick." Running his hand through his hair, Philip smiles nervously. "I can't seem to do this."

"Then don't try. Have some tea, some of the sweets—Cook does them well."

They drink tea and eat a couple of sweets, while gibbons chatter in the trees. She watches Philip sit back and look around. He can look with interest at what God has made, but not at what men create.

"I'm proud of you," he says finally.

"Really?" She keeps her voice neutral.

"You set out to raise your child, and to raise her well, and you've done it. What you wanted to do you did." He snaps his fingers, then falls into another silence, as if the thought has overwhelming implications. "Well. And Sonia—how is she?"

"Beautiful." When he seems about to open his mouth with a compliment for her—ah, with-such-a-mother-how-could-she-be-otherwise— Vera puts up her hand. "And difficult. Her problem is school."

"Doesn't she do well in school?"

"Oh, she's done well, except for spelling, but then, of course, the poor girl is handling five languages. She's chosen to study art, but I don't think she knows yet what to do. I want her to go abroad."

"She should," Philip agrees without hesitation.

"I'm glad you think so," Vera says, her spirits lifting. "I wish you'd give her your opinion."

"Ah, well, it wouldn't have much influence."

"But it would," Vera declares. "You two were always close."

Philip seems delighted by this observation, and it occurs to her that perhaps he'd missed having children. Again her fault. Yet she could not have handled more in her life. She'd had Sonia to raise and this grown child, seated across from her now, to take care of. Even while forming such a picture of the past, Vera suspects it's not altogether true, yet it's her picture, hers; she'll stand by it.

As if looking over her shoulder at this picture, Philip says abruptly, "I won't be a burden."

"Nonsense. I never thought you would."

"I have come back here—"

Vera lifts her hand, asking him to wait a moment. Standing at the edge of the garden is Ah Ping, her slumping figure in black trousers and white blouse a sudden, troubling presence. How long has she been standing there, Vera wonders, with her baggy eyes watching us so forlornly?

"Ah Ping, come here." The old woman steps forward, a dragging walk untypical of someone usually so confident. "You remember—" Well, it's the only name Ah Ping has known or will call him by. "Master."

The old woman bows curtly, turns to Vera. Her hands are inside the sleeves of her crossed arms—where she keeps them when something unpleasant must be reported.

"Oh, Mistress," she begins, stops.

"Is anything wrong? What's wrong with you?"

"Oh, Mistress. I have come from temple. I burned incense, offered flowers to Kuan Yin. She is ruler of the Southern Seas."

There's a look of bafflement and fear in the old face that instills similar feelings in Vera. Leaning forward, she studies Ah Ping, whose lips tremble, whose pouched eyes shift quickly from her to Philip. "All right, you went to your temple. What's wrong?"

"Because I think it's all I can do, Mistress. Kuan Yin hears the prayers of the world. I prayed for her."

Fear runs up Vera's spine like rats' feet. "Where is Sonia? Where is my daughter?"

"Oh, Mistress." The old hands thrust deeper into the opposite sleeves.

On her feet, Vera yells, "Where is she!"

"Gone, Mistress."

"Where? Where, then?"

Ah Ping's hands jerk out of the sleeves and come to her temples, clutching as if to wrench her head free. "Gone forever, Mistress. She left the household of her mother with a bag. She said, 'I'm going, Ah Ping,' and I told her not to go, she is like my own child, my own girl, and I said you can't, you must give him up, but she went to him, I know it, I saw it, I saw her walking to the klong there and she's gone to him. I burned incense. Flowers too, I took those and laid them down for the Goddess, and I told her she must have mercy. I fell on my face in front of the Goddess and prayed and I—"

Philip is on his feet. "Vera!"

Pain has leaped into her chest, squeezing it, until, unable to stand longer, Vera moves back into the chair and looks dully out at the garden, fumbling in the blouse pocket for the vial that contains her little pills.

One under the tongue makes everything all right. Two faces watch anxiously while the bitter taste bubbles under her tongue, and the pain begins to subside.

30 VERA IS LYING on her bed, the door closed. She'll say this much for Philip: He never pestered her for an explanation of what is going on. After helping her upstairs—though she didn't need that, she didn't she didn't—he said, "I'll be in my room. Whatever you want me to do, I'll do." But can she trust him? What he does rarely entails a development. Energy yes, responsibility no. If she draws him into this predicament, depends on him, will he abruptly smell gunpowder and run off?

Wearily Vera rises, testing herself. No chest pain—the little pills work, just as the German doctor who reminds her of Erich Luckner said they would—with qualifications of course, and on and on. Bracing herself on the dresser, Vera stares into the mirror above it at her black hair, mussed now, but still *black,* and at her dark eyes with little pockets beneath them, and at the facial structure, less defined now, with a bit of puffiness around the jawline. *Mai pen rai.*

She'll come back. It's just another weekend in the South with that boy. The idea of it straightens Vera; she opens the door, minces to Sonia's room (noticing that Philip has discreetly kept his own door closed). Glancing around, Vera stares for a moment at the window beside the bed, at its emptiness where once a coconut palm had nearly filled the space. Sonia told her—what was it?—the coconut palm was her astrological tree; cutting it down would bring bad luck. This is bad luck, Vera thinks, as she notices the sandalwood cabinet open. Going to it, she finds it empty of the diaries and the little cross Sonia had made for herself out of two twigs, eschewing the ivory one in honor of the Maid. Vera smiles at the eccentricity, and following this act of love endures pain in its own way worse than angina. She wants her daughter back.

At the doorway Vera shouts for Ah Ping, for Nipa, for Cook to come immediately. Gripping the landing rail, she looks down at the staircase, annoyed to see Rama's smiling face appear first.

"Yes, Memsahib!"

"Go get the women. Tell them I want them here."

Head bobbing like a bird drinking, Rama vanishes. The next head to appear around the kitchen door belongs to Lalawal. "Yes, Mistress?"

"Where are they?"

"Cook is shopping."

"Shopping? She was shopping all yesterday. Today she's cooking—" Hopeless. "Ah Ping?"

The girl shakes her head fearfully.

"You don't know?"

"No, Mistress."

"Nipa?"

The girl shakes her head again.

"Hear me, Lalawal. If you can't find your aunt and bring her to me immediately, tell her she can leave this house for good."

Walking unsteadily back into Sonia's room, she breathes deeply. Pain? No pain. Enough of that, she thinks. It doesn't matter, pain or no pain. Where are the servants? Cowering somewhere, terrified of punishment, moving beads or mumbling to their gods.

Nipa stands in the doorway. "Mistress," she mutters.

"Tell me what you know."

"Nothing, Mistress."

"Very well, Nipa. Think. Or pack your things and leave."

In the next few moments, obviously struggling to remember anything of protective value, Nipa recalls a girl who came to visit recently.

"That's Lamai. She's getting married," Vera says impatiently.

"I am thinking of the other girl, Mistress." Nipa explains that "the other girl" and Miss talked about the girl's brother and about dancing and other things now forgotten, unfortunately, but that's what they talked about. "I know," Nipa announces proudly.

"How do you know?"

"I heard them behind the door."

"You were there listening?"

Emotions run across the woman's face as she assesses the possible result of what she says next. "I was, Mistress."

"They talked about the girl's brother. What was his name?"

Nipa shakes her head slowly. "But her name was Sopita. And she *was*. Pretty."

Sopita: pretty. The name's familiar to Vera. "They talked about dancing?"

"Oh, yes, Mistress. They talked about this girl's dancing." And with the inborn grace of a Siamese woman, for several moments Nipa forgets the circumstances of this interview and breaks into a gentle swaying dance, neck elongated, chest thrown out, arms moving in delicate arcs above her head.

But Vera hasn't witnessed this failure of mood in her servant, for she's busy at the bookshelf, looking for the school yearbook. With little difficulty she finds the name, address, and picture of a determined girl dressed in the high ornate crown of a Siamese dancer. Something further occurs to Vera, who looks up from the book at her servant. "They talked about the girl's brother. What did they say?"

Nipa shakes her head in acknowledgment of a poor memory, but Vera will have none of it. "*Think*, Nipa. I am warning you."

"He was in trouble."

"What kind of trouble?"

"I don't know, Mistress. But the girl told Miss she must never see him again."

Back in her room, Vera takes off her sweaty blouse and puts on a fresh one, and as she lifts her arms to slide it over her head, her gaze fixes on the large teak dresser in the corner. Standing there with her arms raised, as if in a holdup, Vera stares at first without knowing why. Something's wrong. Wriggling into the blouse, pulling it down, Vera takes one step toward the dresser before she understands what cannot possibly be: The porcelain beaker is gone. Rushing to the dresser, running her hands along its burnished top as if conjuring the vanished object back into place, Vera realizes the ink stone is also gone. That ink stone given to her by Shan-teh years ago in Qufu when he returned from Canton. Her prized possession.

He had gone South in search of allies. She had remained in Qufu. Will she ever forget the joy of seeing him again? He'd put the white jade ink stone in her hand, covering hers with his own. Such jade, held tightly, will prevent evil from getting into the mind, he told her. "This jade is so hard a steel point won't scratch it. To grind an ink stick on it will take a long time because the jade's finely grained."

She had meant to use it for the calligraphy she practiced. But after leaving China she'd given up the art, and so the jade was never stained by ink. The ink stone has remained pristine white, as it was the day he gave it to her.

More than once, through the years, she has clutched the stone to dispel evil, and perhaps, so she's told herself, it has sometimes worked.

• • •

Philip didn't stay out of it long, she thinks while they ride in a water taxi through the klongs of Bangkok. And in truth she's glad of it. When she went downstairs, he was behind her, silently but firmly there, so determined to accompany her that Vera never made a gesture of refusing his help. She understands there's no choice. Physically she has lost her freedom. The girl who walked across frozen Siberia is now a woman with heart disease, who must depend on others. *Mai pen rai*.

There are children playing along the canal; the sight of them disturbs her. She doesn't want to look at their happy faces. And yet she does look, stares at them as they carry jars, swing their legs over slatted wooden porches, bang at attap walls with sticks, laugh and shout. She can't help looking at them, because their lives seem nobly simple, blessedly uncomplicated. Out in the villages this late afternoon, boys help with the buffalo, shoo birds from the paddy; girls clean and help with the rice milling. And in a few days the Songkran festival, celebrating the lunar new year, will gladden their hearts in the temples, where they'll pray to Buddha and watch the monks receive offerings; and in the homes, where they'll honor their parents by pouring perfumed water on opened hands; and then at night they'll joyfully throw water everywhere and on everyone, welcoming the onset of life-giving rains.

Pouring water into the hands of their parents.

But of course she has never told Sonia the story of the ink stone, so the theft of it has only financial significance. The girl can't know its sentimental value. In creating the legend of her romance with the General, Vera has exaggerated some details, hidden others. She made him out to be inordinately handsome, never mentioning the gold tooth that flashed rather disconcertingly when he smiled. Perhaps she had made him too heroic. Perhaps unconsciously she had left out the little touches of tenderness, the sweetness of this man who brought her a jade ink stone from the South. And so it is her own fault that the ink stone's gone too.

In a few days, Vera thinks, these children along the canal bank will be scenting water with flowers to pour on the outstretched hands of their parents, honoring them. Pouring water, honoring their parents. Vera stares at them from the low-slung gunnel of the boat: children playing along the riverbank.

Sonia didn't know that she'd stolen a token of her parents' love. At least that.

• • •

They're in a samlor now, entering a narrow alley near Yaowaraj Road. Along one side are Hakka tailor shops, along the other Teochiu pawnshops, and above them long poles draped with laundry—like a forest of banners. When they stop near the sundry goods shop, she asks Philip to wait here; she'll go in alone. She's gratified that he nods without an argument. Once upon a time Philip Embree would have insisted: "I'll go, Vera. You wait here," and ruined everything with his headlong male energy.

In the waning afternoon light the two-story building looks almost identical to the others on the block here, with their gaudy signs in Chinese, their painted shutters, their hopelessly cluttered ground-floor shops, looking as though goods of every description had been shoveled into them, crammed to the ceiling, and with a little push from the rear would tumble out again into the street like an opened jam-packed closet. Stepping inside the store, Vera adjusts her eyes to the dim light thrown by low-wattage bulbs hanging from the ceiling.

A small Chinese man with liver spots on his cheeks is sitting next to the entrance—positioned there to prevent thefts. Although shabbily dressed in coarse blue pants, a wrinkled cotton shirt, and shoes fashioned from old car tires with the soles tied by cord—coolie style—he has an air about him, the arrogance of a Chinatown merchant.

"Nai Chukkrit Napaget?"

After a thoughtful pause, the man nods slightly in acknowledgment.

"I am Nahng Vera Embree." When no flicker of recognition shows in his wary eyes, she adds, "I am the mother of Sanuk—Sonia. Do you know what I'm talking about?"

The man stares at her.

Vera glances at the tremendous load of junk piled high on counters. Another man is coming down the aisle, smiling. "Can I help you, Nahng?"

"Is this man Chukkrit Napaget?"

The other man, frowning, nods.

Turning back to the man on the entrance stool, Vera says, "Do you have a son?"

Chukkrit Napaget is holding an orange squash bottle, nearly empty, in both mottled hands. "I have no son."

"Do you have a daughter named Sopita?"

"Yes, I have a daughter named Sopita, but I have no son."

Vera feels that nothing will break through the iron composure of this man holding his orange squash bottle. But then something occurs to her. "I have a good friend. Perhaps you know him. Chang Kong Chuan, known by his Siamese name as Sri Boon Ruang. Of the Hou-sheng Company."

The man's eyes widen at the mention of Chang and the leading trading firm in Bangkok.

"Nai Sri Boon Ruang has frequently condescended to enjoy my humble hospitality. Such a man graces my little home. He would be pleased to know you spoke openly to me about our problem."

"Yes, I know him well. Please do give him my respectful good wishes," Chukkrit Napaget says quickly.

"Our problem is our children. Yours and mine."

"I have no son."

"Where is he, Nai Chukkrit Napaget? I must know, I *will* know." Her eyes meet his, until finally he glances down at the orange squash bottle, gripped hard in his hands.

"The Communists have taken him from me," Chukkrit Napaget says in a trembling voice. "I disown him. I have gone to the temple and done so publicly. He stole from me, his father, and his ancestors. This evil young man is sought by the police who came here and dishonored me by searching the house in front of my neighbors. I know nothing of your child—"

"My daughter."

"Daughter. But he has stolen money from this family. We don't know his name now, ever. Let the Reds have him. Or the police. It is all one to us."

Pausing a moment, as if obligated to comment—but finding nothing to say—Vera turns to leave.

"I have no son," she hears him murmur at her back.

· · ·

On the return trip Vera sees yet another sight that disturbs her. A young Chinese bridegroom is calling for the bride at her home. Vera cranes her head to look behind the samlor at the awkward figure standing there in a blue flannel coat with boutonnière and white duck trousers. She has a glimpse of the bride emerging from a two-story Chinatown house with her entourage: pink silk, a diaphanous hand-painted veil, a dainty wreath of red paper flowers. She carries a bright crimson parasol.

Turning to Embree, speaking rapidly, Vera says, "I should have read her diaries. They might have given me a clue, but fool that I am, I respected her privacy. This boy is—well, his father is . . . a cheap Chinatown merchant, but arrogant about it, mean-spirited. No wonder the boy's mixed up with Bolsheviks. The father said so. He'll have to get out of Bangkok, I'm certain. He said the police are after them. We'll ask Jim." She waves her hand impatiently. "That's Jim Thompson, partner of mine in business. Jim might . . . listen, Jim will help us check the transportation. Ships, trains, airplanes. Passenger lists." Her own words, spoken crisply, give Vera confidence. After all, nothing's final except death. To plan, to do something, is to start on the road to success —words of Jim Thompson, and he should know. Vera glances at the square, tanned face of the man beside her. Philip's not so bad after all. He's here, right here, sitting right here beside her when she needs him. Everything will be all right. Plans are in motion. There are people to carry them out. "Last year I went to the American Ambassador's Fourth of July party," she continues. "So I know him. Could he help? It was raining all that day. Streets were flooded, and we had to carry our shoes, hoist our evening dresses, and wade into the embassy. Will he remember me? I suppose not," Vera murmurs. "There were more than three hundred people invited. I met him in the receiving line, that's all. Where could they go? Bolshevik? Where does he think he can go? Of all things

—a Bolshevik! We have to find out what ships have left. We could send a wireless, but maybe the ship captains ignore it. And the planes. But what about the trains here? Anybody can just get on and go anywhere —Where will he take her, Philip?" She's leaning against him, crying softly, her eyes closed against his shirt, feeling the warmth of him on her cheek and forehead. "This isn't the way I thought it would end," she sobs.

"Nothing's ended." He has put his arm around her.

"But she's gone, Philip. My little girl's gone."

31 COMING DOWN TO breakfast on the second morning after the girl's disappearance, Philip Embree acknowledges they may have a chance of finding her, although his initial opinion (kept from Vera) had been pessimistic.

The difference between then and now has been the help of Jim Thompson. Embree found his fellow American much as Vera had described him: eager, generous, frank, possibly naïve. When they met at the Oriental Hotel, he'd been charming, only too glad to help. Embree watched him and Vera put their heads together over a list of shipping companies, airlines, and trains. Thompson volunteered to contact every one of them, vowing to get passenger manifests where possible. He was sure they'd have no trouble locating the girl, because if she tried to leave Siam they'd have a passport record of her departure—and he had connections with Government Customs. Embree didn't contradict such optimism by pointing out that she might have obtained other papers— after all, if her boyfriend was a Red, he probably had underground ties —or slipped illegally across one of Siam's borders or simply left Bangkok for a remote part of the country. He was too worried about Vera, who confessed readily (what else could she have done after the episode in the garden?) to "a touch of heart trouble."

• • •

When Philip and Vera were leaving the hotel room, Thompson said heartily to him, "I have someone I want you to meet. Perhaps I can arrange it for tomorrow."

And speaking for him, Vera had accepted the invitation. "Send word. Philip will be delighted."

Afterward, in a samlor, Vera said, "Forgive me. But Jim was some kind of secret agent during the war. At least that's the rumor. So he knows people who might help us."

Embree had agreed. That evening a messenger arrived at the house with a dozen lists, proving Jim Thompson to be as good as his word.

There was a note appended to them: "She's not on these lists, but we'll find her. I have no doubt of that. Please have Phil meet me tomorrow morning, around ten, at the hotel. Jim."

Of course there was no Sonia Embree on any passenger list. Embree watched his wife go through each one with the fastidious care of desperation. He knew better than to interfere, even by suggesting that she rest awhile. So in the late evening he sat with a drink on the veranda, out of her way and mind, waiting for her to finish this meticulous examination of the lists. He might try then to persuade her that a good night's sleep could only benefit their search. And so Embree was surprised when, a half-hour later, Vera appeared on the veranda, after going through hundreds of names, with the announcement that Sonia was headed for Shanghai.

"Then Jim missed her?" he asked. Haggard, pale, Vera took the chair next to his.

"No, he didn't miss her. He was looking for the wrong name." Vera tossed one of the manifests on the veranda table. "Sonia and the boy are on a ship bound for Shanghai."

When Embree picked up the list, she told him to look for "Tang Yu-ying."

"I didn't see it myself at first," Vera said.

"Ah, the 'Tang.' But where did she get 'Yu-ying'?"

"You'll be interested to know Yu-ying was a Shanghai whore I once knew."

"Sonia knows that?"

Vera laughed, shaking her head—a bitter gesture. "I used to tell her about a great Shanghai lady named Yu-ying. A heroine she could add to her fantasies."

Embree watched Vera pick up the manifest, throw it down—again a bitter, desperate gesture.

"Isn't life remarkable?" Vera murmured, as she gazed into the Bangkok evening, with its cicadas whining for rain and its klongs, a network through the city, alive with the splash of oars.

•　•　•

Vera is not down for breakfast yet, so he asks Nipa for the newspaper. After regarding him with a critical eye, she gets it for him. As he remembers the venerable English-language *Bangkok Times*, it was dull and cautious a decade ago. After a quick perusal, he decides it still is, although a short article describes what is called "the long-playing phonograph record," an invention of Peter Goldmark. The news also features something about a horse, Citation, with Eddie Arcaro up, winning the Triple Crown. It has been two decades since Embree set foot in America. He's been gone too long ever to make it his home again. The great athletes of his day must surely be forgotten, and he can't imagine the new heroes in modern uniforms playing for teams he never heard of.

Getting up from the table, he walks into the garden, still dewy-fresh from nighttime. Through the trees he notices a platform with a doll's house on it—the Spirit House. Moving closer, he can see a clutter of little statues inside its wooden walls, and bowls for incense and flowers at the vestibule. It hadn't been there when he left in 1939, although Vera had sworn to put one up. And so she has, and so probably does she pray to it, as a Siamese would, because for Vera, whose religious impulse is enviably simple and direct, unmediated by skeptical ratiocination, what was true in the Russia of her childhood must also be true in the Siam of her maturity. It is the blessed ratio of one plus one equals two, an acceptance of order, faith in design. Strolling toward the Spirit House for a better look, he remembers his own opinion of religious belief in those days: how he sat back amused, detached, sad perhaps, and surely exultant in the knowledge that when non-believers like himself died, when believers like Vera died, there was nothing afterward but zero, a flat no. There was more certitude then than he's known since. At least then he had that implacable negation, that *no*, that morose but comforting monologue, "I'm done soon, I have nothing beyond this, the world has nothing to do with me at all."

And at that very time he was preparing himself to leave Vera, this house, Bangkok, and the past. Not that he realized it—the truth hovered at the edge of his eye then, glimpsed only suddenly and only in part. The preparation began, he supposes in retrospect, with the Japanese bombing of the American gunboat *Panay* near Nanking in December 1937. From that moment on, his imagination fired, Embree read every news report he could find about the Sino-Japanese conflict. He knew what people who've known China always know: that the Chinese have suffered so much they can always take on another war.

He watched, with growing excitement, as both Communist and Nationalist troops resisted the initial incursions of the Japanese. When Chinese troops fought bravely in the streets of Shanghai, he was jubilant. When civilians were slaughtered in the streets of Nanking, he was outraged. When finally the Chinese won a major victory at T'ai-erhchuang, before again being pushed farther from the seacoast of Central China, he was cautiously optimistic about their chances of surviving the Japanese onslaught. Once again he'd been caught up in the tumultuous affairs of China. It was the right place for someone like himself.

Just as he'd left his American past behind in 1927, so he was again preparing to leave something behind in 1939: a wife who didn't need him, a child who wasn't his. A romantic concept of war and loyalty (he knows it now, of course) led him by the nose back to China.

Embree decides against inspecting the Spirit House. He's too troubled by such recollections to be curious about Vera's sacred private symbols, if that's what they are. Whether or not Vera's aware of it, she practices the spiritual insouciance of Asia. Returning to the veranda, he can see her at the breakfast table.

Entering the house, he says, "The garden is lovely."

Vera turns to him with a smile. "I saw you out there. I decided not to bother you." Her smile doesn't fade as formal smiles do, but remains. "You're not wearing the sling today."

"I don't need it any more."

"Wonderful." Her Russian voice speaking English is low, almost guttural, resonant.

He's astonished by her recuperative powers. In the clear morning light Vera looks young for her years, vibrant. Her eyes—always for him Vera's most brilliant feature—are as beguiling as he can remember, even in the early days, when he marked a man for death to have her.

Throughout breakfast, she retains her vitality. There's even a hint of the Vera he once knew—the coquettish Vera, the woman experienced in pleasing men. Sometimes she looks archly at him, puckering her lips at a thought, briefly laughing at some innocuous remark, glancing thoughtfully at him when she knows he'll notice. Yet none of this is for him, really. Vera, in her newfound hope (knowing the name of the ship her daughter's on is reason enough for it), is practicing an old art at which she was once adept, that's all. Yet he doesn't begrudge her anything at this moment. She needs him; that's enough.

Curiously, they have almost finished a breakfast of fruit and tea before Vera broaches the only subject that can have meaning for her. "Now that we know where they've gone . . . You are really going to help me, Philip?"

"I've come back to help you."

"How could you know," she says with a smile, "I needed help?"

"I didn't know. It's my good fortune, that's all."

"Good fortune?" She studies the phrase, her face white and pensive, her eyes almost glazed by the effort of making sense of such *good fortune*. There's intelligence and passion in that face, and Embree understands why, at a certain time in his life, this woman meant more to him than loyalty, self-respect, freedom. "What happens to them in China, Philip, if we don't find them?"

"We'll find them."

"Don't be reassuring with me. Jim Thompson can do that because he doesn't know better. *You* do," she tells him with sudden despairing harshness. "There's a war. How can they go there? How can they do such a thing?"

"There's always a war there. The Chinese can fight in one street while Peking Opera's taking place in the next."

"You were kidnaped in the China of '27," she reminds him.

"And look at me—blond, light-skinned. But these two are different. As I remember Sonia, she could pass for Chinese."

Reaching across the table, Vera touches his hand a moment. "I'm glad you're back. I really don't know why you came back after such a long time, but it doesn't matter. You're back. I need you."

. . .

By eleven o'clock he has seen Jim Thompson and in a water taxi is setting out for yet another appointment. What he'd begun to suspect from the moment Vera told him the rumors about Jim Thompson has now been confirmed: At least some of Thompson's interest in helping Vera derives from his interest in helping the American government.

"I think we have a lot in common," Thompson began, once they were seated on the veranda of the hotel, overlooking the busy waterfront. "I mean the war. Did you know Dick Heppner? He was Chief of OSS, China. What about Lucius Rucker? I think that was his name. Came from Mississippi. I understand he trained parachutists near Kunming in a cabbage patch. You were in Kunming, weren't you? You were never at OSS Headquarters in Washington? Well, let me tell you, the Kremlin couldn't be *that* forbidding. Former buildings of National Health Institute. Brick and limestone. Creaking old hallways, grim rooms—something out of a horror movie."

"I don't know anything about OSS," Embree broke in to say.

"Did a lot out here. First American agents entered Siam in January 1945. They came in to work with the underground—the Free Thai Movement." Thompson sat back, smoking and drinking tea, to squint in the sunlight and recount stories. Embree listened politely while Thompson spoke of OSS-trained Siamese agents, disguised as merchants, carrying STR-1 radios hidden in hampers filled with safety pins, bolts of blue cotton, spools of thread, combs and trinkets, and loaded down with all that junk infiltrating across the Chinese border into Laos. Other agents came by submarine, Catalinas, midnight parachute jumps. The Siamese network was the brainchild of former Prime Minister Pridi, "a man of ability," said Thompson.

The first American agents came by flying boat to the gulf, then to Bangkok by motor launch, then through the city by civilian car in the elementary disguise of broad wicker hats and gaudy shirts. Their headquarters was a two-story yellow stucco house—actually a mansion called the Palace of Roses where ministers often stayed. It had a high tower and a Swiss chalet-type slate roof mottled in white. "Pridi's idea. Our boys lived in a government mansion right in the middle of Bangkok. Of course they didn't enjoy their surroundings. Stayed in a ten-foot-square cubicle and pinpointed the first B-29 raid on Bangkok. It was a good job. The Siamese did a good job too. Too bad for Pridi, though. None of us think he had anything to do with the King's death. But that's Siamese politics." Thompson puffed vigorously. "I never got here until the war ended. I was a parachute volunteer scheduled to be dropped near Laos. Our aim was to prepare for liberation of Siam. Our flight from Ceylon had already begun, as a matter of fact, when we received a radio message that the Japs had surrendered." Thompson lit yet another cigarette. "You must be wondering why I'm telling you all this."

"Yes, I am a little."

"I'm telling you because otherwise you might think I'm presumptuous."

"About what?"

"About broaching certain matters. When I came back to Bangkok, the OSS station chief here was Howard Palmer. I took over from him until they disbanded. The point is I'm still involved, ex officio, of course," he said with undisguised pride.

"Go right ahead. Broach those certain matters."

"Frazer in Madras talked to you about going to China. Are you still against it?"

"I'm not sure." An evasive answer, Embree knew, was a good answer in these circles.

"What's happened to your stepdaughter, does that make a difference?"

"In what way?"

Thompson squinted through the cigarette smoke. "What if she's gone to China?"

"We don't know that, do we." He hadn't told Thompson about someone on a passenger list named Tang Yu-ying.

"But let's assume it. If you went to China and she's there, you could, in a sense—"

"Kill two birds with one stone."

"Exactly." Thompson puffed heartily.

"But what if she's gone, say, to Indonesia or Malaya?"

"Then I'm afraid we—the American government—won't be able to help."

"You've put it on the line."

"Sorry, but I have."

"What do you want from me?"

"What we want to know," Thompson corrected him, "is whether you'll take an assignment in China."

There was nothing to gain by more fencing, Embree decided. They'd know soon enough that the girl had gone to China. "Yes, I'll accept the assignment," he said evenly, "in exchange for help in finding her."

Thompson clapped both knees decisively. "Then I want you to see Jerry Feinberg. He's at the embassy." Thompson looked at his watch. "As a matter of fact, he's waiting for you."

Embree rose, annoyed by Thompson's smug look of triumph, although the deal being struck was, of course, what he wanted. "You were sure of me."

"Yes, I was. Sorry. You see, if the girl's gone off with this Communist, most likely they'll end up in China."

"That's an assumption."

Thompson, rising too, shrugged. "What else is there to go on?" Extending his hand, he said in a gentle, almost shy voice, "If it works out and you do get over there, I wish you all the luck in the world, Philip. I've learned by doing business with Vera what a fine woman she is. A really fine woman. Do what you can."

"Thank you," Embree replied coolly. "I will."

* * *

He is taking a water taxi to the American Embassy.

So they have him where they want him. Well, so what? Gandhi once said, "The quest for truth can't be prosecuted in a cave." Although this quest is for a runaway girl, not the truth, he's damn well going to prosecute it. So they have him, and they know it. Even Vera's naïve Jim Thompson knows it. Less naïve than fervent. The American businessman continues to thrive on the late war. We're alike, Embree thinks, except that Thompson serves memory by doing what his government asks of him. At least there's honesty to that.

The boat is passing alongside a waterfront of slums. The klong water is scummed a milky blue. Trash on the banks is so thick that the slum dwellers can scarcely find room to squat near their cooking fires. He has glimpses of them lying in the dark interiors of their shacks for a benumbed snooze. Enormous water jars sit in the midst of tin cans, ashes, paper. Naked children stare across the choked klong at yet other naked children wedged into the narrow paths between the slanted, dilapidated shacks they may inhabit until they die. Behind the bank is the arching green hood of a rain tree, looming over it, Philip Embree thinks, like a nimbus over the head of Buddha, as he sat in the throes of those early terrible austerities that never brought him enlightenment but that taught him the importance of health in seeking it—health, something these slum children have never had and probably never will. Dogs are running along the bank, as scrawny as those of Benares, but docile-looking, sweet, pitiable rather than fierce. Dogs of Benares. Harry once said to him, "What you do has a destiny." And Harry might have been right about him, and his destiny might be to join the dogs of Benares in the next life. But at least now he has remembered what Harry said, without wondering if Harry has just said it.

Progress, Embree tells himself, watching the slums of Bangkok drift by.

• • •

Embree is escorted by an orderly to the rear of the embassy grounds; a low-slung house is here with a veranda running the length of it and offices facing the veranda. At one of them, door open, the orderly stops.

A short, balding man rises from his desk and extends his hand. "Jerry Feinberg. Hungry? I can use a hamburger, how about you?"

The embassy snack bar is in the same building, in a concrete basement lined with lettered doors, all closed. As they enter the little snack bar and sit at a corner table under a row of fluorescent lights, Jerry Feinberg says, "So you talked to Jim Thompson. Jim's been a help. Right after the war he was unofficial political adviser to the Ambassador. Very knowledgeable about the Laotians. Hamburger and french fries? Guaranteed as good as home. They've got someone back there who makes a great malted too."

A Siamese girl comes to take their order. Hamburger and french fries mean little to Embree, and it saddens him, because this consul obviously derives pleasure from eating food that reminds him of home. What is home? Embree wonders, as he orders the same thing.

Jerry Feinberg folds his arms on the table and leans forward on them. "You haven't been in Bangkok for a while, have you. Well, it doesn't really change. The King dies mysteriously, the Reds print up leaflets, the Chinese grumble, but Siam doesn't really change."

"Why is that?" Looking past Feinberg's shoulder, he watches embassy personnel come into the small windowless room. They talk in a relaxed, confident way that probably upsets the people in whose countries they serve. At this moment Embree feels alien here.

"The Siamese are lucky," Feinberg says. "Don't you think?"

"How so?"

"Well, they live on land that grows things. Few natural disasters. They have more social mobility than most people in Asia."

"Yes, I suppose that's true." Siam is not a place that has much interested Philip Embree.

"On the other hand, so much independence doesn't encourage discipline. They rebel against regularity of effort on a job."

"That's true of the Burmese too."

"Each Siamese goes after his own salvation, damn near unassisted. They're out there scrambling for personal merit, and to hell with the next guy."

"It's a mild form of selfishness."

"Oh, I agree," Feinberg says with a smile. "If they prefer form to substance, at least things go smoothly. You won't find many people who dislike trouble more than the Siamese."

"A plus."

"Definitely. That's why the Siamese have such a peculiar history."

"How so?" Embree notices that all the tables are now taken. Many of the men are blond and ruddy like himself, yet he feels no attachment to them.

"It's a history of minimal violence. Generally bloodless coups. That's remarkable in itself." Feinberg is someone who seems to like sharing opinions; it's less vanity than a desire for fellowship. Or at least that's how Embree chooses to view him.

"The last violent coup," he continues, "was in 1933. They really don't get a kick out of murder."

"I like that."

"So do I. Once the Siamese attempt a coup, it either succeeds at once or they abandon it. They're too sensible to shed blood over a failed idea." Feinberg has on a short-sleeved gaudy shirt; his arms are dark with black curly hair. "Of course, they're rather good at torture. In a certain sense death from a beating is accidental. It's not what I would call out-and-out personal satisfaction, though." He laughs briefly, and Embree joins him. "The government has just picked up a few suspects for the King's murder."

"Did they do it?"

"Well, who knows, but I'm sure they'll be found guilty."

"Last week, when I was in Rangoon," Embree volunteers, "they arrested U Saw for instigating the thing—I'm talking about the assassination of Aung Saw. I guess U Saw figured it was a way of getting ahead in politics."

Jerry Feinberg shakes his head. "That got independent Burma off to a bad start."

"It did. If Aung Saw had lived, he might have pulled the country together." For an instant he thinks of General Tang Shan-teh.

"And of course there's Gandhi."

Feinberg's observation leads to silence, during which other embassy personnel enter the snack bar. There are no more seats at the small, wrought-iron tables that have been flown over from the States to simulate coffee houses in Peoria, Nashville, San Francisco.

• • •

"Anything you want to know about the assignment?" Feinberg asks.

"Frazer told me I'd be going in to have a look-see. You people would want my opinion of current Chinese thinking: what they want and what they think of us and how we can deal with them and whatever else I can come up with."

"That's right."

"A tall order."

"As a help," Feinberg says, "you'll get a briefing in Kunming."

Embree shakes his head slowly. "Never thought I'd see Kunming again."

"We may want you to talk to some people in Chungking, too."

Lunch comes. Jerry Feinberg gives his his full attention. Having liberally covered hamburger and french fries with ketchup, he extends the bottle to Embree. "No? How about mustard? Want some mustard?"

Embree agrees to mustard, without mentioning he has not eaten half a dozen American-style hamburgers in twenty years. Watching Feinberg eat with the gusto of homesickness, Embree is thinking about Chungking, images of it in 1939 and 1940: the Yangtze River flowing past, sluggish and muddy, distinguished visually from the brown city because it moved a little. Brown dusty slopes, their runneled sides fog-covered in winter, the sky over them flat and blazing in summer. In May of '39, yes, it was May, the bombing commenced in Chungking. The population, following the piecemeal arrival of entire factories from the eastern seaboard, flocked to the inland city, swelling it five times its normal size. Air-raid shelters were built of sandstone in Chungking. Red paper lanterns hoisted on poles signaled an air raid. Firebombing left the streets a spindly forest of wooden stanchions; in the poor sections of town, among bamboo huts, there was nothing at all, not even bodies, nothing but a fine black ash drifting into the craters.

That's the Chungking he remembers and never wanted to see again. He remembers the Victory House Hotel. He remembers General Tai Li, a fat little secret service officer who loved Scotch whiskey, his personal ivory chopsticks, and a pretty nurse who traveled with him in Chungking. Ilya Tolstoy, grandson of Leo, was there in those early horrific days of resistance and death. Chungking again? Embree shakes his head in disbelief at the idea of returning there.

"When can you go?" Feinberg asks, smiling at the girl bringing malted milks.

"When do you want me to go?"

"Tomorrow."

"All right." Having eaten half the hamburger, Embree shoves the plate aside. "Now what about my daughter?"

"We'll need a photo of her."

"You'll have it. I'm thinking," Embree says, "she might not be on that ship arriving in Shanghai."

"That's a thought."

"If anybody's helping them who knows anything, they'll change ships in Singapore."

"We'll check Singapore."

"What about these dry-cargo steamers that don't give a damn about papers? Come on, Feinberg. You know Shanghai. They can get in there without a trace. Provided they have help."

"You're worrying about not being there when they arrive?"

"I should be there."

"You're not needed there, pal. We'll cover the harbor. If we couldn't offer anything, we wouldn't have you here right now, would we."

That's true, Embree thinks. On the table he puts a note with Sonia's alias, the ship's name and ETA. "I'll bring the photo tomorrow. When —if—you find her, what will you do then?"

Feinberg sucks lustily on his straw. "We can't pick her up, of course. We'll keep her under surveillance until you get there."

"You can do more than that. You can detain her."

"How?"

"I don't know how. You know how. Customs, immigration, Chiang Kai-shek, Harry Truman—something."

"She's a Siamese citizen."

"It wouldn't be the first time you interfered with another country's nationals."

Feinberg grins. He has a sunny, uncomplicated manner that Embree can't help but like.

"At least you'll get the girl and me out of China."

Feinberg looks thoughtfully at him. "Not you for a while. We'll help the girl, if she wants to leave. Getting her to leave her Red boyfriend is your department. We can't be kidnaping twenty-year-old Siamese citizens."

"I'd prefer going to Shanghai tomorrow. Then when I have her straightened out, I'm ready for Kunming and the rest."

Belching into his napkin, Feinberg shakes his head. "They want to get you started right away. And look at this angle: Her ship isn't due in for a week. By then you'll be briefed, and in Shanghai anyway."

"Maybe."

Feinberg looks first at his empty plate, then at Embree. "One thing. I believe Frazer mentioned the possibility of your wife going. It won't work, pal. You see, your stepdaughter has been seen, as they say, consorting with known Communists."

"The Siamese government is aware of that?"

"They certainly are. They have this police chief who isn't much of a Buddhist. He hurts people until he gets names, places, dates. The point is this: If we get you out of here on military aircraft with your wife accompanying you, the Siamese are going to be unhappy."

"They think she's also consorting with Communists?"

"No. Actually, it's a matter of face. At the moment they'd be annoyed if we flew her out of the country after her daughter has just been naughty. You get the point: We don't want a close relationship with the mother of a fugitive."

"And the father of one?"

"Stepfather. I'm sure they've never heard of you."

Blunt but true, Embree thinks. "Vera can't go anyway. She's ill."

"So that leaves you free to take care of it. Good." Feinberg dabs his lips with the napkin and sits back with a sigh. "I don't care what they say. There's nothing like a burger and fries."

· · ·

Embree doesn't get home until late.

At the embassy dispensary in the afternoon he received inoculations for cholera and typhus, both diseases having appeared in epidemic proportions around Kunming in recent weeks. Then he spent nearly three hours speaking Chinese with an embassy expert. They sat in a hot little room and alternated among Mandarin, Cantonese, and Teochiu as they discussed China during World War II. It was actually a quiz conducted in these Chinese dialects by Foreign Service Officer Roy Atkinson, who spoke English with a thick southern drawl.

What did you think of the controversy between Chennault and Stilwell in the early forties? That sort of question. Embree decided it was a good idea to take them seriously. He replied that at stake was the old philosophical conflict between air and ground warfare. Stilwell wanted to confront the Japanese on the ground and on Burmese, not Chinese, soil. Chennault boasted that his 14th Air Force could defeat the Japanese in China; he won a few victories but ultimately had to watch—as Stilwell predicted would happen—the Japanese push straight through eastern China and overrun the air bases there.

"Where did Marshall and Chiang Kai-shek stand in the debate?" asked Foreign Service Officer Atkinson in flawless Chinese.

So Embree told him in equally good Chinese. Marshall reasoned along with Stilwell that war tonnage carried over the Hump should be used to equip Chinese ground troops, instead of airfields that were, after all, less mobile than men. On the other hand, Chiang Kai-shek wanted American air power to relieve him from the need to reorganize ground troops for a better performance against Japanese infantry. If Chennault's B-29s could release the Nationalist Army for sustained domestic warfare against the Communists, so much the better. Spend American money, save his own strength.

Dealing with such familiar questions, the quiz was obviously designed not to test Embree's knowledge but to discover if he could speak Chinese with the skill promised by his service record.

Foreign Service Officer Roy Atkinson finally left the room and returned a few minutes later with a beaming Jerry Feinberg, bottle of good bourbon gripped in one hand. "Well, pal," said Jerry, "here's to China."

· · ·

After dinner, as Embree trudges wearily up to his room, he is thinking of Vera's reaction to his departure.

"Then that's it," she declared. "We'll have her home in a week." When he tried to rein her in a little—"We'll try for two"—Vera reacted vehemently. "*Two?* Why two whole weeks? You get her on one of those military planes and come back, that's all. Don't be pessimistic." The wildness of her eyes and voice deterred him from mentioning the actual bargain he'd struck: The girl would most probably be coming back by herself. He felt that the entire mission was more complicated than anyone had thus far imagined.

Rama will stay here; at least that is certain. Taking him aside tonight, Embree had asked him, "Do you want to go right home, Rama?"

"I am not keen, Master."

"Memsahib is sick. I want you to stay with her until I get back."

"Not coming with you, Master?"

"I'll make it worth your while to stay with her."

"Those women—"

"Never mind them. Just see to Memsahib."

"When I am going to kitchen for rice, when I am tucking into it, they come yelling at me, Master. I wish they would tone up their ways."

"They've worked for Memsahib a long time. They feel very much in charge. That's the way it is."

Rama had brightened. Straightening up, he said with a broad smile, "Not to worry, Master. Rama will be here."

Outside of his bedroom door, Embree glances at hers. *The Gita* says, "Duty without attachment." Is this at last where he has arrived? Because to both his sorrow and his relief there's no passion left in him for Vera, no attachment, certainly not in a sensual way. Although the young Siamese woman is obviously superficial compared to Vera, he finds himself drawn sexually to her, not to Vera. Is it merely because of Wanna's youth? He thinks not. It's her willingness—the flattery of open invitation—that draws him, whereas from the first moment on the Bangkok dock he's seen the wall surrounding Vera. No wonder people use the term "building a wall around oneself." He saw it rise around Vera Embree as if actual bricks had been laboriously piled up in front of his eyes. A wall, Vera's wall. And here, certainly, age enters into the situation: He's too old to break down such a wall. In his early twenties, when Vera had erected a similar wall, he'd found a way not to smash it down but to bore through it, to get through it somehow, and take her. Now, weary, heading tomorrow to settle a long-standing debt, Philip Embree can do no more than stare impassively at his wife's closed door, then open his own.

· · ·

Two objects, one large and one small, lie on his bed.

The large object is an ax—a metal blade, a wooden haft, and for balance a wooden knob projecting past the middle of the blade. Twenty-one years ago Philip Embree had been given this ax as a gift by a Mongol bandit whose life he'd just saved with it. Twenty-one years ago Philip Embree had chosen to live with this ax, to carry it everywhere, to cherish it as his father had cherished a copy of the Bible. In battle Embree had swung this ax through the air, leaned sideways from a galloping horse, and brained a man. Perhaps he had believed that the ax possessed a kind of magical power, like an amulet, like the word of his father's God. Twenty-one years ago, he had stuck it between his belt and trousers—hidden on his hip by a coat—then with Vera had left China.

Turning it now in his hand, Philip Embree feels for an instant the anticipation of motion that may suddenly end forever. He had used the ax in his first battle.

That had been at the Battle of Hengshui in 1927. General Tang had accepted a rival warlord's challenge to fight—by circular telegram. Like throwing down the gauntlet in medieval Europe. But if the reason for such battle seemed quaint (the warlord accused Tang of making improper alliances and thereby disgracing the Tang clan), surely its conduct was modern enough, fierce enough. While his own cavalry battalion, the Fourth, waited to go into battle, Embree had seen General Tang with his staff gathered on a knoll, watching through binoculars the enemy's artillery bombardment of a wheat field. Embree had thought of Napoleon, but of course he'd often thought of similarities between the two generals—the severity of bearing, the dark, watchful eyes, the altogether taut and potent presence that inspired confidence. Romantic, of course. And yet when Embree went into battle that day, he rode a chestnut stallion to which he'd given the name Marengo, after Napoleon's own mount, and thus expanded the comparison with Napoleon to include himself—at a lower level of fantasy. And that day, yelling "Sha! Sha! Sha!" along with his comrades in a boot-to-boot charge across the wheat field raked by artillery fire, he experienced his first combat. Part of that experience entailed leaning from Marengo and with this ax, the same one he now turns in his hand, felling an infantryman trying to flee. His right arm from wrist to shoulder still remembers the shivering impact, always will.

He marvels at Vera's knowledge of him. She hasn't forgotten the ax, although even before leaving Bangkok in 1939, he'd never mentioned it and surely, had he been asked, would not have known exactly where it was stored in the house. But she knew, and she knew the effect that such a moment as he's now experiencing could have on him. Cunning, implacable woman, who by placing this ax on his bed has tried to make sure he's lost to everything but its promise of action. Vera feels certain this will send him to China.

Embree laughs.

The other object lying on the bed is a photograph of Sonia. At the dinner table tonight he'd asked for one. By the light of a bedside lamp he examines it closely.

The girl is standing in a garden—not a girl now, but a young woman. She is definitely her father's child, a pretty Chinese woman; and yet the more Embree stares at the image, the more European she looks. In her wide-set eyes there's a looking out at the world that interests him. There's a depth of feeling in them that reminds him of Vera; and also a fearless regard that reminds him of the General.

An odd thought: In some indefinable way the young woman also reminds him of his sister Mary. Or once the contrast between blond and brunette is set aside, perhaps the resemblance is definable. Perhaps in the eyes? In a most obvious way the two women are certainly similar: Both ran away from home. When Embree was a child, Mary had run away to New York. He had loved her as much for her rebellion as for her kindnesses to him.

Is the desire to rebel why Sonia has left home? He has not considered that possibility until this moment. For that matter, he has not considered Sonia at all, directed as he has been by Vera's resolve to recover a daughter.

Again he studies the photograph. Posed with hands on hips in the garden, lips drawn into a half-smile as if challenging the world, the tall, slim young woman seems capable of fashioning her destiny without help from anyone. As Mary had been capable of doing too. At the dinner table, years ago, Embree had silently rooted for his sister whose name Father refused to pronounce.

Should he really help Vera stop this girl from going her own way? Yet Vera, surely, has been a good mother. Perhaps nothing more than willfulness has driven the girl to this reckless act. That's good thinking. Or at least good rationalization, good enough to help him make an ironclad decision. By means of this photograph Jerry Feinberg's pals in Shanghai will find the girl coming off a tramp steamer on a Pootung dock. In payment for their locating his stepdaughter Embree will do whatever the government wants. It will be more, surely, than taking a look-see. Sabotage? Not likely, but he'll do that if it's necessary. More likely he'll be called on to confirm what the government has already decided it wants to believe. He'll do that. He'll do whatever is necessary. And he *will* bring her back.

32 Two weeks have passed, no news.
Looking out at the klong from the breakfast room, Vera tells herself it's what she should have expected. Two weeks and not a word from Philip, not a word.

She pushes aside the plate of egg bananas, calls to Nipa for coffee. Again unfolding the English translation of a poem by Yu Hsuan-chi, she reads the penciled words on the smudged paper carefully: "Love and affection should learn from the river how to flow on and on." Pretty little sentiment. Vera had found the paper tucked into a book of Chinese poetry which Sonia had evidently been studying lately, perusing it in the secret world of her room, while Jeanne d'Arc and other heroines and her father and other martyred warriors ran through her young head.

Nipa brings the coffee and sets it down without a word. The servants, even Cook, have been subdued lately, and well they might be. For their failure to hold Sonia in check, she nearly fired them every day for the past few weeks. Now it's too late. They are here and will be here, no matter what they do. That's the judgment of time.

Through a Chinese bookseller Vera has obtained a short biography of Yu Hsuan-chi as an aid in understanding her daughter's mind. Yu Hsuan-chi was a courtesan and a poet, who also lived for a while as a Taoist nun. Heroine for a hopeless romantic.

"Nipa!" she calls out. "This coffee's cold."

The point is—what is the point? She had a thought, a point. Restless, Vera gets up and walks into the garden. Yes, what the girl has actually done, it's painfully clear now, is return to the homeland of her father. It's what Chinese do. Sonia wants to go home, and there's only one home, China, for the Chinese. Anywhere else is where they make money. And this is also true, Vera decides: It isn't the boy she is going with, but the father she is going to.

That, at least, is a thought with comfort in it. One without comfort is the knowledge of what day this is—May 20, her daughter's birthday. Where will Sonia celebrate it, if she does at all? At sea? Or where? Will he give her a gift? No, he won't have the money. Will she even tell him? Perhaps not. About wanting things except knowledge of her father, except courage like his and strength like his, she has always been indifferent. Will she even remember it's her birthday, having embarked on such an adventure?

Vera finds herself at the end of the garden, near the frangipani trees that line the approach to the Spirit House. She hasn't been to it since Sonia left, as if afraid of telling the General's spirit what has happened to his daughter. Nonsense. But in fact she's kept clear of the Sal Phrapum until this morning. Unlike other mornings, she hasn't brought flowers and incense as an offering to the spirits of the property—and to him. Approaching slowly, Vera can see inside the doll-house-sized mansion; almost filling it is the Willow Pattern plate he'd given her. Moving closer to the miniature elephants and horses and dolls, Vera can see through one window the jade buffalo, which stands for him. The buffalo is worth a great deal more money than the ink stone. Yet fearful of the ink stone being stolen here in the garden, she had instead placed the more valuable buffalo here in Shan-teh's memory. For her the most valuable thing she has ever owned is that ink stone—that and the memory of his bringing it to her all the way from Canton. How remarkable life is.

Standing in front of the Spirit House, her eyes level with the figures surrounding its white columns, Vera almost speaks out loud. She laughs at that possibility, recalling how Sonia accused her of talking to the General. Accused is not, of course, what Sonia meant, because the girl often talked to an imaginary person in the sanctity of her bedroom. The servants used to gossip about this habit of hers with round wondering eyes: "Young Miss is in there talking and walking and talking to someone who isn't there!" It was yet another thing the girl had in common with Philip, who used to sit out in the garden, looking across the water, here or in Hong Kong or Singapore, with his lips moving silently in some embattled dialogue. So they lived in their imaginary worlds while she lived in the real one.

Now, standing in front of the Spirit House, Vera speaks too, openly, in a low, distinct voice. "Shan-teh, it's happened. I've failed you a second time. I will say it clearly. Once I ran away out of fear and lost you; that was bad enough, my beloved. Now out of negligence or lack of understanding—I don't know—I've let our daughter run off into the most uncertain of futures. I am to blame. You can't forgive me for this any more than you could forgive me my betrayal. Even so, I believe our daughter is going to China to find you. I believe that. I don't know what, actually, I mean by saying these words, but somehow she is going there to find you. The thing is, as I stand here, feeling both foolish and wrong in talking to a piece of jade in a Siamese Spirit House, I think— I know—in some way you do exist. If I'm right and you do, my dearest, *help her.*"

Turning quickly away, Vera retraces her steps to the house and enters the breakfast room.

"Coffee hot," Nipa announces.

Sitting down wearily, Vera says, "Then bring it."

"Mistress doesn't eat."

"Really?" Vera hasn't thought much about it, but surely she's lost the great hunger. On a plate sits an opened mangosteen, the size of an apple, with its white flesh exposed. Vera can look at it without desire. Is it because of Sonia's disappearance? Of course. And because of Wanna too. She has kept away from the Siamese girl in recent days—ever since Sonia left. They meet only at the shop, formally, over business, although Wanna has tried frequently to rekindle what they had—for what purpose only Wanna can know. Reaching for the mangosteen out of habit, Vera realizes she doesn't really want it any more than she wants her Siamese lover. She pulls back her hand, lifts the coffee cup. How remarkable life is, how remarkable love.

• • •

There's a commotion in the kitchen—rising female voices punctuated fitfully by a single masculine wail of anger. Rama is back. Subdued around their mistress, the women have taken out their frustration on the Indian interloper, who's a perfect target: vulnerable to their insults yet powerless in this alien environment. Vera can't help but smile, hearing him yell out his only Thai—"*Ra wang!*"—"Be careful!"—an admonition that the trio of women surrounding him only laugh at. Vera likes him, has ever since the day of Philip's departure, when he came into the garden with her lime and soda—sent by the kitchen furies—bowing so hard he nearly upset the tray, the sort of accident, Vera suspects, the trio hopefully anticipated.

She told Rama to ignore them, but he stood there scratching his wiry hair and grimacing. When she asked what was wrong, he told her a story. A Holy Man came upon a poisonous snake one day who threatened him. Putting a spell on the snake, the Holy Man commanded it to repeat a mantra, see God, and end its harmful ways. Which the snake did, becoming as harmless as a cow. Once the neighborhood boys realized it would no longer strike, they beat it almost to death. Yet the reformed snake continued to live a disciplined and pious life. One day the Holy Man returned and, seeing the emaciated, injured snake, inquired of it what had happened. Proudly the snake declared that it no longer harmed anything, but lived on leaves. Unfortunately some boys came around now and then to torture it. Hearing this, the Holy Man was angry—not at the boys, but at the snake. "Don't you know how to protect yourself?" he shouted. "I told you not to bite; I didn't tell you not to hiss!" And Rama, grinning shyly, appended to his story this moral: You must never shoot venom into people like those women in the kitchen. But you can hiss at them and scare them off.

Of course, it was nothing but bravado from Rama, who scared them off the way crocodiles are scared off by a bleating sheep tied to a river-bank. Ah, she likes him. Philip did a fine thing by leaving Rama with her. And in he comes, first sticking his head into the room to see if he's welcome.

"Where have you been, Rama?"

In he comes all the way, rolling the brim of a broad-brimmed wicker hat around in his two long dark hands. "I have been talking to men along there, down by the klong. You go around this way quite near. Then you will find them only." He waves the hat in a few directions. "They lodge on that side. Memsahib, if those dashed women—excuse my for-wardness, please—if they were men, by Jove, I would box their ears."

"Well, you know why they do it."

Rama turns the hat. "I do. They move closely, leaving me out."

"That's true, Rama."

"These men lodging on that side, they are telling me about harvest time here. They have biting crabs here coming in droves to paddy, and they bite off shoots. In midday when sun is getting hot, they float through paddy. Not good to eat, but some people are eating them in coconut cream curry. On my side in Madras we have green worms like that. They love young shoots and eat them when they come to surface. But only two weeks of those worms. And we are not eating them. Not waterbugs either like they are doing here. Here take tea, take rest, take those bugs pounded and pickled with fish sauce. I couldn't relish that. We don't relish something like that on my side."

"Do you have family in Madras?" She feels like talking and would invite him to sit awhile, save for the trio in the kitchen, who would curse him and her too for such an impropriety. "Rama? Do you have family in Madras?"

"What is it, Memsahib?"

"I asked, do you have family in Madras?"

"No, that is, I have some but they are shifting away. Drought com-ing."

"Oh, I didn't know that. It hasn't appeared in the papers."

"I have been looking for it," Rama murmurs gloomily. "Mangoes now blooming on my side."

"I'm glad to have you here."

So lost is he in his thoughts that Rama holds the hat without turning it, staring down at his feet.

Vera repeats it gently. "Rama. I'm glad to have you here."

"Thank you, Memsahib." He looks up, able to smile. "I am shaping very well here, thank you. Yesterday I went to one of their temples. It was to see if they had any beastly practices there, but all I am seeing is the true gods—Narayana and Ganesh and Rama and Hamuman in their Buddhist temple, so now"—to emphasize the point, he rolls the hat around again—"I am entertaining new idea about matters on this side. These people are using true gods but calling them by different names. They are saying everything is Buddha, but is also Lord Vishnu and his circle." Heartily Rama slaps one hand against the broad straw hat. "It is one and same. To earn your colors you must think of God as one."

Vera smiles, yet feels disturbed by Rama's rather faulty exposition of what is true here in Siam: Indian Brahmanism has suffused through popular Buddhism. Perhaps her failure with Sonia is linked to the intellectual tolerance—or laziness?—of people they've lived among during the girl's formative years. What Sonia needed to see around her was solidity of values, a firm hold on the verities, such as she might have discovered in Europe. Tolerance, as the Siamese practice it, might really be nothing more than confusion—or worse, indifference.

Thinking of Sonia these days seems always to bring on thinking of Siam. What ruined Siam? The same thing, Vera imagines, that ruined her Russia. In the eighteenth century the Burmans wiped out the Siamese capital. They did such a thorough job that aside from ruins the country has been left quite isolated from its past. War has truncated Siamese history, demolished recollection. And so anything that could fill the vacuum came in—ideas, beliefs, principles rushing into the emptiness left by war. War again. War. Because of war, her own Russia has no history except for the past few hundred years. And today no history, perhaps, that will survive the century.

She falls silent. Rama waits patiently for their conversation to resume, but more noise heralds an event in the kitchen.

The door swings open; it is Ah Ping, her mottled hands gripping an envelope, her eyes glaring at Rama until he backs away a step, holding the hat brim in both clenched hands.

"Hope for good news, Mistress," Ah Ping declares in a rush of anguish, as she reaches across the table with the envelope.

SHE IS NOT ON SHEDULE SHIP STOP
WATCHING ALL ARIVALS STOP
DOING EVERTHING POSIBLE STOP   LOVE PHILIP

Everything possible? Vera crumples the cable, tosses it on her plate. Obviously the boy has slipped her past the American agents. And Philip? If she knows him, he's become swept up in that little Chinese war and forgotten about a child who was never his anyway. Waiting two weeks for this! Vera picks up the cable, unfolds it, and rereads the crinkled misspelled words. *Who* is watching? American agents? What do they know about Shanghai waterfronts? A boy of ten could slip past them.

On her feet, Vera stares at Rama a moment, then says evenly, "We are going, Rama. You are going with me."

"Not to worry, Mistress. Where are we going?"

"To Shanghai."

"Master staying there?"

"I don't know where he is. But we're going."

"Oh yes, Mistress, thank you," Rama says, bowing.

There's no time to think, no time, no time, Vera thinks. Moving with measured steps calculated not to arouse chest pain, Vera climbs the stairway to her room and dresses for the day. It will be a long one.

· · ·

By the time she has reached the shop, Vera has purchased tickets for herself and Rama on a fast steamer to Shanghai via Saigon. She wanted to fly, but no plane tickets were available, and so a week must be spent on the ocean. If only Philip had been more specific—was Sonia on the manifest? If not, did she change ships? He'd been deliberately vague in a misguided effort to relieve her anxiety. Only a man would do that. A woman would never be so foolish as to believe you can make a problem disappear by omission. At the telegraph office she'd sent a cable to him in care of the American Consulate in Shanghai:

ARRIVE SHANGHAI 4 JUNE BOOKED PALACE VERA

That matches him in brevity, Vera thought, sliding the cable form toward the clerk.

Now, weary, she approaches her shop door. So far no chest pain. She concentrates on its absence rather than on her reluctance to see the German doctor once more before leaving tomorrow. After all, she has the pills, and he'd only apologize for making too few tests for a firm diagnosis.

As she reaches the door, her neighbor, the Bombay money changer, gives her a broad grin from his fine corner location, and of course, as usual, she frowns in return. He could have made a good financial deal, but apparently he derives more satisfaction from grinning at her from his tiny doorway. Rama, thank God, is a different kind of Indian.

Opening the door, Vera sees Prakit Chaidee jump up from his desk, just as he does every day. She wastes no time explaining her plans. Of course, he will run the shop in her absence. He will also have complete authority to make whatever financial decisions are necessary. Vera has never given him that authority before, and she herself is surprised at doing it now. His face reflects confusion and surprise. Vera reaches out, gently touches his arm. "Take care of things."

Perhaps I'm not coming back, she thinks.

"Where is Wanna?"

Prakit Chaidee shakes his head. "She has not returned from lunch."

"No? Not yet?" Brushing past him, Vera opens the door of her office. Standing there a moment, she regards everything with a determined sweeping glance, as if to memorize each detail of her life in this room. Foolish. She'll be back. And yet the feeling remains while, at the desk, she examines an invoice, writes an urgent letter.

"Ah, Nahng Vera."

She looks up from the desk at the young woman leaning against the doorway. Wanna's eyes are shining fiercely. Has she been drinking? Vera wonders. The lovely brown skin of her cheeks has a reddish sheen to it, as if tenderly bruised—the girl has come from bed, Vera thinks.

"I'm going to be gone awhile."

"I know, Nahng Vera," the girl says, smiling. "You have heard from Master?"

"It's interesting you should mention him. On the dock that day, when you suddenly appeared, I knew exactly what our relationship was—yours and mine."

Still smiling, Wanna sits down.

"Or I could start by telling you a story. It's famous in China. A young man goes to a courtesan, who refuses him until finally he offers her a thousand gold coins for one night."

"Oh, she must have been a beautiful woman."

"But she declines the offer. Next day he comes to her again and describes a dream of his in which they spent the night together. At which point she demands the thousand coins." Vera smiles.

"I don't understand, Nahng Vera."

"Two people don't always view an experience the same way."

"*Tee rahk*, what has that to do with Master?"

"I saw him as a problem, you saw him as a possibility. Never mind. That's over. But I do appreciate your eagerness to make credit for anything that comes your way."

Vera sighs and looks away from the frowning girl to the ledgers, a bronze from Korat, the little good-luck piece made from a tuber root that sits on her desk. She doesn't want to leave these things, not even for a day. "Wanna," she says, turning again to her, "I've not been fair to you. I bought you. Just as men once bought me. I didn't want to lose you. Frankly, I liked your indolence and easy sensuality. It reminded me somehow of Russia in my youth. Of women like you, quite as free but more refined. When I was a child, I saw them with men who fawned over them and I envied them such attention although I didn't know precisely what they did to get it. Do you understand? What amazes me is my own steadfastness, my desire for commitment. It took you to teach me that, Wanna. I thank you."

"You want me to leave, Nahng Vera?" the girl says, rising.

"I think so. But I can see you're quite ready to leave." She already has someone, Vera thinks.

"You will pay me for this last week?"

"Of course. Prakit Chaidee will have your money—a month's salary."

"Then goodbye, Nahng Vera." At the door Wanna turns, her lips set but trembling. "It's your fault for letting Sanuk do what she wanted. You were with me when you should have been with her."

Long after the door closes, Vera sits there looking at its flat wooden surface, at the image on it of Sonia, a child, running through the garden toward her with open arms.

· · ·

She is home, finally. During dinner there are a few moments when the pain starts, but it goes away before she takes out the vial of pills. Nothing can prevent her from getting to Shanghai and finding Sonia, nothing, not even fate itself.

At her desk, now, she has just finished writing a note to Jim Thompson. Earlier, she'd thought of seeing him to explain her reasons for leaving, but he might very well go to the American authorities with it— and then what? On her return she can apologize. She'll take Philip and they'll have a drink on the Oriental Hotel terrace with Jim Thompson. Because Philip will be with her. Yes.

Philip Embree will come home to stay. That is a given in her plans now. According to him, he has returned to Bangkok to help her, and in his own bumbling way perhaps he's doing just that in Shanghai. And after Shanghai? The debt won't be paid. She'll remind him of that, remorselessly. As Rama is accustomed to saying, "It is time to do the needful." Perhaps age has driven her to such a shameless resolve. It will be good to have someone stand in her bedroom doorway, morning and night, and say "Good morning" and "Good night" and "Did you sleep well?" and "Are you feeling well?" day after day into the unsure future.

Age and the need for security bring her to this view of the future with Philip. Because she and Wanna are terribly alike. Today the girl came warm and exhilarated from someone else's bed; it gave Wanna the courage to dispense with humiliating little strategies for keeping the affair going. And as for herself, Vera understands full well that the reappearance of Philip gave her the courage today to break off with Wanna.

Even so, already she misses the girl, already doubts her own judgment. At a certain age, to give up something is to move in the direction of death. Tonight, at the dinner table, Vera came close to jumping up, hiring a samlor, and riding out to Wanna's small apartment in the north of Bangkok. What stopped her? Perhaps only the suspicion that Wanna would be gone or, even worse, would be there with someone else.

Vera turns the radio on. Lately, at this time of night, the Siamese National Radio Station has been playing an hour of Western music, and Vera has made a point of listening. Wailing out of the speaker at the moment, however, is bamboo music, a powerful concoction of drums and gongs and flutes, which serves only to remind her that tomorrow she's leaving her adopted land. But not forever, of course, and yet forever is possible. Looking back on her life, Vera sees a procession of vehicles leading her always farther from memory.

Nevertheless, the bamboo music, so heavily percussive, draws her back into memory, into the solemn night of Confucius' birthday celebration twenty years ago. All night long the huge drums had signaled up a procession of celebrants moving slowly toward the Great Hall in the temple at Qufu. To this huge sound, in their own dark room, she and Shan-teh had made love.

After lovemaking, unable to sleep in the sound-filled darkness, they talked, and as they often did together in Qufu they talked of their two cultures, of the religions that separated them, of the arts that bound them. That night, Vera finally asked him about his two dead sons. Not until that moment had she dared question him about them. It had been a matter not of fear but of sensitivity. Until that evening he'd merely told her, "My second wife died of typhoid. A month later so did my two young boys." He had not elaborated, and from the anguish he still felt after many years—anguish plainly visible in his eyes—Vera understood that his silence was not to shut her out but to shut his own emotions in.

But on this night of dark and ancient music, having loved him, Vera felt able to ask. As she expected, the boys had died horribly, the older three days after the younger; Shan-teh had been at both bedsides, holding their hands, waiting for sudden recovery or death. She could imagine that; she could also imagine how much he must have wished for his wife then. How can a man lose wife and children within a month and come out of it whole? So she asked him the inevitable question. "Have you wanted more children?"

"No," he said into the darkness.

"But didn't you want an heir?"

"In 1916, shortly after the Republic began, Yuan Shih-k'ai was President. He wanted to become emperor and create a new dynasty. There was much plotting in those days, for and against him. My father was against him. He had my father beheaded, my entire clan marked for assassination. I was a young officer then, stationed in Sian. I went into hiding. The rest of my clan, one hundred thirty-two of them, including infants, were executed. Our ancestral tablets were thrown into the river."

For a while he said nothing more, and Vera wondered if this was all he meant to say. Then he said, "Having survived the clan, I must not have a son to perform my funeral rites."

"Is that custom or your decision?"

"My decision. Funeral rites had been denied to all one hundred and thirty-two."

"So you've punished yourself." When he didn't reply, Vera said, "I'm sorry, but I think you have."

"I have."

"What if we have a child?"

"Yes, I've wondered."

"You've wondered if you would want it?"

"Oh, I would want it. I've wondered how I could acknowledge such happiness."

"A son for your funeral rites. What if the child were a girl?"

"I would want her as much." He touched her arm, moved his dark warm hand up to her shoulder, her neck, her cheek. "I won't have funeral rites. So it doesn't matter, son or daughter. Will you give me a child?"

"I don't know," she said, troubled by this conversation, for the idea of having his child was as difficult to face as the idea of giving him a girl, when everyone knew that a man of China would want sons.

Suddenly the bamboo music stops, and in soft, precise Thai a woman announces the evening's program of Western classical music. Pushing aside the finished letter to Jim Thompson, Vera sits back, and through the pervasive sound of cheeping frogs from the klong she hears the first strains of Borodin's Second String Quartet. When the second movement begins, she's wrenched by the sweet melancholy of the music. It's the language of the outcast. Indeed, the purring woody sound describes her own searing memories in alien lands—and the desire for home: hot tea and cold mornings, fur muffs and sleigh bells, the smell of Father's tobacco, and Mother's cheery cry of welcome below the stairway balcony at the massive front door.

Part Three

33 THEY'RE IN CHINA, but not in Shanghai, their destination when they left Siam.

What Yu-ying remembers most about the long and complex journey is Ho's gambling on the ship bound from Bangkok to Singapore.

She couldn't stop him from playing fan-tan behind the forward cargo hold where men gathered in the late afternoon with their money and loud urgent voices and their visions of good luck. Ho never had good joss, only bad joss, as he squatted on the deck in front of the piled coins to guess at the remainder after they were counted by fours. Yu-ying could see it was a game that took no skill, only a kind of obsessive stubbornness and enough money to support it until good joss appeared —but it never appeared for Ho, who shook his head bitterly at fate and laughed insouciantly when other players commented on his losses. He spoke sharply to her when she hovered near, and later upbraided her for stinginess when she hesitated to give him more money.

Once, standing at the rail with ocean spray stinging their faces, he turned and said angrily, "I shouldn't have brought someone like you along on such an important mission. You're too forward. You should stay below instead of bothering us. And your name, Yu-ying, I don't like that either."

Her name had been an issue between them ever since she told him it was the name of a friend her mother had once known in China. To that he'd said, "I thought you were free of your family, like I am. But you choose a name that keeps yours in mind."

Then he insisted on having her in their crowded little cabin. It was midmorning, and everyone except themselves had gone up on deck for a breath of air. The stifling room had eight wooden bunks sandwiched into a space hardly eight feet high and eight feet long. There wasn't room enough for them to climb into a bunk together, so Ho demanded that she stand against the bulkhead and pull her sam-foo pajamas down. Quickly, in fear of being discovered, she did, and the truth was it felt good when he thrust forward into her warmly and full, but then an old woman burst into the cabin (no lock on the door), and instead of leaving, stood there yelling at them—they had no right to use this place for such a thing!

For a few tense moments, while yanking her pajamas up, Yu-ying hated the young man who gambled away her money and embarrassed her in front of an old woman. But her resentment gave way soon to curiosity as they heard from above decks the cry of "Land! Land!" Going topside, they watched the cloudy blue outline of islands in the Straits of Malacca appear off the bow.

That evening at sunset Yu-ying sat on the fantail. While Ho held a mirror up, she cut her hair. She'd been letting it grow lately (ever since her first rendezvous with Chamlong, when he stroked it feverishly in his pleasure), but now, bound for China, she snipped it at ear-lobe level and straightened the line of bangs a finger's width above her eyebrows.

He said, "I'm sorry about this morning. I couldn't help it."

And with a shy glance she told him, "Neither could I."

But the next day, when the island of Blakang Mati lay off the starboard bow, Ho looked to port at Singapore coming into view and told her that from now on they must be totally dedicated to the mission, because the message he carried was of crucial importance to Nai Pridi Phanomyong, that unjustly accused leader and great hero, in whose hands lay the future of Siam and of the Chinese in Siam and of the Communist Party in Siam. It was a grave little speech, and Yu-ying remembers the way his thick dark eyebrows knitted together, his lips compressed, his jaw tightened, so that once again she looked at him with admiration and hope.

• • •

She will remember that speech of his much later. But she forgot it and everything else in the tumultuous harbor of Singapore. Nothing was possible then except watching the ship glide past the assembly of ships and boats sequestered there: sparkling ocean liners, black tankers, great junks with eyes painted on the bow, Bugis schooners, rusted old coastal freighters, broad-brimmed lighters, and sampans churning the oil-slicked water into a thick brown porridge.

After docking, Ho led her (by her instructions, since he'd never been here before) through the waterfront area to Chinatown.

Here, too, she couldn't think. Too much was going on. But in Sago Street, the Street of the Dead, she thought too much—as she'd done on her previous visit, with Mother.

At that time she had thought of Mother dying. This time Yu-ying thought of herself dying, as she paused to look at the funeral shops. Along this street an entire row of them sold paper models of houses complete with furniture, benches, servants, and dragon clouds. She looked hard, as Ho did, at the lanterns, joss sticks, and paper money to be burned at funerals. Then they squinted up at the second stories of those houses. Yu-ying told him who was up there: the old people waiting to die, lying on bare mattresses for the eventual journey down a flight of stairs to their coffins.

Ho scoffed at the death houses. He was more affected by the sight of men playing mah-jong at the tea shop. For a few tense moments he watched them clicking the tiles and betting. Then, turning to her, he smiled. "You see, I'm serious. I won't ever bet again. Let's go."

They had eaten only rice gruel for breakfast, yet Ho marched them along covered arcades past a Trengganu Street fruit market loaded with purple mangosteens, fat nangka, papaya, hairy rambutans, and five-ridged starfruit. There were one-pot kitchens along "the five-foot ways," serving pork soup, stuffed bean curd, wheat flour noodles; and for a lilting moment Yu-ying remembered how, after their first lovemaking, they had stopped at a little stall much like these. The thought made her blush, as she watched a young woman go by with an infant in a cloth pick-a-back.

On Temple Street, in front of a Teochiu sign—TOW HUAT SIN KEE— Ho said quite fiercely, "Wait here." He entered the shop, which sold woks, dishes, whisks, and jars of spices, eggs, toys. Coming out, he still looked fierce. "Follow me, but if I give you a frown, stop and wait till I come back."

This was not the boy cringing behind a hotel door in Bangkok, and Yu-ying felt happy about it. She nodded submissively and stayed a step behind him, as Ho searched for another address on Temple Street. They came to an open blacksmith shop, where buckets, washtubs, and dustbins were made. A man squatting on a table held a wooden batten and with it was folding the edges of a metal sheet balanced between saw-horses. Yu-ying waited at the entrance while Ho talked to him. A small boy wearing a black skullcap came along and stared at her. He had a face to match his kua pi mao: round, austere, formal. If only she had something to give him, but before she could think of anything, Ho came out of the shop accompanied by the blacksmith, a powerful man in torn trousers and dirty undershirt. She fell in behind them through the markets of Chinatown. Arts and crafts stores, open to the air, emitted the cool pungent scent of sandalwood, and a glimpse inside one of them at its vases and Buddhas wracked her with the sudden pain of remembering her mother's antique store. Mother. The stolen vase.

Yu-ying touched the ink stone in her trouser pocket, just as the two men ahead of her turned into Upper Cross Street.

They went into a second-hand shop—FOOK TECK HOE COMPANY in English and Chinese above the doorway. Yu-ying stood against a green wall and watched three coolies squatting on the ground with their chopsticks flashing over dishes of noodles. Elbows braced on knees, their bare feet parallel, the trio ate with an intensity she recognized. Only the

Chinese eat like that, she thought—with total concentration. Like true believers at prayer. And then she remembered that Mother had once made the same observation about her at the dinner table: "Sonia, you eat like someone praying."

Again touching the ink stone, Yu-ying stared at the shop dealing in waste paper, bottles, gunnysacks. Ho was inside there deciding their next move, while a few old women were bundling corrugated boards in front of the shop.

Mother had Wanna to comfort her.

. . .

When Ho, the blacksmith, and another man left the second-hand shop, Yu-ying fell in behind them and followed through still more markets until, in a tiny lane, they stopped at a two-story house with a sagging balcony.

To her surprise, the blacksmith walked up to her and said, "Come with us. We'll all be equal in the new world."

The words sounded memorized and more ritualistic than felt, yet Yu-ying did not hesitate—not even when Ho gave her a deep, meaningful frown—to enter the house. The air inside was thick with sawdust; three men were fastening canvas straps to wooden clogs, while another trio, sitting on the floor, with long curved knives were shaping blocks of wood into shoes. Behind this room was a storage area, and behind that a dark passageway with cubicles off it—bunk spaces for the woodworkers. As Yu-ying passed by, she saw their belongings: a clutter of boxes, a few articles of clothing hanging on strung lines, some pans, an old mattress. Beyond these woodworkers' cubicles, at the end of the passageway, was a larger room, empty save for a table and a dozen chairs lined against one wall.

Silently the blacksmith sat down. She and Jin-shi sat down too, leaving an empty chair between him and them. As time passed, she began to worry if somehow Jin-shi had been tricked by the blacksmith into believing this was the meeting place of a Communist cell. On her last visit to Singapore she and Mother had listened to an old Britisher in a hotel dining room describe the gangs, both Malay and Chinese, that terrorized the city, that kidnapped people, ran drug and prostitution rings. The Britisher with considerable gusto gave a vivid description of gangs fighting in the streets; often they tossed light bulbs filled with acid at one another.

For two hours she sat next to Jin-shi, scarcely exchanging a word. The stolid blacksmith never moved, but looked straight ahead. Yu-ying was hungry and thirsty. If she and Jin-shi were kidnaped by a Singapore gang, would they at least get tea?

Then two men stood in the doorway, looking around before coming into the room. They pulled chairs away from the wall and sat down, facing Ho Jin-shi, giving Yu-ying the faintest glance. One of the men (he had a lazy eye) made a little speech, then and there. He spoke of the need for armed uprisings throughout Asia. To emphasize the point, he stood up and waved his arms, as if addressing a rally. Here in Malaya, he said, the British imperialists and their Malayan lackeys would soon feel the wrath of Chinese patriots who'd fought against the Japanese only to see their rightful share of the country taken from them in the postwar world.

It was a fine speech, Yu-ying thought. Much like Jin-shi's on the ship. Fine men, warriors.

But she was more interested, really, in the other man who'd just arrived. There was something about him, something unhealthy but fascinating. He had a mean presence, something indefinably frightening. He might be a killer, she thought. He sat stiffly in his chair, hands folded across his chest as if protecting it. His eyes never left Ho Jin-shi. Abruptly cutting into the oration of the lazy-eyed man, he said to Jin-shi, "Let me see that message."

"I can't open it, because it's sealed," Ho said. "But here's my letter of identification." From across the table he handed a folded note to the man, who read it carefully. Yu-ying knew what it was: a letter stating that the bearer, Ho Jin-shi, is in possession of a document meant for Nai Pridi Phanomyong, former Prime Minister of Siam and friend of the people of China; that any courtesy extended to the bearer would be appreciated by the Communist Party of Siam; that the bearer is a patriot and party member. Having read it, the man threw it on the table and curtly asked Ho his plans.

Obviously he was the leader. Middle-aged, his face pockmarked, he had a keen, bright, unwavering gaze.

After Ho explained his intention of continuing to Shanghai, the leader shook his head. "No. That is stupid." He explained himself just as emphatically. Perhaps this Pridi, this Siamese politician, really was in Shanghai, but more probably he had fled the city—Chiang Kai-shek had begun yet another campaign against subversives there. Informers and spies were in the factories, the schools, the merchant organizations, even among beggars and dockworkers. A Siamese would be spotted quickly by the secret police and questioned and disposed of in such manner that no one but God could recognize the corpse.

Yu-ying was surprised to hear such a man mention God.

With arms still crossed on his chest, the leader continued to analyze Pridi's probable course of action. Comrades must have warned him about staying in Shanghai, and if this Siamese politician had any sense, he must have moved northward into a liberated area.

When Ho asked where, the leader shrugged. "Find that out for yourself in Tsingtao," he told Ho. "Because Tsingtao is the place for you to start, not Shanghai. In Tsingtao you'll learn what to do from the cell there."

The man raised his finger in warning, as if speaking to a feckless child. "You must get off the ship you're on," he said. "Get your goods. We'll find you a coastal steamer to Tsingtao." After regarding Ho briefly, he said, "Why did you leave Siam?"

"To get this message to Prime Minister Pridi."

"But why *you?*" the leader persisted.

Before replying, Ho turned to look at Yu-ying, as if seeking advice. Turning back to the leader, he said, "I killed a man. A government agent." It was the first time he had told anyone. Yu-ying was sure of that. He had never even told Wan-li for fear of having made a mistake. She was sure of that, too.

The men, even the blacksmith, smiled. The man with the lazy eye said, "There will be a lot of killing here too before it's done. Here we are, the Federation of Malaya for three months now, but does that mean freedom?"

The leader cleared his throat, indicating the meeting was ended, but the lazy-eyed man continued. "We're going into the rubber plantations, the tin mines. We're going into the jungles and ambush them from there. We'll shoot them from their jeeps, we'll slit their throats in the dark, we'll poison their wells and burn their godowns. The British were thrown out by the Japanese, but now they come back thinking they can take what they want and give the rest to the Malays—*Malays*, who prospered under the Japanese. As for the Chinese, let them work like the dogs they are."

"Let's go," the leader said in a weary voice, unfolding his arms.

"Once I was a member of the Red Dots," the man continued. "I was Grade Five with a good chance of rising to Tiger General. I thought of the old Hung League, the bond of brotherhood, the rebirth, but what we did was keep a whole neighborhood in the palm of our hand, frightened of us—and for good reason. Was this brotherhood? Some of them talked of getting rich and going back to their Teochiu villages, back to Chin Hai or Po Ning or Chi Yang or back to Swatow. I wasn't a *hua chiao*, one of those fools who believe someday they'll return to China. *This* is my home."

"Let's go," the leader repeated in a louder voice.

Everyone was now standing at the door, but the lazy-eyed man sat at the table, continuing to talk at the opposite wall. "I'm not afraid to fight. I'm not afraid to die. The Red Dots think only of money and power. They're wrong. What I'm afraid of is losing who I am. My name, the name of my ancestors. See that? That's what I'm afraid of."

"Let's go," the leader said roughly.

This time, looking around, the man got to his feet, shuffled toward the door.

Later, when they were returning to get their belongings from the ship, Ho said to her triumphantly, "I did the right thing telling them I killed that agent."

"Why?" she asked.

"They didn't understand how a man so young could take on such an important mission. I had to prove who I am. Didn't I?"

"Yes," she told him. And it was probably true, she thought. But her attention drifted from Jin-shi to the man with the lazy eye back there in the woodworkers' shop: He was afraid of nothing but the loss of pride. And the aftermath of such brooding aroused in her a strange new feeling. It was a sense of emptiness, as if something had been taken away from her, plucked away without her knowledge. She felt restless, unable to concentrate on what Ho said or did or where they went for the night in the raucous city of Singapore. She had thought so intensely of pride once before—that time in school, when they tried to persuade her she must wear the cross of people who betrayed the Maid.

That evening, in a squalid room above the night market on Pagoda Street, after Ho was asleep, she stood at the window and in the glow of garish neon wrote in her diary:

> To face north when you rise in the morning, you have bad luck and a shortened life, so they say. But tomorrow I will do it and defy the gods.

She wrote this down in Chinese in the streaky green-and-red glare.

The next morning, rising, she faced north.

• • •

She is thinking now of her defiant act, wondering if she might rectify it here in China by facing east, the direction of power and long life, the next time she rises from bed.

If she has a bed again to rise from.

Things haven't gone well since the coastal steamer arrived in Tsing-tao. A customs official charged her import duty on the amulet she wore, the terra-cotta Goddess of Love on a cheap metal chain. The official insisted it was gold, not terra cotta, and threatened to turn her back when she argued. Having paid ten times the value of the amulet and received a withering frown from Ho in the bargain, Yu-ying emerged from the customs shed to have her first look at China.

She had expected something different. Instead of gray walls and muddy streets under a gray sky, Yu-ying had dreamed for years of the tiny arched bridges, mist-covered mountains, and tiled-roof palaces in the paintings reproduced in books her mother kept on shelves at the store. She used to think of her father in these scenes of the Sung and Ming dynasties: A handsome man in elegant brocaded robes with a long sword dangling from a bejeweled scabbard and a scroll in his hand was seated under a peach tree in front of a red-pillared mansion. Filaments of cloud were trailing down a blue mountainside behind him, and a phoenix, bird of renewal, drank from a nearby pond that reflected on its surface some peony blossoms, an emblem of love. This vision had translated for Yu-ying into a hoped-for China of ancient beauty, not what she saw during her first moments in Tsingtao: real walls peeling, refuse piles, sweaty rickshaw pullers.

There was no time for disappointment, however—they had to find the local Party cell, and when they found it, Yu-ying had to do the talking, since Ho didn't know a word of Northern Chinese and no one here spoke Teochiu. Perhaps because she, a woman, had to conduct the interview with a Party official, they were treated with lack of interest, then impatience. The Tsingtao official had never heard of Pridi, nor did he know where such a man might be found. In response to Yu-ying's insistent plea for help, he suggested they try Hsipiap'o in Hopei Province, where the Communist High Command was located—or was last week. Loyang had just been taken and Kaifeng was under siege, so Mao might want to go to one of those places. The situation was fluid. It was a description Yu-ying would hear often in following days.

Getting to Hsipiap'o was a problem in itself. Hopei Province lay north of Tsingtao; the rail junction leading northward was at Jinan, but train service out of there depended on troop movements. Between Jinan and northern cities like Hsipiap'o the military situation was extremely fluid.

At the railhead in Tsingtao a huge crowd was waiting when Yu-ying and Ho got there. A train in the switchyard stood huffing and sputtering. Steam from the engine sounded to Yu-ying like the breathing of a dragon, and the ring of coals she could see around the ill-fitting lid of the coal burner in the locomotive cab was like the hot red eye of the dragon. She asked Ho if the train didn't look to him like a huge dragon of steel, but he didn't answer, didn't seem to hear her. His inability to communicate in Teochiu had shaken his confidence again, and sometimes she felt on her sleeve the slight pressure of his fingers, fumbling there without his conscious knowledge, but telling her precisely how much he needed her.

• • •

She remembers that too—his hand light as a child's on her sleeve—while they rattle along in the crowded train compartment. Benches have been ripped out to make more room, so it's little more than a cattle car;

a couple of hundred people are wedged together, seated with legs drawn up. Warm air rushes between cracks in the floor, and Yu-ying can feel the airy motion against her cotton trousers. Often she glances at Ho, who in the desperate rush to get aboard was separated from her. He is a few bodies down the way, his head jerking against the compartment wall to the rhythm of the train. He is almost asleep—darker than most of these Northern Chinese, with a longer face and more delicate features. Above his head, framed in the window, is a pair of legs, feet sandaled with tire rubber—on top of the train hundreds of other passengers are riding along. Yu-ying wonders if any of them fall and, if they do, what happens to them. Certainly the train won't stop. People have been talking about their good luck at leaving Tsingtao at all. Last week, because of Communist sabotage along a stretch of track, not a single train ran, and the previous week only troops made the two-hundred-and-fifty-mile journey to Jinan.

A round-faced peasant girl is jammed against Yu-ying, their sides and arms sweaty against one another. The girl begins to talk about visiting Tsingtao, which she'd never seen until now and might never have seen except that her husband, living there, is sick.

"That's too bad he's sick," Yu-ying says.

"No, it's all right. When he's not sick, he beats me. Anyway, he won't beat me any more." The girl leans forward and whispers in Yu-ying's ear. "I am now a member of the Women's Association of the Eighth Route Army."

"Communists are in your village?"

"The Eighth Route Army came through and formed committees. Then they left. I don't know anything about Communists. But he won't beat me any more," she says proudly. Her cheeks glow with vigor, her black hair is tied back in a thick braid. "Now in my village if a man misbehaves, the Women's Association comes after him."

"How do they do that?"

"They tie him up and put him in a storage room for a few days. Then they try him for his crimes. That's what we do in our village," she says, "and in our village we're learning to read. I learn four characters a day," she says proudly.

Yu-ying smiles at the proud girl. "What about the war?"

"It doesn't come our way very often," the girl says with a shrug. "My friend was raped by a soldier one day, and about ten men were taken off to fight, that's all."

"Which side do they fight for?"

"I don't know."

"But you like the Eighth Route Army?"

"I do," the girl says emphatically. "They started the committees and sometimes one of their cadre comes and talks to us about a new life."

Suddenly the girl frowns. "They say we can marry who we choose. They say we aren't slaves to men any more. Do you believe that?"

"I do," says Yu-ying, noticing an old woman staring at them across the compartment floor.

"If my husband doesn't come back, I'll marry again," the girl declares. One broad weathered hand reaches up to the braid and circles it, drawing it through curved fingers sensually. "I'll marry a man who can teach me characters every day, so I'll learn to read like a man does."

"Then I hope your husband doesn't come back."

Giggling, the girl regards Yu-ying closely. "You're not from here."

"Do I speak badly?"

The girl purses her lips judgmentally. "I can tell you're not from here the way you speak. And you speak slowly."

"That's because I haven't spoken your language very much."

"What do you speak?"

"Teochiu."

"I've never heard of it. Are you married?"

Yu-ying hesitates. "Yes, he's sitting over there."

"The skinny one asleep? He doesn't look like he came from here either." The girl leans close to whisper. "Be careful around here. They say the fighting will get worse soon."

• • •

When the train halts, Yu-ying thinks they must have arrived at a station, probably Tzupo, and she smiles across the massed humanity at Jin-shi, who smiles back. But others are groaning and rising. Rising too, at window level Yu-ying can see that the train has stopped in the countryside, without a building in sight. Minutes later, when everyone has debarked, she looks in dismay at the plain stretching flat and brown to the distant horizon. She has never imagined China this way: as a somber immensity that overwhelms even the sky, that seems now to swallow up the hundreds of departing passengers. Even the locomotive seems like a toy in this landscape, as it stands hissing and stalled on buckled track; and the track itself, beyond the section lately dynamited, adds to the illusion of distance, as it runs parallel through field after field and finally converges far ahead, becoming a distant bead of metal flashing in sunlight.

There are a few battered trucks waiting on a dusty road nearby. Some of the passengers—not many—are bargaining for rides, while the majority with their wicker baskets of chickens and old suitcases set out by foot down the road. Yu-ying watches the round-faced girl go that way, broad-shouldered and sturdy, her thick braid swinging to a vigorous gait.

"A few more places!" thunders out a driver, standing on the footguard of his truck, holding up a fistful of bills.

She wants to ask Jin-shi if the truck drivers have ruined the track to get fares or if soldiers did it and how long it will take the railroad to repair the damage, but looking at him, she understands he won't have answers to such questions. He looks stunned, tired, pliable.

The ride is expensive, but the driver's heading for Jinan, so Yu-ying buys their passage. She doesn't even consult Jin-shi, who stands silently at her elbow. The driver won't accept Nationalist dollars, only Renminbi—money printed by Communists in their base areas. Fortunately, the Tsingtao Party official had warned her that in the Shantung countryside you need both kinds of money—that is, he added, for a short while longer. In Tsingtao a pawnshop broker had sold her both kinds in exchange for Singapore dollars.

They climb aboard, but can't find sitting room alongside the other passengers, who gaze at them sullenly as they maneuver their feet into tiny spaces next to the slatted rear of the truck. It's a 6-by-4-foot Isuzu TU 10 with a broken winch platform and bullet holes aerating the back of the wooden cab. With a lurch the old Japanese truck sets off down the road, kicking dust in the faces of train passengers who have chosen to walk.

Through a dust cloud Yu-ying sees and waves at the round-faced girl, who waves back gaily, as if setting out on a picnic. I hope she'll get a man who teaches her to read, Yu-ying thinks. She glances at Jin-shi's face, tightened into an expression of brooding discontent. Or so she interprets his look. Is he skinny? Compared with these husky Shantungese he has a slight, almost delicate build. That peasant girl wouldn't want someone so weak-looking for a husband, even if he could teach her some characters. And not only does Jin-shi, the Golden Lion, lack a word of Mandarin, he can't read very well either. He squints at the characters and mumbles slowly to himself. But it isn't his fault; the father kept him down.

Yu-ying stares at the passing landscape, the checkered fields of wheat and onions, the apple orchards and bean patches—flat, flat, fully exposed to the great hammering of the sun. In Siam the foliage of tree and bush softens the sun's assault, leaves shadowy places to hide from it in, and there's always color, a blossom within sight, and a visual disturbance of things to interest the eye. But here she can take in the entire countryside with a glance. At each rumbling mile she feels more depressed, almost to the point of tears.

A dull pain begins in her lower abdomen. Yu-ying understands immediately what's happening to her. But it's not the right time, is it? She counts rapidly. It is. And if the flow begins before they get off the truck, her trousers will be wet in full view of these people wedged in here. At least her trousers are dark blue.

In another half hour Yu-ying is sure. There's the dull throbbing pain. A sense of fatigue. Nothing in the world could be as good now as a bed and the leisure to lie on it, curled up. Nothing. She looks at Jin-shi, but his thoughts have drawn him deep into himself, deeper than she can reach.

Then suddenly the truck sputters and jerks to a halt. Everyone waits silently while from beyond the truck's cab an old engine tries to assert itself. Again and again the driver turns it over until the battery gives out. With another round of moaning, the passengers rise and start jumping from the truck, just as the driver comes around the side of it. He's holding a pistol.

At first Yu-ying thinks he's a bandit, but when the passengers begin arguing for their money back and he refuses, quite plainly the gun has been introduced to strengthen his claim to the fares, even though—as a passenger estimates—Jinan is still many miles away. The gun wins; fifty people start wandering down the road.

"Too many bags," Jin-shi mumbles, taking up his suitcase. She lifts her own, somewhat smaller than his. They plod after the other passengers down a willow-bordered path, heading west.

The dull pain changes to cramps, sometimes so keen that she has to stop. Finally she takes advantage of a crab-apple orchard to slip behind a distant tree and remove her trousers. She has pads with her, bought in Singapore. Coming back to the path again, she's greeted by a scowling face.

A line from *Romeo and Juliet* comes to Yu-ying while she approaches him. "O! I am Fortune's fool."

"Look," he says, gazing ahead. "They've left us behind, even the old women have."

"The old women are strong peasants." Yu-ying sits down wearily on the ground.

"Is this any time to rest? Are you going to rest now?"

She looks up at him. "I told you it's my time of the month."

Jin-shi sits down too, snatching up a blade of grass. Slipping it between his teeth, he grinds it, spits it out. "Who knows where we are? I've never seen country like this."

"It's so big."

"That's it, it's big, and there's nothing to see. Back there I thought I saw a few little hills, but what they were they were huts. People live in them. This is not like Siam. At least we put huts on stilts. Can you go on now?"

After another few miles, when she sinks down again by the side of the road, bent over from cramps, he says irritably, "I should have left you in Tsingtao. Then when I finished delivering the message, I'd come back for you. Maybe it's best for me to go on alone and you wait there."

The cramps are as bad as she can remember. Yu-ying feels a cold sweat on her brow, a wave of nausea. Yet summoning up the strength to look at him, to speak in a calm way, she says, "All right, go on. But who will talk for you?"

Glaring at her, Jin-shi sits down at her side and gazes morosely at the stolid brown fields rolling on and on and on into the blue distance.

. . .

The rest of the day follows the same pattern—a mile or so of walking, a forced halt, the excruciating cramps, his complaint, a long tense silence. At twilight, seeing a village up ahead and urged by desperation, Yu-ying knocks on a farmhouse door; she asks for food, shelter. After looking at the young couple, the farmer shuts the door. On the third attempt a young woman agrees to feed them and let them sleep in the mule's stable, but for something other than money, she won't take money. Jin-shi produces two packs of Tsingtao Three Castle cigarettes, which she accepts after a lengthy discussion with an old woman lying on a pallet.

The meal of salted pork fat and wheat buns is washed down with hot water. The mule stable is hardly big enough for the three of them, yet the mule, obviously tired, is docile, and the straw feels good to Yu-ying. It's only after she hears Jin-shi breathing in the slow steady way of sleep that Yu-ying allows herself to think past the pain. He's not as true as steel. Tomorrow, given the chance, she will write down that observation in her book—in English, so if he sneaks a look he won't understand. And she'll also write, "O! I am Fortune's fool." How had she ever thought to love him? And yet glancing at Jin-shi in moonlight, she finds him still attractive. His face, all angular, seems pure, clear. Yet she can't trust him, not even enough to confide in him what has excited her throughout the trying day.

She has not reminded the forgetful boy that Shantung is her father's province. Jinan was his boyhood home, and south of Jinan he had died on the sacred mountain of Tai Shan and south of Tai Shan he had fought destiny from his military encampment at Qufu. It is all here, the past of her father. Yu-ying, curling up to lessen the pain, considers her joss to be good joss, miraculous joss, because events, not her own conscious will, have brought her to the place she wants to be.

34 KUNMING.

In the early days of the Sino-Japanese War, before Pearl Harbor changed everything, men of fanatically held opinions and men without any opinions at all, visionaries and losers, adventurers and drifters, found their way to this almost inaccessible town at the far reaches of southwestern China.

In early 1939 Embree had come to Kunming out of the desire for change, disguised from his own understanding as righteous commitment to the cause of Chinese freedom. One day, having read the brief news accounts in Bangkok papers for months, he'd told Vera that he must fight for China against the Japanese. She had shown only faint surprise at his decision, as if she'd expected it long ago. "Philip, we both know you're a mercenary at heart," she'd said, almost airily, and when he protested that money had nothing to do with his decision, she'd added, "What you hire out for, Philip, is adventure."

And so nine years ago he had come here to Kunming by way of Tonkin, Indo-China, to join up with Colonel Stilwell's army detachment. At the northern border town of Laokai he'd taken a small train at sea level, then ascended some wooded foothills into rugged mountains and gorges, from which vantage point he peered down at the rapids of the Nam-ti and Tachan rivers—lines of silver snaking through jungle of more shades of green than he thought were possible to see. The little train, its paint obliterated by constant rain, chugged four hundred miles to Kunming along perpendicular cliffs through countless tunnels. He can remember to this day his first sight of the aboriginals of Yunnan Province, the Lolos: red trousers, silver trinkets, enormous hats of lacquered straw. They walked along the railroad track, looking as though they needed to stay near it for some kind of contact with this century. To ward off cholera, they carried handkerchiefs filled with camphor carved in the shape of tigers and dragons.

This time he returns not by a rickety little train but by military aircraft, but with no intention of joining anything. Seeing the airfield on the brown plain below, he can remember Kunming in the old days: Obsolescent P-40 Tomahawks, painted in green-and-brown British camouflage, mounted with six machine guns and counting on self-sealing gas tanks and commercial radio sets to get them through, were lined up on the field, ready at five minutes' notice to take on the Japanese air force. Those were romantic days. It was a time when Chennault's squadrons were named the Hell's Angels, the Panda Bears, the Adam and Eves, and their pilots, wearing nonstandard flight gear, fought to the death on one-year commercial contracts for a blind organization called CAMCO. They were true mercenaries until Pearl Harbor turned them into patriots. Embree used to drink with them at the Nam Ping restaurant that specialized in contraband stores of American canned soup and steaks. He came into Kunming after stints on the Burma Road, where he served as interpreter between Chinese construction workers and Anglo-American engineers. Getting out of his dusty army fatigues, taking a shower, he then headed for the Nam Ping. Is it still there? If it is, Embree decides quickly, he won't go there. Too many memories of men long dead.

And yet it would be fun to wander alone through Kunming for a while. He can remember a Singer Sewing Machine shop in the eastern part of town, and near it a Kodak shop that never seemed to have film. Hill to the north. Houses roofed with tile and faced with wood of a bronzed red or a blue-green color. In the market he could buy a peach and smell the pungent strings of Yunnan sausages.

When he debarks from the plane, Embree watches a young man in uniform running toward him. "Mr. Embree." After a brisk handshake, the lieutenant points to a black car parked in front of the tiny airport. "This way, sir."

· · ·

In a dingy room he's briefed by officers from MAGIC.

The Military Advisory Group in China has a small unit of half a dozen men attached to the consulate here, and they seem to view Embree with curiosity and appreciation, as if he affords them a little excitement to break the monotony on this isolated post. Taking turns, they explain the civil war in China without first ascertaining what he already knows. These are lectures from men desperate to understand what they're doing here.

A young marine lieutenant (three MAGIC men sit with Embree at a time and solicitously offer him coffee, Coke, whiskey, and snacks from the American PX) begins by explaining the American attempt, after V-J Day, to turn over captured Japanese territory in China to the Nationalists instead of the Reds.

Next, an army lieutenant offers a long rambling account of the Marshall Mission's attempt in 1946 to persuade Mao and Chiang to form a coalition government. The young officer emphasizes the good will and vision of General Marshall, who hoped ultimately for a third party in China, composed of patriotic liberals, that might provide an effective check on the ambitions of the two main factions.

"Patriotic liberals" is what the officer calls men who never came forward in China. It's a phrase Philip Embree would have applied to certain men in China twenty years ago—especially to the man he himself had served: General Tang Shan-teh. For irony's sake he might tell these eager young men that other political analysts had offered liberalism as a solution long before an American general did; that Chinese thinkers, most of them unknown, unmourned, had sought and died for it decades ago. He might even offer a rather grim opinion of his own: that liberalism has never stood a chance in China, because cataclysmic problems—are there others in such a country?—have always created revolutionary solutions.

Instead, Embree accepts the offer of good Kentucky bourbon.

Now an army sergeant gives his own version of affairs. According to him, the ineptitude of Nationalist army commanders has led to the present military crisis. First of all, after V-J Day, the government demobilized entire armies, while the Communists rushed troops into Manchurian cities and secured them. When the fighting started, the Red strategy was to isolate units of the enemy and dispose of them one by one. So what did the government do? Played into Red hands by breaking up units deliberately. This happened because of professional jealousy: High-ranking generals did not want their equals to have better-trained troops, especially those taught and equipped by American advisers in Burma during World War II. Consequently, men trained to fight together were scattered among poorly coordinated units, whose commanders often penalized them for being elite troops by assigning them to guard duty. Thirty-nine crack divisions suffered this fate. In the Manchurian phase of the civil war, many excellent regiments were assigned to isolated garrisons, where Red troops picked them off.

That wasn't all.

The sergeant, a thin morose-looking man, begins to smile. His recital of corruption and stupidity seems to improve his humor.

In the Nationalist command setup there was no provision for augmenting units depleted by sickness and casualties, except by a most primitive method of conscription: Press gangs rounded up young men in villages, chained them together, marched them off. Many of them, unfed and brutally treated, died before ever reaching a military camp. There was no central training area, no replacement system, no logistics program in the KMT organization. What the quartermasters were best at was acting as a transportation corps for the enemy. Many of them got rich selling to the Reds, who were running out of the Japanese weapons turned over to them by the Russians in 1945. There was, for example, that scandal about high-octane gas, lend-leased from the States, which somehow ended up in a Manchurian warehouse for the Red Army—"But that's a story too long to tell," the sergeant says, grinning.

It's enough to say that American lend-lease was rarely used during World War II against the Japanese; it was hoarded by the Nationalists. Chiang viewed it as a gift he could use in his personal war against the Communist bandits.

"As for combat—" The sergeant rolls his eyes dramatically. Because of so much infighting among commanders, none of them wanted to risk his reputation by risking men and weapons. Retreat was preferable to losing face. And then there was the matter of warlords, who took the opportunity of war to regain a foothold in China—like weeds they simply grew back. All looking after Number One. And no wonder, because weakening themselves in battle against the Reds could mean a subsequent invasion by Chiang.

But even the Gimo's own staff wasn't inspired to fight. The G-3 Department, for example, never learned to commit troops and matériel. They hoarded food, troops, and money—most of it American money—even when they knew that by using what they had they might avert a defeat. They just couldn't waste anything—a chipmunk mentality encouraged by Chiang himself. During fallback, G-3 usually left their equipment neatly stored in dumps rather than destroy and deny it to the enemy.

By the end of his recitation the sergeant is beaming happily.

Someone else continues and someone else continues after he finishes, until Embree has polished off three stiff bourbons. Breaking into a tidy recitation of MAGIC's three-year history in China, he says to three agreeable faces, "Is Wen Yi-to still here in Kunming?"

None of them know who Wen Yi-to is, so they send for the ranking officer, an army captain, who has taken the opportunity of so many lectures to sneak back into his office and catch a nap (or so Embree suspects). Minutes later, after Embree's glass has been refreshed, the captain comes into the room (shutters drawn, a grim bank of three green-shaded bulbs providing light, although outside the consulate building Kunming is as bright and fresh as a new morning).

"Who?" the captain asks, looking bleary-eyed.

"Wen Yi-to. He was a poet, a professor who taught at Lianda here. He and his students walked for two months to get out of Jap territory and set up the school here."

"I've heard of him," the captain says dryly. "He made a lot of anti-government speeches. Became a radical after the war."

"I suspected he might." Embree recalls a lecture given by Wen Yi-to, who did the unthinkable in a Chinese academic setting—chain-smoked furiously. He had a great shock of unruly hair, a distracted manner. Students loved him.

"One day he made a memorial speech for a friend who'd been murdered."

"By KMT agents?"

The captain nods. "So that night, when he left the office of the Democratic League, a couple of hoods shot him. Just down the street here. Shot his son too." The captain, clearing his throat, attempts to smile like someone prepared to broach the real subject of a meeting. "Now," he says. "What we'd like you to do is talk to someone. I know you know him, because he's mentioned you in passing." The captain has hoisted his ample rump onto the edge of the desk, his thick legs dangling. "We want him to do a little of what you're going to do—you know, look over this situation here in China. He's been around, like you. So naturally his opinion of certain things would be invaluable."

"You want me to convince him of that?"

"We'd like that."

"Who is he?"

"Robert Grafton, ex-Army like yourself. He lives here in Kunming."

Chuckling, Embree shakes his head. Of all the men he'd known in those early days of Chungking and Kunming, Bob Grafton would be the one to stay on.

"When can I see him?" Embree asks with his first enthusiasm of the day.

• • •

Embree waits four days. Although every day he asks to leave, MAGIC is adamant. They've got him and they know it. If he wants government help in finding the girl, he's going to pay. He can see the self-satisfaction on their faces. Until he talks to Grafton, they'll keep him here in Kunming. The hitch is Grafton, who's been away on business. His eight trucks constitute the largest cartage firm in all of Yunnan Province. MAGIC has been secretive about the time of his return and the arrangements for this meeting. Embree suspects that setting it up gives them something to do. Kunming is as yet untouched by the civil war and therefore its rustic peacetime atmosphere must be terribly stifling to foreigners. Word is finally brought to his room (in the American compound) that Grafton has returned and will see him.

Embree insists on going unescorted to the Hotel du Lac, although a couple of MAGIC personnel seem disturbed by such independence, as if it signals up something ominous. Unruffled by their paranoia—he tries to sympathize with their backwater life here—Embree remains firm in his decision to go alone.

At the entrance to the compound he turns briefly to regard the consulate's stone gate set in a massive wall of red stucco, and its garden with a fountain, no longer used, in the center of which crouches an alabaster Venus (the place was formerly the home of a Chinese provincial governor). What tales that piece of garden sculpture might tell! With a jaunty wave at faces peering anxiously from a MAGIC window, Embree turns away and begins to walk, secure in the knowledge that an inept shadow from MAGIC will be trailing him.

He has wanted to take this stroll alone because a little freedom might shake loose the depression plaguing him these last few days. With nothing to do but read in the consulate's poorly stocked library, he has worried if MAGIC agents will actually honor their part of the bargain and intercept the young couple when the ship docks in Shanghai. He's asked for confirmation from the unit here, with only vague assurances given in return. The captain has intimated, for that matter, that Embree's recruiting success with Grafton may determine how much help he'll get from MAGIC. Well, he won't have it. He'll junk the whole deal and go it alone, if they try that.

It's a gloomy day, perhaps one of the last overcast days before clear skies follow in unaltered procession until late fall. He suspects the boys in MAGIC would just as soon have a few thunderstorms to add some color to their lives. But Kunming is pretty enough, at least in its better sections. Some houses have glass windowpanes, carved lattices, canary-yellow walls, and sea-green timbered second stories. Along the streets of cobblestone herdsmen are bringing their goats to market. The shepherds wear black skullcaps, blue jackets, baggy trousers. They are ageless men with eyes narrowed from a lifetime of too much sunlight.

He can smell the acrid smoke of charcoal fires from tin smelters that lie just beyond the ancient city walls—walls thirty feet high and ten feet thick, walls that keep visitors from seeing another side of Kunming life: the tin mines. He remembers them from the old days, having seen children who worked in them. He won't ever forget that line of exhausted kids staggering down the road with their throats swollen and their skin green from arsenic poisoning. Sold into slavery by their parents, they lived alongside animals in sheds with no running water or even latrines. No wonder they turned to opium, especially since it was the only cheap and plentiful thing in the province.

Now, as he passes some women bent low by bundles of corded firewood, he smells the heavy cinnamon scent of it blowing across the Kunming neighborhood. Half the people in this province smoke opium. He can never think of it without recalling that day in Qufu when Vera on horseback thrashed a fellow Russian—the Red agent—too drugged on opium to protect himself from her riding whip.

China. How many memories it holds for him. Wen Yi-to shot to death on a Kunming street. Behind that news, for example, there's a memory. Embree hadn't told the MAGIC boys about the time he and Wen got drunk together in the very hotel where he's going to meet Bob Grafton.

> Please tell me who the Chinese are
> Tell me how to cling to history
> Please show me the greatness of my people
> But tell me gently gently

That's a portion of a Wen poem, one of Embree's favorites. The last line is especially poignant. How can any country, even one as large and complex as China, afford to lose such men? Ah, watch it, Embree tells himself. Idealism is a form of ignorance and ignorance breeds fear and fear breeds curiosity and curiosity breeds belief, doesn't it. So ignorance ends in belief, and the foolishness begins again in romantic dedication to an ideal. Something like that. Oh let it be.

He's glad to see the hotel up ahead. The hotel used to have an excellent restaurant serving huge black mushrooms and roast duck and fried bees in butter which, in his opinion, was no worse than most such exotic delicacies. "Grafton," he says under his breath while entering the hotel, "you old bastard, heal me."

· · ·

Grafton rises from a table placed in the cobbled courtyard of the hotel. He's talking before Embree reaches him. "When this kid from MAGIC told me you're in town, I nearly fell off the chair. What in hell you doing with those hoopleheads? Jesus, you haven't changed a bit." Grafton shakes his head in wonder. Since they last met, Grafton's hair has become pure white, but he still parts it in the middle like an old-time Ivy League football player. He's big enough to have played football, bigger now that his waist has expanded to match his broad shoulders. But today Bob Grafton wears glasses with thin wire frames and when he smiles broadly, as they shake hands, a gold tooth flashes.

For an instant it reminds Embree of the gold in General Tang's mouth. There's something faintly comic about gold in the mouths of imposing men, he thinks—but it makes them more human, more accessible, he thinks, while taking the seat opposite Grafton at the table, and he tells himself, Stop thinking. Enjoy an old friend.

They order beer—Grafton says it's not bad—and sit back, regarding each other with the curiosity of men who haven't seen each other in a decade. With generosity too, for they'd been together in Kunming before America entered the war. Theirs was the camaraderie of men who were fighting before Uncle Sam's Greeting filled the mailboxes of New York and Texas.

From here in Asia both joined the Army as members of Stilwell's military team; after the General had been relieved of his Kunming command, they stayed on. Both had worked on the Burma Road as interpreters; both had been assigned to Chinese units in a liaison capacity when the Burma campaign began. That's when they'd lost touch.

Grafton does most of the talking; he's become garrulous—maybe from isolation, like the MAGIC officers. He plunges into a reminiscence of Kunming in the late '30s, when Chennault and the American Volunteer Group set up shop here with the old P-40 Tomahawks.

Grafton quaffs half his beer, motions for the waiter in a dirty white jacket to bring two more. "What was their capability, do you remember that? They had a twelve-cylinder eleven-thousand horsepower Allison engine. I remember that much. They could hit 285 mph at twenty thousand feet."

"I forgot that," Embree says, feeling himself smile from the happiness of being with an old buddy.

"They dove at speeds that tore the wings off Zeros. But they couldn't climb."

"Couldn't they? I forgot."

Grafton shakes his head sadly, as if just discovering this particular limitation of the Tomahawk fighter. "Couldn't climb worth a fuck. How did the boys do a thing with such junk anyway? I remember Duke Hedman shot down five Japs his first time out. Did you know I used to paint some of the shark teeth on the nose of their planes?"

"I remember that."

"They said I had a knack for it. I spent more time in Hostel Number Two where they bunked than I did in our own barracks."

"They were plenty of fun."

"They sure were, those shitkickers. I kept track of a few. Dick Ranny, for example. Got a letter from him, well, it was last year, I think. He's with Pan Am, still flying. Sutcliffe's dead. He bought it during the Ichi-Go Operation. Japs got him on the ground during an air raid somewhere in Honan, I forget where. Blake's gone too. Ranny says he died in a car crash in L.A. Poor dumb asshole. He was dead drunk." Grafton leans back, thrusts his long legs sideways from the table. He has liver spots on his cheeks, heavy creases at the edge of his eyes from a life lived outdoors. "What I'll never forget, though, is the ground crews. Remember how they polished the fuselages with car wax? Got ten more mph out of those mothers?"

"I remember." But he doesn't. And except for their names he doesn't remember Sutcliffe and Ranny. He remembers Blake, though—a tall, rough, obscene, and thoroughly alcoholic pilot who feared nothing.

"What I think," Grafton says, finishing his beer, "about the war is this—" Pausing, he stares at Embree. "Do you ever think about the war any more?"

"Oh, yes. Recently I spent time in Burma. I thought about it all right."

"What I think is, the Japs were too offensive-minded. Didn't know beans about protecting themselves."

"Good in small patrols, though," Embree offers.

"Damn right they were. Better than us at night attack."

"Or infiltration."

"That's true. But they were geared to horse traction, when you come down to it. We beat 'em with wheels."

"Remember the Road?"

Grafton chortles. "Do I remember? Drunk or sober, do I remember?

We laid down seven hundred miles in seven months. That's a fact I'm always proud of, Phil. Of course we had a quarter-million coolies helping out. But the job got done, and that's one hell of a miracle."

They're silent awhile, each absorbing his own recollection of the Burma Road. For Embree the most vivid images are of mountains rising shaggy with scrub pine from a switchback road snaking tortuously into Yung Ping, then toward the Mekong River suspension bridge, just wide enough for a single truck, with its heavy cables embedded at each end in concrete buttresses. River flowing a hundred feet below. Dozens of men fell off those cables into the Mekong. And there was the Salween River bridge, then Lung-ling, a town of monsoon mud and broken axles, as he remembers, and munition trucks churning through Mong Shih and Che-Feng, descending into low hills and swamplands—tiger and malaria country. The images are all jumbled, helped by a third strong beer, but most clearly he remembers the pack coolies lugging salt in hundred-pound blocks; they could do eight to twelve miles a day, bless them, with such a load strapped to wooden supports resting on their backs. And he can't forget the road repair gangs either, recruited locally in southern Yunnan. Every one of them was afflicted with goiters the size of golf balls; that had puzzled him until someone explained there was no iodine in the water of this part of the world. And if he can't remember places, he remembers their names: Tshou-Hsiung, Hsiakwan near Tali Lake. There was a marble tomb somewhere, an ancient temple in a grove of cypress. Over everything, it seems in retrospect, there was a filmy curling mist, either lowland or highland, and when you didn't see outcroppings of rock you saw clumps of marsh grass. Wang Ting, he thinks was its name, was that funny little border town with a gate across the road where China ended and Burma began. In this friendly silence of the hotel courtyard, he thinks of what they all accomplished in those days, a few Brits and Americans, thousands of Chinese. Because of that road Burma remained accessible to China. Munitions from Rangoon were shipped by rail to a depot near Lashio, then loaded on trucks and taken across the border as far as Lung-ling, where other trucks took over. Armenians had the truck concessions. Odd thing to remember. The Burma Road—he'd been part of all that. It's true what Grafton said: There's pride in such a memory. So he remembers Kunming and the Burma Road, but not as well as Grafton, who has made the memory of those days the best part of his present.

• • •

"How about it, Phil—can you see me as a married man? The wife's from Tungch'uang. We've got two boys, Yu-wen and Chen-wu."

"Congratulations." Embree is happy for him.

"Are you still married?"

"You remember I was married? Didn't think I talked about it."

Grafton orders two more beers and adjusts his thin-rimmed Chinese glasses. "You didn't. We all figured you came out here to get away from something."

"From a wife?"

The big man shrugs. Embree figures if the day was sunny, the light would shine on that big gold tooth right in front.

Embree answers his own question. "It's true. I was running away from my wife, from boredom . . ." He decides to be honest with this man. "From failure."

"Most of us were," Grafton declares, grinning. He runs both hands through his unruly white hair; the freedom of his gestures gives him a more boyish look than he'd first shown. "Hey, buddy, do you remember how those fucking Chinese truck drivers could bet? Bet on anything? I remember some of those guys, they'd bet on the registration number of the next truck coming over the hill. They bet on how many flies would light on the hood in a minute. Crazy bastards."

"Where were you in Burma?"

"I worked on the Ledo Road."

"The Stilwell Road," Embree corrects him, using the new name for it.

"The old buzzard's road then. They had plenty of interpreters, so they made a construction man out of me. My military career was spent breaking rocks, laying roads, dodging earthslides."

"You make it sound easy."

"It was." Grafton pours his glass full.

"Bullshit, my friend. Everybody knew about those D-4 bulldozers. I heard you people got to be experts on 40-mm. Bofors AA guns."

Grafton shrugs. "At least I got something out of it. My trucks, all of them, came from Ledo."

"How did you do that?"

"Long story, Phil. But every damn one of them came out of the Ledo Road."

They both laugh softly.

"I've wanted to get me a couple of bulldozers, even those lightweight D-4s we used there, but no dice, nothing. I'd buy one from the States —I can afford it now—but Chiang's government won't give me an import license."

"You're lucky to have the trucks."

"Right." Grafton pounds the table with a large scarred fist. "You can't *believe* how right you are. Goddamn country? I've spent more than thirty years here and still don't understand it—and don't want to. For me it's just a place to make a living," he says with a triumphant smile, as if proud of not caring about his home for three decades. Embree knows the symptoms of a China hand fated to live out his life here.

"The way I see it," Grafton continues, "Yunnan is going to need a lot of roads in the future, what with the tin and coal and iron they've got. And *I'll* build those fucking roads. Got to leave something to the family, right?" He waits until Embree replies, "Right." Then he says, "I don't give a shit who wins, the Reds or Chiang. What's the difference." Grafton is slurring from so much beer. "A Shanghai friend tells me they have an influx of counterfeit American dollars there."

"How is that?"

"My friend figures the Chinese are doing it with German plates. They got some terrific German engravers in Shanghai now."

"What the hell, Bob."

"Sure. Engravers were treated good by the Nazis. Made English and American plates for the Third Reich. Now they've got the same engravers out here in China. Can you beat that? Anyway, I'm staying on. Whoever wins is going to need roads, and who knows better how to build them than a guy who did it with Zeros buzzing him every hour. We built five hundred fucking bridges for the Ledo."

Again they're silent. So Grafton and the others understood why I was here, Embree thinks. They knew why when I didn't.

"OK, old buddy, so they sent you to talk to me."

Here we go, Embree thinks. "That's right. They did."

"Well, then, talk."

"They want you to do what I'm going to do—get a fix on what's happening. Maybe they feel a certain reverence for old China hands."

Grafton snickers.

"Anyway, these people would like us to give them some thoughtful analyses of what the Chinese want when the fighting ends and how America can take advantage of it."

"Sure. I could do that all right," Grafton says brightly. "I mean, who knows the tribals better than I do? I know the Yi, I know the Bai, I know the Naxi pretty damn well, and I speak some of their lingo. But what's in it for me? I get cozy with MAGIC and every goddamn Chinaman this side of heaven will know it. So how do I function around here? I got to stay neutral, buddy. I'm surprised at you."

"I'm doing what I'm doing in exchange, Bob. Favor for favor."

"Ah, they're making a deal. Well, that makes sense." After a sip of beer, Grafton says, "One thing, though. Have you kept up on China?"

"Not in the last few years," Embree admits.

"Let me tell you what MAGIC won't. To keep up on China you have to keep up on American politics."

"How does that go?"

"Dewey and the Republicans want to beat Truman, right? So they discredit Roosevelt's deal at Yalta, the part about the Russians going into Manchuria at the end of the war. The Democrats get blamed for Commies overrunning Asia. You got that? OK, then Chiang Kai-shek decides to blame all his troubles on the Russians getting into Chinese territory. So he links up with the Republicans, because they're both on the same side of the issue, and there you are. And then Pat Hurley gets sent over here for a presidential look-see. He's cheek by jowl with Chiang, and when he meets Mao he won't give the Reds the time of day. The American embassy personnel who tried to bring a little perspective into the matter, they got blitzed, fucked. They didn't agree with Hurley, he went back home and called them a bunch of Commies. Made it damn hard if not impossible to give this Chinese civil war a rational look. You even *breathed* Mao's name you were soft on communism. That's how we've been holding on here in China the last few years. Working for Chiang and the Republicans." Grafton leans forward, surrounded by a forest of tall brown beer bottles. "And if you want to understand the drill, old buddy, you got to consider this too: We're close to giving up on this place."

"China?"

"It's true. We're abandoning China. And it makes sense when you think about it. The cozier we get with the Japs, the less we need China. We're going to drop this messy place. And why not? That's the thinking back in Washington. What they want there, they want to concentrate on Europe and forget about here. As long as China doesn't go Red, we don't give a fuck. Right?"

"I don't know much about American politics."

"Sure. You're like me. You haven't seen the U S of A in years. But out of sight, out of mind won't work any more. I get as much info as I can about the States. Because it affects what happens to me here in old Kunming." Cocking his head, Grafton says, "You simple fuck, they're using you."

"I know that."

"These boys in MAGIC are scared of saying anything, and yet if they don't say something or at least have it down on paper, and the shit hits the Chinese fan, buddy, they get the blame at home for not knowing it was going to happen. So this is the way it is: With the ship sinking, they want guys like you—people who know the country—to come in and say, 'Hey, the ship's sinking,' and they don't have to say anything, yes or no, right? It's your personal opinion. They can write it down and when a senator or somebody says, 'Hey, why didn't you tell us it was sinking?' all they have to do is haul out reports like yours and say, 'Here it all is, Senator. You had the information all the time.' And what about you, if you tell the truth out here? Maybe *you're* branded a Red—you *will* be if it keeps going this way. And if you're not, well, what good did you do?"

"Thanks, Bob. But I'm getting something out of it, and I don't give a damn what they call me in the States."

"Sure of that?"

"I'm sure."

"Don't be too sure. There might come a time—"

"I have to do this, Bob. It's an obligation. But thanks for the advice —for the friendship."

Grafton, shrugging, puts both hands decisively on the table. "OK, Phil. You always were a guy who knew what he wanted."

That perverse opinion makes Embree want to laugh. Instead he changes the subject. "Tell me," he says, "how are the tin mines doing?"

"They're about the only thing doing around here."

"And the kids?"

"Still working there. New supplies of them all the time. Nothing's changed."

• • •

At the consulate, Embree tells the MAGIC captain that his efforts to recruit Robert Grafton have failed. He gives no further explanation but demands a report from Shanghai concerning the whereabouts of the young couple from Bangkok. "I mean it," Embree says without smiling.

Late the following day a cable from Nanking arrives, informing Embree that the agents thus far have had no luck. Another cable, time-dated a few minutes later, requests MAGIC KUNMING to arrange a military flight for Mr. Philip Embree, destination Nanking.

• • •

Three, four days pass at the Nanking embassy. Each morning Embree walks between the travelers' palms that flank the central building and enters the Political Section, which is housed in a drab wing behind swinging half-doors. Most of each day he sits in a room with the American flag at his side and a bespectacled Harry S. Truman gazing severely down at him from a black frame. During this waiting period MAGIC gives him something to do: He interviews Chinese who are brought into the shop. "To sharpen up your use of current slang," a MAGIC officer explains.

All of the people have come from Red territory, from so-called Liberated Areas, and possess first-hand knowledge of agrarian reform under the Communists. They describe Mao's ability to mobilize the peasantry for peace as well as war. They explain the skill of cadres in bringing order into villages where only weeks ago there was chaos. Embree soon realizes that MAGIC has selected these people with care for him to interview. Their stories add up to a coherent if biased appraisal of China in the present crisis. MAGIC obviously wants him to see the Nationalists as hopelessly corrupt, the Communists as potentially effective. Conclusion desired? By withdrawing support from Chiang Kai-shek and by maintaining friendly rapport with Mao, the American government can keep a foothold in Chinese affairs.

So Grafton was right. Through a neutral observer MAGIC wants such a report on the records—sponsored by but independent of its organization—to cover any investigation later on into its own competency. Philip Embree is not surprised; from the outset he had supposed that his participation would have as its aim the protection of people in power. Isn't that what a mercenary is for?

And yet ultimately he's indifferent to such intrigue. After all, his is quite another mission. And then a cable sent from Bangkok is transmitted to him from Shanghai:

ARRIVE SHANGHAI 4 JUNE BOOKED PALACE VERA

So bad heart notwithstanding, she has set out to do what he has failed to do.

Embree demands to see the operations officer.

When he and Major Heflin are seated in the operations office with cups of tea and tinned cookies, Embree says, "I made a deal with your people in Bangkok. Favor for favor. So far your boys in Shanghai haven't found the girl, and here I am stuck in Nanking."

Heflin, a slim little man in impeccable uniform, nods pleasantly. "It isn't easy to find someone in Shanghai. But they're trying."

"That's not good enough. If they can't do it, I'll have to."

"I can understand your frustration."

"Can you? The people you have me interviewing have already talked to plenty of Americans. They know what to say, what opinions to have. This is a waste of time."

"I certainly do appreciate your impatience. There was a hitch in Washington about your assignment. I'm sorry."

"Someone doesn't want me running around China?"

Heflin replies with a faint smile.

Putting his cup of tea down, Embree leans forward in preparation for rising. "The deal's off."

"Wait a moment. Please. We did have to check you out. With the language and so forth. You do very well, especially with Northern Chinese. Some Americans know the West and the South because they were there in the war, but once they get out of Nanking and Shanghai, not many of them know North China, certainly not the way you do. And you're politically neutral. We like that. When you talk to people, it won't be with an ax to grind."

For a startling instant Embree thinks of the ax in his suitcase.

"We like the fact that you know China over a long period of time. We like your war record too." Heflin pours more tea, prolonging the interview. "Perhaps you're a hidden patriot, although I understand it's not something you'd admit to. But you could make a real contribution. You're capable of finding out what the man on the street feels."

That imagery amuses Embree. Outside of the large cities there's no man on the street in China; there's the man on the dirt road, the cobbled path, the muddy lane.

"You have no idea what a service you can perform," Heflin adds.

Perform for MAGIC, Embree thinks. But the major's temperate style has mollified him. "I'll carry out my part of the deal, but my stepdaughter comes first. If your men can't find her, I must."

"Your feeling about that is understandable. We'll give you a week on your own. And you'll have access to facilities—plane travel, bank account, that sort of thing."

"Three weeks."

Heflin laughs. "In three weeks the ball game could be over out here. Two."

"I want to begin in Shanghai. I may need to go into Shantung."

"I'll go along with that. But we want you contacting us here or in Shanghai in two weeks. I'm trusting you."

"Don't worry. You'll have what you want."

Heflin, after a moment of thought, returns Embree's smile.

· · ·

Next morning, on a hunch, Embree checks with the communications officer at the embassy about receipt of that cable from Vera in Shanghai. According to the date-time stamp, it had been received more than a week ago. The officer claims that the cable hadn't been sent promptly from Shanghai; it was a failure of transmission. Apology: "wartime conditions." Embree decides that MAGIC NANKING merely held the cable until word came from Washington that they could use him on a mission. They still aren't sure where to send him, however, so Heflin is letting him have a couple of weeks for himself. When he returns to MAGIC, they'll extract from him the kind of report they want.

Heflin made that clear at dinner last night. "We'd like you to go into Red areas. We're not sure which ones yet. The situation is fluid."

"It might be hard to get in."

"Not as hard as you might think. The Reds have been receptive to foreigners so far."

"But the more they win the less friendly they might become. At any rate, what you'll want is for me to talk to people."

"Especially Red officers, company and battalion levels. We want to know about tactics, about relationships among officers and men. We want to know just how effective the Reds are." He paused, waiting for Embree to respond.

And Embree responded in what he knew was the right way. "I think I know how to begin. I mean, I already know their philosophy of combat. They make a breakthrough at the weakest point, then undertake a series of quick battles, and withdraw. They like to isolate enemy units and bring superior firepower to bear. They don't fight battles of attrition."

Heflin lifted his eyebrows in mild surprise.

"Nothing strange in knowing that. The Reds were fighting that way against the Japs back in 1939. There are just more of them now, that's all. But what you want is names, places, actual interviews. You want the philosophy fleshed out. You want it on record that you had specific knowledge of the Reds in the summer of 1948."

Heflin nodded happily. "You're the man for the job."

"If I don't find my stepdaughter, I want your people to keep trying."

"They'll keep trying."

"Then we're really in business."

"By the way"—Heflin sat back in his chair and smiled—"do stay out of trouble when you're looking for your stepdaughter. You could have more trouble with the Nationalists than with the Reds."

"Funny thing"—Embree matched Heflin's smile with his own—"in the briefings your people never told me what happens if I need bailing out."

"Yes, I suspect they haven't. Because there can't be any bailing out."

Embree was not so much surprised as concerned with not showing surprise. He smiled at the news.

"I'm sorry," Heflin said. "With your war record you can appreciate our position."

"Don't appeal to the 'hidden patriot' in me, Major. It may not be there." Embree was still smiling. "If I land in jail or anything else unpleasant, you wash your hands of me?"

"Have to."

"Just so I know." Embree had not stopped smiling, even when he added, "But don't tell me you're sorry."

• • •

Tomorrow he flies to Shanghai, free, as far as MAGIC is concerned, for two weeks.

In these last hours he takes a rickshaw through the wide boulevards of the city. He looks happily at the plane trees on either side of the cobbled way that's shared by his rickshaw with army trucks, horse-drawn wagons, a few cars. It's damn good to be away from MAGIC.

Indeed, recently he's felt the old boredom and frustration of army life. But at least through MAGIC he's obtained a document that associates him with the World Health Organization. Yesterday there was a long discussion among some of the officers about what sort of identity he should assume in forward areas. UNRRA, the old dodge for military agents, has just been disbanded. WHO is new in China; that might upset Chinese officials who suspect anything new. On the other hand, it deals with epidemic control and sanitation; the Chinese will like that even if it is new. So Philip Embree has become a field representative of WHO.

He also has a new citizenship. That, too, was reason for debate at MAGIC. Finally they lit upon a Dutch passport, a logical choice considering that Chinese officials would most likely know nothing about a Dutchman. Someone with a wry sense of humor suggested a name for Embree: Hans Brinker. He of the Silver Skates.

At leisure now, perhaps his last for a long time, Embree drives out to Purple Mountain for a look at the huge mausoleum of Sun Yat-sen. On the way he passes the Imperial Avenue of the first Ming emperor, lined with stone camels, elephants, and mythical beasts. It reminds him of the Kong cemetery of Qufu. Will he ever see it again as he saw it with the General? The Chinese know how to honor the dead not only with stone monuments and poetry but with nature as well; even the trees in a Chinese cemetery look reverent. It's something about these people that Embree admires: their way of suggesting that the dead participate in the lives of the living. And not through nightmare or delusion. They don't have Harrys in their lives, they have philosophers and poets and grand-fathers looking out of the mists at them, speaking gently, gently, as Wen Yi-to would have it.

The immense monument to Sun Yat-sen heaves into sight through a stand of trees. There's a broad tree-lined avenue leading to hundreds of gently ascending granite steps; he climbs them to the Memorial Hall along with a number of other visitors. Many of them are government soldiers in padded blue jackets, faded pants, soiled cloth leggings. A lot of them have the tired eyes and puckered lips that come with malnutrition. Twenty years ago, when China had been even poorer than it is now, the soldiers of General Tang's army were better fed and clothed. The General would be proud of his men today, seeing these. Up through the bright afternoon Embree climbs. Reaching the top, he glances at the white marble walls and blue-tiled roof of the monument, then briefly studies a bas-relief on the pedestal of the tomb, some words praising Sun, some words of Sun. Ideals hacked out of stone, as lifeless as stone, and yet there's something grand and poignant about the attempt to immortalize a man who was a stalwart patriot but a second-rate thinker.

Strolling outside, he enjoys the mountain view across a wooded park. Given a different set of circumstances, he wonders if Tang Shan-teh might not have earned a like honor by now—an imposing tomb on a mountainside.

Embree sits on a step, elbows on knees, head in cupped hands. At a time like this, in the old days, he might have turned to Harry for company, but Harry no longer speaks to him, Harry has become a delusion. But stirred by his mission—the one assigned him by Vera, not by MAGIC—he feels in these moments of relaxation a need for perspective.

What if Vera had left him in Hong Kong and returned to China? What if Tang had lived? What if she had rejoined the General? Damn interesting questions. Answered affirmatively, they might have given him a better chance in life. Looking back at those years with Vera, he regards them as episodes in a dream of inertia such as that universal nightmare in which people slog through mud, unable to move fast enough to avoid disaster. Before meeting Vera, he'd been alive, especially here in China. He'd learned to sleep on a horse, to wield an ax, to thrive in a Chinese army—improbable accomplishments, but all his and true. And yet during life with Vera he drifted through meaningless days, months, years, excoriating himself by doing as little as possible. Thinking of it now, Embree wonders if, in fact, it was something of an accomplishment too—willing himself to be a weak, irresolute man. Thus did he punish Philip Embree.

Getting up, he brushes the dust of Nanking from his trousers.

What he has yet to face is Sonia, if he finds her. If? He will. He must. But then how can he persuade her to return to Bangkok? If Vera is in Shanghai—she could be at the Palace Hotel by now—perhaps she'll think of something. He can think of only one thing to convince the girl: her mother's health. But will Vera let him play on Sonia's sympathy? That woman who refused to speak the French language in protest against French snubbing of the 1920 White Russian government-in-exile? It's doubtful. Vera's pride may well come before anything. Or may not. He can't know this woman. No wonder he once risked everything for her.

With a sigh, Embree descends the stairway toward the waiting rickshaw. On the way down a strange thing happens: Without thinking about it, he pronounces the word "Harry" out loud, as if someone is walking beside him. Has Harry returned? Of course not, he tells himself. Yet in China the dead are never far away. Perhaps Harry is not a delusion after all, but something like a sane, vivid memory.

35 VERA STANDS AT the rail as the steamer comes twisting in along the Whangpoo River toward Shanghai, whose massive buildings shimmer whitely in the morning haze.

A week ago, standing at this same rail, she'd watched the ship enter the forty-mile approach to Saigon. The coastal steamer had glided past the tip of land called Cap Saint-Jacques into the Mekong River's narrow channel. From the rail Vera had shaded her eyes and squinted a long time at spired pagodas rising out of the deep green delta. The huts with garden plots cleared of elephant grass and creeping vines reminded her of klong life in Siam. This, too, was a ripe tropical land, steamy and vast. She noticed evidence of war: French forts with their slimy moats and coils of barbed wire lying against walls pockmarked by bullets. Turret guards showed little interest in the ship, although some of the foreign passengers waved gaily at them.

Dense green walls of stolid mangrove gave way to patches of human motion along the bank. Women in their waterfront huts and fishermen in their sampans halted at work for a brief inspection of the steamer. It chugged through swamp water toward the squat Socony plant, placed like a sentry at the entrance to Saigon Harbor. Docks appeared. Vessels ranging from bumboat to luxury liner were tied to piers or to one another, and the noise of winches grated arrhythmically through the humid air.

Changing to port side, Vera saw the white buildings of Saigon, many with Parisian awnings. Some of them flew the tricolor. In blocky European grandeur the yellow-walled Majestic Hotel stood at the foot of the Rue Catinet, a boulevard lined with chestnut trees and French signs. If Sonia were here, she thought, they'd stand together at the rail and make plans for the day. "They call Saigon the Paris of the East," she'd say. "We'll test that reputation—the stores, restaurants. Until you see Paris, this is the best we have." It might encourage Sonia to yearn for Europe, for the art and beauty of another world.

"Mistress!"

She turned to see Rama rushing toward her. Always to or from. His hair stood up like the bristles of a brush. Umbrella, open, thrust forward like a shield as he ran toward her.

"You will be getting too much sun, Mistress." Raising the flared black object above her head, he stared at the pier sliding toward them. "I couldn't find you out. I looked just down there and up there too." Rama waved his free hand at the ship's bridge. "You must not be getting too much sunshine. In this heat you must take liquid, take rest. You must not be too keen on the sun, Mistress. Not with your skin."

Vera basked in his solicitude. Her mother used to fret and scold in the same apprehensive manner. Odd, but she'd been standing bare-headed in the sunlight; in all her Asian years, Vera had never let her skin go unprotected until now.

• • •

Late that afternoon, on the veranda of the Majestic Hotel, she sipped an aperitif and read a Saigon newspaper in the light still available. The headline loomed at her: LA MENACE DE BLOCUS DE BERLIN! Soviet Russia was threatening to shut down communication between that city and the rest of West Germany. "Bolsheviks," she said under her breath.

On the opposite page was something about escalation of fighting in Indonesia, where Communist and Nationalist groups, while squabbling among themselves, were battling a Dutch attempt to regain full control of the East Indies. Names of the leaders involved and their factions would require a great deal of sorting out, so Vera turned to the next page.

This was local news. Having failed to secure support from French politicians on his recent junket to Paris, former emperor Bao Dai hadn't returned to Saigon. That somewhat puzzling observation led to a general discussion of Indochinese politics. A problem for local Indochinese leaders was their reputation for being inexperienced and corrupt. A predictable observation in this French paper.

Vera turned the page.

Here was news of Korea. The United Nations had sponsored elections there recently. Conservatives under Syngman Rhee had won a majority of seats in the Constituent Assembly and in consequence had promised to write a new constitution, in spite of protests by pro-Communists in the North.

Bolsheviks everywhere. She riffles glumly through the remaining pages.

Chiang Kai-shek had just been inaugurated in Nanking as President of China, even while the Red drive through North and Central China continued. Kaifeng was expected to fall any day to the Communists.

And there were bloody student protests in Shanghai against American aid for the rehabilitation of Japan. Rioting. Bloody. Was Sonia there?

British railroads nationalized.

She put the newspaper down and wondered fearfully if Sonia was in Shanghai. Was the girl walking innocently down a street somewhere? Around the corner cascaded hundreds of angry students carrying banners and brandishing clubs . . .

Picking up the paper again, Vera rattled it vigorously. At least there was a cultural page.

Olivier Messiaen's *Turangalila Symphony* had just premièred in Paris. A new film by Jean Cocteau, *Les Parents Terribles*, was drawing mixed notices. Where was her daughter now? Roaming Shanghai, jostled by berserk students?

And everyone was praising Malraux's *Psychologie de l'Art*. It was a book she must read.

And she was thinking again of Sonia, only not in Shanghai but in Bangkok, long ago. They used to picnic beside the klongs. They played cards and napped under the broad shade of rain trees, so close together they could hear each other breathe, their warm arms touching slightly, making a sweet wet spot between them. Where? In Shanghai? Or perhaps she's now in Shantung Province, searching out the myth of her father. In Jinan? Taian? Qufu? With that boy?

"The news is not worth reading."

She looked up. A tall, bearded man, who had just spoken to her in French, was smiling down.

"Permit me, Madame?" he asked, and before she could protest had seated himself opposite her at the table. "These days it's seldom you find someone worth talking to on the veranda of the Majestic. I thank you for letting me share the end of the day with you. Believe me, it's a privilege."

It was an elegant little speech and drew a smile from Vera Rogacheva Embree. She has always been aware of her weakness for a display of polish, a word of flattery. Yet she has always considered it a small weakness. She judges him to be fifty-five or sixty. Handsome for the age.

The bearded man called to a waiter. "What the lady has, so will I," he said grandly.

• • •

An hour later, after they'd watched the sunset, Vera knew the outlines of his life, because Monsieur Jules Langlais was a talkative if, fortunately, not a boastful man. Half the year he lived here as a supplier of prawns, frogs, and crabs to French provisioners. Half the year he lived in Saint-Cloud, just outside Paris, with his second wife, who repaired antique dolls, especially *baigneurs*, and was famous for reconstructing *têtes en porcelaine*.

Baigneurs. For a few moments Vera remembered lovingly her own French dolls, dressed with care and carried in the crook of her pudgy arm through the rooms of home.

She gathered that Jules and his wife were linked more by finance than by passion, but, of course, men often give such an impression to other women. It was a long time since Vera had analyzed the strategies of men with women, and she found it pleasant, like reminiscing with an old friend.

When, suddenly, in a discussion of Saigon inflation, he asked her to have dinner with him, Vera balked no longer than a few moments before accepting. In her Shanghai days she'd often dangled "Maybe" in front of a man like a carrot in front of a donkey. When he was on the verge of losing interest, she'd accept as if giving him an undeserved gift.

In the trishaw she watched Jules' hands—long, thin, pale, aristocratic. Much like the hands of her father's friends in Petrograd. During her childhood such men had placed her on their laps and given her bonbons, feeding her from long slim pale fingers much like those used by Jules Langlais to light her cigarette.

He had a long, rather somber face but a fine smile. Evening lights along the boulevard brought out the sculptured lines of his nose, cheekbones, jaw. Handsome face, really. She had not often studied a man's face in recent years. Her eyes had been filled with the broad cheekbones tapering to a delicately pointed chin and the soft brown unlined flesh of Siamese girls. As she rode with Jules Langlais, Vera keenly felt his presence. Bulkier seated than he'd seemed standing, Jules was like many of the men with whom she'd driven through Shanghai nights toward restaurants, cabarets, bedrooms. No, not that tonight. Yet she felt herself smiling, as the busy streets of Saigon flowed past their trishaw and he droned on about the little war in Indochina.

Dinner was lovely in a bistro on the Rue Catinet, a boulevard reminiscent of the Paris she'd seen as a child with her mother. On a tinny phonograph an Indochinese waiter played the *chansons populaires* of postwar France. Through the little bistro floated the words and music of war-weary bitter-sweet Paris, of Greco, Piaf, Trenet, Mouloudji, Brassens. The music brought to Vera renewed contact with France. She almost told her dinner partner something strange—which would have been incomprehensible to him: that once upon a time she'd refused to speak French in symbolic revenge against a government that had turned its back on White Russian exiles; that she had spoken French again only to help her daughter get along in the world; but that tonight, here in an Asian city, she again felt the elegance, the profundity, the comfort of her European heritage. Vera said none of this. She drank a good burgundy while Jules Langlais described to her his recent meeting in Paris with a rebel Indochinese leader.

"Have you heard of Ho Chi Minh?"

"He's a Bolshevik?"

"Among other things. His real name's Nguyen That Thanh. But aside from Ho Chi Minh, he's also called the General, Nguyen Ai Quoc, and Mr. C. M. Hoo." Jules Langlais laughed. "He isn't the gangster you might think from so many aliases. I've never met anyone like him. In Paris a ministry wanted someone who knew this part of the world to have dinner with him, so I was one of six chosen. We picked him up at his hotel, the Royal Monceau—quite fancy for a man who'd spent most of his life in jail or the jungle. They say he weighs a hundred pounds, but I'd take away ten of that. Spoke excellent French. Really excellent. Quoted Hugo and Verlaine. They say he did his own laundry in the Royal Monceau. Can you imagine? Well, after sitting with him in a restaurant for three hours, I'd believe almost anything of him. A few bottles of wine, and he debated the existence of God. Was against. Very witty, as I recall. Throughout the evening we all spoke French, so he didn't realize I could speak Vietnamese." Jules poured himself more wine.

He was drinking too much, Vera observed. It comforted her to think Jules Langlais had flaws. Otherwise it would be almost impossible to refuse him, even though she was a middle-aged woman with a bad heart.

"Finally, at the end of the evening, I turned to him and said in Vietnamese, 'If we last through this cold winter, we shall see spring.' The little fellow's mouth fell open. You see, it was a quote from one of his own poems. He'd recited it during a broadcast on *Voice of Vietnam* in December of 1946. I remember that broadcast very well, because it was a call for national resistance. From that moment on, the Vietminh have been formidable. So I recalled the line. Perhaps I was helped by the line from François Villon. Perhaps Ho got it from there—he certainly knows French poetry. At any rate, I quoted it, and I must say, that's the only time in my life I really surprised anyone. But I'd like to try again."

"Try what?" she asked with a smile.

"To surprise someone. Is it surprising to hear I'm attracted to you?"

And so it started.

Eventually, she refused him. In the trishaw back to the pier, Jules Langlais translated his masculine disappointment into political gloom: The French controlled the cities, but the Vietminh had the countryside. He went on with it, voicing two rejections simultaneously: hers of him, the Indochinese people of the French. During the day in Crabs—the latest in amphibious vehicles—Legionnaires scoured the delta for terrorists and rarely found any. What they found were farmers plowing with buffalo. But after dark, many of those same farmers murdered French sentries with bamboo stakes. They threw adders and cobras through barrack windows. They planted crude bombs in open-air cafés. "It's a dirty war," Jules Langlais concluded dejectedly.

As colored lights, strung along the port strakes of her ship, came into view at the end of Rue Catinet, he said, "Are you sure? We've had a wonderful evening so far."

"Wonderful."

"You leave tomorrow. Next week I go back to France. We may never meet again."

"Yes, it's not probable we will."

"There's nothing to lose, is there? And everything to gain—to be together, to have the memory."

"You're a sweet man, Jules Langlais." For the first time Vera touched him—his thin, pale hand. How long had it been since last she'd touched a man with anything resembling intimacy? "I like you very much. But no."

And later, lying in the bed of her cabin, Vera wondered why she'd refused this attractive man. What, really, was there to lose? She had no one to be loyal to—not to Wanna any more, surely not to Philip Embree. To the memory of Shan-teh? No. Unlike her daughter, she didn't live in fantasies of the past. Was she afraid of her heart giving way? Nonsense. She wouldn't fear for her health if love, even a night's love, was at stake.

Perhaps, through the years, she'd been more isolated than she knew. Perhaps, like an inexperienced woman, she had tonight backed timidly away from a sexual encounter, fearful of the unknown. The possibility amazed her. She took from it a new sense of herself, as if by searching for her daughter she was renewing—or she might even say recreating— her own life.

This sense of reawakening takes possession of Vera a week later, when the ship rounds the last bend in the Whangpoo, a river bringing her back to Shanghai. Twenty years ago, in this city, she'd been whore and concubine. Now she looks anxiously past the dock area, as if through the labyrinthine jumble of lanes and buildings she might see old customers, old lovers, the flotsam and jetsam of her youth.

. . .

Waiting for her at the front desk of the Palace Hotel is a message on American Consulate stationery: "Mr. Philip Embree will contact you as soon as he arrives in Shanghai."

As soon as he arrives? Vera is furious. In two weeks he has not yet arrived? Has he, like the romantic young fool he'd once been, put his trust in men who won't lift a finger in his behalf? Furious, she is furious, and for a few distressing moments can feel a constriction in the center of her chest, a little fist tighten in warning.

Later, standing at the window of her fifth-floor suite, looking down at the river traffic on the Whangpoo, she blames herself for being equally gullible by putting her trust in such a gullible man. He, the fool, is out there working for the Americans, maybe risking his life for them in the adolescent belief that they'll help him in return. Or maybe he really knows better, but accepts the premise of mutual aid between himself and the Americans as an excuse for running away again. Meanwhile, Sonia is out there too, as vulnerable as a moth, following a boy far more gullible and therefore far more dangerous than anyone the girl has ever known.

Twenty-one years ago, when there was no Sonia, Vera had stood at a similar window in this hotel and stared down with Shan-teh at a scene that has scarcely changed from that day to this one. The boats and ships, those at this moment within her view, may well be the same ones they had watched before turning to a bed together for the first time. She notices a steamer come chugging along, its motor sounding like an asthmatic dog. That dilapidated old river steamer, with barges secured to its sides, coming perhaps from Chungking, may have taken the same downstream course two decades ago, its hull unpainted then as now, amidships shaded by an awning that must have flapped above it long before the General and she had ever met, the steamer's makeshift toilet still the same hole in the same platform swaying over the stern and enclosed by a canvas screen, the same tattered old canvas screen; perhaps only the goods and passengers have changed. On Soochow Creek, not more than a few hundred yards northward, conceivably even the same lighters are being poled, discharging oil drums and cottons and lumber alongside the same old houseboats lashed together with the same old hawsers; only the drifting wisps of smoke from cooking fires on the sterns have changed; and perhaps even the same trousers and blouses, now mere rags, have been threaded along the same bamboo poles to dry on the bows. Does anything change in China except faces?

There's at least one change in the harbor—a gunmetal-gray American warship, flying the red-white-and-blue flag with its stars and stripes. It's anchored out there among the sculled sampans and web-sailed junks. Americans. She hates them. They have connived to remove what help she might have had in finding her daughter.

Waving her hand in a quick little gesture of thwarted desire, Vera stares at the bed. It was on such a bed in this same hotel that Shan-teh's arms encircled her for the first time; and it was later, while those same arms encircled her, that together they made the child she now searches for. Immense with the implications of a lifetime's history, the thought calms her. It's too huge and complex, adazzle with time and fate and death and hope, for her to consider, along with it, such a fleeting thing as frustration. Vera sits on the edge of her bed and gazes slowly around the room: the brass door plate, the heavy glass counter on the dresser, the threadbare rug, the mahogany door leading to the little baggage room, the dark wall paneling, and finally the ornately framed mirror in which she can see herself—the face not yet deeply lined, but lacking the softly textured skin of youth; the eyes steady and solemn and still limpid enough to hint of sexual promise; but the mouth set in a tight line of control, as if any moment it might open in a scream. Get up, she tells the image. Get up, do something.

So within half an hour, having called Rama from the servants' hotel dormitory, she has returned to the waterfront, facing away from the Bund and its gray Victorian buildings. Sitting on a bale of cotton, with Rama holding up his umbrella to shade her from the afternoon sun, Vera doesn't hear at her back the noise of trams rattling on their wires or of taxis honking; her attention is fixed on the narrow piers, where coolies lug drums and sacks and bales and other cargo from the bowels of docked ships, where passengers debark, each of them examined by her anxious eyes, each of them holding for her the faint, wild hope of being Sonia.

The next day, having stored the other luggage, she sets out with Rama, who carries for them a single suitcase. They are going by train to Soochow, then Nanking, and with any luck northward into the province of Shantung.

Nothing will happen here in Shanghai; of that she's now convinced. If the Americans put two agents at every pier on both sides of the Whangpoo River, they could not reasonably cover the departure of every passenger on ships entering Shanghai. The procedure, clearly, is hopeless. All night she had considered what to do, watching the harbor lights shoot up from the waterfront to streak the ceiling of her room. She watched the patterns of light ebbing and flowing like tides, until thoughts themselves seemed like the motion of water in her mind: ceaseless, unformed, probing. And then toward dawn she sat upright, decisively. It was suddenly clear.

Sonia's heart will lead her to the farmland of Shantung, the sacred mountain there, the birthplace of Confucius. To the myth itself, to General Tang, to her father.

In the black oval of the mirror, as yet unlit by daybreak, Vera sees nothing, yet addressing the unseen image of herself, she says aloud, in a voice of command, "Now do something."

• • •

Experience has taught Vera only too well that travel during wartime is a slow, agonizing process of extracting one mass of people from one place and depositing it, half-dead, at another. She has braced herself for the two-hour train trip to Soochow—anticipating it to feel like two terrible days—yet to her surprise the first-class coach is truly first-class and not fully booked. At least one thing is certain: People aren't desirous of traveling in this direction, toward the site of potential battles in Central China. And so for the courageous few, the travel is deceptively like peacetime on the westward-bound train. The lace curtains are clean; a lime plant sits on the little table between red leather seats; and a coach attendant in white with his buttons done up neatly to his chin serves tea from a porcelain pot.

Rama sits opposite her, tensely studying the *North China Daily News* for reports of drought in South India. Indeed, since arriving in China, he has pleaded with her to check the Chinese newspapers as well for any information. The chance of drought in South India seems to consume his energy, perhaps to the extent, Vera suspects, of preventing him from noticing anything at all during the train ride: groves of mulberry trees and fields of yellow rape weed and ponds filled with water-chestnut plants. She wishes he'd enjoy the best of China: its countryside in the full bloom of summer. She wishes her daughter were here too, beside her, and together they'd watch the river scows being poled along the network of little canals. "Look at him there," she'd tell Sonia, and to- gether they'd have a glimpse of a farmer carrying buckets of water to his rice fields at a quick rhythmic gait, head thrust forward, eyes fixed on the ground ahead, hands gripping the pole that bobs gently, like a twig in the ripples of a brook.

Closer to Soochow there are more waterways, some of them narrow rivers thicketed by slim poles holding up fishing nets, and ancient camel- back bridges, and flat-bottomed barges loaded with cement or melons or timber or vegetables. War? It's still difficult for Vera to believe it can exist side by side with such fecund pastoral charm and utility.

"Look at the trees," she tells the imagined Sonia. "In China there are trees, always trees, set in rows. They aren't great tangled bundles of leaf and branch such as we have in Siam, but they thrust out of the soil here, darling, with thin trunks and delicate leaves, coronas of them. They're clean, bright, slim creatures, aren't they. They create vistas like you'll see in Europe. Let them lead your eyes a long distance outward, a long way. They define the landscape rather than complicate it. Do you agree?"

And Sonia might or might not.

"Rama," Vera says to the dark young man, who is staring at his folded hands. "Look. It's quite beautiful."

"Mistress?" In an instant he recovers himself. "Ah, on this side is quite beautiful. Quite beautiful, isn't it. Do they have droughts?"

"Oh yes."

"Like those on my side?"

"I'm sure they're just as bad."

Nodding, he falls silent again, and the promise of interest fades from his eyes.

"There's no news about a drought in your part of India," she assures him. "Perhaps it won't happen."

"Ah, Mistress, it will be happening. But I am asking God for mercy."

"That's all we can do."

"Yes, Mistress," he agrees. "But when you are praying to God with- out success, you might turn to another."

"How is that done?" she asks with a smile.

"I pray to Narayana. If he is not granting my request, then I might be turning to Lord Shiva," Rama explains defiantly. "Anyway, the gods are one, and they will do what is best. And I am thinking perhaps drought won't be happening too fiercely this year."

On that faint note of hope, Rama turns to the window, trying to arouse in himself an interest in the passing scene, but Vera can see that his attempt will fail, and soon enough he's staring again at his folded hands, seeing visions she would not want to share with him.

• • •

She knows the old saying: "The Heavens have their Paradise, but the Earth has its Soochow." Indeed, as the train pulls into Soochow station, allowing her to see to the northwest, shimmering through the haze of sunlight, the shape of Tiger Hill, Vera feels the sort of traveler's excitement which an old and famous city seems always to arouse. She feels it, although this isn't her first visit here. To the left now, just ahead of the slowing train, she has a glimpse of the nine-story Northern Pagoda.

She had gone there with a man more than twenty years ago. Swede, Italian, Englishman, Japanese? She can't remember who brought her here. So many men.

But, of course—she remembers now. Erich Luckner had brought her here for a weekend in . . . was it the spring of 1926? Purple flowers blooming in fields during the train ride. No one in the compartment, all foreigners, knew what the flowers were. Purple flowers and yellow rape weed—just like today—and then from the train window the same view of Tiger Hill and Northern Pagoda. She'd wanted to see the famous gardens and canals of Soochow—the Lingering Garden, the Humble Administrator's Garden, the Pavilion of Pines, and especially the Garden of the Master of Fishing Nets—but Erich was more interested in the Nanlin Hotel, where they could stay in bed all day and have finely sliced eel with mushrooms brought to their room in lacquered baskets.

Where is he now, with his electric fans and weapons for sale? Perhaps he loved her then, more than the others did. He'd been filled with a dream of going home to Germany. She can't remember where in Germany. But he used to run his hands through blond hair and fret about money needed to get him back there. He would always be short of money, would always dream of saving it, having forgotten the money he'd already spent on her—or she'd stolen from him to protect herself from heartless Shanghai. Where is Erich Luckner now? Perhaps dead, as most of them must be—surely Madam Lotus, that wonderful whoremistress who read Gogol and could have stepped from one of those 1930s movies about an Orient that never existed except in Hollywood and Shanghai; and the girls of that brothel, of other brothels, the chance companions of planned orgies; and of course Yu-ying, the dearest woman Vera has ever known, although a whore like herself and unlike herself an opium addict, whose name Sonia has now innocently taken for her own because it too has come from the glittering maze of legend: Yu-ying, her mother's good friend and a most imperious beauty, who for twenty years has been described as a very great lady of Shanghai, adored by many men, attained by only one! Ah, the folly of storytelling, Vera thinks as the train lurches to a halt.

Before departure, she expects to have less than fifteen minutes for a brief look at the sycamores of Soochow. But a conductor comes through the compartment announcing a delay of three hours. "Trouble ahead," he tells Vera when she asks him what's wrong.

"Train trouble or Bolshevik trouble?"

When he looks puzzled by the Russian word, she asks if the delay is due to Red bandit trouble. He grins.

Three hours. At least three.

She asks Rama to get a trishaw. On the steamer she taught him the Chinese for "hotel" and "quickly" and "how much" and numbers through a hundred. Rama learns fast; to her satisfaction he's displayed a flair for giving commands. In front of the station he waves his rolled umbrella energetically at a trishaw driver, who comes at a trot.

The square in front of the station is filled with people and their possessions: bundles of clothes, pans threaded on bamboo poles, wicker baskets holding ducks and chickens. There are many crying infants and somber children. Men are clicking mah-jong pieces on the stairways. Women sit cross-legged on the hot cement, watching the station as if expecting a miracle to emerge from it. Most of them wear the padded jackets and trousers of northern peasants. Refugees from the interior, from the Northwest? Vera wonders.

Kneeling in front of a woman with an infant strapped to her back, Vera asks where she's from. "From Loyang." "Why did you leave there?" Vera asks. "Because of the fighting." "Where is your husband?" "Dead." "In Loyang?" "Yes, in the street there." "Red bandits killed him?" "No." "Then who killed him?" The woman shakes her head slowly. "He was taking food from a store already broken into. Someone shot him." "Where are you going?" The woman points toward the east. "Shanghai?" Again the woman shakes her head. She doesn't know. Again she points in the direction of Shanghai.

Following Rama into the trishaw, Vera orders the driver to take them to the Garden of the Master of Fishing Nets. At least this time there won't be sex in the way of a long sanity-saving look at the famous garden. Vera glances back at the woman hunched over in the hot sun with a baby strapped to her shoulders—in the shapeless brown cotton they look like an irregular mound of earth. War, Vera thinks. It seems to follow her like a dog. "To the Garden of the Master of Fishing Nets," she declares again with false gaiety in Chinese, and Rama grins in response, as if he has completely understood and has thoroughly appreciated his mistress's keen sense of humor.

. . .

Wang Shih Yuan, Garden of the Master of Fishing Nets. No more than an acre of it, she remembers. Having dragged Erich Luckner to it long ago, she'd walked briskly through its small exquisite courtyards, angry with him for rushing her back to bed. A young and beautiful woman's kind of anger. Today such impatience for love might seem to her more important than art. For a moment she recalls the bearded Frenchman in Saigon, her girlish reluctance.

Leaving the trishaw on a narrow road canopied by sycamores, she and Rama stroll down a cobbled alleyway. An old man, seated on a door stoop, is blowing some green leaves that float on the surface of his teacup. Vera glances back at him while he drinks the steaming liquid through his teeth, straining out a vagrant leaf. The noise he makes is animalistic, hearty. Vera smiles. She's proud of her capacity to find something she can smile at, even at a time like this, when her daughter is missing in a war-torn land. The old man drinking his tea has made her smile. Thank God. It's what the Rogachevas have given her: Endurance. Endurance. Endurance.

Does Sonia have it too?

The garden entrance—a plain-looking doorway giving into a plain white corridor. Here Rama stops and begs to be excused from going farther. He squats in a corner with his umbrella and the suitcase lined up beside his sandaled right foot, as if he's quite prepared to atrophy here through as many centuries as this corridor has guided visitors into the garden.

Vera hesitates. They have come this far together, mistress and servant, companions of the road, and yet here in the face of a mysterious art—certainly this garden is that to Rama—they must go their own ways. Well. She'll respect their need for separation, although as she turns sharply right into a tiny courtyard, Vera understands how close their relationship has become during the last few weeks. She'll miss him on the journey through Wang Shih Yuan.

. . .

An hour later, resting from a short journey through the garden, Vera sits on a low bench in the Pavilion of Clouds and Moon. Projecting on stilts over a small lake, the pavilion has visual command of the heart of the garden: A man-created mountain of Tai Hu rocks to the south; the Hall from Which One Looks at the Pines and Contemplates Paintings to the north; a profusion of trees, shrubs, galleries, and tiled roofs beyond the lake in front of the balustrade on which she leans. Wisteria blossoms float in the water as if an invisible hand has put them there. In such a magical place, anything of deliberate artistic effect seems possible.

For example, she's perplexed and delighted by a covered gallery so constructed that a large cutout section of it seems to act as the frame for a grove of bamboo behind it—a painting that her eye irresistibly composes out of plants and a wall. She tries to decipher the hidden meaning —it must be there—of an ancient cypress, scarred and mutilated by lightning, that keeps its hold on the northern side of the lake, a major branch of it hanging downward, knobby at the end and green, like a cluster of fruit. In every direction she can see *hua chuang*, living windows, so called because within their airy frames are natural tableaux of rockeries, trees, and flowers. Her eye is tricked at every turn; everything is planned to defy the concept of a plan. Below where she sits, the fallen blossoms move in sluggish tides from one section of the tiny lake to another, as if the invisible hand gently guides them. The upswept tip of a reflected roof shimmers in the water—sunlight, at this angle, shoves half of the lake back into a dark jasper shadow, but when she looks again, the water has a waxy carnelian luster, an almost chestnut-brown color that turns, the next time she looks, into a lively sheet of aventurine, pockmarked by little gusts of breeze, into a flecked green.

Her eye never rests, but each moment strays into a new painting, composed of man's and nature's art. The cul-de-sacs and sudden turns keep inconveniencing her eye, forcing it to see, to wonder what can happen next. Each fraction of an inch she moves her head brings effortlessly into view a slanted tree trunk, the ragged edge of a stone, the flat white torso of a wall. Aiding the illusions are large perfect mirrors that throw background into foreground, projecting in front of Vera what exists behind her. Peonies, ginko trees, water creepers, cherry and willow trees—the flora of an isolated world. It's the sort of world she'd known as a child. It's a world of delicate feelings to go with delicate art, a world in which utility drops away like a lowly daily care, a world in praise of the verities, steadfastly opposed to the human concerns of power and progress. The Chinese gentlemen who, for centuries, retired to such places as Wang Shih Yuan were much like her own Russian ancestors. They drank wine, listened to music, cultivated a sense of their own sensibilities as a permanence in the world. Walls are natural to such men.

Goldfish, near the surface of the lake, are sculling limpidly, as though suspended in a soft, warm, gelatinous substance. Are they happy? Vera wonders. They should be happy. They had better be, Vera decides with a kind of jocular grimness, or in the next life they'll be lizards scrambling for shade or appear again as draft horses up to their fetlocks in mud.

Rising, she walks around the lake, crosses a tiny stone bridge with two strides and enters the cool dim interior of the Barrier of Clouds Hall. To the south it's mostly fretwork windows and a round central window through which Vera observes the artificial mountain as if standing opposite it on another mountain. Something happens to her visual grasp of things from this perspective. Has the mountain she is looking at suddenly become a bank of clouds, the interior of the hall a mountaintop? It has. Of course it has. Nothing can prevent it from happening. Whoever designed the false mountain and this little hall has willed the transformation forever. Through the trellis-worked windows, having taken a deep breath as if preparing for a steep ascent, Vera studies the arrangement and size and shape of the Tai Hu rocks ahead of her. Individually they are neither mountains nor clouds solely, but animals as well and flowers and perhaps, with time, with a whole day, they could become universes.

Shan-teh had always loved their convoluted shapes, visual conundrums. He could stare for hours at labyrinthine holes sculpted by the action of swift water rushing for centuries across the surface of such rocks. He used to say such rocks in a garden illustrated the two great principles of Chinese philosophy: the Taoist love of freedom, the Confucian sense of history. He called such a garden the heavens made small, the cosmos reduced to a visible size. How she misses him at this moment. His loss to her is palpable here, even as panels of calligraphy pass before her eyes while she walks. She knows he would have smiled when great pieces of petrified wood, now entangling her vision from their tall redwood stands, entangled his own. No one else should be here with her but that man.

Not even Sonia, who to her knowledge has never yearned for isolated beauty, for the fenced-in contemplation of cherished spots of loveliness. Such a desire assumes belief in retirement from ordinary affairs, in the value of a solitary life, in the possibility of existing within created rather than given worlds. Sonia has never touched the deepest sources of a culture, either Chinese or Russian, although surely she's experienced certain aspects of the Chinese. She eats, for example, with a peasant's intensity—chopsticks poised, eyes narrowed in judgment, jaws working assiduously. Chinese of the street, Nanchang Chinese whose history has been adulterated by years of movement away from the heart of China, those have been Sonia's teachers, not Shan-teh's scholarly Confucians. What a Russian whore and a Chinese general once had so many years ago was a sense of honor, attuned to subtle judgment, delicate judgment, surely romantic and perhaps ineffectual judgment.

"Dear Sonia, do you have patrician endurance?" Vera asks the balmy air of this enclosed garden. That is all, she thinks, aristocrats ultimately have—deep knowledge of cyclical change, the confidence in a wheeling motion of history that someday will bring them back to the only thing that really counts: beauty behind walls.

History is surrounding Vera now. She feels it in the beat of her heart, the slow, steady pulse of centuries. They must have felt this way, the retired officials and great artists who came to Soochow for the air, the water, the rocks, the comforting walls. Today only a few people have paid the caretaker (he walks bent and smiling through the little court-yards) for a walk back into time. Almost two hours have passed, yet she has seen no more than a dozen men, all of them old, in clusters of two or three, silent and thoughtful in their long black Mandarin robes and skullcaps and white cotton shoes. Where have they come from? Has the invisible hand dropped them down here for a while to make perfect the arrangement of lake, hall, tree?

It is with these melancholy thoughts and preciously meaningless questions that Vera ends her journey through Wang Shih Yuan. She feels weary, as if physically the walk through one acre has been demanding. "Shan-teh," she murmurs under her breath, and in this moment becomes aware of something quite remarkable: Since arriving in China a few days ago, whenever she has seen a man (and she sees one now near the entrance of the garden) standing with feet planted firmly apart, torso bent slightly forward from the waist, hands clasped at the small of his back—a common enough stance in this land of reflective people—Vera has been reminded of Shan-teh, always always of him, not dead but as alive as the last moment they were together, her lover and the father of a girl she must take out of this star-crossed country. A destructive thought, surely, leading nowhere. A romantic thought. And a sad thought, appropriate to someone still grieving for a Russian house of order, comfort, permanence. Ah yes, permanence! Vera smiles ruefully.

Returning through the courtyards and galleries, Vera looks down at her feet—they move haltingly across a plum-blossom design of pebble mosaic—and she tells herself that her love for him, after twenty years, is still capable of obliterating the comfort of beauty and leaving in its place a flat gray terrifying void.

There he is—Rama. Still squatting in the corner, but with the um-brella open over his head now, as an afternoon sun beats down against the white wall behind him.

Seeing her, he rises with a smile to smooth out the cotton trousers hanging loosely on his skinny legs. The introspection that accompanied her trip through the old garden abruptly leaves Vera. She smiles back. How delicately balanced life is, she thinks with a mixed sense of regret and hope, when a smile from someone can banish for a time the deepest sense of loss.

36 THEY CAN HEAR the train station before they can see it.
Returning to it in a rickshaw, they halt at least fifty yards from the square. Filled with waiting passengers a couple of hours ago when they left it, the square is now virtually packed with people, with bundles of clothes, sacks of food, trunks of household goods, as if a town in the suburbs of Soochow had suddenly been displaced from there and dropped down here. Vera and Rama enter a crowd milling about with directionless energy. What they heard blocks from the station now surrounds them—the strident clamor of anxious questions. Vera makes out some of them: Where? When? Which direction? Shanghai? Nanking? Attack? Who? Where? When? Train number? Which one? What did you say? What did they say? Attack? Where? What track? Where? When?

Rama turns to say with jaunty confidence, "Don't worry, Mistress. Rama is here!" After which battle cry he plunges—quite literally—into the crowd, jabbing forward with the pointed end of his rolled umbrella and swinging the suitcase from side to side like a club. She's both surprised and cheered by this act of will. Following the path that Rama makes as if hacking through a jungle, Vera reaches the station steps, mounts them behind her champion—no taller than she is, weighing less—who leads her finally into the dim interior of Soochow Station.

Again by flailing away he clears a path to the ticket counter, where Vera sees a piece of torn rice paper slapped hastily with glue on the closed window of the booth: NO TRAIN TO WHUSI AND NANKING UNTIL FURTHER NOTICE. There's something else printed under the notification, but a surge in the crowd, like an irresistible tide, flings both of them away from the window. Holding on now to the collar of Rama's shirt with one hand, clinging to his back with the other, Vera lets him fight their way out of the mob or rather move along with it toward the tracks. She can see the tracks now through the arched doorway ahead, above a sea of fedoras and skullcaps and parcels carried on heads. Stuck here, she thinks. Another wavelike action of the crowd sends her and Rama toward the open doorway. People nearby are yelling "Shanghai! Shanghai!"

She's fighting for balance, aware suddenly that who goes down in this crush may never get up again.

And minutes ago the silence of a walled garden!

War, she thinks, feeling her legs momentarily give way.

Clawing at Rama's back, she finds enough cloth in her hand for a purchase that straightens her up, keeps her off the murderous floor of the station. She's staggering drunkenly forward in the melee. War's a matter of fits and starts. Stop go stop go, she thinks. Vera is gasping for breath as people funnel through the doorway onto the platform.

"Mistress! Mistress!" Rama is yelling an arm's length away, yet she can scarcely hear him, as if his voice is coming from a distance through roaring wind. And then it's drowned out altogether by the heavy chugging sound of an approaching locomotive. Pushed forward on the platform, reaching out and grabbing hold of Rama's black umbrella, she sees the train coming toward them, a great iron monster ramming through a cloud of steam. "Shanghai! Shanghai!"

As the old wooden coaches lurch past the platform, hundreds of people grapple forward. Many of them, wearing the padded cotton of northern peasants, look like great furry insects trying to scramble aboard, when the train finally halts.

Fortunately for Rama and Vera, they've been shoved near the front of a coach door. When it opens, the conductor hasn't time to jump out of the way—half a dozen men fight up the narrow steps, toss him aside, lunge into the coach. As if sucked into their wake, Rama follows, gripping the umbrella and suitcase in one hand, Vera's arm in the other. She is dragged up and aboard, while someone or something jabs her very hard in the back. Within seconds Rama has pushed her down on a wooden seat and found room beside her just before a swarm of people scatter through the compartment, hurling themselves onto the benches, clutching packages and wicker baskets, scowling at others hurtling past them to find somewhere to sit, then somewhere to stand, until the aisles fill up and every inch of space where a foot can be planted has been discovered and secured. Within minutes the coach has become a solid mass of flesh with a tide in it, so that invisibly a ripple of pressure forces the standing passengers to lean now this way, now that, cheek jammed against shoulder, arms spidering out to hold whatever won't yield.

Wedged between Rama and a fierce-looking peasant woman, Vera is aware of her breath: shallow, gusty, rapid. Already the temperature of the coach has risen; already her nostrils are filled with the stench of garlic and sweat. Between two standing bodies directly in line with her eyes, Vera has a glimpse of a child held tightly to the front of someone's padded jacket. Mucus has closed one of the baby's eyes; a steady flow of it runs from nose into open mouth, the upper lip suppurating from long, steady discharge.

War, Vera thinks grimly. War.

With a sudden lurch the train heaves into motion, and the force of it throws the standees backward, forward, backward, as if the earth itself has sent shock waves through the coach. Vera feels her chest tighten. War, she thinks. Glancing at Rama, she notices on his face an expression long familiar to her. She first saw it as a girl of nineteen fleeing Russia by train: Mile upon mile across the frozen tundra until engines broke down, coaches fell apart, women and children surrendered their seats to frightened soldiers, and a new exodus by cart and foot began. Vera regards the set of Rama's dark jaw, the brilliance of his eyes, the beaded sweat along his upper lip. She's seen his face often in trains like this one. If history is cyclical, so is fear. The expression of it never varies, she thinks.

"This will be a short trip," Vera assures him. The effort of saying it leaves her panting. She feels a little pressure on her chest, not pain, just pressure; maybe her blouse has bunched up against it. A man's hip, thrust against her shoulder, prevents her from straightening the blouse. "A couple of hours," she tells Rama.

"Dashed long time," he replies. Once he'd apologized for using the word "dashed" in front of a "white lady," calling it "a bit green." She'd suppressed a smile then, but not now, because she feels no smile.

War consumes the humor of things.

Vera stares ahead, hunching a little, making herself physically small just as she tries to make her mind loop inward into tangled little interior knots, into a thick clogged mass, into an iron fist invulnerable to any force that might try to pry it open. She has done this before, many times, in the long ago days of flight from beloved Russia. Nothing is there ahead of her, not a hip, not a small gap between two bodies through which she can see a child sniffling. There's no discomfort either in her chest, no clothing awry and bunched there to cause a kind of pressure. Why worry? Her breath is only breath, her mind only a series of flashing impressions. Click, click, click—she's counting the wheels thumping over the connected rails. Click, click, click. Each click sends her mind back into itself, coiling back like a snake prepared for rest in a deep cave. She counts: One two three four—until there's no need for counting. All that happens now is the click in her mind, the repetition wished for and satisfied. Nothing's out there; everything's inside. A fist. A click. Vera knows what to do in war.

• • •

It's a dashed long four hours in the coach, all right, especially when she can no longer blame her clothing for the sensation of pressure on her chest. The pressure has grown steadily into something like pain—well, frankly, pain. She's sweating too, but of course so many people jammed within the coach in midsummer have turned it into a steambath. But her sweat is cold, as if a pad dipped in ice water lies across her forehead.

Finally, when the train slows into Shanghai Station, she must fight panic along with the pain. Odd about panic, she thinks. Odd the way it sends everything you think you are outward, leaving nothing inside; it's like people running from a burning house.

This is definitely true: The attempt to loop each thought protectively back into herself has failed. Pain, panic—at last, perhaps, no one can fight them. At least she can't. Reality has always defeated her, hasn't it, and what is wrong right now has an actual location. Her heart is going wrong. A fist is tightening there, but not through her own volition, not through any trick of the mind. This is a fist that lies deep inside her chest, a clenched and bloody fist, unwilling to let go. Managing to free her hand on three occasions during the interminable ride, Vera has got to the vial in her blouse pocket. Three times she's slipped a little white pill hopefully under her tongue. Each time, predictably, there has followed the familiar acrid taste, the slight burning, the rush of what seems like power to the top of her head, the resultant ringing in her ears. But not the cessation of pain in her chest. It remains there, a redoubtable clenched fist. The nitro isn't working, my dear, she tells herself. Panic. Like people inside of her running for exits. They're going to leave her empty inside, and when that happens, she'll yell—if she can yell—and make matters worse. Yes, quite, as the English would say. So don't let them out. Philip should be here with his mystical Indian exercises to help her with the panic. Poor Rama. She glances at him, looking straight ahead. Perhaps life in India prepares the Indian for things like this. At any rate, Rama is good in a crisis. Who would have thought so? Think of that. Think, she tells herself. Define what's happening, pass time. Passing time means everything. What is panic? Panic is, panic is . . . people jumping off an abandoned ship. Out of a burning house. Think of what's happening, inside, in your chest. Something new is going on in there; the fist is opening or rather growing like a plant. Sending out roots. Think of that. Think of pain. What is pain? Pain is . . . growing like something in the Garden of the Master of Fishing Nets. Think of how curious that is.

There's a swell of activity within the coach, as passengers begin the struggle toward the single exit. Why don't they open both doors? Damn Chinese, she thinks, even as the two bodies in front of her, nearly invisible behind bundles and baskets, move aside to leave her with a frightening view of the sick infant—mucus dried into thick runnels down its pale cheeks and chin.

"Rama," she says, hearing her voice come weakly from a distance, "I'm sick. Get me out of here."

• • •

What happened next, Vera Rogacheva Embree will be able to recall only in disparate images, for each of them apparently was separated in her consciousness by pain that forced itself up and into her throat, her left arm, sending out tentacles of a tingling numbness. She was like—it was like—war. Advance troops going through her. Like that, a civil war. Invasion from inside. War, always war, war, war.

Rama was helping her. Somehow he gripped her, although managing as well to salvage the umbrella and suitcase. He was trying to speak

Chinese. "*Kuai! Kuai!* Quickly," he yelled, meaning "Help!" she supposed, but there wasn't strength enough in her to correct him. She held on to the idea that losing consciousness would mean death. He was getting her someplace with the help of two men. She will remember that: the smell of garlic, tobacco—and sweat, hers and theirs.

There was another crush at the exit gate, where many passengers couldn't pay for the journey they had taken, and were standing around or sitting on their belongings, eyes fixed on nothing, mouths shut, hands folded placidly in the long impossible wait for a miracle. But Rama got her out somehow, along with the two peasants.

It was sunny outside, a rather blinding light, which perhaps accounts for her remarkable delusion—or was it? Because there, in front of the station, she saw (will swear to it later) the dark skinny Indian belaboring a heavyset Chinese gentleman with his rolled umbrella in a fierce, really mortal, battle over a single black taxi. The Chinese man fell backward into a gathering crowd, and somehow, but how she will never know, Rama pushed her inside, along with the umbrella and suitcase, and managed to fling coins into the pressing mob, which diverted the curious and the angry long enough for him to climb in beside her, shut and lock the taxi door.

"Palace Fandian! Palace Fandian!" he yelled. "*Kuai! Kuai!* Palace Fandian!" And he gripped her hand.

She'll remember that: the heat of his healthy hand enclosing hers.

And she'll remember saying, "I won't die. I won't die. Not till she's safe."

Somewhere along the route to the Palace Hotel, invading troops overran the defenses. Gasping for breath, she thought the words: I won't die, I won't. She'll remember that: hearing them in her mind before the consciousness she'd fought to protect was swept away.

• • •

Had she been capable of it, Vera would have told Rama to try the municipal hospital instead of a hotel. But his decision—made without deliberation in favor of the only place he knew in Shanghai—probably saved her life.

When the Sikh doorman carried the unconscious woman (recognizing her as a guest he had seen that morning) into the Palace lobby and laid her on a leather sofa, an alert desk clerk brought a doctor, just then in the hotel visiting a foreigner with the flu, to Vera's side within minutes.

Much better than the city hospital is the nursing home in the French Concession, where Doctor Chardon brought her by ambulance. She has a private room overlooking a garden. Rama is allowed to sleep in a corner on a cot, and when the little Chinese nurse who speaks rather good

French is not around, he tends to her—even gets Vera the bedpan, at his own insistence. Being in a place with good medical facilities, Vera well knows, is rare today in Shanghai.

"Narayana," Rama declares frequently, convinced that God has produced a miracle.

Vera won't contradict him. She considers her survival to be the function of a plan beyond her skill to understand or evaluate. Except that somehow it involves Sonia. Vera is convinced, with a Rama type of faith, that her mission in life must surely be to save her daughter for something other than Bolshevik politics. Every day she sends Rama to the hotel to check for a message from Philip, because regretfully she must still count on him. Meanwhile, she focuses her will upon the act of recuperation, as if it's a matter of learning a lesson in school.

When Doctor Chardon comes for a visit, assiduously she questions him about prognosis (guardedly excellent) and medicine and for a few minutes even retains the names of medicine she's given: digoxin, quinidine sulfate, and heparin, among other peculiar things. Now and then she has a distressing pain in her left shoulder and arm, but the doctor says that's common enough. Rest, he says.

Doctor Chardon is a youngish man, proud of having graduated from the Peking Union Medical College. He was born and raised in China, therefore respects her ability to speak not only French with him but Chinese as well. Once he has listened to her heart and taken her blood pressure, Chardon sits on the edge of her bed and talks in the rambling but intense manner of a man eager for companionship. He seems less worried about her health than about the state of Chinese economics. Corruption is reaching new lows; the latest scandal involves the KMT Navy, which has allowed local businessmen to sell goods and weapons to the Communists right out of Shanghai godowns. Junks carrying these contraband goods sail without fear under the guns of Yangtze River forts; patrol-boat commanders accept bribes of gold bars. These shipments into Red territory are actually insured by Nationalist banks!

Chardon, black bearded, sallow faced, shakes his head sadly. You must rest, he tells her, relax and not worry. A Lucky Strike dangles perpetually from his mouth, the smoke curling up into his left eye—always the left eye—making it squint and wink. She can't find him attractive, although he has saved her life.

Every day he brings new tales of Nationalist venality and lawlessness.

Shanghai is on the verge of collapse, he claims. Harassed by Chiang's secret service, teachers are committing suicide, students murdered. Horrible, horrible. And now Chinese from Southeast Asia are halting remittances to families on the mainland, drawing back from the debacle. So are Chinese relatives in America. Everyone drawing back from the

466 ·

horror. Terrible, he says, winking sadly through the smoke. Rickshaw coolies are robbing passengers right here in the city. A hundred people arrested last week as spies. Posters of Mao appear every day on walls. Businessmen are listening to soothing overtures from the Reds, who, they figure, can't be worse than the Nationalists. Hardheaded business-men rushing out of desperation into the arms of communism! Terrible, he declares with a sigh and lights a new Lucky off the butt of an old one. Death of a great city, death of a great nation. Smoke rising into his left eye.

She admires Chardon's passion. In this man there's more love for China than even she can summon from the past. Yet he reminds her of a man more attractive if less committed—Jules Langlais, and the night she might have had in Saigon.

Rest, relax, don't worry. It's easy for Chardon to say, but she'd rather take a thousand medicines than have to cope with such advice—rest, relax, don't worry—so idiotic really. Each day Vera feels a stirring of discomfort in her chest when Rama returns from the Palace Hotel, poking his head into the room with a smile calculated to lessen her disappointment at the news he brings: Master not coming yet, Mistress. And then Chardon with his stethoscope and pathetic advice: Rest, relax, don't worry.

But thank God for Rama. One day he walks into the room sporting a white Congress hat. He wears a pair of billowy white pajamas, a black Nehru jerkin. By this attire Rama is transformed into an Indian, whereas in Western clothes he's been for Vera a dark, indeterminate fellow who muttered the name of an alien god. The Sikh doorman who carried her into the hotel lobby last week has given Rama the address of an Indian clothing store right in the heart of Shanghai. The experience has impressed Rama, humbled him too, for until now he has regarded everything Chinese (and Siamese for that matter) as intellectually infe-rior and spiritually banal. His new clothes, purchased at a decent price, have raised up an entire culture in his eyes. "The farther I am being from home, the more I am wanting my own clothes," he explains. "Bought here in Shanghai. Very good, Shanghai."

He wears them on his next excursion to the hotel. When he returns this time, Vera can see in an instant his smile isn't forced.

"Master is coming. He is on this side now," Rama exclaims, and it takes a long two minutes before he's sufficiently calm to locate a note to that effect, folded neatly into a cube no larger than his thumbnail, and buried safely in his trouser pocket.

It is written again on consulate stationery: MR PHILIP EMBREE ARRIVES IN SHANGHAI SIX JULY.

• • •

Next day she sends Rama to the hotel before sunup.

Waiting is terrible for Vera, especially because by midafternoon there's no Rama, no Philip, not even Doctor Chardon who should be telling her to rest, relax, not worry. She reads one article in an English-language newspaper at least a dozen times and still can't make sense of it—something about the Yung family who are flour (or is it textile) magnates in Shanghai. They ordered millions of dollars of some kind of machinery from the States, but were refused import licenses by the government because they had somehow annoyed Chiang Kai-shek. It has taken most of the day for Vera to get that much of the idea, yet for the life of her she can't remember *how* they annoyed the Generalissimo. Picking up the paper from the bed again, Vera is searching for the answer when the door opens a crack, then swings back to reveal Rama, smiling. "Master is here!" he announces theatrically.

Philip Embree, also smiling—but it's a tentative, guarded smile—comes into the room.

Staring at him hard enough to exclude a show of affection, Vera sees the battered fedora in his hand, the black robe buttoned down the front and slashed at the sides to display a pair of baggy gray trousers. He's wearing cloddish gray shoes. A perfect image of the Westernized Chinese merchant of Shanghai. Philip blends, she thinks. He likes disguises.

He's standing there, hat in hand, hangdog as a bad boy, telling her he's sorry that she's sick and he's sorry Sonia's still missing and he's going to do everything in his power and on and on.

Looking at him in his shabby Chinese outfit, ready as a child for more adventure, she thinks of Shan-teh. He too liked disguises. Perhaps there's something masculine about seeming to be what you aren't.

Philip's telling her where he's been the past few weeks while her daughter is still missing. She doesn't follow much of it, because the fact is that Philip hasn't been here on the spot, watching the waterfront himself. He's saying something about the Americans, about how they're trying, and about how he can devote more time now to the search. He sounds calm, reasonable, and unconvincing.

In a calm, reasonable manner he suggests that Sonia and the boy may already have left Shanghai. Vera nods politely. She finds his analysis worthless and doesn't listen to it. Instead she thinks about men, about the half of the race who bring war and confusion into the world. While Philip continues to assure her that American agents and their Chinese assistants have combed the waterfront, Vera is thinking the masculine mind is incapable of facing the truth, of calling catastrophe by its right name. What men describe as hysteria in women is nothing more than the ability to recognize disaster when it comes along, to react accordingly. But she's been ordered to rest, relax, and not worry. So instead of yelling at him, "Good God, man, you failed miserably and now you come here hat in hand to point out the obvious, while Sonia's out there unprotected in a dangerous, corrupt, suicidal China," she quietly agrees with his calm, reasonable, unconvincing assessment of the situation.

Then Vera tells him that he should go immediately into Shantung and look for Sonia there. He should begin at Tai Shan, where the General was murdered. Sonia will go to the last place first if there's a choice. "Why in that order?" Vera asks the question rather than wait for him to stumble on it. She has thought out the answer during long silences in this bed. Sonia will go first to Tai Shan because she always follows that sequence in discussing her father: first his death, next his life. Naturally Sonia might go the other way around—to Qufu first, then to Tai Shan—but the girl will inevitably, *inevitably*, go to both places. Not out of conscious design, perhaps. She may not even know her destination before getting to it. But the point is, Vera says, *the point is that the girl will inevitably get to Qufu and Tai Shan and Jinan and probably other places that figured in the General's life*—she will simply get there. No matter what the young Bolshevik orders her to do. No matter what happens in China.

Vera feels a turmoil in her chest—not pain, but perhaps the sensation is a warning—yet she can't help declaring in a voice shrill with tension, "My daughter will go to the places where her father lived and died."

Embree breaks into her train of thought to ask again about her health. He's done that more than once since coming into the room, hasn't he—has broken into her ideas with questions about medicine and such—but each time she can't seem to concentrate on what surely is his genuine concern. Poor Philip. He has perhaps deserved better than he got from her, although instinct has always told her that he got only what he deserved. But at this moment, this fateful time of crisis, must he insist on talking about a heart attack and a course of recovery? What can they mean in the face of the *real* problem, Sonia's safety? Can't he see there is only one thing he can do for her, ever *could* do for her, and that is find Sonia? It's as if they had met twenty years ago for that result only—Philip Embree, having led the mother out of China, will rescue the daughter from the same place two decades later.

Rarely, Vera thinks, has she seen as clearly. She wants to break through Philip's questions to the heart of their relationship, which exists and has existed for this reason alone: to rescue Sonia from war and Bolsheviks and from herself. But there's no way to reach beyond his solicitous, irrelevant questions into the truth. Poor Philip. Her mind, having rehearsed to perfection this scene taking place between them, won't have him interfere.

Impatiently she cuts in to say, "Yes, yes, I'll be all right, but there's one thing you must not do, Philip. When you find her—*and* you will—

don't tell her what has happened here. I mean, to me. No, no." Shaking her head to stop his objection, Vera continues. "I want her to come back by her own choice. If she doesn't miss me or the life she once had or can have, then I'll give her up. Yes, I mean it. Even that. Even if it means the death of both of us—hers and mine. I'll give her up if she makes that choice. Because I believe she can make a choice now. By now she's cooled enough to see the Bolshevik for what he is. She can think again. *She'll have a fair choice, and I'm determined to let her have it.* I'll give her up if need be. I will, Philip." She can hear her voice trembling; a weakness like warm thick liquid begins flowing through her arms and hands. "If you tell her I'm sick, she'll come out of duty. And then she'll leave again, hating me. I won't have that. I want her to decide, and I know her decision will be the right one. How do I know? Because my whole life has led her to this decision. She'll choose correctly, I know that, but *she* must do the choosing. So you won't tell her, Philip. You will not tell her. You will not." She watches him shrug his shoulders—a boyish gesture of helplessness. "No, I mean it. You will not. Promise me you will not. Say it."

"Vera. I really think she ought to know."

"Say it."

Again he shrugs. "I promise not to tell her." He adds softly, "But I think you're wrong."

With a sigh Vera sinks back against the pillow. They talk awhile, but it's of little interest to her and doesn't detract from her satisfaction. Indeed, with a kind of wonder she realizes, after Philip has left the room to carry out his mission, that their last spoken words together are already forgotten, lost to her forever, even though something powerful within her consciousness tells Vera that this is the last time they'll ever meet.

But of course, upon reflection, she acknowledges that life has a way of tricking the mind into believing all kinds of notions.

* * *

Each morning the Chinese-language paper comes to her room neatly folded, but the *North China Daily News*, British owned, is crinkled here and there, slightly used.

Rama obviously goes through each page looking for news of drought in India.

And on his daily visits Doctor Chardon becomes increasingly confessional, shifting from talk of corruption in Shanghai to hints of corruption in his own life. His French-born wife has left him for an American businessman who promises to take her to a place called Fort Worth in America somewhere. His Chinese mistress, mother of his only child, has vanished. People say her brother is a political commissar with the Reds in Honan Province. He admits to drinking too much and gambling;

these are painful confessions to hear for Vera, who averts her eyes when his fill up with tears of self-pity. And he presents a bill almost daily—predictable in view of his vices—for medicines and care. Finally this man who despises corruption in Chinese officials admits that most of his medical supplies are purchased on the black market. Rest, relax, don't worry, he declares.

And Rama slinking around with a long face doesn't help either, when her own thoughts drift northward into Shantung Province where Sonia might be—or might not be—for Vera's conviction, now that Philip is bound there, has weakened during each day without news. At night, when the nursing home is quiet, she often hears Rama, snoring in the corner, sputter and cry out. He sleeps poorly. The daytime smile and good cheer only make more poignant to Vera whatever it is that torments him.

One day, into her third week at the nursing home, she asks him openly what she's suspected for a long time: "Rama, have you got a family back in India?"

"Mistress?"

"Don't just smile and say 'Mistress.' I asked if you have a family—wife, children, mother, father, or someone back in India."

"Parents both dead, Mistress."

"Which means you have a wife, children."

Shaking his head, looking past her left shoulder, Rama denies it. "No, Mistress. Not any of that."

"At least tell me what your South Indian droughts are like."

He looks like a small animal backed into a corner. Eyes roll, hands fumble at the Nehru jacket. But finally, seated cross-legged on the cot, he explains in a deeply anguished voice what a South Indian drought can be. When the water dries up in the tanks, outlying villages suffer first. When the wells turn to dust, villagers pack up their belongings and march off to neighboring villages to find water and work. But there isn't work for them to do or water for them to share, so they move on and soon enough the people in those villages that rejected them must also move on, until there is a long trail of them trudging across a countryside that has no water. Children die first.

Some people head for the cities, but they're no better off. Men sell their livestock and women sell their gold bangles to live in the city while seeking work. But of course there is no work. They use up their funds and turn to begging. Drought makes beggars; that's as sure as death.

Rama opens his hands as if signaling up the emptiness and despair he's only hinted at. His smile, usually so bright, has the downward set of pain. "Drought on my side is like that."

"Are you worried about your family, Rama?"

"No, Mistress," he insists. "No family, Mistress. But friends will be having trouble." He manages to smile. "So far no drought, though. Narayana. No flash in the newspapers."

His smile, a mixture of fear and pride and optimism, is painful to see. Vera glances at the open window, a pot of geraniums sitting blood red on the sill. He's lying, she thinks, but there's nothing she can do.

So the days pass, with neither of them receiving news. Often at night she listens to him snore rhythmically, then sputter and awaken with a little groan. At such moments, pitying them both, Vera tries to imagine the Shanghai she once knew. On the Rue Cardinal Mercier the Cercle Sportif Français with its enormous semicircular bar and wonderful rum concoctions. Women there in evening dresses modeled on designs by Molineaux and Chanel. In the evenings, after supper, there were always the dog races at the Canidrome or jai-alai on Avenue du Roi Albert. So many cabarets: the Casanova, the Venus Café, the Ambassador. Didn't she meet Erich Luckner at the Ambassador? Its chandeliers twinkled like those in a Petrograd ballroom. And there was St. Anne Ballroom, where she danced with too many men ever to recall, their hands big and clammy on her bare back, their breaths against her cheek promising a kind of love in the early dawn. There was foxtrotting at the Little Club and a grossly sexual floor show at the Paramount and for a perverse change a stroll through Blood Alley, where escorts took her for a curious look at degradation Vera knew only too well might be her own fate in the end. Shanghai.

She has loved China. The truth of her passion for it surprises Vera, because until now she never realized how wonderfully full and vibrant those days had been; she'd simply regretted living them. She can even think, with a sort of wistful pleasure, of those faceless men who bought her indifferently as a tonic against their own loneliness and defeat. They were all together there in Shanghai, men and women brutal in their desires and needs, like lost children.

Rama coughs in his troubled sleep, while she takes advantage of the darkness to move through imagination and time into Jessfield Park, where concerts used to be held in front of the striped pavilion. She sat on a folding chair beside her faceless escort and listened to the Municipal Orchestra. Did they play—or has she dreamed it—Tchaikovsky's Little Russian Symphony? They must have played it on one of those balmy nights when whores and rickshaw drivers were murdered on the banks of Soochow Creek. The melancholy solo for horn in the introduction to the first movement comes again through Rama's snoring, a clear bell-like note heralding the tragedy of life.

Next day a terrific gust of stormy wind sends the geranium pot crashing to the floor of the room. The crash heralds three days of thunderstorms and gale-force winds, culminating in a typhoon that strikes in and around Shanghai. Thousands are left homeless. She reads in the newspapers that water is waist-high in front of Wing On Department Store on Nanking Road. One thing Vera knows: After a flood or drought has left families destitute in the provinces, there's always an influx into Shanghai of virgins, most of them hardly in their teens. They work the streets as *piao-tzu*. Bodies fished out of Soochow Creek multiply.

Each morning the *North China Daily News* continues to have a rumpled look by the time she receives it. Rama, weighed down by his lie, is silent these days, sitting cross-legged on the cot, waiting without a smile for her to bless him with an errand. Chardon, squinting and stammering, hints of a sexual aberration while sitting on her bed to dispense both expensive medicine and worthless advice. And Vera, through it all, deplores the karma that has put the safety of her daughter into the hands of a callow Bolshevik, the destiny that may soon entrust Sonia to a man who can't help betraying others, especially those who count on him most.

37

JINAN IS HER father's city.

Dust rises in yellow swirls through the streets, and thousands of Nationalist troops march along them, adding to the impression of a grim city. Yet willow trees still line the wide boulevards, and with Jin-shi in tow, she visits the natural springs and lakes here. Jin-shi grumbles that people in wartime shouldn't visit such frivolous places. Indeed, there's abundant evidence that Jinan lies in the path of war. The troops that are bivouacked in the area, when not slogging along in columns, stand on street corners, looking young and lost in their cotton uniforms and straw sandals. There's a tension in their eyes that frightens Yu-ying; it's as though suddenly, on the sort of impulse that follows long boredom, these haggard young men might rush into terrible violence.

She turns a deaf ear to Jin-shi's complaints, because her command of Mandarin has given her an advantage over him that she intends to use. Yu-ying has lost interest in getting the message to Pridi. Her aim now is secretly to absorb the world of her father. Falling in with that plan is the recent loss to Red sabotage of the rail line northward. All that she and Jin-shi can do now to enter Honan Province is use a circuitous route. They must travel first south and then northwest to reach the Liberation

Army headquarters at Hsipiap'o. Going south for Yu-ying means going deeper into the country where her father lived and died.

If only she could confide in Jin-shi, she would tell him what she tells her imaginary confidante late at night: "So in Jinan I saw beautiful carp, all red and yellow and blue, swirling through the clear ponds, and the broad streets with tall willows lining them, but it wasn't enough, you see, because, although I tried to picture a little boy running through the streets, I didn't really see him. The experience wasn't strong enough. Well, maybe because everywhere we went there were these young, tired, underfed soldiers looking at us from dull sad eyes, and I couldn't concentrate. But Mother used to tell me that here, in this city, Father met with great warlords and they intrigued and once a bomb exploded, killing a lot of them, but my father escaped, and right here men were plotting the future of China. But I couldn't see that clearly in Jinan. I had to see more. Do you understand?"

They have a room in a shabby hotel to the north of town. From the window she can see the muscular churning of the Yellow River on its way to the sea. It is indeed yellow, having carried endless tons of silt from Mongolia beyond the Great Wall. Its flooding, during the centuries, has earned for this river the name China's Sorrow. The immensity of suffering goes with the immensity of the land, she thinks—tells Jin-shi this, and he nods without comment. This morning, now that she is "all right" again, as he calls it, he wants to make love, but she's refused. Flatly. "I don't want to," she tells him and watches curiously to see what will happen. Nothing happens, nothing, but he rolls over petulantly toward the wall and does nothing to prevent her from standing at the window alone.

Down below, on a narrow path, a peasant is bringing ducks in a wicker basket townward for sale. They are quacking loudly, as ducks must have done along this same path for a thousand years. Not even the threat of warfare in the streets has made much difference to the peasants who flow in and out of the city gates. So this is what Mother meant when she said, "China has its own way of handling catastrophe."

Turning to the young man lying against the wall, Yu-ying says sharply, "It's time we went south."

Without facing her, he mutters, "How? You heard him at the station yesterday. Trains aren't going south. Trains aren't going anywhere."

"Yes, I heard him. But we're going south."

"How?"

"We'll . . ." She hasn't thought how. But an idea comes at the instant. "We're going to hire mules."

Turning, Ho smiles at her. His smile astonishes her—gentle, shy, trusting—the smile of a child. "And when we get south far enough at that junction, that—" He can't remember the name.

"Hsuchou," she tells him.

"You say from there we go west, then north again?"

"If we can."

Ho sits up eagerly, his eyes alert. "There has to be a way. When Pridi gets this letter, everything will be all right. My fortune is this letter." He taps his shirt where it lies folded in the pocket. It never leaves him, not even in bed. "*Our* fortune," he adds, and pats the sheet beside him. "Please sit here."

"No, not now."

"I don't mean that." He pats it again, his eyes pleading. "Sit beside me, that's all."

Reluctantly, Yu-ying does.

He takes her hand lightly in his and looks past her at the window. "I never thought it would be like this. Where are the palms, the nim trees? I keep thinking that. And no one around here speaks Teochiu. Isn't that Chinese? Where we come from it's Chinese. I don't know. And everywhere you look, people go on about their business, only they seem to be waiting too."

"They are."

"Everything's waiting. I don't know." Holding her hand, Ho Jin-shi sits with his gaze fixed on the window beyond which the great river battles through its banks.

Yu-ying slowly withdraws her hand and smiles at him. "It's time to go. We're going to Taian."

He nods and rises.

• • •

There are three mules heading south—one ridden by a farmer on his way to T'eng Hsien who has agreed to take the young couple as far as the rail junction of Taian. The mules are skittish, and Yu-ying is afraid of hers, but Jin-shi enjoys the ride. His slim legs clutch the barrel sides of the mule, as he urges the reluctant animal into a little trot. The sight of him having fun pleases Yu-ying; after all, he's isolated in his own country. And she has tricked him by silence. What this country means to her is what she hides. After all, if she reminded him that Jinan was the home of her father, Jin-shi would scoff. And if she told him Taian was the city at the foot of the sacred mountain of Tai Shan, where her father met his death, Jin-shi would warn her not to live in the past. Maybe he'd remind her of her promise to forget her family. It's better this way, she tells herself. With the pleasure of guilt, she watches him enjoy the mule ride.

The little caravan goes slowly through the dry, dusty land with scrawny poplars adding a faint touch of green to the white air. And through stands of slim birch trees, now and then, Yu-ying can see wagons shuttling along distant roads. She's surprised how few people can be seen, although thousands must live within the visible horizon. The land is silent, huge; it seems indifferent to being used or changed. On the dry geometric plain the earth itself looks scrubbed clean, nothing inessential on its surface, not a broken twig, a snapped blade of grass. The winds, like giant relentless brooms, have swept the land bone-clean and dry as old wood. It is her father's land.

The old farmer says little, but toward noon he points to the east and mutters, "Soldiers."

In the east now there are mountains, blue and rocky, a low continuous ridge of them, but it takes Yu-ying a long time before she can see what the farmer saw: a tiny line of moving shapes between a feathery row of poplars far off there, on a clay road cut through the fields as if by a knife blade. There's a flash in the sunlight—perhaps a windshield or a pair of binoculars or a bayonet.

"Who are they?" Yu-ying asks.

The farmer shrugs. "I don't know. I don't even know when they're up close."

"I heard south of Jinan the countryside's controlled by the Eighth Route Army."

"That's right," he agrees, looking straight past the stiff ears of his mule. "Sometimes it is."

An old truck passes from the opposite direction. With the hood gone, its engine is exposed, the pistons and fuel lines exuding vapor into the hot summer air.

"We're still in Nationalist country," the farmer observes, looking back over his shoulder at the truck. "When we get into Red country you see trucks with posters on them."

That evening, toward sunset, they see a truck carrying a huge poster nailed against its side. The poster shows huge Red soldiers reaching out to catch antlike KMT troops, huddling cravenly together.

"Now," the farmer says, as they tether the mules for a rest, "we're in Red country."

· · ·

That night they sleep in a kaoliang field, and the next morning they cook a pot of rice gruel under a poplar tree beside the road. A woman and child come along, hands outstretched. When Yu-ying hesitates over her bowl, the old farmer says gruffly, "No."

"We have enough," she argues.

"It is my kettle, my bowls you're eating from, my firewood. No."

She looks at his face under a shabby fedora and says no more, but finishes the gruel. Later, she washes out the iron kettle and three bowls in a stream beyond the roadside. Ho is already on his mule when she comes back. He kicks it into a jittery, stiff-legged trot, and for a moment her heart is gladdened by the sight of an attractive young man laughing in his pleasure.

"Let's go," the farmer mutters. Her mule turns to eye her when she mounts, and suddenly, without warning, the thought comes to Yu-ying that back home in Bangkok her friend Lamai is now married.

In the evening they reach Taian, and Yu-ying scarcely hears Jin-shi questioning her about the railroad station, as she looks up through the twilight at the rocky peak of Mount Tai Shan. It looks sharply pointed in the growing darkness, as if cutting the flat blue of the sky like a huge sword. The mountain seems to come out of memory. Her mother, who never saw it, used to describe the mountain as the Chinese do: most sacred of the five sacred mountains of China, the Mountain Above Mountains, the Gatherer of Clouds, promoted to the rank of Emperor in the Sung Dynasty, at last created a god. Climbing it is called ascending to heaven. All these things her mother used to tell her while they sat in the shady garden not ten feet from a klong in Bangkok, hearing a troop of gibbons swinging in the trees overhead, each imagining her own version of the mountain where husband and father was killed.

Looking at the farmer, who has left them in the city market and is now leading his mules toward the southern gate, Ho says anxiously, "We should have stayed with him. What if no trains are running?"

"We'll find another farmer with mules." There it is, she thinks, the Mountain Above Mountains, Tai Shan.

"At least we better go to the station and find out." He plucks her sleeve. "Did you hear me? Let's go to the station."

"No." It is the Eastern Peak, presiding over life which begins in the east as the sun rises. Tai Shan is the source of life, and when souls die, they meet here at the mountain before rebirth. That's what Mother told her in their garden, while Nipa chopped onions and Ah Ping in her quarters smoked a tiny bowl of opium.

"Then what do we do if we don't go to the station?" Ho persists.

"We go to the station later." Up there on the summit is the temple honoring the Princess of the Azure Clouds. "Let's find a place to sleep. Tomorrow we climb the mountain."

Ho looks up in the fading light at the slopes rising above the city. "That mountain? Why climb it?"

"Because . . ." Yu-ying takes a deep breath; it's time to tell him. "My father was going to climb it when enemies took him prisoner and killed him."

"Your father?"

"So tomorrow *I* climb the mountain." She hears the defiance in her voice.

"Well, then we climb it," Ho says with determination.

Yu-ying looks at his thin face in the last light.

"We climb it," he repeats. "If they killed your father there, then you must climb it. That's Chinese. And that's what we are, Chinese. Aren't we?" He looks down at his feet, as if thinking hard. "I almost forgot that —that Chinese is what we are, no matter what happens. But it's true, even if I can't speak this language. We climb it even though the mission isn't finished. We take the time. We won't stay long, but we'll climb it because . . . because Chinese honor their parents."

Her love for him almost returns.

· · ·

They sleep in the back of a hardware store, along with a dozen pilgrims who have come, in spite of war, to climb the mountain. The storekeeper, having collected his money, kicks them out at dawn. Yu-ying buys some hard-boiled eggs from a streetside vendor near the great Temple of the God of Tai Shan.

"What is that? Do we go in there first?" Jin-shi asks, looking at the Sun Facing Gate, behind which some of the temple buildings are visible.

"No. We're going straight up there." Through heavy mists she's looking in the opposite direction at Tai Shan, its series of peaks obscured by morning clouds, only its rugged gneissic side visible. It's like a huge animal glimpsed in a jungle, just its chest and belly seen—like the tiger in northern Siam she'd once seen on a dawn hillside outside of Chiang Mai during a trip with her mother. From the car they had seen it almost simultaneously: dull in the half-light, huge, moving headless beyond fronds and tangled limbs. Mother said it was like a god, and she said— what had she said? Yu-ying wonders in the Tai Shan mists. But she doesn't tell Jin-shi about the tiger or what her mother said or what she might have said years ago in her childhood.

On the path leading from the temple, a number of pilgrims have begun the gentle ascent toward the foot of the mountain. Some are soldiers in ragged gray, without weapons—young, rosy-cheeked peasants in uniform.

Last night in the back room of the hardware shop, pilgrims had talked casually of the war. Last year, they said, the Communist general Chen Yi camped on the mountain, where the Nationalists couldn't get at him. Now the whole area is in his control.

The casualness, almost indifference, with which the pilgrims discussed the war surprised Yu-ying until she recalled something her mother used to say: The Chinese know that catastrophe turns into good fortune, good fortune into catastrophe, and so they take neither seriously. The pilgrims were big, solid people, the women as well as the men, and she sensed in their slow docility an underlying potential for violence if aroused. Consequently, for fear of annoying them she refused to ask them any more of Jin-shi's questions when he became insistent in his annoyance with their inability to answer simple things: How big were the armies, where did the battles take place, and was there much slaughter? They responded with a shrug, a grin, a blank stare. They reminded Yu-ying of the water buffalo back home. Beat, kick, scream at them for years, and their mouths still masticate like old stones grinding together until, without apparent provocation, one day they trample anything in their paths.

Now, on the way to the mountain, Jin-shi talks excitedly of the future. When he delivers the letter to the great Pridi, everything will change for him. He will rise in the Communist Party either here or in Bangkok. And by telling the Party that she helped him with the mission, she will gain recognition for herself too.

Out of the billowing mist emerges the triple arch of Tai Shan Gate. My father must have passed under it the last day of his life, Yu-ying is thinking. I won't think of them taking him prisoner. I'll think of him starting to climb the mountain. And he'll go all the way to the summit with me.

"You aren't the same."

She turns to look at Jin-shi.

"It's true. You have forgotten the Party, the mission I'm on. All you think of is climbing the mountain."

"Yesterday you said I should climb it."

"Yes, but—" He frowns and looks ahead at the path. "I said we should climb it and that was settled. Why make more of it? But last night when I asked you to take a walk somewhere in the dark, so we could make love, you refused. You aren't the same about that either."

"You said I should climb it because I owed my father the honor. But I think you really said it so I'd make love. Is that why you said it?"

"Well, I don't know."

"Then don't climb it."

"I want to climb it. I'm Chinese too. You think you're more Chinese than I am just because you speak Mandarin?"

"Let's not argue." Reaching out, she touches his sleeve. "It's a long climb."

They walk silently under the narrow stone arch of the First Gate to Heaven. It's a venerable structure, built in the days of the Ming. Yu-ying has seen pictures of it many times. Mother had a book of old photographs, and in the garden together, heads bent over it, they used to stare hard at the blurry black-and-whites, as if intensity of desire might bring to life the image of a man whom she had never seen, whose features her mother could no longer recall.

• • •

They press on in silence through the morning. Of the five miles to the summit, by noon they have walked three. It has been a rather gentle climb through pine groves, past temples. As the morning wears on, they move up the winding stone path beyond the Red Door Palace, the Ten Thousand Immortals Tower, the Dragon Spring Temple, and the Cliff Where Horses Rest. Yu-ying feels history surrounding her; men of the Ch'in and Han dynasties, two thousand years ago, climbed the same stairway, as did Confucius before them. Calligraphy hacked out of the rock, though in characters too ancient or worn for her to read, has left messages from her father's world: the beauty, the wisdom, the exuberance of it, just as Mother told her would be here at Tai Shan. She wishes, as they climb, that her mother could be here too. They'd see what Father once saw; they'd look across the ravine at a distant rock hewn with old praise to the God of the Mountain, and they'd look at each other, knowing for the moment all three of them were here.

But Mother isn't here. Yu-ying glances at the brooding young man who moves beside her on the winding path. If only she could love him again, want him again, but she can't. When did her love vanish—simply leave like an angry guest? Lamai is now married. How does she feel about her husband? I will never marry, Yu-ying tells herself. Swears it, as they climb, a soundless profound vow in this rising landscape of stone-tablet exclamations and poetry. The vow brings her such relief that as they climb she reaches out and yanks playfully on Jin-shi's sleeve —the way a sister might tease a preoccupied brother.

• • •

The approach to the Halfway Gate to Heaven proves steep—but it will get steeper, a panting old woman explains to Yu-ying, who has paused a few moments to rest.

"Are you going up, then, Mother?" They are standing on the last brace of stairs that come before an open space halfway to the summit.

"I am going all the way," the old woman declares. She holds a long thick staff, already trembling in her hand.

Impossible, Yu-ying thinks; the old woman can't get up another flight of such stairs. From this perspective, just past an arch leading to a cluster of buildings at the halfway mark, she can see far in the upper distance a long gray thread leading through a vast ravine to the top of the mountain. The thread is actually the continuing stairway; at this remove it seems like a flat continuous line. Whatever lies at the summit from here has the appearance of a small bead set between sides of the ravine.

"I will see you there, Daughter." The old woman takes a bent step forward, leaning heavily on the staff.

There's a parapet at the end of the last flight to Halfway Gate to Heaven. Getting there, Yu-ying leans upon it, panting.

"Look at them," Jin-shi says, nodding at a group of Red soldiers resting nearby.

They seem so young to Yu-ying, as they pass cloves of garlic around to munch on. Their sunburned faces glow under the noon light. Glancing at her shyly, not one of them seems bold enough to show active interest in her. Yu-ying relaxes.

"When this letter's delivered," Jin-shi tells her, "I'll join the Liberation Army."

She turns to regard him.

"You're different now," he goes on, not meeting her eyes, but staring up at the winding stream of gray stairs above the Halfway Gate to Heaven. "You thought differently when I killed the agent."

"The man we killed wasn't an agent."

Even at this remark he fails to look at her. A boy selling apples comes along. Yu-ying calls him and buys half a dozen, gives one to Jin-shi, who grips it tightly like a ball. "Because I can't speak this language, you lost respect for me."

"I have respect for you," Yu-ying claims, and yet asks herself, Do I? Do I?

"Your mother taught you these languages. You went to school. But all my father wanted of me was work. I learned Teochiu in the street and taught myself to read characters. I don't know many characters, I never had enough school." Now he turns directly toward her. With the sunlight behind him, his eyes are like two holes burned into leather. "In the new world people like me will have a chance, but you don't care."

"I care." Do I? Do I really care? Yu-ying wonders.

Up comes the apple; he bites viciously into it, juice spurting down his pointed chin.

A sudden rush of feeling—what it is she doesn't know—overwhelms her. Beyond Ho Jin-shi the young soldiers are laughing gently together, munching apples too. None of them has a complete uniform, but obviously here and there they have found a tunic, a pair of trousers, a cap —Japanese? Nationalist? American issue? Old warlord army uniforms? But all of them have red stars on white bands on their upper right arms. That unifies them. They are together, whereas poor Jin-shi seems woefully alone. His isolation is accentuated as he stands on this sunny mountain, looking out across vast reaches of flat plain, a little breeze stirring his coal-black hair.

Yu-ying says, "Don't worry." Reaching out she takes his hand in hers; his feels cold, lifeless. Both her hands cover it protectively for a moment, before she drops them. "When we killed that man, our lives became one."

He gives her a puzzled smile.

"I mean we did something together that no one else can understand. What I mean is . . ." Yu-ying pauses, unable to give a satisfactory explanation.

Perhaps this is because a man has stopped nearby, close to the parapet. The soldiers gawk at him when he removes a large conical sunhat. Although he wears a long black Chinese robe, without the hat he reveals something remarkable about himself: His hair is the color of wheat; his face, reddened by sunlight, is that of a Westerner.

With the hat removed, he approaches. She sees a long bluish scar on his forehead, and memory unleashes in her a cry of recognition.

"I wasn't sure," the man says in Chinese. Coming from this blue-eyed man the words sound strange. "You're Sonia?" He has a photograph in his hand.

"My name is Tang Yu-ying," she tells him with extravagant dignity. "But I *was* Sonia." She adds, smiling, "Philip." In English she says, "I remember you." Should I, after all these years, embrace him?

To her relief, he makes the decision for them both. Instead of embracing her, he bows slightly in a formal Chinese way and says, "My karma must be better than I thought. Because I've found you."

38 BUT HAVING FOUND her, what now? Embree asks himself. He has taken them to a little restaurant on Halfway Gate to Heaven; it's in the back of a temple falling to ruin. Looking at her, Embree is surprised that initially he hadn't been sure it was she, even with the photograph in hand. Of course she has cut her hair boyishly short, whereas in the photo it's shoulder length. Even so, at first he'd seen a Chinese girl standing at the parapet. Now he sees the daughter of Vera and the General. There is in her face a racial mixture which has haunted his imagination ever since he first gazed at the infant girl Vera was holding in the Hong Kong hospital. What the black-and-white photograph totally misrepresents is the color of her skin. In some light it has a brownish hue, then in other light an almost ivory cast. Her eyes are definitely Chinese, yet her nose is strongly tapered, like that of her Russian mother.

What's most unusual, however, is the maturity of her expression. He'd expected a girl, not a woman. But seated across the rickety table from him in the dim back room of the dilapidated temple is a woman—studying him warily.

The Communist, on the other hand, seems no more than a boy: thin, sharp featured, quite open, eagerly asking questions. They speak in Teochiu, and with an eagerness bordering on frenzy the boy asks questions. Embree answers them with his eyes fixed on Yu-ying's reaction.

How did he get here? the boy asks. By plane from Shanghai to Jinan, then by wagon and truck. Why has he come here? He's working for WHO now and his assigned territory is Shantung Province. It takes a little time for the boy to understand the meaning of WHO, and during the explanation Embree glances often at the girl.

Her mouth? Her mother's, he finally decides: generous; her lips almost pouted, giving her face at times an abruptly sensual look, at others a skeptical, possibly sullen expression.

Ho continues with his questions. What do you think of the war? Will there be a battle? Where is the Third Field Army?

Embree regards the boy more closely. There's a tensile quality in the dark narrow face he'd ignored at the outset. He tells Ho Jin-shi that it's difficult to say where the Third Field Army is. Once a few divisions were encamped in Taian, after they threw the Nationalists out last winter. But now, as he understands it, only a guard battalion has been left here. Some of its troops are climbing the mountain today for something to do. Usually, however, the Third Field Army is on the move.

"You won't find it easily," Embree concludes with a smile.

"Do you think I'm looking for it?"

Embree shrugs. "Perhaps."

"Well, I *am* looking for it," the boy says, leaning forward, elbows on the table. "I want to join it."

"Yes, perhaps you do."

"You think so?" Ho Jin-shi, relaxing, sits back in his chair. "I'm glad you think so, because that means you understand. I mean, about someone like me. That's because you know war. She told me"—he nods toward Yu-ying—"you fought in Burma. Were the Japanese good soldiers?"

"Very good."

"I saw them in Bangkok when I was a child. They didn't look like much to me. They turned their caps around and wore scarves they wiped the sweat off with."

A small boy brings their lunch, stewed chicken with fungus mushrooms. "I've always heard of this dish." Embree looks at the steaming pot. "They grow a fungus found only up here around the ancient pine trees. At least that's the story. To cook this fungus, you tear it into pieces. Cutting it with a knife ruins the flavor."

"Mother sent you."

Embree hears the statement as he's reaching toward the iron pot with a big ladle. Without looking at the girl, he says, "Your mother wanted me to find you, if I got near this part of the country."

"No, she sent you. She knew I'd be here."

Continuing to ladle chicken and mushrooms onto their plates, Embree explains that since WHO was sending him into Shantung and since she had left home without any word, naturally he'd try to meet her here for her mother's sake.

"You came from Shanghai knowing I'd be here."

"How could I know? It was a guess."

"No," the girl says emphatically. "Mother knew."

Holding a piece of torn mushroom in his chopsticks, Embree blows on it, eats. The small boy brings three cups of water. "This is supposed to be a specialty too," Embree explains cheerily, feeling the girl's eyes on him. "Tai Shan water is the purest, sweetest water in China."

"I'm going to climb the mountain."

Now Embree looks at her. He's startled to see the narrowed set of her lips, because, for an instant, it is Vera he's looking at. "I know you're going to climb it." He smiles. "And so am I." Turning to Ho Jin-shi, he says, "So are we all." After a few bites of the stewed chicken and mushrooms, Embree laughs briefly. "Well, at least the water's good."

• • •

They have set out on the second half of the climb, and above them, undulating in afternoon light, are more than four thousand flagstones that lead toward the brown button placed in the rocky cleft at the summit.

The climb is gentle out of Halfway Gate to Heaven, lovely among cypresses and waterfalls. On the path now are coolies with loads of food and building materials. They carry on long bamboo poles large baskets filled with rice and salt blocks; some carry pots of cement. Ho Jin-shi moves ahead of everyone, irritably eager to reach the top, all of two miles away.

Embree himself feels the impatience of a man much younger. This newfound restlessness interests him. Perhaps he's merely coltish in the presence of such an attractive woman. Responding to nothing more than that possibility, he glances up the trail. The look of it sobers him, and a grim thought follows: How will he persuade Sonia—that is, Yu-ying—to return to Shanghai without breaking his promise to Vera? If Sonia knows that her mother is ill in Shanghai, she'll go right there. And by breaking that promise he will fail again. At least, that's how Vera will judge him. That woman's willpower is a kind of miracle. He has located someone in the midst of war-torn China on the strength of her conviction that he could succeed. Of course, Tai Shan was an obvious place to look first; next he'd have gone to Qufu. And yet a difference of twenty-four hours might have caused him to miss Sonia. Luck bordering on miracle, although Vera never doubted he would find her daughter. And Sonia assumes that this meeting on the mountain was preordained by her mother. Two formidable women. Blessed or cursed with the capacity to believe.

As Embree walks beside her (Ho Jin-shi is out of sight on the twisting path), they establish that Sonia was three months shy of eleven years old when he left for China in 1939. She confesses never to have learned the classical xylophone, *ranad ek*, his gift for her tenth birthday. But she tells him she writes a little—in a diary. And speaks to an imaginary friend.

Halting for a moment, she squints at him in the sunlight. Their eyes are almost on the same level. "I never told anyone that before."

"Maybe you've told me because I talk to imaginary people too. When I was a boy in school, bored with the walk home, I invented a friend."

"Then I'm not crazy?"

"Oh, I didn't say that." He laughs—a strange open laugh less nervous than idiotic. It occurs to Philip Embree that he wants to impress the girl, as a boy might do, by giggling like a fool. For a moment Embree wonders if he's trying to be as feckless as young Ho Jin-shi, who moves far ahead of them like a goat. That would be feckless indeed. But glancing up at the steep mountain, Embree feels a twinge of vengeful pleasure at the knowledge that soon enough the young revolutionary, as slim and keenly muscled as the coolies with their loads, will be slowed to a struggling walk.

· · ·

"You don't know where he was taken prisoner?" Yu-ying asks, as they turn into view of a stone bridge.

"No one knows. But the guess is he was taken at the foot."

"He was going to climb, though."

"I think he was."

"Were you with his army then?"

Embree hesitates; for one dangerous moment he nearly turns, as she'd done with her confession about her imaginary friend, to make a lovely little confession of his own: "By the time he was murdered, I was safe in Hong Kong with your mother." Instead, he says, "No, I was awaiting his instructions in Peking. Look." He points to a waterfall above the Stepping Over Clouds Bridge; in the sunlight, myriad drops of water create a rainbow that dances in the spray a few minutes, then fades. They stand looking at it, then at the turbulent stream below the stone bridge.

Embree tells her about a famous poet, Hsu Chih-mo, who died in a plane crash near this mountain in the early '30s. "He called his sweet-heart 'Little Dragon.' Very much the romantic. He believed only in love, in freedom. He wrote a wonderful poem about departure.

> Silently I'm going
> As silently I came—
> Shaking my sleeves
> Not keeping in them one patch of cloud

Do you like that?"

"It's very sad. But I believe in what he says. When you go somewhere new, you must give up everything."

Embree smiles wryly. Does she mean anything specific by that? Her mother, her home—shaking the past from her sleeves? Sounds like himself long ago, when he did exactly that: left it all behind—home, family, friends, a girl he was supposed to marry, a profession he was committed to; all of it, within a few days, surrendered to curiosity. He might have been hanging by his fingers from a tree and after a quick breath just merrily let go. Life can be changed that way for some people. Is she one of them? Then warn her, he thinks. He'd like to tell her about it, the good and the bad, but can't, not now. "You have your mother's spirit," he says, meaning it.

"And my father's."

They see Ho Jin-shi running down the stairway that towers above the bridge. "Where have you been?" he shouts. "You're too slow!"

Coming up to them, he frowns. "I'm sorry," he says to Embree. "I forgot you're old."

"Where did you get that idea? My God. Not *that* old." But he can feel heat in his face; glancing at Yu-ying, he repeats it. "Not that old."

"Why such a rush? We want to see what's here," she tells Ho Jin-shi, annoyed.

"Well, there's more up there." He sweeps his arm toward the summit. "If we can ever get to it. You should see those soldiers climb. That bunch of them we saw at the Halfway Gate, they're far up there."

With a brisk stride, Philip Embree heads off the bridge for the first flight of flagstones. Ho passes him quickly and maintains a half-flight of stairs ahead of them.

"Now I remember," Yu-ying says abruptly as they climb. "You're a Dragon, like me. But I forget your month and day."

"I was born in August on a Monday. Is that bad?"

"No, you're a Gold Dragon. Jupiter's in your mouth, so you speak wisely."

Does she take astrology seriously?

"But you can be bad-tempered."

Embree laughs—that damn foolish laugh. He swears not to laugh again during the climb, and from the look of it ahead, there won't be anything to laugh at. Already his breathing is labored; his face is getting sweaty. "Come on," he says cheerfully, "let's pick up the pace or your friend will think I'm old."

The girl walks beside him, and with a touch of dismay Embree notices her breathing is almost normal.

• • •

Cypresses are left behind; on the mountain walls to either side of the stairway are cedars and pines. Glimpsed among the foliage are the roofs and pillars of distant temples, isolated monuments in praise of the mountain. Ho returns at The Fifth Rank Pine Pavilion. They sit on the steps of the red-fronted pavilion and look at three scrawny pines, zigzagged over centuries of growth into lightning bolts of brown branch and green needle. During the Ch'in Dynasty, more than two thousand years ago, Embree explains, the emperor took refuge during a storm under a pine tree here. Having served him, it was given the official status of a courtier —fifth rank. During the Ming it was washed away in another mountain storm. These three pines were planted during the Ching.

"And someday they'll be washed away too. Everything is old here," Ho says, rising to his feet. "Except the soldiers. You should see them march on up. Must be all the way now. If I had the chance, I'd stay with them."

"You would," Embree says, rising too. "You're very strong."

"I played soccer in Bangkok," Ho declares proudly. They're strolling together along the front of the pavilion near the winding stairway. "Are you a Communist?"

"No."

Ho looks surprised. "A Nationalist, then?"

"No."

"You have to be something."

"Not in this country." Embree looks over his shoulder at the girl, who has not yet risen from the pavilion step. Perhaps she's thinking of the venerable trees, of the old China her father loved. "But years ago in this country I used to be something."

"What was that?"

"Someone who believed in her father."

Ho looks beyond his shoulder at Yu-ying. "Then he really was a general?"

"Did you doubt it? He was a man born in the right place at the wrong time."

"She said he was a great man." Ho shrugs. "I believed her, but I believe it more hearing it from you. You know war. What do I know? Nothing. What do you think of me?"

The blunt, ingenuous question startles Embree. "Well, I don't know you."

"You don't know her either after all these years, but I know what you think of her."

"Yes?" Embree feels himself straining to smile. "What is that?"

"You'd like to have her. But I don't know what you think of me."

"I think you talk before you think."

"You think so? Come on." Ho steps out and, turning, waves him on. "Don't worry about her. She'll catch up."

Without hesitation Embree falls into stride with him, without even a look backward, and they mount the first flight of stairs almost at a trot.

"Are you all right?" Ho asks when they get to the little landing.

"Yes." He's winded, yet continues alongside Ho up the next flight. Just ahead of them is a stone arch over the pathway. "Wait," he says.

"Tired?" Ho asks with a grin.

"I just want to say something. That arch ahead. It's called the Archway to Immortality. After it there are eighteen flights of stairs, each of two hundred steps. Straight up."

"You better wait here for Yu-ying." The boy turns and strides forward, with Embree following a half-dozen steps behind.

So long ago, he thinks, I did something like this. Only it was in a Chinese army camp, he tells himself as if he's someone else, like Ho Jin-shi, listening in. There were fifteen of us competing in a long-distance run. We crossed a swift river, ran up a steep hill, and returned. A man drowned. Another man, trying to push me over the embankment of that river, I pushed into it, and he too drowned. I nearly won, in spite of injuries. At the finish, in front of a thousand Chinese troops, I lost by two or three feet at the end of a rope ladder. And here I'm desperate to challenge a boy who wouldn't have stood a chance against me then. But he's young, and as he says, I'm old.

These thoughts spur him to an effort that Philip Embree never knew he could make. At the third of the Eighteen Bends he catches up with Ho Jin-shi, who glances at him in surprise. They go up together, more slowly now. The younger man glances at him frequently, as if his ability to keep climbing makes him worth paying attention to.

Huge boulders and fir trees give way on either side to smaller rocks and stubble, while the stairs ascend almost vertically. Old women are groping here for each flagstone, yet with their wooden staffs they make it. Their wrinkled faces, the color of walnut from seasons in the sun, have been turned apple-red by wind and exertion.

His face dripping sweat—running into his eyes, the salt stings, nearly blinds him—Embree, like the old women, goes up too. Yoga, commanding different muscles, has not prepared him for such a gross physical effort. Rowing did, once. His college sculling did. Thirty strokes a minute in a single scull. The scull was cedar, thirty feet long and only a foot wide, so light that an oarsman risked putting his foot through the planking when he boarded. Fast hull speed, of course. Reaching the oar forward for the catch, pulling through for the stroke, and feathering, then recovering for the next catch—that's it. But twenty-five years ago. Pain's ballooning in his lungs, consuming his breath.

He's gratified to see Ho slowing down a little. And every time the boy halts a moment at the end of a flight, his face registers surprise and annoyance, because Embree is not more than a dozen steps behind. That look on Ho's face is worth dying for, Embree thinks. I learned to sleep on a horse, he thinks. I killed a man by throwing him over an embankment into a river. I killed another man in battle with an ax. I survived the jungles of Burma.

But even while bolstering himself with the memory of action, Embree feels his body telling him it cannot be; he must slow down. At the same time his mind says if only he can muster a little more energy, he'll pass the boy.

It's his last delusion. Because Ho Jin-shi, though panting hard too, seems to have found a second wind, and continues upward, without headlong zest, true, but with a quiet new resolve that finds its expression in a dogged, steady pace. The boy won't be caught.

Halfway up the Eighteen Bends, Embree falls twenty, thirty steps behind.

Leaning against a retaining wall on the path, his chest heaving, he looks at the chasm below. Rocks and trees, all jittery in his shaken vision. He can't keep up, he can't. With a glance he sees the slim shape of Ho Jin-shi rise methodically upward. How dare that kid insult him by suggesting he wants the daughter of Vera and the General.

Turning, he looks at the people coming toward him. He asks an old woman, "Are you tired, Mother?"

"No, I don't feel tired," she says, white hair streaming behind her in the wind. Sweat pours down her face.

"We don't feel tired," another coming up tells him.

They stand looking at Embree, who leans against the stone retaining wall of the stairway. "The Goddess of the Blue Clouds gives us strength," the first one says.

Belief.

Embree watches them pick their way slowly, like blind people, up the brutal flagstones. Belief will get them to the summit. But slowly, slowly. Even belief can't give them—or him—the bones of youth.

Now he sees her on the flight of stairs below. She looks Chinese among the Chinese with her short black hair, bangs, blue trousers, plain white blouse. Yet when she looks up and smiles, there's the other person in her face—the tapered nose, the full lips, the mobile expression of her Russian mother. Had he ever seen the woman in the child? Not that he remembers.

As she approaches him, Embree shakes his head. "I'm a fool. I tried to keep up with him."

Yu-ying regards him closely. "Yes, you really are a fool." And she laughs. It's a burst of merry laughter that encourages laughter in him too. People stare at them. "Where is he now?"

"Up there challenging the whole Red Army to a race, I suppose." He has taken up her jocular mood, grateful for it.

"Are you all right?"

"Yes, of course." Embree steps away from the wall. "But we can go slower."

Then something happens.

Yu-ying reaches out to take his arm, but he pulls back as if from a red-hot iron. "No, no," he tells her nervously and steps briskly out. I won't be helped, he thinks. During later moments of leisure he'll recognize the truth: that he feared her touch.

The climb now is sufficiently vertical that they can feel the gravitational pull, the tendency to fall backward. Everyone is bending forward in solemn concentration upon each flagstone. Three soldiers just ahead suddenly halt, and one sits down to vomit quietly between his legs. The coolies with their heavy loads move like somnambulists.

At another stairway platform Embree grips the stone railing and looks across the mountain toward Flying Dragon Rock. "The Emperors climbed differently," he says after getting his breath. "They were carried up in palanquins. When they reached the top, they sat on a throne. Then they drank wine and prayed to the Tai Shan god for a long reign."

"Their way they couldn't feel the climb. It's better to climb Tai Shan this way, isn't it?"

He looks at her; the girl means it as a serious question. "Of course," he lies.

The climb is silent now, save for hoarse breathing everywhere on the stairs. Perhaps this really does duplicate the trials of ascending to heaven, Embree thinks—and shares the playful thought with Yu-ying. She, panting hard, nods in agreement. Now, along the stairway, runs a long iron-link chain for climbers to use in the vertical ascent. Many of the old women are using it, and so are a few of the soldiers. Both Embree and Yu-ying have long since given up trying to locate Ho on the Eighteen Bends. Embree feels gratified that the girl shows no concern for her young companion. But of course, why should she? Ho doesn't need help, Embree tells himself. I do. Up ahead now, a deepening crimson structure in the late afternoon light, is the third and final gateway, called the South Gate to Heaven. The tiny gray bead, the brown button, seen from afar have coalesced into a red arch with a gold-tiled roof.

They stop again. They are stopping now at the end of every flight. Many of the climbers take long rests on the flagstone steps, resting their cheeks against wooden staffs gripped in both hands.

"I really believe for some of them it's a climb to God," Embree says, his elbows on a railing.

"Of course it is."

"You don't question it?"

"No."

It's what her mother would say too.

"Once I was in the holy city of Benares," he begins, letting the thought develop almost without conscious help. "In a boat on the Ganges. I saw this line of three or four hundred Hindus—men, women, and children—unloading a cement barge at the foot of a ghat. You know what a ghat is? A kind of embankment with steps. Anyway, they carried the clay up the ghat, almost as steep as this stairway, which is probably why I remember. The clay was in iron bowls they balanced on their heads. At the top of the ghat they dumped their clay into a construction site. Must have weighed fifty pounds, each load. Now I said men, women, and *children*. I swear some of those children didn't weigh a pound more than the load they carried. It was terribly hot. I got out of the boat right next to the cement barge. Picture this. Barge on the left. On the right was a burning ghat. You understand? Where on criss-crossed logs they cremate the dead. Now just beyond the burning ghat, maybe twenty feet away, half a dozen children were playing in the sand, perhaps because they were still too young to work. When I got there a corpse was burning, and just as I reached land, a foot fell out of the fire. The attendant picked it up—deftly, I recall—with two sticks he kept for the purpose, like giant chopsticks, and tossed it back into the fire. So there I was in terrific heat at midday, looking to the left at a line of people toiling up and down this hillside, and to the right at someone going up in smoke, and beyond the smoke to children playing in the sand. And I thought, Is this life? Is this what it's all about? You're born, you play awhile, you work long hours, you end up with your foot tumbling out of a crematory fire." He hasn't meant to say such things. My God. "I'm sorry."

"Why be sorry? You've seen the world. And you've thought about it."

Turning, he studies her grave, almost defiant face. The look says she's defending him against the world he's seen and thought about. Clearly this is youthful admiration of experience, Embree thinks, but he accepts the thrill of it, even adds to her claim. "Yes. I've seen a great deal of the world."

"When I was a child, I didn't realize that. Mother . . ." She hesitates before revealing something that Embree has always known. "Mother never made much of what you did. She used to say, 'Whatever Philip does, he's always a soldier'—said with a laugh. That's how she presented you."

"She presented me the way I should be."

"Oh no." Reaching out, she touches his sleeve.

Embree pulls the rim of his broad coolie hat down, so his eyes are in shadow. "Your mother just never liked war. She's seen enough of it to know the truth—that the idea of war is to hurt people."

"Yet my father was a general."

"That was different." He can't go on with this conversation, which his own foolish story has created. "Let's go up."

"You see, my mother is always an aristocrat," Yu-ying continues, as they turn to mount the next stairway. "War in Russia took away a lovely way of life for her. So, of course, she hated war. But my father was more than a general to her. He was a man of good family who'd have been welcome in her parents' house. Do you see?"

Embree nods without enthusiasm. Of course what the girl says is absolutely true. The girl who wrote that childishly appealing letter of welcome to him in Madras is not *this* girl. Something has changed her in the interval between the writing of that letter and this moment on the mountain. But that mustn't be his concern. He says bravely, "Your mother's equal to your father. She's a woman of deep . . ." He pauses for breath. "Deep feeling."

"I love her, but I stole from her. I suppose you know that."

Embree nods again, torn between their conversation and his need for rest. Arching his head back, he sees the next platform far, far above them. I won't make it, he thinks. I'll have to sit on the stairway.

To his surprise, Yu-ying sits down first.

Panting, he joins her on the stone step. Embree draws the back of his hand across his forehead, gratified to notice that her face is sweaty too. At her age he could have carried her up this mountain. Well, almost.

"I said, I stole from her."

Again he nods. In a few moments he's able to say, "It doesn't matter. If you think she thinks so, you don't know her."

"Then what matters?"

"You."

Elbows on her knees, Yu-ying looks at her hands clasped between them. "But I can't go back now. I don't want to see her yet."

"Why not? You'd make her very happy."

She turns to him. "You're loyal."

It's not something he wants to hear. Embree looks down at the smoothly worn stone.

"You are," the girl declares. "She never said so, but you are. She always hinted at other things."

"What things? Well, it's not important."

"I don't think it is either. But she hinted at you being . . . irresponsible. Somebody not to depend on."

"Maybe she had good reason."

"Do you think I care? What does it matter what happened in the past?" She looks toward the mountain. "This is beautiful, so this matters. Maybe we all do a lot of wrong things, terrible things."

Embree suppresses a smile. Terrible things? The girl is only twenty. Stole a vase. In the cosmic scheme of things, how terrible is that? He says nothing.

Below them people are struggling, many of them hoisting themselves up with the help of the linked chain. "Look." Embree points across the ravine to a distant rock on the side of which are huge Chinese characters. *"Cautiously approach the region of beauty,"* he reads.

"I can only read some of it," Yu-ying admits.

"And over there. Look. *Pillar supporting the left side of Heaven.*"

Yu-ying squints up in the late-gathering light at the South Gate to Heaven. Now it's a solid red arch only a few hundred feet above them. "So we're close to heaven."

"That's what they said through the centuries—the emperors, the poets, the generals, the philosophers who took the same trip we're taking."

"But most of them were carried."

They laugh, and their eyes, narrowed by the pleasurable exertion, meet almost conspiratorially on this serious climb. Embree can't remember when he has laughed more, when the urge has shaken him so often into brief episodes of laughter.

• • •

It's hard for Embree to believe, when his foot touches the last step, that they've reached the South Gate to Heaven. Looking up at the two-story building towering above them, he reads characters for *The Pavilion That Touches the Sky.* Translating for Yu-ying, he adds, "It certainly feels like it—touching the sky." They look at where they came from: at thousands of twisting stairs which, far below them now, appear to be a continuous sheet of gray water, a mountain stream, just as the pathway above them, when they were in the valley, had seemed to be a waterfall.

"I guess I'm not so old," he says.

"You're not old," the girl maintains with surprising heat. "Don't listen to him. You're younger than Mother, too. She told me once."

"A tribute to her honesty." The girl doesn't react, but stares at the peeled walls, the ruinous appearance of the elegantly named South Gate to Heaven. She'll talk about her mother but won't let him do it. Her relationship to Vera is obviously complex. She must feel a welter of passionate responses to what her mother does. As Vera would have raised her to feel.

They move outside and see where the coolies have brought those crossbar loads. Here on the plateau a road's being paved with rock slabs and cement. Tents are set up everywhere, in front of which, at twilight, workmen are gathering around rice pots bubbling over little fires.

"In the middle of war they're building a road on top of this mountain?" Yu-ying asks in wonder.

"Part of your heritage," Embree says. "One thing about the Chinese. They never let disaster stop them from eating something or buying something or building something. In the middle of a flood, seated on their roof, they'll munch on a wheat bun, buy a piece of cloth from someone floating by on a log, and build a shelter with it." Embree likes what he's said; it has a kind of pert vitality. Or at least Yu-ying thinks so, because she laughs a little. She's sharing his tendency to laugh.

Moving across the rugged plateau, they leave behind the coolies, who are resting beside loads of rice, salt, and clay. Ahead lie a number of temples and stone huts, strewn, it seems, haphazardly among the rocks. With the sun low, what breeze there is has a keen edge, belying the summer season. People seeking their way along the rocky path seem cheerful, having accomplished the climb. Embree feels their triumph.

"It's too late to see the temples today," Embree says, as they follow pilgrims along the path. Ahead is another rise, affording them a view of the actual summit where another building sits, the Temple of Jade Emperor Peak.

"Are there places to stay up here?"

Embree looks at her with a smile. The casual freedom of youth. She has come all the way with no idea where to spend the night. "Yes, of course. Not attractive places, I'm told, but at least we'll keep warm. It'll be cold on the mountain tonight."

"Where has he gone?"

At last the question. Rather irritably Embree says, "It's a large area around here. He could be anywhere."

"I suppose we better find an inn," Yu-ying suggests abruptly.

Embree halts. "There can't be many up here. I'm sure he'll find us." After a pause, trying to keep from asking the question, he asks it. "Will you stay with him?"

"No."

"I see."

"I stayed with him other places. I don't want to stay with him any more."

"I see." Embree glances away from her, as if to find the inn. "Anyway, up here the rooms are probably communal." He feels the pressure of her hand on his arm. Following her gaze, Embree sees the boy coming across the rocky plateau with two soldiers. Has he been arrested? Embree wonders. He recognizes that what he's now feeling is hope.

• • •

"They're veterans," Ho calls out, "and they speak Teochiu!" When he has reached the path—his companions a few steps behind him—Ho Jin-shi smiles at Embree. "Veterans like you. Only they fight for the PLA. For the People's Liberation Army. I told them you're American. I don't think they like Americans," he observes happily. "They say Chiang Kai-shek is the puppet of Americans. That's why Americans give guns to him. But America won't win, my friends say. *We* will."

Embree turns to the two soldiers and speaks to them in Teochiu. Their thin sunburned faces brighten. Embree asks them if they come from the South. They do. Why are they here? he asks. And a conversation starts, while—Embree notices from the corner of his eye—Ho Jin-shi and the girl stroll together down the path.

The two southerners, enheartened by Embree's knowledge of their language, alternate in reporting their history. They were pressed into military service in Canton during the early years of the Japanese War. In Kunming, one says, they did guard duty for two—the other says almost three—years. Then when the Americans dropped the great bomb and the Japanese surrendered, their unit was force-marched to the sea. At Haiphong Harbor in Indochina, they were put on an American boat that looked like a tank—the front fell open. After weeks on this boat, they reached Chinwangtao in Manchuria, where the Nationalists were trying to stamp out Communist troops who'd gone in there when Russian troops left. So there was fighting. They both grin. At Szeping, they were captured by Reds. One says, "We thought they'd shoot us, but instead they gave us food."

The other says, with a little shudder, "It's cold up there."

"Were you there long?" Embree asks, looking past the narrow shoulders of one southerner at the couple walking on the path.

"Almost two years."

"Longer," the other says. "We fought at Szeping and Changchun and Harbin and Mukden."

"Twice at Szeping. Once with the Nationalists, once against them."

"It was coldest around Changchun last winter. My cheek froze against the gun barrel, ripped the skin off." The young soldier claps a hand hard to his cheek and smiles.

The other soldier turns to him. "You had the Japanese gun then."

"No, it was the American. I had one of yours," he tells Embree.

Then when General Chen Yi needed reinforcements here in this province these two men were among troops sent from Manchuria. Came by boat again, only this time by junk across the Yellow Sea from Yingkou. Now they've been fighting with the Third Field Army all spring. "We like it better," one says.

"It's warmer here," says the other.

"You met my friend at the summit?"

"Yes. He's eager to join us."

"He is?"

"We'll take him to our unit. He's come a long way with a message."

"A message?"

They look at him somberly. It's a question these peasant soldiers mustn't answer, not when asked by a foreigner, an American.

Embree offers them cigarettes, which they accept. Soon the three of them are smoking in the brisk wind; the eastern sky is now a glowing orange similar to that at the end of their cigarettes. One of the soldiers has some kind of tumor on his neck. It looks serious to Embree. The other one has a curved pig-skinning knife sticking from his belt, reminding Embree of the ax in his luggage down in Taian.

"You're here with American soldiers?" one asks politely.

"No. With the World Health Organization."

"Fighting against the People's Liberation Army?" He is still polite.

"WHO is not political. It's to help people feel better. Health. It's all we're interested in."

The two grin slightly, as if doubtful whether to laugh or accept a mystery.

Now the girl and Ho Jin-shi are returning—a contrast in moods. He is smiling, she is frowning. He's walking with the zest of someone who has done nothing today to tire himself, and she's slouching along, head down, hunched in thought.

"I have good joss," Ho says gaily as they approach. "Up there"—he points to the summit—"I heard someone talking. I said, 'That's Teochiu, that's the Chinese *I* know.' And when I looked around, here were these comrades. They're going to help me." He beams at them; they give him a restrained smile. "I'm going down the mountain with them now."

"Now?" Embree asks. "It's getting dark."

"Oh, well, I'm young, I can see by moonlight. And they're soldiers who know war. Like you."

"They said you have a message to deliver."

Ho Jin-shi draws himself up. "I can't talk about that."

"I see. You're going with them, and you'll be back?" Embree is looking at the girl, not at him.

"I'll be gone awhile. But I told Yu-ying to leave a message for me at the hardware store where we left our bags this morning. It's all arranged," he says and puts hands on hips. "I might not get another opportunity like this. Where else can I find someone around here who speaks Teochiu?"

"That's true," Embree says. "So you're going with them? Both of you?"

"Oh, she can't go to their army unit. Not yet. I have to prepare everything." Ho cocks his head a moment, smiling at Embree. "*You* take care of her."

When Embree doesn't reply, he turns and goes to the girl. There's a kind of awkward grace, Embree thinks, in the way the young man puts one arm around her shoulder and touches her cheek gently. It's a moment of calm silence. Then Ho claps his hands, as if beginning a game, and turns toward the soldiers. "Ready, comrades?"

They nod.

Without a backward look, Ho Jin-shi leads the way down the path toward the South Gate to Heaven. In the growing dusk his slim figure, between the dumpy ones in uniform on either side of him, seems to move with preternatural speed, as if he's most anxious to leave this place, to leave Embree, to leave the girl who brought him out of Siam.

· · ·

They watch until a slight dip in the path obscures the trio, except the three heads, which seem disembodied in the fading light.

Turning away from them, Embree looks at the silent girl. "Don't worry. If he got this far, he can get farther." Embree steps out, searching along the ridge for something that might be an inn among the makeshift huts, most of which were probably used during the Third Field Army's occupation of the mountain.

When they have walked a few minutes, Embree halts. "Do you want me to bring him back?"

"He wouldn't stay."

Sticking his hands in his pockets—the wind's getting chill—Embree starts walking again. "You're worried about him?"

"Oh yes."

Up ahead, just off the path leading to the final incline of the summit, is a stone cottage with crossed antlers crudely drawn on a sign nailed above the door. Embree slows down, wanting to form a subtle question. Instead he says, "Do you love him?"

"No." There's no hesitation in this reply. "I used to."

"I see," Embree says cautiously.

"But it won't ever be over between us." Yu-ying gives her head an impatient shake, as if clearing it of encumbrances: memories, vows, images. "We're responsible for each other."

Unable to stem the cruelty of it, Embree says bluntly, "You may feel responsible for him, but he doesn't seem to feel that way about you."

"But he does." After a few steps, the girl adds, "In his way."

"The deer sign there means it's an inn." He's trying to sound casual.

"Do you think I should have told him not to go?"

"Well, he'd have gone anyway. You said so yourself."

"I know."

"Here we are," Embree says, reaching for the door.

• ◂ •

After a dinner in a close little room with other pilgrims—a poor meal of tea, wheat dumplings, some fried greens—they go into one of the communal bedrooms. Mattresses are laid on the floor with a foot-wide aisle. There's a narrow window with rags stuffed in the broken panes—most are broken. An old cleaning woman comes along with worn padded jackets and a blanket for each of the eight people who will sleep here. There's a single oil lamp with a long wick, and in this flickering light Embree faces Yu-ying across the room. She looks Chinese now, her bangs straight across the smooth broad forehead, her eyes merely slits from fatigue. But she smiles at him. How young she really is, he thinks, and yet once again he sees in her expression the maturity of a woman. Perhaps that's because she's no longer a virgin. A romantic thought. Embree is amused by his own propensity for the naïve, the romantic view. As she says, he has seen the world—but knowing it is another matter. He doesn't even know himself.

For example, looking at this daughter of Vera and the General, should he not distinguish rigorously between what he feels and what, by circumstances, he ought to feel? After all, he has betrayed both her parents. That should make him uneasy in her presence, yet all she brings out in him is laughter, the easy untrammeled brief laughter of a boy. Well, he is a boy, nothing more. He is, he is.

What is she doing? Smiling?

When she leans forward in the lamplight, he leans forward too. On either side of her sit impassive old women. Most of the guests, having eaten, are already lying on their sides, encased in padded jackets and blankets.

"What is it?" he asks in a whisper. An arm's reach separates them.

"I want you to call me Sanuk. Isn't that what you called me before?"

"You were Sonia in my time."

"I don't want to be Sonia any more. But with you I don't feel like Yu-ying either."

They both laugh gently.

"Mother gave me the name Sanuk. You know what it means?"

"Joy, isn't it?"

"Will you call me Sanuk?"

"Of course." Then, dutifully he asks, "Do you miss your mother?"

"I've missed her since the day we left. But I'm glad to be where I am. Right *here*. I'd be no other place." She's not smiling, and the words strike him as deeply solemn, establishing for him a part of her character hidden until now. She has the gift of acceptance—not a passive acqui-escence to experience, but the power of adjusting to it and surviving. She is Vera's daughter.

"I'd be no other place either," he replies, as if the declaration in itself would give him the same gift of acceptance, which life has denied him and had also denied her father, who died from the lack of it.

After a brief study of him, Sanuk wriggles down from a sitting posi-tion and wraps herself in the blanket. In a few minutes, Embree assumes that the exhausted girl is asleep. He too is exhausted, yet in the crowded room, filled with gentle snoring, Embree treats his wakefulness as a chance to appraise this strange day. Only yesterday he flew into Jinan from Shanghai; only this morning he arrived by truck in Taian. And during the whole laborious journey he never truly believed in finding her. He went through the motions of duty with the well-thumbed photo of Vera's daughter in his pocket. He vowed to climb the mountain and look around, perhaps as policemen do, seeking a lost child they know will never be found. Even when, at the parapet of the Halfway Gate to Heaven, he saw the girl, Embree had not fully believed in the success of his mission. Duty had become an abstraction, something to endure like a penance, without another goal in view. Even when he told himself, "Find her, you must," it was like whistling in the dark. But today there she was, and there she now is, sleeping opposite him, her face real in the lamplight.

And today there were stranger things. On the Eighteen Bends, when she reached out to help him, he'd drawn back, afraid of her touch. Because he wanted that touch.

Because he wants her. The conscious knowledge of his desire is like a shape in front of the lamp wick, a jittery insect flying toward the light. He feels close to panic. But then it occurs to him that his guilty agitation is nothing more than a pose, as so often his moments of success at meditation have been. What he really wonders about, having mentally formed the shape of his desire, is her own awareness of it. Surely the boy, so blind in other ways, was aware of it today. He said, you want her. And it's true. But it's more than simply wanting her.

That's more awareness than he wants to have. He's a child, as foolish as the boy who walked out of her life today.

Embree tries to relax his clenched hands, while staring at the girl, soft-featured and young in the small lamplight. But he clenches them harder.

And out of the past, indeed, out of his childhood, when precociously he set to memory a great deal of the Bible—perhaps the only thing he ever did that pleased his father—Philip Embree recalls a phrase from the first epistle of John: "He that loveth not, knoweth not God; for God is love."

39 THEY REACH THE Summit of the Celestial Pillar before dawn, when the gray light scarcely outlines a small temple on the peak. Pilgrims accompany them up the last few steps to a side hall of the temple facing east—the Pavilion of Sunrise Watching. It is cold; they huddle in the padded jackets and watch the sky undergo a series of transformations: first a wash of gray, then a flush of white, a stream of myriad colors defining cloud after cloud, a burst of gold illuminating the mountainside, and rapidly a flat sheet of yellow light unrolling faster than the eye can follow it along each boulder and peak of Tai Shan.

She smiles at him; he smiles too; everyone around them is smiling, the way people smile after a birth, for it has seemed to Sanuk, surely, that what the sky and sun and earth have just accomplished is a kind of birth, the breaking out of a new world at the expense of tremendous energy. Below them seethes a pristine sea of morning clouds, crushing together beneath the rising sun, now a benign copper circle between this mountain-hovering cloud bank and a higher bank of clouds whose belly seems aflame now, a surging crimson. It is all new, primitive, and with the wind rushing at her ears, Sanuk feels creation must have been like this.

But the world of Tai Shan is also old. When they step down from the balustrade and enter the temple grounds, the iron-tiled roofs seem as ancient as the old pines which they passed yesterday and which Philip said had been here maybe two thousand years ago, before the Great Wall itself was built. They look at the large boulder in the middle of the courtyard with *Ji Ding* carved on its side—the Summit—and then enter a large hall, flanked by bays, where a bronze statue of the Jade Emperor stands. Yu Huang is life-sized, with a drooping mustache and thin goatee. Frescoes around the walls portray the Eight Immortals to the east and wise men studying mystic symbols to the west. She is thinking, Lamai is married.

When they emerge from the little shrine, sunlight has burned off the cloud cover so that overhead everything is a flat, empty blue. They go out to the rocks again for another look below. Sanuk can see a few small lakes—swatches of dropped blue silk—and far to the west a tiny golden thread, which seems to have been tossed carelessly on the brown plain —the great Yellow River moving toward the sea.

She leaves his side. He seems to understand her desire for privacy, because he remains where he is, a medium-sized broad-shouldered man wearing a coolie hat that hides his blue eyes, as blue as the mountain sky now everywhere visible. Sanuk scrambles down a few rocks, seeing a group of soldiers clustered together on a farther rock, scanning the distant horizon for a glimpse of the East China Sea.

She says in a low whisper, "I am talking to you, Lamai. You're a married woman now. What is it like? Oh, you don't have to tell me about the lovemaking—I knew about that when you were deciding to marry. I mean, what is it like to commit yourself to someone? I thought I had done that too. I won't ever make such a mistake again. No marriage for me, dear friend, no commitment. You would love it here, you with your artistic eye. We're at the top now. You should see it, how beautiful it is, like the creation of the world. They were both with me yesterday. Now only one is. Poor Chamlong, I'm afraid for him. He took me aside and talked about his important mission, how it must be carried out *at any cost*, and how these soldiers are his chance to do it. What could I say? If I still loved him, perhaps I'd have thought of something. Poor Chamlong. Before leaving, he touched my cheek and whispered, 'You are my *khwan fa*,' just as he'd done that day in front of the Emerald Buddha—my beloved, my heavenly soul. It was sweet of him, and almost made me cry at the memory of our first time together. Why can't things last? Poor Chamlong. He doesn't know China. He can't see it for the slow and serious place it is. Even though he climbed the mountain quickly, he seemed lost on it. Do you understand? Of course, he was born a Tiger, and that gives him strength. But Jupiter is his heart; he's not a deep thinker. And he's Tuesday's child, born to feel angry. Philip is a Dragon, which I like, but he's also Monday's child. I didn't tell him that means trouble all of his life. He was never my father, never. What I remember of him is a quiet friend who came and went and came and went, always thinking about something not happening where he was. Mother never loved him. Of course, I've always known that, but now I know it was the reason he finally left. Did he love her? Oh, I think he did. Does he love her now? No, not now. You ask me how I know? I know. He keeps wanting me to love her. It's like he's trying to convince himself she ought to be loved by someone. Or something like that. I don't know. But I know he no longer loves her."

Philip is coming toward her; rapidly she mutters, "He too speaks to someone. We're very much alike. We—" But he's too close for her to continue.

At the inn they eat breakfast. It's better than last night's dinner. Hungrily they consume congee, pickled vegetable, and strips of cold bean curd. Leaving their padded jackets (it's warmer now that the sun has risen), they go down steps to the largest temple on the Tai Shan plateau. It's devoted to the Goddess of the Azure Clouds. Entering through the lower courtyard, they walk between high stone walls put there for protection from the wind. Everything seems worn and old in the five halls.

Do I interest him? she wonders. And then a question rises with the rapidity and power of the sun rising an hour ago: Does he love me? He wants me, I know that, even though I don't know why I know, but can he love me?

He says something. "What?" she asks.

"Inside they have statues of the goddess and her court."

She can see his blue eyes under the rim of the broad hat, regarding her closely.

"You don't seem enthusiastic," he says.

"Really, I'm not." And it's true. She's lost interest in these relics; suddenly only the blue of the sky and the shape of the mountain are important. Those natural things and one question.

Old women are coming into the courtyard now with joss sticks and flowers; shuffling along, they head for the main hall of the goddess.

"Then we'll go down," Philip suggests.

Wordlessly, they begin the descent of Tai Shan.

Not far past the South Gate to Heaven, Sanuk notices an old woman hanging on to the linked chain, urging herself up to the next flagstone. It's the old woman she had spoken to at the Halfway Gate.

"Mother, how are you?"

Sweat beads her wrinkled forehead and the silvered mustache above her panting mouth. "Ah, Daughter, I told you we'd meet here."

"Where did you stay last night?"

"On the mountain somewhere."

"Outside? You must have been cold."

"No, I wasn't cold."

"You have only a few steps to go now."

"Did you see the goddess?"

"Yes," Sanuk lies, watching the old woman smile with satisfaction.

• • •

Below the summit as they go down are mists within which crags and pinnacles appear like islands in a foamy sea, but during the descent the mists scatter and a coolness gives way to summer heat. Their calf muscles begin to ache from the jarring descent. A new batch of climbers is on the way, many of them soldiers. One is wearing a potato-masher grenade on his belt; another has a large pistol, which looks to Embree like an ancient Colt .45. Most of them, however, are unarmed, and might well be groups of boy scouts on an outing. Old women leaning on staffs, a few red-faced peasants, even some families, complete the pilgrimage on this bright summer day.

At Philip's suggestion they turn westward at Halfway Gate for a different route into the town of Taian. This is a less traveled way, much of it under towering pines, with the sound of waterfalls in their ears. In the dappled light they move through a succession of mountain forests, smelling of pine needles and evergreen, and emerge suddenly from a downward-winding path at the Black Dragon Pool. White water cascades into a circular basin, where the color of the pool spreads from dark blue to green to brown at the edges. Balanced on overhanging cliffs above the pool are angular rocks, oddly shaped, like the toys of a gigantic child. "That's what they look like to me," Sanuk tells him, "toys," but Philip nods without comment.

He's sitting on a rock, slowly rubbing his sore calf muscles. All morning he's been silent.

Sitting next to him, Sanuk narrows her eyes and listens to water plunge into the pool. It's peaceful here on the sacred mountain of China. They could stay here in a small hut down in one of the ravines, summer and winter, when it was green or snowy. He'd chop wood, she'd gather berries. He'd shoot rabbits, she'd cook them. And they'd watch the seasons change on the mountainside, drink the icy water, hear its music in the rocks. Does he love her?

"I was never a father to you," he says abruptly, then falls silent again.

So he's been thinking of what they were to each other in the past.

"I might have been a father to you if I hadn't known him."

"It's what I always thought—that you never tried to take his place." The sun beats down on them, the water flows through the black rocks, pooling into a bubbly green below their feet. "I was glad you didn't try."

"I always thought you wanted me to try. It was just something I couldn't do."

"What I wanted was a friend—and you were that. But I didn't want another father."

"Was I really a friend?"

His tone of voice startles her; there's a note of pleading in it, as if he has never thought of himself in that role and now, in retrospect, wishes it had been so. "Of course you were," she assures him. "You took me to watch the kites. You bought me sweetmeats on the klongs."

Embree waves his hand dismissively. "Yes, but—"

"And you told me about Bill and Bright Lotus." His questioning look makes her add, "The Chinese princess, Bright Lotus, and her buffalo friend, Bill."

"Oh yes. You liked those stories?"

"They were wonderful." Sanuk clasps her raised knees and puts her chin on them. She can feel herself smiling. "Bright Lotus was a brave little girl, always willing to try anything—and get into trouble. Bill was very serious and practical and his job was to get her out of things. Some of those stories I remember quite well. Dragons in China. Evil sorcerers trying to steal the Emerald Buddha. Bright Lotus chasing a magic butterfly. I always thought you meant Bright Lotus to be me."

Embree nods. "And I was Bill."

"Were we really those two?" she asks, turning slightly to look at him.

"No, not at all. You were a careful little girl. I always felt you needed more daring."

"So Bright Lotus was a hint?"

"I suppose so. And Bill was a hint for myself—to be more practical."

"Maybe we've grown into the characters. When I think back on it, I see you were right. I always felt I had to watch out for Mother. It was my job to protect her. So for a while I became a little old lady. Thank God I've changed."

Embree doesn't respond. There's a long silence. Sanuk wonders if he's taken her remark as critical of his role during her childhood. But then she realizes by his next remark that his silence has meant something else, something better.

"So I was a friend," he says. "I'm glad of that."

She's staring at the waterfall. The hypnotic cascading of water makes it easier to say these things. It's as if she is somehow inside the water, looking out from its spray. From in there she can say what comes to mind, because the roaring tumult somehow protects her. She can say anything on her father's mountain. "Yesterday," she says, "I thought my father would climb the mountain with me. The day they captured him, he hadn't been able to climb it. So now he'd be with me when I reached the top. I was sure I'd feel his presence at the summit. But this morning, watching the sunrise, I felt only the two of us—I mean, you and me. He wasn't there." After a long silence, she adds, "But I want to know more about him."

"Let me show you Qufu, where he lived."

"Where he brought my mother." Her eyes meet his. "When you left, Mother talked about Qufu all the time. We'd sit in the garden, Ah Ping too, and Mother would talk about Qufu, what happened there, and how finally my father sent her to Peking for safety. And how later you took her to Hong Kong at his orders. I've heard it a hundred times, but tell me again. What happened next?"

She watches him swallow hard, as if speaking of it is difficult.

He explains how they waited in Hong Kong for the General to send for them; and how in Hong Kong they learned of his death in the vicinity of the sacred mountain.

"And then you and Mother fell in love in Hong Kong," Sanuk offers, continuing the story herself.

"At least I did."

She smiles at him. "How honest."

"You were on the way then. She needed someone. Really, it's a common enough story."

"I never tire of hearing it."

Rising to his feet—painfully, they're sore—Philip reaches down to help her up. The touch of his hand, strong and warm, thrills her. She can't help it.

"I'll take you to Qufu," he says. "War or no war. I'll take you there."

"When?"

"When you want to go."

"Even if there's fighting?"

"When you want to go."

"Why will you do that?"

"Because it means so much to you. I'll take you to Qufu when you want to go."

• • •

When finally they reach the foot of Tai Shan, he's hobbling, and to a lesser extent so is she. A rickshaw comes along, and they take it down the dusty streets of Taian to the hardware shop where Sanuk spent the last night with Ho Jin-shi among pilgrims in a back room. They have agreed to stay in Taian for a few days on the chance that Ho might return. "But I don't think he will," she maintains. "He won't give the letter to anyone else to deliver."

"He wants to be a hero. I can understand him. Once I wanted it too."

"But not any more?"

"Fortunately it's something most of us outgrow."

"What do you want now?"

Bending down, he rubs his left calf. "To get off my feet."

"But you can't do that," she tells him playfully. "The moon and Mercury are in a Dragon's feet. You're a wanderer, and so am I."

While he gets her suitcase from a storage room in the hardware shop (Jin-shi's little bag is gone), she writes a note in Thai, addresses it in Chinese, and folds it into a square. Inside are the words she formed in her mind during the last part of the descent:

> My Dear Chamlong,
> I hope you get this note before I leave. I will check here before leaving. If you haven't returned, know that I have gone to Qufu. Then where? I don't know. Never forget me. Life has joined our karma.

Having given the shopkeeper the note and some money, Sanuk turns to the cluttered shop. In the wavy glass of a mirror, hanging between hammer and rake, she can see herself. One hand comes up nervously to her hair: It is cut too short.

• • •

They have found a small inn, where liberation has not automatically included communal use of rooms. Even so, if they get separate rooms, Philip explains, they can expect the innkeeper to let the extra beds. She can see his lips trembling when he asks if she will share a room with him. That decision was made by Sanuk during the mountain descent, when beneath the ancient pines and cypresses they walked side by side as if, in her mind, they had known each other longer than a day. Because that's all it has been—one day. They have no past together.

She agrees to share the room, hoping her voice is calm and firm. Because the decision has already been made, not by them, but by their destinies. Perhaps long ago, she thinks. Who knows about such things? Perhaps before either of them was born.

Their second-floor room is tiny, almost filled by two narrow beds on low frames, with bulky mattresses and clean but tattered sheets. A single window overlooks a narrow, turbulent river rumbling off the green shank of Tai Shan. Standing at the window, Sanuk watches late sunlight slanting across rock and pine, where yesterday she first met this man.

Behind her he is talking. "We'll stay two or three days here. If he hasn't shown up by then, we must leave for Qufu. The war could heat up around here. We wouldn't get out. You still want to see Qufu?"

She nods without turning. Can he hear the wild beating of her heart? It seems like a drum in her breast.

"In the morning we'll go to the Temple of the God of Tai Shan. There are only two as great in China."

He's talking to hide his own nervousness, Sanuk thinks.

"And one of the two others is in Qufu. On the temple grounds of Confucius. That one I've seen many times."

Her throat feels so dry that Sanuk is almost afraid to speak. The light slanted the same way that first time she and Chamlong went to a hotel. Slanted like this. Again she nods.

"Then there are other temples."

Finally, without turning, Sanuk says in a small voice, "Why did you return to Bangkok?" She won't turn, she won't, she keeps her eyes focused on the mountain.

His voice comes from behind her. "I wanted to start life over."

"With my mother?"

"Well, I wanted to try."

"Do you love my mother?"

"Of course."

"But I mean—as you did when you were both young?"

There's a long pause. Will he answer? Will he ever answer? Sanuk asks herself frantically.

"I love her as someone who went through a great deal with me."

"That's how I feel about Chamlong."

There is silence, except for a distant rush of water on the mountainside. Sanuk feels they can stay this way forever, not moving or speaking, just being here together in a room. But he's behind her, waiting, and she knows he's waiting. At last she turns. The anguish on his face startles her. "I'm not afraid," she says. "It's all right. I'm not afraid," she repeats, trying to smile, trying to draw him toward her. "I'm not," she says, and for a terrifying moment Sanuk watches him step hesitantly toward her. Then the fear leaves her, as Philip Embree takes her into his arms. There's a desperate roughness to his embrace. He's afraid too. Against his mouth, she is still telling him, "I'm not, I'm not."

· · ·

Awaking next morning to the sound of rain pelting on the roof, she thinks, This is the beginning of my life.

He sleeps. It's a chance to study him in the gray light awash in the room.

A broad, almost unlined face. Mother used to say with a shrug, "He never will age. No matter what happens to him, Philip will look like a boy." Not quite. Unshaven for two days, his beard's a different shade than his blond hair—gray in it, silvery flashes in the gray light. And his body, naked beside hers, is not that of a young man. Not like Chamlong's, so lithe and spare it seemed brittle. Chamlong might break, but never bend, his body all angles and edges, without depths, without what she herself has: soft hollows, unsettled curves. Philip is physically more like herself—with her interior mystery, her mutable definition. That he's past his prime is a comfort. It makes him vulnerable and being vulnerable makes him more accessible to emotion. Indeed, he seems drawn to her own emotions—was last night—so that his entry seemed to go beyond her groin, a leaping and multiple presence she couldn't escape from. Because it became herself penetrating herself into secrets she never knew she had. He surrounded her utterly, moving through the pores of her skin, it had seemed to her in those first startling moments, until, filled by him, she felt the glass overflow that she'd hoped for so often in the arms of Chamlong, the liquid in it at last overflowing the sides in stream after stream of unbearable ecstasy. Or is that really true? Is this nothing more than the recollection of happiness? What she most recalls was his tenderness afterward, his grateful touch and whisper, as if nothing in the world but the gift of herself could please him again.

She wants him again. Running her hand slowly down his chest—gray hair mixed with blond—slowly, slowly along his stomach—not quite flat—to his intricate groin. She hesitates a moment. Have they achieved so much intimacy? With thumb and forefinger she encircles the limp stalk. It's so childlike, such a soft innocent object, lolling between her fingers like the heavy stem of a broken flower. Whenever she'd done this to Chamlong—awake or asleep—life had sprung instantly into her hand. But now, although bringing Philip into wakefulness, it remains for the moment unprotected by purpose, a soft thing like baby's skin. He stirs. Not looking at his face coming out of sleep, managing to turn herself, Sanuk moves along his side, down along it, toward her hand where he's starting to grow within her fingers. He murmurs something, but her concentration remains there, between her fingers. Her head dips; flesh enters her mouth to pulsate there like a plant growing, like the plant of a Bangkok garden burgeoning from sunlight and rain into blossom.

She feels his hand press gently upon the back of her neck, as if telling her, for these moments, he is utterly hers.

• • •

At breakfast she tells him about her discovery of Yu Hsuan-chi. He has read some of the poetry. Try though he does to give a different impression, she can tell Philip doesn't care for it. She learns from this incident how much he wants to please her. It's almost disturbing. In fact, it is. It's perhaps what her mother drew back from—his tendency to please at the expense of candor. Yet he's honest too. He's honest in the sense he believes in honesty. She has never met anyone like him.

They eat congee, pieces of dried sausage, sugar cakes, in the tiny dining room alongside a morose peasant family. These pilgrims have come to Tai Shan to ask the Goddess of the Azure Clouds for a good harvest, lots of money, and no more children, since four of them sit here already. The family came in an ox cart from a village south of Qufu, actually closer to T'eng Hsien. Troops were everywhere. Philip questions the man about this, but for an answer gets only a vague estimate of how many were there and where they were going. But they were Liberation Army troops; that he knows, because they didn't take his food or his wife, who seems much older than he is, much grumpier and depressed. One of the children has a deep croupy cough and feverish eyes. When Sanuk asks if the child is all right, both father and mother stare wordlessly at her.

It's no longer raining when soon afterward Sanuk leaves the inn.

She is waiting for Philip to ask the innkeeper something, and in the heavy summer air, laden with moisture, she feels like singing, although surely with her husky voice a song has never been much appreciated. Mother used to say—

Mother must never have known the pleasure with Philip that she herself has. Mother never knew him. Isn't that strange? Whereas she has known him all her life in a single day. She's proud of her body, of what it can do, of the pleasure it can give and take. She enjoys the sinew and bone that encases her, that each month gives her so much misery. Has Mother ever known the same pride and wonder? Not with all those men. But with Father?

Philip has told her he loves her. Can she believe that? My man is true as steel. Sanuk feels the corners of her mouth turn up in a smile of anticipating belief: He loves her. But it isn't true. He wants her now, he can't love her, not a foolish runaway.

"What's wrong?"

She turns to see him coming from the inn.

"Nothing's wrong," she tells him. "How can it be?"

"Yes," he says with a laugh. "How can it be."

He takes her to Pu Zhou Monastery, the Place of Universal Illumination, where raindrops load down a grove of pine trees. A monk caretaker points out, along one bay of the main building, a room where General Feng Yu-hsiang spent two years during the 1930s, studying not Buddhism but Christianity.

"Did my father know this general?" she asks Philip.

"Oh, yes indeed. They admired each other."

"Is he still alive?"

"I think so. Last I heard he was in the United States, campaigning against Chiang Kai-shek."

Sanuk withholds a comment. Even love can fail, she thinks. He doesn't see that I'm wondering why this man lives and why my father has been dead twenty years. Even Philip doesn't see or he'd touch my arm or say something. Glancing at his face, so intent on the look of balustrades and tile roofs and pavilions rising out of a hillside, for an instant she feels sad, alone, as she always felt with Chamlong in the aftermath of lovemaking.

"What will happen to the monastery now?" Philip asks the monk, who shrugs complacently. "If liberation comes, perhaps there'll be a place for us. Perhaps not. You are Christian?"

Philip looks away.

When they leave the monastery, Sanuk touches his arm, as if to assure herself he's with her. And he is, really. The blue eyes turn warmly to her. It's all right.

A rickshaw puller jogs toward them down the muddy street. "We can go to the great temple now." Reaching out, Philip takes her hand. "Or not go." He repeats that, hopefully. "Or not go."

"That's what I want too," she tells him as they turn away from the rickshaw. With her free hand, without thinking about it, Sanuk presses the amulet at her throat.

$$\bullet \quad \bullet \quad \bullet$$

It's raining again, pelting down on the tin roof of the inn, as they lie side by side, flanks touching.

"What the monk asked me—if I'm Christian . . ."

"You didn't answer." She props herself on one elbow to look at him staring at the unseen rain overhead.

"You, of course, are Christian," he declares.

"I believe in God. But maybe I'm not really Christian. For example, I won't wear a cross. I wear the Indian Goddess of Love." She lifts the terra-cotta amulet with thumb and forefinger, displaying it for his appraisal. "She's good luck in love. That's what the Siamese believe."

He leans forward to inspect it, smiles. "What you learn by living in the East is tolerance. At least where God is concerned. Not tolerance about food or wealth or position in life or property, but about God. At least some of the time. When there's intolerance about God, of course, the violence is as bad here as anywhere else."

"You believe in God too."

He looks shocked, perhaps even dismayed by the claim. "You think so? Why do you think that?"

"Your story about Benares and the people going up and down, the cremation, the children, and you said, 'Is this what life's all about?' "

Philip touches her arm, runs one finger along it from crooked elbow to wrist. As if to get in better contact with what she's thinking. "How does that prove I believe in God?"

"If you didn't believe in God, you wouldn't ask the question, would you? You wouldn't have to."

He drops his hand, as if concentrating hard on what she's saying. So encouraged, she continues. "You would just say, 'Well, life is sad and terrible, but nothing can be done about it.' But you're angry at God because He could change things." When Philip laughs, she smiles at him timidly. "Am I a fool?"

"You make a better argument than some theologians I've heard. You see, there's something your mother never knew about me: I came to China to be a missionary."

Isn't it strange, she thinks. I'm not surprised, she thinks. Can anything he does now surprise me? It's as if I knew everything all along; he needs only to say it and I've known it.

"Did you hear me?" he asks.

"Of course."

"You seem to be somewhere else."

He struggles to understand me. It's something Chamlong never did. So many thoughts assail her she can hardly follow the conversation. "I was thinking I'm not surprised. About you being a missionary."

"Your mother certainly would be. Perhaps that's why I never told her. Or perhaps I was afraid she'd expect too much of me then."

"But you've told me."

Now he says something that rattles her, that will remain with her for a long time, perhaps her entire life.

Turning away, eyes toward the ceiling, Philip says, "You mustn't expect too much of me. You mustn't trust me until I tell you everything, and maybe I never will."

Chilled by his words, Sanuk asks softly, "How will I know if you tell me everything?"

"Oh, you'll know. That will be easy. What's not easy is getting there. Do you understand me at all?"

"Not now." Lying down again, Sanuk folds her arms. He is leaving me out, she thinks unhappily. But when his fingers touch her cheek, caressing it, and his face, serious or perhaps even desperate, looms over her, Sanuk raises hers to meet his, and tells herself, Love him, don't think. Her own fingers touch his face, the slight smooth ridge of scar on his forehead. A soldier in her father's army had shot him there before she was born, shot him during a raid on the camp of bandits who had abducted him. Mother says, "In those days there were such possibilities." And in these days too. It is all a miracle, what is happening here in the land of her father, right now, a miracle, a possibility realized beyond the anticipation of it. Love him, don't think.

• • •

This gray day and rainy night pass again in lovemaking, but when the new day dawns it is searingly bright, as the sky tends to seem after a long period of rain. At breakfast their companions, the family from south of Qufu, are gone. They must have climbed the mountain, with a sick child in tow. The thought of it depresses Sanuk until they reach the southern approach of the great Temple of the God of Tai Shan. She can't stay within herself at the sight of this huge compound with a monumental arch and stone walls towering forty feet above the streets. It overpowers her introspection. Already the ground, quickly drying after the rain of yesterday, has been raked. The indentations sweep along the broad expanse of the first courtyard beyond the Sun Facing Gate. Swallows careen through the bright morning air, defining by missing them the solid spaces where immense Tai Hu stones and ancient steles rise on either side of the Pavilion for Paying Homage from Afar.

"I never cared much for art," Philip says. "Books and languages, yes. But paintings and buildings never meant much to me."

"They do to me."

"Because of your mother. She loves beauty."

"And my father?"

Philip smiles. "Of course. He was a scholar of beauty."

What pleases her so much about Philip is his generosity when he speaks of her father. His attitude enables her to love her father openly. She reveals her obsessive love with the same ease that she gives this man her body. "It's wonderful to be here," she tells him suddenly.

"Though we're in the middle of a war?"

She feels he's afraid of happiness, must break the good mood.

"Don't let the calmness fool you in China," he continues. "Flood, war, fire—they arrive in a moment." Philip stops and looks closely at her. "The threat of war doesn't seem to bother you."

"No, it doesn't."

"I mean it. A battle could start outside these walls any moment. You're not afraid?"

"Of course I'm afraid, but I'm not worried."

"Afraid but not worried?"

"I'm afraid to die, but to be here, in my father's land—and with you —is where I should be. If I'm where I should be, why worry?"

"I think you're your father's daughter."

"You've already called me my mother's daughter."

"I love you for that too. Because I love them both." He looks away from her toward the red-pillared halls ahead.

They stroll among the forest of steles under evergreens, while a group of soldiers crouch in the dusty yard. They're drinking hot water from a thermos and eating wheat cakes. Slurping and grunting, regarding the light-skinned man under the broad-brimmed hat, they eat with the intensity of wolves—blunt-faced peasants, cheeks glowing, their lined skin like veins in rock. Watching them, Sanuk feels an odd sense of companionship, although these men give her long naked glances of sexual interest. They are the men who followed her father, died for him, as they will die again and again in this vast land of sorrow. Yet here they squat and eat among the ancient evergreens and great monuments of a subtle civilization. She's proud to be one of them, takes secret pride in her ability to pass among them undetected as a foreigner, whereas Philip, no matter how hard he tries, how excellent his Chinese, how thorough his knowledge of the people, can never be one of them.

Philip pauses beside a small rock-walled pond in the middle of which stands a Tai Hu rock.

" 'Such rock contains the Tao of the Tao, a something universal captured in the convulsions of stone, an essence enduring yet unseen—' That's what your father used to say. I've heard him say it many times. Quoting a source I never knew. He loved these rocks." Kneeling, Philip stares at some lavender blossoms, torn from a branch in yesterday's downpour and now floating in the pond like cold little boats.

It is here, in the temple called First Ancestor, dedicated to the god of the mountain, that at last Sanuk feels at home in China. And bringing her to this moment has been Philip Embree, the man she loves, and her father, the man she seeks, and those soldiers back there, crouching in the dust.

40 MORNING OF THEIR first day in Qufu.

Is there a sweeter moment in man's life than when he kisses the breasts of a loved woman after lovemaking? Embree thinks not. As his parted lips graze Sanuk's nipples, he senses that this lulling moment is, in truth, the sacred gap between desire and satiety, a tiny unit of time as pure and dear to him as if arrived at through long meditation.

Indeed, meditation. It is with this young woman he's captured what was missing in his spiritual practice—the joy of being *here*. Sanuk: Joy. Through Sanuk he has found it: *Om Tat Twam Asi*. My guru.

Such a flagrantly romantic notion confounds him sufficiently to bring his lips away.

"That amulet you wear," he hears himself telling her, "isn't the Goddess of Love. It's Sarasvathi, the Goddess of Wisdom. All this time you've been honoring the wrong goddess." Belief in something or someone is like that, he insists on telling her: a certainty until found out.

Telling her these things is a needless destruction of illusion, and

Sanuk must feel it deeply, for her body stiffens a little, and when he moves away from her, she lies still.

Outside the inn's tiny room, birds are singing in a morning not yet warmed by sunlight.

Singing, singing, and all's right with the world. Except that once again he's betrayed two people who matter to him: betrayed the General dead twenty years and Vera sick in Shanghai, parents of the girl he held last night in his arms. It is easy to dwell on such betrayals, perhaps fashion from them the elements of good and evil into a kind of myth. A myth or an ethical irony. Something not to take seriously. Because how can he consider what he feels for this woman as an expression of evil? That human love has definable limits is the fantasy of cloistered moralists. He won't let the enforced pieties of childhood take away a fleeting hope of happiness.

But he can't be a fool either. It's best to concentrate, here with this woman, on some kind of reality. He has to get her out of here and back to Shanghai. Check. And somehow confront Vera with his new betrayal —falling in love with her daughter. Check. There's the future; how will he and Sanuk work out their lives together? Check.

How, indeed? In the midst of lovemaking he's aware of his body aging. There's a hollow—a little sag—just above the biceps where arm joins shoulder. His buttocks are flatter now; dressed, he can see his trousers are no longer tight across them—the beginning of an old man. No paunch, but a dollop of fat at his sides between hipbone and rib cage. It causes him embarrassment when she puts her arm around his waist. For an instant, sometimes, he wants to draw away in the shame of having lost the body of his youth, but Sanuk in her own youth is generous: At least she gives the appearance of not wanting him younger.

To have told her about the amulet was an act of gratutious cruelty. Would he have done it at a younger age? At any rate, he can't have the cruelty between them. "But Sarasvathi's a great goddess," he tells her. "She brings knowledge."

Sanuk doesn't reply; one arm flung across her eyes.

"You must always wear it."

She doesn't reply.

For something to say, for anything, he says, "The only object of faith I really believed in was an ax. When I first came to China, a bandit gave it to me for saving his life." After a pause, he adds, "I'm telling you because I think it's pathetic. There ought to be more than an ax to believe in."

She doesn't reply.

"Because I believe in believing in more."

She doesn't reply, arm flung across her face.

"I've never been able to piece together my life. In India I studied

514 ·

yoga, but why? I knew, in spite of certain moments, I'd never find what I was looking for. Because I was looking for faith beyond an ax. I can't leap to the other side, you see. You, your mother, are on the other side to begin with. I see faith over there, where people like you are, but I can't get to it. The leap's too far. I'm stuck on this side for a lifetime."

"I love you." Her arm is still lying across her eyes.

Now it's Embree who doesn't reply.

"That's my faith," she says, remaining motionless.

"Today"—Embree sits up—"I'll take you to see your father."

And he does: They start at the Temple of Confucius, with its six hundred halls and pavilions. All morning they wander through the grounds of the holiest shrine in China.

When they reach the Apricot Terrace, Embree stops. "They say Confucius once taught his disciples under an apricot tree here. Your father used to go into this pavilion and sit for hours."

He watches the young woman study the square two-story building: the red pillars, the triangular pediments on all four sides of the glazed ceramic roofing, the stone benches within. Watching her enter the pavilion and sit down, Embree waits outside until she calls to him. "Come here with me."

Why am I resisting? he wonders, and takes a place on the stone bench beside her.

"It was cared for better then," he volunteers, looking at weeds growing out of cracks in the courtyard paving. Around some of the ancient steles spindly bushes and vines have sprung up. Behind them, one of the marble columns supporting Dacheng Hall has been defaced, its entwined dragons half obliterated by bullets. Someone has been using it for target practice. Never mind, he thinks. Just be here with her.

"This is where he sat?"

"Yes. Often."

"I wonder what he was thinking."

"Yes," Embree says. And what was he thinking when Vera left him? Getting up, Embree leaves the pavilion—it is still filled with the General's presence—and squints, as if truly interested, at some broken tiles on the double roofing. Why did the General take me into his army? A young American with no military experience, no commitment to this land. Why? The General was no fool, and he hated foreigners. But a fatal flaw—curiosity—ah, he had that in abundance! In Burma Embree had once seen a veteran combat man peek when he should have ducked —the action of a recruit, death by curiosity. The General showed a similar lack of caution. Yes. Should have ducked when I came along, instead of peeking. Fear rises from the Other. Fear definitely rises from the Other.

What's she doing? Turning, he stares at the pavilion in time to see her staring at him. Embree forces a smile, he must smile, but he must force it. Don't lose this, he tells himself, and walks toward her as she rises from the stone bench.

. . .

In the afternoon Embree rents horses with two packs of American PX cigarettes from Nanking, and they set out for the Kong family cemetery, a mile out of town. She's not a good rider, so they amble slowly along the dusty avenues of Qufu, passing farmers with baskets of ducks and a few soldiers, unarmed, one of them carrying a hoe. It is hot in the sun, and he can see half-moons of sweat under her arms. She sweats, she is human, he loves her. A feeling of tenderness assures him everything is all right. The past is past. Fear rises from the Past.

And so, entering the five-hundred-acre cemetery of Kongs, thousands upon thousands of them buried here during the past two thousand years, he's put himself into a buoyant mood.

"So many pines," Sanuk exclaims. The grounds are heavily forested, with great blocks of stone lying about—funeral horses, dragons, lions, dogs, goats, and tall sages facing each other as if in eternal debate.

"The Chinese used to line their cemeteries with pine trees, because pine trees are distasteful to Wang Hsiang. Wang Hsiang's a demon who devours the brains of the dead," Embree tells her. "It's a terrifying idea."

"Did you come here with my father?"

"No, on my own."

"I know about this place from Mother."

They have stopped at the riding post that fronts the Avenue of Honor leading to the tomb of Confucius. After a short stroll they arrive at the burial mound of the Sage, covered by summer moss under an old cypress.

"I wonder," Sanuk says, "what they said to each other when they stood here." She turns to him. "I'm sorry."

"It's not painful for me to think of them together. I had a passion for your mother." He pauses, looking at the girl, who stares straight ahead at the mound of earth. "But what I felt for her is not what I feel for you. Otherwise I'd never have left her the way I did."

She hasn't turned to him. "You won't leave me?"

"I want us always to be together."

"Am I too young? Am I too foolish for you?"

"I could ask am I too old for you. And too foolish. But what's happened between us has happened. Age doesn't count. Logic doesn't count. Somehow we've been blessed."

"Yes. I understand that." When they have returned to the Avenue of Honor, she says, "I'll remember always what you said here. When dying happens to me, if I have the chance to think at that moment, I'll remember what you said, here, in this place." Reaching out, she grips his hand. "Somehow we've been blessed."

• • •

From the road, returning to the town of Qufu, he notices a column of men raising dust to the south—soldiers, a few trucks, even a tank. It's a reminder that men are jockeying into position for battles that have nothing to do with memory and love.

There is still enough light for them to visit the great residence of the Kong family. After returning the horses they walk along the ancient town walls to the stone lions that front the Residence. It's been twenty years since Philip Embree last entered here. Then he'd gone to the General's quarters in the West Wing, receiving along with Major Chia final instructions for the military delegation going to Peking. That was the last time he saw the General alive. Sitting at the rosewood desk, tunic buttoned to the neck, Tang had wished the delegation well. They were going to negotiate a meeting with officers representing General Feng Yu-hsiang. Twenty years ago. Tang dead, Feng still alive.

These thoughts occur to Embree while he leads Tang's daughter through a labyrinth of courtyards. He's shocked and saddened by the crumbling halls, the broken flagstones, the desolation everywhere. The Duke Patriarch of the Kong family fled the Residence during skirmishes in town a year ago. Since then troops have bivouacked here. They have hunkered down in old buildings that once served as the Kong family Departments of Seals and Rites and Temple Ceremonies and Music and Civil Administration and Documents and Estates over the centuries. They have lounged in the central yamen where clan offices once handled the business of a family heaped with honors and titles and vast wealth. They have found quarters even in the East Wing, where the Kong family ate, slept, made love, were born and died. Throughout the elegant compound these peasant boys, cold and hungry, have showed merciless indifference to history by treating the halls and courtyards of Qufu as they would a village—by shitting on flagstone and rock garden, burning antique chairs and tables for firewood, scattering paper through the halls where musicians once played at midnight, crushing out cigarette butts on ceramic pots now broken, dropping the flotsam of a wandering army that crouches down for shelter wherever it can be found, that takes no notice of what might be underfoot, the marble floor and pebble mosaic once trod by emperors.

He takes her into the West Wing. It's here the General had his headquarters, near the Hall of Inner Peace. Sanuk walks silently beside him. Along the ruined way (buildings crumbling, weeds climbing trellises once heavy with wisteria) she gazes with an intensity that astonishes Philip Embree, who for a lifetime has run from memories of a father.

They come at last to the General's quarters: door kicked off, shutters ripped from the windows. Entering before her—Sanuk hesitates outside, timidly—Embree slogs through a room filled with tin cans, rags, paper; it smells of ashes and urine; thick motes of dust wriggle in light coming through open windows.

Hearing her stumble through the trash, he turns and tries to be casual. "There was a rosewood desk here. Compliments of the Duke. And over the desk a scroll—well, I don't remember what of. Mountains? Anyway, in that corner hung a punkah. Sometimes his old servant Yao—"

"Is that their bedroom?" Sanuk has walked past him toward another open doorway.

They stand together looking at a floor strewn with refuse. An old dog is stretched out on some rags, and when they enter, it lifts its scabby head to stare a moment. "There were bird cages here. Your father loved the singing."

"I know."

He wants to comfort her, not sure if this squalor can damage a vision she must have created of this place. "There's a back garden where your father used to sit by a pond—he and your mother—and study the reflection of stones in water." It's no good; his words sound flat to his ear, the bland stuff of reportage. He's like a tired, uninterested guide. "There were pomegranates and lilac bushes," he begins again, lamely. "And flowering catalpas. I remember that. There were plum trees near the central yamen. They say Lao Tzu was born under a plum tree. A symbol of long life. That's because its flowers bloom on branches that look withered. Sanuk, it wasn't this way then. It was beautiful, the best of China was here."

"You're patient with me."

"About what?"

"My need to know." Brushing past him, she goes outside to the courtyard. "Is this where they played Tai Chi?"

Embree shakes his head. "I never saw them. I don't think anybody did."

"It can't be here, not where everyone was coming and going." She walks through a moon gate into another courtyard, with him following. They go through two more gates, two more courtyards, before Sanuk halts at last. "Maybe here." It's a tiny courtyard with a pine trunk, sawed off waist-high above the ground, next to one wall. The flagstones, many buckled, are dusted with yellow earth. A broken ceramic tub that must have held chrysanthemums sits in a corner. "Maybe here," she says again. "There's something I've wanted to do ever since my mother told me about them—how they played Tai Chi in a courtyard of Qufu."

"Then do it."

"Will you stay and watch?"

"No. This is yours." He doesn't wait for a reaction, but slips through the round opening of a moon gate into the next courtyard. He waits there, having little glimpses of her passing the gate in the slow elegant movements of Tai Chi. She's in there playing Tai Chi where they once played it.

To love such a woman is dangerous, he thinks. Not much in her life leaves her. What happens to her hangs on, so that she's loading herself down with memories, symbols—and someday, because of them, with demands. Ah, he knows her. In common with those who speak to people who aren't there, she has the tendency to let the past keep dragging her down. They're alike, although in his own youth he avoided what hangs on, while she plunges into it.

In a quarter of an hour she emerges from the courtyard, frowning. "I'm not finished," she tells him, lips trembling. The slow, calming exercise, done in that atmosphere, has merely agitated her. "There must be more. I want to know more."

"What you want is people who knew him."

"Please help me."

"All right. We'll find them."

• • •

It's not that easy. Next day Embree scours the shops of Qufu for anyone who had once served with the General twenty years ago. Most of the shopkeepers pretend they've never heard of General Tang Shan-teh. Perhaps they're afraid of a foreigner at a time of war. At last, however, toward noon, Embree enters a tiny restaurant near the Drum Tower where twenty years ago he'd seen Vera Rogacheva beat a man from horseback with a whip—White avenging herself on Red in a dusty Chinese town.

Inside the restaurant, however, this memory fades, even as the light does. For a while he can't see in the dim room. Then appearing through the murk are half a dozen tables and one man seated in a corner chair, smoking a foul-smelling bamboo pipe.

Pushing a back curtain aside, the owner—quite fat—comes into the room. "We don't have food yet," he shouts, waving his hands. "Half an hour. Come back then, you can have anything except fish. No fish today, no pork either. It's the war. No wagons come in when troops are moving. It's—" Thrusting his sweaty neck forward, he squints at Embree.

"Is it *you?*" he asks, eyes rounding. "Ax man? Man with the White Ax?" Leaning forward, he stares hard; then, laughing, he shows a mouthful of rotting teeth.

• • •

Embree, Sanuk, and the old soldier take chairs at a table; they lean forward to talk.

"Do you remember me?" the old soldier asks, wiping his forehead with a pudgy hand.

"Yes, I think so," Embree lies.

"Easy to remember *you*. With hair that color and the horse you had—they say you could sleep on it—and that ax. Do you still have it?" When Embree nods, the old soldier cackles. "You were never without it. In those days men did strange things, all of us. Remember the foot race? I was there watching near the end of it. You almost won." Turning to the young woman, he says, "He almost won," and to Embree again, "Is this your woman?" He leers at her. "Young." He cackles again. "Do you remember the Battle of Hengshui?"

"Of course," Embree says.

"I was a Chia man—Second Regiment, First Qufu Division. Remember?"

"Of course."

Thoughtfully the fat shop owner looks from man to woman. "What are you doing here in Qufu?"

"I've come to remember how it was then," Embree explains.

"Well, that's good, but it's the wrong time to come here. All the armies around—first Reds, then Nationalists, then Reds again. Who's next? They come and go, wrecking the fields. Most of them boys. We were young, but not that young. Those Nationalist troops from Anhui and Chekiang—here last year—they'd steal the shoes off your feet when you were walking in them." Enjoying the image he'd just come up with, the shop owner laughs. "Not like our army, not like the army of General Tang. There was no army like his."

True, Embree thinks. For that time it was a great army, but then too there were dirty, hungry boys toting guns for the General. Aside from the well-trained special units, they were a rabble pushed into soldiering by fear. The best of the day, perhaps, Tang's army, but men died in it for lack of medicine and good diet and weapons that worked.

"Was he a good general?" Sanuk asks, arms crossed, leaning on them.

"None better. When a soldier raped a girl, the General had him shot. You did wrong, he put you in the cangue."

"What is that?" she asks Embree in English.

"Your head is put in a heavy wooden yoke. It's a neck stock, worn as punishment."

"He wouldn't use quicklime in the killing cage," the soldier declares boastfully.

At her insistence Embree explains that the killing cage was a narrow upright coffin-shaped structure in which the victim stood with his head in a neck stock. Bricks under his feet were taken away one by one, each day, until he strangled. In some killing cages they poured quicklime over the last few bricks, so his feet dangled in it.

Sanuk blanches.

"A scholar, that's what he was," the old soldier claims. "Wouldn't use quicklime. But when he had to, he'd use that bamboo spike of his."

"What's that?" Sanuk asks.

Before Embree can explain, mildly, in English, the shopkeeper moves his pudgy hands through the air, describing a small cage in which a man sits on a stool, hands bound behind him, with a sharply pointed bamboo stake, driven into the ground between his knees, touching his throat. "If he moves forward—" The soldier jabs his thumb upward into his own jowls.

When she turns helplessly to Embree, he shakes his head. "It was used. That was the times." To the soldier, he says crisply, "It was not used often."

"No. And if a man told what it was he knew, the General let him go. Not a better general in China." He leans toward the young woman, eyes slitty in fat. "Your man here and I served with the best of them. Paid wages too, when there was money."

"Why was he killed?" she asks in a small voice.

The fat shopkeeper shrugs, wiping his face with a rag. "Tea?" He yells at the curtained back room, "Bring tea!" Bending, he spits on the floor, then with a deep sigh turns to the young woman. "There were always enemies. Nobody knew why he was killed. They ambushed him somewhere around Tai Shan. Don't the good ones always die? I've heard that. Anyway"—he is speaking to Embree now—"a few months later Chiang Kai-shek came up from the South and people either joined him or ran away. I ran away."

"Who would your General support now?" Sanuk asks. "Nationalists or Communists?"

Grinning, the soldier turns to Embree. "This woman of yours talks a lot. Who would he support? None but himself."

In English Embree says to her, "He wouldn't support the Nationalists. They're too corrupt. He was too much the Confucian to accept that. Probably he'd support the Reds." After a pause he adds, "No, not them either. He used to say communism was a foreign idea."

Replying in English, she says, "Then he'd have been murdered in today's world too."

"Oh yes," Embree tells her, watching the insight bring sudden tears to her eyes. "China's not ready for him." He wants to reach over and touch her hand, but can't, not in front of the grinning ex-soldier. "Friend," Embree says to him, "there was an old man who used to read the yarrow stalks for the General. I suppose he's dead."

"Alive. Must be almost ninety now. Every day he sits over in the north side of town, near the old arch. Remember that arch? He reads the stalks for people."

"And there was the General's servant."

"Old Yao. Yes, everyone remembers him. He lived almost a year after the General. He smuggled the General's songbirds out of the Residence, so no one else could have them. They say he boarded them in a farmhouse at his own expense. Rose before dawn each day and went out there to clean their cages, feed and water them. He groomed them every day without fail. That's what people say who knew him. And they say until the day of his death he took them in their covered cages for a walk, swinging the cages for their exercise, just as he did in the General's service and in the General's father's service. Old Yao, yes. And I know something else."

Tea is brought by a hunched woman, possibly his wife, to whom he speaks sharply when she pours a cup too full. "There was that foreign woman. Remember her? I bet she liked to eat bean curd." Laughing, he winks at Embree. "Whatever happened to her?"

"I think she left China."

"Good for her. It's been nothing but war, nothing all these years. Lost my first and second wives to the wars."

In English Sanuk asks what the man means by liking to eat bean curd.

Pausing a moment, Embree says in English, "She was passionate." Then, blowing on the hot surface of his tea, he asks the shopkeeper, "What else do you know?"

The old soldier belches. "I have some good pork back there, fresh, with noodles, if you give me a little time for the cooking. It's my pleasure."

"We're unworthy of such an honor."

"My pleasure."

"You see, friend, we haven't much time here."

"That's true. They'll start shooting again before we know it. Came through here last year fighting. I'm glad to be done with all of that." He pats his belly. "Too old and fat now. What was I telling you, friend?"

"What else you know."

"Ah, yes. Thinking of Yao made me remember, because he hated women. I know where Su-su is."

Embree tries to remember who Su-su is. "Tell me about Su-su. I don't remember."

The shopkeeper shakes his finger at Embree, teasing him. "You remember me and everyone else, but you don't remember that pretty woman? Su-su was here before the foreigner came," the old soldier explains. "Then when the foreign woman came, the General sent Su-su away, and they tell me he gave her money for a dowry. That's how she got the farmer."

"Where is she now?" Sanuk asks quickly.

"Out of town there." He waves his arm behind his head in a southerly direction. "Maybe two li, no, three. On a farm beside a duck pond. There's an old stone fence on one side, half fallen in. It's been like that for years. Married a good worker, though. Lucky for her. Su-su's done well."

"She was the General's woman before the foreigner?" Sanuk asks.

Studying her a moment, the shop owner says, "You speak with an accent. You aren't from here. You speak his language too. Where did you get her?" he asks Embree. "I like them young myself. Is she from the South?"

"No," Embree says. "She's from here. She's just been away a long time."

In a few more minutes, Embree rises, thanks the old soldier effusively, and takes Sanuk away. It's occurred to him that too much contact with the past might reveal what's better left hidden. His own betrayal of the General, for example, although few people must have ever known of it, surely not common soldiers. Glancing at Sanuk's determined face, however, he understands nothing will stop her from speaking to the old diviner and especially to her father's concubine of twenty years ago.

Outside, she turns to him and says, "Those cages. My father used them?" When he hesitates, Sanuk says, "Yes, I understand." Meeting his eyes, though her lips tremble, she adds, "I'm not a child. That was his world."

Just as the food shop owner described it, an old man is sitting by an ancient stone arch leading north toward the cemetery. They might have passed him earlier on the way back from there, yet who would notice this frail figure wrapped in rags, sitting beside the dusty road on a broken keg in front of a rickety bamboo table?

"Do you recognize him?" Sanuk asks.

"Absolutely. He hasn't changed much. Twenty years ago he was old; now he's merely older. I'd recognize him anywhere."

"You said he was an opium smoker."

"I suppose still is. Some people thrive on it." To the old man—squinting, perhaps going blind—Embree says, "We knew each other, Grandfather, years ago, when the great General lived."

Milky eyes turn toward him; cheeks sunken back against toothless gums blow a little—a sign of surprise. "Ah, the General." The voice is distant. "It was not correct the way they did it. They had to bring some of him back or he wouldn't get proper rites. I told them, bring back whatever you can find, even if it's a finger or a shoe. We can bury that and give it rites. Then he can go to the Land of Ancestors without trouble. But no one found anything—Ah, I know you. That foreigner with the ax. You slept on a horse." He laughs—the dry rustle of paper. "Who is he with you?"

Embree glances at Sanuk. "A friend, Grandfather. We want you to read the oracle for us. One reading for both."

The old man frowns. "That can't be done."

"Yes. That way our fate will be the same."

"Did you read for the General?" Sanuk asks.

"I did, boy, many times. He gave me money for the landlord."

"The landlord," Embree tells her in English, "is opium."

"What did you say?" the diviner asks.

"Tell us about the General's oracles."

The old man shakes his head sadly. "I've forgotten them all. I knew them once, even after he was dead a long time. But the trigrams get mixed up in my head, and the Commentary of the Duke of Chou. But I remember, when his officers were pestering him and war was everywhere, he'd still have time, like his father before him, to see me and ask for the oracle. He always gave me money."

"Now read ours," Embree says.

They watch the feeble old man take up a trembling handful of dried yarrow stalks and count them slowly, discard some and hold others, discarding and holding until he has created the numbers for two trigrams. Staring hard at the stalks, he mutters, "Heaven and fire. Do you know the lines, boy?"

"No," Sanuk says.

"The six lines of an oracle tell what happens and they stand for changes, for how things are moving from one state to another. Honorable Sir," he says to Embree, "you have money?"

Embree holds out Nationalist money, which the old man peers at closely, then shakes his head. "No, the other kind." Once he has a few yuan of People's money slipped into his dirty blouse, the diviner continues. "Fire is order. Heaven is strength."

"Can you read your book, Grandfather? Or can I read for you?" Embree asks.

"No need for the book any more. At the end of my life I know it all. Fire in heaven. In this hexagram you have five moving lines, one fixed. The fixed one in second place is the gate of understanding and accomplishment. The moving line in the fifth place is the ruler. The lower trigram means weapons, the upper is advancing toward it. Success for great armies."

"Which great armies?" Embree asks with a smile, but the old man seems not to hear. His rheumy eyes rove slowly over the strewn yarrow stalks. "Nine at the bottom; that's friendship at the gate, with no blame. No secrecy. Everything open is best. Don't lie. The six in second place and the nine in fifth place want union. They're prevented by lines in the third and fourth place. This hexagram is about movement upward. Fire and heaven both mean upward. That is good. And the heaven's brighter when fire reaches it. That means fellowship and love. The second and fifth place, remaining true to each other, will overcome the obstacles." He pauses.

"Then it's a good hexagram," Sanuk declares.

"It's a sad one, because the lines aren't noble enough in this arrangement. The third and fourth places are too strong and in the end will break everything apart. The good lasts only a short time." Irritably he pushes the stalks together in a heap. "Order and strength, brotherhood and love last only a short time here."

• • •

That evening, when they have returned to the inn and eaten a poor dinner of watery pork soup and fried cabbage, Sanuk looks from the open window of their room into the drowsy summer town. "I want to see her tomorrow, then I'll quit."

Lying on the bed, watching her, Embree says, "Quit only when you're satisfied." He won't tell her again that more warfare in the region is likely. He has warned her frequently. Each time she nods as if he's just told her it might rain. It's what he'd expect from her mother, too.

"Can I be satisfied with the past?" Sanuk turns. "Any more than be satisfied with how much time I have with you? We all want memories."

"Do you think so?"

"At least I do. I want them. I never knew how much until now. Thinking back on my life in Bangkok, I've lost most of it. My friend is married now. I remember Ah Ping, Nipa, Cook—not Cook very well, except for the scowl. But most of it seems gone already, even the look of the house and where things stood and their size. It's fading, and I hate that."

"It comes back."

"Does it?"

"Of course. Even when you don't want it to."

Coming to the bed, she kneels on it, not ready to embrace him. "Tell me what happens after tomorrow."

"Come to Shanghai with me."

"Is Mother waiting there?"

Embree tells himself he should have known all along that she knew. The diviner said, No lies. "Yes, she's waiting there."

"I see. You came to get me."

"That was the original idea. My darling," he says in English, "obviously things have changed."

"And I'm to go home with her?"

"You're to *meet* her. But after that you and I will go somewhere together."

"Not to Bangkok?"

"Not there. I don't know—somewhere."

"In China?"

"I don't know." Holding out his arms to her, Embree hopes she'll come to him, and she does. But passion hasn't yet drawn them beyond words that can dominate feeling. Gently he enfolds her, waiting for more of them.

"That oracle" she says, "was very sad. It sounded so good, everything rushing upward—heaven and fire, love and brotherhood—but then he said it won't last."

"You must understand: With the oracle everything always changes. That's why they call it the Book of Changes."

"What he remembered about my father was the money."

Embree laughs, moving his hand down her arm. Her breath is warming the hollow of his collarbone. No time to talk of sad oracles. "Kiss me," he says.

• • •

Again they rent horses for the trip southward to the farm. It's a gray morning, a pall of thick-bellied clouds hanging above the peanut fields and pear orchards of Shantung. Embree glances at the young woman, who's been grimly silent since they left their room. It occurs to him she might never leave this country. What he said yesterday could be true: She comes from here; she's just been gone a long time. And if she remains here, so will he. Will he? That he loves her is clear. That they can make a life together is unclear, no matter what he tells her. The diviner said, Don't lie. Yet perhaps love is built on a foundation of lies, illusions, fantasies. A very old, old thought in this world, as grim as her lovely face is now.

After two, no, three li—the old infantryman who served under Major Chia is right—there's a duck pond near the road and a stone fence, half fallen in. The farmhouse is typical: mud-walled, thatch-roofed, with a silo of wicker behind it, and in the front yard, rutted from mud and oxen, an immense grinding stone lies on a stone table. Before they can even dismount, she's there in the yard, among chickens: a squat woman in shapeless black trousers and top, squinting at them myopically, her hair, still black, in a bun secured with bamboo pins. Her bound feet in cotton shoes look like tiny blocks of wood.

They have not discussed how to introduce themselves, so Embree is surprised to see Sanuk go up to her and declare, without hesitation, "I am the daughter of General Tang Shan-teh."

For a moment the woman frowns, then dips her head in obsequious little gestures.

Now it is Sanuk's turn to be surprised. To Embree, she says in English, "I didn't say it for that. I don't want that."

"Never mind. Talk to her."

So while he stands back, not far from a huge pink pig tethered to an iron post, the two women move toward the house, leaning toward each other in conversation. They stand at the entrance—Sanuk tall and slim, with bobbed hair; Su-su short and dumpy now, with long hair severely managed. With more bowing, the older woman ushers the younger one inside.

Embree wanders about the yard, seeing in a distant field a solitary figure leaning behind a yoked ox. That must be Su-su's farmer. More clouds are rolling in, like the caissons used for carrying ammo in the old days here—gray, rumbling objects over the flat plain. Will he ever command enough courage to tell her the truth? That he betrayed her father—took her mother out of China when his own plot of assassination failed? Of course, men and women live with secrets as dark as his, live well with them, knowing the truth can ruin everything. And yet. With this woman there must be truth. Must there? Why is this young woman so special on the deceiving earth? Because to him she is. Until he tells her, "I betrayed your father to have your mother, and yet I love you. Forgive me," there's no chance for them, none at all. Because the truth, the truth, the truth is what she wants and always will. Yesterday she said of her father's punishments and tortures, "I understand. I'm not a child. That was his world."

But not yet. There's time for the truth. He must be patient, right? Embree takes a deep sigh of satisfaction at his eminently sane decision to wait a while. There's a stump on which the farmer chops wood. Sitting on it, Embree watches the clouds roll in like an army. Love finds a way. Isn't that also an old, old thought?

He waits a long time before the two women appear again at the entrance to the farmhouse. Sanuk has taken the older woman's hand, holds it, smiling. But when she lets go of Su-su's hand, the farm woman bows rapidly, deeply, and remains staring at the ground until, mounted, the two riders have left the compound.

The farmhouse is out of sight before Sanuk begins talking. When he sees tears in her eyes, Embree keeps his own straight ahead.

"She was once a gift from a big landlord to a mayor," Sanuk says. "Then the mayor, wishing to please my father, gave her to him as a gift. She said my father was very kind to her."

"Yes," Embree says.

"When my mother came to Qufu, my father told Su-su to leave. He might have given her nothing—he owed her nothing, Su-su said. Su-su was very clear about this. Instead, he gave her a fine sum that she used for a dowry, like the soldier told us."

"Yes."

"We talked about my father's death. She said if they didn't find and bury him properly, his spirit would howl in space."

"Many peasants believe that."

"To do something about it, she became his unofficial mourner."

Embree glances at her.

"In a back room of the farmhouse they have a little table with clay tablets on it."

"Yes, ancestor tablets."

"She picked up one and handed it to me. She'd brought it into the household as the tablet of her mother's great-uncle. That way her husband wouldn't know it was for my father. Every day she prays to the tablets, my father's among them."

"Yes," Embree says.

"But now she believes he's not really dead. That's right. She believes he lives as a god. He was killed on Tai Shan where the gods are. It was fated, she said. She said he's up there now, one of the gods."

They ride in silence.

"She has no children," Sanuk says after a while. "Her husband is good to her, but dull, I think. She's out here alone. There must be nothing else to do but wonder what might have happened if my mother hadn't come along."

"Yes," Embree says, not knowing what else to say.

 NEXT MORNING BY OX cart they travel the bumpy highway from Qufu to the rail junction at Yanchou. The road crosses the Wenhe River by means of a broad stone causeway on which fishermen are casting balloon-like nets from overarching bamboo poles. Sanuk is interested in the fishing, looking over her shoulder at the skillful throwers until they fade into the distance. Last night she'd been fiercely passionate, as if knowledge of the General's life has somehow given her the freedom to live her own.

Sensing her freedom, Embree looks for his own. Freedom from his own past. On this sunny day, traversed by strong but balmy winds, he decides they can wait a long time for the whole truth—maybe a lifetime.

Why should he ruin her faith in him when the man who betrayed her father was a young, foolish, uncertain, and rebellious twenty-four-year-old? Not Philip Embree today. As he bounces along in the wagon, watching her watch the fishermen, her bobbed hair shaking from the wooden motion, her skin freshened by breezes, Embree thinks the logic is inescapable. Love gives him a reason for deception. Had he loved Vera so much twenty years ago? No. But enough to deceive her too.

At Yanchou they have good joss—a freight train is leaving for Taian. What space is left after the loading of food and ammo, however, is taken by PLA troops. Yet on the top of one car there's space for two more riders. Good-naturedly some peasant soldiers help the foreigner and his woman up. They settle down in the midst of staring troops for the fifty-mile ride to Taian. With a great puff of steam and a shrill whistle, the old locomotive gets under way at last. Troops yell in triumph; so do Embree and Sanuk.

The countryside of Shantung rattles by, and Embree feels a sudden elation, much like he felt during his first train ride in China so many years ago.

And the excitement, the freedom shows in her face too.

Then through the rush of air, Embree hears a testament to that independence, that freedom: Abruptly Sanuk tells him she's not ready yet for Shanghai. "Not yet," she repeats, "not yet!" In her face, he sees the willful child who's tasted freedom and wants more. Not yet to face her mother. Not yet to face tomorrow. She reminds him of the Philip Embree who left his passport and Bible and entire past in a train compartment twenty years ago and walked into the first freedom.

Halfway to Taian, Embree notices to the west a road curving toward the railway track, and on it, close enough to see clearly, a large column is moving—Red troops, from their arm bands. Those in the train wave gaily to their comrades. Sanuk waves too. He wonders, would she wave if they were Nationalists? In her mood, probably. To emulate her he joins the waving, while at the same time gathering impressions of the force.

It's far better equipped than he would have imagined. Men are carrying both Japanese and American arms. He notices a BAR, a 6.5-mm. Taisho light machine gun. It's hard to say whether they have more M-1 carbines or Type 38 Arisaka rifles. What he'd been told by MAGIC about the Red talent for accumulating weapons from the enemy is evident here on the road heading north. Along come a couple of Staghound Chevy armored cars, with twin 50-cal. Brownings and a three-inch howitzer. Compliments of Uncle Sam. There are mortar squads ambling along the dusty road, with 60-mm. M-2's. Waving men have on their belts Mark II A-1 fragmentation grenades, heavily serrated, with mousetrap igniters, which on occasion he has thrown himself; and Jap grenades, copies of the German *Stielhandgranate*, which on occasion he has avoided when thrown.

And this PLA brigade is not done surprising him. Light Japanese trucks with slatted rear compartments and canvas cab tops are rumbling alongside the infantry. There's a Dodge three-quarter-ton, and another, and another, and a line of jeeps, all of the occupants waving gaily at their comrades in the train. It's like a parade. Glancing at Sanuk, he sees her waving without letup, lips parted like a child. Lo and behold, farther along the line he sees a tank, American, M-22 Locust, with one of its crew proudly waving from the hatch. Then a Sherman M-4, then two, three in series, all clanking up the highway toward Jinan, a couple of hundred miles away.

Leaning toward Sanuk, he shouts in her ear, above the noise of train and motorized brigade, "They're going to take Jinan under siege!"

"Yes?"

"You don't understand. We have to get out of Jinan as soon as we get there."

"But not to Shanghai."

"Whatever plane we can get, we must take."

Sanuk frowns. "Not to Shanghai. Not yet. I want time alone with you. Mother can wait."

If he mentions the heart attack, Sanuk will change her mind; of that he's certain. Change her mind and infuriate Vera. Both women live by a code that seems romantically stern, even to him, a romantic as well. How many betrayals must he live with? Promises and duties—what he runs from always come back to him. Irritably he shoves the dilemma from his mind in contemplation of this splendidly equipped army of peasant boys, who have managed to wrest from Nippon and the U.S. of A. the finest weapons in the world. There is always irony, he thinks, to keep one smiling.

That was early afternoon. Now the shadows of their train lean far to the east, darkening the weeds at edges of wheat and peanut fields. For the troops, at least for those clinging to the roofs of boxcars, the euphoria of feeling the rush of balmy air across their faces and of waving festively at comrades on the road has dissipated as time and shadows lengthen. Certainly the elation is gone from Sanuk's face; yet the fatigued set of her mouth changes when Embree looks at her. She smiles, tries to, and he tells himself this is the first woman who has ever loved him. But that's not true. His mother did, confined though her emotions were by his father. And there had been Fu-fang, a camp follower of White Wolf's band. But had she merely appropriated him in a mountain fastness where men treated horses better than women?

Riding on top of the boxcar, with streams of smoke flowing about them, now and then, almost timidly, he reaches out to touch Sanuk's fingers gripping the handrail.

And Vera? What will she say to this turn of events? Ah, that's obvious, he thinks grimly—

Men are shouting, pointing, from the car behind them. Embree squints into the sky, which seems spotless for a moment. Then, following the gaze of others, he finally sees a speck, off to the west and coming, it seems, from the sun itself.

"What is it?" Sanuk asks, but hardly are the words out than he has flung himself over her, clutching the handrail on both sides of her waist, as if in brutal sexual assault, and within seconds the whirl of an overhead engine turns his head up so he can see the P-51 Mustang swooping down obliquely toward the track.

There's a rattling sound, a yell, and the Mustang gains altitude, coming around again for another high approach, which again ends in a few rounds of .50-caliber bullets slamming into the top of a freight car. It's the one just ahead, and Embree watches two men slump over the side onto the railbed, like sacks of potatoes thrown overboard. This time, when the Mustang returns for another canting attack, some men in a coal car give it a burst of machine-gun fire. They can't elevate that high and so they miss badly, but the plane doesn't get off a single shot this time; instead, it ascends with a straining roar to get lost in the rays of the afternoon sun.

Rising from her, sitting cross-legged on the wooden roofing, Embree mutters, "Bloody fool." When she looks at him, puzzled, he says, "Came in across us. A child would know he's got to come in parallel. Bloody coward too. If that's the Nationalist air force, I pity them."

Color returning to her cheeks, Sanuk laughs gently. "Yes. You really are a soldier."

Just then the train shuffles to a halt. Steam pours into the sky with a hissing sound, and troops begin to climb from the boxcar roofs to the ground.

"What's happening?" Sanuk is staring down at them, as they crouch or stretch out along the railbed.

Rising, Embree tells her they better get off too, so down the ladder they go. He pulls his coolie hat far over his eyes, leading her away from the train into a peanut field. When they're a few hundred yards from the track, he says, "I've seen that before in China. A train stops somewhere and that's it, it stops. For a long time. Maybe the boiler's leaking or a gauge is broken or the fireman's tired. We can't wait for a Chinese train. Anyway, we must be near Taian now. Give me your suitcase."

"No."

"Give it to me. Mine's light. No? Well, so be it."

Suitcases in hand, they walk across the field, along the narrow furrows between rows of peanuts. Near sundown they come to a village.

Turning to her before they enter it, Embree says, "One thing about villagers. If they're eating well, if they're not threatened, they let you alone. But with the war heating up, things may be different around here. They're liable to take sides. All right?" He opens his suitcase, rummages under some clothes. Pulling out the ax—the wooden haft sits in a grooved hollow of the blade—Embree sticks it in his belt. "Not much of a weapon today. But like I said, it's what I have faith in." He rummages again, this time coming out with a holster and a Colt M 1911 semiautomatic. Weighing it judgmentally, he says, "Bit heavy, but the best pistol ever made." As he fits the holster to his belt, Embree says, "I'm Dutch from now on, not American." Once again he rummages in the suitcase, breaks off two packs of Lucky Strikes from a carton and puts them in his pocket. "You have a Siamese passport?"

"A Chinese one too."

He slips on a light cotton coat, loosely ties it with a piece of cord, hiding his weapons. "From now on you're a Siamese national."

Entering the muddy lane of the village, they see first, nailed to the brick side of a little house, a large poster, spanking new. Depicted on it in garish color is a gigantic Red soldier; with a bayonet he's pushing back a tiny warship carrying a Japanese naval officer and a red-nosed General MacArthur, both of them intent upon rescuing a drowning Chiang Kai-shek. Under the cartoon is a large inscription: OPPOSE AMER-ICAN IMPERIALISTS OPPOSE SUPPORT OF JAPAN OPPOSE AID TO CHIANG KAI-SHEK OPPOSE AGGRESSION AGAINST CHINA LONG LIVE THE PEOPLE'S REVO-LUTIONARY ARMY!

Slowly they move down the narrow street, with mud or brick houses on either side, functional, spare, close to the earth. Embree has always liked peasant China, the practical marshaling of energies toward a single goal—survival. God doesn't get in the way. Although ancestors do sometimes: complaining through village mediums about taxes and the poor farming of their land.

Abruptly two men come out of a hut, one holding a pitchfork.

"Comrades," shouts Embree, holding his hands out. He explains they're Dutch and Siamese citizens, trying to leave the war zone. They work for the people, he adds vaguely.

"What do you want here?" the man with the pitchfork asks.

"Food and shelter, comrade. Then tomorrow we go."

"What do you have?"

"Foreign cigarettes."

The man lowers the pitchfork.

"One thing, comrade," Embree adds pleasantly, as they follow him down a lane along which gawking faces appear in doorways, "The First Regimental Leader of the Second Division of the Third Field Army knows us. He's coming through here tomorrow. If anything happened to us, he'd be unhappy. We're doctors, and we saved his life. Understand?"

"Doctors?"

Embree waves his hands. "No more medicine. We can't do anything without it."

Sullenly the man nods. "Here." He points to a hut they're approaching—thatch-roofed with windows shuttered, although it's still too warm for that. "You eat here," he explains, "and sleep there," nodding toward a dilapidated stable beyond one corner of the hut. He walks inside; they follow into a dim room smelling of garlic. A fire in a little stove glows under a big black iron pot that hangs from the ceiling. A woman, seeing them, steps back against the wall. Roughly he tells her to get bowls for these people, turns to Embree. "The cigarettes?"

Embree takes out a pack of Lucky Strikes.

"No," the villager says. "Two of those."

"One."

"Two."

Finally Embree shrugs. "You take everything I have," he declares, handing over the second pack.

Turning the packs around, picking at the tight cellophane with a thick finger, the man says, "American cigarettes?"

"Dutch."

Turning, he shouts at the woman who has put bowls out on the *kang*, a raised platform along one side of the mud wall. "Hurry up there!" To Embree he says defensively, "All we've got is some vegetables and gruel. We're a poor family." Turning again to the woman he raises his hand, threatening to cuff her. Ignoring him, she continues to stir the pot.

With a smile, he sits on the *kang*, next to Sanuk, whom he looks over with open interest. "You're Siamese? Where is that place?"

"South of China."

"I don't know Siam," he observes sourly. "The army comes through tomorrow?"

"Yes," Embree says. "The regimental leader told me to stay at this village until he arrives."

"Ah," the villager nods emphatically. "You, woman, hurry! These are important guests." With a smile for Embree, he says, "When your wife's angry, beat her. When you're angry, beat her. That's the way to happiness."

• • •

The sun is setting, but already they are bedded down in the hayloft above the stable, which at present is occupied by an old mule, a pig, and a few rats who are skittering around the baseboard of the old wooden structure, rustling through the hay. Embree has blocked the door by jamming a rake against it and tamping the end into the loose earth of the stable. He explains if anyone tries to get in, at least they'll have a warning.

"Is it dangerous here?" Sanuk asks. They're lying in a heap of straw, with a tiny loft window letting in the last rays of orange light.

"I don't think so. They're expecting my friend from the Third Field Army tomorrow."

"Do they believe that?"

"When what you tell them is about an army, they believe it. They can't afford not to. I don't think precautions are needed in this village. But people do strange things when a war reaches their doorsteps."

"Now I know another part of you," Sanuk tells him. "I used to dream about warriors, about being one myself. Like Jeanne d'Arc. The Rani of Jhansi. Riding beside my father into battle. But now, having seen you, I'm not sure it's what I want."

Laughing, Embree leans forward and kisses her warm cheek.

She backs away, serious. "There's something in you that frightens me, even though I like it. I'd have felt the same with Father too. I know it now. You enjoy the danger, the idea you might use that thing." She glances at the pistol hanging in its holster over the hayloft's railing.

Earlier he'd stripped and cleaned the gun with a little oil he kept in a vial. Sanuk had watched, fascinated, as he loaded the magazine with seven 230-gram bullets, and then, with a metallic click, locked the barrel to the slide with the pivoting link. "I'm a coward. I never thought it possible, but now I know I am," she declares.

"I doubt that. Or we're all cowards if we stay with it long enough. A friend of mine, he's dead now, saw the coward in me."

"I don't believe it."

"Both the fool and the coward. And I'll tell you another thing. Today, when the plane attacked, I was terrified. You see, I've never wanted to die from the air. It's a silly attitude—considering if you die fast one way or another, you're lucky—but it's mine. I want to see my man. Or at least know he's shooting me from my own level. But up there—"

"Don't," she says, and picking up a fistful of hay throws it at him. He throws some back. Looking at each other, they start to giggle; fistfuls of hay fill the air. Next—Sanuk does it first—they reach out to grapple with each other, roll into the snapping hay. With the dry earthy smell in their nostrils, the dusty straw gently scraping their faces and arms, they begin kissing, and the mule below them shifts nervously as they become silent, intent, lost in each other.

Later, as they lie side by side in darkness, Embree says, "None of this could have been dreamed of."

"I know that."

"I feel very sane." Embree pauses, considering whether to take the path now leading through his mind. He says, "I believe I was quite mad in India," and tells her about Harry. Everything about Harry. "And there in Pagan on the temple terrace I tried to contact him." She has been silent, absolutely motionless while he told the story. Now he feels her hand against his shoulder.

"I hope I would have done the same."

Embree turns but can't see her in the dark. It makes him feel as though she's a disembodied spirit, a voice coming out of the void. "Why would you hope to act like a crazy man?"

"I believe in boldness. And after all, there was nothing else you could do but go up there and challenge your demon."

Embree takes her in his arms and holds her until at last she falls asleep. He knows that he has never loved anyone as he loves her now. How could he not love her? To rid himself of a demon he had confronted it in Pagan. Perhaps it was the most significant thing he has ever done in life—to face the demon within. And perhaps the most significant thing anyone has done for him has been done by this woman tonight. She has believed in him in his strangest hour.

• • •

It is not yet daybreak when Embree shakes her. Quietly they slip out of the stable, down the lane, into the morning fields. Dew wets their legs. A brilliant planet in the east harbingers the brighter light of the sun, which doesn't appear until they're far beyond the village.

"A journey of a thousand miles begins with a single step," Embree says as they slog out of the field onto a road.

"Who said that?"

"Attributed to Lao Tzu."

"I wish he was here to take some of *my* steps."

"Do you love me?" Embree asks suddenly. She looks new, he thinks. Young and fresh in the Chinese dawn.

"I'm glad you ask," Sanuk says. "I mean, at this moment."

"Why?"

"Because I was thinking the same thing: Does he love me? And by asking me the same thing, you let me know you do. Yes. I feel the same. I love you."

It's said with a conviction that frightens Embree. Too much happiness is a danger. That's a truism in every language. But pessimism is, perhaps, the worst of habits to fall into. When you have faults, Confucius said, don't be afraid to abandon them. Small wonder the Chinese still listen to him, Embree thinks.

Taking her hand, he steps forward, the heavy shape of the holster thudding against his hip. They'll make it. They love each other. And sure enough, by the time the sun has climbed halfway to noon, in the distance he can see a blue conical shape emerging from the haze: Tai Shan. Soon they'll be in Taian.

• • •

It isn't the same place they left a few days ago. Entering the town, they see troops everywhere—not lounging around or eating sugar cakes on the street or preparing for an excursion to the mountain. These men are walking in columns, creating a sound only too familiar to Embree: the rhythmic clank of an army on the move. Trucks rumble down the streets, raising a dust that jitters in the sunlight. Coming to the Temple of the God of Tai Shan, Embree glances once through the gate, seeing within there a cluster of soldiers inspecting their bed rolls, their sausage-shaped cloth bags of rice, their American and Japanese weapons. The temple's become a marshaling yard.

"We'll try the train station," he suggests.

Coming into sight of the tin-roofed structure, he notices a train in the station and at least a thousand troops waiting in the hot sun. Pulling his hat down, tightening the cord around his coat, he warns her again, "You're a Siamese national." They push through the waiting crowds of soldiers to the main platform, where a number of guards, armed with rifles, are standing. One of them, noticing Embree, approaches. "Who are you? What are you doing?"

"I'm Dutch. I'm with the World Health Organization," Embree says. "She's my colleague. We need transportation."

Looking them over, the guard guides them out of the station to a jeep parked on a side street off the square. There are two officers sitting in it, one behind the wheel. Embree tells them the same thing. The one behind the wheel has a fat, open face and tremendous hands.

He says, "What are you? One of those spies trained by General Ma Tu?" But he says it pleasantly, with a smile.

"General MacArthur is American. I'm Dutch. I'm working for the people."

"What people?" the officer asks in a sharper tone.

"Whoever's sick. That's what WHO does."

"Never heard of it. Heard of the other one. Yu Ha."

"UNRRA is finished now. We're the new one. Could you give us transportation toward Jinan?"

"What do you want to go to Jinan for?" The big man behind the wheel laughs and turns to his companion, a sour but equally big man. "They go there to get killed."

"To get a plane," Embree says. With a shrug he adds, "If we get killed, then we can't bring medicine back when the PLA wins."

"Nobody ever gave us medicine in the past. Why should they now? But we don't need your help. What you give the Nationalists we take from them anyway."

"True," Embree says. "But after you finish them, you'll be the only ones left to get the medicines and the cots and the bandages."

Both men nod. The commander turns over the engine. "Giving a ride to an American," he says.

"I'm Dutch," Embree corrects him politely.

"Foreigners these days are all Americans."

"I'm not American."

"Giving a ride to an American. Isn't that nice?" He puts the car roughly into gear. "Well, come on, get in. We'll give you a ride to a village not far from Jinan. Then it's up to you to get into the city by yourself. The Nationalist bastards are so scared they'll probably shoot you on sight." With a roar the car moves. "Even if you are an American or a Dutchman or any kind of foreigner."

• • •

As the staff car rattles along the dusty road between Taian and Jinan, the officer at the wheel honks his horn gaily at almost anything he passes, including parked vehicles and seated men. Embree understands why the staff car isn't chauffeured—the big muscular company commander likes to drive it. He's also democratic about using it—often stopping to give soldiers a lift for a few miles, letting them out and picking up others, wedging them next to Embree and Sanuk in the back seat. Nothing pleases him as much as this jeep, yet after praising its engine, its tires, its metal chassis, its steering wheel, he turns from his driving to glare at Embree and claim the people don't need such cars. "You Americans all have them, don't you. Every family has one, but we don't need them. Look—" He points to a couple of farmers, in tandem, with ropes straining against their shoulder pads, pulling a wagon along the road; it's loaded to bursting with gravel. "We do it ourselves," he says proudly.

"I'm not American."

Honk honk honk. The commander nearly cuts down an old man bent double by a load of roped faggots. "Do you think I care if you're American? Do you think that means anything? We don't need you. We don't care what you give those Nationalist fuckers. We just take it from them."

"I'm not American."

"All men with hair your color are Americans. Is it true your emperor, Fu Da Re Rufuzi, lives in a white palace?"

"I think that emperor is dead now. Now it's a man called Truman. I've never seen their white palace."

"I never heard of Dutch people in China. You're American." Having settled the matter, he becomes amiable again, honking ecstatically as they pass a column of farmers—at least two miles long—bringing up supplies for the army. Mule-and-man-drawn wagons carry bags of grain, piles of loose onions, sacks of corn, stoppered jars, ammo boxes, cartons of blue cotton shoes, chickens in baskets, pigs in slatted cages. "We pay for everything," the commander declares, honking furiously. "Those farmers give their service free. That's how the PLA wins against Chiang's running dogs."

Squeezing Sanuk's hand in his, Embree looks across fields of kaoliang now ripening on either side of the road. Their cornlike grain is clustered around the plant tops asway in a brisk wind. He points it out to her: "Kaoliang." Conical haystacks go by. Peasants look up at the sound of an engine while they're hoeing vegetables, gathering manure for the fields. China goes on, war or no war.

In two hours the jeep roars through the gate of a crumbling village wall. Apparently this is a forward command post, because the dusty lanes and streets are clogged with Red troops, all of them armed, some even wearing pot-shaped Japanese helmets.

Two men are lugging an M-18 recoilless rifle. Another carries its tripod. We had them in Burma, Embree remembers: 57 millimeters, fires a canister or HEAT round more than 4000 yards, good penetration. He imagines the Reds will use it against the walls of Jinan.

Ahead of the jeep an American 105-mm. howitzer on a self-propelled carriage is clattering through the marshaling area of the village—a cement threshing square.

"This is as far as we go, American," the big commander says, getting out of the jeep. Three soldiers, recently picked up on the road, hop out and so does the other officer, who sat next to the driver in complete silence the entire ride.

"I thank you, comrade," Embree says, when he and Sanuk get out too.

The big man, towering over him, grins. "Jinan is that way"—he points north—"about an hour's walk. Don't stay there too long, though, or you'll see me again."

. . .

Once out of the village, Embree tells her they aren't going into Jinan, but directly to the airport about four miles west of the city. She nods without comment. He knows what she's thinking: I won't go to Shanghai, not yet, I won't face Mother until I've had more life of my own. He knows what she feels—the elation of freedom. In twenty years he hasn't summoned the courage to face his own father, if indeed his father still lives. But with Sanuk he holds an ace in the hole: her mother's sickness.

A mile beyond the village there are no soldiers, no trucks, no supply wagons. It's silent enough for them to hear the kaoliang rustle like paper in winds sweeping in from interior China. They cut across plots of wheat separated by stone fences. Swallows dip out of the sky to skim inches above the burgeoning tassels.

"Let's go to Nanking," Sanuk says abruptly, turning in the wheat, waist high now, to smile appealingly at him. "I once read it's beautiful."

If they could, he thinks. Nanking with its roads lined with sycamore, pine, and cypress. It's a city of trees—cedar, evergreen cork, nut-bearing giant hickories, cherry and parasol trees. The City of Plum Blossoms. She'd love the look of Nanking, its spaciousness and greenery.

When there to see MAGIC, he stayed at the Nanking Hotel. Thought nothing then of the azaleas in the garden, the wisteria, the Himalayan pine near the entrance. But now, with her struggling alongside him through kaoliang fields toward a mutually uncertain future, he wants very much for them to be together in that garden. They'd eat in the hotel restaurant: blood-red curtains, pillars a shade of ivory. There's the ballroom too. Parquet floor. American couples from MAGIC were dancing there. Some of Chiang's officers and their wives too, decorously. Sat out the fast numbers. Sat beribboned on chairs, smiling, afraid to say anything that might be overheard and reported back to the Gimo. Does Sanuk dance? He'll teach her, though he himself hasn't danced since college days. They'll learn together in the ballroom of the Nanking Hotel, with its revolving fans and enormous red lanterns along the walls. Mahogany panels in the big room, giving it a warm deep glow. She'll like that. They'll dance to the Filipino band there, if it hasn't already fled China.

Then, tired of dancing, they'll go to their room.

He recalls his room, except in his mind now they are there together: a large armoire, a mirror over the dressing table with a glass top. He'll buy things for her to set on it: perfumes, something pretty in silk, and one of those boxwood combs the suburb of Shangchou is famous for. There's a balcony overlooking the pines and magnolias. Two beds. Well, they'll push them together. A marble bathroom, chandelier, a ceiling fan to cool their bodies sweating from love. If it's cold, they can lie in bed and hear the massive, ugly radiators hiss and knock. They'll lie awake at night and hear the wind rushing against panes of their balcony doors.

"Really," Sanuk says, bumping him playfully. "Nanking."

"We'll take what we can get out of Jinan."

"You sound angry."

Halting, he puts his arms around her waist. There's a thin mustache of sweat along her upper lip. "Not angry. Frustrated we're not in Nanking now." Bending toward her mouth, sensuously he licks the moisture off.

Drawing back, Embree tells her they must go faster now; they have only an hour of sunlight left.

. . .

And so they reach the Jinan airport—airstrip really—a macadam surface with a single runway, a low-slung control tower, a couple of sheds, one hangar. It's in front of the shed labeled FLIGHT INFORMATION, in both English and Chinese, that they'll wait, along with three or four hundred other people, in a line stretching from one shed to another. Will wait that night, sleeping on the ground, will wait all of the next day, as only two planes land and take off, one bound for Peking, the other for Shanghai. Grinning hawkers come around with food. People hold places in line for those who use the latrine: a couple of V-set flagstones placed over holes in the ground behind the hangar. The shed area becomes a campground, with debris piling up at the edges—paper, bits of food, cigarette butts—while strangers become neighbors in Chinese, English, French. It's a flat hot space, harshly glaring, in which they arrange a serpentine sloppy line of preference leading to the FLIGHT INFORMATION door.

On the second day Embree and Sanuk are not even halfway down the line. Most of the time the shed door is closed. When it opens, applicants for a flight are taken according to their position in the line, although many people want only one destination or another. That means a last-minute reshuffling of positions—some people moving forward, some backward—with voices rising, with pushing and shoving, and angry words exchanged in languages not always understood. Inside the shed passports are checked, often accompanied by interrogation, so that the question of a domestic air flight becomes one of customs and immigration as well. Fear and opportunity work in concert to break down the last vestiges of law. Once passports are checked, passage is paid. This is a difficult affair, since the airport officials won't accept the inflated currency of their own government. However, they'll take Renminbi, Communist Area money; Embree chuckles when people go up and down the line complaining of such unprincipled behavior.

No one, he thinks, is as practical as the Chinese. They elevate pragmatism to an art.

The best way of paying for a flight is through barter: jewelry, watches, fountain pens (highly prized, an object of authority), even clothing and cigarettes. "Thank God," Embree says, "the Chinese love to smoke." Once payment is settled between applicant and official, the ticket (a blank piece of rice paper) is duly stamped, the passenger leaves the shed by a back door, boards the plane, breathes a sigh, and gets the hell out of this doomed city.

If Embree could use his connection with MAGIC, they'd commandeer passage on a military flight: The Chinese 26th Air Force has its landing strip adjacent to this one. Surely the Americans still have some credit left with the Nationalists. All day long planes are flying in and out over there, carrying officials from Nanking and Shanghai and Peking to Jinan in a last-minute effort to save face for the Generalissimo by somehow saving his force of a hundred thousand men now bottled up inside its walls. But Embree knows the rules of the game. If he attempts to get through to MAGIC in Nanking, authorities here will suspect him of colluding in a dire American plot. A few Americans have already been turned away from the shed on the pretext of some irregularity in their papers. They have been seen boarding trucks for a ride into Jinan and God knows what fate. People in line say the Nationalists in Jinan are charging Americans with giving aid secretly to the Reds.

All right, so the Chinese wouldn't look kindly, Embree thinks, on his attempt to contact Americans in Nanking. And even if he got through to MAGIC, instead of helping him the boys there would deny they ever heard of him. MAGIC will remain politically invisible.

Rumors multiply all day long among people waiting on the hot tarmac. Many of them walk about, wiping their faces with towels. Others try to sleep through the nightmare, sprawl out with newspapers over their faces. Still others huddle under umbrellas, squinting into the light and smoking cigarettes. Some are Chinese, either wealthy merchants or landlords, who sit quietly in family groups, morosely listening to Europeans castigating the Yellow Race. Some of the Europeans, however, wait as patiently as the Asians.

There's an elderly English couple within speaking distance of Embree and Sanuk. They exchange pleasantries and sometimes the English couple strolls over for a bit of conversation, as if assembling for tea. The woman wears a tweed skirt in this hot weather and high hiking shoes. The man keeps on a rumpled seersucker jacket. Both wear solar topis above their sun-reddened faces. They have been here collecting ancient clocks and astronomical instruments for a museum somewhere—Embree misses its name the first time around and feels too embarrassed to ask again, for the old couple are obviously convinced that nothing is more important to the world than their expedition for collecting gnomons and armillary spheres and early versions of Chinese clepsydras.

The woman, hands on hips, tells about it. "We have found a very old clepsydra only twenty kilometers from Jinan in a farmhouse."

"Not quite twenty," her husband adds.

"Are you acquainted with the clepsydra?" she asks Embree and without hesitation embarks upon a lecture, while heat waves rise from the tarmac like the sea: Inflow clepsydras appeared in China before the Christian era—

"Long before the Christian era," her husband adds.

She describes how the clock works by letting water flow into a container at a standard rate, with a float indicator and a pointer on the vessel's neck. Very accurate timepiece.

"The later ones were quite accurate," her husband adds.

She praises the testimony to their accuracy recorded in a document nearly eighteen hundred years old—that of Huan Tan, a court official from the Han, who described how these water clocks were regulated in both water flow and temperature—

"To control the rate of evaporation," her husband adds.

Later Sanuk grips Embree's hand. "This is the right place for it."

"For what?"

"For Bright Lotus and Bill to have an adventure."

"How will it go?" Embree asks with a smile.

"Well . . . Bright Lotus won't leave the airport without Bill but the authorities say he can't come along for two reasons: because he's a water buffalo and because he's too big. She insists until they say she can't fly either. So . . ." Rubbing her nose thoughtfully, Sanuk continues. "She waits until dark and smuggles Bill into the cargo section of a plane and puts a tarpaulin over him. He warns her there'll be trouble. But Bright Lotus just says, 'Don't worry. They won't find us until we get in the air.' And Bill says, 'What if they want to throw us out?' And Bright Lotus tells him—"

"Wait. I know. She says, 'I'll think of something.'"

"So you do remember!" But there are other stories, grim ones, now coming out of the tin-roofed shed: Chinese officials are starting to grill the applicants about anything under the sun—their education, their loyalty to Chiang Kai-shek, their propensity to drunkenness and licentious acts. Inspectors have ripped open suitcases, wrecked goods in a furious attempt to find contraband. Army officers, standing by, have whimsically accused certain people of espionage. A slow answer, a wrong glance, a slight deviation from what's expected—such things have resulted in one out of ten people being turned away for flights.

On the third day, after a flight to Peking has loaded and left, Embree and Sanuk are sitting on their suitcases, as some protection against the heat of the unshaded tarmac.

She breaks a long silence. "I've been thinking about the old diviner and our hexagram. That we can succeed by remaining true to each other."

Embree nods. He won't point out the ultimate pessimism of the reading: that the two places aren't "noble" enough to hold against opposition. "Yes," he says. "Fire in heaven."

"In case something happens," she continues. "If there's trouble, I want you to know something. Something I've done."

Sounds like a confession coming, Embree thinks. God, no. Last thing he needs is a confession from her—the challenge to reciprocate. "It isn't necessary to tell me."

"But you have to know."

"Past is past. Really. It isn't necessary," he says, feeling close to panic.

"But you said it yourself: Unless you told me everything, I mustn't trust you. Someday you'll tell me and till then you'll worry it and worry it, because it stands between us. I know you, darling. Maybe because I feel the same." She is speaking Teochiu in case anyone in the line might overhear them. But the "darling" she says in English. "Let me tell you."

Embree sinks back, looks down at his feet. She is brave, he thinks gloomily. Most people preparing to confess would choose a better time than high noon in blistering heat; they'd wait for sunset or darkness— or maybe, he thinks hopefully, what she has to confess is nothing more than a prank. Cautiously he says, "All right, then. But don't ask me to judge you."

"You?" She smiles. "The only person you ever judge is yourself."

And so in blinding sunlight, hunched on a suitcase, while heat waves surge up from the tarmac, Philip Embree hears the story of two young people who strangle a man on a moonlit beach. It is a sad tale, because most probably an innocent man died, and a pathetic tale too, because only the young and the untried could have reacted in such a heedless way with such a dismal result. It's also a tale of courage, because however wrongheaded the act they committed, they committed it without faltering and learned to live with it thereafter. Perhaps it's a comic tale, in the philosophic sense of outraging the order of things without destroying it. To kill a man, he knows only too well, is not difficult. Perhaps not ultimately significant. It's a momentary ripple on the surface of ordinary events. Yes indeed. Yet the poor girl has harbored this sad, pathetic error as if the existence of the world had been threatened by it. That's part of the comedy—the lack of proportion in her assessment of what youth has done. The other part is the imagined sight of them farcically grappling with the victim in the ocean, all three of them struggling toward a conclusion as old and foolish as humanity itself.

But Embree knows the real truth of his callous reaction to her truly anguished confession: It has taken an act of will for her to make it and has made her older and braver than he can be. And where is his own offering of truth? Can't make it yet. On the plane, maybe, or after they've stood in front of Vera and confessed to something else. But not now, not yet, not in this harsh glare of noon on the tarmac of a ramshackle airfield.

He tells her, of course, with all the tenderness he can show, that her confession means a great deal to him, that it speaks in full measure of her love for him, that it establishes for them a standard of truth and faith. But does she realize how stiff, how ungiving his words really are? Does she have an inkling of how anxious he is to pretend satisfaction with what has just happened, with what, in fact, has shattered his self-esteem and marked their future together for more grief than even he can imagine? They are holding hands, staring ahead. One glance tells him that the tears in her eyes are tears of relief.

How lucky she is, he thinks.

A man in khaki pants and a bush shirt comes along the line, mopping his sweaty brow. "I have just learned," he says, "another plane is due in shortly. Returning to Shanghai if you're going there. Better get yourselves sorted out," he adds, looking at Embree's section of the line. "You might make this one. I bloody well won't."

Getting off his suitcase, Embree opens it and digs through the clothes, coming up with four and a half cartons of cigarettes. "Open your suitcase," he tells her.

"No."

"Open it."

She does, reluctantly, and he shoves the cigarettes inside, then closes the suitcase himself.

"If you're asked a difficult question, shove over a carton of these. If that doesn't satisfy him, shove over another."

"No."

"Use them all. Don't be shy about it, either. The men in that shed won't be shy about taking them."

"The plane's going to Shanghai?"

"Don't be shy with the men in there. Send over the cartons one by one."

"Mother can wait. I'll make peace with her later. I don't want to go there yet. Not Shanghai."

"We must go."

"Not Shanghai. No." She's shaking her head with a child's determination.

"All right then." Embree sighs. "I'm going to tell you something. I'm going to tell you about your mother."

"I know. I treated her badly. I made a terrible mistake. I owe Mother a real apology. And so do you—for letting this happen. Is that what you're going to tell me? All right. But not Shanghai, not yet."

"Listen to me. She raised you with little help from anyone. She built up a business on her own, while I sat around dreaming. Your mother's a survivor, but something's happened that even *she* can't handle."

"My running away?"

"Whether she knows it or not, she can handle that. Your mother's had a heart attack."

He feels Sanuk's eyes searching his face for a sign of the truth.

"I wasn't going to tell you until we reached Shanghai."

"So you did come to take me back."

"I came to take you back."

"Do you love me? Is that true?"

"That's as true as anything in my life. But we're going to Shanghai. Your mother's ill." Embree hears a distant droning in the air.

"You've told me this story to get me on the plane for Shanghai? I know your loyalty to Mother."

"I'm telling you to get you on the plane. Because it's a true story. Now, wait. *Listen* to me. She's in a nursing home. The Aurore Nursing Home in the French Concession. Your mother said, 'Don't tell her. It's got to be her choice to come. I forbid you to use this.' I swore I wouldn't tell you." He can hear the plane drawing closer. "So I'm betraying a trust. Because there's no choice, darling. If we don't take the flight, we could be here a long time. And maybe she doesn't have that much time. We're going now."

Sanuk looks down at the tarmac in wordless acquiescence.

• • •

A twin-engine plane appears over the hills southeast of the airfield. Embree is familiar with the type—a Curtiss C-46 Commando—indeed he is. They used to parachute supplies into the Burmese jungle. Perhaps this one ferried Chinese troops from Rangoon at the end of the war.

Everyone in line is standing, even those without a chance of making the flight. The number of passengers will be determined by how much other cargo is loaded. So far, every flight has concentrated upon boxes and steamer trunks—personal effects of local politicians and staff officers.

The shed door opens, a soldier comes out and stands at the entrance, carbine in hand, to keep order. Then three people at a time enter the shed, while at the loading door on the Commando's port side great trunks, boxes, and objects of different sizes wrapped in gunnysacks disappear into the plane's belly. Here too a soldier stands with his carbine ready, as a column of sweating coolies bring more cargo to the tarmac.

"How will you get through?" Sanuk asks suddenly, as they approach the head of the line. "You don't have cigarettes to give them. You gave them all to me."

He raises his arm to show his wristwatch. "I have this and plenty of Renminbi. I'll let them have the Colt too. They'll like that."

"Nothing will go wrong?"

"Of course not." She looks so young at this moment. Does worry make a young person look younger, an old person older? At times her youth frightens him. As lovers they're equal, but at a time like this her inexperience separates them. Not that she's wrong to worry. Oh no. Because something might go wrong.

Now there are half a dozen people ahead of them. Minutes pass, as heavy and slow as the aircraft getting loaded out there. "You're a student from Siam studying the Chinese language. Don't say more than necessary."

"I love you."

"Remember to shove a carton forward, one at a time. If he asks a question you can't answer, shove another forward." Reaching out his hand, he grips hers, feels the nervous chill of it. "Get ready."

At a curt gesture from the guard, Sanuk enters the shed. She does not look back. Good, Embree thinks.

• • •

When it's his turn to go in, Embree doesn't look directly at her. With a sweeping glance around the shed he locates her standing at a far table. There are a couple of naked light bulbs dangling overhead, no other illumination in the room. A rattling old fan, just one, circulates what little air there is. He's called by a seated customs official to the middle table of three. Wearing a white shirt open to his navel, the man is sweating profusely. He squints up as Embree hands over the Dutch passport. Embree can see a coin-size bald spot on the official's head as he hunches over the booklet.

Another glance her way.

Embree sees her take from the open suitcase a carton of cigarettes and shove it across the table. Good girl. Smiling faintly at her, the official takes the carton and throws it into a box at his feet. Then he puts his own hands into the suitcase and comes out with those diaries of hers that she keeps tied with ribbon. Methodically the official unties each one and thumbs through the pages.

What does she write in her diaries? Embree wonders. On the tarmac she hunched over pages in one of them, scribbling intently. Does she write, "I love him"? He's never asked her; her only reference to keeping diaries: "It's something I can't help doing."

Sanuk takes another carton and moves it across the desk toward the official. Putting aside the diaries, untied, he asks her more questions, his face severe.

"You speak English, Mister Brinker?"

Embree nods. His questioner speaks excellent English. Is that good or bad for him as a Dutch citizen?

"What are you doing in China, Mister Brinker?"

Giving the man his letter of introduction from WHO, Embree explains he's a dietitian, studying the food habits of the Chinese populace. "I study what people eat," he explains. It sounds fine to him, not too technical, yet somewhat sympathetic. He has forgotten his own dictum: that when you think the Chinese are becoming predictable, they prove you wrong.

Glancing at Sanuk, he's heartened to see her tying a ribbon around one of the diaries.

Shoving his chair back, Embree's interrogator gets up and holds a quick conference with an army officer seated in the back of the room with his crossed feet encased in leather boots—a rare sight in China—high up on a desk for everyone to admire. Coming back to the table, the interrogator is smiling. He slips Embree's passport into his pocket. "I'm sorry, Mister Brinker, but the quota for this plane is filled."

"Wait a minute." He glances at Sanuk, who's closing her suitcase while the man there stamps her ticket. "What's the problem? I'm with WHO—World Health Organization."

"You can wait in Jinan a few days, Mister Brinker."

The army officer is sauntering over. "What do you do?" he asks Embree roughly.

"I study what people eat, you see. For the World Health Organization. We check water supplies and study epidemic control and start vaccination prog—"

"Never heard of it. UNRRA, yes."

"They've stopped UNRRA. WHO is taking its place." Beyond the officer's shoulder he can see her moving along with suitcase in hand. She's staring his way.

"Open your suitcase," the officer tells him. When it's open, he shoves Embree aside and rummages through it, coming up with the Colt. "We must confiscate this."

"But other people are carrying pistols."

"Why are you carrying one?"

"For safety, what else would—" Embree checks himself.

"Weapons of this size must be confiscated."

"That's an American gun," points out the customs official with a frown.

"Sold throughout the world. Look, I have money, whatever kind you want. An alarm clock somewhere in there—"

"What's this?" The officer has pulled out the ax, turning it curiously in the dim metallic light. Sweat from his chin drops on the blade. "What do you have this for?" he demands of Embree.

"It's an old friend. I mean I carry it everywhere."

Tossing it back into the suitcase, the officer scowls, as if contemptuous of someone who'd carry such a primitive weapon. "We have to check your papers. Do you supply the Red bandits with radio transmitters and codes?"

"WHO supplies medicine."

"To the Red bandits?"

Carefully Embree chooses his words. "To people who are starving and sick. That's the idea, you see. We don't supply bandits anything."

"You're the first Dutchman we've had here," says the seated customs official in a tone that sounds accusatory.

"I'm expected back in Shanghai," Embree insists. She has halted. Don't panic, don't come over here, he thinks. "World Health Organization is what I work for. I'm a Dutch citizen working for health. Frankly, you have no right to detain me. I can pay for my ticket. This is a civil flight."

"This is a battle area," says the army officer. "We do what we must to protect the people of China."

"Then get me to Shanghai." Embree has been speaking Chinese to the officer, but turning to the customs official he says in English, "What can possibly be wrong with my papers? My government will protest this treatment, I assure you. And so will WHO."

"Your English is very good," the customs official observes. "Where did you learn so well?"

"In England. Mine's no better than yours."

"Better."

"I have Renminbi, lots of it," Embree says, while slipping off his wristwatch.

"No," says the army officer, pushing away the watch extended to him. "You wait a few days. We check, then you go."

Embree studies him. There's profound decisiveness in the square jaw, the narrow eyes. Opening both hands out, Embree says, "Very well, then. What am I to do? Wait out there again?"

"We can take you into Jinan," the officer says. It's not an invitation but a statement.

"I see."

"Take your goods and go over there." After picking up the Colt and jamming it under his belt, the officer points to the desk where he'd propped up his stylish feet.

She's at the exit doorway, lips parted, waiting for him. Chancing it— he must—Embree walks toward her. Even before reaching her, he's talking. "Go," he says. "I'll be held up awhile. Go on, go now. Hurry before they change their mind."

"I'll wait."

"Sonia," he says. It sounds odd, a stern word out of the past, her mother calling for her, "Sonia! Sonia! Child, come here!" He wants to touch her, but mustn't. There's such a yearning for explanation in her face, but no time to give it. "I won't be long," he tells her with a little shooing gesture. Irritably he says, "Get on the plane. They're damn touchy right now. Don't stand here. Go on out. *Do* it."

Half-turning from him, hesitating, Sanuk says, "I'll wait for you. In Shanghai?" Turning fully toward him, she adds, "Or where?"

"Don't worry about that now. Shanghai. Peking."

"Peking?"

"Depends how I get out of here."

"When? *When?*"

Embree glances at a soldier regarding them closely. "I won't leave China without you," he tells her.

"But how will you get out of here? How?"

She seems very young, with the round eyes of a troubled child. He recalls her somber little face staring at him as he sat beside her near the klong and took them both on another wild adventure, Bright Lotus and Bill, setting forward into infinite possibilities. "I'll think of something," he says, confidently. "Now go."

She goes.

SHE FEELS MUCH older than she was yesterday, older than she was this morning when the plane left Jinan Airport. Walking down the dim corridor of the Aurore Nursing Home, she wonders if it will ever be possible to feel older than she does now.

While the little Chinese nurse is reassuring her that her mother is making excellent progress toward recovery, Sonia senses in her own body the inertia of age. She'll never be young again, not even when she's back with Philip. Together they'll be old: he made old by years, she by a few months.

Will they be together again?

He said, "I won't leave China without you."

The nurse continues to reassure her. "And Doctor says in her favor is a strong will. She's had no more *crises cardiaques*." The nurse, proud of speaking French, speaks a little. "Each day makes complete recovery *de plus en plus certain*. You see? Please don't frown so! Smile when you see her." With this advice, she stops along the corridor and opens a door wide.

Propped up on pillows is her mother. Seated on the edge of the bed is a dark young man with unruly black hair, wearing clothes worn in the Indian bazaar of Bangkok. The two hold playing cards, and look up from their game with startled expressions.

Sonia won't remember rushing across the room or what they said to each other, but she won't forget the feel of her mother's cheek against hers, the sense of being a child again, held in those familiar arms. They're saying words of relief, giving little exclamations of joy, and Sonia feels prepared to tell everything at once, holding nothing back, not even her love for Philip Embree.

But then she feels her mother's body stiffen, draw away.

"Where is he?" Mother asks.

Sonia looks into the eyes of a woman who in youth must have been truly beautiful. Indeed, illness has served to emphasize the shape of her mother's face, so that Sonia can see clearly in it an outline of the past: eyes set wide apart, wide cheekbones tapering to a small but full mouth, a catlike chin. What's missing in this pale, parched face is the wondrous skin; it must have been wondrous.

Breaking free when her mother does, Sonia glances at the dark little man, who has risen to stand in a corner, like a servant.

"I said, where is he?" Her mother's voice has a sharpness of command in it that's also familiar.

"Philip's still in Jinan. They won't let him out yet."

"I mean the *boy*. Where is he?"

"I don't know."

Her mother nods approvingly, sinks back on the pillows. Thus relieved, she introduces Rama. He bobs his head in her direction to acknowledge the honor of being introduced, then bobs it with similar enthusiasm at Sonia.

"How did you find me here?" Mother asks, frowning.

"We thought you were at the hotel." It's a lie she worked up on the flight—to protect Philip. "When I went there, they told me you were here. And what had happened."

"We? Who is we?"

"Philip and I."

"Philip?"

"He's still at the airport."

"What airport?"

"In Jinan."

"That's right. You said Jinan."

"They won't let him out yet. I got on the plane, but they held him."

Mother waves her hand dismissively. "Don't worry about him. He'll take care of himself. What's important is you're safe. You really are safe. Here, and safe. Nothing else matters."

They look at each other. Sonia has rehearsed an apology, but here, with her mother's avid eyes on her, she feels it's too studied, without heart. And yet when she does speak, the unrehearsed words seem just as stiff, but less coherent. "I'm so very sorry, Mother," Sonia begins. "The whole thing is painful. What I mean is—"

"We won't speak of it again. You're here and safe. It's over." She crosses her hands, waving them back and forth as if flagging down someone going too fast. Sonia notices how thin those hands are, how fragile. Indeed, her mother seems fragile for the first time she can remember, but along with fragility there's a keen, feral expression in the green eyes.

"I didn't mean," Sonia insists on continuing, "to steal like a—"

"Don't say *steal!*"

"I didn't mean to steal. I didn't think of it that way. I didn't mean to be a thief, but I was desperate. You see—"

"It's over. Forgotten."

Again Sonia glances at the Indian servant, surprised that her mother allows him to stay during such a conversation. "It's not forgotten," she begins again, "it can't be. I'm sorry for the way I did it, but I'm not sorry for doing it." Their eyes meet until her mother looks away. "I thought I loved him. I thought what we were doing was right."

Her mother looks almost serene, exercising restraint. "I admire your honesty. Now it's over. You're here and safe."

• • •

In fits and starts over the next few days, Sonia describes the journey she and Chamlong took from Bangkok until Philip Embree met them on Tai Shan. Her mother responds with questions and remarks calculated to sidestep emotion. "And then where did you go? How long did you stay? Ah, China hasn't changed. Yes, I see, but it would have gone worse in the old days." They might have been discussing a vacation taken by Sonia with a classmate. It proves disconcerting, prepared as Sonia is to defend or at least explain her emotions. And in this puzzling mood, neither defensive nor giving, she in turn discusses the medical aspects of her mother's voyage to Shanghai. "When did the pain first start? How many pills do you take? What does the doctor say? You mustn't try too hard. When? Thank God you're strong."

Tension increases between them as they run out of factual questions, banal remarks. At the end of that first day, Sonia insists on finding a hotel room, although the nursing home would provide one.

She decides that until her mother knows everything, they must behave like polite strangers. On this intuition she keeps her distance. She finds herself a dormitory bed in a *dian*, a mile's walk away. Each morning she comes to the nursing home, where between them a battleground is laid out, and across its silent expanse they observe each other, waiting.

Meanwhile she gets acquainted with Rama, and indeed, during these daily visits her only moments of relaxation are spent with him. He likes flowers. He wears a holy stone; they compare amulets. He's a vegetarian, although admittedly during this long trip there have been occasional . . . he lets a pause here damn him rather than a spoken confession, as if words alone might bring down punishment on him for having tucked in a piece of meat here, an egg there. A pause is his confession—and a muttered "Narayana," which becomes as familiar to Sonia when she is with him as her own breathing. He talks with his hands, chews betel (purchased in an Indian store right here in Shanghai, Narayana), complains of gaseous food here on this side, and picks his nose. Even on a cloudless, rather balmy afternoon, one of his hands is always clutching the black rolled umbrella. Having gone to a mission school, where he learned English, Rama considers himself a modern man. Someday he'll visit Home (she discovers he means England), because it is there that the Indian Educational Service was founded. She's able to ask him questions about Philip. It thrills her to hear Rama in his singsong voice exclaim, "Ah, Master is very good man!" When they discuss Master between them, for her it's as if he is only around the corner, soon to turn it and be with them.

Often Rama expresses what she does not: "I am worried for Master. Very clever man, but this is strange country. Here they bury the dead like is done in Burma cemetery. Nurse telling me the Chinese don't want burning, because they appear before ancestors in bodily form. Very strange. On this side even a clever man, a white man like Master, is not certain. Here is uncertainty each way your head turns."

And every day that passes without a word from Philip, she feels uncertainty pressing in on her. Is Mother aware of it? Those green eyes seem more alert than ever, compensating in their quickness for a body confined to bed. Soon, Sonia feels, she won't be able to contain her anxiety, and if fear pours out, so surely will the secret of her love—pour out pell-mell, at a time not prepared for. Because Mother, in this delicate state of health, needs to be prepared for such news. That's more certain every day. Never before has Sonia understood the depth of her mother's dislike, perhaps even hatred, of Philip Embree. It's evident in her callous indifference to his prolonged stay in a threatened city. It shows in her sneering references to his involvement with "spies and secret agents who've been shuttling him around China for weeks." If Sonia wonders out loud why he hasn't returned yet to Shanghai, Mother comments archly about "his love of wandering through the countryside with that ax shoved in his belt like a wild American cowboy." Sonia is saddened to realize that the man who brings out the best in herself brings out the worst in her mother.

And without reassurance she begins to doubt his love for her, fights the impulse, but sometimes succumbs to it. Perhaps he's already in Shanghai with no intention of seeing her. Perhaps he's had second thoughts about a woman who murdered an innocent man. Did he merely pretend to justify her action, while in truth harboring contempt for it? Did he in fact deliberately separate from her at the airport? Of course not, of course not, of course not. Yet these are questions that remain with her like the memory of a dead man's face in a moonlit ocean.

A week has already passed without word. Each day she pesters the nursing home staff for any message he might have sent. Each day, perusing the papers of Shanghai, she looks for news from Jinan. The few reports coming from there are mere references to "a fluid situation in the area."

Another week passes, nothing.

Each day, watching Mother grow stronger, Sonia grows more restive, then fearful. She can't hold the secret in much longer; this self-knowledge encourages her to avoid Mother, to spend less time at the nursing home, to retreat from the battleground. Yet that, in turn, awakens feelings of guilt and deceit. She must do something, make contact with Mother in a deliberate way, or else misfortune will overcome them both.

Until now they have only waited. Clearly Mother has been waiting for some kind of truth to emerge from their bland days together. And for herself, Sonia has been waiting for the proper time to do two things: tell the secret and return the jade ink stone which, unlike the porcelain vase, she didn't sell. Both events are linked in her mind as the opposing ends of an emotional spectrum, but she decides only one should occur now—return of the ink stone. She'll give it to Mother with love, as a substitute for truth, and withhold a confession that can wait until Philip comes back.

• • •

Puddles left by the recent typhoon rains have long since dried up, and the surface of mud turned hard and dusty has been lifted by breezes into a gritty suspension, a delicate film in the bright air this Shanghai morning, when Sonia enters the nursing home.

Rama is out on an errand, which is fortunate. She doesn't want him around—though they've become friends—when the ink stone changes hands. Wordlessly, after a quick embrace, she places the wrapped object beside Mother on the bed. There's a gasp of surprise, the hesitant pulling away of colorful rice paper, the ink stone emerging.

She watches her mother turn the oblong of grooved jade slowly. Tears welling up.

"I don't think you know what this really means."

"I'm afraid it means I didn't sell this too."

"It means you've returned to me the thing I value above all else. I can see that surprises you."

"I never knew its value." Be honest, she tells herself. "It was there, so I took it."

Turning the stone, the bedridden woman says, "Its value is sentimental. Your father gave it to me. Someday, when you married, I was going to give it to you. I remember the day he gave it to me. He'd returned from the South." Pausing, as if unsure of saying it, her mother says, "You haven't talked about him. I've been waiting for it, but you never mention him any more."

"I've been waiting too."

"For what?"

"For the right time to talk about him. I saw where he lived and died. Philip took me everywhere in Qufu. He showed me everything, the town, the temple, the cemetery. He showed me where you lived, where Father worked. I played Tai Chi where you two played it. We met people who'd known Father."

"And was he the way I told you he was?"

"Yes." Only a partial lie. In Qufu and on Tai Shan the legend of her childhood had been realized. Yet Su-su and the old soldier had also given her a separate image to think of—that of a generous if fickle lover, a soldier capable of torture yet beloved by his men, a complex personality beyond the reach of legend. Philip had shown her the man. "Yes," she repeats. "Thanks to Philip, I saw everything."

Putting the ink stone in her lap, Mother smiles tightly. "You give Philip a lot of credit."

"Which he deserves."

"Does he? He told you I was ill, didn't he. That's why you came. It was the only thing he could think of to get you here and away from the boy."

"Isn't that what you wanted him to do—to get me here?"

"He promised not to tell you. Can you understand, darling? I didn't want you to come out of duty. It's something he wouldn't understand."

"He wouldn't understand love?"

Mother doesn't reply; she has picked up the ink stone again, turning and turning it, gently, like living flesh. Her eyes fill again. "Someday you'll meet a man you'll love as I loved your father." She's smiling through the tears. Radiantly. "I believe you will. I believe you have it in you to love like that."

And now Sonia does what later she will look upon as the outcome of pure folly or profound miscalculation. It is because so much emotion plays across her mother's quite lovely face, because expressed there is the untrammeled capacity for love, that Sonia makes a decision—walks boldly onto the battleground.

"I *do* love like that."

The words catch her mother in a smile. It remains, as if frozen by the shutter of a camera, when she says, "You love like what?"

"Like you loved Father. I love a man like that."

"That boy? I thought you said—"

"I love Philip, Mother. I *love* him."

"Yes, well, let's be serious. You love him, but who is this man?"

"It happened in Taian. It happened. I love him, we can't help it."

Gripping the ink stone hard, Mother stares. A new smile playing about her lips gives her the look of imprisoning something in her mouth. "You can't be serious." After a pause, in a low, awed voice she says, "But you are. I see it. You're really serious. Well."

The room fills with silence. Someone is walking with uneven steps down the corridor. Sonia, who's been standing, sits in a corner chair, gripping her hands and staring at the floor. She can't bear to look at her mother's anguished smile.

"Life is full of surprises," her mother says finally. "Yes. But they never tell you how many. It's true?"

"Yes."

"But you don't know Philip Embree."

Sonia looks up. "I know him better than you do."

"Let me point out something. He's my husband. My daughter is talking about being in love with my husband. You bear his name."

"He was never a father to me, and you know it. I don't think of you married to him."

"And if you don't think it, then it's not so? That's terribly young, Sonia. You really are terribly *young*." Again silence. With a sigh her mother murmurs, "Of all men."

"I can't help it."

"You've slept with him, of course."

Sonia doesn't answer.

"Has it occurred to you how stupid I've been? To admit my past? To an impressionable girl? Are you trying to follow in my footsteps? Is that it? In the worst way? But, Sonia, don't you see the difference? I did it for money! I did it to survive! It wasn't fun, it was never adventure. But you're taking up with anyone who happens along."

Sonia rises. "I'm going."

Her mother leans forward as if preparing to scramble out of bed.

Frightened that the sick woman might do it, Sonia sits down again.

"I was wrong to say that." Mother is breathing hard. "This isn't easy for me to think about." Her breath slows, but her face, drained of color, still alarms the girl. "You know nothing, Sonia." There's sudden strength in her voice. "Not about the past. I have a perspective you can't have. Do you understand that?" Her voice is strong but not angry now. Her eyes have lost the luster of anger. She wants to persuade, Sonia thinks.

"Perspective is what time gives us. It's why I see this differently. That name you put on your passport—Yu-ying? She wasn't a great lady of Shanghai. That was fantasy. Yu-ying was just someone I knew. She was a cheap, sad little whore who took opium and died from it. I made a lady out of her for the story."

Sonia can't help this cry from the heart: "What have you done, Mother, since I was born, but lie, lie, lie?"

The sick woman sits back against the pillows, looking abruptly old and frail. Sunlight pouring into the room gives her skin a waxy dead sheen. "I can't answer that. Well, maybe. Just maybe I can. You see, it was you and me against the world. That's how I saw us. My loveliest memories are of us in the garden. You would sit on the grass in front of me, and I'd have my drink on the table, and it would be twilight and we'd see boats coming down the klong through the undergrowth. Remember? And Cook would be humming in the kitchen. Ah Ping would be setting the table. Never did know where Nipa hid herself at sunset. Did you? She was always gone." Mother wets her lips, smiles. "We'd be there with dusk in the leaves, and you'd ask me for a story about your father and our life together and where we'd been and who we were. A story about things binding in life. But after childhood my own life had been terrifying. I'd been a whore. You had no relatives living. Your father was dead. Out of all this what could I pull together to make us happy? I added something to the truth, invented, changed things around until we could see him, General Tang Shan-teh, coming through the garden. A great man. Ours. And then other people joined him from memory. Out of my desire, I suppose, for better memories than I had. So I told you lies. Yes, I did that." She pauses for breath. "Now let me tell you," she continues, "you may think you know Philip Embree, but you know nothing about him. Nothing about my past with him. You always thought we left China together *after* your father died. That's what I wanted you to believe. But it's not true. We left before. Sonia, we left *before* your father died. We ran away and left him. I did it because I was carrying you. I feared having you in China. Especially with your father in such trouble. They were out to get him, and I was frightened for you—and for myself. I betrayed him. As for Philip, he wanted me and didn't care how he got me. So he betrayed your father too. He persuaded me to go with him, and I did, and we've lived with what we did all these years. Can you expect me to trust, not to say love Philip Embree? I see in him my own contemptible self."

It's not something Sonia thinks through or she might not have said it, but without thinking she says, "Philip is honest, I love him, and you tell lies." Now is the time, Sonia thinks angrily. It's the time to tell Mother what happened years ago when the door was ajar: two women in bed; light slashing across their naked bodies. Now's the time. Now?

"At least today hasn't been a lie," her mother says. "You have the truth now, whatever you think of it. It's what you never had till now." Lifting one hand in a gesture not completed, she lets it fall back into her sheeted lap. Her eyes turn to the open window, focus on sunlight flecked with Shanghai dust.

Sonia rises again. "I'm going, Mother." This time, without looking back, she walks from the room.

• • •

That night she writes in her diary, using Thai since it's the language she writes with ease.

> I confessed my love for him today. She was furious as I knew she would be. But she was more than furious, she was filled with spite and hatred and I feared for her heart. She accused him of being untrustworthy and deceitful. She claimed he betrayed my father by persuading her to run away with him. It's a terrible thing, if true, and I think it's true. It's terrible if you look at it her way. But there's another way too. He loved her then as he loves me now—without limit, without caution, without any thought of right or wrong. Because that's the way he loves me, I know it as surely as I know anything. He loved her the same way, enough to do anything to have her. What she will never understand is his honesty. Instead of being deceitful he was passionate and that made him impulsive and being impulsive made him blind to consequences and that made him almost childlike—innocent—not deceitful. Innocent! Always, always! She never saw in him the sad and tender man he'd been all those years with us, a man who suffered terribly because of what he'd done without thinking—on the impulse of a child! Father would forgive him now, I think. Father would say to him, "You were a young fool, but you paid for it. Now live." She can't understand why he's done what he's done, but I can understand him because I love him and because I'm no longer a child who believes everything she's told. I won't see her again until he comes back. If I see her the fight will continue, and if it continues I know she will die. He said: "I won't leave China without you," and I believe him.

· 557

• • •

The next day, waiting near the nursing home entrance, she intercepts Rama on an errand. "How is she?" Sonia asks anxiously.

Rama's angular dark features tighten. The umbrella is tucked under one arm like a drill sergeant's stick. "Ah, Miss, she has gone down."

"Mother told you of the fight I had with her?"

"You must not worry yourself. Rama is here, seeing to it."

"Let me know how she is. You must. Every day."

"I will come over where you lodge," he says grandly. "I will find you out and say everything."

"Has she mentioned me today?"

"Oh, indeed she has. She is keen on seeing you."

"No, Rama. Not now."

"You could come round at evening. Or I might collect you," he suggests, cocking his head.

"No, Rama. It has to be this way. And don't tell her we met."

Digging into his pocket, Rama comes out with a handful of nuts. "Will you partake? Very healthful. Pakka nuts, Miss."

She feels herself near tears, but takes a few, holds them as if not knowing what they're for—her hand straight out, clutched. "You mustn't tell her we met. But every day let me know how she is. You must."

"You are too much worried, Miss. God will provide. And for your Ma—" It's the first time he has used this familiarity between them. "I will assist her out of difficulty."

"Thank you, Rama."

"Thank you too, Miss. God bless you. God bless you both. Narayana. He will provide."

And she watches him set out, swinging the umbrella like the cane of an English gentleman on a stroll through the lanes of London.

• • •

In the days that follow, Sonia has time to learn what waiting means.

She goes to the U.S. Consulate, where a young consul stoutly maintains they've never heard of Philip Embree. At the Dutch Legation they laugh when she talks about someone issued a passport under the name Hans Brinker—and continue their packing, for the legation is pulling out of Shanghai. Twice a week she returns to the young American consul, insisting that Philip Embree—a bona fide national of the United States who nevertheless carries a Dutch passport—is being held in Jinan. Each time now, when the consul sends out a Chinese clerk to tell her he's not in, she can see the Marine guards smile knowingly.

To kill time while waiting, Sonia reads Chinese, acquiring new characters every day, and writes little essays in English with the aid of her dictionary. She writes about Shanghai, the city that was once Mother's and is now becoming hers.

She walks for miles, getting to know the public gardens, the markets, the waterfront. Hours are spent along the green promenade of the Bund: docks and ships to one side, gray buildings and trolley buses to the other. Hours are also spent in the concessions, down narrow lanes crammed with rickshaws and bicycles, where the manswarm of Shanghai ekes out existence, a task increasingly difficult because of an influx of homeless people from the countryside. War has brought these thousands of peasants in their padded jackets here to the Lucky City, where they mingle with soldiers in faded yellow KMT uniforms and with whores and opium addicts and with factory workers who loiter on the streets because industry is closing down without raw materials from the countryside from which these peasants have fled. Newspapers in Chinese and English carry headlines about spiraling inflation, while government posters blame it on Communist conspiracy. She reads that since the typhoon hit Shanghai its water mains are full of eels. She reads that Hsuchang and Pingdingshan have fallen to units of the Red Army. She reads there are fifty thousand beggars now in Shanghai. She reads of spies being executed without trial, on the spot of their capture.

Turning a corner one day, she notices on a telephone pole halfway up the block some curious nodules, the size and shape of pumpkins, protruding from its side like fruit from a branch. Getting closer, she realizes they are human heads spiked into the wood. Horror must show on her face, because small boys nearby begin to giggle and point at her.

She writes that down in her diary. She also describes an itinerant dentist who worked in the street with a foot-pedaled drill.

> He reminded me of the first time I met Somchai. He had gone to a Cantonese dentist who sawed off a tooth at the gum with tools taken from a biscuit tin. Now poor Somchai lies in prison somewhere, frightened and sick. Or maybe he's dead. I remember the day he played Push Hands Tai Chi with Chamlong in the Temple of the Emerald Buddha and how clever and quick they were and how I was afraid a guard would throw them out. Every time Somchai opened his mouth, the bloody hole showed, and he didn't like me at all because I came between him and his friend. But later he liked me. Later we became friends enough for me to understand he was very shy and afraid of girls. Strange, but for that bloody mouth of his I can't picture him now. I can picture Chamlong, though. I always will. I will never forget his sharp jawline and his clear bright eyes and his soft pretty lips and his scowl. And we are linked together by what we did. Wherever he is now, I wish him good luck. I wish him *every* luck.

> I love him in my way. We are brother and sister. We are comrades in the most terrible thing of all.

Many of the Shanghai entries are devoted to the dormitory which she shares with a dozen other girls. It would be enough space for three or four people, but with cots of string wicker and bamboo jammed together, leaving aisles so narrow the girls walk sideways, the room is terribly crowded. There are no dressers, not a single mirror; the girls must go down the corridor to the latrine—two holes cut in the floor—where a small mirror dangles from a nail. Their belongings go under their cots when they're in the dorm, but otherwise stay in a baggage room. Even so, now and then a theft occurs, usually during the night. Sonia keeps her suitcase on the cot, which takes up a fourth of it, making sleep difficult. And yet the rent is cheap enough to warrant staying here.

Sonia is learning about money. She still has some Communist Renminbi to sell on the black market, and Siamese bahts which she uses for barter. Even if she didn't have money, she wouldn't ask Mother for it, that is certain. There's no communication between them, not now, not yet, although every day she meets Rama at a tea shop for a progress report. He comes along in his Congress hat and Nehru jacket, carrying the rolled umbrella, giving her good news because she knows he knows she wants to hear it. Twice a week she intercepts the little Chinese nurse, who gives a more accurate report of what seems to be a strong, steady recovery.

Each day brings Sonia closer to the girls in the dorm. They are Chinese, Tonkinese, and Filipino girls, and Sino-Russian daughters of women who, like Sonia's mother, fled to Shanghai during the Russian Civil War. Aside from Sonia and a young musician, they are all *piao-tzu* and each evening at sunset go out to work the streets.

Sonia (or rather Yu-ying, for she has again taken the name) becomes a good friend of Anna, a Jewish girl from Munich, who sings and plays violin in Frenchtown night clubs. Anna is sixteen. Her family fled Germany in the winter of 1937–38, coming to Shanghai because papers weren't required for entry in those wartime days. Of their three children only Anna survived a cholera epidemic that ravaged the city soon after the family's arrival. Then Anna's father, a pharmacist turned waiter, died of TB when the Japanese held Shanghai. Anna's mother, a professional violinist, worked in the dance halls and restaurants, in her spare time teaching the girl how to sing and play. Now that her mother has also died, Anna is on her own. Sometimes, while the girls lounge on their cots, Anna stands in the doorway (there's no other place) and sings and plays her battered violin. Her thin but eager soprano is undaunted by "Shoo-fly Pie" and "Doin' What Comes Nacherly" and "Zip-a-Dee-

Doo-Dah," all of which she renders in precise, heavily accented English. Her violin interpretations of "Almost Like Being in Love" and "Papa, Won't You Dance with Me" are brisk, confident, filled with eighteenth-century ornamentation.

Some of the girls are jealous of her, especially after she announces one day that she's landed a night-club job in Manila. Someone asks if she has to sleep with the customers, to which Anna replies indignantly, "I'll sleep with the owner if I have to, but I won't sleep with the customers. I'm an artist," she declares proudly. "I can sing in German, Yiddish, French, and Chinese now and English. American songs are what they want today, so I sing a lot of that. I don't have to sleep with customers when I can sing 'Come Rain or Come Shine.' " She has pale skin and large waiflike eyes. No one knows better than Anna where to buy the cheapest and best sugar cakes; by telling no one where she buys them, she keeps a measure of power in the dorm. Anna always comes home with sugar cakes for Yu-ying, who rewards her with tales of Siam, to which the other girls also listen. When she's with them, Yu-ying feels herself smiling and the sense of it lifts a dead weight of age from her mind until she's almost young again. But not quite. At least not as young as she'd been six months ago in Bangkok, idly playing with golden finger guards and confiding in imaginary friends.

Here in the Shanghai dorm she confides in real ones. She tells them about Chamlong; about the flight from Bangkok (nothing, though, about their association with Communists, or someone might inform the secret police) because he (not she with him) killed a man; about their entry into China; about the reunion with her mother's husband, an older American, who promptly fell in love with her and she with him; about her escape from Jinan and his detainment there; about her determination to wait for him here.

Sitting on their cots, the girls bite their fingernails and laugh and frown and offer advice. "It's good he's so much older than you are. That means he'll die sooner and maybe leave you something." "Not if his wife can help it," observes another, and they all laugh. "This man's your father, if he's married to your mother. In my village I was taught if you have anything to do with him, it's the worst thing possible, and your ancestors won't let you into the Great Hall. You can't do that," a girl maintains stoutly, but another argues, "You can do anything except sleep with the man who made in bed with your mother. Look at me. My mother sold me to her rich cousin and later, when my parents needed money again, my mother slept with him too." A Tonkinese girl says gently, "Maybe he'll take you to America. Then when you get there, run away." Most agree that if he returns, Sonia must stay with him because he doesn't beat her.

By telling her what to do, they talk about themselves. She hears about the notorious Futze-miao District in Nanking, where peasants bring their wives and daughters to sell; about the huge multistoried brothels of Shanghai where each floor emphasizes a different sexual specialty; about young girls, kidnaped in the countryside, who are brought into brothels, chained to beds, tortured until they submit.

Now and then the owners of brothels come to the dorm on a recruitment visit. Fortunate is the girl they select, because she'll have a room of her own sometimes and protection from the streets. Twice Yu-ying is approached. Then one afternoon, after looking hard at her, a fat little madam declares, "Pretty, but too old." Afterward a girl explains to Yu-ying that the woman has a house famous for whores younger than fourteen.

And Yu-ying writes this down too in her diary, learning about life in Shanghai as she waits for her lover to return.

. . .

One day, when she meets Rama, he tells her that Mistress can go unassisted down the corridor to the Ladies' for a call of nature. He waits outside in case she needs help back to the room, but Mistress always pushes him away. He laughs. He's happy about such progress, not forcing a smile but letting it command his whole face. Then, reaching into his pocket, he comes out with a piece of newsprint so thumbed and creased that Yu-ying must look closely to decipher words through the worn paper.

Madras, India. August 14—
The drought threatening much of South India has been averted by unexpected thunderstorms during the last week. They anticipate the regular monsoon rains by many weeks, and local pundits call them "a miracle," answering the prayers at many temples during the last few months. Authorities say the rains have filled the wells and reservoirs adequately enough for emergency demands until the monsoon arrives. The estimate is that thousands of lives have been saved.

"A miracle!" Rama exclaims, carefully refolding the little article. "Ganesh has done it, that is my feeling. He is remover of obstacles. Rain coming now. Great miracle."

"You have friends there, Rama?"

"Oh, yes, Miss. Good friends."

"But no word from Master?"

"Not hearing yet. But God will provide."

It is Rama's faith that encourages her to visit a nearby Catholic church on Rue Mazarin.

In the small chapel she prays for Mother, for Philip, for Lamai, who may even be pregnant now. Holding her cross made of two twigs, Yu-ying recites parts of the Missal as she learned them in school long ago. The Latin sounds very important and serious to her ear as she mumbles, "Kyrie eleison. Gloria in excelsis Deo." Thinking of Philip somewhere in this war-stricken land, she intones, "Dominus vobiscum. Et cum spiritu tuo." He was once a missionary; that's easy to believe, even though anyone can see he's also a soldier. He's a man for causes of the heart, and that's why she loves him. One reason. And at lovemaking he's tender with her in a way that Chamlong never was. He's a man of honor, like Father, and therefore a tortured man, a man filled with God and violence. Sometimes when she thinks of Philip and Father, she thinks too of Jeanne d'Arc.

In the dim chapel, where she can hear two priests speaking French near the altar, Yu-ying recalls her Bangkok schooldays and the obligatory prayers at assembly, even though half the girls were Buddhists, who mouthed the alien words with the mechanical indifference of eating their morning rice. Is Lamai happy with her husband? Her life must be very circumscribed, quiet, rhythmic. Do miracles really happen? Mother can walk around now; she will certainly recover. How do miracles happen? Surely not how Rama believes. Or perhaps not at all.

Life in Shanghai is deteriorating each day, and she duly records it in her diary.

> I hear the rickshaw pullers can't work very long because of malnutrition. There is rioting in the stores, because merchants refuse to sell their goods at the inflated rate. People carry suitcases of money to transact business now. The government is issuing new currency, but no one believes it will do any good. Yesterday I saw a woman sifting through the dirt outside a store. She was looking for stray kernels of rice after rioting inside had ended in looting. I heard that the owner fired into the mob with a shotgun, but they rushed him anyway and crushed his head in. I read that refugees from North Jiangsu tore up dozens of vegetable patches in the suburbs—just to get rid of their anger. They can't buy a pound of rice with their life's savings. I am learning things. Where is Chamlong? Has he delivered the message to Pridi? Does he really believe in the Communist cause? What do I believe in? Philip. I believe in Philip.

Often now, when she goes to the chapel, Yu-ying prays for the girls in the dorm. Looking at them, Yu-ying tells herself she might be looking at her own mother twenty years ago. She tries to make friends of the girls with Russian blood, but they are particularly rude, bitter, and defensive—girls without futures, caught between worlds. Perhaps her mother was like that. Seeing them go out each evening, she marvels at her mother's capacity for survival. She regrets, too, the petty quarrels which marred her childhood with such a remarkable woman. Yu-ying understands now that she'll never tell her mother about the door ajar, the two women in bed together. That can hardly matter now.

Not until she herself has really loved has she understood what is owed to her mother. To her father she always felt she owed the desire for intense belief in something, and someday she would give her life to it—an ideal, a cause, a vision. She felt the strength and will of her father within her veins, and often wondered what there was in her of her mother. And all the while it was her mother who gave her the daily affection that had shaped her young life. What Yu-ying had been ashamed of—oh, she can admit it fully now—her mother's love for other women, no longer seems shameful. Loving Philip the way she does, Yu-ying can imagine the possibility of other love as well—even, perhaps, her own love someday for another woman. Is this the way of love? That by loving once, you learn to love again and again? Her mother has that capacity. As for herself, however, she is sure her love will stop with Philip. It would be impossible for her to love anyone else as she loves him. What she has achieved, nonetheless, is the ability to imagine a love that encompasses more than one possibility. It's what her mother was teaching her all the time.

· · ·

Yu-ying is returning from the Bund when Anna and one of the Sino-Russian girls intercept her on the street. "Don't go back to the dormitory," Anna warns. "They're looking for you."

"She means the Te Wu," adds the Sino-Russian girl, who goes on the street by the name of Evening Flower.

The Te Wu is the Special Service Section of the Bureau of Investigation and Statistics—secret agents, dreaded in Shanghai.

"I've done nothing."

"We had to stop you," Anna says breathlessly, "from going back there. You'd be arrested."

"Let's not stand here." Evening Flower herds them into a tea shop. At a table she leans forward and explains what has happened. About two hours ago a man in a Western hat came to the dorm and looked inside. At first they thought he was a brothel owner or maybe just someone who wanted a girl, but when he asked for Tang Yu-ying—by name—it was clear who he was.

"Did you know they carry little bars of gold to pay informers with?" Evening Flower says with a smile. "I knew a girl who used to sleep with one of them. He had a piece of silk with his SSS number on it. He carried an American gun and a piece of thin wire—he'd never tell her what he did with it, but something awful. Each time he turns someone in, he gets a bonus. So, anyway, the one who came to see you, I started talking to him—acted like I was interested in him. He asked me if I ever went to the American Consulate too. Not me, I told him and slipped out of there." She leans closer to Yu-ying. "He got your name and address from someone who works at the consulate. Do you know someone there?"

"An American consul."

"Who's got Chinese working for him. Little bars of gold." Evening Flower smiles faintly. "I'd be tempted to tell on somebody myself for those bars of gold."

"But you wouldn't."

The girl laughs. "What does it matter."

She might be saying *Mai pen rai*, Yu-ying thinks, staring at Evening Flower, a rangy girl, ripe-looking, with features too large and dramatic for her Chinese eyes. A pretty girl. Having similar blood, Yu-ying has always wondered if she's as pretty as Evening Flower.

"So I told him you didn't know anybody at the American Consulate, unless it was to sleep with. But I don't think he believed me."

"Thank you for trying."

The girl shrugs her broad shoulders. Until now she's hardly spoken to Yu-ying. Trouble has made her a temporary friend. "You better get out of Shanghai. When they start looking for you, they find you."

"I haven't done anything."

"You've been going to the American Consulate."

"Yes, I've done that."

Evening Flower opens out her hands in a gesture of finality. "They'll want to know why you went there and who are you and what you're doing and pretty soon you'll find yourself with wires jammed through each tit and joined together and the current turned on. That's what they like to do. I know a girl who's got scars to prove it."

"Come with me to Manila," Anna urges. "I'm going in two days. The night club sent me some extra money. I can help pay your passage."

Yu-ying reaches out and squeezes her hand. "I have to stay in China."

"Better get out of Shanghai," Evening Flower says. Her deep voice has a flat, factual tone, as if events in her life have taught her never to speak with animation or hope.

• • •

She meets Rama one more time and pulls him into a tea shop on Rue de Paris.

After listening to her, Rama shakes his head. "You must be seeing Mistress one more time."

"I can't risk that. By now they know I've been going there." She hands him a folded piece of paper. "Give this to her. Tell her I brought it to the nursing home." The note is very short and deliberately vague, in case someone intercepts it: 'I must leave Shanghai. You'll hear from me when possible. I love you. That has never changed. Forgive me for disappointing you in so many ways. If he comes to Shanghai, tell him I am waiting. Yours.' She doesn't sign it either. To Rama she says, "Tell her I love her."

"Ah, Miss," Rama says, "you must be seeing her one more time."

Looking around anxiously—for the last day she's seen an agent in every man who wears a fedora—she hears Rama's voice, trembling and shrill, come at her now across the table. "Ah, Miss, it is terrible when you go away from them!"

When she turns toward him, Rama says, "It is true, Miss! You will see! I went away from wife, two sons. God forgive me. Because before time I did not see them, and now I think always of them. Even without drought coming. And I think, better I die here in strange country than know what they were feeling when I went away from them."

"Rama," she says. Suddenly it's clear: He has been living with something as haunting as her own memory of a dead man in a moonlit ocean. Reaching out, she touches his dark brown hand. "Whatever you did, you suffered for it. You've done good things too. Think of me, of Mother, of Master. You've been good to us."

"Good?" He laughs nervously, pulling his hand back. "It is said: Who is busy doing good finds no time to be good. No, no, I am not being good." Rising, he stares down wild-eyed at her. "You must be seeing her one more time."

"Tell her what I said—I love her. And give her the note."

"If you see Master, tell him Rama is praying for you both."

Next day, after a tearful dockside farewell with Anna, who boards a steamer for Manila, she will find passage for herself (under the Siamese passport) on a coastal freighter to Tianjin. From there she'll get a train to Peking, which is still accessible to travelers. Three weeks now, and Philip hasn't reached Shanghai. Perhaps, as he suggested at the Jinan airport, if not Shanghai, they'll meet in Peking. Seeing the girl of sixteen leave for an unknown future in Manila, Yu-ying tells herself, No one can stay put for long. We must go out, we must live.

She waves at the small white face above the ship's rail. Something edges into her mind from the shadows. How did it happen that she forgot to count during her days with Philip? The truth is she never forgot. One day she counted and it was the wrong part of the month, but she pushed aside that fact because what was happening to them must never end, must not even be interrupted, and now she is past her time. She is certain of it. And yet *mai pen rai*. There is nothing to regret.

Philip said, "I won't leave China without you."

If not Shanghai, then Peking.

43 By sending Sanuk back to Shanghai, he's paid his debt to Vera.

It does not, however, prevent him from rejoining Sanuk, and he will. What worries him was his failure to make specific plans for meeting her in Shanghai. They had time before entering the airport shed. Surely he could have planned to meet her at the Cathay or Palace or at one of a dozen other Shanghai hotels in case they had trouble with the Kuomintang authorities here in Jinan. So their parting was rushed, vague, frantic rather than purposeful. He let it be that way. Perhaps he wanted it that way. That's what worries him.

Has he escaped recklessly from pattern once again?

If so, it's an escape that can be rectified. The KMT officials have trucked him into Jinan and put him up temporarily in a mission-school house. They claim he'll have air transport out of the city in a few days. Right now all flights have been requisitioned by the military. They don't even bother to interrogate him further, having forgotten he's possibly a spy. Men in control of embattled cities tend to become whimsical, zealous, and phlegmatic by turns. At present they allow him to go where he wants; he's just a foreigner who won't get a flight out of the city. If he wishes—Embree knows this too—he can escape to the other side. The Kuomintang would probably regard a foreigner's defection to the Reds with benign indifference: After all, they wouldn't have to house and feed him any more, although he does pay for room and board at the mission school, as do a half-dozen other foreigners in the same predicament. What he does is of no concern now to the Chinese government; that is clear to Philip Embree. The authorities ignore him because they think he's an American. That he claims Dutch citizenship and belongs to a suspicious organization is of less importance than his actual nationality. In this final crisis, the American government won't help the Nationalists, so the Nationalists won't help an American. Even in embattled cities men can still use logic.

And Jinan is surely embattled. General Chen Yi's Third Field Army has surrounded the city, bottling in more than seventy thousand Nationalist troops who are subject to artillery and mortar fire within a few kilometers of the ancient town walls. In the mission school's sector of Jinan, the 84th Division of the 66th Army has set up defense works. Last year they were hit hard, while on their flank the 74th Army was nearly wiped out near a village in West Central Shantung, and earlier this year the 84th Division lost a third of its men in the South.

Each day Embree strolls along the barbed-wire emplacements, watching the troops in their yellowish brown uniforms loll against sandbags. They look young, tired, apathetic. And from what he knows about war, if the siege is long, they'll need a strong sense of commitment to maintain readiness for battle. But they seem to have lost theirs already; and as if already responding to their lack of spirit, officers are punishing them on the spot for minor infractions of discipline. During a single morning's walk, Embree sees three young soldiers beaten, one severely on the bare buttocks as two men hold him over sandbags and a lieutenant barks out the number of lashes a third man delivers with a bamboo cudgel.

Yet the government equipment is impressive: Jap machine guns and mortars, U.S. jeeps, howitzers, and antitank guns. If morale holds up, the battle of Jinan may be a hotly contested one. That's a judgment he makes with bland confidence, as if the outcome of it has nothing to do with him. But he thinks it will have a lot to do with him. He has no faith in getting out of Jinan by air. Perhaps, therefore, he ought to make plans for getting out some other way, but the days pass with nothing done, or even considered. He wanders through the city of natural springs and parks. No one, he thinks, can accept war like the Chinese. Alongside troops and military vehicles that choke the streets of Jinan are coolies pushing their wagons to and from soybean-processing plants, lumber companies, flour mills. Men stand in doorways smoking; women hang laundry on window poles. He thinks, Indomitable.

In the afternoons he often goes to the Fountain Spring Pavilion, where twenty years ago he accompanied General Tang as a bodyguard. It was at the Fountain Spring that Embree had asked for a transfer to the cavalry. The request had been granted because only the previous day Embree had saved the General's life on Thousand Buddha Mountain, just outside of Jinan. He had hurled his own body against Tang's, knocking both of them out of a temple bay at the moment of an explosion. Embree has often recalled that morning at the temple. A dozen men died in the assassination attempt on the General, yet what he remembers most vividly is a gilded bronze statue of Kuan Yin, lying face down in a pool of human blood. So once he'd saved the General's life, even as once he'd tried to take it.

He spends hours at the Fountain Spring, walking beneath the willows, staring at the carp that trail their spurts of color through a bubbling pond.

On the streets, going back to the mission house, he watches the trucks and artillery rumble toward positions, as rumors have the Reds attacking this or that sector, although thus far no attack has come. Each day, put there by a mysterious hand, posters appear on Jinan walls extolling the Reds and ridiculing the Nationalists. Most intriguing are the large sheets of white paper, nailed to telephone poles and shop doors, which display in big black characters the poetry of Chen Yi, the Red commander in charge of the siege. Embree always stops to read and study the latest effort. Some of the poems are quite good, done in the *tsa-yen* style, using lines of mixed lengths:

Now I see my comrades riding home together on horseback.
To whom does the Yangtze Valley belong?

And:

When old friends meet you and inquire about me,
Tell them to look at the desolation at the enemy's rear.

At night Embree walks along the canals that traverse the city. Lamp-lights are fuzzy, haloed from a darkness full of dust. During the morning he listens to children reciting English nursery rhymes from their long narrow classroom across the schoolground. They sing out in strident little voices "Jesus Loves Me" and "Onward Christian Soldiers." He listens, rapt, for in this besieged city what these Chinese children are doing he did in his own childhood.

Father, are you still alive?

Then one morning the schoolground is still; lessons have been suspended as the city girds itself for siege.

Meanwhile, Embree spends his time on the street or in the mission-school dormitory trying to meditate or in the dining room playing cards with other foreigners who also await transportation out of Jinan.

• • •

But what he does is not really meditation. When alone in the dormitory lined with wooden cots, Embree sits in a corner facing the wall and just thinks about meditation. Why hasn't it really worked for him? Why does fear still rise from the Other?

In these sobering moments, seated with closed eyes in a corner of the dormitory, paralyzed into a thoroughly Western contemplation of motive and goal, he can no longer use the techniques learned in India. At times during his Indian years he had reached zero while meditating; of that he's certain: For moments or for a minute, perhaps even longer, he had achieved an altered state characterized by loss of ordinary consciousness and by an awareness of something else too, deep within whatever it was that made him aware. But if he had been at zero, where had he been? He could answer in two ways. He had been at the heart of mystery in touch with the cosmic I. Or he had been nowhere save in a mind stunned and tricked by self-hypnosis. This was and remains his tragedy—Philip Embree can't decide.

Perhaps he never had a potential for the spiritual life. Perhaps none of the Embrees did, not even his father, who spent a lifetime serving the Lord. What the Embree clan seems to have had abundantly is energy and will, but both directed toward goals other than spiritual. Embrees have wanted knowledge or success in their ventures; they have wanted to convince others they were right; they have pursued adventure for its own sake in the guise of religious fervor. None of their desires, when he thinks back on Embree history, have had much to do with God. Where was the humility? That's the secret. No humility, no surrender of the ego, no closeness to God.

Not only does he concentrate on his failure at meditation while sitting in its classic pose, Embree uses these glum occasions to judge his recent behavior. When Sanuk made her confession about killing a man, he might have reciprocated. By lacking the courage to do it, he remains in limbo, unable to escape either Jinan or his conscience. Conscience? Well, that's the worst of it. That's why he is so content to be here in this beleaguered city, far from the woman he loves. This way the moment won't come when he must reciprocate by telling her that he once tried to kill the man whom she has sought all her life.

Such desolate thinking drives him away from the dormitory corner to spend more time among his card-playing companions in the dining room. He hates cards, yet plays or watches or sits at a round table with someone over Chinese beer. The days and nights pass monotonously this way, a not unpleasant way for Philip Embree.

Only once is there excitement. One of the foreigners brings in a Shanghai paper, bought from a staff officer who just arrived on a military flight. With an intensity that surprises him, Embree reads each item, hardly able in his eagerness to differentiate the important from the insignificant. The paper is a month old, yet it seems to him that it contains the history of the world. The Security Council of the United Nations has passed a resolution ordering a ceasefire in the Indonesian war between nationalists and Dutch colonials. Syngman Rhee's conservatives in South Korea have won a majority of seats in the new Constituent Assembly, and Rhee has been named the first president of the Republic of Korea.

Then there's an item of real interest to Embree: Ex-General Feng Yu-hsiang died on the *Pobeda*, a Russian ship on its way to China from the United States by way of the Atlantic and Black Sea. A film projector caught fire on board, and the General was asphyxiated.

Embree had taken Sanuk to the Taian monastery to which Feng had once retired in the 1930s. Feng had survived war and intrigue for thirty years. His recent, highly critical remarks in America about Chiang Kai-shek surely infuriated the Nationalists. They might have bribed someone aboard the Russian ship to murder Feng before he could return to China.

What is of such interest to him goes back twenty years. A meeting scheduled with General Feng in Siam had been the occasion for the abortive ambush of General Tang—for that event which keeps Embree from finding a way back to Shanghai and Sanuk.

Of the six men in the mission school, only one is obnoxious: an Indian trader from Bombay, Gopal Tilak, who waited too long to take a plane out of Jinan, driven by greed to seal a final contract for bulk flour. He's a swarthy, fat man, perpetually in a sweat; loud, aggressive, suspicious. Each day in the dining room he questions the others at length about their prospects for getting a flight, terrified that someone may get out before he does. Each day he goes to military headquarters to complain about the food in the mission house (he's a strict vegetarian), about the long wait for a flight, about the government's inability to ship out the flour he's contracted for.

"It's a wonder they don't give him a flight just to get rid of the whining." This is the judgment of his companions, most often made by Bernard Petter, who is here on assignment for a leftist French journal. Petter is a pale, narrow-chested Parisian in his mid-twenties.

"Wasn't the man who shot Gandhi from Bombay?" he asks Embree as they sit together in the small dining room. At a far table two Englishmen play chess as they usually do in the evening.

"I don't know. I don't know anything about India. I've never been there." He's hiding his knowledge of India, especially from Tilak, who'd surely try to use their Indian bond for some kind of advantage.

"I thought you knew India. I've seen you sitting in the dorm, facing the wall. Yoga or something." Petter, true to his profession, is observant, in his own way as nosy as Tilak.

"I learned that in Thailand." They are speaking French now, although at times they shift to English, especially when Embree, who hasn't spoken French for years, has too much trouble with verb forms. Petter is well educated and wears his learning with European insouciance, except when political theory is the subject. Then he flaunts a wide reading in Marxist literature and harangues his companions with leftist polemics until one by one they find excuses to leave the dining room.

Embree has admitted to Petter and the others that he's American— you can't fool Europeans long about a European language you don't know or about a farcical name like Hans Brinker—although he maintains the pose of working for WHO. He rather enjoys these evenings in the gloomy dining room either at cards or just sitting with a warm beer, allowing a bit of conversation to finish off another day.

Aside from Gopal Tilak, there's another source of tension in the mission-school house. That's the friction between Petter and a German who's under contract to the Kuomintang as a tank adviser. During World War II, Dietrich Mueller was a tank commander with the Panzer Group Eberbach. Caught in a pincer movement between Patton's Third

Army and the British Second and Canadian First, he was captured in mid-August 1944 by elements of the U.S. Fifteenth Corps near Falaise in Normandy. He's precise about details. Released from prisoner-of-war camp after the Allied victory, Mueller like many of his German comrades, joined the French Foreign Legion. Sent to Indo-China, he tired of barracks life in Tonkin and deserted at the invitation of a KMT agent who recruited him to work for the Nationalist Army.

A heavy-set, florid man, Dietrich Mueller likes to sit over beer in the dining room and reminisce. The British sit with him, a pleasant trio discussing battles and the death of old comrades, and so does Embree, who enjoys the company of veterans, whatever their loyalties. Indeed, he especially enjoys someone like Dietrich Mueller, whose enthusiasm for the Panzerkampfwagen VI Tiger—its fifty-six tons, its Maybach V-12 water-cooled engine, its TZF 9b binocular telescope—is like a child's for a favorite toy.

After a week of beers with Mueller, Embree and the two Englishmen know nearly all there is to know about the Tiger tank: how many rounds of mixed HE and APCBC it carried, how many forward ratios there were on its gearbox, where the ammo bins were located, the width of its combat track (precisely 724 mm.), and the firing statistics of its 8.8-cm. gun. Petter never enters into this discussion of the Tiger's performance, although at times, when one more is needed for bridge, he reluctantly sits with Mueller for a few hands.

At first Embree and the Englishmen take Petter's dislike of the German as a legacy of the war. But they soon discover it has nothing to do with World War II, everything to do with the civil war in China. Mueller hates the Reds and Petter admires them; that's the problem. Embree and the two Englishmen make their own indifference clear. Tension in the dining room has no source in memory but in current politics.

Tonight, as Petter and Embree are sitting in the dining room, the German walks in. "We will not hear more of his tank," Petter mutters in English, rising.

There's a sullen Chinese boy who handles the bar—a wooden case of beer bottles. Having got a beer and made a check mark on a torn piece of paper the boy thrusts at him, Mueller sits down with a sigh at Embree's table. "Attack has begun," he says. "They have taken airport."

"That just leaves the city airstrip then," Embree comments. "Not that the 26th Air Force will use it anyway."

At their chess board the two Britons lift their heads thoughtfully a moment, then return to their game.

"We'll hear the guns soon," Embree says.

"I will not be here long now any more. My last tank went out today and did not come back." Mueller has been here to oversee the performance of the 66th Army's Sherman M-4 tanks. "Do not take offense, friend," he continues, "but your Sherman was never match for German armor."

"Maybe not for the Tiger, but what about the Panther?"

"No, I am sorry. No match for Panther either. Panther had even lesser—fewer—shock traps than Tiger. And more speed—30 mph. I like Tiger cannon best—in battle the .88 is much much the better than .75. But Panther was good tank. Your Sherman could not match either of them." It is said courteously in the neutral tone of a professional commenting on facts.

"I heard that," Embree says, cocking his head.

"So did I too."

"What was it? A .105?"

"I think it was. There is nothing here for me now. They will send me out soon. Back to Shanghai."

"Will you join a new unit?"

Mueller shakes his head. "I am done with KMT. They cannot fight. They had good advisers in the 1930s, but did they listen to them?"

And Mueller, drinking beer, talks about China from the German point of view. It's really a view of Germany in China. In the '30s the chief foreign advisers to Chiang Kai-shek, according to Mueller, were German staff officers. And he had names to prove it: Wetzell, von Seeckt, von Falkenhausen.

"Were they good?" Embree asks.

"Of course they were good. They were German staff officers."

Had such men had more time, according to Mueller, the Reichswehr might have succeeded in making an ally of China and changing the course of war in Asia. They instituted German-style helmets, the use of Mauser-designed Gewehr '98 long rifles, Krupp-designed PzKpfw I tanks, and 2-cm. Flak 30 antiaircraft guns mounted on two-wheeled Sonderanhanger-51 trailers. Goering sent General Milch to aid the Chinese air force in modeling itself after the Luftwaffe. A U-boat expert became chief naval adviser. General von Reichenau appeared on the scene as Hitler's personal representative. Had the Japanese postponed their invasion a year or two, they might have faced an army capable of defeating them, an army trained by the Third Reich, their ally. Mueller chortles; he's a man who enjoys irony.

"We could have made something of the Chinese," Mueller concludes.

That's how Americans talked in Kunming when Embree was there with Stilwell.

"Aggressive war has never appealed to them." Embree offers an explanation for Chinese reluctance to follow German tactics. "They think in long periods of time. They believe in protracted wars. They know how to wait."

Mueller grunts distastefully. "Then how did these Red bastards learn to fight so good?"

"By trial and error," Embree suggests. They hear a few distant sounds, like a boy chucking pebbles into a pond. "Yes, those are .105s."

"Damn Red bastards," Mueller grumbles, yet his spirits lift as he talks about Red tactics, which are more to his liking. He has learned a good deal in six months here. Enough to have contempt for the standard Chinese habit of allowing an escape avenue for defeated forces. Historically they like to leave a corridor so the enemy won't feel cornered and consequently fight hard. It's the pragmatic way the Nationalists conduct war.

As Mueller sees it, the Reds follow a more European—a more German—attitude toward battle: total commitment to victory. For example, the Reds willingly take losses in order to destroy their opponent. "We taught offense to Chiang Kai-shek in 1930s, but did he listen? Who listened was the Reds, those swine bastards." Leaning forward so the Englishmen at their chess can't hear, he says, "I can get you out with me. You are veteran too, so I tell them we work together." Mueller smiles broadly. "Then you go home."

Later, thinking about it, Embree will be surprised and appalled by his reaction. Instead of accepting the offer, he draws back. "Give me a little time, Dietrich."

The brawny man sits upright, glances at the Englishmen, then at him, and frowns. "Time? Who has time? Tell me *now*."

"No, tomorrow," Embree insists.

Later he will think, "How irrational," and even later, facing the dormitory wall with his eyes closed, meditating on motive rather than cosmic consciousness, he will understand just how rational his irresoluteness was. Otherwise he'd have had to keep that rendezvous in Shanghai.

The next day, by late afternoon, Dietrich Mueller is gone, and for the two Englishmen and Philip Embree there's no more tension in the dining room. Out of the tank commander's shadow, Bernard Petter talks almost as relentlessly about the coming glory of communism as Gopal Tilak complains about animal matter—eggs, a few shreds of pork—in the evening meals, the long wait for a flight, the shipment of bulk flour that sits on a railroad siding, and the injustice of letting a German war criminal leave Jinan before he, a citizen of Independent India, is given the same chance.

• • •

Next evening before dinner, Embree sits next to the Englishmen's table and watches them play chess. They're both sandy-haired men with full mustaches, polite but aloof, generally taciturn. Having just won three games in a row, however, one of them—Adam—becomes sufficiently expansive to undertake a little conversation with Embree.

"Too bad about the German leaving that way. Rather miss him."

"So do I." Embree is looking at the other Englishman, who's intently studying the next move.

"Much better to have sent off the Indian, don't you think?"

"Definitely."

The conversation is suspended while Adam, after a swift glance, counters the move made by his opponent.

"At least the German knew weapons," Adam says. "It's a bit of a shock, though, to realize you were in Normandy at the same time, potting at each other."

"When do you think you'll be leaving?"

"Damn," Adam mutters after studying the board. His opponent smiles, then frowns, when Adam moves B-N5. "Suspect we'll be here to the end. Frightful prospect, but they don't much bother with bean oil exporters." That's what the two Englishmen do—buy vegetable oils in the East for British paint and plastic companies.

"The end is in sight," Embree remarks. All day the guns have been booming in the south. Rumor has seventeen Red columns ringing the city, outnumbering the Nationalists almost two to one. Clearly the Communists are entering a new phase of their campaign; they're changing from guerrilla to positional warfare. Embree feels sure that General Tang would have admired their flexibility as he would have despised the ineptitude of Nationalist forces. Or rather Nationalist leaders. The General had been Confucian in that he believed a state or an army, or any organization for that matter, depended on the moral quality of its leadership.

During this period of enforced leisure, Embree thinks often of the General. Few Chinese in the 1920s were able to shake off Taoist reluctance to act, as Tang had. Although he understood and respected the Taoist principle of giving way to outside force, he'd been able to set aside that traditional way of thinking; he'd challenged fate in a Western manner by fighting for principle. Died for it. Yes, that too.

Today there have been Red posters all over Jinan, assuring citizens that small private businesses will be encouraged to remain; only corrupt officials will suffer. School will open again in a few days after the People's Victory.

Once again, checkmate.

Adam with a smile turns away from his opponent, who's diligently setting up black pieces for another try. "I say, when will you get out?"

Embree shrugs.

"I rather think we'll all be here at the end," Adam says. "But I should think he'll get out."

"Who?"

"Frenchie. Petter. All it takes is a bloody good bribe. He can buy his way out whenever he wants." Having set up his own men, Adam sits back a moment and stares at Embree. "Don't you know, old man? He's the nephew of Charles Petter."

Embree smiles in acknowledgment of his ignorance. "Charles Petter?"

"Of the Petter Pistol. French Army used it as their Model MAS all through the war. A fine little weapon."

The other Englishman adds, "It's rather like your Colt 1911 with the Browning swinging-link design for recoil action. Only better, the French say."

"I don't know French weapons."

"Nor do I," Adam admits. "But during the last show this 7.65-mm. was very popular. Had an eight-shot magazine. Very solid little weapon. The point is, old Charles Petter invented it. Got rather wealthy when a weapons company produced it. At Chalet, I think."

The other adds, "Chalet in Alsace. Your move."

After brief study Adam moves P-K4. Then he says, "Young Petter has inherited the estate, you see. Filthy rich now."

"How do you know?" Embree asks.

"One night before you came here, he got rather tipsy and sat here condemning his uncle for inventing such a weapon. Vilified his uncle for bringing more death into the world. That sort of thing. Said conscience has brought him here to see Imperialism and Communism in action."

"That sort of thing," adds the other Englishman.

"But he's not given up on his uncle altogether. You see, he's not being paid by the journal who gave him this assignment. I gather since he's come out here on his own, they'll see if he can handle the drill."

"Bought his own passage."

"With his uncle's money," adds Adam.

Both Englishmen smile and turn to the chess board. When Adam sees that his opponent is mounting a Scotch Opening, he shifts his attention fully to the game.

• • •

The next morning, while Embree stands in the dusty courtyard of the mission school, listening to the distant thunk of howitzer shells in Jinan suburbs, Bernard Petter joins him.

"What do you think?" Petter asks guardedly.

"Actually, I'm thinking of something I heard years ago. There's a park in Loyang with peony beds so beautiful it's worth getting there at the risk of your life to see them. I'm sorry. You meant the siege. Well, the shells are dropping closer this morning. Maybe we have a week. Maybe less."

"The way Mueller got out is not the way we should get out," Petter says.

"How should it be done then?"

"Through the Reception House just across the Yellow River. General Chen Yi welcomes anyone who wants to come."

"You mean, Kuomintang deserters?"

"I mean soldiers who no longer want to fight on the side of imperialism. I mean—"

Petter delivers one of his polemics, while Embree takes a stance of listening without hearing one word, his attention solely for the English ivy that climbs along the schoolhouse wall. When a breeze ripples each five-lobed leaf, the entire side of the building looks like thousands of little green hands waving goodbye.

Suddenly Petter says, "Tonight I am leaving for the Reception House. Will you come along with me?"

"You mean, over to the Communists?"

"I am quite aware," Petter says with exaggerated dignity, "you don't believe in the cause, yet I also believe you're a man of principle. Unlike Mueller or the Englishmen. We need more men like you, men who can explain to the world what is happening here."

What a boring speech, Embree thinks, yet continues to smile at the narrow face of the young Frenchman, who's running desperately from his inheritance.

"Let me think about it," Embree tells him.

"I will leave here at midnight. Sharp. There is little danger, from what I'm told. The Nationalists have no interest in what we do."

"It's not danger I have to think about."

All day Embree walks through the city, hearing snatches of rumor while the pace of life finally quickens. It has taken Red entry into the suburbs to arouse the citizenry. People bustle about with their belongings piled on wagons, trucks, bullock carts, on their backs. Reds have broken through the western sector of town into a business district. The divisional commander has surrendered—or did he defect?—somewhere in the southwestern part of the city. Two Red columns, supported by tanks, are hammering at an isolated government outpost a few miles east. Throughout the day, planes go in and out of Jinan's air space, carrying people out and supplies in. Refugees stream toward the northern gate, while heavy black smoke begins to rise over the northwest. Someone shouts that Reds have blasted the Gate of Perpetual Safety with mortars and are pouring in there. A police regiment guarding the railway station has also defected.

Not a week, Embree figures. No more than another day.

When he returns to the schoolhouse, Embree discovers that the English-men are gone.

Granted flights that afternoon, they left with a few minutes' notice, taking their chess board along. So there are only three foreigners left in the dormitory. As he strolls down the hallway, past the tiny washroom, Embree hears a remarkable sound from behind the closed door. It is Gopal Tilak, singing. What makes it remarkable is the poignancy of his deep baritone. Although Embree can't understand the words—they must be in Marathi, the language of Bombay—he's transfixed by their sadness. It's as if the moment of death has been located in sound. Halt-ing in the corridor, Embree waits for Tilak to sing more, but hears instead a resonant belch, the burbling noise of lips fluttering against the surface of water, a following cacophony of splashing and burbling and throat clearing, as the little Indian goes about his noisy ablutions, the song forgotten.

That's like Indians I've known, Embree thinks. It's an affectionate thought. They can throw life away, life and death away, with a shrug, a song, a splash of water. They can shrug off emotion as if they never felt it. They, alone, can do that. And they can do that because for them there's really no future, there's only the moment and God.

It's how Rama thinks, isn't it? He looks at the world from those big clear eyes as if for the first time. He lives in the moment, this moment, and then steps pristine pure, like a newborn child, into the next mo-ment, and each succeeding moment breaks free from those gone by. What is pain, suffering, death? All yesterdays or tomorrows. Every-thing comes round again, so what's the difference? God will provide.

And so, to Embree's way of thinking, the Indian—Rama, Gopal, so many others he has known—takes a special journey through life. He balances on each moment like a man crossing an ice floe, each piece of it breaking off, having no connection with others floating past. Precar-iously he moves from one shifting cake to another, alert and optimistic, but quite prepared at the next step to slip and plunge into freezing water.

India has no future, Embree thinks. The idea comes with the force of a blow. India has no future, not in the sense that nations and peoples usually envision a future. India has no progress in mind. He has always known it, yet until now he hasn't cared. Not even Gandhi, so attached to his spinning wheel and the cottage industry he dreamed of unreeling from it, not even that brilliant man had a worldly view of the future. Or so Embree thinks now, at this very moment, this Indian moment, with the sound of Gopal Tilak still in his ear. And perhaps the sound of artillery drawing closer has brought him back to the future, away from

God. Because the sound of it means tomorrow. The sound of it connects pain to suffering to death in the inexorable linkage of events within time.

Walking back to the dormitory, he looks at the blank wall without sitting down, eyes closed, in front of it. But the Chinese have a future, he thinks, and it's here. On earth. They're too busy with that future to bother much about gods and the next life, if there is one. They can be helped to go from here to somewhere. He's had proof of that in three experiences of this awesome country. Such practical people can be helped. Whereas the Indians, full of music and soul, can't be helped by anybody, even by themselves. Staring at the wall, he decides against sitting in front of it, eyes closed. That's not his world any more, never was.

Before dinner, he seeks out Bernard Petter in the dining room. "Very well," he says, "I'm going with you."

• • •

An hour after midnight they stand on the bank of the Yellow River. They've been halted only three times by sentries; two of whom, seeing they are foreigners, wave them on. Petter quickly bribes the third guard (turning his back, like a suspicious rich man, so Embree can't see how much money he hands over). Below them in the moonless light they can hear the gentle sloshing of something against the riverbank. A light suddenly flickers, dimly illuminating the outline of a scow loaded with gunnysacks and bales. A score of young men huddle along the gunnels —KMT defectors. Even a half-hearted river patrol could prevent such escapes, but the Nationalists are now too panicked by disaster to worry about individuals breaking rules to save themselves. The Reds have deliberately left this section of the Yellow River untouched until more deserters have crossed over to augment the Third Field Army. Perhaps tomorrow the Reds will ford it here and attack the northeastern suburbs. Tonight, however, boats go in the other direction, as a dozen ferries head for the "Reception House" on the opposite shore.

"I have friends," Bernard Petter boasts. "They'll help us on the other side. Long live the revolution."

The little fool, Embree thinks. Petter doesn't know the real war he wants to fight is against the memory of his inventive uncle, who has left him with more responsibilities than he can handle.

By this act, Embree thinks, as Petter starts down the embankment toward the scow, I move farther away from Shanghai, from conscience, from Sanuk.

But he steps forward in the darkness, following the dim flicker of the lantern held on the riverboat's stern. Left behind in the Jinan school-house is Gopal Tilak, awaiting the conquering Red troops, sitting alone at a table with his complaints unheard, with the receipt for a boxcar of spoiling flour in his clenched hand, with religious songs to console him that he learned as a Chitapawan Brahman long ago, in the Bombay of his youth.

44 IN THE FOUR months since descending Tai Shan, a lot has happened to Ho Jin-shi, the Golden Lion of Bangkok.

Accompanied by the two Teochiu-speaking infantrymen from the South, he stumbled through darkness the last part of the descent and together with them left Taian before dawn. They proceeded by foot to an encampment outside of Yangchou, where Ho told their squad leader of his important mission. Unable to judge the significance of Ho's letter—and unable to read it even if he had dared break the seal—the squad leader sent him on to the battalion commander at HQ. This young officer had never heard of Pridi, hardly of Siam, but the mystery of these exotic names encouraged him to send Ho, along with one of the Teochiu soldiers, by train to Third Army Headquarters in Chining.

Ho waited there for a week in a regimental camp until word came through from Hsipiap'o to send him on to Linch'ing near the Hopei-Shantung border. Again accompanied by his interpreter, Ho took a freight train to Linch'ing. Through the open doorway of a boxcar hauling grain and cabbages to the Third Field Army, he stared at farmers knee deep in their fields. He didn't know what they were harvesting, city boy that he was, but the plants, ripening, looked as stiff as bristles, and healthy—even he could see that. Dirt paths led his eye beyond the fields into little villages which looked, from afar, like so many cardboard boxes, the kind piled up behind stores in Bangkok's Chinatown.

Meanwhile, Yu-ying was no doubt still back there somewhere looking for her father, traveling with an American because he was an American and because those people have power in China. Ho felt well rid of her. Traveling with a woman took time and patience—neither of which he had, not while on a mission. Later, somehow, he'd find her and take her back. Not that she'd be faithful to him until then. Women never were, although he wouldn't have to worry about the American touching her. The man was too old, and anyway, he was her father, married to her mother, so he was her father, and whatever god you believed in, that sort of thing was not right. She won't let him touch her.

Fortified by that analysis, Ho watched the fields go rattling by, the countless squares anchored sometimes at one corner by a village, but the landscape unfurling almost without variation, without teak forests breaking the horizon into tiny pieces or golden chedis needling the sky.

At Linch'ing the PLA staff decided to send him farther with his strange message, its seal still unbroken. Another small-gauge track got him by train to Techou and then, crossing over into Hopei Province, a large-gauge track got him by troop train to the city of Shihchuachuang, a major center of Red military activity between Manchuria and the Yangtze River. An officer there sent Ho and his interpreter, Lu Ting-fang, by truck to a place near Pingshan called Hsipiap'o.

From this dusty little town Chu Teh and Mao Tse-tung directed the Liberation Army campaign in Central China.

Once again Ho and Lu waited in a crowded barracks near the train station. Day and night for almost a week the young man from Bangkok listened to whistles heralding the arrival of trains from places whose names he couldn't pronounce. He stood by the doorway and watched American tanks and trucks pass along the bumpy street, raising clouds of red dust. He watched the officers and soldiers waddle along behind the motorized vehicles, no distinction of rank on their collars. They all looked bottle-shaped in uniforms which were full in the hips and buttocks and narrow at the trouser bottoms, making their feet look small, almost too delicate to balance such gray-colored bulk. He grew accustomed to the Chinese always munching something, often a big piece of bread, as big as a skull, their white teeth tearing off a hunk and methodically chewing. Cigarettes, tea with the leaves floating on the surface, and hunks of bread.

That was the Chinese, and in their presence he felt foreign, more so than when he'd first arrived in this country. Perhaps not being with Yu-ying made him more aware of other people. Perhaps it just took time to feel unwanted when he so much desired acceptance. He was conscious of their apple-red cheeks, of such bright color on faces much lighter than his own. Would these rough-hewn, robust people accept him? His chance was in the mission. Every day, accompanied by Lu, who was always cheerful and patient about it, Ho camped in the waiting room of HQ, asking for Nai Pridi Phanomyong, former Prime Minister of Siam and friend of the People of China.

One morning, rousted at dawn by a PLA officer, he and his interpreter were put on a southbound train. Destination: Handan, where a number of "foreign friends" were staying. This time, on arrival, Ho was met by a thin little man wearing the uniform of a Siamese naval officer.

Until the man addressed him in Thai, Ho did not realize just how homesick he'd been for many, many days.

• • •

It was somewhere on a tree-lined street. Chamlong was too excited by the prospect of meeting Pridi to remember how he got there. There was a building and a small room with a heavy sofa, chairs, a marble-topped table—he remembered that; it was the kind of cramped, stuffy room his father would like. There was an ashtray on the table, a lamp, a coat rack with a white scarf draped over one of its arms. And then the naval officer entered the small room with another man wearing a plain Chinese uniform. Stocky, his short hair bristling, he held a cigarette.

Leaping to his feet, Chamlong shouted *"Chaophraya!"*—Siamese title of highest respect for anyone save the king.

Nodding, Pridi puffed on the cigarette and scrounged in his jacket, coming out with a crumpled piece of paper. "Is this the only message you carried?"

"Yes, *Chaophraya!*"

The politician-in-exile turned to his aide. "Take care of it."

And Nai Pridi Phanomyong was out of the room before Chamlong had a chance to shout once more, *"Chaophraya!"*

"You," said the naval aide severely. "Can you read?"

"Yes, I can read." But it was with difficulty that Ho picked out the meaning of this letter from the Central Committee of the Communist Party of Siam to His Excellency Nai Pridi Phanomyong. Filled with praise for the virtues of the ex–prime minister and assurances that his followers in Siam hoped for the day of his return, it ended then with a flowery close. That was all. Looking up at the aide, Ho said, "What does it mean?"

"They had you carry compliments all the way here."

Chamlong looked down at his feet, thinking. "Compliments? What does it mean?" he repeated softly.

"It means you can go now."

"What?" He stared at the thin man with a severe face.

"You can go now." The naval officer made a motion as if getting rid of a child. "Go now. Go."

Outside the building, where Lu waited for him, Ho repeated the question to himself again again again: What did it mean? He had been there in the presence of the great Nai Pridi Phanomyong with a message brought all the way from Bangkok and then Pridi had left without a word for him and then the naval officer had mentioned compliments from Bangkok. Compliments? What did it all mean?

He and Lu walked in silence a long time. They had walked back to the shed, where they were bunking, before the terrible truth struck him:

His friends in Bangkok had used the message to get rid of him. They had sent him out of the country with nothing but a few empty compliments written on a piece of paper, and the great Pridi, instead of rewarding him, had turned him away in contempt. He was ashamed and humiliated. It had been a trick, a joke!

They had done this to Ho Jin-shi, who once played soccer for the Bangkok Friendship Society.

"Are you all right, friend?" Lu asked.

"Me? Of course. Except—" And the truth of this also registered with the force of a blow. "I don't know what to do now. I don't have any place to go or anything to do."

. . .

That was four months ago.

Today he has something to do, although Lu, his friend, does not. Lu is dead.

Lu had persuaded him to join the People's Liberation Army, because there was nothing else he could do. What was so obvious to his Teochiu friend became obvious to him. He walked out of a bad joke into one of those baggy uniforms—a short, dark young man who seemed more frail than ever, lost—as he murmured—completely lost. But Lu stood beside Ho in his moment of despair, exclaiming in a burst of oratory, "You have come here from the South, as I have, to fight for Liberation!"

Returning to Lu's unit, they moved north a few days, toward Jinan, which was under siege. Then they turned south when word came through that Jinan had fallen.

He had been in Jinan once—walked its streets with Yu-ying. Jinan had fallen, and maybe Yu-ying was still looking for the history of her father. If his father had been a general, maybe he'd do the same. He'd like to know everything about such a man, but his own father hoarded money, that's all, in safes that were opened only when a concubine wanted baubles. He envied Yu-ying her father. And for a time, after joining the Third Field Army of the PLA, Ho Jin-shi wondered if he might appropriate hers for his own. He might tell his new comrades, "My father was a general—of this province, too!" Except he couldn't answer the questions they'd ask.

The desire to tell the foolish lie vanished after his first firefight, because he kept pace with Lu across the hard-packed ground and pulled the trigger of his Japanese rifle twice, and afterward sat there panting like the others. He didn't need a general for his father any more.

Then last week in a skirmish with Nationalist forces, Lu took shrapnel in the stomach. There weren't enough bearers with their shoulder poles to clear away the wounded and get them to an advance collecting station, much less to a main dressing hospital. Ho had pleaded with another soldier to help him carry Lu back to an open-air first-aid area. Fortunately the man knew and liked Lu, so he helped, and together they got the little Teochiu to a lunar landscape, stark and bare, pitted with shell craters, where the wounded, wrapped in blankets, were lying among empty boxes and drying blood.

Ho couldn't get a doctor to come around; there was only one in the area. So he just knelt beside Lu and waited. The sun moved slowly down the sky, while Lu breathed rapidly. As time passed, Ho had the strange feeling that the motion of the sun was governing Lu's life, and when it set, Lu would die, and that's what happened.

When there were only a few streaks of light in the west, Lu reached out and clutched his hand—they'd spoken hardly a word the whole terrible afternoon—and said, "Chu-chin, get me water, I'm thirsty."

He didn't say any more, he died. And it was very strange, because he'd never mentioned a woman to Ho, yet a woman's name had been on his tongue at the last moment. It made Ho think of Yu-ying, there in the gathering darkness among groaning men, many of them dying like Lu, helpless and cold in the chill wind.

One of these days he would find her, he thought.

Then some men came along and picked up Lu by the hands and feet, spread-eagling him, as they moved sideways toward a mass grave. Getting to his feet, Ho remembered an old saying: Yellow gold is plentiful compared to white-haired friends. If Lu had lived, that was what they'd have been—friends into old age.

Because I won't die, Ho thinks. Ever since joining the army, Ho has secretly known that he will come out of it. He has one rifle, two hand grenades, eight clips of ammo, one blanket, one rice bowl, chopsticks, and one serving kit. With these things he will survive. This is his closely guarded secret.

• • •

Already Ho has a new friend, who learned Teochiu during his army days fighting the Japanese in South China. Lao Chang began his soldiering at T'aierhchuang ten years ago—one of the few battles the Chinese won during World War II. This distinction earns him respect today in the Liberation Army. Old Chang is squat, hairy for a Chinese, and always hungry.

Out of quixotic good will, the older man has taken Ho under his protection. "I like you," Lao Chang says with a guffaw. "You look like a bird with a broken wing."

Ho follows the veteran everywhere and through his encouragement begins to learn Mandarin. Chang gets him a book used by children to learn their characters. Written in rhymed sentences of three characters by General Feng Yu-hsiang some years ago, it is called *Resist Japan*.

Ho learns well enough to get up at a political meeting, held when his unit is pulled out of action for a few days, and declare in a loud voice, "My father was a capitalist landlord! I ran away! Long live the Revolution!" Such a statement brings a round of applause. He feels tears of pride and wishes his father could see him now, a brave man of China.

With Chang translating for him, he entertains his comrades with dirty stories from Siam, learned from the easygoing companions of his childhood. There's the one about three wishes. A demon gave a poor man three magical wishes. The poor man thought of all the riches he might have, but his wife wanted him to wish only for pretty clothes and trinkets for herself. Angry at her selfishness—just like a woman, Ho observes with a knowing shake of his head—to spite her, the poor man wished that his whole body was adorned with cocks, both limp and erect ones. He wondered what she'd think of that! Fancy, was she? How fancy would she be with a man with cocks sticking out all over him!

Ho's comrades laugh.

When she saw what he looked like—a forest of cocks waving around—his horrified wife begged his forgiveness for being so selfish. He forgave her, and when she pleaded with him to wish all those cocks away, he used his second wish. They all disappeared—his own included.

Ho's comrades roar.

So the poor man had to use his third and final wish to restore himself to normal manhood and was no richer than before. With such droll stories from the back alleys of Bangkok, a young man never known for wit at home acquires the reputation for it among these peasant soldiers of China.

. . .

Army life also gives Ho Jin-shi the chance to gamble again. He frees himself from the promise (where had he made it? Ho can't remember now) to Yu-ying that he'd never gamble again. Some of the men carry mah-jong tiles, and their clicking brings him running. He plays fan-tan too, and learns to bet on grasshopper fights. When they're placed in a bowl and agitated, Ho is there, judging their ability, claiming a talent for estimating the skill of insects.

He hasn't seen much combat yet, only a few skirmishes like the one in which Lu was killed, but Ho has found in himself a courage which he never realized was his. This is what the army has given him—a good feeling about himself. And it gives him more: clothes, food, friendship, and ideas. By piecing ideas together he fashions for himself the big idea of communism, something he'd never done in Bangkok. Into this idea he crawls like an animal looking for shelter. What had been a way out of his troubles in Bangkok becomes that and more in China. Because it's everything. Communism is good against evil; it is a divine mission; it is complete dedication of self to cause, which he'd always told Yu-ying it was without knowing what he meant; it is faith; it is the need for his own reform into a better man; it is the creator of heroes like Mao Tse-tung and Chu Teh and the generals under which he himself is serving —Liu Po Ch'eng and Chen Yi. He memorizes the Three Main Rules of Discipline: Obey orders, don't steal, turn in what's captured. And he learns the Eight Points of Attention, barking them out in faulty Mandarin: You must speak nicely! Buy what you take! Return what you borrow! Pay for damage! Refrain from beating people! Avoid trampling crops! Resist the temptation to harm women! Treat prisoners humanely!

From having nothing to do he has everything to do. A cruel joke in Bangkok has led him, so Ho Jin-shi thinks, to his salvation. Even his trouble with language has become a kind of blessing, because isolation brings him in contact with his own thoughts. He likes his own thoughts and what his eyes tell him about the world. For a few months now, on the march, he has seen China. The Chinese think the world is China, and because he's Chinese, he is finally seeing the world.

· · ·

As the Third Field Army proceeds southward, meandering like a stream toward the strategic city of Hsuchou, the young man from tropical Siam learns what the North is and how people live in it. The geometry of the Central Plain takes getting used to. The roads are mercilessly straight. They go on and on, giving the traveler no illusion, by curve or obstruction, that the journey is less long than it actually is. At daybreak, squinting past fields of clover and rows of tall poplars, he can see the horizon they'll march to by sunset. Such distances trick him. At a considerable distance, for example, it's hard to judge whether a village has been shelled in a firefight or has been left untouched—the outline of mud huts and piles of rubble are visually similar. Of course, when his column approaches the distinction is evident: On one hand there will be homes with children staring at the soldiers; on the other, collapsed walls, a severed little arm, lying in what was once a hearth.

It gets colder. Buildings on the landscape are no more than a story high, and that one story flatter than higher—unlike Siamese houses on stilts—hugging the ground as if in fear of the frigid Manchurian wind that brings with it a wall of stinging dust. Even the wildlife looks cold. Ducks on ponds have a cold metallic sheen to them, and herds of ivory-colored goats have a tense jerky motion as they cross a path, as if they're as cold as he feels on this windy plain.

He begins to understand what Lao Chang tells him. "The old sage, Confucius, was asked what three things a man must have to rule. The sage answered, 'Food, faith, and weapons.' Which one can you do without, if you must? the sage was asked, and he answered, 'Weapons.' That's Mao too. He gives us food and faith but not weapons."

"Without weapons he can't give you food or make you believe he's a good leader," Ho argues.

Lao Chang shakes his head. "You don't understand, southerner. He sees to it we get something to eat and we get justice. After that the weapons just come."

"How?"

"We take them from the enemy." They are at a campfire during this discussion. Lao Chang rips off a large hunk of bread from a round loaf. "The old sage used to say what a people need is a good leader. We've got him and the other side hasn't. So we'll win." Lao Chang chews lustily. "It's that simple."

There's always something, each day, that reminds Ho of Mao Tse-tung. There are crudely drawn pictures of him on unit flags. Once in a rail yard he saw a painting of Mao on cotton cloth draped over the boiler of a disabled locomotive. And each evening, around campfires, the men sing revolutionary songs, which slowly he begins to learn. One he can already sing lustily, at least the first verse:

> The sun is rising red in the East.
> The earth has given us Mao Tse-tung.
> He fights for the good of the people.
> Ai! Ya! Yo! He's the savior of China.

Lao Chang not only explains Mao Tse-tung to him, but other things as well. Ho begins to wonder if this man hasn't been destined to be his proper father. If only Yu-ying were here, she might tell from astrology if it is true. Lao Chang reads, writes, and remembers almost everything. Munching a wheat roll, his belly popping over the rope belt of faded gray pants, Lao Chang tells him about the old days, even before the Japanese came.

In those days the Turtle Eggs (his name for landlords) ruled this province with a fury even the Japanese couldn't match. He shakes his head at the memory. "It's true. The Turtle Eggs used to bury people alive. If you didn't pay your debt to a Turtle Egg, he had you murdered. No good asking for protection from the magistrate, because the Turtle Egg *was* the magistrate—or his brother or cousin was. So for some old debt you got buried. Or maybe you got buried because you didn't give him your pretty daughter. You dug half the night, and when the hole was higher than your head, they started throwing the dirt back in on you. Didn't do any good to scramble out. They bashed you back in with a shovel and kept filling the hole. When I was a little boy, I used to think a lot about that: how it would feel to be inside the hole, all covered up, unable to see or breathe, and I wondered if you could hear them up there laughing."

He tells Ho about joining the Red Spear Society. On one of their secret raids against landlords he murdered a couple of Turtle Eggs. It was the most fun he ever had in his life, watching them squeal like pigs when he stuck them.

And he tells Ho about running away when the Japanese came and about joining the Eighth Route Army. Fighting was hard then, not like now. Men fell from marching and were eaten during the night by dogs and pigs. "We fought in small bands. There weren't battalions and regiments like now—just a leader and some men. Nowadays we have bandages, cotton, and pills sometimes, and iron pincers to take a bullet out, and thread to sew you up, but in those days, if you got a head wound or gut wound, you lay there and died. Your comrades couldn't waste a bullet on you. And they couldn't bear to use a knife on someone they knew or strangle an old friend. That was too personal. But if you were in bad pain, you tried to persuade someone to do it for you. It was hard to convince anybody, because if he did it for you, then he'd be called on to do it for someone else, and so he'd end up finishing off his own comrades. So you probably lay there and died the hard way. Unless a Jap patrol came around. Then you were lucky. They'd shoot you or bayonet you. We used to say, if we got wounded badly, we hoped the Japs would come along. Hand me a piece of that bread. No, the whole thing." He asks Ho about life in Siam.

Strangely, Ho can't give him clear answers. The South and its lazy charm elude his memory. Siam is only a green image, a green unformed shape in his mind now. Reality is this flat earth of the North, which reveals its mystery each day he marches through it. As the temperature falls, Ho Jin-shi has his first look at frost—like finely shattered pieces of glass lying across the sheared fields, stubbled, gray, swept by freshening winds from the north. But he tells Lao Chang of the Siamese government that's against the Chinese. He mixes together the memory of his father with Phibun, both men unjust and tyrannical.

"So my mother was Siamese. That meant I didn't belong in my father's Chinese house. I was never sure of our Chinese ancestors the way Father was. He knew them. He burned paper to them and said the ancestors watched this smoke go up. I never saw them watching. Maybe they wouldn't let me see them, considering who I was. I don't know. I was one of them, but not one of them. I believed the ancestors hated me for having Siamese blood. I still believe it."

"Don't believe it. You can forget your ancestors here."

"So my father and the ancestors treated me rotten because of the Siamese part. But the Siamese hated the Chinese part. When Pridi was prime minister, it was all right to be Chinese. Not any more."

Lao Chang nods solemnly. "You're better off here."

Better off here? Ho's convinced of it, except that sometimes he thinks of Yu-ying. Someday he'll take her back, because . . . well . . . he can't form the conclusion of such a thought until a number of intervening distractions—the way something looks, hunger, the adjustment of his pack—catch his mind off guard and allow him to finish the admission: He likes Yu-ying better than any girl he can imagine. He loves her. Yes, that too, although a man shouldn't waste time on such thoughts. He once stood in front of the Emerald Buddha in the Wat Phra Keo, with his eyes closed and his hands held in a respectful *wai*, and he'd taken an oath, even though he has never believed in the Buddha, "I love this woman and promise always to love her." He'd made this vow in front of her, too. What more could a woman want? Someday he'll have her back, that is certain, even though he mustn't waste time thinking of such things.

And there isn't time to waste. Units are gathering and moving south now at a fast pace, although Lao Chang maintains it isn't fast. "When General Chen Yi wants to get somewhere fast, you'll know what it is to march. Right now we're just wandering around until he knows where he wants to go."

Now, on either side of the fields, Ho can see columns moving south, funneling together into a swelling gray tide through the cold November light. The Third Field Army to the east and the Second to the west are moving across the fallow countryside, shattering clods under the tread of thousands of straw sandals.

Someone comes along with news. "Mukden has fallen!"

When Lao Chang translates this for him, Ho stares into the distance. He doesn't know what Mukden is. Something flashes in the distance, something with glass in it. Binoculars? Spectacles? Windshield of a truck? "Ours?" Ho asks breathlessly.

"Theirs," Lao Chang says, just as the squad leader orders them to move forward at a crouch. Their steps on the crusty earth make a crunching sound that's lost soon in the firecracker sharpness of small-arms fire, then the whistle and boom of artillery.

"Where are we?" Ho asks.

Lao Chang shrugs.

We don't know, Ho thinks, and moves forward with his secret intact: If a battle's coming, he won't be killed.

· · ·

A few days after the Communist capture of Mukden in Manchuria, Harry Truman defeated Thomas Dewey at the polls and was reelected President of the United States.

Ho Jin-shi doesn't know this any more than he knows his unit, along with others, is headed for the bloodiest, most important battle of the Chinese Civil War. A million men will struggle for two months in mud and snow around the city of Hsuchou, a junction for the east-west Lunghai Railway, near the Hwai River.

Historians will call it the Hwai-Hai Campaign.

Generals on his staff have warned Chiang Kai-shek not to meet the Reds here, but to withdraw southward to the Yangtze, where supply lines will be shorter. Instead, the Generalissimo brings up armies from the South under the command of Tu Yu-ming and Liu Chih, both fresh from defeats in Manchuria. As field commanders, he assigns generals who belong to the Whampoa clique. They refuse to cooperate with one another, and persist in dealing individually with the Generalissimo rather than following a chain of command. What Ho and Lao Chang and the thousands slogging toward confrontation on the plain around Hsuchou do not know is Chiang's determination to hold here, at any cost in men and matériel, with the last of his thirty-nine elite divisions supplied with American equipment.

At this gateway between North and South China nearly half a million combatants will be killed, wounded, or taken prisoner.

· · ·

Days later, how many he doesn't remember, Ho Jin-shi's battalion is withdrawn from the front lines. It is snowing. Everything is white. He stares dully at some ducks sitting on a pond, its surface blown into rippling agitation by Siberian winds. An hour later he notices a rabbit skittering across the flat snow, and toward sunset, along a frozen farm road, his unit strolls by an American weapons carrier, with no top, broken rear crossbars, dented mudguards, and its engine blown away. Two Nationalist soldiers are lying beside the cab. One has no head.

Ho has learned something about death. If a dead man is whole, he looks dead. If a dead man is in fragments, he looks like a kind of machine that's broken, each isolated piece of him not necessarily integral to what had been a man, but just a thing there, something that belongs to machinery.

He has learned this and more. For example, what he thought was a closely guarded personal secret doesn't exist.

He learned it during his first major battle, when an officer blew a whistle and the whole line started to run across the pitted ground. He saw men fall, saw them knocked backward or tumbled sideways, but his secret was still intact until someone within arm's reach yelled out and clamped hands to his face, falling down bloody and writhing.

At this moment Ho Jin-shi understood the enormity of that lie he'd told himself. The lie was that he'd live through all of this. So his secret was nothing more than a lie. He didn't have any secret to hold on to, not when he was out here in plain view and with men falling through the smoke. He felt himself running, but on legs that could buckle any moment. His throat was drier than ever in his life; the thirst was like something alive, crawling down his windpipe. Without the secret, Ho knew he was going to die out here, exposed, in the noise and smoke and with these men around him flopping to the earth, crying out, bursting open, wriggling and groping and lying still. And then ahead of him other men were running, only away from him, their baggy shapes in the windy morning easing through smoke, some of them falling too, some of them shattering like clods of earth thrown against rock.

That was the first time.

Since then one day has followed another without his holding the secret, at least that one. Now he has another secret: He's afraid, he's a coward, he can't feel his legs when the whistle blows and everyone rises from the earthwork ridges. Always the thirst too; that's part of the new secret. And when they halt awhile, the strange thing is he isn't thirsty at all. He's just tired, and what he really wants to do is count the members of his squad, to make sure they got across the battlefield alive.

That's what he thinks about—who is and who isn't alive—not about the battle itself.

He doesn't know that by attacking the weaker section of government forces northeast of Hsuchou, General Chen Yi has encircled and isolated the Nationalist Seventh Army Group, avoided the main force held northwest of the city, and in effect completed the first phase of a campaign designed to isolate and destroy the enemy piecemeal. He has no understanding of Red Army hit-and-run tactics, made classical by long employment of guerrilla warfare during the past twenty years. What Ho Jin-shi knows is thirst, and the harboring of a terrible new secret.

The unit has, in Mao's military usage, "withdrawn to a terminus." It means a little rest from the shelling.

They sit outside a village in bright November sunshine and watch some farmers hitching horses to wagons. Sitting on top of gunnysacks of wheat, the farmers wave and yell out their intention of going to market. None of the soldiers stop them.

These are peasant soldiers who understand a peasant's need to plant, to harvest, to sell what is harvested. "What market can they be going to?" Ho asks Lao Chang.

The older man, munching on a turnip, replies simply, "They'll find one."

"In the middle of a battle?"

"They'll find one."

And after thinking about it Ho understands, because he's beginning to understand the peasantry of his own blood. Because through generations these peasants must have found a way to sell their goods during war and disaster. They'll find a way; they'll create a market somehow, he thinks. Perhaps over the rise there, they'll meet an old merchant whose wagon is filled to brimming with hoe handles and cotton shoes, maybe a few battered flashlights without batteries. Ho wonders at their capacity for doing what they please. They'll haggle while the bombs whistle overhead; and from the improvised marketplace, to their mutual satisfaction, they'll drive off while within earshot men are slaughtering one another.

I understand, Ho tells himself. This is how China survives. And I am one of these people, he thinks proudly. A man of China. Young Ho: Shao Ho.

• • •

The respite is soon over, and his unit joins with other units of the Third Field Army to move southward, under Chen Yi, toward Pangpu. Coming from the West is the Second Field Army led by Liu Po Ch'eng, who lost his left eye to a grenade. Their mutual objective is to cut off the Thirteenth Army in Hsuchou from reinforcement. While the pincers close, the Nationalist Twelfth Army under Huang Wei is isolated and surrounded twenty miles west of Suhsien by divisions detached from the Second Field Army. The Generalissimo orders him to wait there for rescue, although Red troops are encircling him with trenches and mine fields. Three armies, sent by the Generalissimo and commanded by Tu Yu-ming, are repulsed in the attempt to relieve Huang Wei and afterward are pressured to retreat southward.

"Where are we?" Ho asks his friend one cold evening, the wind stinging their faces. They're huddled around a small fire; in the distance they can see tiny dots, the fires of men they will fight in the morning.

"I don't know. Somewhere in Anhui. I think T'aierhchuang is around here somewhere."

"Weren't you at T'aierhchuang?"

"I was."

"When was it fought?"

"Some years back." Lao Chang spits into the fire. "I forget."

"Were the Japanese good?"

Lao Chang nods. "But we surprised them then. I think T'aierhchuang is somewhere around here."

In their heavily padded jackets and Mongolian fur hats, taken from Nationalists shipped down from the Manchurian debacle to their death, they look like small bears.

"I think it was somewhere around here," repeats Lao Chang. Scratching his chin, he adds, "But you can't tell where a battle was."

"Why not?"

"You're too busy staying alive." He hunches his shoulders. "It doesn't matter, though. I never worry about where I am. When I think about the years of fighting, what I remember is the forced marches and who died. When I was down South—that's where I learned your Teochiu—I marched thousands of li through those provinces, but I don't remember any of it, except one time we marched without a break for two and a half days. I remember friends who got it. I remember that. When you're soldiering, you shouldn't do more."

"Why?"

"If you wonder how the fight is going or what the name of a town is or where you're marching next, you get confused because you're thinking. Then you try to guess what the generals will do. What generals do shouldn't interest you. Your interest is staying alive. Let Chen and that other commander, the One-Eyed Dragon, do the thinking. Don't get tired because of thinking. I like thinking. But not while soldiering. It's no good wasting your strength with thinking. I know how to live through it, you see, and it's not by thinking. You have to hoard yourself up. Like this." Lao Chang hunches more, making himself into a ball-like shape.

Next day an officer yells through a tin megaphone at the opposing troops. "Chinese shouldn't be killing Chinese! Come on over! We won't kill you! We're brothers! If you don't like us, we'll give you train fare home. You know that's true. It's what we've been doing a long time now. So come on over! We won't kill you."

Through a dreary mist Ho Jin-shi watches the bulky shapes emerge at a slow, hesitant walk. Hands are up. There are dozens, then hundreds of men surrendering along the line. They are cold, wearing rags across their faces, and they know the truth: that if they fight here against Red troops who've maneuvered into numerical superiority, they will die.

That night in front of disarmed Nationalists, who've been fed and given blankets (most of which were taken a few days earlier from their dead companions), Ho gets up and shouts at them what his company commander has drilled him to shout: "I am from Siam, a country south of here! My father was a capitalist landlord! I ran away! Stay with us, brothers! Long live the Revolution!"

• • •

In the weeks that follow, in spite of alternating episodes of rain and snow that slow down the mobile Red forces, their tactic of isolation and encirclement continues to succeed in the Hwai-Hai area. Propaganda leaflets, churned out of Japanese mimeograph machines and a single press using hand-set type, are smuggled through Nationalist lines, promising amnesty and a better life. There are wholesale desertions. In one instance an entire division goes over to the Communists.

Meanwhile, General Tu Yu-ming's army groups, fleeing southwest, are trapped by Red troops at Yung-cheng in Honan Province and destroyed. There's a final attempt by the Generalissimo to relieve Huang Wei's Twelfth Army; the Sixth and the Eighth move northward from Pangpu, but meet stiff resistance.

Involved in that resistance is Ho Jin-shi, who slogs forward, carrying his pack and rifle and secret fear. What Lao Chang told him proves true: He remembers the marches and those who die. Three men in his twelve-man squad have got it so far. The young soldier from Siam is convinced that one of these days he'll join them in death. Yet what can he do? Like the crumpled dead on the daily battlefields, he can't escape destiny. What he can do, however, is imagine being seen on such battlefields by the gamblers who caught him outside the boxing stadium and made him admit his Siamese heritage. What would they think of him now, fighting alongside heroes of the People's Liberation Army? If they caught him now, he wouldn't bend; he's sure of that. Every day he goes out with his fear and comes back with it every night, yet between times he fights in spite of it. A soldier of China. Those Siamese gamblers could take him into the alley now and threaten to kill him, but he wouldn't deny his Chinese blood. He'd say, "I am Chinese," and await their knives.

As the daily battles take place, leaving the burning wreckage of American tanks and weapons carriers everywhere in sight, something new happens within Ho's battalion: Down to the last man they all know that the PLA is winning, that Chen and the One-Eyed Dragon have the Nationalists completely on the run.

From a mood of fatalism Ho Jin-shi emerges with guarded hope. He just might make it, along with Lao Chang and their comrades.

And if he does, he'll find Yu-ying again. As for the American, that old man won't have her. She saw who climbed the mountain faster, who was stronger, and anyway, the foreigner was old, was her father, married to her mother, and so anything between them would be wrong in the eyes of the gods or Buddha or the Christian god whose name Ho has forgotten.

But if he never finds her again, he'll accept the loss. Nothing will hurt him again, as long as he has his comrades. What the Liberation Army —and communism too—have come to mean is simply that: his comrades. The truth is, Ho Jin-shi spends little time on the theories shouted by political commissars attached to the regiment. Even when he has a translation of their words, Ho doesn't waste thought on what they say. How far you march and who dies—that's what interests him. He feels a powerful bond between himself and the men of his squad. It's forged by danger, intensified by the possibility of sudden death. Between the abyss and his life stand these men, and only these men—fathers, sons, brothers, yes, and mothers and sisters and lovers as well. They are everything.

For the first time in his life Ho Jin-shi belongs.

One morning, as the line sets out across a field dusted with fresh snow, he says to Lao Chang, "You are my father now."

The older man laughs, chewing on a stale wheat bun.

Ahead, through the snow lifted into whorls by a brisk wind, they see the enemy, a ragged silhouette of tiny objects moving in the distance. Clatter of machine-gun fire. He hears nearby a familiar grunt, like a pig makes when it trots—familiar because he's heard it often lately: a man receiving the impact of a bullet.

Lao Chang is lying on the ground, face up, eyes open.

Ahead of Ho the attack continues, with men moving slowly forward through the mists of dawn, but he kneels beside the fallen man and shakes him by the shoulders. There's nothing in the face to make an answer. In one piece, but with a bubbling well of blood pumping from his throat, Lao Chang is dead. He is a whole man, a dead man.

Rising to his feet, Ho stares down a moment, then rummages at Lao Chang's waist, unfastening the ammo belt. Throwing it across his shoulder, he turns to join his comrades. He's running with the sound of frost crunching beneath his feet. Ten or fifteen yards ahead of him three men go down, shattered by a shell blast into fragments of bone, flesh, cloth. He smells the acrid smoke, moves on through another nearby concussion that stirs the earth beneath him. Ho hears himself screaming. It's not a word emerging from his mouth, but a long wailing animal cry of fury and exultation. Exultation because he has no fear, at least not for this moment, none at all, and around him his comrades are running into pain and death, all of them together, he with them, and the noise pouring from his throat joins theirs in one immense sound of victory over fear, over caring for anything save this terrible, this fierce, this passionate moment together.

• • •

By early January 1949 the Nationalist Thirteenth Army, trying to flee Hsuchou, is hunted down in open country fifty miles southwest of the city and annihilated. Chiang Kai-shek has lost four army groups, seven full divisions, and the celebrated Armored Corps commanded by his son. The battle is over. The belly of Nationalist China lies exposed to further attack.

The Third Field Army proceeds toward Nanking.

45 RAMA SPITS. Betel juice splashes on the ground. The heavy stream of it is dark red, made especially dark by the spicy filling of marsala put into the sirih leaf by the panwalla from whom Rama always gets his morning chew. It's a hot February morning in Singapore. It's the festival day of Thaipusam, dedicated to the glory of Lord Murugan, Son of Shiva, General of the Celestial Army.

For the occasion Rama has marked his forehead with ashes. Ashes avert evil, cure rheumatism and liver trouble, as well as increase potency. He feels secure, almost happy during his walk to the temple on Serangoon Road. And why not? He has a new job that will let him save money, so he can fetch his family here, *lah*. Until now, doing odd jobs in the pickle factory, he's scarcely made enough to buy food. Of course, when Mistress left him in Singapore and returned to Siam, for his services she gave him a bonus large enough to send for them. But if he sent for them and they arrived, how could he rent lodgings and buy food for four? What to do? For two months he has pondered this disparity between the desire to send for them and the inability to support them.

Today, taking darshan of Lord Murugan at the temple on Tank Road at the climax of the festival, he will have much to be thankful for. The drought did not materialize. Narayana. Mistress recovered sufficiently to leave China and bring him out of that cold country with her. Narayana. And now he has a job that pays enough for him to bring his family here.

Not that he'd thought of doing it when Mistress brought him to Singapore. That had occurred to Rama only after he'd wandered during his second day here into Serangoon Road, where immediately the long-lost smell of familiar things overcame him: onions frying in ghee; paratha bread smoking on chowki griddles; Madrasi coffee steaming in street stalls.

In wonder and increasing excitement he had wandered through the center of Little India. Here was the comforting sound of Tamil being spoken, the mridangan drum of South India being played in a second-story room over a garland maker's shop. It was not exactly Madras or his village, but here was India, the mother bountiful with her markets, her panwallas, sari retailers, astrologers, goldsmiths, and provisioners, selling things to the shrill cry of hawking and the clang of hammers.

He was home in an instant.

All morning Rama walked, that second day in Singapore, through comforting memories, as he smelled the pungency of sandalwood from stores that sold images of the gods he loved; as he watched the catties of green and black dal being weighed in old brass balances; as he listened to spices sizzle in a kwali before pulse and vegetables were also tossed into the pan. The profusion of goods bewildered and gladdened Rama, who closely studied what the Nattukottai Chattiyars had for sale in their crowded little shops: cigarettes, sweets, batteries, magazines in his beloved Tamil. With Usha and the boys beside him, Rama could be happy here. That realization came by the time he had traversed Serangoon Road but once.

And as the days passed and his familiarity not only with old Indian ways but also with new Singaporean ways deepened, Rama became convinced that here, indeed, was the place his karma had selected for him—and for his family. After a while he didn't mind the incessant banging of Chinese drums from the direction of the Hokkien and Cantonese settlements in Telok Ayer Street. He learned to eat ice cream from the three-wheeled Magnolia Push Carts, whose vendors wore white topis. He discovered the public toilet in Gemmill Lane with its pinnacled roof and stolid brick walls, like a British fortress. He became accustomed to reading signs unavailable in Madras or in any of those Chinese cities on the mainland where everything was written in those incomprehensible chicken scratchings. Here he could read the large impressive billboards for Carlsberg Beer and DeWitt's Antacid Powder. He liked to think that someday he'd buy a ticket at the Alhambra Theatre on Beach Road, at present showing an American movie, *Yolanda and the Thief*. He stared with national pride at Gurkha policemen with their kanda sticks and rattan shields and shiny traffic whistles. He loved to stop at a sarabat stall for ginger tea and sweetmeats. He even liked to stand in front of the Fish Head Curry Shop and sniff the fish-house specialties in there, although God forbid he'd actually touch such flesh. Narayana. But then he could always go down the street and eat syrupy payasam and drink cool lassi. With or without money, a man, even an Indian, could live well in Singapore.

In Singapore he learned fast. There was, for example, always some place, no matter where you were (he never counted Chinatown as any place), that served heaty food like South Indian ediyapam and coolie food like thairu. He discovered exceptionally good thairu on a street so tiny it was nameless, where an old woman ladled the yogurt from a bucket set on an overturned orange crate.

Long ago, in this section of Little India, Rama was to learn, there used to be knacker yards for skinning and tanning, stables, and cattle sheds. But for many years, no longer permitted to keep their cows in town (a worldwide epidemic of rinderpest settled that), dudhwallas have pulled their walking dairies through the streets at dawn, selling fresh milk from door to door for strong morning coffee.

Today there's a forest of brick kilns on the periphery of Little India, run by Tamil contractors, who have showed Singapore that Indians can be more than cowherds, servants, laundrymen. Rama has learned, however, that among their Chinese neighbors there are many who hate the Indians for cooperating with the Japanese during the war, especially through the Indian National Army under Chandra Bose. But what is that to him? Singapore is a pakka town, and someday he'll fetch his family here.

And then came that day, two weeks after their arrival, when Mistress summoned him to the Palm Court of Raffles Hotel. Rama was quartered a block away in a servants' dormitory, and each time he came into the hotel, awe overtook him at the spendthrift luxuries of white people. There were overhead revolving fans stirring air above huge water jars in which enormous palms sat, and there were teak staircases, chandeliers in the pillared corridors, courts and arbors, a bronze cupid sitting on top of a large porcelain urn. And Mistress fit perfectly into this scene of opulence. Illness had, if anything, given her extra beauty, because her skin was even paler now, a kind of glowing white that any Indian girl would give half a lifetime for. She had come up, he thought, from where she had been, but she was still pulled down because of losing her child. How would he feel, losing his own?

Rama came, Congress hat in hand, past the coconut palms, across the manicured lawn where she sat at a marble-topped table. He made his way hesitantly, worried about the look of his Nehru jacket in the open space between the arcade and her table. From the balconies, facing the Palm Court, perhaps white men were staring down with disapproval upon his progress toward the handsome woman—toward the pallid woman in a white cotton dress, sitting with one soft hand cupped around a tall glass with ice in it and a concoction of fiery Western liquors.

She gave him a broad smile. In their way, he thought, they were friends; surely he'd felt a paternal affection for the woman during her days of suffering. White people in pain had to be cared for.

"How do you like Singapore now?" she asked, no doubt recalling his reluctance to accompany her here.

To that question he could make an easy answer, because it was not the question she really wanted to ask. "I am liking it here. They aren't too pushy. They laugh around and have a jolly good time. Serangoon Road is very good."

"Do you think of going back to India, Rama?"

"I am not wanting that, I don't relish it."

"So you still feel Independence won't work?"

"I believe in it, but it won't work, no, Mistress, until communities calm down."

"You mean castes?"

"I do, Mistress." He shook his head judgmentally. "Bapuji is dead.

Nehru is giving Moslems too much. There are strikes, riots, and no good coming of it."

"Then will you come back to Bangkok with me?"

This was the question he'd been waiting for, and his answer was ready. "No, please, thank you, Mistress. I am keen on staying this side."

She smiled at him in a way he'd seen his Usha smile at the boys sometimes, when they'd done something wrong. "What will you do here?"

Turning his hat around in both hands, rapidly, he said with pride, "I passed out of school nearly ten years ago. I am educated. Good work will be coming."

• • •

And so, finally, it has. Only yesterday, at the Singapore Railway Station on Keppel Road, he sat in front of the man at the desk and answered questions and then, after a long wait outside the office, he'd been called back in and given the job of assistant conductor on the Express Rakyat, which leaves Singapore daily at 8 A.M., stops at Kuala Lumpur, and travels on through Malaya, arriving at the terminal for Penang in the evening—or it is the next evening? Not that the length of the trip matters. Like his own father, he will travel by train, day after day, seeing the sights and following a schedule. He is fiercely proud to be selected—he, a Kling, a South Indian—over the other applicants, both Chinese and Malay, who had sat beside him for hours on the hard bench, awaiting their own interviews.

My English did it, he thinks happily.

Rama is joining the crowd that lines the way to Perumal Temple. I am lucky man. I will fetch them someday, *lah*.

Rama has learned to use the Malay *lah* for emphasis, even in his thoughts. He knows some *bahasa pasar*, market talk, and the Chinese for "that one" and "how much" and "too much." Singapore is his home, he thinks contentedly, while watching the procession gather for the long day.

He sees a man stagger out of the temple; cheers go up riotously along the lined road. That is someone, Rama thinks enviously as he stares at the man, who will have a terribly long, difficult, and ecstatic day.

• • •

The man wearing a loincloth carries a kavadi, which is a heavy cage (Rama has heard that some of the cages weigh sixty or seventy pounds, half his own weight) of wire struts, resting on his waist and shoulders; from the arched strips of the cage hang at least half a hundred thin chains that loop down to the man's chest and back where they are hooked into his flesh with barbs. The complex frame is garlanded with flowers, giving him the appearance of a grotesque insect imprisoned in golden filaments spun from the gut of an immense spider. Running through his cheeks and tongue are thin silver skewers, whose ends are ornately fitted with trident heads and magical designs. There is no blood. The man stares ahead fixedly, while friends or relatives following him chant shrilly "Vel! Vel!" They encourage him to step forward, heavily, with the cage swaying about him, the flesh of chest and back pulled away from his body with the consistency of rubber. But no blood. This man and other devotees carry their kavadis in an act of penance or in appeal for a favor or in gratitude for a boon granted by Lord Murugan.

Rama presses forward in the crowd which seethes alongside the pandals—temporary stalls lining the procession's route. The precise course has been posted in Little India for days, and even Rama, for whom Thaipusam is not an important ritual, knows all of its details. The celebrants will proceed slowly through Serangoon and Selegie roads, down Dhobi Ghaut, to Clemenceau Avenue, and from there Murugan's divine image in a silver chariot will lead the way to New Bridge Road. There prayers in the Vinayager Temple will be said in praise of Ganesh, the Remover of Obstacles. In the evening the celebrants will continue to Tank Road's Murugan Temple for the climactic ceremony: There the kavadi carriers will be relieved of their burdens, and their wounds lovingly treated with ashes and lemon juice as they receive the blessing of priests.

Although a devotee of Vishnu, Rama feels the excitement of this event among so many followers of Murugan. The hair on the back of his head stands up when a kavadi carrier passes in front of him, eyes half closed in abandonment to religious ecstasy while the tongue, protruding, is threaded by two crossed skewers.

Steepling his hands, Rama murmurs, *Om Sri Skandaya Namah.*

He knows the story of Murugan. What Tamil doesn't, although the story varies. He knows the version told to the boys of his village by their pundit. Once upon a time Shiva and Parvati were locked in the embrace of love for many hundreds of years, but so violent was their lovemaking that they shook the earth and frightened the other gods, who asked them to stop. Shiva agreed, spilling his love juice on the ground, but there was too much of it and so the forests and lakes were inundated, threatening the existence of the entire earth. The gods asked Agni, God of Fire, to swallow it, and so he did, carrying the love juice of Shiva for five thousand years. But finally it turned him yellow. To rid himself of Shiva's seed, Agni persuaded the River Ganga to take it from him, and so she did, opening her mouth and letting him spit it into her body, where it germinated and formed the divine child Murugan, who was born the way he entered—through her mouth. His image has six faces, honoring the six goddesses who suckled him.

Now Rama finds himself yelling in unison with the other spectators, many of whom are banging drums or tin cans to sustain a deafening noise. A man comes along with limes hanging from barbs dug into his back and stomach—they sway easily like green balls, stretching the bloodless skin from his bare torso. Slowly he twirls, making the limes follow a long smooth arc of motion, raising nodules of flesh that refuse to bleed. They refuse to bleed, Rama thinks, feeling the eyes roll in his own head. It is beautiful to go to God.

But then, among the carriers, he notices a young woman who balances on her head, with the help of both hands, a large milk pot decorated with flowers and fruit. Her head never bobbles, but her hips undulate under the blue sari; on her forehead there's sweat, her lips glisten. Rama can't take his eyes off this beautiful girl, and follows her alongside the procession, until the crush of onlookers squeezes him out of the front row. She vanishes into the surging mob.

Rama can feel the sweat pour down into his eyes, the salt stinging them. It's beastly hot, he thinks irritably, and glances at hawkers behind him in the pandals. Displayed on one of them are Chinese windup toys, some of which move jerkily along: bears, dogs, and dragons. His boys would like them, Rama thinks. And at another stall a man is selling cheap novels in Tamil. On one cover a young man and a girl are staring mournfully at each other; it's entitled *Their Sin*. He'd like to buy it, but is ashamed in front of all these people, under the watchful eyes of small boys who congregate around the pandals.

That girl with the milk kavadi was beautiful, he thinks. There are many girls in the crowd, festively decked out in their best silk saris with gold borders and jasmine entwined in the slick black coils of their hair. He covets them all. Suddenly, just as the wonder of religious devotion had raised the hair on his head, he now feels great battering waves of lust course through his body. Glancing sullenly at two girls, one in yellow and one in red, who stand nearby, he feels his loins fill with the blood of desire.

In the past few months he has often wanted a woman. He has even thought of brothels in Chinatown, although Chinese girls aren't attractive to him. Their slanted eyes are nothing compared to the big black limpid eyes of Tamil girls. And he's been shy of going to a Chinese brothel. What would they think of him there with his dark skin and big nose? Those delicate Chinese girls with their ivory skin and little noses would not like him, even for money, and charge him as much as a white foreigner.

There's always one of the brothels in a street off Serangoon Road, but he won't go to any of them. He has never gone to a brothel in his life, but if he ever did, Rama would not degrade a woman of his own country that way. It's a decision he has often explained to himself. And yet one night recently, he'd stood outside one of them and looked up at the second story, where girls in chemises passed the brightly lit windows. Leaning her elbows on the sill, a girl looked down at him and said pleasantly, "Don't be shy. Come on up. Ask for Kamla." On either side of the girl, laundry was hanging over the shutters to dry. A white flower was tucked into her hair. She smoked a cigarette and blew the smoke down at him. When he turned away, then turned back, Kamla giggled but said nothing when he turned away for good this time and strode down the street.

Kamla. He's remembered her name.

He can't stay here, Rama tells himself. Not among these women screaming in ecstasy, sweating, wearing flowers in their hair. Breaking free of the milling crowd, Rama wipes his brow—it is soaking wet—and turns toward home.

. . .

Home is on Veerasawy Road above a cattle shed converted a decade ago into a pickle factory, where Rama has been working as a handyman the last two months. He pounds on the barred door until it opens a crack, and a long-nosed little man peers myopically out at him.

"What's wrong with you?" the caretaker asks sternly. "Why aren't you at the festival?"

Rama brushes past him without answering.

"I don't see why I'm stuck here, while *you* get off and don't even go to the festival." He adds querulously, "What are you doing?"

Ignoring the little man—of a caste he'd not associate with back in India—Rama glances at the gingelli-oil press. It's a bulky iron machine that daily squeezes the oil from unroasted sesame seeds, adding a deep syrupy fragrance to air already pungent from the pickle vats where limes and mangoes are mixed with chilis, ginger, lotus stem, bishop's weed, karonda and dela fruits, a variety of spices.

"What are you doing?" Rama hears at his back as he mounts the stairway to the dormitory on the second floor, where most of the employees and a few tenants bunk. Ascending wearily, as if he's just put in a long day of work, Rama comes level with the floor, then above it stares at the narrow room flooded with morning light. Charpoys line both sides of it with an aisle running up the middle. On each of the hemp-string cots a wrinkled sheet is either folded or strewn. Clothes hang over lines stretched above the charpoys from one end of the room to the other; this single line is dresser and closet. Rama goes to his own charpoy and stares at it, broken down at the center, like a depression in the earth, with a faded sheet bunched at the foot. He looks around the room, as if expecting something from it, but aside from the clothes hanging on the line and the cots themselves, there's nothing here. If the clothesline and charpoys were removed, the room would be empty.

Bending down, he rummages under the bunched sheet to see if his umbrella is still there. He hadn't taken it with him this morning for fear of losing it in the crowd. Better take a chance in the dormitory than in the midst of a festival. It is there. Satisfied now, Rama lies down on the hemp strings, which give softly with his weight. Feeling exhausted, he pulls his legs up to his belly in a fetal position. His eyelids flutter and close his vision down to a furry slit. I will tone myself up, he thinks, but not now. Perhaps if he were hungry, he could go down to the backroom kitchen and make himself something. The cook, a friend, allows him to use the small brazier and kettles. He keeps his own tin of rice and another of dal on a shelf there in case he wants to cook something. Then he could bring it on a banana leaf up here and eat on the floor beside his charpoy, just as he does every night. Then he could smoke a Beedi, one of those potent little cigarettes he likes so much every night after eating.

That would be nice, but he won't move, not yet. Images swim softly in and out of his half-closed eyes: Miss Sonia in Shanghai, her face pinched and white, as she asked after her mother; Mistress in the nursing home, her face pallid too but not pinched at all—serene, masklike, because she was too proud ever to ask him where he thought her daughter had gone. Poor woman. Narayana. He recalls helping her down the hall to the Ladies' and waiting for her until the water flushed with a tumultuous cascade and she reappeared at the door, putting her hand out for him to take. His dark hand holding her white forearm on the way back. She was like a child then, a white child, but when her health improved, once again she was Mistress. And the anguish on the girl's face each time she asked about her mother. And where is Master? Dead, probably. Narayana.

Take food, he orders himself. But his eyes close altogether, so that everything is blotted out except for a wayward procession of images coming and going until he floats into a waking dream of golden light in a Tamil countryside. It is sunset, and a dark slim woman in a blue sari is balancing a brass jug on her head. She walks among the palms between flooded paddies. The brass jug, flashing in the sun, sends slivers of yellow back into the blue sky. It's like tiny explosions following the woman's progress through the fields. Her soft figure is stately; it halts and stands as poised as an egret beside the limpid surface of a paddy.

It is Usha.

Rama opens his eyes wide, then closes them again, so tired now that he lets his consciousness go in an instant, and he sleeps.

He awakes tumescent, his first thought for the girl carrying the milk kavadi in the Thaipusam ceremony. She had prominent curves, and while her head stayed motionless with the jar upon it, the rest of her moved liquidly down the street, as if there were no bones at all support-ing the buttery brown flesh.

Father once told him something the great Tagore had written: "Chas-tity is a wealth that comes from abundance of love."

Father said it was what a man looked for in a woman—chasteness, the ability to set aside temptation. Or how could you put trust in your children? Is Usha tempted? Surely she's one of the most handsome women in the village, lah, and he knows men of his acquaintance who would surely like to take her some balmy night into the fields and lie with her in the crackling stubble of the last harvest. The idea so angers and frightens him that Rama loses the tumescence immediately.

Usha is plucky. Narayana. If she were here today, he'd buy her a garland of jasmine threaded with colored tinsel at the big stall. And at other stores, if she stopped to look at something, he'd buy it for her. He'd buy sandalwood paste and rub it into her skin (how sweet the paste on her skin) and bottu, made from roasted sago, for her to mark her forehead with. He'd buy her bangles, hair clips, and on this particular day he'd buy her a peacock feather in honor of Lord Murugan. Together they'd study the silver and gold jewelry at the shop on Chitty Road, and perhaps there he'd buy her a locket embossed with the image of Lakshmi, if it weren't too expensive. Someday when he's rich, he'll buy a betel-nut silver set. It'll have a box with a concealed drawer for keeping the sirih leaves along with iron shears for slicing areca nuts. In the set there will be two round boxes for sliced pieces of tobacco or cloves, a goblet, and a cylindrical container for lime paste. He saw the perfect set in a store last week on Bamboo Lane.

And if they were living here with a place of their own, they'd shop together for spices, for coarse attar and refined Maida flour, and buy ghee and spices at the places he knows now. He'd buy her a pretty cotton choli, very close fitting across her breasts, and she'd look at him deeply from her large black eyes. Chastity is a wealth that comes from abundance of love. Narayana.

I will tone myself up, he tells himself.

How are the boys now? The youngest is ready for Upananyana, the ceremony of taking the sacred thread. Village boys must rag his sons for not having their father home. Boys can be cheeky chaps. He doesn't fancy his boys getting a ragging.

It's almost time for the mangoes to bloom again back home. He missed seeing them last year and now a second year will pass without him seeing them. Maybe he'll never again see the mangoes of his village. Rising to a sitting position, Rama cups his chin in his hands and composes a letter in his head.

Dear Wife Usha:
   You will kindly note I am sending rupees sufficient for your passage to Singapore and for those of the boys. I am thankful to you for obeying your husband.

He must write it in elevated language, because Uncle will surely read it and look for errors and vulgarity. But can he write such a letter? He has their passage money, but what if his new job on the railroad goes bad and after they arrive he can't make both ends meet?

Rama gets up.

Taking off his clothes, he hangs them carefully over the line and then from it takes a newly washed dhoti. With lightning speed his skilled hands tie on the triangularly folded loincloth, while holding one end with his teeth. Once the other two flaps have been tied around his waist, Rama takes this third end and pulls it under his crotch and into the crack between his buttocks. Then he folds the end under the cloth at the top of his buttocks. Neat as a pin. Done in twenty seconds. He slips on his best pair of sandals, ready now to go out. But where? As the caretaker would say, "What are you doing?"

Rama doesn't know. But having thrown off the morning's lethargy, he feels the need to go out, go somewhere, do something.

• • •

Rama wanders for a long time, so long in fact that the sun is glowing with a late mellowness against the white *chunam* plaster of Singapore walls, when finally he halts.

From the distance comes a low murmuring sound which, he knows, up close is the ecstatic chanting of thousands. Perhaps the celebrants have reached Vinayager Temple, and Brahman priests are paying homage to Sri Ganapati, the elephant-trunked god, in his sanctuary, scented by bruised flower petals and smoky from camphor burning in puja lamps.

I can be there, Rama thinks, and take darshan of the god. But later.

He stands in his white dhoti and white shirt, one hand grasping the rolled black umbrella, on the corner of a street deep in Little India. His throat is dry and gets drier, as he continues to stare at the three-story building. Frequently he says to himself what *The Gita* says: "What does God care for man's sin or righteousness?" It is true; man is nothing compared to God.

He is staring at the second floor, where the bottom set of wooden shutters at most windows are closed. It is too early yet for the girls to fling the shutters wide open so they can be viewed easily from the street. He remembers the exact window from which she'd leaned. It is that one with the upper half of the shutters pushed open, but with the frayed curtains hiding from view what's inside. A striped towel hangs over the lower shutter. Is it her towel?

Outside of the house two girls are squatting and talking. He can see them clearly from the corner. One girl wears jimikis of silver. His Usha would like to have long dangling earrings like those. Holding the idea of his wife in mind while staring at these whores so confuses Rama that he turns and strides away. Yet he doesn't go half a block before returning to resume his watch on the corner. A stout young woman comes out of the house carrying a naked baby on her hip. The three women chat and laugh together, although each of them, at intervals, returns Rama's stare and smiles invitingly at him.

Then, suddenly, he is walking toward the house. Without thinking, he is walking. What he feels is the constrictive dryness in his throat, a pulse throbbing at his temple so loudly that he wonders if people hear it. Fortunately, almost everyone in Little India is at the festival. Caretakers and whores are about the only people left at their posts. As he approaches, all three women rise and smile at him. The one with the child shifts it on her hip until its bare bottom faces him.

"Are you coming to see me?" she asks.

Wordlessly, he shakes his head and walks past them, hearing one say, "Imagine coming so early and on a festival day," and another say with a giggle, "He must really want it." Rama almost turns to run away, yet somehow he's set himself on this course, won't or can't deviate from it.

Just inside the doorway there's a dark hall. The sunlight follows him only a couple of steps into it, and he squints to see where to go.

"Over here."

Rama's sharp face hardens in concentration as he peers through the gloom in the direction of the voice. Then he sees a very large, very fat woman standing at the end of the hall. She swings a door back, illuminating with a shaft of electric light the hall and her purple sari and sagging face.

"You're early," she says in a pleasant, surprisingly thin voice. "Didn't you go to the festival? I thought everybody went except us and the Chinese." When he gets near, she smiles. "I thought for a moment you were Chinese. Sometimes they come on festival days, because it's not crowded. Leave it to the Chinese to think of that." Opening her pudgy hands out in unison—a gesture of helplessness—she exclaims, "What a way to live! I get so furious thinking about it, and I've been thinking about it all day, because there's nothing else to do. I pay the rent for this place *every day*. I mean, I pay each and every day." She backs through the open doorway, beckoning him in. "I rent from this Bengali who comes for his rent every day of the world. Won't even give me a month at a time, not even a week, but he lets the bitch on the third floor pay every month. Why is that? It's a good question. I don't know. Do you want anyone special?"

"Kamla."

Dabbing at sweat on her brow with a lace handkerchief, the madam nods with a broader smile. "You've had her before?"

Rama says nothing, but looks at the four-poster bed that takes up nearly all the room, save for a chair and a large iron safe and a wall closet with all four doors open, revealing a jumble of boxes, clothes, newspapers, even a couple of brass pots.

"How much?" he says, trying to control the sound of his voice. He holds out the imitation-leather change purse he bought last week in a Chinatown market.

"Pay her directly. That's how I run my house. Don't you remember?"

Nodding, he looks around in a rising panic.

"You don't remember. This is your first time here. Up those stairs," the madam tells him, giving him a curious look. "How do you know Kamla?"

"I spoke to her from the street once."

"She's a good girl. Second room on your right." Going to the door, the enormous woman cups her ringed hands at her mouth and yells, "Kamla! Customer!"

Rama is looking down, not straight at the big woman. He sees gold rings on each of her toes. As he eases past her, he notices watches on both wrists. A rich woman, he thinks.

Now he must climb the narrow stairway. Feeling weak in the legs, he supports himself at each step by placing his hand on the unsteady banister. He smells the deep woody fragrance of sandalwood upon reaching the upper floor. This aroma (sexual in memory because Usha used to smear such paste on her body when she came to him in the darkness) sends Rama forward, trembling in anticipation. In dread, too. Along the dark peeling wall a festive string of colored lights has been strung, leading him to the second room on the right.

The door is open, so he stands just outside it and looks at the girl sitting on a wooden bench. In one hand is a powder puff and in the other a round mirror. Her naturally dark face has been turned by powder into a ghostly white under a naked light bulb. Meeting his gaze, the girl says without changing expression, "Don't be shy. Come in."

"Don't be shy" assures Rama that she's the same girl. But he continues to stand there, staring at her and asking himself the question that the caretaker at the pickle factory might ask, that Usha and Lord Vishnu and Lord Murugan and Lord Ganesh might also ask of him: What is he doing?

"Are you coming in?"

He steps in. "Do you remember me?" he mumbles.

"What?"

In a louder voice he repeats it. "Do you remember me?"

"No," she says bluntly, but looking him over, after putting the mirror and powder puff on the bare wooden floor, she smiles. The girl is wearing a plain white choli and a half-slip of a blue and white check. That other time, seeing her from the street, he'd imagined her thinner. Now, as she sits there on the bench, he can see a little fold of flesh above the half-slip, her navel embedded in the brown expanse of her belly, and calves thick enough to vanish with hardly a curve into her ankles. The cushiony look of her abundant flesh excites him. Rama smiles timidly.

"You're lucky, you know," she tells him, leaning back on the bench against the wall. With a quick motion she pulls the slip up and spreads her legs wide. She is wearing nothing underneath the slip, and a patch of darkness there excites him further. "Everybody's at the festival, so you don't have to wait. Usually you have to wait on the bench here. Come on."

He follows the girl behind a curtain, which divides the room. The ceiling is high, so that the confined space, containing a bed and a wall closet and painted a dark green, seems like a shaft. In what little area is left there's a cement drain and a large jar of water.

"Did you see any of it today? I thought everyone went to the festival except us. I get tired of the same old place. People say I talk too much, but that's because you have to do *some*thing. We never get off but the one time she takes us to the movies each month."

He looks at her face closely for the first time. She has seated herself on the edge of the bed, over which is draped a bright yellow-and-red coverlet. She has a tiny nose jewel on her left nostril and a tinsel flower pinned to her swept-back hair. Her nose is flat, wide, her lips heavy and bruised looking. But he likes her eyes, even though they don't seem to be looking at him when they look at him.

"Did you see it? Did you see them carrying the kavadis? Why doesn't it hurt them? Are they drugged? Some people say so. Some people say it's because they pray to God. Did you go?" she asks again.

"Lah, for a little while."

"If you walked away from it just to come here, you don't believe in God, isn't that so?" There's a teasing tone in her voice.

"Narayana. Of course I believe in God."

With a little shrug, Kamla reaches back to unbutton the choli. When she yanks it off, her small firm breasts waggle a little. The sight galvanizes Rama, who leans down to embrace her, but she pushes him away. "Wait now," she says and removes the tinsel flower from her hair. "Remember, I don't let men kiss me on the lips." Still sitting on the bed, she lifts her buttocks and pulls down the slip. Folding it carefully, she drops it on a narrow shelf running above the bed, stretches lazily, and turns to Rama with a thoughtful smile. "You must want it pretty bad to miss the festival for it. So come on," she says, wriggling her tongue at him.

. . .

Rama turns modestly away to untie the dhoti, still keeping his white shirt on until the girl orders him to take it off. "You'll wrinkle it," she tells him maternally.

Now he doesn't hesitate, but falls upon her, and also without hesitation she opens her legs wide to make penetration quick and easy. She grunts at the impact and whispers against his ear, "Go slower, we've got plenty of time. You're lucky."

At first Rama thinks it will be over soon, because the warmth and wetness of her, coming after months of celibacy, surprises and excites him. And he wants it to be over soon. Working rapidly in her, he tells himself, Quickly quickly, and almost as quickly he remembers the village pundit telling the boys, "You are allotted only so many shootings and if you exceed your limit, you shorten your life." What if today he goes beyond his own limit and dies? Dies here in her arms, shaming his father's name? There's someone upstairs who is pacing back and forth in a steady rhythm similar to that he's using against the body of this girl. And a baby crying.

"All right, handsome man. If you want to so much, go on and shoot."

He works faster, wondering if this time he might die, and then suddenly the curtain is pushed back. He turns his face toward a girl standing there, one hand on the curtain, the other holding a cigarette.

"Can I borrow your necklace?"

"Which one?" Kamla asks, shifting a little to look at the girl, but keeping Rama inside.

"That one with the round locket on it."

"It's in the tin on top of the suitcase."

The girl moves over to the wall closet as Rama, motionless above Kamla, lifts his head in trembling curiosity to watch what she does. The girl opens the closet door, revealing clothes hanging on hooks and a shelf containing among its clutter a brass puja lamp, a garish poster of Lord Krishna as a child with his herd of cows, and a faded photograph of an old man. Holding the cigarette away from the hanging clothes so as not to burn them, the girl bends down to a battered suitcase tied shut with a rope. She opens a spice tin sitting on it and rummages around, coming out with a locket and chain. "This is the one. Thanks."

Rama watches her pull the curtain with a smile and hears her soft tread on the creaky floor and the door close.

"Come on, handsome man. What's wrong?"

He feels himself fall out, shriveling as though, on a cool morning, he has just splashed himself with cool water. Turning away from her, he draws his legs up to his chest.

There are only so many, the pundit said. He mustn't die here in shame.

"It's all right," Kamla says with a sigh. "This way I don't have to get up and wash right away. We can talk. We're lucky, we have the time."

He is staring at the curtain, hearing someone upstairs pacing rapidly.

"What kind of work do you do?" Kamla asks, her voice livelier now that they are lying side by side. When he sullenly replies, "Railroad," she throws one arm over him and puts her face right above his. "I like that. I wish I could do that. You travel around?"

"Yes." His eyes meet hers, then lower away from her face. He notices for the first time a tattoo on her arm, a word in a language he doesn't know. "What is that?"

"My name in Marathi."

"Are you from Bombay?"

"I was born and raised in Bombay. Bombay's my home." So Kamla begins talking in the rapid disconnected manner of someone who's afraid of being left. Years ago her father took passage from Bombay and set out to make his fortune. He worked on a rubber plantation in Malaya, then came here to Singapore with savings enough to set up a sarabat stall for ginger tea and in his letters he said it was very good tea, the best on the street, and so he could finally send for them, only by that time her mother was dead and she had been working on Falkland Road, but of course she didn't write her father that.

Falkland Road—it's a name young Indian men know. That's where the famous brothels of Bombay are. Three of his friends went there once, and the stories they told in the village drew whistles of wonder.

When she arrived on the dock in Singapore, her father hadn't been there to meet her. She found him dying of fever in the flat he'd rented for them, and after he died and the money ran out, she'd come to work here. Her boyfriend beats her and takes her money and picks pockets on Orchard Road. She doesn't care if the police catch him, lah, and she doesn't believe in God either, because why would a good god put her in a place like this if he cared for her?

Rama stares at her face, dark as Usha's now with the white powder rubbed off. He's been making love to a godless woman. "You can't look at God that way," he tells her anxiously.

"It's the only way I can." She raises her head in a gesture indicating the closet. "I keep the image of Lord Krishna in there, but I don't do puja any more. Lord Krishna never helped me, not once, and I was going every day to the temple and doing puja there too and spending all sorts of money on camphor and incense. It was too much money if I didn't get something in return."

"Try another god," Rama suggests. He wishes for eloquence, like that of the village pundit, but he thinks only of telling her she can't look at God that way. "Don't pray to Lord Krishna for a while," he says. "Try another god. Lah, he might listen to you." A godless woman. What have I done? Rama asks himself disconsolately. He's been holding a godless woman in his arms! What will happen to him? Rama shifts away, pushing her arm aside, extricating himself from contact with her.

"What's wrong? We have plenty of time. Want me to suck you?"

Rama sits up, facing away from her.

"You don't like me."

"Of course I like you." But he swings his legs around and sits on the edge of the bed, preparing to rise.

Kamla sits up too. "Don't be angry just because you didn't shoot. We have plenty of time. You're lucky today."

"I have to leave now." Getting up, he ties the dhoti around his waist and under his crotch and secures the cloth tail.

She's sitting cross-legged on the bed, her mouth turned down. "I talk to the girls a lot, but what do they know? They don't go anywhere, they don't see anything. They don't travel on trains like you do. Will you come back later? Will you tell me about it?"

Rama tries smiling at her, a godless woman, while buttoning his shirt.

"You don't like me."

"Yes, of course, lah. I like you."

"You wanted me but now you don't."

"That's because I have to leave now." He is opening his little money purse.

"Give me two ringgits. I'm honest, I won't cheat you."

Paying her the money, Rama stands there wanting to say something about looking at God in a different way.

"I split it with the Mother," Kamla explains. "One for her, one for me. She's the best Mother around here, but she's not having it easy," Kamla says in the rapid manner of someone trying to detain someone. "The Mother upstairs, she only pays once a month and throws in a girl for the owner when he wants one. But our Mother has to come up with money every day. Otherwise I wouldn't charge you at all."

Rama looks at her curiously. "Why?"

"Well, you didn't shoot." With a smile she adds, "And I like you. It must be wonderful to travel on the railroad."

This compliment returns him to good humor. For a moment he hesitates, thinking, well, why not? As *The Gita* says: God doesn't care for man's sins or man's righteousness. But a godless woman? What if he should die in her bed, shaming his father? "I have to leave now."

"You're lucky, you know. There won't be customers until after the festival, so you can come back and stay with me a long time, lah. We can talk about traveling. I'll see that you shoot, don't worry. It won't cost you either."

Rama feels the smile freeze on his face. "Thank you, I'll come back," he lies. If he comes back, in the next life he'll be one of those leeches he hates that come out after the monsoon rains, waving their feelers, shiny and slick as blood.

"You won't be long, will you? I haven't anything to do until the festival's over. It's lonely here on a festival day. You'd be lonely too, cooped up in here. Look how cramped it is. I never see anything except once a month when she takes us to the movie. Last month we saw an American movie. They had words in Tamil under it," Kamla tells him, kneeling on the bed, hands on her thighs, leaning forward so that the nipples of her small firm breasts tilt downward. "When you come back, lah, you can kiss me on the lips."

As he turns to plunge through the curtain and run out of there, he hears at his back, "Don't forget your umbrella."

• • •

He hasn't rushed more than three blocks away from the brothel before, on the street ahead, Rama sees a very old man seated against a shop wall with a bird cage on a crate next to him. The old man sees Rama at the same time and beckons. "Come here, young fellow. Vasu can tell you what you want to know."

This is no time for fortunetellers. He's still absorbing what he already knows: that a few minutes ago he was making love to a godless woman in whose arms he might have died. Yet the way lies near the fortuneteller's feet, so Rama keeps coming.

"That's right," the old man says with a nod. He wears a dirty white turban and a rumpled dhoti drawn up around skinny legs blackened by the sun. Something green is hopping around in the cage. "Vasu tells me you need help. You have money problems."

Struck by the accuracy of this remark, Rama stops.

The old man grins up at him. "That's right. You have some money, but not enough. Isn't it so?"

Rama nods.

Holding up a pack of well-thumbed cards, the old man says, "Vasu's the best fortuneteller in Singapore. Do you read? I have testimonials." Starting to rifle through folded bits of paper on his lap, the old man continues. "I understand Vasu's chirps, and he said, 'The young fellow coming down the street has money problems. He has some money but not enough.' "

"Not enough money for what?" Rama asks, wanting to be cautious.

"To provide."

"That's true."

"Cost you a ringget."

"I haven't got it."

"Half a ringget."

Rama, squatting, watches the old man shuffle the cards, then lift the cage door and thrust his hand in with the cards fanned out. A green parakeet shifts on its perch, cocks its yellow head, and stares from one black eye at the cards. Then with a fluttering of wings it lurches forward, grips a card in its beak, and is back on the perch in a single whirring instant. Taking the card from it, the old man turns to Rama. "Vasu's the best bird in Singapore. You can count on that, young man. You saw the testimonials. It's a nine. See?"

Rama looks closely at the card.

"That's good, a nine," the old man says. "You will marry, have sons."

"But I am married and I have two sons."

The old man nods vigorously. "That's what I'm saying. You will have more sons." The parakeet is chirping.

"When?"

"Vasu won't say when. But you'll solve your money problems and someday—Vasu says it—you are going to move closely with big shots on Serangoon Road."

"I'll have more sons?"

"Vasu's never wrong."

Minutes later, continuing down the street, Rama hears from the second story of a house two women arguing in Tamil. Back home in his village his two boys, unless asleep, are probably arguing in the same dear language. And Usha will be close by, working at something, with the smell of sandalwood hovering about her thighs and breasts. Narayana. She would like the flowers here in Singapore. She likes flowers almost as much as he does, and once, when he said to her, "Wouldn't it be nice to talk to flowers?" instead of laughing at him, she'd nodded solemnly.

Overhead it's clouding up, is clouded up in another minute. He has been heading toward the harbor, why he doesn't know, and he reaches there just as the storm breaks. Opening his umbrella, Rama stands on a deserted pier and looks out at the harbor; the water is like milk in the downpour, a churning mass of whiteness, neither land nor sea nor sky distinguishable, but just this moiling milkiness out of which, in a couple of minutes, tugs and liners appear. The savage pelting on his umbrella slows down to a steady musical rhythm. The water is gunmetal gray, and clouds of blue-gray have pink bellies as they lumber out to sea. Out to sea. Liners, tugs, ferries emerge on the horizon. Smoke rising from a stack becomes mixed with the clouds, gray into gray, a colorless steamy muck above the water of Singapore. Going out to sea. The rhythm on the cloth above him slows to a few soft beats, and the sky lightens perceptibly. Bows of motorboats plowing through the green water wear white mustaches, and when the rain completely stops, there are patches of blue in the sky. The edge of a single cloud pulls free from a swollen mass of them and defines the position of clouds in front of and behind it, until the whole sky appears to be swinging into motion and twisting free of the storm bank, breaking up the immense force into myriads of little clouds, and then a burst of intense sunlight slants down on the water, making it a brilliant sheet of emerald, like a polished gem he'd like to buy Usha, a gem he'd seen in a store, and God has spoken to him, Narayana. Because this is a sign, here, on the water, where the boats are bobbing and preparing for sea and where the sky has just revealed the almighty power of God.

"I will tone myself up," Rama says aloud in English, as if that language adds gravity to the vow.

Folding and tightly rolling his umbrella, Rama squints into the late afternoon light, made especially brilliant by the glitter of wet walls and streets. He will tone up his life, he will move out of ordinary circles and be a glory to his community. He will make both of his ends meet somehow, hadn't Vasu said so? And someday he'll move closely with big shots on Serangoon Road. And if it doesn't work, well, then it doesn't. That will only mean his karma hasn't been good enough this time for him to get the result he desires. Then he'll simply pray to Lord Vishnu and Lord Murugan and Lord Ganesh and Lord Shiva and the other gods, forget his ambitions, and wait for the next time around. Meanwhile, the world's ahead of him. He'll have them take passage on one of the boats that appeared out of the mist in the harbor after the storm. It was a sign. He will tone up and provide for them when they come. And he won't die as Kamla's father did and leave them waiting on the pier with their suitcases, bewildered and helpless. He won't shoot with other women and tempt fate. He'll tempt fate that way only with Usha. When she comes to him, her skin smelling of sandalwood, he'll put himself in God's hands because that's all a man can do.

And he'll do more.

Rama quickens his pace, swinging the umbrella and heading for Tank Road, where the festivities will end this evening at the Murugan Temple.

Because he must do more than send for them, even more than provide. He must show God what he feels. He has much to be thankful for. For example, drought not coming, a miracle of God. And the money given him by Mistress to pay their passage. And the railroad job just like his father's, so he can travel but come home too. He has already seen so much of the world and in the company of white people, who found more in him than another cowherd or bearer. He has seen things and learned what it is to lose what matters most, the woman of his bosom, the children of his loins. He's lost them and must find them again.

If he sends for them tomorrow, maybe they'll be here for Deepavali, the Festival of Lights. Deepavali means freedom, doesn't it? A new life. The four of them, together, will have a new life for as long as it lasts. There is no time really, there is only the conflict between good and evil and it lasts forever, so time doesn't count. Time does not count. It is all in *The Gita*. Only what the heart does, only that counts. He won't ever be a *jnani*, a realized soul. At least not in this life. But next year, if they come safely to him here, he vows to carry his own kavadi on Thaipusam Day.

At this very moment he vows it: If they come to him here, he will honor Lord Murugan by carrying a *slav kavadi* of his own. He can see himself now, buying the paraphernalia at a specialty shop and having the boys help him assemble it. Both boys, even the little one, will help him attach peacock feathers to the frame and a flower arrangement on top of it and then the tinsel-and-jasmine garlands along each metal strut and then help him lift the whole complex frame to rest upon the yellow pads on his shoulders and fasten the supports into the leather girdle at his waist and then—they won't cry, they won't falter—they'll help him place the dozens of hooks securely into the flesh of his back and chest while he praises Lord Murugan and Lord Shiva and Lord Vishnu and all the gods, Narayana, and then the boys will steady his head while someone drives the skewers through his outstretched tongue and through his cheeks, but without blood, because his mind will be on God, Narayana, and because he'll be thanking God for holding back the drought so these boys wouldn't starve and because he'll be doing penance, too, for running away like the coward he was because he couldn't bear to see them starve, and so there won't be blood or only a little of it because of his devotion, *Om Bhagavate Namah, Om Namo Narayanaya*, and he will carry sixty-five pounds, half his weight, through the streets of Singapore with metal barbs hooked in his flesh, because God is a great pleasure and the gods give us pleasure, Narayana, if we please them.

Rama quickens his pace through the late afternoon, anxious to see the kavadi carriers stagger the last few paces into the temple on Tank Road.

46 FOR THE FIRST time in thirty years Vera Rogacheva Embree is alone. Of course, there are the three old servants in the house, but essentially she's alone—no lover, no husband, no child.

It's hot now in Bangkok. The warm days and cool nights have merged into one steaming twenty-four hours followed by another, so that the teak in the house no longer creaks from expanding and contracting in response to a temperature change; there is no temperature change. It's hot in the morning, even before sunlight has risen into the top leaves of a tree where that old hoolook gibbon and his mate sit, picking lice from the folds in each other's neck.

Vera sits under them at a shaded lawn table with a view of the muddy klong straight ahead and of the Spirit House to the left, through a grove of mango trees. With a handkerchief she wipes her forehead, dabs at sweat along her upper lip. It is the hot season, all right, and her German doctor has warned her to keep out of the sun. She tires easily, but there's no more of the shoulder pain that plagued her in the early months of recovery.

I will survive, Vera thinks, looking at the sluggish klong between interstices in the vegetation. I will survive, but to what purpose?

On the table sits a bowl of purple mangosteens. Her appetite has returned with a vengeance. For breakfast this morning she had water apples, soft and juicy within their waxy pink skins, and tart mangoes and a piece of bland papaya. But that hadn't been enough. She'd gone into the kitchen just to stare at other fruit awaiting her today: starfruit, brown egg-shaped chiku, and thorny durian, and jackfruit as big as rugby balls, and hairy red plum-sized rambutan. Her mouth watered. Cook grumbles a lot these days, having little to do but shop for fruit and argue with Ah Ping, who has become tyrannical in the household since Mistress returned from China a cripple. Or at least that's what Ah Ping thinks—a cripple.

But Vera feels in herself a steady renewal of energy; soon she won't even be feeling tired from climbing the stairs. She will survive, although to what purpose without someone to look after, to think about, to love? Picking up the newspaper, Vera forces the grim question out of mind.

Much has happened lately in the world beyond this garden. The new state of Israel has signed armistice agreements successively with Egypt, Lebanon, Trans-Jordan, and there's a report that another will be signed with Syria. So they'll have peace there, she thinks. The Middle East is solving its problems, unlike Asia, where conflict increases daily. Folding the pages carefully, Vera reads each column with a deliberately achieved sense of leisure in the enclosed garden. An American jet has flown across the United States in three hours forty-six minutes. Britain has devalued the pound sterling from U.S. $4.03 to $2.80. Richard Strauss has died

—she never liked his music very much. Colette's *Le Fanal Bleu* has just appeared. Vera will have her agent in Singapore get a copy for her. Now that the Berlin airlift has ended, Europe seems to be quiet. Good. Apartheid has been established as the official policy of the governing Nationalist Party in South Africa. What will that lead to? Nothing good. But nothing worse, probably, than what's happening out here. China, Malaya, Korea—apparently lost to reason and order.

There's a long article this morning about the Dutch Foreign Minister announcing from The Hague that the Indonesian government's sovereignty will be recognized as soon as guerrilla activity ceases in the islands. But it won't cease, will it, Vera thinks, and the killing will continue. It always does. Bao Dai has established a new government in Saigon. What will that lead to? Nothing good either.

And nothing good will come of the Bolsheviks taking over China. That is beyond dispute. And now Taiyuan has fallen. Mao and his pack of Bolsheviks have taken up residence in Peking, while the Nationalists have moved a lot of their offices from Nanking to Canton, a sure sign they expect the capital to fall soon. Vera lowers the paper, letting it crinkle up on her lap. From the klong comes the sound of oars splashing through the hot syrupy water.

Nothing good will happen in China when the Bolsheviks assume power. Nothing good has come of the Bolsheviks since 1919, when they destroyed Mother Russia.

It has been more than four months since she left Shanghai, and nothing good can come out of that place for a generation, even if, by a miracle, the Bolsheviks don't grab it. Because war has destroyed the city even before troops have clashed in it. Shortages of coal and electricity and rice, coupled with incredible inflation, have destroyed Shanghai as effectively as fighting in the streets might have done.

The memory of Shanghai during her last days there, in late November, convinces Vera that there's more than one way to murder a people: You can murder them simply by taking away the value of what they own. You can do it by telling people who have scrimped and saved all their lives that their savings aren't enough any more to buy a pound of rice. And you can kill people by smothering them in money, just as Chiang Kai-shek did before Rama got her on a ship and took her out of that hellish place, out of the Shanghai of her youth, the Jewel of the Orient no longer, where a newspaper cost $25,000 Chinese, and the cost of printing $10,000 exceeded the note's value.

Every day in the nursing home, sitting in its garden with a shawl around her shoulders, Vera had read about the death of a city, the looting of it as if rampaging soldiers had entered its streets. She read with horror about the riots, the executions of officials ordered by other officials, the suicides of helpless women and despairing merchants, the ensuing famine that claimed children as its first victims, the breakdown of any authority except the gun. She read daily about devastation fanning out from the business district into the suburbs until uncounted corpses lay festering in the cool mornings of November with no one to remove them—as if a tremendous battle was raging in the streets of Shanghai.

And so she'd once again left the China of her youth, a land of art and poetry but also the scene of war and suffering beyond measure, crushed finally not by armies but by fiscal policies created from the need to have armies.

No good will come from the Bolsheviks any more than good came from the Nationalists.

Vera throws the newspaper on the ground. Up in the tree the gibbons are stirring, and she looks at them in time to see the big male swing across to the adjoining tree, his long arms like ropes thrown gracefully through the air, his black-ringed eyes as big as an owl's. The female lunges, airborne, and joins him. We down here should envy them, Vera thinks. Where is she? Where is my daughter now?

• • •

Ah Ping is coming across the lawn, her pouched eyes wide and wary, as if she's a general in the midst of a campaign. "Workmen with that thing have come, Mistress."

"That thing" is a telephone, which at Jim Thompson's insistence Vera is having installed. Ah Ping doesn't believe in the contraption, arguing that if messages need to be sent, she can do it or Nipa can run them along or Nipa's niece or Cook if need be. It's dangerous to put trust in something undependable like electricity or whatever runs that thing. And aside from Ah Ping's objections there's the cost; it's very expensive to have a private telephone in Bangkok. But Jim's right—without it she's cut off from the world, especially now when she goes to the shop only two or three times a week and spends most of her time right here, in the garden of her house. Not that she minds staying home. It's a luxury after years of struggle. A weak heart is enabling Vera to look at the world calmly for the first time since her girlhood.

"Tell them to get started," Vera says.

Folding gnarled hands in front of her paunch, Ah Ping hesitates. "Then you will have it put in, Mistress?"

"Yes. You can tell them to get started."

"They have tools for breaking down walls."

"For making a few holes, Ah Ping."

"For breaking down everything, Mistress." After a pause she drops her hands and sighs. "The thing will make noise, it will go ding ding ding in the middle of the night."

"Tell them to get started."

Glaring a moment longer, the old woman turns and heads across the lawn, her feet slightly turned in, giving her a jerky gait.

Soon Vera hears Ah Ping's voice raised in high, querulous protest and a deeper male voice replying.

They will have at each other all morning, Vera thinks. It's good to be here in this garden. And with "that thing" giving her new access to some of the world, at least. Jim has been a good friend as well as a fine business partner. The silk company is a going concern. All of the Moslem weavers are now using foot-operated shuttles and color-fast dyes from Switzerland. Orders from abroad have started to come in, thanks to Jim's flair for merchandising. Clearly she stands to make a great deal of money on her impulsive investment, but to what purpose? She has enough for herself from the proceeds of the shop. There's no daughter to send abroad now for an education, none of those exciting expenses involved in selecting clothes and luggage.

Vera picks up a piece of fruit, holding it absently in her hand while dreaming of Sonia on the deck of a liner, waving from the rail as it lumbers away from the dock, blowing clouds of smoke into the air, bound for Europe or America, taking her into the sort of adventures a pretty and intelligent woman ought to have in her youth.

Perhaps Jim will come around today to check on the phone installation. He's like that. Yesterday he showed up with some of his new designs, exuding the enthusiasm of a child. "Someday I'd like to have a house like this," he said, glancing around.

"Not like this. Better," she'd told him. "Yours will be better." And it's true that he has a strong aesthetic sense, if not yet well articulated. He's bought a Khmer clay sculpture, a Ching vase from her, and she has had to restrain him from buying other, less worthy things. Jim takes pills for a gall-bladder problem, smokes too much. She fusses over him like a mother, and he loves it. Jim's a good friend in his brash American way. He returned recently from a trip to Indonesia to see the batiks there. Called Sukarno an opportunistic swine who plays Moslem against Red for his own political ends. "It's explosive," Jim declared.

"Dear Jim, everything's explosive to you."

"Because most things out here are. Except in Siam—Thailand."

His slip was understandable; everyone, including Vera, slips once in a while. Prime Minister Phibun has recently changed the country's name again from Siam to Thailand as a tactic for stimulating nationalistic fervor. *Mai pen rai.* What it has meant to Vera is the need to paint a new sign above her shop: THAI ORIENTAL ARTS instead of SIAM ORIENTAL ARTS. So much for Thailand—land of the free people—even though Jim Thompson constantly urges her to pay attention to politics. Well, she's tried. She knows a few things. Phibun's new constitution has removed nearly all authority from the National Assembly. She knows the governmental agencies are dominated by the army, which bribes and cheats its way to election victories. In return for financial deals many Thai bureaucrats serve on the board of directors of Chinese firms that otherwise can't get licenses from the ministries. What more should she know?

But Jim will come over, mopping his forehead, staring from his startled eyes, lighting one cigarette from another while fulminating over the vagaries of Thai politics. From her point of view, it's nothing more than comic opera—the only politics she can abide. At nineteen she ceased to believe in political systems; at almost fifty, she has no intention of putting her trust in them again.

Comic opera—that's what she called it when Jim Thompson came roaring in a couple of months ago with the latest news: Quite out of the blue, Pridi Phanomyong had appeared on the Thai scene again. Disguised as a naval warrant officer and wearing a full mustache, Pridi entered the University of Moral and Political Sciences on the grounds of the Grand Palace along with Lieutenant Vacharachai, the aide who had escaped with him to China, and at least two dozen navy men. Another group took over the radio station in the Public Relations Building and announced that a provisional government had installed a new prime minister who would restore a democratic constitution. Pridi hoped for support from the marines and navy against the army, but most of the junior officers in the navy pulled out of the coup attempt, and so it failed. Nor had Prime Minister Phibun been captured by Pridi and the insurgents. In fact, Phibun managed to surround the Grand Palace with artillery and tanks, although not in time to prevent Pridi and his comrades from escaping and seeking exile again in China.

Vera's reaction? She laughed, much to the dismay of Jim Thompson, who persists in taking it all seriously.

Poor Jim. Poor men, all of them, who play at politics with the same feckless naïveté as boys play at war. All of them: the men whose mistress she'd been; her longtime German lover, the weapons salesman Erich Luckner; and Shan-teh, who of them all seemed most capable of transcending the brute instincts he needed to survive; and then Philip Embree, doomed to pursue senseless adventure; and even this dear harmless man Jim Thompson, who sweats Thai politics as if it has some kind of meaning.

. . .

Now she hears banging within the house. Perhaps Ah Ping is right; these workmen, trying to install the telephone, may well be breaking down the walls. And that, too, is the way of men—a broad thrust of energy without definition, indifferent to consequence.

Ah Ping is coming across the lawn again, this time with the tiny figure of Prakit Chaidee following her. Although he comes to Vera almost every morning for consultation (often it's nothing more than a courtesy call), Ah Ping insists on bringing him out to the garden like a proper guest.

And with his own sense of decorum Prakit Chaidee insists on standing in the presence of his employer, while telling her in detail what's happening at the shop. Workmen have knocked out the wall between their place and that of the money changer from Bombay, who finally sold her his corner location. A new shipment of art objects has come from Burma, including iron opium weights in the shape of elephants, birds, and gods; mother-of-pearl inlaid screens; and some ivory covers for palm-leaf manuscripts, quite rare. A shipment from Singapore has also arrived. Vera's agent there has sent Formosan coral, brass and crystal, Japanese pearls, and rather crudely done wood carvings from Malaya, along with a letter suggesting that increased tourism in the East should encourage her to buy cheaper things in bulk as well as expensive items for sale.

Vera knows this already. She intends to stock the corner annex with the sorts of things uninformed tourists will want to take back from Thailand. With no more effort than following the implications of this single insight, she can be exceedingly successful. Of course.

And that's the plan she will follow, but to what purpose?

There's a note from Professor Silpa Bhirasri; he's called a Friday meeting for the Committee of Citizens to Preserve Thai Art. Topic: preservation of dry-fresco murals in wats. He has also invited Vera to attend a lecture of his own on mural technique. Topic: the use of ki-lek leaves to remove salt from wall surfaces in preparation for applying chalk and tamarind-seed binder.

She will go to both the meeting and the lecture.

Her Chiang Mai agent, Pakhoon Chirachanchai, has found another priceless relic in a field.

Vera laughs.

Even Prakit Chaidee, generally cool and impassive, can't suppress a smile. Then he produces a letter from Germany. A collector from Heidelberg wants a set of paintings on koi paper, a *thotsachat*, representing the last ten births of Buddha. She doesn't have a *thotsachat* available, but Prakit Chaidee reveals that a west side monastery does. Moreover, the abbot needs money, so he'll sell it to her. How lucky she is to have Prakit Chaidee: loyal, industrious, cunning. But to what purpose is she lucky? To succeed in an enterprise that has no discernible goal save the accumulation of wealth? And yet wealth brings power, and power is not boring. Perhaps that's what motivates her, Vera thinks: the fear of being bored in the face of being lonely.

Having finished business, Vera reminds him to put a flower at the foot of the tuber root figure, *wan nang kwak*, that sits on her desk for good luck. Within the house there's insistent banging. How big is the telephone they're installing? Vera wonders ruefully. But she mustn't act concerned in front of Ah Ping.

As the noise increases, she smiles at Prakit Chaidee, who stands in the shade, looking cool in his white shirt. The flame-shaped tattoo on his left forearm seems almost too physical for his delicate features. He's a good man, she thinks. Prakit Chaidee and Jim Thompson, two good men. And her own household contains women vigilant in their protection of her. Does she deserve them all?

After Prakit leaves, Vera bites into the water apple, savoring the released flavor as warm wet fibers give way under the pressure of her teeth. Food. What is there for her now except its pleasures? Since returning to Bangkok, she's never asked for the whereabouts of Wanna, and no one has volunteered any information. She won't ask, ever. Does she still care? Of course. What frightens her is the possibility of learning by accident where the girl is and with whom.

Ah Ping is coming across the lawn again, this time almost running, her mouth opened in an O of astonishment.

• • •

"It has come, Mistress, it has come, I know it!" The old woman is waving an envelope. "I know her handwriting! It's hers, I know it, it has come, Mistress!"

Frantic with anticipation, Ah Ping continues waving the letter, although Vera has her hand outstretched to receive it. Unable to give it up, Ah Ping stands beyond the circle of shade under blazing sunlight. Her mottled forehead is sweaty, and strands of iron-gray hair have come loose from their bun. "I can tell her handwriting, I know it. It's hers. She has written, Mistress. I know it!"

"Ah Ping."

"I know it, Mistress, it's hers! Finally! I *told* you it would come!"

"Ah Ping!" Leaning forward, she stretches out both hands to take it.

When Vera has the envelope—thin, torn along one edge, the address smudged almost into illegibility—she just stares at it, hearing the little servant continue the stunned, boastful, expectant commentary.

Rama used to work in the Indian postal service; Vera remembers that now. Such lean hands, dark as mahogany—sorting letters like this one, letters that hold destinies in their folded, harmless-looking pages. There's joss inside this crinkled envelope. Joss good or bad.

"I told you! I knew it was coming! I said to Nipa—you know how she believes nothing—I said to her it will be coming very soon now. I said that only yesterday. But you know Nipa. When I said it, she—"

"Ah Ping."

The old woman makes no move to leave. Her sandaled feet look planted in the lawn, rooted there until whatever the letter contains is fully hers.

"I want tea, Ah Ping."

"It's her handwriting, isn't it, Mistress? I knew it was coming. That girl won't forget us. I said—"

"*Tea*, Ah Ping. *Now. Please.*"

Watching the old woman shuffle reluctantly across the lawn, Vera puts the letter down on the table, picks it up, puts it down again. Ah Ping has had more faith in this letter coming than she herself had. She'd never expected to hear from her daughter again. Or at least she'd steeled herself never to expect it. And now here it is.

Picking it up again, Vera holds the letter a few moments in both trembling hands before carefully slicing the envelope open with the fruit knife lying beside the plate of apples.

Dear Mother [in English],

It has been so long, yet you must not believe I forgot or was indifferent or never wanted to write you. I have waited until now because it seemed the right time. [Right time? The girl forgot to date the letter. When was it written?] I am now living in Peking. I was here last month when the People's Liberation Army entered the city. [Last month? That means late January; she must have written and mailed this letter in late February or early March.] There were bands, truck floats, congratulatory banners, armored cars, columns of infantry and cavalry, and truckloads of waving soldiers. It was exciting. And I saw Chairman Mao standing up in a jeep. There was no bloodshed at all, and the change of city government took place without incident.

I am happy to be here. [Fool, Vera thinks, lifting her eyes away from the paper a moment, as if reading it has become unbearable. Happy to be among Bolsheviks!] It is a wonderful city. The light is yellow from the dust carried in it.

I am happy here. There is so much to say, but to put it all in a letter would be impossible. I miss you. That is one thing I can say easily and truly. The longer I'm away the more I realize how close we've actually been. You were always good to me, Mother. I won't forget that, ever. Don't worry about me here. I am managing very well. Because of my languages I have got a fine job translating materials for a news agency. I will be moving soon from my present lodgings. They are tearing down the section of town where I live in order to build new housing for workers. You see, already the new China is rising. [Fool. Mouthing their Bolshevik slogans.] When I am located, I will let you know the exact address. If Philip contacts you, let him know too. [There it is! Philip!] We haven't made contact yet, but it's only a matter of time. He might try to reach me through you.

I know how you feel about that. [Do you really? Can you possibly know?] But I have never asked you for anything I wanted more than your help in finding him again. I know he's here in China. I know he's trying to reach me. We belong together—that is one certainty in my life. If only you knew. [Knew what? What is there about this situation I don't know?] Please trust my judgment, and if he contacts you, let him know where I am. They say we will be relocated soon on the west side, near the Tartar City. I will send you the exact address. [Second time she's mentioned that.]

If he comes to Peking, I know everything will work out for us and I know that when it does you will understand and accept it. [What I can hope for, Vera tells herself, lowering the paper to her lap and looking across the lawn, is Philip's fatal indecisiveness.]

I hope this letter gets to you, Mother. Mail is leaving from Tientsin regularly now, but they say the Nationalists have set up a blockade in the China Sea. I will let you know where I am. And I beg you not to hate Philip, because I love him and he loves me and fate somehow will bring us together again. I believe that as much as I believe in your love for me. You must know that whatever happens, my love for you is still as strong as it ever was. If you see Lamai, tell her I love her too. Tell the servants I think of them. I think of all of you.

Yours,
Tang Yu-ying

• • •

So she loves me, Vera thinks. Has there ever been doubt of that? Curiously, that has always been certain in Vera's mind. Their mutual love has been fixed, a given in the midst of chaos and folly.

Vera gently folds and unfolds the letter. She smiles. No mistakes in spelling. Sonia must have used a dictionary. An English dictionary in revolutionary China. Proper young woman writes proper letter. A concession? But there's no concession in the closing use of the assumed name Tang Yu-ying. She might just as well have written, "I am Chinese, as I claimed to be at the breakfast table when we argued about my nationality. I am my father's daughter, whatever you say. And whoever once used the name Yu-ying, whore or great lady, it is now mine."

Stubborn, Vera thinks. Like me.

Clenching the letter, she stares at the brown patch of klong visible between the leaves.

Don't think about the letter, she tells herself. It's too important to think about too quickly. Casting about for something else to think about,

Vera remembers something that happened in Singapore when she stopped there on the way out of China in December. Her agent had come to Raffles for a talk, after which Vera had nothing to do. Calling a taxi, she rode aimlessly through the streets of Singapore—or so she thought, but somewhere along the way she must have given the driver an address familiar to her from the time she lived there.

Getting out of the taxi, she stood in front of half a dozen shops that sold pet birds. In the old days, drawn here by memories of Shan-teh, who loved songbirds, she had strolled past the varnished bamboo cages and wondered which of the larks and canaries and finches he'd have preferred. A morbid pastime. It had always sent her home to Philip in a mood of bitterness.

Visiting the bird shops on that last trip to Singapore had been no different: She'd returned to Raffles doubly weighed by the loss of Shan-teh and of their daughter. At a table in the Palm Court, under sunset clouds riding the sky in a tormented orange glow, Vera had hoped to have Philip once more in her presence to assure him of his profound success in ruining her life.

One of Vera's first acts upon returning to Bangkok was to sell the mynah bird, Taksakan, whose vocabulary had consisted of one word, *"Choei!"* No more screeched-out warnings of trouble. Think of that, not of the letter. Think of birds. But thinking of birds is a way of thinking of Sonia's father and Sonia's lover and so Vera comes around to the letter again. What of everything in it is most painful? Her daughter living so far away? And in a country of uncertain future? With Bolsheviks?

Each of these things is painful. Yet the most pain comes from the girl's desperate infatuation with Philip Embree.

She can feel the heat closing in, drawing an invisible band around the greenery of the garden. Yet it isn't heat that causes her to rise and start for the house. She must go to Sonia's room. Now, this minute.

The banging has stopped in the living room, where they're installing the phone (Jim says if she likes it, then she must also put one in her bedroom), and after a glance at the workmen huddling against the wall with both Ah Ping and Nipa hovering critically above them, Vera slowly mounts the stairway. She no longer becomes short of breath before reaching the top, although today, perhaps because of emotion, Vera feels lightheaded, slightly dizzy, by the time she opens the door to Sonia's room.

Steadying herself against the door frame, Vera looks around. She's kept everything in order, so that Sonia might walk in here tomorrow and feel at home again. There's one change, of course: The sandalwood cabinet that had contained her diaries is now empty, the doors to it deliberately swung wide open. On the walls the framed batik paintings.

Bed with a brocaded coverlet. Thai dancing dolls in their ornate dresses and rhinestones, set, all eight of them, on a bench along one wall, just as they'd been there when Sonia got too old to play with them any more.

And the *ranad ek*. Vera walks into the room and sits down in a chair beside the French desk, feet wide apart, elbows on knees. She stares at the classical xylophone that Philip gave Sonia for her tenth birthday.

Vera remembers him coming in with the *ranad ek*, grinning happily.

"She won't play it," Vera told him.

Sonia had never shown musical ability, much to her mother's disappointment. Vera herself had studied piano in a childhood marked by the need to play Chopin's études, however poorly.

"She won't play that thing," Vera said, grimacing at the bow-shaped instrument of polished wood.

But Embree had insisted on carrying it up to the girl's room.

And it has been there, untouched, ever since. Vera can't recall the girl even picking up the mallets, let alone striking the wooden blocks with them.

Now Vera stares at the *ranad ek*. The Thai diatonic scale is composed of seven full tones within the octave. Where did she learn that? The mind becomes filled with meaningless information. Getting older, she thinks, you have to pick through garbage to locate a valuable idea, carelessly flung in with the trash. Perhaps Philip told her about the diatonic scale. His mind has always been a trash dump of worthless facts.

Vera stares at the *ranad ek*. What she does know about it is this: In a *piphat* orchestra it usually plays variations; the principal melody is assigned to the *gong wong yai*. She knows where that bit of meaningless information came from—from Wanna. But Wanna, raised on an orchid farm, never played a musical instrument, so where did she learn something so esoteric about music? No doubt from a lover. Because most of what the lovely girl knows has been learned in bed.

A mean-spirited observation, Vera thinks.

She rises and stands over the *ranad ek*. They play it sitting cross-legged on the floor. Reaching down, she picks up a mallet and hefts it in her hand. Sonia never tried to play it, not once. Sound never interested her. What she liked was to write secrets in a diary and hide them away or to carry on imaginary conversations that the servants pressed their ears against the door to overhear.

Bitterness and loneliness are twin demons, she thinks.

Lightly she strikes the mallet against one of the resonant wooden bars; it emits a deep, pure tone, giving the illusion of coming from a distance. Cocking her head, Vera listens until the vibrations, wavering, fade and vanish. Then she strikes another wooden bar, another, another, and without thinking about it, Vera brings down the mallet on the rim of the instrument with enough savage power to snap its slim wooden handle.

Then she's kicking the *ranad ek* in the side, kicking until it falls off its small square pedestal. Reaching down, Vera gathers up the xylophone, an awkward armful, and half pushes, half throws it against the wall. Without hesitation she lifts it again, again throws it. This time, one whole frail side is bashed in. Driving her foot against the percussion boards, she springs loose a couple from their leather ties. Once more she lifts the instrument and throws it, releasing the ties from their end moorings and thereby freeing a group of wooden bars to spill from their frame, like teeth knocked out of a mouth.

Vera is puffing now, feeling heat in her face, the pounding of her heart. Nevertheless, she bends once more to lift the *ranad ek*, now a jumble of splintered wood and leather thongs. In spite of shortness of breath, she manages once more to hurl this mass against the wall, dislodging a framed batik print.

Vera sinks to the floor, panting hard. She glares at Philip Embree's broken gift.

A band of constriction around her chest prevents her from rising to throw it again. Turning slightly, she notices in the doorway both workmen, mouths agape, and Ah Ping and Nipa, all four of them crowded into the narrow opening for a better look at what's going on.

She manages to smile a little. "Don't worry," she pants. "It's all right." Glancing back at the ruined xylophone, she says at it, "I'll survive." Working to get her breath, Vera mutters, "And she'll come back."

Starting to rise, she waves off the two servants who come toward her. "No," she tells them sharply. "Let me alone." Sinking down again, Vera sits cross-legged. Turning her head slowly, she looks at the wreckage. The sight of it brings a smile to her sweaty, pallid face. "I'll be here. I will. I'll survive."

47 DURING HIS FIRST days with the People's Liberation Army, Philip Embree was often interrogated.

One Red officer insisted on using English, although his English was less effective than Embree's Chinese. It became clear to them both that he was more interested in practicing a language than in learning anything from Embree. Another interrogator, more serious, questioned Embree in Chinese about a Manchurian espionage network that he claimed once operated out of the American Consulate in Mukden. "Were you part of that operation?" the officer asked.

"I've never been to Mukden."

"Did you supply radio transmitters and secret codes to KMT operatives?"

"I've never been to Mukden. I've never been to Manchuria."

"Why is the American government persecuting the people of China?"

"I don't know anything about that."

The man chain-smoked; each time he took out a cigarette, however, he offered it first to Embree, who always refused. "In 1944 the Chinese Communist Party celebrated your Fourth of July. Did you know that? Chou En-lai invited your ministers to visit Yenan. Did you know that? General Chu Teh was willing during the World War to put Communist forces under American command. Did you know that? Chairman Mao asked for a meeting with your president, but was turned away. We tried very hard to make friends with your government. Do you know these things?"

Embree nodded. Thanks to MAGIC briefings, he knew these things and more. Many Americans were convinced that without Russian aid the Chinese Reds would be forced to accept Nationalist terms. That was a mistake all right. And then there was Marshall's naïve hypothesis that America could arrange an accommodation between the warring factions; that two decades of hatred and bloodshed would be set aside in the interest of a democratic dialogue. There were probably more Western theories about China than this interrogator had ever heard of.

"What do you think of these imperialist actions?" the interrogator asked angrily.

"I think American policy demonstrates some errors in judgment."

"Is that all?"

"Errors coming from ignorance. Isn't that enough?"

"Do you support Chiang Kai-shek?"

"No."

"Then are you a Communist?"

"No."

"If you are not a Communist, then you support Chiang."

Embree shook his head, watching the man furiously light another cigarette. "As a matter of fact, I think China will be better off if you win."

"Why?"

"Because anything's better than the present regime."

"Anything?"

"Anything."

"That doesn't say much for Liberation."

Embree says nothing.

"You dislike communism?"

"I'm suspicious of Marxist ideas."

"What do you think of the People's Liberation Army?"

"I'm beginning to think it might be a great army."

"It's a Communist army."

"Very well, a Communist army. And maybe a great one."

"If you believe in our army, you must believe in our goals."

"I draw a distinction between your army and the government that's going to come out of it."

"Why?"

"Because you're fighting for your lives. When you've secured them, I wonder if you may not find a way to waste them."

"You don't make sense."

"Yes, that's possible."

Throwing a New China News Agency bulletin on the desk, the officer pointed to it. "MacArthur has sent special American agents from Japan to spy on us. You can read it here."

"I think that's an unproven allegation."

"What are you here for? To spy on us?"

Embree thought about what sort of answer to give. There was a good chance he might push WHO right past them, go even as far as insist on his Dutch citizenship. But stirring in him, as it had almost every day since he put Sanuk on the plane at Jinan Airfield, was the familiar wayward impulse of his youth, when just to see what might happen next he'd disregarded the basic rules of self-preservation. Was he a spy? Embree took another chance. He said, "In a sense."

"What do you mean?"

Embree shrugged. He looked at the fancy pistol belt this officer wore. It was all that distinguished the man from a young soldier guarding the door. "In the sense I want to go along with your army to see how it works. To see if it's really great."

"Are you an intelligence officer?"

"No. I left the army in 1945."

"Are you a journalist?"

"No."

"You must be crazy."

Embree doesn't reply.

"What exactly are you looking for?"

"I don't know. Everything. How your men feel, react, go into battle. I know about battle, I can judge it, believe me. I'm curious. I'm a student of warfare in the philosophical sense." He was only half joking.

"Would you go to the American government and tell them what you saw?"

"Yes, I probably would."

"So that would be your purpose. To spy on us."

"I'm not interested in statistics or exact deployment of troops. That's what a spy would want."

"Do you expect me to accept your word?"

Embree says nothing.

"If you're not a spy, why would you tell the American government anything?"

"I'm a citizen. If they asked me what I'd seen or thought, I'd tell them. But my own purpose in studying your army?" Embree looks at the wall in front of him, peeling, with an old calendar of a pretty Chinese girl on it. "My own purpose would be to learn the truth. To learn why you've won against odds."

"Who would you want the truth for?"

"Myself."

"But what would you do with the truth once you had it?"

"I would just have it."

That ended the interview. Next morning the officer returned, smoking a cigarette. After offering one to Embree, who refused it, he said in a shrill, aggressive voice, "If you want to spy on us—well, *do* it! We don't care. Do what you want. You Americans can't hurt us any more."

"Does that mean I'm free to come along?"

Nodding, the officer draws hard on the cigarette.

It's difficult for Embree to know what the man thinks of this decision, made obviously at a higher level. "Are there restrictions?"

"Do you think we're afraid of you finding something out? We have nothing to hide. You can do what you like." The officer puffs smoke into the air for emphasis. "But you must pay for transportation, food, the use of anything. We're not a rich people. Otherwise, go where you want. Nobody will stop you. We'll even give you a letter authorizing travel."

"You'll do that?"

"That's how afraid we are of American spying."

And that was the end of the interrogation. Embree had taken a calculated risk, counting on two Chinese characteristics: respect for the objective observer and curiosity. He'd appealed to the Chinese love of a philosophical view of any activity—including war. He'd relied on the Chinese interest in reflection and their capacity for admiring whoever has such an interest too. And what, indeed, did they have to lose by letting him come along? They were practical people who judged matters from an immediate perspective as well a historical one. That he was a white foreigner was less important than his outspoken, imprudent, and therefore believable goal of learning the truth about an army they were fiercely proud of. No hysteria, no paranoia, just a cool assessment of the situation. He must seem to them an experienced and educated man—after all, he does speak Chinese—who might learn something of distinct advantage to them. Of what sort of advantage to them? Perhaps they didn't know any more than he did. But without risk to themselves, they could take a chance on it. In any case, he could do no harm, not when flushed with victory they had every prospect of more victories in the offing. Therefore, let him come along—that was the idea. Just as scholars throughout Chinese history had accompanied the shapers of great events. So apparently he'd guessed right.

• • •

Soon after their arrival at the Reception House across the river from Jinan, Bernard Petter left. Warfare being distasteful to him "as a political statement," he'd persuaded Red officials to send him behind the lines to areas of agrarian reform. That was what he told Embree when leaving. "I want to see Chinese Marxism in action," he declared. "Not on battlefields but in villages, where the true revolution's taking place. Where I can see the Chinese mind at work."

"You've already seen it at work," Embree suggested as the little Frenchman packed his gear. "The Reception House, for example."

Bernard Petter nodded gravely. "An illustration of humanity."

"Of practicality. They offer amnesty to men sure of defeat, even set up a reception center. So what happens? They decrease the number of troops they have to fight. And they increase the size of their own forces in the bargain. I understand they're forming the defectors into a new army within the PLA. The 35th. It'll be called the 35th Army of the People's Liberation Army, no strings attached. And led by General Wu Hua-wen. Conveniently, they've forgotten he was a puppet administrator under the Japs and a recent crony of Chiang Kai-shek." Embree laughed.

Indignant, Bernard Petter chose his words carefully. "I'm glad I helped you get out of Jinan. Because now you'll see the future as it really is, instead of how imperialists generally see things. You'll see this is a new world you're living in. These men are different. They don't think like people did in the past. They have vision."

"All men are brothers," Embree said, half mocking, half wanting to believe it.

"Exactly. Don't let cynicism blind you to the truth."

A nice line, Embree thought, watching the young Frenchman stagger under a heavy pack that would soon have to be lightened, unless the PLA gave him an aide to carry it for him, which they might do if he continued to talk like a Marxist hero.

• • •

Within a few days Jinan fell. The Reds gave rice to citizens who volunteered to remove corpses from the streets. Looters were shot summarily, including troops of the entering Third Field Army who were caught at it. He heard that some of the soldiers, fresh from the countryside, didn't know how to turn on electric lights in the buildings. Thousands of KMT troops were being fed salted pork fat and greasy vegetables while cadres harangued them about the joys of joining the PLA.

Philip Embree put his freedom to the test. He got a ride on a truck into Honan Province, where Liu Po Ch'eng, the One-Eyed Dragon, was marshaling the Second Field Army for a push southward. Embree was stared at wherever he went, but nevertheless traveled freely, sometimes with troops, sometimes with supply vehicles (paying for the transport), moving farther away from the eastern seaboard, where Sanuk might be waiting for him. He immersed himself in details of *ko ming*, the transfer of Heaven's Mandate from one source of power to another. Destiny had brought him to this place at this time, and Philip Embree resolved to make the most of it, while putting aside the real question of his life: Is there a chance for him and this young woman? He put it aside and followed the Red Army toward its own destiny.

● ● ●

That was half a year ago. It is now the spring of 1949.

The Liberation Army is poised for a final push to Nanking, and Philip Embree is still with it, accompanying a unit of Red infantry. He's been with these thirty men through the hard winter of Central China. Mukden has fallen. The flower of Chiang Kai-shek's army was destroyed during the Hwai-Hai campaign. Red troops entered Peking almost a year to the day after Gandhi was assassinated. Two weeks later Tientsin fell. T'aiyuan has fallen. Since then, the Third Field Army under Chen Yi and the Second under Liu Po Ch'eng have skirmished their way through Honan and Anhui provinces, hunkered down during winter storms, and beginning in April have maneuvered toward a major confrontation with Nationalist forces on the Yangtze.

In spite of deficiencies in armament and tactics, the Liberation Army is a force, Embree has come to believe, that stands comparison with the world's best. What would General Tang Shan-teh think of it? Surely that stern professional would approve of its tenacity, discipline, and commitment. Surely the General would like this army as it is now—before victory brings political responsibility—the look and motion of its young columns, the optimism in the wind-burned faces of its peasant soldiers. Tang would like this army.

And if ever the Americans come up against it, the Liberation Army will give a good account of itself. That's what Embree will tell MAGIC, if MAGIC still exists. He rather doubts it. If he knows anything about the military, they have packed their bags and slipped out of China, avoiding last-minute confrontations that could embarrass the American government.

But then he'll describe the Liberation Army to anyone else who wants to listen, or if no one wants to listen it doesn't matter. What matters to him is recapturing the feel of China that gripped him in his youth. These past months he's sat around many campfires, hearing his companions slurp and belch their way through meals as companions did twenty years ago. He had almost forgotten that—that and the hacking cough in the morning and the smell of garlic and the bad jokes and the uncomplaining fortitude on marches. All of it comes back to him in a good way, like the memory of a comforting touch on the arm or the look of a room in which sleep has been sound. Traveling by truck or on foot, Philip Embree has seen in the young men plodding determinedly along these endless roads the faces of old friends. Now and then, disconcertingly, he notices a certain stance or facial structure that reminds him of someone long dead whose death he'd forgotten in the intervening years. It is like rolling back his own personal history to travel with these men.

And then there was the day in February, bitter cold under a crystalline bright sky, that he saw, while passing a column by truck, a small thin figure huddled in a padded jacket with a rough blanket wrapped around the shoulders, a young soldier distinguished from the others by a dark complexion, as if lifted from the tropical South and set down among them, a jungle plant in the midst of a wheat field—Ho Jin-shi. Or so Embree thought at the moment, but in the rattling truck there was no time to establish the identity of the dark young man, lips set tightly against the bitter wind, the eyes large and round and punished by the weather. But even had Embree taken the time—after all, he could have jumped off the truck and gotten another one later—he'd not have wanted to know with absolute certainty that Ho Jin-shi had survived. The Siamese boy was no longer part of Sanuk's life or his own, Embree decided and turned away. Winter moved into spring, and with this pleasant transition he's forgotten the existence of Ho Jin-shi.

So many things have given him pleasure recently: a temple, for example, with its guardian lions coming through a mist at daybreak, advancing toward the column of marching men, while cheeping birds, just awaking, herald that advance. Only last week he saw a bent old man walking through a field with a hoe slanted across his shoulder; the sight eased Embree back through centuries, when the old man's ancestors, if not running from bandits or armies surging through the countryside, also carried hoes, just like this one, aslant their shoulders through the same young fields of spring. Poplars with their tall straight trunks conform to the mathematics of the region; so do canals and roads. Only a single mule browsing in a distant field of stubble may betray a curve, as the line of his neck arches down to the shorn stalks his nibbling lips are after. This is the China that Philip Embree remembers. In spring the tiny brilliant-yellow wisteria and cherry blossoms along the road. There's a breadth, a massiveness, an expanse to this long corridor between Peking and the Yangtze that dwarfs the individual yet lifts the spirit, certainly lifts his, because it's a brisk, salubrious land, generous and open, nothing hidden or mysterious about it, but laid out for all to see.

And in recent days the fields have been light green, stretching northward all the way to Peking, the cold city that has so often resisted invasions and even more often assimilated the invaders. Peking, as capital of a new China, will return China to herself. That's the talk he hears around the campfires.

Embree sits among these soldiers in a mood of watchful serenity. Within a few more days Nanking will fall, and with its fall he'll move on to the next phase of his life. In his youth he didn't look back. Surely he didn't when a single impulse once carried him beyond the limits of his twenty-three-year-old past—when, with one swift motion, he turned away from everything he'd known until then, including his dedication to God, to cast his lot with an embattled warlord. He wiped the slate as clean as a man is capable of. He'd been like the righteous citizen who kisses his wife one morning, turns the corner of the block, and walks out of her life and away from his job and beyond his identity forever. But now, middle-aged, Embree notices with satisfaction a new tendency in himself: After an impulse has carried him away from everything he's become, he can look back at what that was. And he can think of the possibility of returning to it. Each time he looks back, the face of a young woman comes into view. As the Liberation Army has pushed southward, he's looked back more frequently, seeing her there.

What has he done? The question can't be pushed aside any longer. He's run away. Again.

And what must he do? He must go back to her, if she's there in Shanghai or Peking. Will she be there? Perhaps, perhaps not. No perhaps not. She'll be there.

And without the hesitation of a single moment he will confess to what has kept him from her. After half a year of seeking the courage to say it, he will say it outright: To have your mother I conspired in the ambush of your father. In only one respect will he seek pardon for what he did. What he did did not lead to the death of her father.

As Embree slogs through the melting snow of Honan with the Red column, he tries to imagine her response. But when this proves impossible, he attempts an analysis of his confession. There are two parts to it. The first is: I took your mother out of China because of love. Sanuk might accept that part, even if it involved the betrayal of her father—at least it's romantically human. The second is: To pay for getting your mother out of China, I conspired in the attempted assassination of your father. Aye, there's the rub. She can never accept the second part of the confession. Or if, through terrible effort, she manages to accept such a truth in order to rescue them both from it, she will never be able to let go of it. She will clasp it to herself until it eats into her heart.

We were doomed, Embree thinks, twenty years ago in Peking.

So he won't confess. But someday in a weak moment he might do exactly that, and then what? Their life together will be like walking through a mine field.

But they'll have a life together. Somehow. It must be. Why? Because it is part of a pattern.

. . .

It is mid-April on the approaches to the Yangtze, where a great clash should take place between 120,000 Nationalist troops and an equal number of Communist forces. But it isn't going to take place—at least not a *great* clash. Only a small one. Many factors have led to this more pleasant prospect.

Chiang Kai-shek has been busy transporting troops, supplies, the government's gold reserve, and national art treasures to the island of Formosa, leaving him little time and less inclination for interfering in the conduct of a lost war on the mainland. That has given aides and commanders a chance to save themselves through defection, bargaining, or running away. A few days ago General Ku Chu-tung, Chief of Staff of the Central Army, entrusted command of Kiangyin Fortress to a subordinate, who promptly turned its formidable guns not on Red gunboats but on the government's own naval squadron, forcing it to surrender to the Communists—probably with the well-founded expectation of amnesty or even acceptance by the Liberation Army as a newly recruited staff officer. A number of army units assigned to resist a river crossing have been withdrawn by secret order of General Tang En-po, although he has publicly boasted that Nanking will be a second Stalingrad.

And so the Liberation Army, assembling on the bank of the Yangtze opposite Nanking, does not expect stiff opposition. It has come through ripening spring fields in the last few days, and along canals where river boats, gray with age, plod up the channels on the strength of two lean scullers. The columns move briskly along the road of spring, past a long row of twisted old cypresses exploding with the power of new life, their gnarled branches ending in bursts of greenery, thirsty and throbbing in the soft wind. Ponds are filled with lotus and water-chestnut plants.

Flocks of ducks and egrets rest on the tranquil surfaces. Humpbacked hills, heavily wooded, appear on the horizon. Pine, fir, orchards, and gray-stoned villages line the way of the Red columns.

In the midst of such a spring, Philip Embree feels his spirits lift like sap in a branch. The Other moves pleasantly past his eyes: oxen pulling carts; wooden braces shaking; spades catching the light dully; poplar leaves turning; cottonwoods; a network of clay lanes through villages; pear trees; apple orchards; sheep and pigs. The images break around him like spume, the noiseless surf of his childhood when to swim was to be in heaven.

His pleasure is not lessened because he's heading for a battle. On the contrary, that prospect enhances his sense of well-being. Not because he loves violence and death, but because in war he's found something no better realized in meditation as he's practiced it: a heightened sense of the ineffable. As *The Gita* once told him: "Certain is death for the born, and certain is birth for the dead. Therefore, over the inevitable you should not grieve." Easier said, of course, than done. And yet in war there's more than death, something beyond the violence and horror. It's what Embree has known and it's what he suspects soldiers always know but never talk about: a terrific sense of life being lived, given up, passed on, the whole history of the world encapsulated in moments of frightening clarity. Looking at the young PLA soldiers with canteens banging against their thighs, leggings half unraveled, billowy pants dusted by the fine earth of China, Philip Embree remembers that time in Madras when devotees during a festival seemed to be threaded together by a fine wire. Not that the same hallucination occurs now. After all, he was plunged into it then by too many gimlets at the Adyar Club. But in this most terrible of human endeavors, there's sometimes a similar feeling of communal oneness. Men engaged in saving their lives don't find God in prayer but in acts of both bravery and cowardice and in abject fear and in hope and in suffering, for then a whole lifetime comes down to the events of a single moment, the insight and love and hatred hurtling into the intense zero of an instant.

Or so he might say. And quote *The Gita:* "He who takes the Self to be the Slayer and he who thinks he is the Slain, neither of these knows. He slays not, nor is he slain."

It's perhaps easy to find in such words indifference or a blatant excuse for violence or facile abstract philosophizing or just plain naïveté. At least the fourth possibility is wrong, in Embree's opinion. There's no ivory tower in *The Gita*. Indeed, one of the great religious dialogues of the world takes place on a battlefield.

And so I might say, Embree thinks, just as he hears from the front of the column a shout of "Yangtze! Yangtze ahead!"

It's altogether possible—indeed, the thought has been with him often the last week—that he'll return to America. For what reason? To tell people what he knows of this new China. And, of course, Sanuk will be with him.

It's a wild romantic vision, only too fitting for someone who has wandered his adult life in search of an idea, a belief, a lover, or a god. Perhaps this, too, is part of the pattern, the dawn of a new morning in his life. The General would approve, surely. If I go back to America, Embree tells himself, and talk about China, it will be the one thing I've done since his death that I'd want the General to know. And it would be payment of my debt to him. Yes, that too.

Perhaps it's only a happy thought, soon forgotten in the bright lights of Shanghai or Peking, when at last he finds Sanuk. But it's a good thought, one to cling to. He imagines himself standing in front of a lectern (not unlike Father delivering a sermon) and speaking to an audience of Americans in a university or a forum. It won't be easy; after all, twenty years have passed since he last saw a group of Americans in anything but military uniforms. Will people listen to him? Is there still freedom in the country of his birth? Will the China Lobby, through the press and Congress, attempt to silence him in their support of Chiang Kai-shek? Let them try. Surely there are people to hear him out. He'll say, "We *must* recognize the Communist government of China. Not because we agree with its ideals, but because diplomatic recognition will help us remain in Asia and have a stake in what happens there. The Soviets will have less influence in Peking if we're there too, our diplomats countering the Russian moves. We can maintain trade with the Chinese and keep our businesses in their cities for mutual benefit. By establishing diplomatic relations we'll encourage the Chinese Reds to follow a policy of moderation. We can't afford to lose contact with one-fourth of the world's people. We must learn to live with the Communists of China." On lecture platforms and in magazines he'll make these claims. And doubtless face a storm of protest from those who see global evil in a policy of accommodating Communists.

Surely, Embree knows, he could lose everything—what money he has, a comfortable life with Sanuk. Yet to risk everything for the truth (how strange for him) would bring into his life—surely into hers, too—the excitement they both crave. He'd write articles, give talks. He'd get into trouble, he'd be called what he isn't.

So maybe it's part of a pattern. Twenty years ago the pattern took its initial murky form, and now, faster and faster, is reeling out into a design of clarity. Foolish thought. Reckless. Embree is buoyed by it, even as his column comes off the road onto the bank of the Yangtze.

He stares at the broad brown river and imagines it must be something like the Mississippi of his own country, although he's never been farther west than Connecticut. He's seen much of the world, surely in the

Orient, but no more of America than the Eastern seaboard from Boston to New York. He couldn't show Sanuk America; they'd discover it together.

Now on the Yangtze a flotilla of watercraft has assembled: junks, barges, scows, rowboats, sampans. They bob on its vastness like so many pieces of debris. A convoy of barges, pulled by a single tug, is loading troops, while across the surface of the river, sparkling in morning light, puffs of smoke above thick gray walls suggest that some kind of resistance has been mounted in the city of Nanking.

Embree's unit moves down to the shore.

They begin to board a river scow with prominent curved strakes, its gunnels nearly awash. As Embree climbs aboard, he notices a small boy squatting over the bow, shitting calmly into the agitated water, while around him thousands of men in battle dress prepare to cross the Yangtze. The squad moves along the deck, past the wheelhouse covered with canvas, past the stubby mast and its furled lug sail amidships. Embree finds himself near the bow, starboard, next to a big hawser fender, and in sight of the anchor windless, metal chocks, coiled lines, and the small boy wearing only a shirt. Embree smiles at him. The boy stares back solemnly at the foreign man with blond hair sticking out from underneath a tan PLA cap with a cracked bill.

The noise of a clattering motor comes from the stern. Looking over his shoulder, from where he sits braced against the braided-hemp fender, Embree sees an entire company of soldiers seated among stacks of timber that will have to wait awhile for delivery.

• • •

The fleet of river craft fill the Yangtze as far as he can see. Light reflected from the churned water hits up against sail and engine and fixed bayonet, glinting against metal, giving wood a soft tannish glow. Ahead, from where he sits near the bow, Embree can see balls of smoke puffing up behind the city walls of Nanking. But it's not much of a show.

Embree can't help enjoying the anticipation that comes with the fear of approaching combat. Not that he'll participate, but he intends to be in the middle of it. Like a fool. Like an addict. He touches the stone head of the ax stuffed under his belt. As always. He touches the ax as a sort of formal gesture, acknowledging the good offices of Luck.

Coming from the east, across the city, is an airplane, which he hears before he can see it in the sun's glare. Then it comes out of the glare, high above the river, too high for him to see its distinguishing shape, let alone markings. Goddamn Chinese pilots, he thinks. A tactical bomber hung up there in the sky like a toy lantern on a pole. Too high for anything but saturation effect, although this guy probably carries no more than three or four bombs at the maximum. He releases one now —from that distance it looks to Embree like an eagle's turd. It crashes into a cliff a couple of miles north. Maybe it takes out a bird's nest, a footpath, with luck a fisherman's shack or two. Why doesn't the guy go home? Embree wonders. He hasn't the stomach for a fight or he'd bring the plane lower. So why do it at all? Maybe his commander instructed him to drop every bomb before returning—where didn't matter. The pilot up there is either following a directive like that or he's a coward or an idiot.

Embree grins at the boy seated on the other side of the hemp-rope fender, then points in the direction of the plane. Now the boy grins too. They're becoming friendly through the ineptitude of a bomber pilot.

The plane, having made a wide curve high in the air, circles back, this time from the west, so that Embree has enough of a look to recognize a Douglas A-26B with solid nose and drop tanks. What in hell would that plane need with drop tanks? he wonders. It's not going anywhere. This might well be its last run of the war; then it'll fly to Formosa and join Chiang Kai-shek. Still too high for anyone below to see its ground-attack armament, the A-26B drops what is probably the last of its load. A hundred yards away a sampan disintegrates in a blinding flash of yellow. And another shell blasts into a nearby junk, ripping it apart, scattering shrapnel along the starboard side of Embree's boat, and showering a little scow a few yards ahead.

The concussion has driven Embree back against the fender, across it against the small wooden housing on the bow that contains some winching gear. He's been hit. The force sending him back that hard tells him. He doesn't feel pain. He's just shaken up, trying to account for his body landing propped up against the bow housing, the calf of one leg curled under the other thigh. Straightening his head to the vertical, looking around, he sees the boat boy next to the hawser fender, back awash in blood, one arm sheared off. He hears screams and moans. Looking down —he delays doing it for moments that expand, spread out, carrying him forward into the delusion that everything's OK—making himself do it, Embree sees where the wound is. Piece of shrapnel in the gut. Piece of shrapnel right in the gut. Ripped right across it like a knife, exposing the whole thing.

Like Harry.

God, this wasn't supposed to happen. Gut wound in a scow on a lovely morning. And not much of a show going on. Can't happen, a gut wound, a bad one. Can't get rid of you, Harry, he thinks. It's the first time he's talked to Harry since coming to China. First time since Pagan. He tries to think about that instead of what has happened below his chest. Because it's bad, it really is. He feels the sweat pouring from his face, drying and cooling in the river air as the boat keeps rattling along. It's going to give him trouble soon. He's scared. He feels fear like a sudden sensation, like ice put against his forehead.

One bit of good luck: Everything's staying in place. That's not funny, he tells himself. But wasn't meant to be.

Lowering his eyes, Embree takes a quick, cautious look. It is all terribly open. A coil glistens in the red mire. That's the worst of it, what it looks like. There's no pain at all, not yet. If it falls out, he'll scream in horror and cry like a baby. He knows he will. If he doesn't breathe too deeply, maybe he won't shake the gut loose. But his breath is coming in quick, frantic little gusts, just like Harry's did, just like yours did, Harry. Harry, you fucker, is this your doing?

Poor Harry. Dead but blamed. It's starting to hurt a little, like a funny throb in the gut—something I ate that could just cause me more trouble than I need. What about it, Harry? I never really lost you, old boy, now did I.

I'm not going to get up and walk away from this. But I won't think about it, I'll think while I can think about something else. But what? What else can be important?

A Buddha with its eye shattered—where had he seen that? Somewhere, anywhere during these years. Through the throbbing pain he manages to see it. Kidding myself, Harry? Yes, but it's true. Embree sees the face of that Buddha as if just this morning it appeared by the roadside, a bullet smashed into its stone eye—

Ah, this isn't fair. He won't see her again; it isn't fair. But then this kid here—not fair for him either.

Embree shifts a little, terrified of the pulsing coil in the middle of his body springing loose and slithering down his groin, Jesus, like a butcher gutting a hog and letting the bowel quite casually dribble down the front of his apron. He'd seen that once, when his father took him to visit a church member, an old butcher who never missed a Sunday. He'd watched silently, then excused himself, walked outside and vomited, embarrassing Father.

Quite casually dribble down the front of that apron. If the stuff comes out like the stuff from a hog, he'll cry like a baby. Or he'll stuff it back in. But can he? He feels numb, as if arms and legs had fallen asleep. Trying to move his fingers, he's saddened to see them grope a little, as if frozen, then stop moving. Now he knows how Harry felt, propped against the tree, unable to reach the gun to put himself out of it, having to count on a cowardly friend.

Nothing's going to move again. Is it, Harry.

Now it's hurting a lot, a deep throbbing pain radiating up, down and sideways. If the stuff falls out, it'll still be you, attached to you. It *is* you. But *The Gita* says— Fuck *The Gita*.

This can't be happening. It's not part of the pattern. It's breaking the damn pattern.

Sanuk— No. He can't talk to her.

"Behold," he quotes—aloud, he thinks. "I show you a mystery; We shall not all sleep, but we shall all be changed." That is . . . what is that? Corinthians. Forget chapter, verse. Funny. Remembering Bible now. If it isn't sleep, then what is it? That's the mystery all right. But he's not ready for it, not now, not yet. Shall all be changed. Sure, a rotten bag of bloody guts. Shall all be changed. Where's the technique he meditated with? Shut down the I Maker. You are that. *Am Twam* whatever it is. The Other. There is no goddamn Other. Or there is. *Tat Twam Asi Tat Twam Asi*. The *ahamkara*, shut it the fuck down!

Hurts too much. Can't.

He's glad to die on water. It sort of compensates for being killed from the air. Compensates? Hell it does. But he's not dead yet, he's not going to die, because that's not part of the pattern.

Ah, it hurts now, *really*.

He thinks of her; they've only just begun. He's paid his debts, hasn't he? So it's his turn to live. No guilt attached. He'll find her somewhere, in either Shanghai or Peking, and they'll go wherever she wants, or she'll want to go with him to America where he can make a fool of himself and she'll love him for being a romantic fool, Sanuk, Harry— ah, Jesus, it hurts. Something alive's below his navel, snapping with red-hot teeth.

For a few moments he concentrates on breathing. Breath in Breath out Breath in— Except this isn't spiritual. He hears them—can't turn to see them behind him, amidships—groaning and crying and screaming. He turns slightly, or thinks he does, and at the corner of his eye there's the burning wreckage of the sampan. Or a dog lying on the water, its teeth on fire. He listens now, intently. That's nothing but pain in his ears, and with no little surprise he realizes that his own noise has joined theirs—a soft whimpering groan steadily following the pace of his quick breaths.

He hates this, fears it. If he goes around again, will it be as a dog? A Benares dog? He dreads both choices—life or no life. He needs time to choose.

It would be nice to grow old and have Sanuk beside the bed, holding his hand at the end. Not like this, not alone. That's the way people should die.

She doesn't know I'm dying.

The abysmal enormity of that truth frees him from pain an instant. He'll be dead without her knowing. The idea's extraordinary.

He's not yelling any more. His teeth are chattering; the only part of him that moves. It would be nice to change positions, just a little. In fact, there's nothing in the world he wants more than to shift the left leg curled under him. He's immobilized the way he'd been in the village with those farmers sitting against the opposite wall like crows on a fence, ready to help him into the old car. No Other then. There's something from *The Gita* he's trying to remember, but it gets loose, floats off on the pain.

The sound of the river-boat engine and the noises of wounded men are blown away by a brisk Yangtze breeze. Sunlight dances on the water; he watches it through pain that burgeons into a huge iron balloon. It's inside of him, growing bigger, unbearably bigger, taking up the spaces of his body, pushing everything aside, swelling and swelling and swelling, squeezing the rest of him into flat tiny pieces, white hot, like slivers of hot glass.

Harry, he tries to whisper. You should see her eyes.

His chin manages to lower slightly, or so he imagines. At any rate, he can see the gut, and is comforted to realize it's still balanced there above his groin, like a snake sunning itself on a branch. It won't fall out, it won't come tumbling out of him until he's gone.

Am I going? Is there something more or is this all? He doesn't know, so not yet, he can't go yet, he's got to stay. But something's going, he feels it going, it's going now.

See—

Ah, Father—

Her eyes . . .

As it's going. It's going now, and now everything for Philip Embree, the sight of himself and of the water and of the daylight and the feel of himself and the I Maker itself, all of these things fall away from him. What remains against the bow housing breathes in and breathes out a while longer, then is still.

48

"TODAY IS 1 October 1949," she writes in Thai.

"Chairman Mao will proclaim the establishment of the People's Republic of China today, and I, the daughter of General Tang Shan-teh, will be in T'ien An Men to hear him." She is writing in Thai in case the diary is looked at; no one will be able to read it. And when finished with it this morning, she'll replace the diary under the loose floorboard of the room along with the others she brought from Bangkok. No one in the apartment building knows about them; at least, she hopes not. Although she can't think of anything in them that would trouble the authorities, common sense tells her to keep them hidden, if she must keep them at all. Chu-chin, her comrade and friend, would tell her not to keep them, but Yu-ying has decided to hang on to them whatever happens. She needs them to tell her about the past, which each day seems to recede with terrific speed into a great mist.

Our group, the Progressive China News Agency, will assemble at Hsi Tan Market and march together to the square. It is getting cold, but not so cold that I can't take him with me. Then someday he'll be able to tell people, "I was there. My mother took me with her when Chairman Mao read the proclamation from the Gate of Heavenly Peace." Perhaps I should write Mother about everything now—appropriate, surely, on such an occasion—but it'd be better to wait until Philip comes for me. Then I can say, "The three of us are all right, because there are three of us now, our son too, born in the Year of the Ox." How strange it seems that I've waited nearly half a year since last writing her. I should write now, and yet knowing what Mother will think prevents me from doing it. If Philip hasn't come for me by now, she'll think he never will. *But he will.*

Yu-ying looks up from the page at the cold shaft of early light slanting across the fat square face of the baby, who gazes at his pudgy fingers coming together as if gathering the sun rays.

• • •

Minutes later, she's hurrying through the morning with him in a sling facing her. Wrapped in a quilt, he looks like a package; only his eyes, nose, and mouth are visible. His blue eyes watch her from Chinese folds.

Ahead, on the left, is the British Cemetery—or what's left of it. Before Liberation, Kuomintang soldiers demolished the cemetery walls, removed marble slabs, and vandalized graves which might contain something of value. She's heard they did the same to the Russian Cemetery. A horse drawing a rubber-tired wagon filled with lumber comes along the street. The peasant switching it has a sun-darkened leathery face, and from his impassive expression you'd never know, Yu-ying thinks, an event of importance was taking place today. Yet everywhere there are red banners hanging from windows, celebratory posters nailed to walls. A torn one on the corner of the lane ought to be taken down; it's past history now: a crude drawing of Chiang Kai-shek as a turtle on which a white-bearded foreigner in a cutaway coat and stovepipe hat is riding. The President of America?

It's quite possible that a PLA unit somewhere is holding Philip. That's what some of the workers at the news agency think, but when she applied for information at military headquarters, they just stared at her and told her to go home. People tell her it's better to say nothing until things settle down. She's resisted asking Mother for help, but maybe it's all she can do now. She can write: "Mother, I know how you feel about Philip, but I am desperate. Is there any way you can start a search for him through the American Consulate in Bangkok?" But is Mother in Bangkok?

Is her mother alive?

Yu-ying fumbles with the quilt until only the baby's mouth is still visible. Then she pulls a scarf across her own face; a stinging dust blows straight at the crowds funneling through the lanes toward assembly areas.

She can get a letter out all right, if she decides to write Mother again. That fellow with the *Progressive Daily* got out the first letter and has promised to get out more for her. She knows he wants to have an affair with her, but she won't do that. Philip will come for her.

Now she's passing through the district where she lived when she first came to Peking. So far nothing has replaced the old buildings that had been vacated and torn down by zealous planners within weeks of Liberation. Only rubble remains, and signs on posts: OUT WITH DISORDER! and VICTORY TO THE PEOPLE! Students in black jackets are marching down the streets, lustily singing revolutionary songs and carrying huge portraits of Mao and Chu Teh. Mao looks grim; Chu Teh is smiling.

It will be a long, difficult day for the baby in this chill weather; yet he must be able to tell people, "I was there." It's what Chu-chin told her. "He's a healthy baby. Take him, so he can say he was there on the First of October."

Everyone at the agency agreed, and it's to Yu-ying's advantage to please them. She is very lucky; everyone knows it although no one says so. But Chu-chin and some girls at the agency have warned her not to stir up envy. After all, she's the youngest translator on the staff, without experience, and practically free to do what she pleases, because no one else in the agency can read Thai. Her job consists of translating Thai newspapers and journals that come through fitfully from South China. Most young women her age work at hard labor, but language has given her a great opportunity. Of course, her translations, especially those that go to the various ministries, must be rewritten and she must share her stipend with the older man who "cleans up this mess" for her, as he calls it. A former journalist for a KMT-controlled newspaper, he is bitter, caustic, obviously disgusted by the new regime. Never mind him, Chu-chin tells her. A running dog of the capitalists like him won't last much longer anyway; Chairman Mao wants loyal people on the newspapers. I will be loyal, Yu-ying tells herself.

Although she can't hold imaginary conversations out loud any more, in rare moments when she's alone, Yu-ying has carried them on silently. Only last night, just before sleep, she imagined herself in medieval France. She was the Maid, kneeling in front of the Dauphin and in a ringing voice telling him, "Most noble Dauphin, I have come from God to help you and your kingdom."

There are vendors along the way, selling ice sticks from handcarts. Stiltwalkers wade above the crowd in red and yellow costumes, a startling contrast to the people heading for the celebration—everyone dresses shabbily these days, rejecting the bourgeois past. On first coming to Peking, she'd seen a lot of fedoras, but they're rare now; most men wear billed worker caps to go with old raincoats and torn sweaters.

Some young people come along chanting the "Eight Points of Chairman Mao." From a narrow lane Yu-ying emerges into the Hsi Tan Market; brilliant blue sky stretches over the rumpled canvas of the sheds, and sunlight dances in a charge of dust particles. Her own group is standing across the way; two young women wave gaily, urging her to join them.

When she gets to them, one of the girls wants to know where Chu-chin is, and Yu-ying tells them the poor woman has a terrible cold. Yu-ying likes one of the girls especially. Last week they attended an art exhibit together. The paintings were big, awkward, garish portrayals of peasants in fields, laborers in factories, soldiers fraternizing with civilians, Mao leading a charge under a red banner. Walking down the row of crude paintings, Yu-ying remembered her own student days at Silpakorn University. But the memory faded quickly. Too much is happening these days for her to spend time on memory. Except the memory of Philip.

Even as the girls chatter excitedly about the celebration, she's quoting under her breath those lines of Yu Hsuan-chi, "I know we'll not meet again in the season of flowers," lines that appall and frighten her. She reaches out and tenderly touches the scar on Philip's forehead. "So at last you've come. Sometimes I lost hope."

She tries to smile in the crisp air, while they all turn to watch the People's Republic of China flags being carried past the group—rippling in the wind with a large white star and four smaller ones changing shape across undulating cloth.

A girl takes the baby for a while, allowing Yu-ying to rest. She catches the old journalist's eye. He's standing near a group of men, and she can overhear some of their conversation about the "New Democracy." On the brisk wind she hears snatches of their rambling talk: "rural class enemies" and "lenient treatment" and "a check on excesses," and each time she glances their way, her eyes meet those of the journalist, who stands at the edge of the lively circle, smirking gloomily, as if already judged and sentenced.

· · ·

They wait all morning in their assembly area. The sun heats up the air until coats are opened, sweaters removed. The celebrants sit on the ground to wait and wait and wait, munching rice cakes sold by hawkers clever enough to recall that parades never begin on time but marchers always get hungry. Some members of the news agency wander over to the market sheds and study old phonograph records and fancy clothing which none of them has the money for, much less the daring to buy. But it's a novelty to see mirrors and porcelain and curios laid out just as they'd been in the days before Liberation. Now shops have started to change their items for sale: industrial chemicals instead of pewter, shoes instead of mirrors, fountain pens instead of curios, yellow laundry soap instead of porcelain. In half a year opportunistic Peking has become utilitarian.

Toward noon the baby cries, his face turning red with anger. With girls sitting on each side of her, Yu-ying turns away from the men to unbutton her coat, her blouse; pulling him closer, she gives him her breast. The girls praise him, yet Yu-ying feels they are critically studying his blue eyes. But he looks Chinese, doesn't he? He does, of course he does, but those eyes unsettle the impression his features otherwise give—unsettle, but do they destroy it? No, no, he looks Chinese; and he'll have a Chinese name too. So far she has called him only "baby," waiting for Philip's return when they can select a name together. Yu-ying smiles at him while he sucks. No baby came into the world with greater ease; she firmly believes it. The pain, not much of it really, lasted only an hour; then he came. She breathed deeply, pushed, and he came into the world. Yu-ying tells everyone who will listen how quickly he came into the world, how much he wanted to be here. What actual pain she suffered is lost now in the legend of a painless birth.

Glancing at the girls, Yu-ying looks for an expression of their disapproval. Are they just being polite? Later, when she's out of earshot, will they say, "Did you notice them? Blue as the sky?" Both the *Glorious Daily* and the *Liberation News* carry public notices almost every day that have to do with foreigners: apologies for misdeeds and abject confessions of petty crimes committed by foreigners who still live in China. But the child was born in China, and her own father was a great Chinese general. Isn't that so? They are not foreigners. And yet Chu-chin says, "Don't make too much of your languages, except Thai, and Thai only in connection with your work for the People. I know everyone's happy these days, but it's better to be cautious." Chu-chin befriended her from the first day at the agency, when Yu-ying answered a job notice pinned to a bulletin board in the Information Ministry.

Behind her, as the baby sucks, men are criticizing someone missing from the celebration. This man persists in calling the city Peiping instead of Peking, although Chairman Mao has officially changed it from "Northern Peace" to "Northern Capital" as a symbol of the New China. And this child, she thinks, will be part of it, the New China of the People. Child of the Ox. The moon's in his mouth; he'll be sharp-tongued and proud. Mercury is in his heart; he'll be clever. And with Saturn in his loins, sensual. He'll have many wives, according to the Brahma Jati, because he's an April child, the Wild Ox whose element is the sweet earth. A noble bull, but difficult to control. Cruel sometimes. Yes, that. Like his grandfather.

Handing him to one of the girls, Yu-ying arranges her clothes, seeing from the corner of her eye the aging journalist walking with hands behind his back to the verge of the assembled group, staring above the tiled roofs. What's he thinking? Yu-ying wonders, the question filling her with dread. It's terrible to be alone, cut off. Behind her they're still castigating the missing comrade for continuing to say Peiping instead of Peking.

It's like Siam being changed to Thailand, a patriotic gesture, a giving up of the past in hope of the future. Comparing Thailand to China always gives her vague discomfort; there are too many ironies for her to weigh. When she lived in Thailand, Yu-ying knew little about it. Now she knows more about that country (even secretly she never thinks of it as her homeland) than she ever did while living there. When Pridi attempted his coup, she read all about it—long after the fact, of course, and only in the official version—but she had a keen sense of his coura-geous if ill-planned landing in Bangkok, along with those brave men who'd followed him to exile here in China. How often, during their own escape from Thailand, had she and Chamlong talked about the loyal men who followed where Pridi led. On their passage from Thailand to Singapore, they had speculated on the importance of the message Cham-long carried until, for them, it assumed a special urgency, a contribution to a dimly envisioned victory over evil.

Had Chamlong—Ho Jin-shi—been instrumental in helping Pridi re-turn to Thailand? Had the message he carried been part of the plan? Had Chamlong actually delivered it? How proud he must have been!

Yu-ying smiles at the thought of him standing ramrod straight, his angular features narrowed in concentration, while the great man Nai Pridi Phanomyong praised him for his courage. Where is he now? Is he still alive? Or did he, one way or another, gamble his life away? Poor Chamlong. He made the wrong choice of a woman, the wrong choice of a homeland too, because had he remained in Thailand, by now he'd probably have given up politics and settled down to work for his father.

For herself, however, Yu-ying is glad she left Thailand. She has only one regret, but one crucial enough to determine the course of her life—leaving Philip at the Jinan airport more than a year ago. A year. Is it possible?

Behind her some men from the agency are discussing the Cultural Control Committee which has just been established. They agree, every one of them, that it's vitally important in the New China to ban performances of superstitious and feudalistic plays. She hears someone say, his crisp voice carrying on the wind, "We must trample the old ways, we must never again be slaves, we must show the world!"

Stirring words to Yu-ying. She is wholly Chinese now, at least in her loyalties, in her thoughts—or so she wants to be. Last night she even felt ashamed of imagining herself as Jeanne d'Arc. From now on, Yu-ying vows silently, while settling the baby in the sling, whenever she imagines herself as anyone, it will be as a revolutionary fighting for the Chinese People.

Someone is calling out. It's time to assemble and move by columns into the procession heading toward the square. Soon Yu-ying, alongside the girls and directly behind the aging journalist, is marching through the windy afternoon toward T'ien An Men. A whiff of pungent smoke blows across their column. She has smelled it before and didn't know what it meant until one day Chu-chin explained that people were choosing cremation these days instead of burial, because it's cheaper, cleaner, and takes less space. But on Proclamation Day? There must be many to bury, Yu-ying thinks, as the column swings onto the wide boulevard, past unpainted houses which in the years of civil war have become dilapidated. From the head of the long bobbing column comes the sound of firecrackers. On the right Yu-ying sees another old poster peeling on a storefront. Beneath the portrait of a huge PLA soldier reaching over the wall of Nanking to seize a bald and babyish Chiang Kai-shek cringing on a pile of skulls, there's a blood-red inscription: STRIKE ON TO NANKING AND SEIZE THE TYRANT ALIVE!

The square itself comes into view. Thousands have already found their positions chalked by number on the flagstones. Hovels had stood east and west of the railroad tracks which dissect the square, but they've been razed for the celebration; and the hawkers and fortunetellers, who daily used to stake out territory in front of the Forbidden City, have melted into a gray throng awaiting the dignitaries. A month ago Yu-ying watched kites flying in the square—blackbirds and dragons zigzagging above the Avenue of Emperors. They'd reminded her of kite fighting on Pramane Grounds, but today the memory eludes her almost as it comes, and with thousands of others Yu-ying raises her voice in the cry

"Mao Tse-tung wan shui!" Her eyes are misty, as she places one hand behind the baby's head to brace him, while her own body trembles from the effort of shouting.

"Mao Tse-tung wan shui!" echoes off the scarlet walls of the Gate of Heavenly Peace. Yu-ying shouts it along with the massed ranks of Chinese in the square of their capital city. She is Chinese, wishing her leader a life of ten thousand years.

• • •

Looking down at the baby, she sees his eyes narrow from the impact of the noise, his mouth open as if ready to scream, but after a pause he stares gravely at her and his mouth closes on a bubble that breaks into drool. She wipes it away with her finger, leans and kisses him just as another shout of victory rampages through the square. And for a long time then, hours—she'll never know how long—Tang Yu-ying is caught up in celebration.

Delegates arrive in their gray and brown uniforms, plain save for big red buttons attached to long red ribbons. The news agency group is near the front, so Yu-ying has a good view of the high balcony on the Gate of Heavenly Peace, where the great men of the revolution stand waving at the crowd: Mao Tse-tung and Chou En-lai and Chu Teh, holding his rolled speech and grinning like a boy, and all the rest of them, great heroes like Jeanne d'Arc and her own father, waving at the assembled thousands until a hush falls and a huge flag runs up a tall white pole, snapping free, a great swath of crimson with five yellow stars. As it ripples above the shouting crowd, howitzers salute the PRC's flag (the baby snivels when they go off, then lapses into sleep, although noise continues: the national anthem's swelling chorus of "You Who Refuse to Be Slaves, Arise Arise Arise!").

Yu-ying watches Chairman Mao step forward in his plain brown uniform; the others back off, allowing him full glory, and for a moment she thinks it could be her father receiving the adulation of all these people, of herself too, for along with them she's shouting hoarsely, *"Mao Tse-tung wan shui! Mao Tse-tung wan shui!"* And she hears him declare that the Central Governing Council of the People's Government of China on this day assumes power in Peking. It's already late afternoon by now, and the air itself has a fluffy weight, as if it could be pressed together into something as bright and porous as a cloud. A feathery presence, it holds the sunlight tremulously when the entire square goes mad with jubilation—Chairman Mao has just shouted into the microphone, "We have stood up to the world! Nobody will insult the Chinese people again!"

The parade begins, moving in waves under the high balcony of the gate. There are tanks with red stars on the metal flanks—"American tanks!" someone yells, causing people to laugh—and armored trucks and cannon and sailors with fixed bayonets and peasant guerrillas carrying red-tasseled spears and cavalry in round helmets—"Kuomintang helmets!" someone yells, to more laughter—and long columns of troops with backpacks and crossed straps and leggings and with mounted officers distinguished not by insignia but by dispatch cases and field glasses, all of them clattering past the reviewing stand at the southern gate of the Ming and Ching emperors. And then, to great applause, the students, Chairman Mao's "second army," march by in clumsy rows, their affiliations barked over the public address system.

The sun has lowered behind some of the old Manchu buildings in the west, so that the delegates clapping and waving from the gate turn into blue figures without faces. But the parade continues, featuring more American and Kuomintang equipment, more shouts of recognition, more defiant and victorious laughter, and when finally the fireworks break over the Forbidden City, illuminating the ceramic figures on the ends of roof tiles, Tang Yu-ying feels she's left everything behind her that was not Chinese. Swept by a cold wind, while sunset fades into the hollows of T'ien An Men, she warms the baby at her breast and smiles at the aging journalist, who turns to regard her somberly. "I won't forget this day," she tells him.

Without smiling back, he nods. "None of us will."

He is lost, she thinks. A good man lost. In such times there must always be good men who fall by the way. Like my father. Like Philip? No, he won't fall, he'll come for me.

And when the celebration ends and large red lanterns in the shape of stars bring light into the vast square, Tang Yu-ying heads out alone, thinking of Philip coming for her. And he too will want to stay here, because this is a new land—old but new, as new as the life now sleeping in the sling she carries. He knows Chinese well; perhaps he too can work at the news agency. There must be untold opportunities, even for foreigners, in such a new world. And if he doesn't want to stay, then she'll go with him elsewhere, anywhere.

The crowds, dispersing, hunch through the gathering darkness. Drums are pounding, firecrackers going off. On one street a few students are doing an impromptu Yang-ko dance. Now that the sun is down, Peking is cold; blowing dust burns against Yu-ying's face as she leans into the wind from Central Asia.

Passing two men, she overhears one saying, "He lives in the Pavilion of South and Central Lakes."

She knows what they're discussing: where Chairman Mao lives. It's known but rarely spoken of that he's taken up residence deep within the Forbidden City, where the Ming emperors once lived. Glancing back, she sees that both men are elderly, perhaps the same age as the journalist who's doomed in the new world.

"Wait! Wait!"

Yu-ying turns and in the final light manages to see the features of a girl from the agency.

"I thought it was you. I saw the bundle." The girl reaches out and picks up an edge of the quilt, peers in with a smile. "Did he sleep through it?"

"Through most of it. Are you going this way?"

"Yes, I'm meeting people at a restaurant. He's a good baby. Everyone says so."

They walk in silence, while around them the noise of firecrackers increases, and a whistling rocket appears in a blast of crimson over a nearby roof.

"He's a good baby not to be upset," the girl remarks.

"He'll be able to say, 'I was there.' "

The girl is silent awhile, then, halting, turns to Yu-ying. "I was asked to speak to you, but I haven't had a chance."

"Asked to speak to me?"

Again the girl hesitates. "You wear something around your neck."

"Yes, an amulet." Yu-ying touches her throat and smiles. "I used to think it was the Goddess of Love. Now I call her the Goddess of Hope. It's just a cheap thing from Bangkok."

"People say it's decadent."

"What?" Yu-ying is still smiling, trying to see the girl's shadowy features. "This?"

"I was asked to tell you. I'm sorry. But we must get rid ourselves of old things. Chairman Mao says we must stand up."

"Chairman Mao said we *have* stood up."

"People say the thing around your neck is decadent. I'm sorry."

"You mean, I mustn't wear it?"

"I'm sorry."

"Then I'll take it off."

"Everyone sacrifices for the Revolution. I'm sorry."

"I won't wear it tomorrow."

"That would be better. Here is where I leave you. The baby is brave and pretty. See you tomorrow."

• • •

Yu-ying is still thinking about the amulet when she mounts the narrow stairway toward the second-floor room she shares with Chu-chin. Maybe she'll take the amulet off but keep it hidden, because otherwise, if she gets rid of it as the girl suggested, what will she have that's hers?

A booklet of Thai astrology, the diaries, an English dictionary, the cross of twigs, that tortoise-shell comb from Chiang Mai. Northern Thais claim that such a comb brings happiness, and by next year she can use it to comb the baby's hair. In the meantime she'll hide it too. And that's all she has, aside, of course, from memories of Bangkok, of friends like Lamai, of the servants at home, of her early love for Chamlong. She has Mother and Philip still, if Mother's alive. And he will come for her.

Opening the door—there's no lock—Yu-ying sees her roommate sitting on the bed against the west wall, reading by the light of a hanging bulb. A middle-aged woman, Chu-chin has a broad Mongolian face, a squat, powerful figure. Looking up, she smiles and puts the book aside. Blowing her nose into a rag, she asks how the celebration went.

Yu-ying sits down wearily in the one chair they have. Their room contains the chair, two beds against opposite walls, a desk, a dresser. Down the hall there's a lavatory. They share a little kitchen downstairs with two other families.

Still holding the baby in the sling, she describes the parade and the speeches and how Chairman Mao looked, what he wore, how he waved, and the fireworks at dusk that lit up the eaves of the great roofs within the Forbidden City and the Yang-ko dancing and the late cold wind.

Chu-chin nods. "The cold wind. I'd not have survived it today. At your age I'd have gone out with a Peking cold, but not now."

She translates Russian articles for the news agency. A Communist cadre in the late '20s, Chu-chin once lived in Russia. She followed Mao to Yenan after he made the Long March, fought against the Japanese, then the Nationalists. She holds a degree from Peking University. Her husband and two children are dead. She's never told Yu-ying how they died.

"How did he do?" Chu-chin asks with a smile, looking at the baby now lifted from the sling.

"He was brave," Yu-ying declares, and while talking more about the great day changes the boy's diapers. Finished, she puts him on her bed, against the wall—that's where he sleeps. "I'll cook soon."

"I'll help."

"No, you rest."

They smile at each other. Then Yu-ying reaches to her throat and removes the amulet on its cheap metal chain. Both of them look at the terra-cotta image of a woman with four arms seated on a lotus. "I was told today this is decadent."

Chu-chin nods. "Yes, I can understand that."

Looking at the crudely carved figure of Sarasvathi, who she once hoped would protect her from sorrow in love, Yu-ying throws it on the desk with a sigh. "I won't wear it any more."

"Good. That's best."

"That's what I was told." Feeling a surge of defiance, however, she leans forward in the chair and picks up the amulet. "But I'll keep it anyway. I'll—hide it."

"No," Chu-chin says, shaking her head.

"Why not? If I don't wear it, what's wrong in keeping it? Just to look at? For memory's sake?"

"No."

"Why not?"

"Because they might search the room."

"Can I keep the chain? Look how cheap it is."

"Well, I think so. For now," Chu-chin estimates.

On the instant Yu-ying decides to keep and hide the amulet as well as the chain. "Who could search our room?"

"That's hard to say. But remember, you come from another country."

"Maybe I do. But I'm Chinese."

Chu-chin blows her nose loudly. "Of course you are. I believe that. But no one is safe. Not me, not you, not anyone. Don't ask me why. I don't know. But China will be a strange place for a long time." Coughing, she looks at the small dark window. "A strange place," she repeats. "Everything's new. We've won, but what happens next? I've been with this movement nearly twenty years, yet I can't answer that question. I know the celebration is wonderful and the victory is very great—earned with so much blood. But everyone's gone from the square tonight, and the fireworks will stop, and Chairman Mao and the others will have tomorrow to face. So will we all. And it's a tomorrow we know nothing about. Believe me, nothing is known." Chu-chin, eyes red and watery, blows her nose and shakes her head again. "Nothing is worse than a Peking cold. It's the dust. There is something I've wanted to say." After a pause, she continues. "People wonder if you might want to meet some men—young like yourself."

"No. I'm happy this way."

"You're very young," Chu-chin says with a wan smile. "You can't let your life end because of him."

"He'll come."

"Yu-ying." After a fit of coughing, Chu-chin looks hard at her. "He might be dead." It's not the first time she's mentioned that possibility.

And it's not first time Yu-ying has replied as she does now. "No. He's not dead. He's a soldier, he knows how to take care of himself. He's been captured or held somehow or he's sick or . . . or there's something he must do before coming here. But he'll come. I know it's been a long time, but I can wait."

With a rueful laugh, Chu-chin moves her head from side to side. "Only a young woman could say that."

They are silent, listening to the distant noise of firecrackers exploding, as if Peking were again under siege instead of enjoying peace for the first time in years. Chu-chin has said it, the girl thinks: What happens next? What happens next? The question hammers in her head—what happens next?—until mercifully the baby cries.

Getting up, Yu-ying goes to the bed and picks him up. He yells lustily in hunger. Baring her breast, she's relieved of the question for a while. Calm descends.

As he feeds, she considers a prediction from the Brahma Jati: Women born in a Dragon Year will have reliable sons.

He digs at the nipple. In wonder she stares down at him: his square face pinched red by the wind, his blue eyes watching her, his mouth seeking life from her body.

About the Author

Malcolm Bosse lives in New York City with his wife and son. He has lived in India and traveled extensively throughout Southeastern Asia, in Japan and Taiwan, and in China.